**ALBANY COUNTY
PUBLIC LIBRARY**
Serving the Laramie Plains since 1887

Laramie, Wyoming 82070

PRESENTED BY

Friends of the Library

COME
TWILIGHT

By Chelsea Quinn Yarbro from Tom Doherty Associates

COME TWILIGHT

A NOVEL OF SAINT-GERMAIN

Chelsea Quinn Yarbro

TOR®

A TOM DOHERTY ASSOCIATES BOOK
NEW YORK

A Tor Book
Published by Tom Doherty Associates, LLC
175 Fifth Avenue
New York, NY 10010

www.tor.com

Tor® is a registered trademark of Tom Doherty Associates, LLC.

Library of Congress Cataloging-in-Publication Data

Yarbro, Chelsea Quinn.
    Come twilight : a novel of Saint-Germain / Chelsea Quinn Yarbro.—1st ed.
        p.   cm.
    "A Tom Doherty Associates book."
    ISBN 0-312-87330-1
    1. Saint-Germain, comte de—Fiction.   2. Spain—History—To
711—Fiction.   3. Vampires—Fiction.   I. Title.
PS3575.A7 C65 2000
813'.54—dc21

                                                                00-031710

First Edition: October 2000

Printed in the United States of America

0 9 8 7 6 5 4 3 2 1

for

Stephanie Moss

Author's Introduction

Most of us in America have a tendency to think of places—particularly in Europe and Asia—as being sociologically monolithic, that is, ethnically and culturally intact for as far back as we can imagine. Demonstrably this is not the case, as even the most rudimentary education in history makes clear from the start: borders have changed, invasions have taken over entire regions, whole populations have been displaced, ethnic identities have been blurred, and societies have evolved to accommodate these events or they have been supplanted. Few places in western Europe make this more apparent than the Iberian Peninsula—that is, Spain, Andorra, and Portugal. Native groups have had, over time, to contend with Phoenicians, Carthaginians, Greeks, Romans, Visigoths, and Moors, to mention the most obvious. Each invading group left its mark on the people and the culture, creating a multilayered ethnicity and culturality that still have impact in Spain today.

The region of Spain now known as Catalonia has had more than its share of cultural bludgeons over time; as part of the natural barrier between what is now France and Spain, and wedged against the Mediterranean Sea, Catalonia has been struck by every invading wave to hit Spain with the possible exception of the Vikings, who generally confined their raids to the northern coast. Often the embattled established populations of the region would withdraw into the Pyrenees, into remote valleys and inaccessible peaks in an attempt to preserve themselves from the campaigns of the newcomers, a pattern that has survived into this century. What today looks like rich cultural diversity was seen at the time it began as oppression and social calamity, a perception that supported the virtual lockdown on the country by the Catholic Church once the Moors were finally expelled from the country at the end of the fifteenth century. Stability might demand a high price, but given what the country had endured, most of the people were willing to pay it.

The notion of a Spanish identity did not begin to evolve until the middle of the eleventh century; before then, regional, ethnic, and familial loyalties created the sense of place in the world for most people on the Iberian Peninsula; the primary loyalties remained with kingdoms but the understanding that all the kingdoms were Spanish had finally begun, a dramatic change from the patterns of the past. Even during the Roman occupation, the people native to the region were never fully Romanized; they remained strongly committed to their various ethnic groups and lacked the cultural cohesion that would have made such a transference possible. To be fair, neither Romans nor the Iberian peoples sought such assimilation, for the Roman policy was to disrupt the society as little as possible, to keep down impulses to insurrection. Later, during the Visigothic period, the people had no reason to identify with their Germanic invaders; nor did the Visigoths themselves support the notion of a national identity—theirs, or the native populaces'—although the early Church tried to promote a spirit of shared responsibility, both as a measure against paganism and heresy, and as a means of protecting those who were formally Catholic; it was also an attempt to assert an authority that the Roman Church, at that time, did not possess. As a remnant of the Roman period and the presence of the Church, Latin remained an official language of the Iberian Peninsula well into the eighth century, but it was a Latin battered by declining education and the influence of Gothic structures; without the Church, even such minimal cohesiveness would have been lost. Additionally, rules of spelling and structure faded almost into nonexistence in the thousand years between the end of Roman occupation and the establishment of a new, recognized national language. For those periods, I have opted to use the most common forms of place names in use during that time—occasionally imposing a regularity that did not, in fact, exist—and forms of personal names that are most consistent with the usage of the time. In regard to the place names, I hope the maps will help reduce any confusion created by language drift.

The advantages of the Church affiliation vanished for most of the Iberian territory upon the successful invasion of the Islamic Moors, who pushed the Visigoths north beginning in 711 when Tariq defeated the Visigoth King Roderick. This event was not met with the kind of resistance some of the populace expected due to the lessening of the Byzantine presence in Spain; the Greek-speaking Byzantines had garrisoned soldiers in Valencia and Barcelona the century before, but had

troubles of their own with the expanding forces of Islam by the time
the Moors commenced their conquest in Spain, so were not available
to help to stem the tide. And what a rapid conquest it was: in 719, the
Moorish forces reached the Pyrenees, and many Christians and pagans
saw the wisdom of conversion to Islam, although this occurred more
often in cities and large towns than in villages or rural areas; outside
town walls, the single biggest pressure put upon non-Islamic persons
was the burden of double taxation—for many, incentive enough to
change religious affiliation. The Moorish conquest went largely unchallenged until the middle eleventh century, when Ferdinand I of
Castile and León began a reconquest, taking back lands from the
Moors; his policies were continued by his sons Sancho II, el Fuerte,
and Alfonzo VI, who, with the aid of Ruy Diaz de Bivar, known as El
Cid, drove the Moors back as far as Valencia which Diaz took in 1094,
turning it into virtually his own kingdom, and where he died in 1099.

In the eleventh century, as an offshoot of this vigorous military expansion, the beginning of the Romano-Moorish language known now
as Spanish occurred. More than force of arms, the spread of language
united the Iberian peoples into an identifiable group, and created a
cultural commonality neither religion nor armies had been able to
achieve. It became the single most unifying factor in all of the efforts to
cobble a national identity out of so—to use the current word—diversi-
fied a population. The importance of this can be seen in the rapid
spread of documents in the vulgate [popular-tongue—Spanish], and
the consequent regularization of personal, familial, and place names.
The social upheaval of the war against the Moors was profound, and
lasted from around 1055 to 1492, when Isabella the Catholic finally
conquered the last Moorish strongholds.

The emergence of the Spanish language was an important part of
the reconquest efforts, for it created a common cultural vehicle to
begin developing a sense of nationalism among the Iberian peoples. By
conducting business and recording other communications in Spanish,
the reconquest forces brought about a new level of commonality in society. Far more than religion—which quickly became dangerously po-
larized—the spread of language brought the country together and
created an identity that endures to this day.

The shifts in language and ethnicity play roles in this novel; the
changes of names reflect the evolution of language as well as the presence of various invaders in Catalonia. It is through these changes in

names that cultural shifts and the impact of time are measured. In studying records of Catalonia (Gothalunya, Cotalunya), divergence in ethnicity, ecology, travel, and belief systems are reflected linguistically; I have followed these historical disturbances as much as possible in telling this story, and although many records are scanty at best, I have done my best to follow the form of the changes when specific vocabulary was not available. Going from Roman words to Visigothic, to Moorish, to Spanish in the course of the novel may be confusing to some, but the changes are appropriate to the four periods of the action; I have, in fact, as noted above, imposed a standardization in each section of the story that did not exist at the time, spelling rules being a long way in the future from the events in the novel. For example, the city that is first identified as Caesaraugusta on the banks of the Iberus, becomes Zaraugusta, then Zaraguza and is known today as Zaragoza on the Ebro; and the Roman town of Osca becomes Usca, then Usxa, at least in the most consistent sources, and is today known as Huesca.

Part IV concerns itself in part with two kings, one living, one dead, with the same name—the Romanesque version of Alfonzo. Both of them used many spellings of their names, none of them preferentially or exclusively; I have selected to refer to the living king with the most popular spelling of his name at the time: Idelfonzuz, of Aragon and Navarre. For his late father-in-law, I have used another spelling of the name: Adelfonzuz, of León and Castile.

In the case of Csimenae, Chimenae, Chimena, Ximene, the language-drift as well as cultural influences account for the changes. Csimenae is pronounced Tsih-MAY-nye, Chimenae is pronounced Chih-MAY-nay, Chimena is pronounced Chih-MAY-nah, and Ximene is pronounced with the Old Spanish X, a softer, slightly slurred version of the *ch* sound, thus: Spanish Xih-MAY-nay. For post-Roman-Spanish, as for most languages, writing was phonetic until the printing press made certain regionalisms the standard for the language wherever it was spoken. Once the phonemes are learned, the spoken tongue is accessible, and that is true in this book as it was in the few written records that provided references for the linguistic development found in the story.

As always, there are thanks due to a number of people: to Father Joseph Avila for providing information on Visigoth Spain, particularly the role of the Gardingi; to Eleanor Westfield for access to her impressive library on the break-up of the Roman Empire; to Harold Pinkser, for the use of his maps and photographs of Catalonia, particularly his records regarding erosion and soil chemistry; to James Castion for material on the Moorish invasion of Spain; to Annemarie McNaughton for her expertise on the development of Spanish agriculture during the Moorish occupation; to A. G. for information on folklore traditions on sacred blood and Grail legends; to Philip Krasny for explaining the problems of deforestation in Catalonia during the Moorish occupation; to Pat Lee for the opportunity to read her thesis on the politics of the Christian resurgence of the twelfth century, particularly in regard to trade routes; to Shaneesia Chaney for her records on Islamic and Christian intermarriage during the Moorish occupation of Spain; to Dana Henniger for architectural information on the Moorish period in Spain; to J. Westfield for references on the development of Early Spanish and language "drift"; and to Wallace Bruchmeyer for sharing his expertise on Mediterranean economics during the height of Moorish power, and the vacuum following the Moorish withdrawal from Spain. Errors in fact or opinion are certainly not the fault of any of these good people.

Thanks are also due to Bryan Cholfin and Melissa Singer, my editors, and the other good people at Tor; to Lindig Harris, for the newsletter (*lindig@mindspring.com* or P.O. Box 8905, Asheville, NC 28814); to Robin Dubner, my attorney, who protects the Count; to Eugene Smith, Carla Serrano, and Paul Shaw, who read the manuscript for accuracy; to Maureen Kelly and Sharon Russell (with an extra thanks or two for other reasons), who read it for fun; to Wiley Saichek, for keeping tabs on the Internet and on my publishers; to Tyrrell Morris, for keeping my machines working and set up and maintaining my Web site (*www.ChelseaQuinnYarbro.com*); to those bookstores that continue to keep Saint-Germain on the shelves; and to my readers, for persevering in their support of these adventures.

Chelsea Quinn Yarbro
Berkeley, California
May 1999

PART I

CSIMENAE

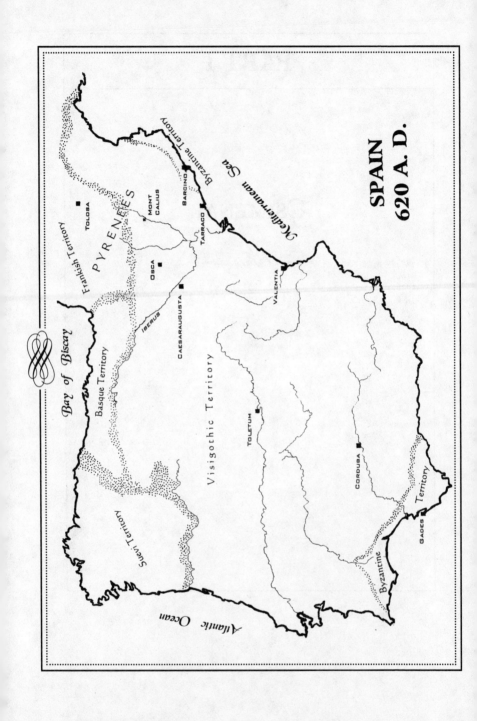

Text of a letter from Bishop Luitegild of Toletum to Gardingio Theudis of Aqua Alba in Iberus and Exarch of Aeso.

To the most esteemed Gardingio Theudis, the blessing and ave of Episcus Luitegild of Toletum on this most sacred occasion of Advent, when all good Christians pray for the redemption of sin and the coming of Grace, for surely it will not be long before the Son of God comes again to raise up the righteous and cast down the mighty as Holy Scripture promises us.

This is to inform you that the bearer of this tomus is a man worthy of your good consideration, for he is of high rank and reputation, esteemed by noble, merchant, and clergy alike. Nothing ill is said of him by any who have dealt with him. All praise his conduct. He enjoys the highest positions available to foreigners in Toletum, and we view his departure as a misfortune that will give us cause to lament his absence for many years to come.

It is his departure that prompts me to write to you, for you have immediate contact with Caesaraugusta, which is across the river from you. As the Gardingio of the eastern side of the river, it is in your power to speed or hinder the departure of this man and his servant when they present themselves at your fortress. You would be doing a Christian service to ease this man's passage through your territory; I would re-

*member your kindness in my prayers for a full year, and I would inter-
cede with the local authorities here in Toletum to the benefit of those in
your region who remain obdurate in the Aryan heresy or in clinging to
the pagan ways of the past. Surely such concessions will move you from
your usual adamantine posture in these matters.*

*The man of whom I speak is one it would behoove you to receive
well, with the courtesy due one who has been a companion to those of
highest positions in the world. He has traveled much and can instruct
you in many things that will prove useful to you as well as entertaining.
He is educated and erudite, with the comprehension of one who has
journeyed widely. Let me encourage you to listen to him and benefit
from his wisdom. He is also skilled at healing and may be induced to
treat any suffering from injury or disease at your fortress. You would
do your dependents a disservice not to avail yourself of his talents in
this regard.*

*To facilitate this introduction, I will include a description of the
man, so you will not be abused by an imposter: his name is Franciscus
Sanct' Germain. He is of high birth and carries the winged eclipse as a
badge of degree. He is somewhat above middle height, sturdily built,
his actions are decisive and energetic, his features are pleasing but a bit
irregular, his hands and feet are small and well-made. You will be taken
by his eyes, which are of a blue so very dark they appear black. His hair
is fashionably cut in the Byzantine manner, has some curl to it, and is a
dark-brown color shot with ruddiness when struck by light, and he is
clean-shaven. His voice is mellifluous and he speaks eloquently, but
with an accent that I have not heard in anyone but him. His manservant is a thin man of middle years with sand-colored hair and pale-blue
eyes; he answers to the name of Rogerian.*

*While he has lived here in Toletum, he has gained high regard for his
skill as a jeweler and goldsmith, and his devotion to civic works. He also
has some skill with medicaments. In these capacities various he has
earned the good opinion of the city's Jews, who have praised his abilities and integrity in terms they usually reserve for their own; that does
not mean he dealt only with Jews, for it is not so—he has been useful to
everyone in Toletum, I would have to say. However, being a man given
to study instead of contemplation, it is to the Jews that Sanct' Germain
is entrusting much of his property, including his house and a small villa
outside the city walls, as he is bestowing his household goods upon the*

poor of our faith, along with a donation to Sancta Virgine and the monastery Sacramentum.

I know that those Gardingi living away from Toletum, as you do, are not often minded to extend yourselves for those of us here, but I ask that in this instance you do as I have asked you to do. It will redound to your benefit in this life as well as in the life that is to come when God returns to judge all mankind; you will not want it said of you that you failed in your duty as a Gardingio and a Christian, as must surely be the case if you pay no heed to my bidding. You will not be the only Gardingio to whom I write, and if you decide to give no regard to my request, your peers will learn of it, and of the disgrace you have brought upon them.

Weather permitting, Sanct' Germain should present himself to you before the Paschal Feast. He will be traveling with a small escort whose maintenance he will vouchsafe. It is my hope that you will extend your duty to providing him further introduction to those of your fellow-Gardingi who control the roads to the east of you, so that Sanct' Germain may continue his journey unimpeded. To that end, I am sending with this tomus my seal impressed on a writ of passage in the certainty that you and all other Gardingi will honor it in accordance with your vows of fealty.

May God give you good health, good fortune, and good fame. May you deserve and receive the confidence of your peers. May your children all live to hardy old age. May you never face a foe you cannot best. May your loins always be fruitful. May your fields and herds be bountiful. May you be spared the catastrophes of famine, flood, and war. May your women be faithful, chaste, and devoted. May your heirs be worthy of your accomplishments and uphold your dignity. May your name be remembered with awe. May your family be held in high honor from this time until God summons us to Judgment. Amen.

Episcus Luitegild
of Toletum and
the Seat of Sanctissimus Resurrexionem

Written and sealed on the first day of Advent in the 621st year of man's Salvation, in the calendar of Sanct' Iago's reckoning.

1

Darkness, like a malign shepherd, came striding out of the east, storm clouds dogging its heels. All of Toletum huddled down against the sides of the hills as if hiding from the approaching winter night; as the wind picked up a freezing mizzle settled over the city, promising snow before the night was much older. Drafts sniffled and moaned at the door and windows, while a leaching chill prowled the streets with a persistence that made many pray to Heaven to protect them from the insidious cold.

"When do you think this will let up?" asked Rogerian as he laid his hand on the shutters in the library. He looked more concerned than his master did; he was visibly fretting, which was unusual in a man of habitual composure.

"In a day or so, I hope," Sanct' Germain answered absently: he was standing over his athanor, waiting for the hive-shaped oven to cool enough to allow him to open its door. He was dressed in Byzantine fashion in a long-sleeved black silk paragaudion picked out with silver thread over narrow Persian leggings of knitted black wool. A thick-linked silver collar held his eclipse device, the workmanship his own.

"Then our departure will be delayed again," Rogerian said. "I am sorry, my master." He spoke in the Latin of his youth, a tongue that was now six hundred years out of date.

"No matter," Sanct' Germain said in the same archaic language. "The storm is a timely warning. I would just as soon winter here, safely indoors, than out on the road."

"Not that we have not endured worse than storms," said Rogerian with an attempt at humor.

"All the more reason to remain here for a while longer," said Sanct' Germain. "Our earlier experiences have shown us the folly of undertaking unnecessary hardships. And fortunately," he added with a half-smile, "there is no pressing reason for us to leave, at least not yet. We have a few months before claims are made against us, or so the Episcus assures me."

"I am sorry that I insisted we abide here for so long," he said, his voice dropping to a near-whisper. "You tried to warn me, but . . ."

"I hoped you would not be disappointed," Sanct' Germain said, his dark eyes compassionate. "I know that I was when I made a similar attempt, long ago. You must not be surprised that you can find no trace of your descendants."

"Yes." Rogerian nodded his agreement, tugging at the sleeve of his old-fashioned dalmatica; he had augmented its warmth by adding a long tunica of boiled wool; both garments were mulberry-color, appropriate to a man of Rogerian's position. "But winter is here, and that is a danger in itself. Those on the road may have the more obvious hazards, but a town has its own risks. But you seem worried about staying on here."

"So I am." Sanct' Germain said calmly. "And I worry about the traveling, too. For many others than for us." He glanced at the window. "Since it is necessary, I can arrange a delay."

Rogerian looked startled. "With Episcus Luitegild's safe conduct, shouldn't we travel while—"

Sanct' Germain chuckled. "We have no reason to think that he will withdraw his endorsement simply because we do not leave the moment it is handed to us. He is abrupt but not unreasonable. Who knows: waiting awhile before going might surprise the Praetorius enough to delay his claims; he could not declare me a fugitive if we do not leave at once. Episcus Luitegild may not have much power, but he could stop the Praetorius from seizing my property." He studied the athanor a short while. "The Exarch might see it differently, of course."

"You mean he might not accept an introduction delivered so long after it was issued? Do you think he would deny the Episcus the hospitality requested?" Rogerian was apprehensive. "Is there a good reason to suppose—"

"I have no notion," said Sanct' Germain. "But these Exarchs—and there are so many of them these days—tend to claim all manner of rights for themselves by virtue of having a Byzantine title, just as the town leader calls himself a Praetorius, to make it seem he holds his position from the time of the Romans." He paused, his brows flicking together. "You were right, old friend. The longer the Byzantines have been gone from the region, the more of the nobles have claimed that title for themselves, and squabble over territories that overlap, and the townspeople have adhered to the Roman honors."

"But they could return," said Rogerian, his eyes very bright. "The Byzantines, not the Romans, could they not?"

"They might, if it were to their advantage," Sanct' Germain allowed. "But I doubt they have any interest in these barbaric places; they have barbarians enough of their own to contend with, and so long as the ports are safe, they can use their soldiers to better purpose." He considered the possibilities in silence.

Rogerian looked at Sanct' Germain, perplexed. "You have told the Episcus that Constantinople will surely reinforce Hispania if it becomes necessary."

"And I meant it," said Sanct' Germain. "But I did not mean the necessity would be the Episcus'. If Constantinople sees its own influence being compromised, they will tend to instill the respect they demand; at least they have done so in the past. The Episcus might find the aid he desires comes at a ruinous price. It would not be the first time that the rescuers proved to be more unwanted than a foe." He brushed his palms together and walked a short distance away from the athanor. "The Episcus is in an awkward position, having so little official authority in the world. If he has reservations about our remaining here a little longer, I will send him a pair of these new rubies I am making: that should smooth over any difficulties that might arise."

"Can you spare them?" Rogerian was startled at this suggestion. "I supposed you intended them for our travels."

"And so I do. But I will have time to make more, if the weather continues to worsen," Sanct' Germain pointed out. "If we wait until spring, I can amass a tankard of jewels; doubtless they can be put to good use, at least among those men who value jewels over weapons. There are many who would be glad of jewels, and would not mind waiting awhile for them." He managed a slight, ironic smile. "The Episcus would not begrudge us a few weeks for such an exchange."

"True enough," Rogerian said, and went to the fireplace to add another log to the rest. Once the new fuel had lit, he turned back to Sanct' Germain, saying, "I had not thought it would matter so much to me."

"Finding your descendents?" Sanct' Germain inquired. "Why should this surprise you, old friend?"

"I thought I had put that part of my life behind me. When I was made a bondsman and sent to Rome, my family was lost to me, in any case." He shrugged. "After so many years. Why should it trouble me that our name has been forgotten? Since my grandchildren left Gades, it was likely that our family would disperse."

"But you hoped they would not," said Sanct' Germain. "There was certainly no harm in looking."

"It still troubles me," Rogerian said quietly.

"That you have not found them, or that you wanted to look for them?" Sanct' Germain asked, his dark eyes compassionate.

"Some of both," Rogerian answered after a short, thoughtful silence. "I thought I had accepted that they were lost to me; I came back to that again and again, and it troubles me anew each time I grasp it." He shrugged. "Repetition will not change anything." He folded his arms. "I cannot keep from believing that I should not have undertaken this search."

"Because it turned out in ways you did not anticipate?" Sanct' Germain went back to the athanor, a slight frown between his fine brows.

"I suppose so," Rogerian said ruefully. "More foolishness."

"Hardly foolishness," said Sanct' Germain. "Loneliness, more likely." He saw the shock in Rogerian's eyes and knew he was right. "The peril of long life is loneliness."

"So you have said," Rogerian allowed. "And I thought I understood. I did not, not until now." He took a long deep breath. "When did you go searching for your family? You have said little about that." Over the centuries, he had found Sanct' Germain's reluctance to speak of that time of his life puzzling. At first he had not minded, but over time he had become both curious and wary about Sanct' Germain's taciturnity.

Sanct' Germain's single laugh was immeasurably sad. "I had not that luxury for many, many hundreds of years. I was enslaved, and then, when I took vengeance for what was done to us, I had no thought to find my family's descendants, for the few there were had also been made slaves and their names lost, and I was consumed by bitterness and despair. Once I was captured, I was taken far away. By the time I returned to my homeland, thirteen centuries had gone by, and all traces of my people had been lost except as figures of myths. It is nothing like your desire to find your family." He stared into the middle distance.

"Do you regret any of it?" Rogerian knew the answer from Sanct' Germain's demeanor, but needed to hear it spoken.

"Of course. There are many things I would rather now I had not

done. No one lives long without having something to regret." Sanct'
Germain lifted his hands in a philosophical gesture. "But that is what I
believe now, and had I not done those things that I now deplore, would
I have the understanding to regret the actions?" He shook his head. "It
is the storm, I think, and the delay, that fill our minds with such fruitless reflection."

"Fruitless, no doubt," said Rogerian darkly.

"Thought is always of value, and memory, no matter how painful,
can illuminate life. It took me centuries to realize these things, and
centuries more to be convinced they were so, but I am persuaded
now." He touched the athanor gingerly. "Not quite."

Wind screeched in the chimney, blowing smoke back into the
house. Rogerian batted at the air with his arms, coughing; he glowered
at the fireplace as if accusing it of deliberately failing. "Again!" he muttered. He made a gesture of exasperation. "This will not do." Turning
to Sanct' Germain, he said, "I am going to climb onto the roof. I think
the chimney-cap has blown off."

"See you go carefully," said Sanct' Germain, who agreed with this
assessment; that was one Roman invention he was pleased had not
been forgotten. "The roof will be slippery."

"I will take no chances: I have no wish to fall into the grain emporium next to us," said Rogerian, and hurried into the corridor to the
narrow wooden stairs that led to the loft in the rafters and the roof
beyond.

Sanct' Germain stood beside the athanor listening to Rogerian
work. He realized he had not offered Rogerian the consolation he
sought; he stared at his athanor, his thoughts ranging far into his past,
to the centuries alone, and the immensity of loss he had experienced
over the thirty-five hundred years he had walked the earth. Rogerian
deserved better from him, he knew; there was so little he could do to
lessen the self-condemnation his old friend embraced. He was keenly
aware of Rogerian's grief, and knew beyond all doubt that time alone
would mute its fury.

A clatter and scramble overhead announced Rogerian had completed his task; the smoke in the room began to dissipate as the chimney recommenced to draw properly once more. Clambering footsteps
traced Rogerian's progress back across the roof to the trapdoor, and the
sound of him coming down the stairs to the attic. He came directly to

Sanct' Germain's library, his clothes wet and spangled with melting snow. "It was the cap," he said. "It's taken care of."

"So I perceive." Sanct' Germain rubbed his chin with his thumb. "How is the storm?"

"It is growing worse. The wind is as cold as if we were once again in the Celestial Mountains." Although they were far away in the fastness of north-western China, the memory of the autumn a century ago when they had crossed that branch of the Old Silk Road brought back sharp recollections of marrow-chilling bitterness. "Not a good sign, such weather."

"No," said Sanct' Germain slowly, continuing. "If there were no snow in the mountains, I would still try to leave now, but as it is, we must winter over somewhere until the passes are clear, and this is a better place than the villa of a Gardingio we do not know, and who may not be pleased to have strangers under his roof." He sighed once. "So it is probably just as well that we wait here a few months."

"You are not angry?" Rogerian asked, suspicion in every aspect of his demeanor.

"Not at all. In fact, given the severity of the storm, I am grateful; this would have been an unpleasant surprise were we traveling," Sanct' Germain replied with a trace of amusement in his attractive, irregular features. "I have no wish to be abroad in such weather."

Rogerian did not say anything for a long moment, then remarked. "I do not like storms, either." As if this concession was as much as he could offer, he turned, prepared to leave Sanct' Germain to his alchemy. "I shall send a note to the Episcus, to inform him of your postponed departure."

"Thank you," said Sanct' Germain tranquilly. "Inform him also that I will call upon him in a few days, to review my plans."

"Of course, my master," said Rogerian as he withdrew.

By the time Sanct' Germain emerged from his library, the first, feeble glow of sunrise was struggling to disperse the clouds; the library hearth was cold, and the athanor had been emptied of its treasure; the house was cold enough to make him glad of his heavy tunica beneath his dalmatica. Despite his satisfaction with the accomplishments of the night, Sanct' Germain could not rid himself of a vague, persistent unease that had taken hold of him as the storm came on; he had not been able to rid himself of it; he had stayed in Toletum longer than was wise, and might yet regret his delay. As he went along the corridor to his private apartment, Sanct' Germain weighed the pouch he carried in his hand, trying to calculate the value of the stones he had made; five rubies, two opals, two sapphires, and an amethyst, more than enough to pay for the journey into Frankish lands. He had just stepped from his sitting room into his bedchamber when he heard a rap at his door. Slipping the pouch under the clothespress near the foot of his bed, Sanct' Germain went to open the door.

"My master," said Rogerian. "I do not mean to disturb you—" He stopped himself, unable to go on.

"What is it, old friend?" Sanct' Germain asked after Rogerian fell silent. "Is something the matter."

"I need a word with you," he said. "I would rather not wait until you arise in the afternoon."

"All right," said Sanct' Germain, no sign of dismay in his manner. He stepped aside to allow Rogerian to enter. "Tell me what is troubling you."

"I had a most . . . disturbing caller," said Rogerian, and then took a deep breath, delivering his news in a single rush. "Ithidroel came a short while ago, immediately after his morning prayers, to warn me that there was going to be an attempt to seize your house and goods after Mass on Sunday, because you do not attend the holy services. The Praetorius' scribe told him the whole of it. Your apostasy is the excuse they intend to use." He held up his hands before Sanct' Germain could speak. "Ithidroel said that it is not enough that you come to the synagogue to discuss the writings of the Prophets and Patriarchs, for you are not a Jew any more than you are a Roman Christian. The Praetorius is short of money, and you are rich."

Sanct' Germain shook his head; his apprehension now had shape and meaning. "I suppose I must be grateful for that introduction Episcus Luitegild provided, after all; although it was probably one of the Episcus' slaves who passed on my need of the introduction. The Praetorius' intentions are not coincidental, I suspect, with our plans to depart. Praetorius Chindaswinth may not have a Byzantine garrison to protect him any longer, but he is not entirely powerless, either, and his coffers may well be empty. It is not surprising he would think of me, for I am a foreigner and he knows I have gold and property." He fell silent for a brief moment, then spoke as calmly as if he were arranging for feed for his horses. "We will have to move our goods outside the city over the next two days, as unobtrusively as possible. We can explain our need to have the villa well-stocked in case the storm should cut it off from Toletum."

"And if this is forbidden?" Rogerian asked without any significant change in his demeanor.

"I cannot be the only resident of Toletum who has to provide his country house for the winter," said Sanct' Germain calmly. "Everyone who keeps a villa will be doing the same thing; to refuse me would expose the Praetorius' intentions before he can put them in motion. I doubt he would be so foolish. If he wants my property, he will have to justify his seizure or risk having his court rebel."

"Would they do that to support a foreigner," Rogerian wondered aloud.

"It has happened before," Sanct' Germain pointed out. "The Gardingi withdrew their men-at-arms from the city and taxed the Praetorius for it. No, we have a little time, and we must make the most of it."

Rogerian had been with Sanct' Germain long enough that this swift shift in plans did not astonish him. "What do I tell the servants here?"

"Tell them that they will not suffer on my account. I will pay them two years' salary and grant writs of manumission for all slaves as well for when I leave. I want none of them to starve, so I will also provide— through the synagogue—to have money enough to maintain this household for some time to come. I suppose Ithidroel will be able to manage that for me, I will visit him this afternoon and make the arrangements, including a suitable donation to the monastery when I have settled matters with Ithidroel." He strode about the room, stopping beside a red lacquer chest of Roman design where he kept his medicaments. "Choose such items as you know I will need, and prepare the rest for storage. This must come with us. I will attend to the athanor myself." He paused. "A pity I did not have time to make more jewels. These, and the gold I made last week, will have to suffice."

"Then you do not doubt that the Praetorius will act once he is ready?" Rogerian asked.

"Certainly not—if I did, I would expose us both to consequences neither of us wants. And the Jews have the most reliable information about such matters. The Episcus does not concern himself with the

Praetorius' authority; he cannot afford a clash of wills and purposes."
He flung up his hands to show his exasperation. "I should have known
this was coming. I should have realized that as soon as the Episcus issued our introduction, that the Praetoris would be informed and would
demand some price for my departure. Three days to depart—fewer
than I would like, but it is better than no warning. It is my lapse. I
should have been more vigilant."

"The Praetorius is greedy, the Exarch is greedy; they are all greedy,"
said Rogerian, his voice level; only the light in his faded-blue eyes
showed how condemningly he meant this.

"As I knew, and as you reminded me," said Sanct' Germain, dismissing this. "This is not the first time we have ever had to deal with
such a man as Chindaswinth." He looked at Rogerian. "We will need to
get the strongest horses out of the stable, and the best mules. At least
we can move them to the villa without questions being raised."

"I will see to it," said Rogerian.

"Give me time to trim their hooves before taking them out of the
city; if I leave such tasks until we reach the villa, someone will remark
on it." Sanct' Germain pointed to the clothespress in the next room. "I
will need my sturdiest garments, and so will you. Be sure you take
some that are for ordinary wear, or the guards at the gate may report
what we are doing."

"Do you think they will bother with such concerns?" Rogerian did
not wait for an answer; he supplied his own. "We must suppose they
will."

"You comprehend the matter," said Sanct' Germain, approvingly.

"I, too, remember," said Rogerian with a hint of a smile.

Sanct' Germain nodded. "I will rest for an hour and then call upon
Ithidroel. I do not want to be so hasty that the servants remark upon it,
not with our departure near at hand. I would appreciate it if you would
be good enough to let it be known that I am planning to restock the
villa as part of my winter preparations. That should provide a cover for
our true purpose."

"Certainly," said Rogerian. "I will also choose two or three slaves to
accompany us to the villa. That will show that we are not trying to escape."

"We will make more than one trip to the villa and back in the next
two days, so the guards will become used to what we are doing. Go and

return at the same time of day, and they will accept the routine. When you return from the villa this evening—you are planning to go there today, are you not?"

"Yes. I think we might set out at mid-day, when the sun is highest. The storm is not diminishing, but we will have the most light then." Rogerian waited, clearly anticipating the rest of Sanct' Germain's instruction.

"When you come back into the city, take the occasion to complain of repairs needed. You may lament my strict requirements in such circumstances, saying that I will not listen to reason. Tell them that I insist on prompt repairs, and that I am not willing to be satisfied with less than full compliance with my orders. In weather like this, the rectifications must be done quickly or worse damage may ensue." Sanct' Germain was already pulling off his silver collar. As he set this down on a low wooden chest with a pair of Burmese dragons carved on its panels, he pulled the hem of his paragaudion up, tugging the garment over his head and turning it inside out with the same movement; he tossed it aside as he reached for his black linen kalasiris in which he slept. "If I have not risen, wake me in an hour; I cannot afford to lie abed very long, so be accurate in your timing. Use the old water-clock, in the atrium." This relic of the Roman occupation had proven one of the most useful devices in the house; it was one of the things he would miss when he was gone from Toletum.

"An hour; very well," said Rogerian, preparing to leave the room.

"Oh, and Rogerian," Sanct' Germain said, stopping Rogerian in mid-motion. "I will need a gift for Viridia; nothing elaborate, but enough for her to remember me with kindness."

Rogerian considered the matter for a moment. "Would some of the silk do? There are six or seven bolts of it left in the storeroom. It does not promise too much, but few women in Toletum can boost of wearing silk from China."

"An excellent notion. Perhaps we should take a few of the bolts with us. Not of fine cloth, but good, sturdy wool and thick linen. No doubt they would make welcome gifts for our hosts in our travels." He bent to remove his leggings, and when he had put them aside, he added, "Cut them into generous lengths, enough for good-sized garments. They will be more easily carried off the bolt, and we will have more to give, having smaller portions."

"As you wish, my master," said Rogerian.

"You are very good, Rogerian. Thank you." He watched the door close, then went into his bedroom, a chamber of such austerity that it might have been a monk's cell; it contained Sanct' Germain's bed atop three large chests, the clothespress near the foot of the bed, and a stand for books which just now held an unlit lamp and Pliny's *Historia Naturalis*. Sanct' Germain pulled back the black coverlet and lay down on the thin mattress, falling into a sudden and profound sleep, taking restoration from his native earth in the chests below.

When Rogerian rapped on Sanct' Germain's outer door an hour later, he found Sanct' Germain just risen and finishing shaving; clothes fresh from the press were laid out on the low couch in the sitting room. "You should have summoned me," said Rogerian.

"You have more urgent tasks," said Sanct' Germain as he wiped the last of the oily soap from his face with a length of old cotton. "I have shaved myself for many centuries without needing my reflection to guide me."

"Just as well," said Rogerian. "I have taken a bolt of bronze silk from the storeroom; it is in the library. Your gray gelding is saddled and waiting for you in the stable."

"How are the other preparations going?" Sanct' Germain asked as he picked up the horseman's dalmatica of black wool. This Roman garment was more than a century out of fashion but it was of superior quality, and no one would regard it as inappropriate for the foreign alchemist to wear such clothing. "I need my high boots."

Rogerian opened one of the chests against the wall and pulled out a pair of tall Mongol boots lined in goat hair. The heels and soles were thicker than was usual for Mongols, a detail that no one in Toletum would know. "The preparations are going well. I believe we will have two wagons ready to go by mid-day." He handed over the boots without comment.

"Very good," said Sanct' Germain, taking the boots. "I will attend to the horses and mules as soon as I return from my errands." He continued dressing.

"Will that include Viridia?" Rogerian asked without inflection.

"I think so," said Sanct' Germain after a short silence. "I will present her with her gift, and the deed to occupy this house in my absence. Once I have seen her, there will be no way to keep my plans secret; her slaves barter every scrap of news they come by." He gave a wry chuckle then added, "Fortunately Viridia does not allow them to watch her at her pleasure, or I would not be safe with her, no matter how accommodating she may be."

"Will she say anything of that when you have gone?" There was nothing in his question to reveal his own uncertainties.

"With tenancy of this house settled on her, she would be foolish beyond imagining to do anything that would compromise me. She might, if there were advantage in it, but it would mean more danger for her than I think she wishes to bring on herself. If she speaks against me, no man after that would trust her enough to lie with her except by force. It is no easy life to be a woman of her station—better than a common prostitute, but not quite a courtesan. She will be very careful how she deals with all she knows; she has no wish to end up branded and in prison, and there are those who would be glad of a reason to condemn her." Sanct' Germain shook his head. "She is not inclined to play into the hands of the envious. That would be ultimate folly for her."

"Might her slaves decide to sell what they know . . ." Rogerian suggested, leaving the possibilities open.

"If they were trying to gain advantages for themselves at Viridia's cost, they would be more likely to carry tales of her other lovers, men with position and power greater than any I could have here. They are far more vulnerable than I am, having place and reputation to lose. I am an oddity among her patrons, a foreigner with little influence in the city, and so I do not offer the advantages the others can." He fastened the lacings of his boots and straightened up. "I will need my pluvial," he said; the heavy cloak of heavy waxed linen would be necessary for many weeks to come.

"Yes, you will," Rogerian agreed. "It is in the vestibule."

"I will take it as I leave," said Sanct' Germain as he gathered up his belt and pouch and buckled them into place. "How long are you going to need to pack the wagons?"

"For the first trip to the villa?" Rogerian asked. "As I have said, we should be ready to depart by mid-day. When I return, I will spend more time readying your goods for travel."

"I need not have asked," said Sanct' Germain with an apologetic wave of his hand. "I am preoccupied, or I would not have done."

For the first time Rogerian frowned; it was unusual for Sanct' Germain's attention to be distracted. "My master," he ventured. "What is troubling you?"

Sanct' Germain picked up his long Byzantine dagger. "I dislike being pressed," he said curtly as he thrust the dagger through his belt. "Still, it is not the first time, nor will it be the last."

Rogerian had to be content with this observation; Sanct' Germain went out of his private rooms leaving his manservant to begin the task of packing his belongings for travel.

By the time Sanct' Germain reached Viridia's house, afternoon was closing in, the storm-clouds looming overhead, the wind whooping down the narrow streets; the people of Toletum had been driven indoors, so few curious eyes watched as Sanct' Germain was admitted by Viridia's single slave, a middle-aged woman from the north. "Is your mistress busy?" he asked as he removed his pluvial, letting it drip on the rough paving-stones of the entry. He took the large, brightly colored sack from under his arm, preparing to present it as custom required.

"She will be pleased to see you in her private reception room," said the slave, taking care not to look at him directly, or the gift he carried.

"Thank you," Sanct' Germain said as he handed her a silver coin. He climbed the narrow stairs quickly, and stepped into the central hall of the house. The private reception room was on the left; he paused before entering the room.

Viridia sat on an upholstered bench near the fireplace; she was dressed in Byzantine splendor; her dalmatica of mulberry silk and fine woollen palla were heavily embroidered with gold thread, and her elaborate gold earrings—gifts from Sanct' Germain—set off her lovely face and russet hair. She had been waiting for him, and now she smiled, extending her arms to him without rising. "I did not know whether or not you would come," she said, chiding him gently.

"Nor did I," he responded with more candor than she had expected. "The Praetorius is making matters difficult for me just now."

"I had heard something of that," she said, still waiting for him to approach her.

Finally Sanct' Germain went to her, and made a proper presentation of the sack. "I regret only that this is not sufficiently fine for you," he said, as good manners required.

"I am sure you honor me too much," she said, equally formulaically.

"I am humbled by your high opinion." Taking the sack, she opened it, and for the first time her smile was wholly genuine. "Oh, *oh,* Sanct' Germain, it's beautiful. Where did you ever get such silk?" she exclaimed as she ran her hands over it. "Let me look at it," she went on before he could answer.

"I brought it from the other side of the world," he said, recalling his long journey on the Old Silk Road.

She laughed as she spread out the shining fabric, measuring it with care. "There are lengths and *lengths* of it," she approved as she caressed the silk as she spread it out around her. "Oh, thank you, thank you, thank you." Wrapping herself in the fabric, she flung herself into his arms. "This is wonderful. *Wonderful.*" She kissed his chin. "How did you know to bring me this?"

"You have said you like silk," he said indulgently.

"Well, yes; who does not?" She slipped away from him, almost dancing. "I will have the most *beautiful* dalmatica made from it. I have fifteen gold coins that can be sewn into a tablion for it. That would be magnificent."

"I am pleased you are satisfied with my gift," he said, making her a reverence.

"I am *delighted,*" she told him as she came back to his side. "You make me sad that you are leaving."

Sanct' Germain shrugged. "I am not wholly jubilant about it, either," he said, his eyes enigmatic. "But it would not be wise for me to remain. It would be dangerous for you, as well."

"The Praetorius is not interested in women like me," she said, dismissing his concern. "If I sold myself in the marketplace, he might imprison me, but I am discreet, I have only a few lovers and I see them here. What danger is there in that?"

"There could be, if the Praetorius believed you were . . ." His voice trailed off as he watched Viridia gather up the silk he had given her, put it into a chest against the wall, and then begin to remove her palla. "The Praetorius is not the only danger you face."

She let the palla drift to the floor. "If you mean the Episcus, I do not fear him."

"No," he said as she slowly shrugged out of her dalmatica, letting it puddle around her feet in a shimmering mass; now all she wore were her felt house-shoes and her earrings. "I mean that I can be dangerous to you, that even if I were not leaving this place, it would not be wise for me to continue to . . . visit you."

"What nonsense you talk," she said as she stepped out of the pool of silk and came toward him. "You have done nothing to hurt me. You do not beat me. You do not tup me. Where is the danger?" As she reached him, she put her arms up to his shoulders and leaned against him. "I'm cold, Sanct' Germain. You must warm me." She glanced toward the curtained alcove where her bed was.

"This will be the fifth time we lie together. It is the last time, Viridia," he said gently. "More than six times, and you would have much to fear." His kiss was light and persuasive at once and it stirred her need as well as his own. Their second kiss was longer, more involved, and it left Viridia breathless.

"Come," she urged him. "I am eager for you."

"But not too eager to savor this time together," he said as he lifted her into his arms and carried her toward the alcove.

She held onto him, a little breathless in anticipation. "I wish you did not have to leave," she said as she nuzzled his neck.

"I would have had to, eventually," he said softly, an expression in his eyes that was unlike anything she had ever seen before: longing and loneliness and compassion, and something more than all three—a kind of endurance that baffled her.

"Will you miss me when you are gone?" She asked it lightly enough, but there was apprehension in her voice that her flirtatiousness could not disguise.

He stopped still and looked down into her face. "Yes. I will."

She snuggled closer to him, taking comfort in his surprising strength. "Then I will not be too angry with you for leaving."

"Thank all the forgotten gods for that," he said, and kissed her brow as he resumed walking. As he carried her beyond the curtain into the alcove, he felt her shiver. "Are you still cold?"

"A little," she admitted as he put her down on the heap of wool-lined silk blankets that were strewn across the raised platform which two banded chests supported. She reached out for him. "I will be warmer in a little while."

He sank down beside her pulling one of the blankets around her so that she was wrapped snugly in it. "Your cocoon," he said. "You are about to emerge as a butterfly." His smile was intriguing, and it roused her appetite.

"All because of you," she said, and drew his head near so that she could kiss him. "When you kiss me, that is all you do. The world might well vanish and be gone. You think of nothing but me, and the kiss," she marveled as she released him, beaming with delectation.

"What would be the point of kissing you if I did not pay attention?" he asked, almost playfully, as he began to explore her body, starting at her feet; he removed her felt shoes, tossing them away as he took one foot in his hand, stroking the arch with a firmly gentle touch. "You have such pretty feet."

"Do you really think so?" She stretched the other, flexing the arch. "They say if a woman's feet are too big, she will always stray."

He laughed quietly. "It is not the feet that stray, it is the heart, and the soul." There was no condemnation in his tone, only a kindly resignation that made her wonder briefly how he came to believe that. Then she stopped all contemplation and gave herself over to the enjoyment of all the sublime sensations he awakened in her, to the passion that she did not often experience with her other lovers. He moved gradually up her body, finding the secrets of her legs and thighs, and then the center of her flesh. He was elating and he was patient; nothing he did—no touch, no kiss, no caress—hurried her or seemed intended to force her response. His mouth was as inciting as his hands, and she succumbed to the luxury of his touch, from the stroke of his finger on her breast to the numberless kisses he bestowed all over her, now tantalizing, now tender.

Her ardor consumed every part of her, thrilling her to her core. Everything that Sanct' Germain did—every kiss, every caress—summoned her most intimate rapture, and as she felt herself carried to the culmination of her exultant delirium, she clasped Sanct' Germain more closely, holding his head to the curve of her neck; there was a moment of keenest ecstasy that made her tremble with fulfillment as she succumbed to rapture. When she came back to herself, she held Sanct' Germain tightly, wanting to hang onto the ephemeral elation she had felt, but as cold needled her skin, the last of her bliss faded. Finally she released him, once again wrapping herself in the blanket. "Almost a butterfly," she said at last.

Sanct' Germain met her gaze steadily. "Surely, for an instant, a butterfly."

Viridia sighed, "I want to think so," she said, and blinked as he rose from her side. "I hate to see you go."

"I fear I must," he told her, bending down to kiss the corner of her mouth one last time, aware of her nearness with all the poignancy of loss.

She caught his hand before he could turn away. "Sanct' Germain, what is it you long for?"

"Something those of my blood may never have," he replied, the kindness in his voice making her want to weep.

"What is it?" She held his hand more tightly. "Tell me. *Tell* me."

He shook his head very slightly. "It would not be wise for you to know."

"You mean it could be dangerous to you?" she asked, hoping to provoke him into answering her.

"No, Viridia," he said calmly. "It would be dangerous to you."

"Oh!" she exclaimed, releasing him. *"Oh!"* She refused to look at him so that she would not have to see him go.

Text of a letter from Ithidroel ben Matthias to Episcus Luitegild of Toletum.

To the most respected Episcus Luitegild, the greetings of Ithidroel ben Matthias, spice merchant of Toletum.

In accordance with the instructions of Franciscus Sanct' Germain, I am sending to you the sum of fifteen gold Apostles as his donation to your good works in the city, and your continuing protection of his former slaves, whose writs of manumission you and I both witnessed. It is the intention of Sanct' Germain to continue his donations annually until he himself, or one of his descendants, shall return to claim his holdings. I have among the instructions Sanct' Germain has given me the conditions of identification that must be met when and if one of his blood comes to claim his estate. I or my successors will be responsible for verifying the identity of anyone attempting to establish himself as Sanct' Germain's heir. This sum may not be taxed even though it is held and administered by Jews.

I commend you for your intercession with the Praetorius. Without your timely arbitration all of Sanct' Germain holdings within the city walls would now be in the hands of the Praetorius and the fighting men who surround him. Your efforts have been noted by all who live here and are praised everywhere; you found an authority in your position that the Praetorius had to honor. Had you not succeeded, I would have been powerless to protect Sanct' Germain's holdings no matter how persuasive my position might be, for I would not have had the additional jurisdictional influence you bear by right of your position within the Church. The devotion of the Praetorius Chindaswinth to your faith has at least been of benefit to more than himself or his court. It is to your credit that you have been willing to extend yourself to the benefit of someone who is not of your flock.

Those of Sanct' Germain's servants who are continuing to care for his house and villa are now protected from any claims against their master. You will have no reason to fear that you might have to provide for them from the donations Sanct' Germain has made to your Church. I have just received the necessary signatures on the deeds that ensure their position and their livelihood. Since money is not an object in this instance, the servants will not have to worry that their situation might be suddenly changed on account of debt. I am pleased to see how beforehand Sanct' Germain has been in his planning. This speaks well of him, on that you and I can agree, I am certain.

In that Sanct' Germain has granted lifetime residence to Viridia, a high-ranking whore of the city, you and I may deplore his decision, but it is as binding as any of his other donations, and to question his generosity would result in all his gifts being diminished; this is provided in the terms of the grant he has left in my keeping. He has stated that she has been good to him, and as such, deserves a sign of his friendship. As I have no desire to deprive my people of the beneficence of this foreigner, I will not endanger the good he is doing by questioning this one lapse in judgment, for that way lies many losses. So I will see that his wishes are carried out in regard to this woman and I will advise you to acquiesce in this, or face the prospect of having your donations cut in half, a result you cannot want.

I have taken the liberty, which has been granted to me by Sanct' Germain, to make a contribution toward the repair of the Roman Gate and the public cistern. This will not diminish the donation made to your Church, but it may decrease the money to be given to the beggars of the city, at least for this year. I judged that water and protection were more urgent needs of Toletum than tending to those who beg; there are other places charity can be found than from Sanct' Germain's purse. I do not mean that you should carry the burden wholly, only that I am convinced that it is appropriate to put the welfare of the city ahead of the welfare of its beggars. If I have failed to do as Sanct' Germain would have done, I will tender him an apology upon his return, and I ask you to record this letter in the archives of your seat, Sanctissimus Resurrexionem, so that his heirs might have the opportunity to read it, should the title to his holdings pass to them before he himself returns.

May the God whom we both adore guide and protect you, your wife, and your children. May you suffer no ills of the world. May you never know the sting of ingratitude nor the pangs of doubt. May you always be worthy of your high office, and may God prepare a place for you in His Sight.

Ithidroel ben Matthis
Merchant and teacher

the Red House, Roman Hill, Toletum, ten days after Christian Epiphany, in the Christian year 622

2

Sunset lay behind them, reddened by the wind that chafed the plateau which rose from the eastern bank of the Iberus toward the mountains that were little more than a jagged line beneath the ominous clouds gathering ahead. A few stands of tattered oaks provided the only shelter from the wind, but the road ran straight between them, leading toward the old Roman town of Aeso and its grand estate, Aqua Alba in Iberus. Behind them on the western bank of the river sprawled Caesaraugusta, a Roman town around a ferry crossing that was the merchants' gateway to the central Iberian Peninsula: Sanct' Germain and his escort had passed three days there before the weather improved sufficiently to allow them to travel.

"How much longer?" Rogerian had to yell although he rode only an arm's-length from Sanct' Germain.

"I don't know. We will need shelter soon. The wind is getting worse; it is almost dark." He squinted at the five out-riders who led the train of mules and provided protection for them. "I think Wamba is ill. I have watched him and he is pale and sweating," he remarked as he gave his attention to Rogerian once again. "Either he is ill, or he is carrying a skin of wine instead of water."

"Wamba is given to drink, as we saw in Caesaraugusta," Rogerian agreed, struggling to hold his Mongolian mantel around him, the wool side turned in, to keep him warm. "I do not entirely trust him."

"I do not trust any of them, old friend." Sanct' Germain wore a hooded Roman paenula of black Persian lamb over a Byzantine paragaudion of heavy-strand embroidered black silk that had weathered far worse conditions than these; his leggings were knit lambswool and his Mongol boots came almost to his knees. "But they are eager for gold, so I am willing to believe they will do no ill while we are on the old roads. Once we go into the mountains, I am not certain we will continue to be safe in their company."

"The Exarch at Caesaraugusta said that there is a monastery on this road that will take in travelers for a donation," Rogerian reminded him, holding the lead of the mule behind him with force; the animal had been trying to lag behind for some time. "The escort resents having to travel at night." He had not intended this observation to be a warning, but as he spoke, he felt a niggle of apprehension come over him.

"I know," said Sanct' Germain. "They are afraid of demons."

"Demons," echoed Rogerian, and cracked a single laugh as he tugged on the lead once again. "Wolves, more likely. At this time of year, there could be packs about."

"These men are not shepherds, or goatherds, to be afraid of wolves," said Sanct' Germain, but wondered if Rogerian might be right.

"If there is a howling," Rogerian began, leaving Sanct' Germain to finish his thought.

"It is the wind," said Sanct' Germain. "Once we get into the mountains, then there may be wolves, but out here, on this plateau, the winter is not hard enough for wolves to come so far out into the open." It had been more than three centuries since he had seen wolves running loose in the open in winter; the memory was not a comfortable one.

They went on for another two or three thousand paces, and then Childric, who rode in the van of the party, held up his hand. Swinging around in his saddle, he shouted, "Building ahead! An old outpost by the look of it!"

"Any sign of occupants?" Sanct' Germain called back.

"Nothing!" Childric answered in his blunt way. "We're tired! The beasts are hungry!"

"Time to stop!" Wamba joined in.

"Is the outpost safe?" Egica asked, his voice rough from shouting. He swung around in the saddle, hanging on to keep his seat.

"Why should it not be safe? What is there to fear?" asked Recared, his voice pitched a bit too high.

"I need food and drink," shouted Egica, and ended his demand with a harsh cough. "If the place is safe, why not—"

"If the outpost is deserted, there is no point in stopping," said Sanct' Germain at his most reasonable. "Let us press on; the monastery is not more than two thousand paces ahead."

Childric glowered and put his hand on his sword. "I say we stop."

"And I say we go on." This came from Leovigild, the sartrium for the escorts. "The patron is right. The outpost will give shelter but very little else." He was older than the others—over thirty—grizzled, scarred and proven: he commanded them with the ease of long experience. "Two thousand paces, even in this wind, is not so far."

"We should see the monastery," Recared exclaimed. "Where is it, if it is only two thousand paces ahead?" He was one of three men other than Rogerian who held leads in their hands, and guided a short string of mules with them.

"Probably in that stand of oaks," said Sanct' Germain, taking care not to challenge the men by this observation; they were touchy of their reputations and could find any questioning of their competence an insufferable slight. He shifted in the saddle, renewing his grip with his calves, and pointed ahead. "It is about two thousand paces to that grove of trees."

The men grudgingly accepted this. "As far as the trees, then," said Childric. "If we find nothing there, we will come back here and make camp for the night. I don't want to have to fight any of the people hereabouts. They're not fond of us. They are treacherous fighters, given to ambushes and traps. And with all these laden mules, we'd be singled out for a fight."

"They weren't fond of the Romans, either," said Sanct' Germain, recalling the many accounts he had heard from Legion officers of battles with the various tribes of Hispania. "Nor of one another."

"Then we will find shelter for the night," Wamba said, glancing back at the fading light. "We haven't much longer until it is full dark."

"Shouldn't the monastery have a travelers' light?" asked Egica. He, too, held a lead. "I can't see one."

"Let us keep moving," Leovigild said, urging his horse to a jog-trot. "It won't take long to reach the trees if we don't dawdle. Wamba. Sit up, man. And keep a grip on the lead. The mules could get away."

Wamba righted himself, gathering up his mount's reins and doing his best to look prepared for a long ride. "I am not myself, sartrium."

"All the more reason to be alert," said Leovigild, and brought his horse alongside Wamba's. "This will be over soon."

Childric grumbled, but fell in just ahead of Sanct' Germain. "I can't see very much," he warned. "If there is no travelers' light . . ."

Sanct' Germain waited a moment, then said, "I see fairly well in the dark; those of my blood have such talent." In fact, he saw almost as well at night as he did in the day, but he knew such an admission would bring suspicion upon him. "I can make out the road, and if there is a travelers' light, I will not miss it."

"If you say so," said Leovigild, apparently reserving judgment. "Keep a keen watch, then. It is going to rain tonight, or snow."

"Yes, it is," said Sanct' Germain. "And the wind will get keener."

Leovigild pulled his mantel more tightly around him. "In the morning, we will need pluvials." This was a concession, for it was rare for any man-at-arms would admit that any man not a soldier could reckon such things; not even peasants were thought to know anything about weather.

Rogerian pulled on the lead again. "The mules are getting restive."

"They are taking it from our escort," said Sanct' Germain, and once more looked toward the trees. "There!" he said. "A travelers' light."

Leovigild checked his horse. "Where?"

"Just there," said Sanct' Germain. "It's deep in the trees and not easily seen, but—there it is again." He pointed, and hoped that Leovigild's eyes were able to make it out.

"A flash," Leovigild conceded. "Are you certain?"

"Yes," said Sanct' Germain. "No peasant puts a lamp on the roof."

"True enough." Leovigild hesitated. "Might it be a trap? Wouldn't robbers try such a ruse?"

"Perhaps, but I doubt it, not on a main road, and not at this time of year." He looked about at the others. "If there are robbers, we are armed, and they would be fools to attack us."

The men gave half-hearted agreement, and Rogerian made a warning signal to Sanct' Germain.

"There has been fighting in the mountains, they say," Wamba muttered.

Sanct' Germain shook his head. "If you have to fight anyone tonight, I will pay three Byzantine Emperors to each of you, beyond the fee we have agreed upon. My Word on it."

Childric grinned, the wind whipping his hair about his face as if he were one of the ancient storm gods; he drew his sword from its scabbard. "Well and good. Let us be about it, then." He tightened his seat on his horse and picked up the pace to a fast trot. This gained the attention of all the men-at-arms and they, too, readied themselves for a skirmish.

"No faster!" shouted Leovigild. "Think of your horses. No faster! If your horse goes down, you ride a mule!"

This disgraceful prospect curbed the men to a jog-trot once more, and the mules on leads did their best to slow the pace to a walk.

"We will be there soon enough," said Childric, still showing his enthusiasm for battle by waving his sword. "Any robbers would be wise to flee while they may."

"Do not distress the monks!" Sanct' Germain ordered. "They will refuse you shelter if you do." He had the satisfaction of seeing Leovigild nod in approval. "You want hot food and a bed tonight, do you not?" Without waiting for an answer, he went on. "If you ride in like the robbers you are ready to fight, will the monks not turn you away?"

Childric said nothing, but drew his horse down to a fast walk. "You may be right. Monks are as easily frightened as women."

Egica patted his sword. "If I need it, I can draw it," he said, paying little or no heed to the sharp look Childric shot him.

In the wake of sunset the sky was dulling in the west as night closed in; the travelers' light was now more readily seen against the darkness.

"Should someone ride ahead?" Leovigild asked after they had gone on a bit further. "The turn-off is not far, and it might be wise, there being so many of us, to alert the monks before we arrive."

"A prudent notion," said Sanct' Germain, and gave his attention to Rogerian. "Will you do that for me, old friend? Will you ride ahead? I'll take the lead you hold."

Rogerian nodded once. "Of course I will," he said, holding out the lead to Sanct' Germain. "I will not race, but I will go as quickly as this horse can trot as long as the road is smooth." He tightened his hold on the horse's body and wiggled his heels against the animal's sides; in response the gelding extended his trot, quickly pushing to the front of the group, then pulling ahead of the rest; Rogerian's garments flapped around him like winged shadows. The sound of the hoofbeats carried back to the others even as Rogerian and his bay horse became indistinct in the gathering night.

"Watch where he goes," Sanct' Germain said. "He is showing us the way."

"If the monks will admit us, then well and good," said Egica gloomily.

"They dare not refuse," said Childric. "We are their champions." He put his hand on his sword again, as if to assure himself he could pull it from the scabbard at the first whiff of trouble.

The men-at-arms were growing more restive; the mules, laden as they were with crates, chests, bags, and sacks, grew fretful at having to keep up this pace. One brayed in protest and was struck across the nose with a whip.

"Don't do that," said Sanct' Germain quietly, but with authority that stilled Recared's hand as he prepared to lash out again.

"The animal is impertinent," said Recared. "He must be submissive to—"

"If he is to be struck, I will do it," said Sanct' Germain levelly. "But I have heard far worse from you and your companions than I have from that mule, and no one has wanted to whip you."

"If you want disobedient animals, what is it to me?" Recared asked the air, lowering his whip. "He is your mule."

"That he is," said Sanct' Germain, thinking of how many mules he had left behind at his villa just outside Toletum. He had sustained many losses over his long, long life, but each loss had a poignance of its own, and the mules and horses he had been forced to leave were no exception.

"The turn's coming up," said Leovigild, this observation more convincing to the men-at-arms coming from him than from Sanct' Germain. "There look to be ruts on the side-road."

"Then we will have to walk the beasts," said Childric, sighing with disgust. "If it starts to rain, I will curse Heaven for it, and the monks will not stop me."

Sanct' Germain kept a steady hand on the lead as he pulled his handsome Lusitanian gray onto the road to the monastery; he listened to the wind in the trees and had a long moment of discomfiture as he imagined what he and these men would do if they had to fight on the churned-up road in the middle of the grove. He tried not to be uneasy, though the speculation was worrisome; he reminded himself that this was Hispania and not the Greek mountains, that no enemy forces waited ahead. Taking a firmer hold on the lead, he tugged the mules secured to it to keep them from balking altogether. "Keep moving," he called out, as much to the mules as to the men-at-arms as he pressed on.

As they reached the first of the trees, there was a sudden flare of light ahead of them as the monastery doors were flung open, and half a dozen monks surged toward them. Two of the horses whinnied in dismay, and one of the mules almost sat down like a dog in an attempt to halt.

"All is well," cried out Rogerian. "Hold your hands!"

"Weapons down!" Sanct' Germain ordered. "You are in no danger here." He urged his horse to the front of the group, the mules for once responding to the pull on the lead with alacrity, sensing the end of the day's journey; their jarring trot shook the burdens strapped to their saddles noisily adding to the milling confusion.

The monk in the lead stopped still. "When your weapons are sheathed, you may come in." His voice was that of a man used to command, and he stood as straight as any captain would. "These Fraters will see to your animals. You must dismount before you enter our monastery."

Childric glowered but slid out of his saddle. "I'll lead my own horse, thank you. Fraters," he muttered as he dragged his red-roan's reins over her head. "Tell me where your stable is."

"Frater Roderic will show you the way," said the senior monk, and motioned to one of the others to tend to this task. "Lead one of the strings of mules, Frater Roderic," he added before he came up to Sanct' Germain. "You were wise to send your manservant ahead to us. Now that night is fallen, we would not have opened our gates to you."

"A monk refusing to shelter the stranger or feed the hungry?" Sanct' Germain said with mild surprise. "What would your Episcus say?"

"He would commend us, since four monasteries on this side of the Iberus have been sacked since winter began." He stepped aside as one of his monks went past leading a string of three mules.

"Then why shine the travelers' light?" Sanct' Germain asked in a carefully respectful tone.

"It is part of our Rule." He ducked his head. "I am Primor Ioanus."

"I am Franciscus Sanct' Germain of Ragoczy," he said, using everything but the two titles he could claim in this part of the world. "My journey began at Toletum," he went on, thinking that this was hardly the truth, but it would do for now. Then he was dismounting and preparing to lead his horse and mules within the monastery's gates. "I thank you for admitting us."

"Your manservant is a most convincing fellow," said Primor Ioanus. He turned toward the open gates as his Fraters secured horses and mules. "If you will go along to the stables, I will send word to the kitchen to prepare meat and bread for you." He cocked his head. "You are fortunate: we slaughtered two goats yesterday."

"For which we give thanks," said Sanct' Germain. "I ask only that you feed my men-at-arms; I have provision for myself." This was also not the truth but he knew the Primor would accept it without reservation.

The monastery was built around an open court, with the monks' dormitories on the north, the hostel dormitories on the south, the chapel to the east, and the kitchen and stables on the west side. A small, low building adjacent to the kitchen Sanct' Germain took to be the refectory, for there was the unmistakable chimney of a bake-house at the far end of it.

"I will see it is done." He motioned to the monks to hurry. "There are only three other travelers within our walls tonight, and one of them is suffering from blackened feet." He crossed himself.

Sanct' Germain stopped still. "How severe is the blackening?"

"It is bad enough that the man has no feeling in them. He has put himself in God's hands." Primor Ioanus shrugged. "We are praying for him and keeping him abed, not that he can rise unaided."

"How long has he been here?" Sanct' Germain asked, aware that once feet blackened and lost feeling the whole body was at risk.

"Four days. When he came, he said robbers had taken his boots as well as his donkey and goods. He was cold to touch, but claimed to be warm except in his feet." He pointed to the stable at the far end of the long, rectangular court. "There are many empty stalls, and hay in the loft for the animals."

"Very good," said Sanct' Germain, and led his horse and mules in that direction. He had almost reached the stable when Rogerian caught up with him. "You have done well for us, old friend."

Rogerian waved his hand in dismissal. "It is going to be a hard night. The weather makes demands of all of us. None of us wanted to be in the open, not with rain and cold coming on the wind." He lowered his voice. "There are between forty and fifty monks here, and room for as many travelers."

"The Primor says that they have few guests tonight, and that one has blackened feet," Sanct' Germain remarked as he stepped inside the stable, and glanced at the long rows of stalls on either side of the central aisle; Childric had already claimed the stalls across the way and was busying himself with giving his horse a quick grooming.

"Yes, so I understand," said Rogerian.

Sanct' Germain halted. "But you doubt this," he said, having caught a note of disbelief in Rogerian's tone.

"Yes, I do," said Rogerian. "I know what the monks are saying, and they are frightened. Why should blackened feet frighten them?"

"Some say the Devil causes blackened feet," Sanct' Germain reminded Rogerian; he started moving again, pulling his horse and mules with him. "A few steps more and you will rest," he said as he coaxed the animals along.

"Primor Ioanus has made this his fiefdom, or I know nothing about it," Rogerian added quietly.

"So I think," Sanct' Germain agreed. "He may be a younger son, or a bastard." He considered the matter. "A younger son, I presume from his manner. Or a stepson. Yes," he went on, thinking aloud, "a stepson, raised with all the trappings of power but with no way to gain it for himself: except here."

Two monks had come into the stable, each with horses and mules in tow. Rogerian indicated a row of empty stalls. "These should do," he recommended. "We will look after them."

"As well we should," said Sanct' Germain, and gave the mules' lead to Rogerian, then pulled his gray into the nearest of the stalls. "I'll tend to the packs as soon as I am finished with my horse."

"I'll secure their halters," said Rogerian, and went about his self-appointed task with the ease of long experience.

By the time Sanct' Germain set about removing the pack-saddles and their loads from the mules, the monks had left the stable; Childric had gone before the monks, and now only Sanct' Germain and Rogerian remained to tend to the animals and what they carried. Two small oil lamps provided a faint, luminous glow to the center aisle but did little to mitigate the gloom beyond.

"Bring me that barrel," Sanct' Germain said as he struggled to unfasten the breastplate on the tallest mule. "I need somewhere to rest this that will not break the saddle-tree." He had removed his paenula, leaving it hung on the end of the gatepost that closed the stable in for the night; if the cold bothered him, he did not show it.

Rogerian hastened to obey, rolling the barrel close to the stall and securing it with an old paving stone so that it would not rotate once the packed saddle was set upon it. "It is ready," he said.

"Let us hope no one is watching," said Sanct' Germain as he lifted the laden saddle in his arms and carried it to the barrel. "I would be hard-pressed to explain why I am able to—"

"The Primor is coming," Rogerian interrupted him.

"Just in time," said Sanct' Germain; he settled the pack-saddle atop the barrel and went to gather an armload of hay for the mule. He lowered his head in a sign of respect as the Primor came down the central aisle toward him. "Thank you again, Primor, for letting us stay here for the night, for giving my escort a bed, and for providing for my animals."

"It is as God commands us," said the Primor, not quite able to conceal his satisfaction at this expression of gratitude.

"I will shortly finish with feeding the mules. The horses are already attended to—brushed, watered, and fed—and the mules will be shortly."

"Do you actually brush your mules?" Primor Ioanus exclaimed.

"Yes. I do not want them hindered by the saddles riding badly on their coats." He went to the mound of hay that had been forked down from the loft, gathered an armload of it, and went back to the mule in the stall. "Here you are," he said to the animal as he put the hay in the long trough that served as a manger.

Primor Ioanus watched with mild astonishment, shaking his head in disbelief. "You do this yourself when you have a servant to attend to it."

"My servant manages the tack, I care for the animals," said Sanct' Germain as if this were the most ordinary arrangement in the world. "This way if my horses or mules come to grief, I have only myself to blame."

"Ah," said Primor Ioanus in comprehension. "You do not trust anyone but yourself. In that case, I can understand why you might decide to do these things." He sighed. "Would that others were as vigilant."

Knowing it was expected of him, Sanct' Germain asked, "Why do you say that?"

"Oh," Primor Ioanus said in an off-handed way, "that there are unscrupulous men who prey on travelers, pretending to provide aid and actually preparing the unsuspecting man for disaster. They are active in many places in the mountains, where the steep valleys and deep forests give them protection. They are cruel to their victims. We see many such at this place, men who have been robbed, often beaten, and left to live or die as God pleases."

Curious to know where this was leading, Sanct' Germain responded, "My manservant and I are no strangers to the hazards of travel, but I am obliged for the timely warning."

"A man abroad with as many goods as you carry would be well-advised to exercise care in all you do: robbers long for the opportunity you provide. You have men-at-arms, but they are not always proof against the bandits. There may be other means to guard what you carry." He put his hands together in silent prayer. "If it is not overbold of me, may I recommend another precaution to you?"

"I would welcome it," said Sanct' Germain as he picked up the stiff brush and began to go over the mule's coat.

"I am half-brother to Gardingio Witteric, whose estates are east of here. If you would avoid the perils of the road, may I recommend you go to him and ask for hospitality until the thaw? You might find the road too hard if you try to get through the mountain passes." He indicated the mules. "These are fine animals, but even they would not be proof against the cold. My half-brother is a most worthy man; his donations have supported this monastery for many years."

Sanct' Germain studied the Primor for a long moment, then said, "I had thought to pass the winter with the Gardingio Theudis, although that may not be possible now. I have an introduction to him from Episcus Luitegild of Toletum." He watched to see what response this information would evoke.

"Aqua Alba in Iberus," said Primor Ioanus, nodding. "A most worthy man, but one much burdened by a visitation of the Great Pox. He is receiving no travelers until the miasma has lifted from Aqua Alba."

"The Great Pox," Sanct' Germain said studiously. "I had not heard that it was abroad."

"The Exarchs have decided not to bruit it about, for fear of making the Pox worse." He crossed himself, and waited until Sanct' Germain put down his brush long enough to do the same. "One who has traveled as much as you must have seen how speaking of Pox brings it upon the people. I should not have spoken of it had you not said you were bound for Gardingio Theudis' estates. I will pray tonight that God will forgive my lapse and spare my monks."

"I thank you for the warning," said Sanct' Germain, his expression grave, for he had seen what the Great Pox could do more times than he liked to remember; he had also seen the cruel scars it left behind on those fortunate enough to recover from it. "I will consider what you have told me," he assured Primor Ioanus, resuming his brushing of the mule. "Are my men-at-arms being fed?"

"Yes. We have bread and baked cheese and a bean-and-rabbit stew. It will warm them and give them strength against the cold." He coughed gently. "It will be a hard night."

"All the more reason for me to care of my animals," said Sanct' Germain, going into the next stall to start brushing another mule.

"You will be hungry," said Primor Ioanus.

"I will bear it as well as I am able," Sanct' Germain said philosophically. He was ironically amused at his predicament, for he would find nothing to sustain him in this community of monks. "Tell me more about your half-brother." He hoped his prompting was not too obvious.

"He is a man of substance, highly regarded by all who know him," said Primor Ioanus, his family pride tinged with envy. "He is a stalwart man, known for his strength. He maintains a suitable court; not so grand as some, but good enough to do him honor. He keeps a household of forty fighting men, and controls more than two hundred peasants. His estate is in the mountains, so he has not gained the fame that some have, but the holding is a Roman one, fortified, and it has served him well."

Sanct' Germain heard him out as he worked, thinking that this Gardingio was probably a bully given to exploiting his dependents and abusing his inferiors, as most of his kind were inclined to do; with a fortified villa, he could live in safety while he preyed on the countryside he controlled. But, he asked himself, were any of the others much better? and knew the answer better than he liked. He paused in his brushing as he reached the mule's flank. "If the other Gardingi are worried about travelers, why should I suppose your half-brother would receive me and my escort?"

"A discerning question," said the Primor, not quite smiling. "You would have to rely upon my powers of persuasion in the letter I am willing to write for you, and the honor of our family." He waited a short while, then said mildly. "You need not decide yet. You will be kept here for at least one full day. Tell me if you want my aid before sunset tomorrow, after you have had time to rest and pray." Without waiting for Sanct' Germain's reaction, he blessed the stable before he turned and left it.

The monastery was almost silent by the time Sanct' Germain left the stable; freezing rain was pelting down through the trees, driven by a demented wind. As he closed the stable door and put the bolt in place, Sanct' Germain had the uneasy sensation he was being watched. He had pulled his paenula around his shoulders and was puzzling out where he should go when Rogerian came out of the travelers' dormitory, an oil lamp shielded by his hand.

"My master?" he said quietly.

"Have they all gone to their beds?" Sanct' Germain inquired. He moved into the small overhang of the doorway. "Wretched weather."

"That it is," Rogerian agreed. "And likely to get worse."

Sanct' Germain nodded. "Did the monks say anything about the Great Pox? The Primor told me it has broken out in the mountains ahead of us."

"Nothing," said Rogerian, but there was a hesitation to his answer that kept Sanct' Germain silent while Rogerian considered the question. "One of the monks did say it was more dangerous to travel than we knew. The others hushed him at once."

"They're afraid to speak about disease." He sighed, thinking how far the western world had slid in the last three centuries; had there been a report of an outbreak of Great Pox in the ninth century of the City, the Romans would have instituted a quarantine, offered prayers to the gods, and sent physicians from the Legions to survey the problem. But that was four hundred years ago, and those times were gone.

"The Great Pox is terrifying; you cannot blame them for being afraid," Rogerian observed. "If it has broken out, that would explain why the hostel is nearly empty. The weather cannot be the entire cause, nor the bandits in the mountains." He looked toward the monks' dormitory across the courtyard, his faded-blue eyes narrowing. "I will try to learn more, come morning."

"Very good," said Sanct' Germain. "In the meantime, where shall I rest?"

"I have set up two chests of your native earth in the last cell on the second corridor. I doubt the men-at-arms will venture there." Rogerian muttered a curse as the wind blew the little flame of the oil lamp out. "We had best get within," he advised.

Sanct' Germain made a sign of agreement, but did not move. "Rogerian," he said in the tongue of his long-vanished people, "have you noticed anyone watching us?"

"Do you mean as the monks have done, or something more covert?" Rogerian had opened the door, but half-closed it in an effort to hold in what little heat the building contained.

"I have had the sensation of being monitored since I went into the stable." He did his best to shrug off this unwelcome intuition; he glanced over his shoulder as Rogerian swung the door for him, and then he was gone into the dark corridor and on his way to the earth-filled chests that served as his bed.

Text of a report from the monastery of Archangeli near Roncesvalles, entrusted to lay-brother Terio for delivery to Gardingio Theudis on the 28th day of January, 622; never delivered.

To the Gardingio Theudis, the greetings of the monks of Archangeli on this most dreadful day, with the prayers that you will be spared what God has seen fit to visit upon us for our impiety and failings.

As soon as the weather clears, this message will be carried to you with all dispatch. I have already chosen who is to carry it, and with God's Grace, he shall reach you before the end of February, for I have told him this work is urgent, and he must travel from sunrise to sunset on every day the sun can be seen in the sky, for this tomus is of importance not only to us, at this monastery, but to you and your family.

It is the sad duty of this monastery to inform you that your cousin, the Primor Gaericed, has been called to the Throne of God to answer for his life. He has the company of many of the Fraters of this monastery to comfort him, as the Great Pox has claimed many lives here, but none so much valued as that of your cousin, for whom those of us who remain alive pray night and day.

There is no way that we, as religious, may abandon our place here, and so we will remain, to honor our Primor and our vows. Should the Great Pox spare us, we must hope that God will not let us die of hunger, for there is so much death about that no one ventures to bring food to the monastery; it being the depths of winter, we have only our onions and turnips and cheese to feed us. God has laid His Hand upon us heavily, and it is for us to bear the burden rather than be cast down by it, for in such wise, we fail our God as much as if we had placed the Crown of Thorns upon His Head. We will submit to God's Will, and His Mercy, however it may be shown, and praise His Name.

Your cousin is ready for burial, and we have sung his funeral prayers, but he cannot yet be buried, nor can fourteen other monks, as the ground is yet too hard. We have disposed all the dead in their winding sheets and placed them in the smaller chapel, so that they may be in a holy place and safe from storms and thieves and wolves alike. As soon as the snow has gone, we will seek to lay all of those who perish, to good, Christian rest.

The Frater-tertiary who carries this to you will vouch for all I have said here. He is a simple man, and humble, but his devotion to truth is beyond question. On behalf of your cousin, who brought the Frater-tertiary Terio to Archangeli, I ask you to house and clothe and feed him in your cousin's memory. You will find him reliable and faithful; God has given him great strength of body, that he may make his way in the world. I should tell you that he is easily frightened and therefore unsuited to the battlefield; his strength is best employed in building and similar tasks.

I have charged him to make note of all he sees in his journey to you, and to make a full and faithful account to you, telling only what he himself has witnessed. There are rumors everywhere, and in each of them, the Great Pox is worse; what Frater-tertiary Terio sees he will tell you, no more and no less. You may rely on him to report aright, and without guile, for so he is charged to do, on pain of eternal damnation. You may find such information useful as the seasons warm and the sickness is absorbed into the air from the infected earth.

May God reward you for your charity to Frater-tertiary Terio. May He open the doors of Paradise to your cousin, our Primor, and show him God's Peace. May you not suffer the visitation of the Great Pox. May all your family remain untouched by it. May your lands be in good heart. May your fields and orchards be bountiful. May your herds and flocks thrive. May you live in favor with your peers. May your enemies be struck down. May your coffers fill with treasure. May your name be spoken with respect from now until God comes again to deliver His People from the pains of this world.

> *Frater Morduc, Scribe*
> *Half-brother to Episcus Honorius of Caesaraugusta*

at Archangeli monastery near Roncesvalles, written on the 21st day of January in the 622nd year of God's Incarnation, in the calendar of Sanct' Iago.

3

A band of jugglers had arrived the day before Sanct' Germain and his escort, and so the villa of Gardingio Witteric was filled with activity: musicians playing bladder-pipes and drums rushed about, creating noise, their half-masks transforming them into otherworldly beings as their fantastical clothing flapped in the icy wind. There were soldiers and men-at-arms lounging in the central courtyard—a heavily fortified addition that had been erected after the Romans left—laughing at the musicians and watching the entertainers put their talents to balancing and throwing and other feats of skill. Two large braziers provided as much smoke as heat to those who crowded around them, seeking their warmth even as they batted at the soot and coughed. A dozen large dogs watched all this uneasily, occasionally growling when one of the musicians ventured too close. Servants and slaves did their best to continue at their tasks in spite of this distraction: a few actually succeeded.

The sartrium at the gate looked over the new arrivals, accepted a few silver coins from Sanct' Germain, and agreed to introduce him to the Gardingio at once instead of demanding the usual delays. "Your men may put their mounts in the open stalls—the box-stalls are for our horses. They'll have to curry their animals themselves, and see to their feed and water—Gardingio Witteric does not care for the animals of those not in his household, or of his invited guests." He laid heavy emphasis on the word *invited.*

This was not unusual, although Sanct' Germain knew his escort would complain. "Well enough. My bondsman will supervise the rest, if you have no objection." He paid no attention to those who stared at his black pluvial over a black-and-silver Byzantine hippogaudion riding habit and high boots of red leather.

"If that is your wish," said the sartrium. "Gerdis will show them the way." He whistled through his teeth and shouted for a young man-at-arms. "Take them to the stable. Let them have a measure of hay for each horse and mule, and time at the water trough, as courtesy to travelers." His scowl cut off any protest from Gerdis, who gestured at Leovigild to follow him. "See you do well by the Gardingio," the sartrium called after them.

"I will return when I have made an appropriate introduction," said Sanct' Germain to Rogerian, and went after the sartrium. "You are in charge of the horses and mules."

"That I will, my master," said Rogerian as he dismounted and signaled the men-at-arms to do the same.

"We are hungry," said Egica. "And we are cold."

"That will be attended to as soon as I have presented myself to Gardingio Witteric," Sanct' Germain said over his shoulder as he continued through the disorder of the courtyard.

The sartrium paused just inside the door of the central villa, his expression severe. "You are not expected."

"No. I have an introduction from Primor Ioanus that should reassure Gardingio Witteric; they are kinsmen, as I understand it." Sanct' Germain showed no sign of distress as he spoke but he could not keep from wondering what kind of welcome he might expect to receive in this place in so hard a season. "No doubt there are many who trespass on the Gardingio's hospitality, but you need not fear I am one such. I do not bring my men here to sup and drink without obligation. As a stranger, I am beholden to his generosity as no relation would be. You may tell your master that I am prepared to offer recompense for his courtesy."

"Oh, if you can pay he will be glad to have you in his court," said the sartrium. "And your men-at-arms seem worthy sorts; not laggard and not swagger." He nodded once as if to indicate he was satisfied, then he continued toward a U-shaped inner court that had once been a proper Roman atrium but was now as much a fortress as the outer walls around the villa. Among the other changes wrought upon the villa was a second story, cobbled on in a rougher style than the original building, with narrow slits for windows and an array of chimneys that smoked like miniature volcanos.

Sanct' Germain kept up with the sartrium, remaining a respectful two paces behind him as they entered the villa. The light was halved, and the smoke from the fires burning in braziers and on the hearths of two enormous fireplaces did little to alleviate the gloom; the fireplaces had been added to the villa recently and were made of rough-hewn stone, not the marble the Romans had built with. The few windows were covered with thin-cut alabaster screens, providing a diffuse, milky illumination that did not penetrate far into the chamber. Here there were more slaves, many of them women, and not all were working at tasks; a group of children ranging from age three to about ten were in one corner near the vast, smoking fireplace in the main chamber, playing with paddles and balls where they were watched over by two elderly women with widow's veils over their plaited hair. There were half a dozen slaves in the chamber, most of them preparing the long table for the prandium, which would be served before the next canonical Hour. In the corner opposite the children was a dais of two stairs, and on the dais stood an old Roman chair; a ruddy-haired, scar-faced man of early middle-age—perhaps thirty or thirty-five—was sitting in it, legs set wide, one hand holding a staff of office, the other thrust deep inside the enveloping fur robe of the young woman who stood beside him, smiling distantly.

The sartrium saluted as he faced the man on the dais. "Hail, Gardingio Witteric. May God show you favor and advance your—"

"Have mercy, Ruda," said the Gardingio, cutting off the sartrium, and revealing a mouth full of discolored and broken teeth. "You are a faithful man, and for that I am grateful. I have seen proof of your loyalty. You need not call Heaven to witness it." He pulled his hand out of the robe and patted the young woman, a lazy, sensual smile almost negating the severity of his scars. "This is not for you, woman. Go away until I call for you."

She lowered her head and departed, going toward the door that led to the inner rooms of the villa.

Ruda straightened up and began in a formal voice, "This is Sanct' Germain. He is traveling over the mountains with an armed escort and a servant. They have horses and mules and good tack, so it is not as if he is a criminal escaping. He says he has a letter from your half-brother—"

"Which one?" the Gardingio asked sarcastically.

"Primor Ioanus," said Sanct' Germain before Ruda could speak. "My men and I stayed at his monastery some days ago on our journey from Toletum, and he was good enough to provide me an introduction to you." He did not mention that he had another introduction to another Gardingio, for that might give offense to these men, or add to an already existing rivalry.

"Primor Ioanus," said Gardingio Witteric in mild surprise. "Who would have thought that he . . ." He let that thought drift away. "So you are going over the mountains? What is your destination?"

"Tolosa, on the far side of the mountains," said Sanct' Germain at once. "I have a blood relative there." It was near enough to the truth that he spoke confidently: Atta Olivia Clemens had holdings there where he would be made welcome, whether Olivia herself was there or not.

"Is that your homeland?" Gardingio Witteric demanded sharply, leaning forward as he asked.

"No. My homeland is many, many thousands of paces to the east, in the hands of invaders." It was true enough as far as it went, and Sanct' Germain did not add that the conquest of his homeland had happened more than twenty-five hundred years ago, for invasions were common enough in these times, and needed no explanation.

On the far side of the room there was a sudden burst of activity among the children, then shouts and angry sobbing; the two widows bustled around the children doing their best to restore order.

After casting one fulminating glance in the direction of the commotion, he looked squarely at Sanct' Germain. "So you came west," said the Gardingio approvingly. "Will you return?"

Sanct' Germain knew the answer that was expected of him. "In time." That he measured his time in centuries he kept to himself.

"You want the help of your kinsmen," said Gardingio Witteric, satisfied. "Thus you go to find them, to rally them."

"It may come to that," said Sanct' Germain. "I must get to Tolosa first to find out. I ask your aid to do this."

Gardingio Witteric laughed aloud. "Clever, too." He slapped his free hand down on the arm of his chair. "I cannot fail to show you courtesy, since my half-brother asks it of me and you claim you do not come to join my household. I could not receive you into my Court as you must know. But barring that, you are welcome to be my guest. You should have the opportunity to do as you wish as one received in my half-brother's name," he announced. "You may remain here until word comes that the passes are open. You will need only to pay for the food your animals consume."

"That is most gallantly done," said Sanct' Germain. "But I would be less than honorable if I did not offer you more than that: I have three jewels that I would want to give to you to acknowledge your courtesy.

As a traveler, I am beholden to the charity of lords like you to aid me in my journey. It is fitting that I show my appreciation." If the Gardingio accepted the jewels, Sanct' Germain knew that his horses and mules could not be confiscated when he left.

"Let me see them. You may come up to me," said Gardingio Witteric with a grand gesture.

Sanct' Germain reached under his black woolen pluvial into the leather wallet that hung from his belt; he drew out an emerald and two diamonds, the emerald as large as the end of his thumb, the diamonds somewhat smaller. "Here," he said, placing them in the Gardingio's palm. "Better are not to be found anywhere. Set your artisans to polishing them and they will add to the treasure of your House."

Behind Sanct' Germain, Ruda the sartrium let out a whispered oath.

"These are very good," said Gardingio Witteric, his eyes shinning with greed. "Yes, very good."

They are yours for the kindness you show to me and my escort and bondsman, and our animals. I would be an unworthy guest if I did nothing to express my gratitude for your hospitality." Sanct' Germain made a gesture of submission and moved back a few steps down the dais.

Gardingio Witteric held up the emerald and squinted at the play of light through it; in spite of the dimness of the room, he liked what he saw. "Very fine, truly very fine. This is first quality, as good as any I have seen," he approved as he studied the gem. "Where did you get it?"

"I have sworn not to reveal that," Sanct' Germain said. "I must ask you to let me honor my oath."

"So it is stolen," said Gardingio Witteric, shrugging to show his unconcern. "What is that to me?" He looked next at the diamonds, his attention less focused. "These are very fine, also." Weighing them in his palm he considered the gift. "All right, foreigner. I will accept these on behalf of the villa, and I will remember your munificence when you depart."

"I am doubly grateful to you, Gardingio," said Sanct' Germain, lowering his head in a show of deference.

"In winter, any traveler is at the mercy of the storms and those of us with walls to protect them," said Gardingio Witteric complacently.

Ruda the sartrium intervened. "What about the mules and horses? They are going to eat and drink more than the men."

Gardingio Witteric laughed. "These jewels will buy a summer of hay, and our wells have not run dry. Let them have what they need and do not press them about it," he ordered, his joviality gone as swiftly as it had come.

Aware that there was no point in belaboring the matter, Ruda saluted and turned away, pulling Sanct' Germain's elbow to pull him along. "You have men to attend to," he said to account for his abrupt actions.

"And you have duties, no doubt," said Sanct' Germain, only mildly offended by this brusque treatment; had the sartrium been a Roman servant, it would have been another matter, but these western Goths lacked the grace of Roman society and could not be expected to conduct themselves otherwise.

"You will have to put your men in with our household guards," Ruda told Sanct' Germain as they neared the outer courtyard once again. "We have no quarters to spare for them if we are to provide for you."

"I doubt the men will mind," said Sanct' Germain with a trace of irony. "They enjoy their own kind."

"As do all men," said Ruda pointedly. "You cannot suppose that tending to a foreigner brings them honor."

So that was it, Sanct' Germain thought; these men-at-arms did not want to compromise themselves by remaining too devoted to a man who could not advance them. "Ah, yes," he said, "but I pay very well."

"Money does not bring honor, and cannot hoise us," said Ruda bluntly. "If you were not foreign you would know that; foreigners always think the world is set right with gold. No one can say that riches are better than favor and advancement." He glowered at a juggler who approached them, a long sausage balanced on his nose. "Come. I will show you where you are to stay."

"Very good," said Sanct' Germain quietly, not willing to continue a debate that could only lead to greater acrimony.

One of the jugglers was standing atop a stool placed on a barrel and was spinning a dish on a stick, his face rigid with concentration. the plate leveled out and the juggler took a second stick, and using his shoulder to brace the second plate, began to set that one spinning as well. He had just got the plate moving when a bull of a soldier deliberately lurched into the barrel, setting the juggler, the plates and stick, the stool, and the crowd around him scattering. As the juggler landed, he screamed as his collar-bone broke.

Sanct' Germain motioned to Ruda to stop. "The man is hurt," he said when Ruda expressed surprise at the foreigner's concern.

"He's a juggler," said Ruda as if speaking to someone addled in his wits.

"All the more reason to help him; his arms are his living. If he should lose the use of one, he might as well take up a begging bowl and be done with it." Ignoring the look disbelief the sartrium shot him, Sanct' Germain went over to the juggler, who was now lying curled into a ball of agony. "I am going to look at your injury," he informed the juggler as he dropped to his knee beside him.

The juggler shrieked as Sanct' Germain touched him, and kicked out feebly; a few of the men who had run off now came back to see what was happening, looming over the juggler and the foreigner as if waiting for more entertainment.

"Ruda," said Sanct' Germain, "would you be good enough to send a servant to fetch my bondsman? I assume he is in the stable." He could see the shine of sweat on the juggler's face and the white line around his mouth; in a little while the man would begin to shake from cold, and then it would be more difficult to help him.

Ruda sighed with exasperation. "Why bother?" he asked.

"Because he is suffering," said Sanct' Germain, and tried again to touch the juggler. "You have broken the front of your shoulder, the bone that is at the top of your chest," he said, doing his best to calm and reassure the man as he made another attempt to examine the injury; he sensed more than saw blood, and realized that the broken bone had penetrated the skin. "Can you lie back?"

The juggler whimpered. "The pain," he whispered.

"Yes," said Sanct' Germain, "But it will be no worse if you will lie on your back." He was not sure this was the case, but he knew that he could not treat the man if he remained huddled in a ball.

One of the men-at-arms of the villa whispered a crude joke to his companion and the two men laughed; the juggler who had been balancing the sausage rushed up, his face pale with worry. A moment later, the senior juggler was beside him, worry in every aspect of his demeanor. Neither man dared to speak.

"If you three will move back?" Sanct' Germain said to the men-at-arms whose shadows were falling across the disabled juggler; reluctantly the men complied, one of them grumbling that now he could not see what was happening.

Then the crowd was shoved aside as Leovigild pressed through the knot of men, dragging Rogerian behind him. "What's this?" he demanded as he caught sight of Sanct' Germain on the ground beside the juggler. He came nearer, arms akimbo, his brow thunderous as he stared down at his foreign guest. "Have you been slighted? Did that fellow offer you an affront?"

"No," said Sanct' Germain patiently. "He had the misfortune to be thrown from his perch and has broken a bone from his fall: this one, here, in the front of his shoulder." He pointed to the place on himself as he looked about in the hope that some of those watching would understand the severity of the situation; what he saw did not encourage him. "Rogerian, would you bring my red chest? I believe I have medicaments that will help relieve his hurts."

Rogerian acted promptly. "Of course, my master; immediately," he said before he hurried back toward the stable, shoving his way through the gathered men-at-arms, jugglers, musicians, and slaves. By the time he returned with the chest, the juggler was lying supine, Sanct' Germain's black pluvial covering him. Rogerian had to force his way back to Sanct' Germain. "What do you need, my master?"

"The anodyne paste in the green vial," said Sanct' Germain, not looking around. "You know the one."

"That I do," said Rogerian, opening the chest and taking out what Sanct' Germain had asked for. "What else?"

Before Sanct' Germain could answer, the senior juggler spoke up. "Is he going to die?"

"I hope not," said Sanct' Germain. "If he takes no putrid humors, he will recover." He did not want to admit how worried he was; the juggler was clammy and his breathing quick and shallow.

"But you will treat him?" The senior juggler clasped his hands together, imploring the black-clad foreigner as if Sanct' Germain were lord of the villa and not Gardingio Witteric.

"I can tell you nothing more until I have dressed the wound. I will need a good-sized table to lay him on if I am to set this bone." He smeared some of the pasty substance from the vial over the bleeding, torn skin. "It must be set if he is to have any chance of recovery."

"It is not fitting that a juggler should be taken into the villa," said Ruda stiffly. "He is not sworn to the Gardingio."

"Perhaps not," said Sanct' Germain, "but Gardingio Witteric has received the jugglers and let them entertain his men-at-arms: he has some obligation to see to their well-being while they remain. If he fails to treat them well, his reputation will be damaged, and that would be intolerable to him." He stood up. "Find me a table I can use, and I will undertake to set the broken bone."

Ruda stared at Sanct' Germain in angry disbelief. "You cannot give orders here. You are here on sufferance as much as much as they."

Sanct' Germain glanced toward Leovigild. "Sartrium, can you find a table where I can do my work?"

"That I will," said Leovigild. "You will have to answer to the Gardingio if I act against his will." With that warning, he pushed through the crowd, shouting to Wamba and Childric to aid him.

"You are an ungrateful guest," said Ruda, and spat to show his contempt.

"He is not," said a loud, hoarse voice from the entrance to the villa; Gardingio Witteric strode forward, those gathered around the fallen juggler moving back to open a pathway. "If he can help this man, let him show it."

Everyone hearing this knew Sanct' Germain was being tested; two of the men-at-arms muttered bets with each other on the outcome, spitting and slapping their palms to seal the wager. As if aware of this additional excitement, the senior juggler made a wretched attempt at a smile, ducking his head ingratiatingly, first to Gardingio Witteric and then to Sanct' Germain.

"A table first, then," said Sanct' Germain, his manner composed as if he were unaware of the challenge he had been issued.

"Let him have what he wants," said Gardingio Witteric, and the men around him sprang into a action to obey.

In short order, a trestle table had been assembled of saddle stands and planking near the entrance of the single open room in the outer walls that had been allocated to the jugglers' use; the crowd watching had grown, and the women of the household had gathered in the narrow windows of the second floor of the villa to see the excitement.

"Shall we lift him for you?" Leovigild asked, not quite able to conceal his reluctance to render such service to a mere juggler.

"Never mind," said Sanct' Germain as he knelt and carefully took the semi-conscious man in his arms; he did his best to shift the juggler's torso and arms as little as possible, doing his utmost to minimize the pain he gave, and to minimize the additional damage such moving could inflict. He stood slowly so that the juggler would not be shaken or jarred, and laid him on the improvised table. This uncanny display of strength gained the awed approval of all the men who saw it, a circumstance that troubled Sanct' Germain, who preferred to keep this capability to himself whenever possible. As he adjusted his pluvial around the juggler, he asked one of the man's companions. "What is his name?"

The senior juggler hesitated. "Alboin," he said at last. "He is a Lombard."

Gardingio Witteric chuckled unpleasantly. "And fallen so far; named for a King and reduced to wandering the world with a pack of vagabonds," he mused aloud. "Well, the Lombards are always inclined to take on more than they can accomplish." He took a wider stance as if preparing to defend himself against attack. "Still, do what you can for him, Sanct' Germain."

"It is my intention," was Sanct' Germain's answer. "If your people would step back a bit, my task would be easier." He addressed himself to Gardingio Witteric. "If I have no room to work, I cannot help this man."

"Oh, very well," Gardingio Witteric sighed. "Do as he says." He gave a single, fussy gesture to indicate his men-at-arms should do as Sanct' Germain requested.

Leovigild stood his ground. "If you have need of me," he said stubbornly.

"Not just at present, sartrium," said Sanct' Germain as he folded his pluvial back from Alboin's injury and inspected it for bleeding; the blood flow was lessening and becoming tacky to the touch, although there was already heat in the wound. "Rogerian," he said, "take his left arm, stretch it out and hold it firmly. He will probably fight you, but do not let go until I tell you."

Rogerian paid no notice to the new wave of excitement that passed through the crowd; he took the juggler's wrist and stretched out his arm, holding it though Alboin moaned and struggled against him.

"There are pieces of bone in the wound. I will have to pull them out later, after the break is set," Sanct' Germain said as he took his position to realign Alboin's collar-bone. When he moved, he was so swift that any watching him were certain he had accomplished the feat by magic: he tugged the juggler's right arm out and up with his right hand, and with his left, pressed the bone back into position.

Alboin screamed and fainted.

"You have killed him," Ruda said with grim satisfaction. "The Gardingio will have your life for it."

Sanct' Germain moved aside. "You will see he is still breathing." He motioned the senior juggler to approach. "Verify it for yourself. You as well, Ruda. Come look at him and tell me if he is dead or not."

The senior juggler put his hand to Alboin's mouth, and nodded. "He breathes. The bone is in place."

Reluctantly Ruda came to the side of the table and stared down. "He speaks truth. The man is breathing."

There was a general sigh from the crowd, some in relief, some in disappointment; the jugglers exclaimed their thanks aloud and the senior juggler crouched down to kiss Sanct' Germain's foot.

"That's not necessary," Sanct' Germain said at once, trying to conceal his distaste. "I have done nothing more than any other physician would do." He saw Gardingio Witteric was studying him attentively. "I have only set the bone," he said to explain himself. "The man has not yet recovered. There is time for gratitude when the man can practice his skills once more."

"You set the bone and he is still alive," said the Gardingio. "Not even the farrier could manage that."

"Possibly not," Sanct' Germain said, bending over Alboin, his fingers pressed lightly to the unconscious man's neck to check his pulse. "He has a way to go before there is cause for hope." This was nothing more than the truth, but it served as a warning to the jugglers and men-at-arms alike.

Leovigild spoke up. "Sanct' Germain cured Wamba when he was taken with fever, and gave ease to a traveler who had blackened feet. I saw it all."

"The traveler did not live," Sanct' Germain reminded the sartrium.

"Who does, with cold-blackened feet?" Leovigild asked, and was answered with muttered agreement. "At least he was not screaming, or shaking himself to pieces in spasms." His pride in Sanct' Germain's accomplishment was obvious and his boasts were listened to by everyone but Sanct' Germain himself.

"Did you do this?" Gardingio Witteric demanded, coming toward Sanct' Germain impulsively. "Have you the power to assuage the agony of blackened limbs?"

"Sometimes I can provide an anodyne," Sanct' Germain said cautiously: he had given the traveler syrup of poppies, and that had made his passage out of this life less arduous than it would have been without the ameliorative slumber the syrup of poppies bestowed.

"You can do this for other hurts?" Gardingio Witteric asked before anyone else could speak.

"Sometimes, yes; it depends on the injury and the nature of suffering. Not all ills may by relieved in this world." He wanted to give his full concentration to Alboin, but knew that if he refused to answer the Gardingio, he might well be expelled from the villa without his men-at-arms, horses, mules, or any other possessions. "There is suffering that only a man's God may treat."

"True enough," said Gardingio Witteric, beginning to pace around the table where Alboin lay. "Well, we shall see how he goes on. In a few days, if he has not taken a fever, it may be possible to tell if he has any sensation in his hand."

The senior juggler clapped his hands to his face in a show of horror. "Nothing so terrible as that."

"We will not know for a time," Sanct' Germain warned. "It would not be wise to hope for too much until then." He was aware that Gardingio Witteric was dissatisfied with these remarks, and added, "There are things that cannot be rushed, any more than a blossom can be rushed on a branch. When Alboin is able to tell how much he can move his hand, then we will know something."

"And if the man has no sensation in his hand, what then?" Gardingio Witteric challenged.

"Then we must wait until the bone knits to find if he has any strength in the arm. If he does, he can learn some new skills. If he does not, then . . ." He let his words die away. When he spoke again, his manner was brisk. "The sooner I can pull the splinters from the wound, the sooner his shoulder can be bandaged and the greater his chance for recovering the use of his hand and arm."

"Oh, very well," the Gardingio fumed. "Tend to the juggler. If you have need of anything from my household, send your servant to fetch it, and if it is not unreasonable, it shall be yours."

"That is very generous of you," said Sanct' Germain, who knew he should not ask for anything beyond the most minor aids. "A pail of hot water and a small brazier would be very useful, and three men to carry this tabletop to the quarters you have assigned to me." In response to the startled look on Gardingio Witteric's features, he added. "I will tend him."

"Why should you care for a juggler?" asked Gardingio Witteric. "You can put him with the others and tell them what to do. You are not a player, going from place to place."

"No," said Sanct' Germain bleakly. "I am an exile." There was something in his aspect that silenced the Gardingio, and set the men-at-arms to whispering as they watched the black-clad foreigner.

Gardingio Witteric cocked his head, considering Sanct' Germain's remark. "Yes. A man may travel for many reasons, I suppose. Pray you have no need to regret your traveling." He made an abrupt sweeping gesture. "There is nothing more to see here. Go back to your tasks, all of you. Ruda, the braziers are low on fuel: bring more wood to keep them well-lighted." Without another word to Sanct' Germain, the Gardingio stumped away toward the entrance to his villa.

Those around the table hastened away, leaving Sanct' Germain to deal with Alboin on his own. "Do we know which quarters are ours?" Rogerian asked when all but one soldier and an old slave were left nearby; he spoke in the language of Sanct' Germain's long-vanished people.

He was answered in the same tongue. "No. But if someone is bringing water. I trust he will guide us." Sanct' Germain looked down at Alboin. "I do not like his color. He is too pasty."

Rogerian considered the juggler, his expression hard to read. "He is very cold."

"Exactly," Sanct' Germain agreed. "I fear we may not be able to keep him from fever, for the longer he is cold, the hotter he will burn." He had learned that lesson long ago, in the Temple of Imhotep, and although experience had modified his opinion, he still regarded the teaching as sound. "He will have to be watched: closely."

"Yes," Rogerian agreed. "As soon as there is a brazier lit, I will take up that task." He regarded Alboin's waxen features. "There is one sure way to restore him."

Sanct' Germain shook his head emphatically. "Turn a young man like this out into the world as one of my blood, unprepared, with no knowledge of what he has become? This is not Kozrozd; he would not comprehend his nature. He would be stoned or burned the first time he tried to satisfy his need. That is hardly restoring him, it is only trading one misery for another." He went silent, then said, "I am sorry, old

friend. I know you meant that to his good, but you know how dangerous it would be, for all of us."

Rogerian nodded and was about to turn away. "Do you not long for
those of your blood?" he asked wistfully.

"I long for the knowing, the touching," Sanct' Germain said, his
voice distant. "I cannot have either with those who have come to my
life." He shook his head. "We had best get this man inside, before he
becomes colder. Finally," he said in the language of the western Goths
as a young slave came up to them, carrying a pail of water warm
enough for faint tendrils of steam to be rising from it. "Lead the way."

The slave lowered his head and pointed. "Over there," he said before he went on.

"You'd best take one end of the table-plank," Sanct' Germain recommended. "I want to keep speculation about my strength to a minimum."

"Of course," said Rogerian, taking the foot of the plank in his hands
and lifting it as Sanct' Germain raised the head of it; with Alboin suspended between them, they followed the slave toward the east side of
the villa.

Text of a report from the scribe Aspar for the records of Gardingio Witteric.

*On my life and on my honor, I swear this is a true account of the ac-
tivities at the villa of the Gardingio Witteric in the Paschal Season in
the 622nd year since God came to earth for the salvation of Men.*

*In accordance with the teachings of the Episcus at Caesaraugusta,
the Gardingio duly ordered the slaughter of pigs for the last night before we give up meat and ale to show our devotion to the Sacrifice. All
of the people of the villa and its region showed their veneration of the
Resurrection by vowing to eat no meat from this feast until the priests
tell us that God has departed the world yet again. In that spirit, there
was feasting and dancing, and the jugglers who have spent half the
winter at this villa entertained everyone with their antics.*

*Two of the Gardingio's women are with child, and have been sent to
their quarters until their babies come. One of the women, the one sent
by the Iacetani clans, is showing signs of distress; slaves have been ordered to wrap her feet in hot tarragon leaves twice a day and to mas-*

sage her belly with wool-fat. The priest's wife has been ordered to pray at her side morning and night, and to place the Gospel under her pillow in the night. With such excellent care, surely she will be safely delivered of the son she has promised to give the Gardingio.

Messengers have come from the east to inform the Gardingio that although the Great Pox is abating, it has not stopped its ravaging of the villages up the mountain, and that the presence of the Pox has kept travelers from venturing toward the passes, not for fear of cold and snow, or robbers, but of the Pox. When word comes that travelers have completed their journeys without falling ill, the Gardingio will send his men-at-arms to secure the countryside again.

There have been more rats, mice, and other vermin in the storehouse, and slaves have been set to the task of guarding the grain and clubbing to death any such creatures as they may see. Also three small dogs have been kenneled outside the storehouse to prevent more of the rats and mice from entering and adding to the numbers already stealing the food from the villa. These dogs are said to be adept at the killing of vermin, and for that reason they have been entrusted with the task of killing those rats and mice that seek to deplete the stores of our villa. The cooks have offered to bring their cats to the storehouse, but Gardingio Witteric has said he will not have such malign animals protecting his grain and other food.

One of the jugglers, a man who suffered a broken bone, has at last succumbed to fever. The foreigner who undertook to minister to him, Sanct' Germain, has been sent away from the villa with his manservant, two horses and two mules, an act of great mercy, for Gardingio Witteric might have had Sanct' Germain's life in recompense. With the death of the juggler, it was the Gardingio's judgment that the foreigner had forfeited all right to his men-at-arms and their mounts and supplies. The juggler lasted for nearly a month, far longer than anyone thought he would, and for a time he appeared to be on the mend. But his fever returned and he abandoned his life nine days since. The foreigner and his manservant made no protest to the ruling of the Gardingio; they departed four days ago with the assurance they will not remain in the lands of Gardingio Witteric any longer than it must take them to leave.

The shepherds from the village six thousand paces distant have brought three lambs for the Feast of the Resurrection; they will be fat-

tened while we fast, and when the priest proclaims the sacred day, the lambs will remind us of the Gift of Life as we eat their flesh in memory of God.

Nine men have been executed by hanging alive in chains for their looting of houses of those who have died of the Great Pox; they were condemned by the Gardingio and the priest for what they had done, and their execution was duly carried out over the main gate of the villa's outer walls. The strongest of them took four days to die—by then his eyes had been pecked out by kites and he was raving. These robbers have shown themselves to be beyond the redemption of religion as well as the salvation of law, and as such, can make no appeal to Episcus nor Gardingio to excuse their actions or their goals. Gardingio Witteric said this would warn all other such criminals of what will befall them, if they do not honor the Gardingio's authority.

The cooper, Duvoric, was ordered castrated for fondling Gardingio Witteric's second wife. The family of Duvoric was cast out of the villa and sentence was carried out by the farrier; Duvoric subsequently took a fever and putrescence from the wound killed him, a warning to all who trespass on the family of the Gardingio.

This spring has begun with heavy rains and the rivers are bursting their banks in the valleys. Homes have been demolished by the flood, as have been roads and bridges. There are reports of landslides higher up the mountains, some wide enough to bring down stands of trees and bury small villages; we have not seen such catastrophe here on the plateau. The ground everywhere is shining with water and the roads are seas of mud from the rains. As soon as the waters have receded, the banks of the rivers must be rebuilt so that the farms and villages of this region will not be swept away entirely. The Gardingio has declared that all peasants must give one day of labor each week to this rebuilding. If he should fail in this duty, his lands will be seized and given to those willing to be worthy of it.

Submitted on this first day of Paschal Mourning,

Aspar
Scribe to Gardingio Witteric

4

Skulls of horses hung over the broken gates of the little village tucked away among the oaks and pines of the narrow mountain valley; the slanting rays of the westering sun imparted a glow to it that was belied by the shallow graves on the lower slope of the hill where spring had laid its first, tentative touch with pale new grass and a few white flowers. Marks painted hastily on the stone walls around the village indicated that the Great Pox had struck the place and that many had died.

"The rest have probably fled," said Sanct' Germain to Rogerian as they drew up at the gates; both of them rode a horse and led a mule. "That has been the pattern. When the Great Pox arrives, the people hide or die." This village was on a secondary road, one not often used by travelers bound for the pass into the Tolosa region of Frankish lands; the main road was reported to be flooded out higher up the mountains, so Sanct' Germain had decided to attempt the crossing by lesser routes; he had not anticipated finding abandoned towns and farmholds, yet this was the second such village he had seen in as many days.

"So it has," said Rogerian. "And if the village is empty, we can shelter here for a day or so. The animals need rest."

"As do we," Sanct' Germain agreed. "You are right." He slid out of the saddle and caught his horse's rein as he approached the gate. "No locks, no bolts. It will not be hard to open."

Rogerian also dismounted. "How many died, would you say? And how many fled before they died?"

"There are twenty-three new graves on the hill, on the other side of the town from the olive orchard. Judging from the number and condition of the houses, the village may have had as many as three hundred occupants: at least five families, perhaps six or seven." He reached for the gate and took hold of the iron brace, lifting it and leaning into it; the gate moaned as it opened.

"There could still be people here," Rogerian said.

"There might be," Sanct' Germain said with a nod. "We shall try to find them if they are here; there is only a faint smell of smoke in the air—no one has burned a fire for at least one full day." He pointed to an old well just ahead of the gates. "See if the water is wholesome and give it to the horses and mules if it is." He glanced at the skulls over the gate. "This is a very old village, if those are any indication."

Rogerian paused in his attempt to drag the well-bucket up from the depths. "The people here in the mountains have kept to their old ways; no one has changed them."

"For many centuries," said Sanct' Germain. He glanced at the stone buildings with their plank-shingled roofs. "The men here are foresters and hunters, by the look of it. The orchard isn't large enough for more than oil and olives for the village."

"That is the way in these mountains," said Rogerian as he finally pulled the well-bucket onto the stone rim; it was large, its wooden sections bound by rusty iron, and water sloshed as he sat down. He cupped his hand and dipped it into the water to taste it. "Good enough. Not brackish and without bitterness."

"Let the animals have it," Sanct' Germain said, somewhat preoccupied as he contemplated what he could see of the village. "No dogs," he remarked. "If they fled, they did not go in a panic, or the dogs would be left: and hungry."

Rogerian had let the larger mule drink first and was now holding the bucket for the second mule. "Just as well," he said with emotion born of memory.

"No chickens or ducks, either, judging by the silence. Sheep and goats and pigs could be turned loose in the forest to be recaptured later, but not chickens and ducks. They would have to be taken away, or eaten." Sanct' Germain looked down one of the two cart-wide streets running through the town from the front gate; a number of smaller alleys radiated in all directions, but Sanct' Germain gave his first attention to what were obviously the most important corridors in the village. "There is probably a market square at the center of this town," he said, starting along the nearer of the two streets.

"Do you intend to go there? to the market square?" asked Rogerian; Sanct' Germain's gray and his own red-roan were nudging at him for water.

"It might give us a better notion about where everyone has gone," Sanct' Germain said.

"Do you think sickness has chased them out?" Rogerian went back to the well to get a second bucket of water.

"It is the most likely explanation," said Sanct' Germain as he glanced down an alley. "If the sickness had remained here, we would know." His expression combined distress and compassion. "The odor would be undeniable."

"Truly," Rogerian agreed as he lowered the bucket. "Where do you suppose they have gone?"

"I have no notion," said Sanct' Germain. "No one is here to tell us. We saw few travelers as we came up from Gardingio Witteric's holdings; certainly nothing like a whole village on the move."

The mention of Gardingio Witteric brought a frown to Rogerian's face. "His gratitude left much to be desired."

"He had no reason to be grateful," said Sanct' Germain. "The juggler died of fever. Not I, not anyone could have prevented it. The bone was too badly splintered. The sickness had gone too deep. The sovereign remedy was not enough to preserve his life." He swung around to look directly at Rogerian. "And do not tell me my blood would have spared him: I had no time to prepare him for my life even had he sought it." He thought briefly of Nicoris, who had ultimately refused the gift he gave her; she had died the True Death not quite two hundred years ago but the memory of her loss was still a stern rebuke within him.

"He need not have died," said Rogerian stubbornly.

Sanct' Germain came back toward his bondsman. "Many others have died before now and you did not resent it; there is little place in the world for those of my blood: we are tigers, not wolves, and our nature makes us solitary by necessity. Those who are prepared to live as vampires must are few in number and far apart, for their own protection as well as the protection of those around us. You have understood this from the time you first learned what I am. What was it about Alboin that was different?"

Rogerian pulled up the bucket before he answered. "I do not know. Perhaps it was his youth. He seemed so . . . so cheated by life."

"Ah," Sanct' Germain said, nodding his understanding. "He had that about him, did he not." He went toward the other street in swift, long strides. "I will find a place we can shelter for the night, and then I will go into the forest and find a meal we can share: blood for me, flesh for you."

"That would be welcome," said Rogerian, giving water to Sanct' Germain's gray.

Sanct' Germain stood still for a short while, then said, "I am sorry I could not save him; the sovereign remedy is usually sufficient to stop fever, but this time it could not."

"That does not mean he had to die," said Rogerian at his most blunt.

"No, it does not," Sanct' Germain conceded. "If I had more time, and an athanor to make more of the remedy, he might have lived." He looked about the village. "You cannot doubt that I have done all that I could to preserve the lad."

"Oh, I know that," said Rogerian with uncertainty. "But the fact of the matter is that I expected your skills to save him, and if you did not, that your blood would bring him to life again."

"And you are angry because of it," said Sanct' Germain.

"Not angry: disappointed," Rogerian allowed.

"For that I am truly sorry," Sanct' Germain said before he started down the second street; this one was slightly narrower than the first, and the stone houses huddled together like a flock seeking companionship and warmth. They had the look of sudden desertion about them.

"Mind how you go," Rogerian called after him.

Sanct' Germain nodded, although he knew that Rogerian could not see this. He kept his senses alert and his thoughts marshaled to the exploration he had undertaken: there was a mounted whetstone in front of one of the houses, Roman in design, which told Sanct' Germain that this place had not remained wholly isolated while the Romans held the region. This, he told himself, was an excellent sign. He hoped that if he found an inhabitant, they could understand one another well enough to converse, for if they could not, he had no doubt that he would have to move on. The whole village still had the faint odor of humanity about it; the occupants had not been gone more than two or three days at most. A half-dozen steps farther along the street he came upon a vat lying on its side. Stopping beside it, he was aware of the penetrating savor of olives.

A half-open door flapped in a sudden gust of wind; the sound made Sanct' Germain jump as he realized that there was something moving inside the house; this was confirmed by a soft clatter, as if a chair had been overset. "Is someone there?" he called out first in the Visigothic dialect and then in Latin. "Is anyone there?"

His question was met by a whimper and a low cry that made Sanct' Germain move forward hurriedly, for he could tell that the voice that made the sound was human, and that the human was in distress. He took his Greek dagger from its sheath as a precaution just as he crossed the threshold into the dark interior of the house.

The house consisted of two rooms separated by a large stone fire-place open on the front and back, flanked by plank walls, with a loft above the far chamber. There was a long table in the nearer room, with a long bench drawn up beside it. Two chests, standing open and empty, were against the west wall, mute testimony to the abrupt departure of the household; a basket that had once contained bread lay on its side and open on the floor. On the far side of the hearth eight cooking pots hung on brass hooks, showing the residents had some wealth. Sanct' Germain stood facing the fireplace, listening intently. Finally he heard a soft moan coming from the loft.

"Are you ill? Are you hurt?" Sanct' Germain called out, beginning in Latin this time, and repeating in the language of the Visigoths.

"Ill," said the voice in Latin, panting with the effort of talking; the voice was low and cracked, more a croak than speech.

Sanct' Germain was already looking for a ladder to gain access to the loft. "I will come up to you."

There was a silence, and then the voice spoke again. "I . . . I have . . . a knife."

"A knife?" Sanct' Germain hesitated as he picked up the ladder that lay beneath the loft. He wondered briefly how long the ladder had lain there, and if the person in the loft had been trapped there because of it: or had it just been kicked over, and that was the sound that had attracted his attention? "I will not hurt you; I mean you no harm."

"I . . . have . . . knife," the voice repeated.

"You need help," Sanct' Germain said as he put the ladder in place. "I am going to climb up to you. I will not hurt you."

". . . knife . . ." the voice breathed.

Sanct' Germain went up the ladder slowly, talking as he went, hoping to reassure the person in the loft, "My bondsman and I came here on our way toward Tolosa. The main road is not passable, and we were told that there was another way. It led to this place. We found the village empty. People and most animals were gone. There was no one guarding the gate. I saw the new graves, and I supposed that the place had been struck by sickness."

"Great Pox," the voice said just as Sanct' Germain climbed into the loft. "I have—"

"—a knife. Yes; I know," said Sanct' Germain, ducking his head to fit into the low space. He could smell the sweat from the huddled mass of bear-skins and rough-woven blankets. "You have more than a knife. You have had a fever."

"It's gone," the voice told him.

"How long?" Sanct' Germain asked; he crouched down, waiting for his opportunity to move forward. "When did it end?"

". . . Two days?" There was a flash of metal as the person brandished the knife weakly.

Sanct' Germain reached out and with surprising gentleness took the knife. "You will not need that."

The person in the bed gave a distressed cry and flailed out with one arm, knocking over the ewer of water that stood on the little shelf beside the wall; water spilled onto the bed. As if trying to escape, the person hunched back against the wall, the bear-skin an engulfing-but-cumbersome protection. "I am pregnant," the voice announced with as much strength as the speaker could summon.

"All the more reason to accept my help," said Sanct' Germain after an infinitesimal pause. "Come," he went on persuasively. "You cannot want to remain here in a wet bed. You are probably hungry and thirsty." When he received no answer, he added, "You cannot remain here forever. Let me help you down the ladder. I will start a fire to keep you warm and my bondsman will make you a meal as soon as I have gone hunting."

The woman peered suspiciously at him, her large, black eyes bright with emotion. "I am . . . hungry," she admitted at last.

"If you are pregnant and recovering from a fever, this is not remarkable. It is also necessary that you eat, for the sake of your child as well as your own," he said dryly. "Keep the bear-skin, if you like. I would not want you to take a chill." He held out one arm to offer her assistance. "Lean on me. I can hold you."

"If you will?" She stared at him, sensing his foreign clothes. "Who are you?" Her voice cracked half-way through the question and she had to ask it again.

"Sanct' Germain," he said. "You will tell me who you are when you are downstairs and fed. That is our first concern—to see you are not starving. And you will tell me how it happens that you are in this deserted village." He steadied himself on one knee and held out both hands to her. "Come."

She was just about to take his hands when Rogerian called out from the doorway, "Is all well, my master?"

The woman retreated as far up the bed as she could, hunkering down in the bear-skin.

Doing his best not to show his exasperation, Sanct' Germain answered Rogerian over his shoulder. "I have found someone. If you will build up a fire and start it burning, we can help this unfortunate woman to restore herself." He glanced at the woman. "You would like that, wouldn't' you?"

The woman made no move. "Are there . . . more?"

"My bondsman and I, and our horses and mules: no one else." He tried to reassure her. "You must not fear us, good woman. We mean you no harm."

She glared at him.

"I cannot think you want your babe to suffer," Sanct' Germain said, taking the chance that she would be more protective of her unborn infant than herself. "Let me help you down the ladder and let my bondsman tend to you while I hunt. It will be night soon, and without a fire, you will surely be cold." He continued to hold his hands out.

After a long moment, the woman sighed with exhaustion as she gathered the bear-skin close around her and began to move toward Sanct' Germain.

Sanct' Germain waited for her to take his hands, making no further move that might frighten her. "I will back toward the ladder; you may watch as I do it," he said as he began to guide her; he could feel her shaking as she gripped his hand and arm. "I will go down ahead of you, and you may come after, so that if you should slip, you will not fall. That should reassure you."

There was a soft light coming from below; Rogerian had found a number of oil lamps and lit them; the scent of olives filled the air.

As he reached the edge of the loft, Sanct' Germain hooked his foot over the top rung of the ladder to make sure it was still in place. When he was satisfied, he began his descent, taking care to guide the woman's hands to the ladder.

"I am going out to get wood," Rogerian called up to Sanct' Germain.

"Very good," said Sanct' Germain a bit distantly, his concentration on assisting the woman down the ladder. "Your foot will need to be a little lower, and you will have to kick it free of the bear-skin," he warned as he went down another rung. He could see by the way she moved that her pregnancy was well-advanced; she was probably in the seventh month. "Hold on tightly," he said as he guided her foot onto the next rung.

She made her way gingerly down the stairs, shaking with the strain of it; she clung to the bear-skin as best she could, and dragged it closely around her when she finally reached the floor. "Cold," she said, her voice hardly audible.

"Rogerian will build up your fire. Never fear." He smiled at her, trying to ease her apprehension. "Is there somewhere you would like to sit?"

"Chair," she muttered, and pointed. In the lamp-glow, her face looked yellow but Sanct' Germain did not let this alarm him; morning light would tell him if she was jaundiced.

"You will have food in a while. Is there anything here I can give you now." Sanct' Germain took a step toward the covered shelves he assumed held food.

"Gone," said the woman. "Cowards. All cowards. They ran and left me here." She had found the chair she had wanted and now squatted on it, trying to make herself as comfortable as she could. Snuggling into the bear-skin, she watched Sanct' Germain narrowly.

"Did the others take it when they left?" he asked as he opened the shutters to reveal empty shelves.

"Not all," she answered, and grunted, rubbing her belly where her baby had kicked her; she sighed as her discomfort eased.

There was more to be learned, but he did not want to press her. "You need rest," he said. "If you can doze there, I will instruct my manservant to see to your comforts. I must go hunting if we are to have sustenance before midnight." He did not add that he would dine first, on the blood of the animal he caught.

She yawned and looked about anxiously, obviously struggling to stay alert; the climb down from the loft had sapped what little strength she had.

"You are not to worry," Sanct' Germain told her, understanding her distress. "We will do nothing to harm you." He had said so already, but realized she had not believed him then, nor did she now.

Rogerian came back through the door, a load of wood in his arms. "There is plenty of this; they left most of it behind, by the looks of it." He set the pile down in a heap and turned his attention to the hearth. "I put the horses and mules in the barn behind this house. I've given them all some grain. I will find hay for them later."

"Very good." Sanct' Germain rubbed his jaw. "I should not be too long. Night is coming on, and there will be deer about."

"And wild boar," Rogerian reminded him by way of warning. "You should be wary."

"What about wolves and bear?" Sanct' Germain asked lightly as he slipped out of his pluvial and handed it to Rogerian; he wanted nothing to encumber him on the hunt, and cold did not trouble him nearly as much as wet did. "They run in these mountains as well as boars. Something is always hunting, old friend." He shrugged, showing his acceptance of the danger the animals posed. "I will try for deer and be back as quickly as I can. See that the woman stays warm."

"That I will," Rogerian said, and began to lay wood in the fireplace.

Sanct' Germain slipped out into the dusk; he went to the village gate and let himself out onto the hillside, tasting the coming night. Moonrise would be late tonight but that was no inconvenience to him; he saw at night as readily as a fox. The nearest stand of trees was just beyond the new graves and he made for them at a speed that would have astonished anyone seeing him, for now that the sun was down, all Sanct' Germain's strength flooded through him. The forest promised game and good hunting. Once into the trees he stopped to listen, his senses extending into the darkness as if to embrace every living thing on the mountainside.

An owl drifted past him on huge, hushed wings, and for an instant the wood was silent. Then the wind ruffled through the branches and movement returned: insects bored and flittered and hummed, badgers trundled along in the underbrush, martens scrambled in the branches, a sounder of boar rutted among the roots of the trees some short distance away, wild cats prowled in solitary pursuits of prey, higher up the slope careful deer minced under the trees. Then there came the bleating call of a wild goat, and Sanct' Germain moved off toward it, quiet and agile as a shadow.

Four wild goats grazed in a small meadow; a short distance away an old male stood guard over the four, his shaggy coat matted with shedding hair.

Moving carefully with the skill of long experience, Sanct' Germain crept up on the goats, knowing he would have one chance to catch his prey without a chase. The goat nearest to him was a young male with a scar on his nose; the animal was good-sized and well-fleshed for this time of year: he would supply meat for Rogerian and the woman for several days. He concentrated on the goat, using his ability to influence animals to lull the young goat into a stupor, just dazed enough to give Sanct' Germain the opportunity he sought.

His rush at his prey was so sudden that the other goats barely had time to look up in alarm before the young male was gone, rendered unconscious and carried away by something swift and powerful. The old male on guard let out a challenging squeal as he came rushing down, head lowered, pursuing Sanct' Germain and his prize. But Sanct' Germain sprinted at a speed that the goat could not match, and in a short time he had outrun the herd leader and began to make his way back toward the village with his prize, seeking out the paths the animals and shepherds used.

He came to a broad path at the edge of the forest, one that was intended to carry oxen and carts and wagons. Thinking this must lead back to the village, Sanct' Germain set out on it, glad that he could move more quickly. He had gone roughly a thousand paces when he saw something lying in the road ahead, looking like a heap of tattered leather and smelling of dried blood. Approaching carefully, he saw it was the remnants of a man, one who had been cruelly killed, for the man's abdomen had been abraded away, leaving internal organs exposed and worn. Broken ribs like barrel staves stuck through his chest. The head was nothing more than a mass of shattered bone; the face had been obliterated, the eye sockets crushed, and part of the jaw gone. Only the legs were relatively intact, and the feet were almost black, the ankles still bound with rawhide strips.

Sanct' Germain decided he would have to return to bury the body— he had to get the goat back to the village now—to keep it from being devoured by cats and wolves. He stepped away from the hideous corpse and continued on toward the village. As he neared the walls, he took what he needed from the limp goat before breaking its neck and killing it; only then did he feel a pang of regret for what he had had to do, for it reminded him of the battered dead figure out on the road.

Carrying the goat slung over his shoulders, he went through the gate and down the street to the one house that had light behind its shuttered windows. At the door of the house, he put down his burden and called out to Rogerian, "I have food. He will need to be hung and dressed at once."

"Of course," Rogerian replied without any sign of urgency or worry.

"I will come tend to it at once." He emerged from the house a moment later, carrying a long skinning knife in one hand and a wide, flat pan in the other. "A goat?" he said as he looked down.

"It was near," said Sanct' Germain. "It's good-sized."

"So it is." Rogerian nodded. "I will have my portion as I dress it. That will leave the rest for the woman. Shall I save the skin?"

"Of course; she cannot afford to waste any of the animal," Sanct' Germain said. "And smoke the rest; it will last longer that way. If you roast it, it will be useless in a week. I will hunt again in a night or two, and that will also be smoked for her. This woman will not be able to provide for herself until the end of summer. She cannot hunt as laden as she is with child, and once the babe is born, it will be many weeks before she can leave the infant unattended." As he helped Rogerian to shoulder the goat, he asked, "Has she said anything?"

"Only that her man died of the Great Pox. She disdains speaking to me because I am a servant," Rogerian said without rancor. "She believes she is above servants and slaves, and probably anyone born beyond the walls of the village." He prepared to move off, but added, "Still warm. You came back quickly."

"If I had thought I would be much longer, I would have gutted him myself. I did not kill him until I was almost at the gate; the smell could bring cats or wolves, or bear. I do not intend to waste any part of the meat: it would insult the animal and it would be foolish." Sanct' Germain folded his arms. "Olive-wood should give the smoke a pleasant savor."

"So I thought. I will make a smoke-house tomorrow morning if I cannot find one in this place. Oh, there is a spot of blood on your cheek." With that he wiped it away, then turned and was gone down the narrow alley between the houses.

Sanct' Germain paused as he prepared himself to face the woman, knowing he would have to reassure her; he ran his hand over his chin, then went into the house. "You will have goat to eat," he announced.

She was still in the chair where he had left her, but she no longer sat with her knees drawn up as far as her belly would allow; she slumped with fatigue but there was no trace of defeat about her. The bear-skin draped around her more for warmth than protection; the fire was lively enough to provide warmth as well as light. She looked up at him, showing him black eyes sunk in dark circles. "You did come back."

"Did you think I would not?" Sanct' Germain inquired lightly. "My bondsman, my horses and mules, and my belongings are here. Why should I not return?"

"The Great Pox drives everyone away, if it does not kill them." She stopped to drink from a cup in her hand. "Your man mixed hot water with honey for me."

"Your throat isn't dry," said Sanct' Germain, wondering how Rogerian had convinced her to drink the preparation. "This is all to the good." He glanced toward Rogerian and nodded his approval.

"Not dry anymore. My voice has returned. It is most useful, to have my voice again." She looked at him for a long moment. "I am Csimenae," she said at last, as if making a tremendous concession to him. "My man was—" She stopped herself before she spoke his name. "He died of the Great Pox after almost everyone was gone from here. They made a grave for him before they left."

"So you—" Sanct' Germain began, only to be interrupted.

"I dragged him out to his grave and rolled him in and covered him with earth. My babe moved within me the whole time. Then I was overcome." The condemnation in this admission surprised Sanct' Germain.

"Who would not be?" He came a step nearer to her. "Did everyone leave but you?"

She glared at him. "I would not abandon my man. They would not leave anyone with me. Nor did I need anyone. I saw him die and I buried him." Her voice rose and she stopped to drink again. "If they come back, I will not let them in."

Sanct' Germain realized he had to be careful. "Because they left you alone."

"Not me: the babe I will have. I have managed for myself, but the child is powerless. They said he would be born poxed, but I will not believe it." She tossed her head in scorn and the long black braids plaited around her head, already loosened, swung free. "I would think nothing of my welfare, but this"—she laid her hand on her swollen abdomen—"is as helpless as stranded fish. For that they deserve to be shut out."

"Even those of your blood?" Sanct' Germain asked gently.

"They most of all," Csimenae declared, and stopped to cough. "They should have cared for the babe. As it is, I . . ." She faltered, her black eyes filling with tears. "I may have to make a grave for him, too. I took no Pox, but his father did, and it may have penetrated my womb."

"If the child is still moving, it is probably alive, and if it is alive, it should not be poxed." Sanct' Germain hoped he was reassuring her; nothing in her expression showed any emotion other than defiance.

"I do not want to bury this child; he must thrive and be worthy," she said stubbornly. "This village will be his, when he is grown. I will see that he comes to rule here, for he will deserve to rule. It will be his because all the rest ran away, and so it falls to him by right. He must have the strength to hold it. My grandfather was unable to hold the village—my son shall restore us to mastery here." Her hands were fists, and she almost kicked out at him.

"If that is what you seek for him, who am I to deny him," Sanct' Germain said quietly. "Let us see him safely into the world, and then, perhaps, you may decide on his fortune."

She said nothing for a long moment, staring at him defiantly. "It is the right of my blood to rule here. I have remained here when others fled. I have proved this is ours once again. My grandfather shamed us, and they dragged him behind a horse until there was nothing left but his legs: my son will vindicate our honor." Then she lowered her eyes. "If I had a horse left, I would kill it to ensure my son is safe."

Aware that her hopes might be in vain, Sanct' Germain asked, "And what if you have a daughter; what of her?" He thought of the body lying in the road, and he knew he, too, had been dragged, face-down, behind a horse.

"God is not so cruel to give me a daughter, not after my man is dead." She shook her head repeatedly. "No. I will have a son. It is my right to have a son."

"That may be," said Sanct' Germain. "But many a mother has loved her daughters as well as her sons."

Her laughter was harsh. "I scorn such women!"

Knowing Csimenae was overwrought, Sanct' Germain kept his thoughts to himself; he hoped, for the sake of the child, that the babe was male. "You should not tire yourself," he said gently. "You need your strength."

"To keep my son strong," she agreed as she drank the last of the honied water. "He will be ruler here, and all the other villages will show him honor. I will see to it, or I will die defending him." She sat upright, a martial light in her eyes and determination in every line of her body. "No one will slight him."

It would be easy, he knew, to give her an easy answer, to agree with her desires for her child, but she might as readily take offense at such a remark as be bolstered by it, so he said, "Time enough for that when he is grown."

"He will be lord here before he is grown," she announced. "Mont Calcius will be his when he is sturdy enough to run around its walls."

"Is that the name of this place?" Sanct' Germain asked. "Mont Calcius?"

"The Romans called it Mons Calcius," she replied evasively. "As do the other villages in this region. It has an older name."

"No doubt," said Sanct' Germain, picking up a length of wood and adding it to the fire.

Csimenae looked at him as he tended the fire. "You have a servant to do servant's work," she said.

"He is busy with dressing the goat I killed." He was silent for a moment.

"Does it shame you to kill a goat? There are deer and boar to hunt as well." She gave him a genuine smile. "You did not much dishonor yourself. Even Gardingi hunt the goats in this region. You need not trouble yourself on that account."

He knew she would not understand his ambivalence about killing, so he said only. "I am not troubled."

She almost grinned. "To have meat again! I have lived on onions and cheese for days." She threw back her head and shouted out three hard syllables in a language he did not recognize. "There. I will do it properly at the edge of the trees once my babe is born, but this will do for the time being. The spirits will respect what you have done, now. You may hunt without fear of them."

"You are good to do this," he said; whatever she believed about the animals in the mountains, he was willing to accept it.

"I have my son to preserve; nothing else matters so much as he." She folded her arms. "I am still thirsty."

"I will fetch water from the well and heat it for you," Sanct' Germain offered, wondering at the sternness in her face.

She nodded to acknowledge his service but said nothing more.

As he went down the dark street, Sanct' Germain cogitated on what Csimenae had revealed as well as what he had inferred; drawing water from the well, he decided to remain in Mont Calcius at least until Csimenae was delivered of her child, for it took the sting out of his need to travel.

*   *   *

Text of a letter from Episcus Salvius of Tarraco to Episcus Gerundol of Corduba.

To my most esteemed peer and Brother in the Church, my greetings and the assurance of my prayers to guide and comfort you in this time of travail. We are being tested, and beyond all question, our souls will hang in the balance when our ordeal is ended.

Your tomus has been put into my hands, and I read with dismay of the spread of the Great Pox. It has not yet come to Tarraco in any great force, for which I must thank my good Angel, for it is God's goodness that preserves us. It is not so for much of the countryside. I am told by travelers that the mountains are filled with it: indeed, the pestilent vapors are so powerful that many of the Gardingi are refusing to repair any damaged roads, fearing that will bring the Pox more quickly. Nothing that the Exarchs have ordered has been carried out, nor will it be until the Pox is gone from the land.

Byzantine ships have refused to take cargo from any port west of Massilia, saying that to do so would carry the Pox to Constantinople, which they will not do. This is making for hard times among the merchants of this city; they must watch their goods spoil in warehouses or face empty ones, with none of their goods delivered. Because of this, many men have been unable to find work and are now asking for charity of the churches here, saying they face starvation. We have extended ourselves as much as we are able, but we, too, have been deprived of goods, so our position is perilous.

I implore you, as a worthy Christian, to consider making work available to men from Tarraco if they can get to Corduba. With the Great Pox killing your people, surely you will have need of strong and willing workers. If you will but assure me that you will be able to secure them employment, I shall recommend that able-bodied men depart from here as soon as you think prudent. I am aware that it will take time for your reply to reach me, so I will tell you that I would want to be able to send these men on their way before Midsummer Day. It would be best for them to travel in good weather and long days.

The Episcus of Caesaraugusta has already said that there will be no work until the Gardingi authorize the rebuilding of roads, and so I cannot recommend that these men go there, although it is closer. I have sent requests also to Saguntum and Toletum, but have not heard from either Episcus. I beseech you to do as much as you can to find employment for these unfortunate men: in Tarraco we are at the limits of our resources and God has not yet seen fit to end our tribulation. If you will but give me a sign of hope, I know those who come to the church for succor will be thankful and more sure of God's goodness than if they are left to languish as beggars. Many men do desperate things when they are in such straits as these men are. Several of them have seen their wives and children die of hunger, and without help, there will be more called to the Throne of God.

You may think that because we have not been much visited by the Great Pox that God has spared us, but I tell you it is not the case. The Great Pox is a subtle and deadly enemy, capable of any ruse to bring down men. Each of us must bear burdens, as Christians must to be worthy of Salvation. Here we have starvation instead of Pox, but both are equally deadly. I cannot offer hope to those without bread and whose fields are barren. If you will only consider letting me send these men to you, I know your act will redound to your benefit in Paradise.

In return for your generosity, I will send with the men the olive-wood crucifix from Jerusalem that has long hung in our church. This is a most holy object, doubly sanctified by the place it was made and the Sacrifice it exemplifies. You will find its presence imparts a sanctity to all that come near it. All of Corduba will know it is your greatness of heart that brings such a treasure to your people, and it will strengthen their faith.

May God show His Face to you in this and in all things, may your children never abandon the ways of virtue, may your wife do you honor, may your flock always hold you in esteem, may the Church reward your fidelity, may you never falter in devotion to Christ, may your dedication never flag, may you never neglect any pious act, may you be fearless in the cause of God's Right, may you never have reason to regret any act you may perform, may your body be preserved from all ills, may you live in wisdom and die in grace, and may your name be heralded in Heaven.

In the Name of Father, Son, and Holy Spirit,
Salvius
Episcus of Tarraco

on the 9th day of April, in the 622nd year since the Coming of Our Lord

5

Her delivery had been hard after a day and a night of labor; the child had come at last shortly after dawn, red, wrinkled, and outraged. Now Csimenae lay exhausted on the straw-filled mattress, her face wan, her hair damp and tangled, but her eyes shone like burning embers, and she managed a smile that was all teeth. "I said I would have a son," she told Sanct' Germain defiantly as she looked down at her infant. "I should have sacrificed a horse. I should have drunk its blood."

Sanct' Germain nodded, showing no dismay at her wish. "You have your son." He had a bowl of warm water in one hand and a soft cloth in the other. "If you will let me wash him?"

She held the baby more fiercely. "No. You will take all his strength from him. He must have all the juices of his birth upon him, to guard him from death. He should be washed in horse's blood." She put a protective hand over her son's head. "You must give me the cord you cut. He will have to wear it around his neck until he is five years old. And I must keep the afterbirth preserved in oil until he marries, or he will not be fruitful."

"And the cord? What benefit will it provide?" He knew better than to argue with her, although he had never learned that such a practice served any worthwhile purpose.

"He must be strong," she said as if he were a fool. "You are a stranger, and you do not know anything."

"That I am a stranger is beyond question," said Sanct' Germain quietly, "but it does not follow that I am wholly ignorant." In his long centuries at the Temple of Imhotep, he had learned about difficult births—the only kind the priests ever saw, for all others were handled by midwives—and knew that fatigue would soon overtake Csimenae; she would require careful nursing to regain her resilience. "Your babe will need you to restore yourself if you are to be able to tend to his needs; he will be hungry in a short while, and he must be fed then, or he will lose strength. You would not want that to happen." He indicated the partitioned room beyond the hearth where she lay, thinking again that it had been wise to move her into the largest house in the village;

here she felt safe as well as confident of having the greatest power in Mont Calcius. He saw her hand shake from exhaustion. "You will be able to gain stamina only if you rest.

In his improvised swaddling bands, the infant began to fuss, soft, harsh cries indicating his dissatisfaction.

"He will be a mighty leader; all the signs point to it," she said, trying not to yawn. "He is full of promise." She smoothed his forehead and blinked slowly as sleep began to take hold of her. "When the others come back, they will . . . They will own him the lord here." Sighing deeply, she struggled to keep awake. "Do not wash him."

Sanct' Germain carefully said nothing. He signaled to Rogerian. "You had better make a strong broth for her. The venison would be best. Add garlic and tarragon and a little of the angelica root to clean her blood."

Rogerian looked away. "And you? What of your blood, my master? How long as it been since you—?"

His response was hardly more than a whisper. "I would never seek a woman in her state; I could harm her, and give her more distress than joy. It would put her at risk, and perhaps her child as well. I could not have that on my conscience." He looked at Csimenae for a long moment. "The animals will suffice for the time being," said Sanct' Germain brusquely, then went on in a kinder tone. "I am grateful you are concerned for me, but, truly, you have no reason to worry."

"So you tell me," said Rogerian, plunging on, "and yet, you have said that when you do not have—"

"She'll hear you," Sanct' Germain warned as he moved toward the table where Rogerian was chopping herbs with his dagger.

Rogerian went silent at once. When he had finished with the tarragon leaves, he looked directly at Sanct' Germain. "You will have to seek touching eventually, or you will suffer for it."

"Perhaps," said Sanct' Germain, being deliberately evasive. "Let me know when she begins to stir, or if her infant wakes again. Both of them are tired, but Csimenae is worn out. With so long a labor and so hard a delivery, she may be feverish. She is worried for her babe, which is not astonishing; soothe her if you can. Be sure she has plenty of broth and water, and a little toasted cheese, if she wants it, but do not give her other food until tomorrow. If she seems too depleted, tell me." He had raided the cheeses from the other houses in Mont Calcius; there were still five good-sized rounds left; in another month there would be new ones from the small flock of sheep he had acquired.

"And if she takes a fever, what then?" Rogerian asked. "If she is ill for long, her child may die from it."

"Keep your voice down," Sanct' Germain cautioned. "It is important that she not be distressed." He rubbed at the short beard he had grown over the last seven weeks. "I am going to tend to the stock, and then I am going to try to find some eggs for her. I should not be long."

"The sun is strong today, and it will grow stronger until mid-day," Rogerian pointed out, giving an oblique warning. "You will have to have new earth in your soles soon."

"Yes; you are right about that," said Sanct' Germain as he went out of the house into the street; he made his way toward the only real barn in the village where his two mules and two horses were stabled, and the three feral nanny-goats he had managed to capture were penned inside high walls. Birds nesting in the loft twittered and screeched as he came inside; he paid them no mind as he checked the water in the stalls, and then in the pen. "You'll all be fed," he told the animals. "No need to fret." Using the rickety ladder he climbed into the loft and grabbed two armloads of hay which he threw down to the goats. Then he gathered the same again and carefully backed down the ladder. He fed the mules first, then went up once again to get hay for the horses. Once the fodder was in the mangers, he went and fetched a skin of olive oil, and poured a little onto the hay for the horses and mules, to help their coats stay healthy. Those chores done, he took a large armload of hay and strolled out of the barn, thinking as he went that he would have to trim his horses' and mules' feet soon. He dropped the hay into the village sheep-fold and smiled wryly at the occupants' bleating; he chided his own longings, commenting aloud, "If only I were so readily satisfied," before he went on about his self-appointed chores.

There were three places where the newly arrived wild geese occasionally laid eggs, and he checked each place; the geese and any eggs were missing. He frowned, trying to decide what to offer her instead—honied goat's milk, perhaps—when a movement above him caught his attention. A hawk flying high overhead skreed to its mate, and was answered from another part of the sky. The wind was picking up, coming in from the south-west smelling of wild thyme and juniper. From far down the slope came the distant, unmusical sound of a bell: a goatherd was leading his flock out to feed; it was a reminder that Mont Calcius could expect visitors from time to time, and that some preparation should be made to receive them, whether friendly or hostile. The villagers who had left might also decide to return, and Csimenae would insist that they be humbled for their desertion; she spoke of her intentions often, taking pride in her anger. She would make them bow to her and to her son or she would shut the gates against them. Sanct' Germain decided to make an inspection of the wood-and-stone wall that surrounded the village in order to be certain it was in good repair, and went out the gate to attend to it at once. On the north side of the wall he found half a dozen timbers were loose, leaning at an angle: these would have to be replaced, and soon. As he went around to the eastern side, he discovered two of the broad planks had fallen completely, and a whole section of the remaining wall listed at a precarious angle—one good rainstorm and it would all come down.

Sanct' Germain reproved himself that he had not bothered to check the wall more thoroughly before now; returning from the hunt, he usually approached from the west, and had not paid much attention to the state of the wall. He would have to go to work soon: that night, he told himself, he would bring back logs from the forest instead of meat. Continuing around the outside of the town, he was relieved to find the south side of the village wall was intact, and he had already repaired the gate on the west side of the village. If he did the work at night, when he was strongest, he could have the whole of it refurbished in a matter of two or three nights: Csimenae's apprehension would be assuaged by the restoration of the wall and it was an easily done task.

"My master?" Rogerian was calling as Sanct' Germain came back through the gate and set the heavy wooden bolt in place.

"Here, Rogerian," he answered. "Is anything the matter?"

"The baby is awake, but Csimenae is not. I put him to her breast to suck, but he is fretful." Rogerian appeared at the end of the street.

"Hardly surprising after such a delivery," said Sanct' Germain quietly as he lengthened his stride. "Is he well otherwise?"

Rogerian shrugged and fell into step beside Sanct' Germain. "He is only a few hours old. I cannot tell."

Sanct' Germain raised his brows in speculation. "How does he appear to you? Is his color good?"

"I would know more if she would allow us to wash him and swaddle him," said Rogerian with a slight frown of concern.

"I am not certain swaddling is much use. Those I have seen over the years have not been helped by such confinement: babies will grow straight or crooked according to their natures, not because they were swaddled or not." He was almost at the door of the house where Csimenae now lay. "Whether or not she will let us bathe the child, she must certainly wash as soon as she is awake again."

"And if she refuses?" Rogerian asked.

"We must convince her it is for the good of her child." He stopped, his hand on the latch. "Which it is: it will do the boy no good to have his mother ail."

Rogerian nodded. "Is there anything I can do for her now?" He paused. "She wants to wash him in horse's blood."

"I know.' Sanct' Germain considered briefly. "Milk the nannies, then, this evening, heat the milk with honey and a little of the wine in the pantry here. Then give her broth again. It is fortunate that there are ewes in the sheepfold at last—we will soon make a fortifying cheese for her. For now, we must make do with what we have." Sanct' Germain was about to step inside, but Rogerian halted him once more.

"What of the Great Pox? Has the child escaped it?"

"He is alive and his skin is clear: I must assume he has. He cries readily and he is active, so it would seem he is well enough." He went through the door without giving Rogerian a chance to speak again. The odor of sweat and blood was still strong in the room in spite of the aromatic branches Rogerian had thrown on the fire. For a brief instant, Sanct' Germain felt a pang of esurience that was all the more poignant for its brevity. He stilled the need as soon as he was aware of it, chagrin taking its place.

"Rogerian?" Csimenae's voice was thready, hard to hear.

"No: Sanct' Germain," he replied as he went toward her partitioned room. "Rogerian has gone to milk the goats. He will be back when he is finished." Then, in order to keep her interest, he continued, "I went to inspect the walls of the village, to be sure they are strong. I will shore them up where it is needed."

She blinked in an effort to bring his features into focus as she held her son against her nipple. "I am so tired," she said to account for her drowsiness.

"You had an ordeal to bring your son into the world." He took a step nearer. "What shall you call him: do you know?"

"It is not time to speak his name," she said, doing her utmost to be severe. "If I say his name before he has been alive for three days, the old gods will surely take him from me. He is in their hands for the first three days. The God of the Church guards him after that, and the gods of this village . . ." Her face was darkening with effort.

"Shh," Sanct' Germain said, calming her. "Your ways are not my ways, and I have no children. I did not know this."

"How could you not?" she demanded, her agitation communicating itself to her infant, who began to wail. She immediately clutched him in her arms and tried to roll onto her side to shield him with her body.

Sanct' Germain took a step back. "Care for him, Csimenae. Then rest."

"I am no weakling," she snapped before curling protectively around her squalling son. Only when she felt his mouth at her nipple did her anxiety diminish.

There was nothing he could say that would comfort her now. Resigned, he went to stoke the fire so that she would not become chilled; she might easily take any sickness that lingered in the village, for the effort of delivery left many women prey to all manner of debilitation; he had seen such collapses many times before. The fire would keep her warm, he reminded himself as he put the cut branches on the wood that already burned. That done, he took the largest cauldron from the cabinet next to the pantry and prepared to carry it out to the well: it would not do for Csimenae to bathe in cold water; she would have to remain in the bath for a good while in order to loosen her muscles to alleviate the discomfort she felt. He was sorry no Roman bath remained at the village, for it would have been an easy task to fire up the holocaust and heat the caladarium. As it was, he had a fair amount of work ahead of him. Making his way to the well, he studied the sky, noticing the high clouds and marking their course, for the weather would dictate much of his work.

By the time Sanct' Germain had filled the barrel with hot water and aromatic herbs, Csimenae was awake enough to be curious about what he was doing. Holding a length of linen across her body, she sat up to watch him, curiosity flavored with suspicion. She still carried her son close to her, but she no longer looked as if she expected the infant to be torn from her hands. She smiled to show her inquisitiveness was untainted by leeriness. "This is an unusual thing—washing a mother before her birth-courses have stopped."

"You will find you and your babe will benefit from it," said Sanct'

Germain in a tranquil tone. "Come. You will want to make the most of the warmth."

She faltered. "You will not hurt my son, will you?"

"Of course not," said Sanct' Germain, more worn than surprised by the question, for he had become familiar with her deeply held suspicions. "You have made your wishes clear and I will honor them: I will not even attempt to wash him, although I believe it would be to his good to do so."

Csimenae shook her head emphatically. "He would suffer if you were to do such a thing. It is bad enough he is not bathed in horse's blood." She glared at him. "I will curse you if you betray your Word, and phantom horses will trample you and the fires of the sky shall burn you."

"I will not betray my Word," said Sanct' Germain patiently, recalling the dead man on the road.

She did not appear convinced, but she carefully rose from her bed and, wrapped in a length of rough linen, made her way toward the barrel, all the while glancing back at her son, who lay in a pile of bear-skins half-asleep. Csimenae smiled at the boy, a tenderness in her face that she reserved only for him. As she reached the improvised bath, she said, "You must not watch. Turn away. It would be dangerous to my child if anything weakens me." There was resentment in her voice, and a deeper emotion that was more than anger. "You are too close, foreigner."

"Would you not like my help?" Sanct' Germain asked as if he had not heard her.

"I will climb on the stool. That will suffice." She glowered at that item of furniture as if she were accusing it of being in league with Sanct' Germain. "You must not come near," she said with emphasis as she dropped the linen cloth on the plank-topped table and tugged the stool up to the barrel. "Turn around. You are not to look at me."

This command struck him as absurd, but he said nothing as he complied with her order; he listened as the stool rubbed against the stays of the barrel and heard the splash as Csimenae let herself down into the water. "Now you may turn back."

"That I will," he said as he did.

"It is very warm," she announced, not imparting approval or condemnation in her tone of voice.

"Do you think so." Sanct' Germain hitched one leg over the far end of the table and half-sat there. "The herbs will help you to regain your strength and to add virtue to your milk. When you are done, I have prepared a little wool-fat to ease the cracks in your skin, and your lips. When I have caught more sheep, I will prepare more for you. I told you about the sheep." He had found five sheep wandering in the hills a few days before; one had been belled and all flocked around him, so he had brought them back to the sheepfold near the market square.

"I remember," she said, turning in the barrel so she could watch him. Her black hair spread out like trailing vines around her and she almost smiled. "You have promised new cheese."

"That I have," he agreed.

"The rest will be jealous when they return, to see that I have not died." Her satisfaction showed in her smile. "Perhaps we should bar the gate and keep them outside the walls until they have owned my son their leader."

"Why not wait until they come to decide?" Sanct' Germain suggested. "You may have to suit your intentions to the purpose of the others." He had cautioned her before and each time she had scoffed at him. This time, she cocked her head in consideration.

"You may be wiser than I have supposed," she conceded after a long moment of consideration. "Have you seen anyone in the hills?"

"A goatherd or two," Sanct' Germain said, "And I think there may be a band of robbers nine thousand paces to the north of here."

"A band of robbers?" she repeated uneasily. "Why did you not tell me?"

"Because I am not sure they are robbers. They may be villagers driven out of their homes by the Pox." He did not think this was the case; the signs pointed to robbers who preyed upon travelers. He said nothing of the dragged corpse.

"Then they might be from here," she said and flicked water off her fingers to show her contempt for them. "They could be villagers."

"If that were the case, I would have thought they might come this way before now. The weather has been good and there has been no word of Pox, and if they supposed the village was empty, why should they not come." he said calmly. "You said your people went to the south-west when they left. These robbers are north of here."

"Still, they might be from here, keeping themselves by robbing before coming back," she said stubbornly just before she sank down in the barrel, ducking her head under the water. As she emerged, she wiped her face and looked at him. "You do not know the people of this village."

"True enough. But the robbers have bear-skulls mounted on their walls, not horse-skulls as you have here." He let her consider this, then went on. "If your people come back, I would expect them to come from the direction they left, and I would expect them to have their flocks with them."

"They could have gone to the north as well," she said stubbornly, her chin beginning to quiver.

Although Sanct' Germain did not agree, he said, "It is possible," and let the matter go.

For a little time there was no sound in the house other than the quiet lapping of water. Then Csimenae spoke up as if they had been conversing all along. "You do not want to let in anyone who comes here, of course. This is to be held for my son."

"As you wish," said Sanct' Germain. "If someone should arrive, I will send for you at once and you may decide what is to be done."

"And no one will be permitted to claim this house. It is mine by right. I remained in the village, and that makes my son lord here. No one can deny me this." She had raised her head as if she expected him to challenge her. "Well?"

"He is very young to be lord," said Sanct' Germain carefully.

"Do you mean he is not worthy of being lord?" Her voice rose with emotion and furious tears stood in her black eyes.

"No; I mean he is very young to have enemies," Sanct' Germain replied in a level voice. "If you seek to have him advance, you will have to hold the position for him. You must have thought about this, Csimenae. You have talked about your hopes for your son often enough. You are capable of doing much for him, as you have shown already." He did his best to reassure her. "You have prevailed. You have brought your son into the world. You have held the village for him. You can keep him from harm."

"He will rule in this village. He may extend his powers throughout the mountains." She nodded to herself. "It is his right."

"As you have proven," Sanct' Germain agreed; he sensed her exhaustion under her assertions. "I will bring you a clean cloth to dry yourself."

She shot him a stern glance. "You will leave this house while I do that."

"If you wish," he said, not wanting to offend her. "I will dispose of the water as you instruct me."

"You will," Csimenae said bluntly. "There is blood in the water, so it must be poured away from the house, otherwise you will bring trouble here." She slipped under the water one more time. "I will need my comb," she said as she emerged again.

"I will bring it with the drying sheet," he said, and went to fetch the large square of clean linen for her. Her comb, he remembered, was on the shelf over the bed where she had delivered her son. Taking care not to disturb the sleeping infant, he retrieved the comb before he went to the barrel where Csimenae was wringing as much water as she could from her hair, and struggling to keep herself wholly upright as she did. "Your comb," he said as he put it on the table. "And your drying cloth. There is an open dalmatica on the chair for you to put on. You may reach it without difficulty. Do you need help getting out?"

"No. It is unfitting that you assist me. Leave the house," she responded, and remained still until she saw him leave. Emerging from the barrel, she was careful to be sure none of her birthing blood got onto the floor; she wadded one end of the drying sheet between her legs and used the other end of it to blot her skin dry, then tied it in place. Finally she picked up the old Roman garment and tugged it on, shrugging to adjust its drape; the material was old and soft with use and little as she wanted to admit it, she liked the feel of it on her skin. She went back to her bed, comb in hand, ready to work the knots out of her hair and braid it once again in the fashion of married women.

"Csimenae?" Sanct' Germain called from outside the door. "May I tend to the barrel?"

"Yes," she said as she gazed down at her son. How proud she was of him, and what great things he would do! Taking pains not to disturb his rest, she dropped down next to him. "Do not make noise," she whispered.

Sanct' Germain saw her stretch out and smiled faintly, knowing it would not be long before she was, once again, asleep. Standing so that she could not see what he was doing, he lifted the barrel and started for the door. The blood in the water was a tantalizing reminder of all the need he had kept in check for so long; he did his best to keep from yearning too much for the intimacy he missed. If she had shown any inclination to welcome him, he would have been overjoyed, but there had been no sign of such willingness, or any desire for more than he already provided her. Her strength fascinated him as much as her vulnerability awakened his protectiveness, though she sought neither of them, and would fervently deny both. He made a small gesture of resignation and went about his self-appointed chores. As he stepped out into the debilitating light of early afternoon, he had to admit that the blood of animals was to him hardly more than bread-and-water to the living.

Rogerian was working in the shed that served as a creamery; he looked up from his panning as Sanct' Germain went by, bound for the midden. "She bathed?"

"Yes." he had almost reached his destination but stopped, setting the barrel down and sighing. "How much more native earth do I have in the chests?"

"The smaller chest is still full, the larger has perhaps a third of its contents remaining." He set the broad, shallow copper pan aside and considered Sanct' Germain carefully. "You do not have enough to last more than two years, if we are careful and you find a lover to help sustain you."

"Two years should be long enough for us to reach Roma. I have more than enough of my native earth there. Olivia has ten chests of it at her estate and I have the same at Villa Ragoczy." He looked toward the east.

"You assume nothing has happened to the chests," Rogerian said firmly. "But there have been armies at Roma, and they have looted and robbed, as have all armies before them. You cannot be certain that your chests are still intact, or that they can be found, not now." He gave a worried stare at Sanct' Germain. "Your homeland, too, is filled with barbarians."

"As it has been for more than two thousand years," said Sanct' Germain with a tranquility that Rogerian found disturbing. "Looting armies care nothing for chests of earth, and even if they should do, half of the chests are well-hidden." He smiled fleetingly. "It is good of you to think of it."

"One of us must," said Rogerian, more abruptly than he had intended. "Since she has not chosen to accept you as her—"

"Exactly. Her what? She is concerned wholly for the well-being of her child. It is all that matters to her—securing his position." Sanct' Germain picked up the barrel and carried it the rest of the way to the midden. He tipped it over gingerly, making sure the water did not run too fast. When he was finished, he righted the barrel and returned it to the shed where Rogerian was once again panning milk. "I am not entirely a fool," he said genially.

"Not a fool, no," said Rogerian. He set the pan down on the rack above the others and laid a rough, damp cloth over it. "Fools are not the only ones who . . . But you do not always . . ." The words died out.

"Possibly not," said Sanct' Germain with an ironic inclination of his head. "But I have not yet died the True Death. And I am in no immediate danger of doing so." He righted the empty barrel. "We go on well enough, old friend."

Although he nodded, the trouble did not leave Rogerian's eyes.

Text of a letter from Atta Olivia Clemens to Sanct' Germain at his manor near Tolosa.

To my oldest, most treasured friend, my eternal greetings from the Eternal City, as this poor embattled place fancies itself.

It has been too long since we have exchanged news of our lives. To set an example, I will tell you that the eastern Goths are in charge here still, pretending they are managing as well as the Caesars did, and all the while intimidated by Constantinople. They have changed the walls of the city and do not maintain the aqueducts as they should in order to keep the water pure. They have let the baths go to ruin because they do not often bathe. This is not the place you remember, Franciscus, not even as it was fifty years ago. Most of the city seems to be cobbled together out of the old buildings from my youth. It saddens me to see so many fine buildings of all sorts turned into heaps of brick and marble rubble, and that rubble used to make houses my father would not have thought adequate to stable his mules. To hear the people of the city point to that golden statue of Nero in front of the Flavian Circus, saying it is Apollo, and calling the Circus the Colosseum for the statue puts me near laughter. Niklos understands some part of my amusement, but not as you would do if you were here.

Which brings me to ask why you have left Toletum. From all you have said in earlier letters, I would have thought you would have come back to Rome or gone to Constantinople or Alexandria. When your letter finally arrived—taking seven months to reach me—I was startled at your decision. I can truly comprehend why you might want to go into Frankish territory, but it would seem more prudent to seek out more genial places. From what you have said of the Franks, you might not be entirely welcome in their territory. Not that the Byzantines would welcome you open-heartedly. They are so caught up in their Court-life and their Church, that it would not be easy for one as foreign as you are to be able to manage without suspicion falling on you. So perhaps the Franks are safer than the Greeks.

It has been a hard winter; there have been more storms than usual and the roads are in dreadful disrepair. If the rest of the world has suffered as we have, no wonder it is taking months for letters to come instead of the weeks of five hundred years ago. Do you recall how swiftly a letter could travel from upper Gaul to Rome? Eighty-five thousand paces a day. That, I fear, is long-lost. Say what you will about the Empire, it did move the mail quickly and well.

Mind you, I am not prepared to hail old Rome as the epitome of all cities, nor decry it as the sink of debauchery some claim it was. It was never as fine as some say, nor as decadent. Rome was a happier place to live when I was still alive. I can say that in spite of my own wretched state at the time, for I know the difference between my suffering and the society that was around me. When I came to your life, Vespasianus was Caesar, and the law avenged me. Today no one would say anything if I were treated now as I was then.

Enough of this. I am sending this along to your estate near Tolosa in the hope you will be there to receive it. I am also sending four crates of your native earth from your stores here, in case you have not enough of them. In these times, with the fortunes of the world so unpredictable, I believe it is wise to be prepared for misfortune as well as to anticipate a need rather than be surprised by it. Do not think unkindly of me for doing this—you have done the same for me in times past and I know it is fitting to repay you for your attentive concerns. I will not dispute the matter with you. It is not my intention to make decisions for you, but I am keenly aware that you may be left in difficult circumstances if you do not have your native earth readily to hand.

Tell me how long you will be near Tolosa; I may decide to pay you a visit, that is, if I cannot persuade you to come to Rome for a time. I am willing to wait for letters to arrive, but not forever. So I will tell you how long I am prepared to remain here, expecting your answer: if I have no word from you by this time next year, I will gather my chests and come to Tolosa myself, to see if you are well. I would hope that I have news of you before then, for just now I abhor travel, having done *more of it than I wanted a century ago—conditions have not improved since I left Constantinople in a miserable fishing boat. To subject myself and Niklos to the horrid roads just to ascertain you are well is a trifle more than I am eager to undertake, so you had best answer this before the year is up.*

Since it is foolish to implore gods or Heaven to look after those of our blood, I will only assure you of my continuing affectionate devotion, which the Church is beginning to claim for itself alone, insisting that piety is for God and not for human souls; it seems to me that humans need that affectionate devotion more than any god ever has. You have been more constant for me than any Saint or Emperor, and so you have my fealty, in such a way as I demonstrate fealty.

May this find you well and in no danger. May you know the happiness you seek. May you continue to thrive. May all the usual end-of-letter benefices be yours.

In the old Roman sense of the word, piously,
Olivia

at Rome, June 1ˢᵗ, Christian year 622 according to the Pope and the 1575ᵗʰ Year of the City

6

There were nine people at the gates: two men, a woman, two boys— one with the mark of the Great Pox on his cheeks—two girls, a toddler and a babe-in-arms. All were thin and pale enough to make it apparent that they had not fared well in the last months; their garments were worn and fraying, and two of them were barefoot. They came, empty-handed, up the narrow, rutted road to Mont Calcius, all seeming to be at the end of their strength.

"This is our place," said the older of the two men as he reached the gate and faced Sanct' Germain, who waited just inside the newly repaired gates. "We are trying to return to our homes."

"Perhaps," Sanct' Germain replied steadily in Latin, as the man had addressed him. He knew his black hippogaudion and dark-red Persian leggings of Damascus silk marked him as a stranger as much as his accent, the silver eclipse ornamenting the fibula that held the shoulder of his clothing, and the Byzantine dagger through his belt. He kept his expression cordial as he regarded the nine over the top of the gates.

"It is," the man insisted, his hand on the hilt of a short, wide-bladed sword that had seen better days. "We have lived here for generations."

"You left it," said Sanct' Germain in a level voice; out of the corner of his eye he saw Csimenae hurrying toward him.

"But we have returned," the man said, desperation making his tone sharp. "It is our home. We have come a long way. We want to . . . There are others, too. They will come here before summer is done."

The afternoon sun was bright, shining like brass in the sky; beneath its rays, the land hummed with heat so that even the dust drowsed.

"Will they?" Csimenae laughed aloud as she reached the gate. "Rogerian told me," she said to Sanct' Germain, then, without waiting for anything he might say, she addressed the people outside the gates. "Let them come. They will face what you face. They will have to kneel to my son."

The younger man stared at Csimenae. "Your son?"

"Aulutis. He is named for my father," she said defiantly in a mixture of Latin and the ancient tongue of her people. "You will have to promise him your fealty if you are to be allowed to return here."

The younger man laughed. "How can you keep us out?"

"I have weapons and men to use them," Csimenae announced, smiling.

At this Sanct' Germain intervened. "You did not come all this way to fight, surely. You wish to come back to your village, as what man does not?" He glanced at Csimenae. "You must be willing to have your neighbors back without making a contest of their presence. They should have no reason to refuse giving loyalty to your son for the sake of the village, and you will need their help to keep the place going."

"They left. They left me to die." She pointed to the younger man. "You. Tacanti. I remember what you did. You took the last of my meat when you left."

The younger man looked away. "It would have been wasted. Your husband was dying, and you . . . You could make no use of it, not with a husband to bury. How could I know you would find robbers to help you?"

"Robbers?" Csimenae laughed, merriment mixing with spite. "This man is many things, but he is no robber. He has taken nothing from the village; he has brought good things. He has kept me and my son alive through his skills as a hunter, and has made the walls stout again, so that beggars like you, yes, and robbers, cannot come here without my leave." She glanced at Sanct' Germain. "You will not let them harm me, will you?"

"No," he said. "But I have no wish to harm them, either," he added, anticipating her displeasure.

He was not disappointed. "You will do as I tell you, or you will leave this village; no one comes here now, but on my sufferance," she said sharply. "I will allow no one to diminish my position, for that will harm my son. He is master here now, and you will have to acknowledge him so." She pointed out through the planks of the gates at the returning villagers. "I will have water brought out to you, and you may think about what you wish to do." She turned and called out to Rogerian to fill two buckets at the well. "These will be yours," she said, addressing the nine once more.

"But," the older man said, "we have nothing to eat. We have gone two days without food." He held out his hands. "Surely you will not deny us something?"

"You were ready to deny me food. You left me almost nothing to sustain me—a few cheeses, a half-dozen barrels of flour, a few strings of onions. You took everything else and you knew I was pregnant, so you were willing to condemn my child, too." She leaned against the gates. "Weren't you?"

The older man shook his head unhappily. "You proved us wrong. You lived and your child is alive. You understand, then, how we feel."

"I certainly do. All the more reason to consider my terms," said Csimenae, her black eyes shining. "You say you want to come back inside the village, yet you bring nothing but your appetites with you. Is your fealty so much to ask, when you offer so little?"

The older man lowered his head. "It is our home, woman, just as it is yours. Can you find nothing useful in our presence?"

Sanct' Germain wanted to speak up, but held his tongue; Csimenae would not welcome any interjection he might make during this bargaining.

"I am a builder," Tacanti reminded her. "You have building to be done, haven't you? You have need of me. And my nephew, Blada, he has tended flocks before. You will want to have a herdsman for your flocks, won't you? You cannot keep your flocks penned all through the summer; they will sicken if you do. They must be let out to graze and to run. We are willing to do what needs to be done." He held his hands out to her. "It was wrong to take food from you, I will say so. But if you hold me in contempt for doing it, how can you refuse to take us in?"

"So you have studied the village," Sanct' Germain remarked, and saw the quick look the two men exchanged.

"We feared robbers," muttered the older of the two.

Csimenae's temper flared. "You mean you decided to see if you could sneak back. You thought I would be dead along with the rest." Her accusation was so stern that all but the infant looked abashed.

"Then you will not let us in," said the woman, hopelessness showing in every line of her body. "You refuse to let us return to our home."

"But I do not refuse," said Csimenae directly to the woman. "Ione, I cannot let you displace me and mine from our station, though you have drunk the blood of horses. You left and my son and I remained. I found a defender for the village and I have kept it safe with that defender. You cannot discount what I have done." She looked at each of the people standing before her on the far side of the gates. "If you swear allegiance to my son, and kiss his foot in token, you may come into the village at once. I will assign you a house and see that you have food. But you must swear allegiance to Aulutis or you may not enter."

Tacanti sighed as he wiped his brow. "I had a house of my own in the village—"

"You will take the one I give you, or you will have nothing," Csimenae said, cutting him off. "This is my village now; I hold it for my son."

The older man nodded. "She has the right. She has the right. We cannot deny it. When we left, she stayed here—"

"Did she?" Tacanti interrupted. "Or did she flee and then return?"

"I was *pregnant,*" Csimenae reminded him. "How could I flee? It took all my strength to bury my man when he died. How could I have gone away, then come back before you, with sheep and goats?"

"As you said, you had that man"—he pointed to Sanct' Germain— "to help you."

"He came to this village with his servant," Csimenae said, her head coming up. She cocked her chin in the direction of the well where

Rogerian had just begun to fill the first of two buckets. "You know how I was. You, Tacanti, have no right to say I did not remain."

Ione laid her hand on Tacanti's arm. "It is for her son that she holds the village. We cannot deny her his authority."

"Perhaps not," said Tacanti, his features sullen and his voice truculent. "*If* she has truly not left the village."

"If you would take my Word," Sanct' Germain interrupted, "I will swear that she has not left the village since my servant and I got here, and that was very soon after you left."

"Ha. An easy thing to say, when you hold the village," Tacanti countered.

Sanct' Germain smiled faintly. "Why should that concern me? This village means little to me. I have no reason to lie to you."

"You have a woman to lie for," Tacanti accused.

In answer, Sanct' Germain laughed. "Not I," he said. "Nor would Csimenae do anything that would compromise her son. She still grieves for her man, who died after you left." He folded his arms. "I am not some proud Gardingio, to claim women as a ram claims ewes. My servant and I came upon Mont Calcius by chance, and stayed for . . . convenience. You impugn Csimenae's devotion if you say otherwise."

Tacanti was about to speak again; his demeanor crackled with indignation; but the older man put his hand on Tacanti's shoulder. "For now we will accept what this stranger says, Csimenae. Later we will talk again."

"Oh, no. You are not through the gates yet," Csimenae reminded him. "Rogerian, give them the water. We will return after we have tended to the animals. You may say then what you have decided to do. And if you are allowed in, that will be the end of it. There will be no discussion, only your oath to my son." She stepped back from the gates to allow Rogerian to open them sufficiently to hand out the two buckets of water. As Sanct' Germain closed and bolted the gates again, she leaned back against the heavy planking, saying, "Nine of them. We can keep them off if we must."

"Yes, for a time." He nodded to a place along the wall where the stones were higher and thicker than near the gates. "They will not be able to overhear us as readily."

"Oh," she said, glancing uneasily at the gate. "Yes; they could listen."

Sanct' Germain motioned to Rogerian, indicating he should go along to the barns. "You know what has to be done."

"That I do," said Rogerian, and strode away from the gates.

Csimenae had not paid much attention to this exchange; she took hold of Sanct' Germain's wide sleeve. "We can hold them off, keep them out, can we not?"

"So we can," said Sanct' Germain, "if that is what you truly want."

"What do you mean?" she asked, her frown as startling as it was intense. "Why would I not want to keep this village for my son?"

"I only mean that it seems wise, at least to me, to admit these nine. They will make their vow and they will then have to defend the village against others who may return. If you do not admit them, then they might make common cause with the rest. I agree it would not be hard to keep those nine from coming in, but double that number, or triple? If more should come, I would not want them to add to our opponents." He gave her a long moment to think over what he had said. "And if they should attack as a group, they would surely kill Aulutis and you when they break through the walls."

This last held her attention as his other observations had not. "They would not dare," she said with more bravado than conviction.

"Do you think so," he said. "They were willing to let you die with your man. What would stop them from killing your son? Or you?" He waited while she began to pace. "It would be useful to have a herdsman, to look after the sheep and goats. Then these people will want to defend the village."

"That Tacanti will try to hurt my son. He is too proud. I do not trust him." She held up her hands in a gesture of frustration. "He is despicable."

"He may be." Sanct' Germain took a step away from the wall. "Yet it might be most prudent to have him where you can watch him than leave him to work against you where you cannot touch him." He took a step closer to Csimenae. "If he gives his vow to Aulutis and then breaks it, the other villagers will see that he pays the price. If he gives no oath, then he will be able to do away with you and your son without disgrace."

She studied him in silence for some time. "You do not know how he is."

"I have some experience of treachery," Sanct' Germain said, a sardonic edge to his voice as he recalled the assassins in the Temple of Imhotep, the uncle of the Farsi warlord, Led Arashnur in Rome, Nicoris' half-brother at the Hodiopolae . . . "Tacanti may be unknown to me, but perfidy is not."

"Then why should I not refuse to let him in?" She was growing petulant, seeming very young. "You see for yourself that he is—"

"I see that he must be watched. I see that he may well prove unreliable. But I see also that it is better to have him where you can see him than where you cannot. If you exclude him, then he becomes your declared enemy and those who are of his blood may side with him against you," Sanct' Germain said, keeping his tone low and steady. "If he gives his vow of allegiance, his family will be bound by that even if he is not."

Slowly she nodded. "Yes. I see that; I had not thought of it," she said, condemning herself for her lack of foresight. She straightened her shoulders. "Very well. If he will swear fealty to my son, I will allow him to be in this village again. But he must be housed as far from me and mine as he can be."

"That would put him near the gates," Sanct' Germain pointed out. "That could prove unwise if he should decide to admit your foes."

Csimenae stamped her foot. "Very well! What do you suggest?"

Sanct' Germain paused before he answered. "Where was his house before he left?"

"Near the market square, the one with the grinding stone beside it." She caught her lower lip in her teeth.

"Let him return there. Rogerian and I can keep watch on him there without seeming to." He shrugged. "He may be satisfied with having his house again."

"Do you think so?" She watched him out of the corner of her eye.

"No," he admitted. "But it will give him less opportunity to complain, and his complaints will not be as much heeded." He was not entirely convinced, nor was Csimenae, but they were both satisfied for the time being.

"Then, if he says he will give his oath to Aulutis, he will have his house back again. Otherwise I will bestow it on one of those who is willing to kiss my son's foot, to show how loyalty is rewarded." She almost clapped with satisfaction, then her brow darkened once more. "If he will not swear, then I will send him down the mountain. Let him eat berries and mushroom and bark as the wild pigs do."

"You do not want him to have good reason to act against you, for that would persuade others that he was right in his opposition," Sanct' Germain said, still doing nothing that would appear argumentative. "Think of the long years before Aulutis is grown and what you will need to do to keep him safe. The more of your villagers you may draw to his cause, the better his chance of ruling here for many years to come."

She stared at him resentfully. "You have no reason to help him. You are not of this village. You have told me you will not remain here. So what use is your advice?"

Sanct' Germain was ready to answer her. "It is useful *because* I will not linger here. I have nothing to lose and nothing to gain from his success. This is your home, not mine, and so I have no ties to this village that might color my thoughts." He managed a smile. "You may doubt me, but I give you my Word that I wish nothing but success to you and your son."

"You helped him into the world," Csimenae allowed. "That should bind you to him as his protector."

"If you like," Sanct' Germain said, his memories stirring. "He has nothing to fear from me: nor have you."

She studied his face, shading her eyes with her hand, the better to read his expression. "I will think about what you have said," she announced before she turned away from him and walked back toward the gates.

For a short while Sanct' Germain remained where he stood, his thoughts far away; the sun bore down on him as relentless as an invisible flood, sapping his strength and making him tired. Recollections of the desert outside Baghdad—only thirty-five years ago—drove him into the shelter of the creamery as much as the brightness did. He busied himself with tending the ripening cheeses until he heard Csimenae calling his name. He set aside a clothful of new curds and stepped out into the blazing afternoon where he found her waiting, Aulutis in her arms, a clean cloth wrapped loosely around him.

"I have told those outside the gates that they have until sundown to make their decision. Two of them want to come in now." She squinted against the light. "I want to know what you think is best. I may not agree with your recommendation, but I want to hear what it is."

"Well enough," Sanct' Germain said. "I would allow any to enter as soon as they say they are willing to swear fealty to your son. It is often such concessions that wear down the most obdurate will."

Csimenae made a single nod. "So I think. Henabo has said he is willing to kiss Aulutis' foot this instant."

"Henabo?" Sanct' Germain asked.

"The older man. He and his daughter Pordinae have asked to be admitted. So has Blada, but Tacanti says he will not permit it." She laughed aloud. "It shook his pride, to have his nephew speak so."

"You would be wise not to gloat. That would turn some of the others against you. Particularly Tacanti—he will hold such satisfaction against you." Sanct' Germain saw her glower. "You said yourself that he is a proud man. Why make him angrier than he is? You will only put Aulutis in danger if you do."

"Why do you say so?" Csimenae demanded, her voice so sharp that Aulutis wakened and began to fret. "There? You see what you have done?" She bent over the baby, rocking and whispering consolations to him until he dozed again. Then she addressed Sanct' Germain, her tone a threatening murmur. "If you cause any ill to my son, you will regret it."

"I mean him no harm, Csimenae," Sanct' Germain said gently. "I mean none to you."

She watched him narrowly; when her scrutiny was over, she said, "Come with me. I need to have you at my side when I hear what those outside the gates have to say to me. They must see that I am not alone." Without looking to see if he obeyed, she set off down the street, holding her child as if he were a talisman of profound power that commanded her devotion; her determination was apparent in every movement.

By the time Sanct' Germain reached the gates, Ione, Pordinae, and Henabo were pressing against them, calling to Csimenae. He took up his place next to Csimenae, saying in an undervoice, "Have you made your decision?"

"I have," she told him as quietly. "I will let Henabo come in first. He is the oldest and his oath will mean the most. Then Blada, if he wishes to be admitted. That will sway the others, I think."

"Perhaps not Tacanti," Sanct' Germain warned.

"Perhaps not," Csimenae said coolly, "but the rest will heed his swearing, and they will remember." She indicated the horse-skulls over the gates. "And they will know who has sworn."

"What do you want me to do?" Sanct' Germain asked.

"Be sure they come through one by one. They are not to be allowed to pass in greater number. I will not be rushed by these people. They will do as I demand or they will remain outside." She took a deep breath. "Very well. Open the gates enough to admit one." Raising her voice, she called out, "Henabo, you may come through. My son is waiting to receive you."

Sanct' Germain drew back the heavy bolt and eased the right side of the gates open far enough to admit the older man, then swung them closed again behind him, keeping the rest outside.

"I will vow fealty to your son, Csimenae," Henabo declared as soon as he was inside the gates. "I will kiss his foot to seal my oath."

"That you will," said Csimenae as she held out her baby to the old man; in response to this disturbance, Aulutis began to squall.

"He is a lusty boy, and you have shown yourself able to defend him," Henabo approved as he bent and touched his lips to the infant's right foot. "Very well, I will accept the terms. I am his until death."

"It is witnessed," said Csimenae, unable to keep the triumph from her voice. "Blada, you may come next."

There was a fierce, whispered squabble the other side of the gates, and then Blada shouted out to be let in. "I will swear!"

"You fool!" Tacanti bellowed, the pitch of his voice rising half an octave in choler. "The boy is still at his mother's teats. She is only a woman. He is not yet walking. What use to swear to him?"

"I will be back in my village," said Blada as Sanct' Germain eased the gate open for him.

"You are being foolish!" Tacanti shouted. "All of you are."

In response to this, Aulutis made more noise, and his face turned an astonishing shade of plum.

"You! Tacanti!" Csimenae cried out. "Be silent or I will never open the gates to you, no matter what vows you offer. You are offending my son!" She began urgently to soothe her distraught infant.

"How can you swear fealty to that?" Tacanti scoffed. "I would be ashamed to do it."

"You do not have to," Csimenae yelled back. "You may remain outside the gates until you starve." She held Aulutis close to her, making hectic efforts to quiet him.

During this exchange, Sanct' Germain eased Blada through the gates and nodded in the direction of Csimenae. "Make your vow before her. She will tell you where to live once you kiss the child's foot."

Blada made a sign to show he understood. As he approached Csimenae, he lowered his head. "I swear fealty to your son, from this day until I draw my last breath," he said before he kissed Aulutis' foot, then went to stand beside Henabo; he looked relieved as he smoothed his dusty tunica.

"That is two," said Csimenae. "Who else wishes to come? Ione? Do you want to enter the gates? Does Pordinae?" She waited for an answer, and smiled when Ione conceded. "Admit her, Sanct' Germain."

Ione brought the toddler, Gratio, in through the gate with her, and carried the baby who was not yet a year old. "His parents are dead, and his two sisters are married away from Mont Calcius. They cannot take him, and he has no others to claim him. I will care for him, and I will see that he honors his vow. Gratio will stay with me as well, if you will permit it."

"Poor child," said Csimenae in a tone that was in earnest. "It is good of you to take him in hand, Ione," she went on as if conferring great honor on the two. She went on, "As you have no man with you, your vow will bind you."

After that, Pordinae came inside the gates, and finally Rilsilin, the pockmarked youth, came to kiss Aulutis' foot.

"What do you think, Tacanti?" Csimenae called out, and was mildly surprised to hear nothing in answer.

"I think he has gone into the woods," said Rilsilin, sounding embarrassed. "He said he was disgusted with . . . with having to honor an infant." His face flushed, and the scars stood out on his skin.

"Gone into the woods," Csimenae repeated as if slapped. "How can he have done that?"

"He did not want to come here," said Rilsilin, his face almost purple from his intense embarrassment.

"May he die of hunger," Csimenae said loudly enough for everyone to hear her. "May bears and wolves fight over his bones."

There was a long silence after that, and then Rogerian came from the alley that led toward the sheepfold. "I have finished putting out the evening feed," he reported to Csimenae as if he were wholly unaware of this discomfort around him.

"Very good," said Csimenae. "We will now assign houses to my son's new allies." She smiled at the eight who had gathered around her.

"As you wish," said Pordinae for all of them.

"Yes; as I wish on behalf of Aulutis." With that, she started toward the market square, the others tagging along behind her.

The assigning of houses took very little time, even though Csimenae did her best to make the occasion a momentous one. Walking along the street, she offered her assessment on each of the buildings she passed, letting the others chafe with impatience. Her confidence increased as she went on, and she became less critical. She promised that no one but Aulutis could evict them from their houses now, and added that their chores would be assigned to them tomorrow.

"And for tonight?" Henabo asked, making a point of screwing up his courage so that the others would pay close attention.

"There is smoked goat-flesh and new cheese. I will order a fire made in the center of the square and we can all gather there." Csimenae beamed at them. "You will be glad you have returned here."

Watching this from the edge of the market square, Sanct' Germain was troubled by the way in which Csimenae reveled in her position. "Her character has force," he said to Rogerian in the language of his own, lost people, "but I fear she lacks the ability to stand alone."

Rogerian shrugged. "Why would she stand alone? She managed with the two of us."

"That is what troubles me. We will not always be here, and if she is ever at odds with these people—and oath or no oath, it is possible— then she may be swayed by her own loneliness."

"Is that so great a failing?" Rogerian asked, his face revealing little of his thoughts.

"If it betrays you, yes," Sanct' Germain responded, his dark eyes distant.

"Do you think it would?" Rogerian's faded-blue eyes were perplexed.

"I do not know; that is why I am troubled." He looked north-east, to the mountains rising behind them. "Perhaps I am seeing the anxiety of an abandoned woman—and one with child—and that is what makes her so vulnerable."

Rogerian considered this. "Is it the vulnerability that worries you, then?"

Sanct' Germain shook his head for an answer, and resumed speaking in the admixture of Latin and the local tongue. "This village could be hard to defend, if it came to that, with only the people she has admitted so far."

It was not an answer to Rogerian's question, and he knew it, but he accepted it for the dismissal it was. "Could it come to that?"

"I suppose that depends on Tacanti," Sanct' Germain said after a brief silence. "If he decides to gather others around him to try to seize this place, it could lead to very real danger for everyone inside the gates."

"And do you intend to do anything about it?" Rogerian inquired, vaguely aware that Rilsilin was standing nearby and listening.

"I do not yet know what *to* do," Sanct' Germain confessed. "I suppose I will have to remain alert to more than prey when I hunt."

"Then you are planning to continue hunting?" Rogerian was not entirely surprised, but he was keenly aware of the greater risk this could entail now that Tacanti might be in the forest.

"I must," Sanct' Germain said. "We cannot feed these people without meat. If we kill the goats and sheep we have penned, most of these people will starve by the end of summer."

"Do you plan to try to find more goats and sheep for the flocks? That could ease the situation for the village." Rogerian was certain now that Rilsilin was paying close attention to everything they said.

"If I can. We must somehow find a village down the slopes where we may purchase grain, or trade for it. There are only two barrels of flour left, and they will not last long."

"Truly," Rogerian said.

"If not a village, perhaps a monastery or an estate," Sanct' Germain went on. "With the Great Pox on the wane, there will be markets again."

"Will there be a market here, do you think?" Rogerian asked, making a covert gesture to Sanct' Germain, indicating Rilsilin was eavesdropping.

"Possibly not this year, but if all goes well, perhaps next year," Sanct' Germain answered, his fine brows lowering.

Rogerian considered this response. "Will Mont Calcius be ready to open its gates to unknown visitors then, do you think? She cannot hold a market if she insists on letting in visitors one at a time."

"No," Sanct' Germain agreed. "And she will need more people in the village if it is to thrive."

"Is that likely to happen?" Rogerian scraped his thumb along the bristles of his cheek. "Tacanti might not be the only villager who is unwilling to give an oath of fealty to a baby."

"He might not be," Sanct' Germain seconded.

"And where does that leave Csimenae and her new allies?" He shot a quick look at Rilsilin, who had slid closer to them.

Sanct' Germain frowned, and responded obliquely. "I believe Csimenae is confident she will be secure now, that the people she had allowed to swear fealty will honor their oaths, but I am not as convinced as she is."

"Do you plan to warn her?" Rogerian doubted that Csimenae would welcome any such remonstrating as Sanct' Germain might offer, no matter how gently he phrased it.

"It would be expedient to do so," Sanct' Germain said. "When the opportunity presents itself, I will."

"And how soon do you think that will be?" Rogerian studied Sanct' Germain's face.

The answer came in the tongue of Baghdad. "Before that youth reports to Csimenae."

Rogerian managed to smile a little. "Yes," he said in the same language. "He may well do that."

Sanct' Germain gave a single chuckle, and said in the language of the village, "I am relying on it," as he carefully avoided looking in Rilsilin's direction. "In the meantime, I should prepare to hunt tonight."

"You will have to be more careful hunting, now," Rogerian said, more intent in his words than was apparent to anyone but Sanct' Germain.

"Yes," said Sanct' Germain with full understanding. "I suppose I will."

Text of a report to Episcus Salvius of Tarraco from Episcus Luitegild of Toletum.

To my most respected and worthy Brother in Christ, my greetings and prayers of thanksgiving that God has spared you from the Great Pox in this time of dreadful trial which must surely mark the beginning of the Last Days and the return of Our Lord to the world He saved.

I was grieved to learn of the death of Episcus Gerundol of Corduba, for it had seemed that God was inclined to spare that city from the Great Pox. When I received word of his Call to Glory, I realized that it was left to us to bear witness to this calamity and the truth of our great teaching that all is in the Hands of God. I have ordered the monks of Sanctissimus Resurrexionem to say Masses for the repose in Grace of Episcus Gerundol's soul, and the souls of all Christians who have perished. It is the one thing we may do for them now, and the one thing

God requires of us at this time. No one can doubt the importance of worship in the face of such proof of Judgment Day approaching.

It is altogether suitable that religious men put away their wives during this time of preparation, dismissing them to convents, or to the life of service that is the lot of women since the Fall of Eve. As we have been so wisely admonished by Sanct' Paulus, women are to be silent in their devotion, acquiescent to their husbands and fathers, who have dominion over them. Yet there are those, who, in their zeal to purify themselves, have put the females of their families to death, the better to cleanse themselves before being brought to answer before the Throne of God, for they believe that so long as they have women in their houses, they are stained by the Sin of Eve. Therefore, I have issued a tomus to the Christian men of Toletum not to kill their wives or their daughters, for although no punishment awaits them in this world, God is a strict Judge and there is no blood-money in Heaven. If God wishes to lay His Hand upon the women, then we must bow our heads in submission. But if He spares them, then so must we, and pray for the redemption of women through the Magna Virgo et Mater.

To honor those of Toletum who have died, I have authorized the donation of houses left empty by death to fellow-Christians who lack shelter. This is in accordance with the instruction of the Evangelists, and it has the approval of the Jews, who are most powerful in this city, and who have the position to see to the administration of its laws; they have done much the same for their own people, and I am assured they will not stand in the way of any such distribution among us. In anticipation of a favorable decision, I have submitted lists of available dwelling places which I am informed will be given approval for occupation at once, with one exception: the house of Sanct' Germain, which he entrusted to Viridia, has been left empty by her death, but as she was not the owner of the house, it must remain as it is until instructions from Sanct' Germain should reach us, or Ithidroel ben Matthias. It is a shame we can do nothing with the house, for it is handsome and well-fitted-out; had I some notion of where Sanct' Germain might be found, I would seek out a courier to take a message to him, wherever he may be, and ask that he let his wishes be known. But I have no means to find him: it may be that he, too, has been taken to Grace and if this is so, then his wishes are known only to God, and until they are revealed by vision or prophesy, there is nothing more I can do.

We have been able to provide shelter for over sixty Christian children left without parents or family to care for them. The boys will be apprenticed when masters can be found for them, but it is not fitting they be made slaves, for once sold, they could be made to serve those who are not Christians. This would not do honor to Our Lord. In finding a place for these orphan boys, we will serve God well in this sinful world. The girls will be married to Christians or taken in as nuns, to serve the monks and priests as handmaids and to provide for the comforts of those who have given their lives to Glory.

According to the few travelers who have arrived here since the Paschal season, the roads are more empty than usual, and many are in ill repair, so that those on the road take much longer to reach their destinations than was the case before the Great Pox came. Some of the Gardingi have set to mending the roads and charging tolls for their use. They enforce their claims with armed men, some of whom make demands beyond those of their masters. This displeases many travelers, who already have much to contend with as regards the rigors of travel: to risk all the goods they seek to trade in order to use a good road is a poor bargain for them. It may be necessary to appeal to the Gardingi who have levied the highest tolls to reconsider their actions, for if travelers are so preyed upon, few will hazard the journey to our cities. Those seeking to make a pilgrimage for the good of their souls will also be reluctant to risk being detained and pressed into service of a Gardingio who takes his tolls in vassalage.

I beseech you to consider making a similar stance on behalf of the Christian souls of Tarraco. You, too, are subject to the rule of Exarch and Gardingio. You, too, have long relied on trade to keep your city wealthy and safe. You, too, have a city that thrives on travelers and the goods they bring with them. To permit the Gardingi to do as they wish, taxing and detaining travelers as suits their whims is to grant them a power that could yet compromise our people and our faith. With God's Aid, we may set an example that will sustain our flock and our Church in these parlous times. I have urged my fellow-Christians to make a stand. If you do not believe that Tarraco, with its seaport, can come to harm because of these policies, I beg you to consider the fate of travelers who seek to bring their goods inland, and who depend on greater markets than the port cities can offer.

May God show you His Will in this and all things. May you always *seek to do the Will of God. May your sons do you honor, and your wife be given a place to serve God in Heaven as she served you on earth. May your city be spared from war and want. May your flock never stray from the path God has set for them. May the examples of the Saints always inspire you and your Christians to the acts and thoughts that are most pleasing to God. May no worldly power hamper you in your devotion to God. May all you do bring Glory to God and favor to you and your flock. May you stand with the Sheep at the Final Day.*

With my prayers and blessing,
Episcus Luitegild
Sanctissimus Resurrexionem

at Toletum, the summer Solstice and the Mass of the Redeemer, in the 622nd year of man's Salvation, as given in the calendar of Sanct' Iago

7

Over the next few months as summer swelled and began to wane, another twenty-seven villagers returned, and twenty-five of them were willing to kiss Aulutis' foot and swear their allegiance to him in order to stay. The two who refused cursed Csimenae and swore vengeance upon her, promising terrible ruin for her and her son, who had not been bathed in the blood of a sacrificial horse; they had come at the end of summer, and Csimenae had assumed the threat of winter would incline them to make their vows to Aulutis. When they refused, she had pointedly ignored them, laughing as they execrated her name and the whole line of Aulutis. Only when they had gone and she was alone in her house did she give way to the tears that had almost overwhelmed her. She sat in the single chair and held Aulutis close to her while she did her best to stifle her sobs.

"You have been very brave," Sanct' Germain said to her as he came through the narrow rear door that led to the barn and the sheepfold.

"What are you doing here?" she demanded, her voice shaking with her effort to control it; she put both her arms around Aulutis.

"I have finished my chores and I feared you might be in some distress. Rilsilin told me what happened at the gates." He had expected such a confrontation, but had not thought it would come so soon.

She looked up sharply, glowering as she wiped her eyes. "I am angry. I weep when I am angry."

"No doubt," said Sanct' Germain. "Others before you have done the same."

"No one should see me cry," she said earnestly, still glaring at him. "They think when women cry, it is a sign of weakness, not of fury. If I had horses, they would know better. I would make a sacrifice that all would remember." She began to rock Aulutis, calming him and herself at the same time.

"Rilsilin said that five men refused to make their vows to your son," Sanct' Germain went on.

"Five? What five would be so defiant?" She did not quite laugh, but the barking sound she made might pass for harsh amusement to someone listening outside. "Two; just two. One was Dantho, who keeps . . . kept the olive trees. He said he is entitled to rule here, not my son. He says as long as the trees are growing he has the right to rule."

"And did he rule here before the Great Pox?" Sanct' Germain asked, watching her more closely than she knew.

"His cousin did. Occathin. He and his father before him. My grandfather was lord here until he brought a foreign wife to the village; he was disgraced by her. Before then, it was the old priests who ruled here. Occathin's father changed that, more than my grandfather could. He was head of the woodsmen. Dantho says that Occathin lost his sight and has gone to a monastery where the monks will take care of him. The other was Barago, who trapped animals for their hides. He has no importance here. No one will mind if he stays away." She had mastered herself now, and she sat up straight. Her face was alert and she spoke with banked emotions. "Occathin's sons have gone to one of the Gardingi, to find a living for themselves. His daughters have been given to their men." Her chuckle was more successful than her laughter had been. "The horses did not hold much honor in his sacrifice, and those men have no interests here, not with Occathin gone."

"Did Dantho say so?" Sanct' Germain could see the corners of her mouth pull down and the edges of her eyes tighten.

"No. Dantho says that all of Occathin's blood will come to claim what is theirs. As if they have a right to any of this." She held up her head. "You do not know what scorn I feel for all of them."

"I may have some idea," he said, his tone lightly ironic as a way to shore up her flagging spirits; some of his own memories were equally harsh, but he did not speak of them.

She wiped furiously at her eyes. "I do not want them here. If they despise me, let them live in the forest, with the rest of the beasts." Her face tightened. "The signs are for an early winter. Perhaps they will starve."

"Perhaps they will have to ask you to take them in," Sanct' Germain suggested, his gaze enigmatic.

She let out a single exclamation of derision. "Let them in? Why should I do anything so foolish? They have chosen their way." As Aulutis began to cry, she rocked him automatically, but did little else to comfort him.

"It might be prudent to show them clemency, should they ask for it, for the sake of the other returning villagers," he said, taking care not to argue the point. He glanced at the shelves that served as a pantry, and noticed that there were very few bits of bread left. "Have the monks sent any more flour?"

"Not yet," she said, not looking at him. "We have not made a donation, so they—"

"If you need a few coins for the donation, I will provide them. You will want the flour shortly, or the rains will make it hard to fetch the barrels up muddy tracks." He realized he should have tended to this on his own, that she would never ask anything of him for fear of being beholden to him.

"Why should you pay for flour when you eat no bread?" she challenged, daring now to look him full in the face. "It would be better to let me have one of your two horses, for a true sacrifice."

"I want the flour for the sake of the village," he said quietly. "I do not plan to leave here before spring, and perhaps not then. Why should I want to see all of you starving simply because my appetites are not what yours are." He came a few steps closer to her. "Tell me you will let me do this for you, as a sign of my devotion to Aulutis."

Her voice and her manner were sharper. "Why should Aulutis have it as a sign of anything?"

"Because he is a baby; one day soon he will eat bread and cheese, as you do. It would be best if you have bread to give him when that time comes. You have not enough of a crop planted to provide bread for more than a week or two after you harvest it." He did not change his demeanor, but something in his compelling gaze convinced her.

"All right. Since you will be here until spring, and perhaps longer." She cocked her head. "Why do you want to stay so long? You do not have to remain, and yet you do. There must be a reason. Are you seeking a haven from the Gardingi, or the Church?" It was the first time she had broached the matter so directly, and she regarded him with interest as he answered.

"I am sure there are Gardingi who would be pleased to detain me because I would be of use to them. And I am certain there are monasteries where the monks would be glad to command my skills. But I left Toletum with the good-will of the Episcus and the Jews, and no one has countermanded their good words—no one that I know of." He sighed, knowing she expected more. "I told you that I am an exile, that I am going to Tolosa where I have holdings. I have a blood relative in Rome, and I may visit there to show honor to—"

"Yes, yes," she said impatiently. "But it is still odd to me that you would prefer to stay in this place than go to Tolosa."

"If the roads are in bad repair, I would have to stay in another village on another road in another part of the mountains. This one is as good as any of them." He smiled briefly. "And here I have been made to feel welcome."

"Because you are useful," said Csimenae.

"Fetching flour is useful," he pointed out.

"I will believe you because it suits me to believe you," she said at last, stroking her child through the worn linen of his tunica. "And because my son will need bread come spring. So will the villagers. In better times this would not be necessary, for the villagers would have planted enough grain to make bread of their own to last all through the winter. Well. They have sworn allegiance to my son, and in his name I must take care to see they are taken care of."

Sanct' Germain saw her quick frown. "Do you want to send word to the monastery at Templo Antica? It is near Osca. They have flour to sell."

"If you will go there and bring back what we will need, I will be grateful. I will not ask for either of your horses if you do this for us. And

if you go and do not return, I will know you for a miscreant and a liar."
Csimenae showed her teeth. "Your manservant will remain here, of
course."

"Of course," Sanct' Germain echoed, and busied himself with tending to the herbs hung out to dry on the doors of the pantry. He thought
of her precarious situation, wondering what else she could do if she
was going to maintain her authority. "I will tell the villagers that this is
your wish that I fetch the flour."

"Why?" She was suspicious as well as surprised.

"Because this is your home, as you have reminded me often." He
gave her a long moment to consider this. "I am a stranger here, and
anything I do is questioned: you are not the only one to have doubts
about me, Csimenae. I know I am not wholly welcome among you. I
am useful, which gives me some credibility, but not very much. I am little more than tolerated. Yet the villagers comprehend your wishes, and
respect them; anything you do is to ensure your position and the position of your son for the future. No one questions this. So your decisions
are not regarded as suspect."

In the silence that followed, he left her alone with Aulutis while he
went out to the market square, searching for Rogerian; he looked
about the village until he found his manservant in the creamery, washing curds and turning the ripening cheeses on their shelves. When he
finished explaining the mission he was about to undertake, he said, "I
will send a few letters from the monastery while I am there. I should be
able to find men willing to carry them for me if I pay them for the service; if I am careful in my choice of messengers, one or two should
reach their destinations."

"Why do you do this for her?" Rogerian asked in ancient Greek.

"She is fighting a very lonely battle, and the odds are against her,"
Sanct' Germain replied in the same language. "I know how difficult
that can be."

Rogerian said nothing while he tapped one of the cheeses. "It is almost ready. There is an ample supply here."

"Good," Sanct' Germain approved. "The winter is going to be hard,
I think. The more foodstuffs we can prepare, the better."

"And you?" Rogerian inquired. "What plans have you made for providing for yourself during the winter?"

"I will hunt, as I have done," said Sanct' Germain calmly.

"It is not sufficient, not if you limit your feeding to animals. You have said as much yourself, many times. You may not wish to admit it, but you are losing flesh, as you do when you are deprived of . . . touching. Why do you remain here if you are reduced to this?" His eyes were worried. "Do you seek that from her?"

Sanct' Germain understood his deliberately vague reference; he shook his head. "It hardly matters: she does not seek it from me."

"Then why do we remain here?" Rogerian persisted bluntly, unaware he was echoing Csimenae's question. "This place is the edge of nothing. You could be in Rome, or in Tolosa, or in your homeland, for that matter, and you would be—" He broke off, seeing something haunted in Sanct' Germain's dark eyes.

"I would be as much a stranger there as I am here. I would have to find a means to make myself acceptable. At least in this place I am useful. And there are no invaders pouring down the slopes, or harrying up them, for that matter, and no barbarians seeking slaves and livestock, as there are from my homeland to the Frankish uplands. You recall what it was like there, only twenty years ago; there is no reason to think it has improved. Here, at least, I have no greedy men watching me in the hope of increasing their riches through claiming mine. I have no one watching me and reporting to others for his own benefit, as we had in Toletum. We tolerated it because it was necessary, but I am pleased not to be perused so relentlessly. There are few havens we could find as accessible as this one, and both you and I know it. If I must live on the blood of animals for a time, what harm is there?" His wan smile was vastly troubling to Rogerian, who spoke to him in Latin.

"When do you plan to leave to get the flour?" It was a safe question, and one that could be overheard without causing alarm.

"In a day or two: within a week, most certainly. I have to hunt tonight, I think; tomorrow I will make arrangements." Sanct' Germain did his best to encourage Rogerian. "Do not fret, old friend. We will be gone from here soon enough. A week, a year, both are gone in no time."

This did nothing to reassure Rogerian; he continued to work with the cheeses. "When that time comes, I will be ready," was all he allowed himself to say.

"I take your meaning," Sanct' Germain assured him, doing his best not to feel tired, although a sensation like fatigue insinuated itself through him. "And I will consider your apprehension."

For an instant, Rogerian hesitated, then asked, "Do you miss Viridia?"

Sanct' Germain nodded. "And Nicoris, and Olivia, and—" He made himself stop. "I could not bring Viridia to my life; that does not mean I have no love for her, or that I have forgot her."

Rogerian kept himself from saying anything more, for he knew it was of no use. He went on with tending the cheeses, finally saying, "I will see your horse is ready when you need him."

"And a mule," Sanct' Germain recommended. "I will need both if I am to bring back enough barrels to carry the village through the winter."

"As you say," Rogerian conceded.

Sanct' Germain spent the rest of that afternoon in the house Csimenae had allocated for his use; he busied himself making compounds of herbs and olive oil and wine that could be used to treat many ills, and which he supposed would be necessary to get the village through the winter, for he knew from long experience that cold and pernicious coughs traveled together, as heat and bad air did. This activity satisfied him, for it provided him with the means to occupy himself as well as demonstrate his value to the people around him. Over the centuries, he had been calmed and soothed by preparing medicaments; the afternoon faded quickly as he went about the familiar work. By twilight, he had done as much as he could with the little equipment he had, and reluctantly he put his materials away, thinking he would soon have to gather herbs or accept more shortages still. Now he missed his athanor and his reductio almost as much as he missed having moldy bread, from which he made his sovereign remedy against all fevers. At another time, he might have built a small athanor, but in Mont Calcius, he doubted the villagers would tolerate so foreign an object being used inside their walls, no matter what its potential benefit might be. So he would have to content himself with the compounds he could cook up in a pot over the fire. At least, he told himself, he would soon have moldy bread; it was a consolation of sorts.

Night sent the villagers indoors, and the odor of cooking filled the dusk. Last chores were done in pens and the barn as the livestock were bedded down for the night. One of the villagers walked down the two streets calling out the names of those inside, and making a record of all replies. This was soon followed by darkness in the houses, and a breathing silence that was as familiar to Sanct' Germain as the pull of blood. When Rogerian came in from tending to the animals, Sanct' Germain greeted him in passing. "I am going after goats tonight, I think."

"I will be ready to dress your kill, as soon as you bring it back," said Rogerian. "There is not much meat left in the village."

"I am aware of that," Sanct' Germain said, adding, "If there is time, I will try for a second animal."

"Good hunting," Rogerian said without a trace of irony in his voice.

Sanct' Germain slipped out into the night, his black hippogaudion and black Persian leggings making him one with the shadows and the dark, his movements flexible as a cat's, as fluid as a shadow. He knew his way through the trees now, and he went swiftly toward the glades where the wild goats could be found; he was anticipating an easy kill, one that would feed his hunger and provide for the village, allowing him half the night to find other game that would serve as surplus, and one that was much needed if winter came early. Before he reached the little meadows, he sensed something was wrong—the night was too still, and the air too alive. He approached the clearing cautiously, testing the air as he went. Then he stopped moving, his attention fully on the sounds that came from the place where he expected to find goats, for he heard men's voices instead of bleating, and in a short while he saw the wavering light of a single torch.

"—could burn the gates down," one of the men said, raising his voice to be heard.

"It would have to be at night," said another. "There aren't enough villagers to keep a proper guard. They do not watch after the mid-point of the night, and that watch is kept by one of the foreigners."

"Not . . . for the baby," quipped a third, some of his remark so quiet that Sanct' Germain could not hear it; whatever he said was seconded by laughter.

"We'll roast him on a spit," said the second speaker, his tone venomous.

This was met with chuckles and muttered approval from more than a dozen voices.

"And that mother of his, we'll—" This speaker broke off, laughing nastily.

"Save her for an offering," suggested a man with a gravelly tone. "After we have done with her."

The others chuckled again, more angrily; Sanct' Germain took advantage of the sound to move a little nearer to the clearing.

"Tomorrow night, then: we're agreed?" This was a fourth man. "It's time we took back what is ours. Occathin's kin should rule in Mons Calcius, not this stupid woman."

"We must drink the blood of horses," said the gravel-voiced man.

The rest muttered agreement.

"Then we must get our weapons in order. A pity we have only the one small ram, but it will knock down the sheepfolds and the barndoors." The second man relished what lay ahead. "Those who fight us will die or be our slaves."

"That's right," the first man declared. "It should have been ours all along."

Sanct' Germain slid back into the forest, skirting the clearing; he would have to return to the village by a round-about path, in case these men should decide to venture up to the walls in preparation for their coming attack. He paid only cursory attention to game in the forest, telling himself he would hunt later, after Mont Calcius was ready to fight off the men in the woods.

As he scaled the walls, he was struck by an unpalatable thought: the men in the forest must have someone inside the village to keep them informed of what was happening in the town; they had known he and Rogerian patrolled the village at night, and the implications of that knowledge burgeoned in his mind. As cautious as he had been, he now felt he had been careless. He landed near the house he occupied, and waited a moment until Rogerian came out of the main door. "There is trouble," he said quietly.

"So it seems," said Rogerian. "You bring no game."

"It may be a fortunate thing that I do not; I have come upon something more important than meat in my hunt," Sanct' Germain said, going on steadily. "There are men gathering in the forest who plan to attack the village. I found them in a clearing and overheard some of their talk." He paused. "From what they said, they have at least one spy inside the walls. I had hoped we were done with spies."

Rogerian did not look astonished. "They have blood ties to the people here," he said. "You, of all men, should appreciate that."

"I do," Sanct' Germain said with irony to match Rogerian's.

"What do you think? Are those men in earnest?" Rogerian prompted. "What are you going to tell Csimenae?"

"About the coming attack?—as much as I can. About the spy, I have not made up my mind. I do not know what she will believe." He began to pace. "My accusation would mean little, since I am an outsider. But she must be alerted to the presence of the spy, or it is useless to plan our defenses."

"Then you are going to help her fight," said Rogerian, his certainty so strong that Sanct' Germain paused in his pacing and stared at him. "You could leave, could you not?"

"Of course I could, but I will not," he replied sharply. "Why should I put the village in danger because I fear for my skin?"

Rogerian did not quite smile. "Apparently you do not think that reason enough to leave, though nothing holds you here." He touched his forehead lightly in a gesture of acquiescence. "I am not surprised."

"You know me too well, old friend," said Sanct' Germain.

"I have had time to know you," Rogerian pointed out. "I would have been surprised had you decided to leave."

"That is a compliment of sorts, I suppose," said Sanct' Germain. Making up his mind, he started off toward Csimenae's house. "Come. She should hear of this now."

"Will not waking her in the dead of night alarm her?" Rogerian suggested as he followed Sanct' Germain.

Sanct' Germain walked a bit faster as he answered, "I should hope it would."

Csimenae answered her door promptly enough to suggest that she had not been sleeping; her eyes were brilliant and she moved decisively to block their way. She held Aulutis in the crook of her arm as she regarded Sanct' Germain uneasily, her face faintly illuminated by the single oil lamp that burned just inside her door. "You have no game," she said, making it an accusation.

"No; I have something of greater import than that." He did not try to cross her threshold, in case someone else should be awake at this hour, and watching.

"You must, to come to my house at this hour. If the villagers find out, they will say my grandfather has cursed our family again." She lifted the edge of her tunica so that Sanct' Germain could see the long knife thrust through her belt. "I will not let you do anything that would call me into question."

"Nor would I," Sanct' Germain said. "It is not my purpose to discredit you." He saw her eyes sharpen. "Yes. You must hear me out: there was more than game in the forest tonight," he told her, and went on to relate what he had stumbled upon. "I think there are a fair number of them; a dozen or perhaps more. Mont Calcius is not the only village to lose its people. It is possible a number of them have banded together with the intention of claiming this place as their own."

She stared at him, outrage distorting her features. "How *dare* they?" she demanded of the darkness. "I gave them the chance to return, and they do this to me." She lifted her son up so that his head was on her shoulder. "They would deprive Aulutis of what is his."

"They want the village," said Sanct' Germain. "They will not hesitate to kill you—and your boy—to claim it. They know they must do that or fight again." He saw her flinch, and added, "They would do the same to anyone holding this place if they wanted to make it theirs."

She nodded. "We must prepare. You were right to warn me, Sanct' Germain," she said, her manner transformed again, this time by diligence. "Will they come tonight?"

"No," Sanct' Germain assured her.

"That is good," she said. "I will have a little time to ready my people to withstand the attack." She was about to go inside her house when Sanct' Germain stopped her.

"You will not want to be too obvious about what you are planning," he said, and, as he saw her frown, he continued, "They expect to attack an undefended village. It is best that they continue to think the place undefended, for that gives you an advantage against them, for they will be surprised, not you."

Csimenae stood quite still as she considered this. "An undefended village. Yes. You have a point," she conceded at last. "I must think about this, to decide what is best for Aulutis. At least we have your horses, and your mules: better than nothing. If we must, we will take one for a sacrifice, but only if we must. You did well to come to me, and to give me your thoughts. Now it is for me to decide what is best for my son." With that she closed her door, leaving Sanct' Germain and Rogerian in the darkness.

After a while, Sanct' Germain said, "I had better hunt in a different part of the forest tonight."

"You are going out again?" Rogerian was almost shocked at this calm announcement.

"Because there are desperate men in the forest does not lessen our need for sustenance." Sanct' Germain shrugged. "They will need meat if they are to fight."

"And you will need blood if you are to endure the daylight," Rogerian said, turning away and starting back toward the house they occupied.

"Yes," Sanct' Germain said before he sprinted for the walls. "I will."

Text of a letter from Frater Morduc, Scribe of the Archangeli monastery to Episcus Honorius of Caesaraugusta.

Now may God be praised for your delivery from the Great Pox, my half-brother, and may He continue His Favor to you for all of your days. Amen.

We of Archangeli monastery have prayed day and night for all Christians struck with the Great Pox, and finally, our faith has prevailed. Amen.

There has been no new case of Great Pox for more than a month, and the few travelers we see at this place have all given testimony that the Great Pox is everywhere in retreat. No one has come here to escape the Great Pox in more than a month, as well, and we have heard no tales of more outbreaks. For this we are most truly grateful. Amen.

To the most eloquent Episcus of Caesaraugusta, Honorious, the greetings of Frater Morduc, with the assurances of my continued devotion to the Church we both serve and the family whose blood we share: your own plight was reported to us some months ago, and therefore we have been diligent in the exercise of our faith in the hope that God would spare us, and you, and all those worthy souls who must guide the work of God before the Last Days are upon us. It was most troubling to learn of your ordeal, for if God visited so much upon you, who are known for the holiness of your life, what could such men as ourselves expect? We have striven to endure our travail in patience and in humility. Our own numbers are decreased, although we rejoice that so many of our Fraters are called to see God's Face; we have much to do to maintain this place with so few monks remaining to do the tasks once shouldered by half-again as many as now abide here. Not that we do not thank God for our lives every day, for we do not question His Wisdom, nor do we seek any attainment beyond the fulfillment of our vows to Him, and to Holy Church.

It would ease our conditions if you would encourage the Gardingi on the road between Caesaraugusta and Roncesvalles to allocate men to rebuild the road, for as it is now, few travelers are able to transverse

these mountains. Ours is not the only monastery left in isolation be-
cause of the neglected roads. We have heard those few, intrepid men
who have made the journey in spite of all, say that without immediate
efforts, the passage will be more arduous next year. If the road were in
better repair, we might have more men to use it, to bring alms to the
monastery, and to add their tolls to the coffers of the Gardingi. You are
in a most favorable place in this respect and I beseech you, my dear
half-brother, to prevail upon the Gardingi and Exarchs of your region
to participate in this necessary work.

Certainly the Great Pox has robbed the Gardingi of men, as it has
robbed this monastery of monks, but it is fitting and right that the road
be restored, for without it, many of the villages along the way will lose
their ties to the Church and the Gardingi, and become what they were
before Salvation—wild tribes of savages preying upon one another and
upon any who venture into their territories. This cannot be seen as any-
thing but the triumph of the Devil, and the denial of the Greatness of
Our Lord. What benefit could that be? Yet if the Gardingi do not act, it
could yet come to pass, and that would be a great misfortune for us all.

We are informed that the men of Tolosa have ordered their portion
of the road restored to full use; you cannot want it said that Franks will
do what Goths will not. I am certain that if the Gardingi and Exarchs
know of this, they will strive to see that the road is again in as good re-
pair as when the Romans of old first laid its foundations. Pilgrims and
merchants alike will benefit from the road being repaired, and so will
the Gardingi, whose men will not have to make their way along the
goat-tracks that pass for roads among the people of the mountains. This
will be useful to everyone.

You may well fear that the Exarch will not be willing to grant money
for such a task, and that may be true, but he can assign men to the work
as part of their vassalage. We here at Archangeli have a few monks and
tertiaries working on our portion of the road, but there is not much we
can do, given our numbers and our lack of equipment. The road-bed
has washed away in some of the steeper sections, and until we can re-
store the bed-work, the problem is going to continue; to fill in the dam-
age is useless, for it will only wash away again with the first rains. No
one can keep the road in repair for its underpinnings are gone. Tell
your Gardingio and Exarch that there could be an avalanche that
would bring down the whole of the road that would render it unusable

and unrepairable for years to come. Such an avalanche could also dam-age various forts and watch-towers if it struck a wide enough part of the mountain, which would mean trouble for the Gardingi as well as for the Exarchs. It is a danger that is very real, as we have seen with our own eyes. May God spare us from such a calamity. To that end, I im-plore you to impress upon the Exarchs and Gardingi the necessity of seeing this task attended to in good time.

Without the road, these mountains are as remote as the hills of Jeru-salem. It may be that there is protection in such remoteness, for the Franks of Tolosa cannot bring armed men over the mountains without roads, but neither can merchants nor monks nor scholars travel as they are wont. If the road is left to wash away, all the mountains will become the harbor of wild men and the bands of robbers who even now roam the crags and valleys for the purpose of looting and killing. Surely the Exarchs cannot want this. Surely the Church cannot support so ru-inous a policy. I urge you, in the name of the family to which we both are bound, to prevail upon the Gardingi and Exarchs to act now, before there is complete disintegration in these mountains, to commit them-selves to keeping the road open, maintained, and safe. To do otherwise would leave the Church exposed and the markets empty of goods, which serves no purpose but to return the country to a state of bar-barism. As great as the dangers have been in the past, if the road is in poor repair, there will be worse for all to bear who live along the road.

May God send you to know the right in this and in all things. May He reveal Glory to you, and bestow His Grace upon you and your sons. May He maintain your community of Christian souls in virtue. May you live in favor and die in Salvation. May you know honor in this world and the exaltation of Paradise in the next. May your flesh be proof against all illness and sin. May your prayers have the power of the Saints in them. May your name by praised from generation to gen-eration until the Last Days. Amen.

Frater Morduc, Scribe and kinsman

at Archangeli monastery near Roncesvalles, on the 29th day of August in the 622nd year of God's Incarnation, according to Sanct' Iago's calendar

8

"It has been more than ten days, and no one has attacked," Csimenae said to Sanct' Germain late in the afternoon of the mid-point of September. It was hot; the languid breeze hardly moved the air around, though all of the barn doors stood open. Odors from the creamery on the south side of the walls mixed with stench of the midden, to the north-west, away from the little stream that leaped and shimmied down the hillside a hundred paces beyond the village walls. "Are you certain of what you saw in the forest?"

"I am," he said as he stood up, letting the mule's hind leg drop. "They said they were going to take Mont Calcius." The barn was lit by the slanting rays of the setting sun, burnishing everything; the animals were lethargic with the heat, only flicking their tails to be rid of flies, but otherwise drooping as Sanct' Germain went about tending to their hooves.

"But they have not come," she persisted; she held her son in an improvised sling, and as he struggled to free himself she confined him again. "Might they have meant another village and you misunderstood them?"

"It is unlikely. Their intentions were plain, though they have not acted yet," said Sanct' Germain as he went around to the off-side of the mule and lifted his hoof, straddled his leg and began to wield his rasp; in spite of the warmth of the barn and the effort of his task, there was no trace of sweat on him.

"Perhaps they will not come, after all. Perhaps the horses have kept them away. We have enough men to hold the gates, and we have weapons to fight with. They may have seen that we are prepared to fight and have looked for easier game," said Csimenae with enough emphasis to make it apparent she was no longer convinced of the danger.

Sanct' Germain paused in his work. "Perhaps. Or it may be that they know more than you think." It was risky to venture so much, but he thought it judicious to draw her attention to the possibility of a spy in the village.

"Do you mean they watch us?" She nodded, absent-mindedly

stroking Aulutis' arm. "Yes. I suppose they would do. They will know we have strengthened our walls. I still think they may have decided not to bother trying to take the village. They may choose one that is not as well-defended."

"Or they may be waiting until you drop your guard," Sanct' Germain said. "They may be watching more closely than you know."

She glared at him. "You think there are spies inside the walls, don't you? Do not bother to deny it. I can read it in your face. You are certain that there are spies." She caught Aulutis' tiny hand in hers and held it. "You believe that there are men in this village who will betray their oaths."

"Yes. I do," he said, looking up from his work. "And so do you."

"No!" Her eyes glittered. "How can you imagine that I would hold such thoughts about anyone in the village? You should know better than that, Sanct' Germain. I have accepted the vows of all who live inside the gates. How can I believe that they are foresworn?"

"Because they are men, and they are not alone in the world. You would be foolish not to have some doubts," said Sanct' Germain at his most unperturbed. "You would not guard your son as you do if you were as certain as you claim to be." He finished his work with the rasp and let the mule's foot down.

"You are wrong," she said with a show of indifference. "You are not one of us. You do not know—"

"I have been about the world, and I have seen men swear fidelity with treachery in their hearts. Even the most honorable of men can turn to perfidy if he is driven to it." Most recently had been outside Baghdad, and had led to the death of nine men, as well as his own ordeal of heat and sun. "You may be right, but if you are, you have a village of honor beyond any I have ever encountered."

"Well, and so I do," she asserted. "You have let yourself be misled by those who are greedy and untrustworthy. Here we know what an oath means. If I fail to keep my pledge, may I be dragged behind a horse to my death."

"I hope, for your sake, that you are not put to the test. But I encourage you to keep the night-guards patrolling." He went to the next mule and lifted her on-side front foot. "Think about all you have done for Aulutis, and measure your decisions against that."

"You want to make me afraid," Csimenae said.

"If that will keep you safe, then yes I do." He used the rasp as he went on. "I also ask you to observe your people. Some of them have ties to those outside the gates, and they may feel that their obligations of blood outweigh the vows they have given to your son."

"You are a horrible man," Csimenae declared, turning abruptly on her heel and starting out into the glowing afternoon.

"Possibly. But I may also be right," he said as he continued his work.

That night passed uneventfully, and the next, but the night after that there was a disturbance at the edge of the sheepfold that brought the night-guard running into the market square to pound on the brass shield that had been hung up for that purpose.

"Thieves! Thieves!" Henabo shouted, bashing the shield one last time. "They're taking our sheep!"

"Taking sheep?" came the sharp cry from Csimenae's house. "They shall have none. By my blood, they shall not!"

The uproar increased as the village roused from sleep into confusion. Shouts and alarms began to summon everyone from their houses. Rushing out of doors, the women milled around the market square, trying to keep their few children from panic. The men were not much better: they held clubs and knives but were irresolute in their manner, and one of them was already behaving as if he had been bested in battle. Frightened and dispirited, the villagers responded to Csimenae's outrage with a lack of enthusiasm that boded ill.

If Csimenae was aware of this, she did not reveal it in her activity; she made her way to the center of the market square and climbed onto the bed of a low wagon that stood there. "You know there is danger!" she shouted aloud. "You know that we are set-upon by evil men. You must rally now, and fight them off, or you will be their slaves and worse than slaves."

"They are of this place!" Rilsilin protested.

"Not if they come to take it with weapons and kill us." Csimenae took the nearest torch and extinguished it. "We will not make it easy for them. Let them have as little light as possible to guide them."

"That was clever." From his position near the barns, Sanct' Germain marveled at Csimenae's steadfast demeanor. He held his Byzantine sword in one hand and a Roman dagger in the other. He was listening for the next rush the attackers were about to make, sensing that they were not quite ready to charge the walls.

"Let each of you stand to his place by the walls and use the flails on

the attackers. Break their shoulders and their heads and you will have
the victory, for there are fewer of them than there are of us." Her voice
was a clarion, strong with purpose. "If you defeat the attackers, you will
be rewarded for your fealty to Aulutis. If you fail, you will receive no
mercy from the men outside the walls."

Rilsilin lifted his head and shouted, "Do not fight! They are our
kinsmen. They will do us no harm."

"Do you think so?" Csimenae demanded. "There are no enemies as
bitter as kinsmen. But if you want to take your chances, you may slip
away through the sheepfold, and pray you will be welcomed with gratitude." Her laughter was harsh and condemning.

There was a muttering among the others, and finally Henabo
shouted out, "We must fight. If we do not, we will be disgraced." He
climbed up beside Csimenae and raised his fist. "Get your flails and
your axes and your hammers and take up your positions. The woman is
right."

For a long moment no one moved, and then Ione shouted, "I will
take a cudgel."

That ended the reluctance: the men and youths surged forward, all
trying to show their courage as they shouted their new-found determination aloud.

Sanct' Germain kept his attention on the sheep, watching their nervous behavior, their surging from one side of the sheepfold to the
other, listening to their bleating; they were as useful watchmen as dogs,
or geese. "Not yet, not yet," he said quietly, wondering what the attackers were doing that kept them in the trees.

There was a flurry of movement as the villagers hurried to take up
their posts, weapons at the ready. Everyone was excited, their senses
keen; they kept their fear at bay. Csimenae shouted to them, putting
them on their mettle, exhorting them to be vigilant, not to slack in their
purpose.

But the men in the forest did not move for some time; the village
defenders grew edgy, then sullen, at last becoming sleepy and inattentive. As exhaustion seduced them, their fears returned as they waited,
their imaginations increasing the number and ferocity of their enemies
with every suppressed yawn. As the delay lengthened, two of the
guards drowsed off into fitful slumber.

Csimenae had gone back into her house to tend to her fussing son
when there was an eruption of men at the edge of the trees, and more

than a dozen of them charged the walls, a log slung on ropes between them to use as a battering ram. Those awake enough to cry out did, and in the space of two quick breaths all was confusion.

One group of attackers made for the gate with the intention of breaking it open while a second group ran at the barn with axes swinging. Wood splintered and a mule screamed as a curved blade bit through the rough plank, embedding itself deeply in the animal's flank; the mule kicked, breaking the wall open for the men outside. The second mule brayed and began to strike out with her hooves, her teeth bared in warning. The horses milled in their end of the barn, eyes showing whites and necks craning as they sought to flee.

Sanct' Germain moved quickly to the edge of the barn, his weapons ready to swing. The long Byzantine sword hummed as he sliced the air with it. Then he turned and brought the sword up in a smooth, backhanded stroke that stopped as it struck one of the marauders who had hidden in the overhang of the barn roof. In the next breath, Sanct' Germain had brought his dagger into play, driving back a second man before the first had finished screaming. He advanced on the men—there were four of them on their feet—his sword driving them back. One of the attackers landed a lucky blow on Sanct' Germain's forearm, and was rewarded by a thrust from the dagger that left him on his knees before Sanct' Germain, his eyes dazed and blood spurting out from between his fingers. Sanct' Germain ducked an axe-swing that caught the kneeling man on the temple; he went down without a sound. The third attacker shrieked and struck at Sanct' Germain with a long-handled axe. Sanct' Germain slapped the axe away with the flat of his sword and then lunged with his dagger. The metallic odor of blood was thick in the air.

Shouts and shrieks filled the night as the fighting continued; one of the two torches lit in the village was doused, so that most of the skirmishing was done in darkness. When two of the attackers attempted to scale the walls, the guards fell on them from their watches above them and brawled with fists and feet with as deadly intent as those with actual weapons in their hands.

Sanct' Germain continued his progress along the side of the barn, driving back the attackers as he came upon them. Two more men lay wounded by the time he reached the creamery door and signaled to Rogerian to admit him. He paid little heed to the wound on his forearm, and none at all to the blood that dripped from it; there would be time to heal after the town was safe.

Rogerian noticed the wound, but said only, "The villagers are holding their own."

Nodding, Sanct' Germain said, "They will prevail if they do not let fear overwhelm them. The attackers are not prepared for resistance."

At the gate there was a sudden shout of dismay, for the attackers had smashed one of the horse-skulls that hung over it. The omen was plain and the villagers all but lost heart as the skull was battered to shards by the men outside.

"Go," Sanct' Germain said to Rogerian, cocking his chin in the direction of the market square. "I will brace this door."

"Do not falter now!" Csimenae was shouting. "If we fail now, then we deserve to be slaves! We deserve death!"

There was a bit of a rally, a few of the defenders taking up her challenge; the rest were too disheartened.

Then Rogerian came running up with two new torches in his hands. "You must uphold the horses," he shouted to them. "Their spirits will not spare you if you do nothing to preserve their home."

In the creamery, Sanct' Germain had more trouble: two men were chopping down the door with axes. His brace was not enough to withstand their assault, and so he took his sword and thrust at the men through the gouges in the wood.

One of the men cursed, but the other fought all the harder, reducing two of the door's boards to kindling in five desperate blows. His companion continued to hurl imprecations at Sanct' Germain and the village he defended. The man with the axe started to climb through the opening he had made. Sanct' Germain swung his Byzantine sword, letting the weight of the blade carry it deep into the man's thigh.

The man bellowed and scrambled back, leaving a wide spatter of blood behind. He and the man with him staggered away from the door as Sanct' Germain pushed through the wreckage of the door to make sure the two did no more damage; they might be injured, but they could still be dangerous. One of the men brandished a dagger as he strove to escape. Sanct' Germain had no difficulty seeing the fleeing men in the darkness, but the confusion of the fighting made it hard to keep track of them as the attackers began to mill, their own disorder bringing more disarray to the villagers. He kept after them, occasionally glancing back to see if any of the other attackers had discovered the gaping hole where the creamery door had been.

As Sanct' Germain dispatched the second of the men he chased, he heard the renewed shouting from the gates—the villagers had begun to fight once more, and their resolve was once again high. They began to shore up the gates as the younger men took baskets of stones and climbed to the top of the walls to hurl these down on the men outside.

Csimenae began to chant; the words were harsh, in a language Sanct' Germain did not recognize, and the melody confined itself to three notes, but it was stirring to the villagers, and soon most of them were chanting with her, shouting on every eighth syllable.

Now the attackers hesitated, and two of them broke and ran; the slower of the two was brought down by a cudgel thrown by one of his fellows. One of the attackers did his best to shout over the chanting, "This is deviltry! They are praying to demons! What do we have to fear? There are monks praying for us!"

Rocks showered down. From his vantage-point at the side of the barn, Sanct' Germain saw the attackers withdraw a short distance. He took advantage of this lull to hasten to Csimenae.

She was still leading the chanting, and a few of the villagers were flushed with premature victory. "How many did you rout?" she asked as she reached the end of a cadence in the chanting.

"Four," he answered. "Two of them are dead and we will have to bury them."

"Oh, no," she said. "Not until the kites and crows have picked their bones." She grinned her fury. "They must show what happens to those who come against us."

A few of the villagers added their support in vigorous shouting.

Sanct' Germain knew better than to press the matter with her now. Instead he told her, "I think they will make another rush, and soon."

"No," she said. "They will vanish into the hills and we will never see them again." The last words were cries of triumph.

"I fear they are not beaten yet; they may return for another assault," said Sanct' Germain. "Keep ready until sunrise. In case they have not accepted their defeat. Remember they have wounded to retrieve—"

He got no farther. "Wounded?" She pointed to Henabo. "Take one of the men with you and kill the injured. We have no use for them here."

"Kill them?" Sanct' Germain could not stop himself from exclaiming. For the first time he felt the ache in his arm where the blood was finally beginning to dry. "You cannot kill them."

"Yes. We must. Kill them. They would have done as much to us. We haven't food enough to keep them as slaves—you know that as well as I do. So they must die." Csimenae held up her arm and the men around her shouted agreement. "Go; do what you must."

"At least wait until morning," said Sanct' Germain. "Your men could be—"

Csimenae ignored him. "Kill them. Now."

Henabo pointed to Namundis. "You. Come with me." He hefted an iron-headed sledge-hammer and strode toward the gates.

Namundis nodded, swallowed hard, and took a stout cudgel before going after Henabo, his cheeks flushed beneath his fuzz of youthful beard.

"They will swear vengeance on you and on this village for—" Sanct' Germain protested, only to be interrupted.

"Let them swear whatever they like," Csimenae declared, and spat. "We will kill all who come against us." She smiled as the villagers made loud cries of assent. "They will not dare to attack us, no one will dare."

Pordinae shouted, "Let them die!" and the others took up her call, repeating it until it, too, became a chant.

"There is no benefit in this," Sanct' Germain said, but no one heard him.

An appalling sound rent the night—part shriek, part sigh, it came with a pulpy thud.

"That is what will become of all who attack us!" Csimenae shouted, and was echoed by a second fatal bludgeon.

The villagers cheered. Then the cheers turned to screams as a second wave of attackers came rushing out of the woods, their axes and hammers already swinging.

Namundis, who had been straddling a wounded man, gave a cry of dismay, then fell under the first onslaught as the men rushed at the walls.

"Fight!" Csimenae shouted. "Fight! Kill them!"

The people of the village struggled to overcome their burgeoning terror. Pordinae reached for a big iron rake and started to climb onto the wall. "Strike them down!"

"Strike them!" The shout encouraged the villagers, and they strove once more to fight off the outsiders.

It was a fast, ferocious skirmish: the attackers rushed at two sides of the walls, their hammers striking stones and flesh alike. The villagers clambered onto the walls and used rakes, hoes, and flails to batter at the men charging their stronghold.

Sanct' Germain climbed onto the roof of the house nearest the gate and called out where the attackers were. "Someone close the creamery! Brace the door from within!" he ordered, knowing it was the weakest part of their defenses. "And someone guard the barn! And the sheepfold!" He was shocked at how few men there were, and he realized how desperate they must be; he was at once more sympathetic to their plight and steeled against them, for they had very little to lose in this battle. Along with the sweep of the fighting, he could sense the coming dawn, and knew his strength would diminish with the light.

Three of the attackers managed to climb onto the wall, and one of them used a shepherd's sling to hurl rocks at the defenders until one of the villagers managed to batter him off the walls with a pig-goad. One of the fallen man's fellows was able to loose three more stones before he, too, and his remaining comrade, was driven from their place.

When the end came, it was quick; the attackers lost their impetus, faltered, then fell back rapidly, dragging their wounded with them, and pulling Namundis' mangled body after them. Inside the walls the villagers rushed to watch the retreat, confused by the suddenness of the withdrawal.

Sanct' Germain came down from the roof, weariness possessing him like a ghost. He leaned against the wall of the house, his arm aching, and his soul in despair. The villagers who hurried past him paid him no heed.

"My master." Rogerian's voice cut through the commotion and caught his attention.

He straightened up. "What is it?" For he could see from Rogerian's face that something was wrong.

"Csimenae," said Rogerian. "She has been . . . hurt." He said this last in the language of the Mongols on the Old Silk Road. "Ione has her."

"Hurt?" Sanct' Germain repeated in the same tongue. "Badly?"

"Yes." Rogerian glanced about uneasily. "Come with me."

Sanct' Germain squinted up into the night sky that was just beginning to fade. "I will," he said, knowing he would soon have to be indoors or suffer for it. He made himself walk with Rogerian as if he had
all his strength still. "What happened?"

"One of the rocks in the slings—it struck her. Here." He laid his
hand on the side of his head, above and slightly behind his ear.

Sanct' Germain frowned. "The skull?"

"Is broken," said Rogerian, and paused while Sanct' Germain considered this. "Not terribly, but broken. The side of her head feels . . .
soft."

"Is she conscious?" Sanct' Germain asked as they reached the door
to Ione's house.

"When I came for you she was, but her pain was great and she
was . . . not herself." He indicated the villagers who had come to the
market square to assess their losses, and said, "They do not know yet."

"Ah." Sanct' Germain closed his eyes a moment, then opened them,
saying, "You had best bring my chest. I will do what I can for her."

Rogerian nodded, turning away before the crowd could understand
their purpose. "I will be circumspect," he promised as he went off
through the reveling villagers.

Behind Sanct' Germain, Ione opened the door. "Come in. Hurry.
There isn't much time." She tugged him inside.

"Is Csimenae failing?" Sanct' Germain asked as the door was closed
sharply.

"I fear," said Ione, pointing to the huddled figure beside her hearth.

Sanct' Germain went to her at once, dropping down onto one knee
and leaning forward to examine her wound; he saw she held Aulutis
close against her, and said, "Will you let me take him?"

"No!" Her voice was weak but there was no mistaking her determination. She looked blearily at Sanct' Germain. "Don't let. Them."

"She is afraid of what they will do to him," Ione explained.

"Why should they do anything?" Sanct' Germain wondered aloud as
he inspected the side of Csimenae's head.

"They swore fealty to him," said Ione as if there was an obvious conclusion to this.

"Yes. Why should he fear them if he has their oath?" He saw the
matted blood in her hair and the slight depression where the bone had
broken; without his sovereign remedy it was only a matter of time be-

fore contamination of flesh would exhaust her body and she would suc-
cumb to fever. At least, he thought, he still had syrup of poppies to ease
her pain.

Csimenae licked her lips. "Thirsty," she muttered.

"May I have some water?" Sanct' Germain asked Ione before once
again attempting to take Aulutis from his mother. "I will not harm him;
I want to treat you. Surely you can trust me to do this."

"No," she whispered, clutching her son so fiercely that he whimpered.

Ione brought the water. "It is the villagers," she said as she handed
him a ceramic cup. "They will have to kill him if they want to end their
fealty. They will drag him behind a horse. And her as well."

Sanct' Germain did not falter in holding the cup for Csimenae, but
he looked around at Ione, startled. "Why should they do that?"

"If Aulutis cannot lead them, they will have to find someone who
will. If Csimenae dies, they will kill her child for the good of the village." Ione studied Sanct' Germain. "Is she going to die?"

"Her injury is very grave," he admitted as he took the cup away; Csimenae had managed to drink half of it. "But killing the boy—"

"They must," Ione said as if any other possibility was unthinkable.
"And Csimenae."

"And if Csimenae lives, what then?" He touched the mass of hair
and blood as lightly as he could; there was no doubt the bone was broken.

"Then they will not abjure their oaths. But she would have to be
strong enough to raise him, and to bring him to manhood." She took a
step back. "If she is weak, or simple, they will kill her and her son, so
that they may have a proper leader to support."

"If she needs time to recover, will she have it?" He was vexed with
himself for what he was thinking; he had sworn when Nicoris had decided to die that he would bring no more of the living into his life; she
had shown him that for most, his gift was worse than a scourge and he
had realized then that he must not impose himself again on anyone. Yet
he knew beyond question that if he did not offer his life to Csimenae
she, and her child, would be lost to the desperate villagers and the attackers beyond the walls: it was unbearable. He heard Rogerian's rap
on the door, and turned with relief. "If you will admit my servant."

Ione pulled the door back a little way and peered out. "It is he," she
said as she opened the door to let him in.

"Very good," said Sanct' Germain as he rose to take the chest Rogerian carried. "Thank you," he said.

"It is little enough," Rogerian responded with a slight nod in Csimenae's direction. "That injury is . . . dire."

"I fear you are right," Sanct' Germain said as he opened the chest. "Syrup of poppies and the pansy anodyne, I think." He spoke remotely, as if his thoughts were far away and this work was done by rote.

"And willow bark," Rogerian suggested.

"It will ease any swelling," Sanct' Germain agreed. He looked at Ione. "Do you have a small bowl I could use? I want to make a treatment for Csimenae."

Ione's expression was skeptical, but she went and retrieved a small copper bowl from her pantry shelves. "Will this do? And what of the boy?"

"She will not let him go," Sanct' Germain said, aware of the force with which Csimenae held onto Aulutis.

"Not yet," said Ione, her meaning clear: when Csimenae was dead, Aulutis would be sacrificed.

"She's almost crushing him," Rogerian said, his concern making his austere features look forbidding. "Can you persuade her to release him?"

"I do not know," Sanct' Germain said as he took two small jars and a vial from his chest. "I will need a bandage for her. Something light, with that loose linen from Corduba."

"If there is any left," said Rogerian.

"If there is not, then make strips of my old silk tunica; you know the one. It is light enough." He went about his preparation with the ease of old habit. "Ione, will you keep watch for us?"

She hesitated, then said, "I will. Unless she fails. If she is dead, I must tell the rest, or they will kill me for my silence."

Sanct' Germain nodded, knowing that Csimenae could not last very long no matter what medicaments he provided. "That is kind of you."

Ione said nothing in reply; she kept her position, looking nervously from the door to Csimenae and back again. She bit her lower lip as the noise outside increased.

As soon as Sanct' Germain had prepared his herbal paste, he gave the vial to Rogerian. "Mix this with wine for me, if you would. Not too much. She is too weak for much syrup of poppies."

Rogerian took the vial. "This will not—"

"Do it," Sanct' Germain said softly.

"There is one thing you can do to save her, my master. You cannot restore her, as you did me, for you haven't all the material you would need. But you can save her." Rogerian went about diluting the syrup of poppies as he spoke.

"You know what coming to my life has done," Sanct' Germain said, his voice brittle.

"You mean what it did to Nicoris," Rogerian said evenly.

Sanct' Germain began to spread the paste on the side of Csimenae's head, covering the whole area; she moaned and mumbled a few scraps of protest, but was unable to gather strength enough to stop him; she paddled the air with limp hands and stared out at Sanct' Germain with glazed eyes. "What do you mean?" He gave Rogerian his full attention as soon as he had finished.

"I mean that Nicoris was not Csimenae, and that what Nicoris found a curse would be salvation for Csimenae. Think of what will happen if you do not." Rogerian spoke bluntly, meeting Sanct' Germain's dark gaze unflinchingly. "Do you think Olivia finds her life a curse?"

"Csimenae is not Olivia: she has no notion of what I am, or what my life is," Sanct' Germain said as he scrutinized Csimenae, trying to read her pale face.

"At least if you save her, she will have time to learn," Rogerian handed him a cup with the syrup of poppies. "It would mean her son would live. She has done so much for her son." Beneath his stern self-control, Rogerian felt a pang as he remembered his own children, now centuries dead.

"That she has, and with scant reward," Sanct' Germain said, comprehension in his response. "All right. For the sake of her son, and for you, old friend."

Csimenae muttered, "Horses."

Rogerian made a formal reverence. "I will see to Ione," he offered, and went to the woman at the door. "Will you help me? I have silk to cut." He added, "It will be to bind Csimenae's head."

She made a gesture to the door. "If anyone should come inside."

Aulutis began to wail, his tiny fists waving in his struggle to get away from his mother's convulsive hold on him.

"Set the bolt," Rogerian recommended as he put action to his suggestion. "That should keep them out."

Ione shrugged, and gave a tug to her stola. "It should, for a little while."

Wriggling, Aulutis managed to work himself out of Csimenae's arms; he lay beside her, his eyes tearing from the effort of what he had done.

"They may not even try it," Rogerian assured her. "It is almost dawn and they are exhausted. They will tire, and then no one will disturb us." He led her away from the door and the place where Csimenae lay.

Sanct' Germain looked down at Csimenae's curled body and gave a tiny shake to his head. Then he began to peel back the scab on his arm, letting the blood well as he went down on his knees next to her. Very gently he took her head in one hand and guided her mouth to his own wound, holding his arm so that his blood ran over her lips. "Drink, Csimenae," he urged her, and felt her swallow once, twice, and then several times; she murmured a disjointed phrase, and finally began to suck on her own. As she did, her body began to relax, opening from her tight position to an attitude of peaceful half-slumber; although she remained pallid, the shine of sweat went from her brow, and she held onto him gently, taking what he offered without distress, her ghost of a smile revealing her satisfaction. After a while, there was a small trail of blood running from her lips to her chin. Only when his arm stopped bleeding did he rock back on his heels, knowing that she was now protected from death. "Rogerian," he called out softly, "It is sufficient."

Rogerian came to his side. "She looks better."

"I suppose so." He rose unsteadily to his feet then paused, listening intently. "The villagers have retired. And the sun has risen." His dark eyes were livid with exhaustion. "I must rest."

"I will tend to the livestock and then—"

"The mule will have to be killed if he isn't dead already. Smoke the meat." His voice was soft and when he took his first step, he nearly stumbled.

Ione, who had picked up Aulutis and was rocking him in her arms, stopped, regarding Sanct' Germain with alarm. "Are you ill?"

"No," he said. "Only tired." He looked at Ione for an instant. "You will have goat's milk for the child before morning is gone. Rogerian will bring it. I will return later in the day, when I have restored myself. I will watch Csimenae. In the meantime, do not worry at her condition. I expect there will be a crisis some time today. She may enter a very deep swoon, and her breath might be hard to detect. By tomorrow at this time, she will be recovering." He did his best to calm her fears. "She will rise from her bed, I promise you."

"For the sake of this boy, I hope so," said Ione, making no secret of her doubts.

"Let no one see her until tomorrow. I do not want the others to panic because Csimenae is injured." He made himself stand straighter. "Rogerian will leave my chest here for today in case I should need any medicaments to treat her tonight."

Rogerian, who had gone to the door, now inclined his head to show obedience. "It is time you retired, my master," he said. "Leave me to my tasks."

"Well enough," said Sanct' Germain, and nodded to Ione. "You will be rewarded for your kindness."

She held Aulutis up in her arms. "Milk for the boy, and soon, will be reward enough," she said, certain that if Csimenae survived she would be shown favor far beyond any she might have expected before this night.

"I will bring it directly," said Rogerian as he opened the door. Sunlight streamed in, brilliant and powerful.

Sanct' Germain lifted his arm to shield his face from the light. "Let us hasten," he said to Rogerian, feeling as if acid ate at his skin.

Rogerian complied at once, doing his best to keep between Sanct' Germain and the early morning light. As they went through the debris of the market square, he said to Sanct' Germain, "You did well, my master."

"Did I." Sanct' Germain told himself his uneasiness came from fatigue and sunlight, not from Csimenae's unprepared passage into his life. There might be difficulties for her, and for him, since only she had tasted blood; he had gained no knowledge with his bond to her. He would have much to tell her when she wakened that night; she would have to learn quickly. Vampiric life had immediate demands she would have to understand; he hoped she would not be repulsed by what she had become, that she would understand the necessity of what she had become. Entering his house, he sank down gratefully on the largest chest of his native earth, and as he lay in a stupor for most of the day, none of his misgivings troubled him.

Text of a letter from Episcus Luitegild of Toletum to Episcus Salvius of Tarraco.

To my most esteemed Brother in Christ and the Church we both serve, my prayerful greetings from Toletum on this most fortuitous day, when all Christians must give thanks to God for the bounty of harvest and the fulfillment of prophesy, and when it is agreeable in God's Eyes that we Episcus Brothers inform one another of the events occurring since the Paschal Feast; in such devotion I tender this to you, as I will provide similar reports to our fellows.

On this day, at the Feast of the Virgin, there has been word brought to this city that the Gardingi have finally agreed to rebuild the road to Tolosa in the spring. That will not have any benefit for this year, but winter will soon be upon us in any case, and any repairs that could be made will be of no use in this season. While we of Toletum may rejoice in this decision, you at Tarraco may have less reason to thank God for moving the Gardingi to action, for it may mean fewer pilgrims will sail from your port than have done this year because they could not travel on the road. It is still to our benefits that the road will once again be open, for whatever the case, it is of importance to all of us; once the road is repaired, Christians may once again undertake to walk to Rome to pray at the Tomb of Sanct' Petrus and seek the blessings of the Pope. Those who are going to Jerusalem are still going to arrive at Tarraco to take ship for that most sacred place.

The Praetorius of Toletum has announced a tax on all travelers, including pilgrims. I have appealed to him to remove the tax, but he has remained adamant. I warn you of this, for many of the Gardingi have also begun to levy such taxes, and it is possible that you, in a place where pilgrims gather, may find your flock equally burdened. The tax must be reduced for the sake of our faith. If your Praetorius is not willing to excuse pilgrims a tax, you may find that many more pilgrims will decide to travel by road rather than spend what little money they have on the taxes of Praetoria and Gardingi.

We have been told that there have been fewer Greek ships coming to Gades; have you seen a similar reduction in Greeks? If you have, do you know the reason why there has been such a reduction? There are rumors here, but I can discover no part of the truth. I have spoken to the Jews of the city, for they are powerful and their trading ships go everywhere, but we are too far from the ports for them to know anything more than what we have been told. If the Greeks have found other ports more to their liking, it would behoove us to know which ones they have decided to favor. The price of good cotton is rising in the *markets and if that is to continue, we will have to provide other woven goods to our religious communities in this region. The Greeks have made cotton their own, and we have no choice but to pay their price for it or make our own linen. Would it be possible to grow cotton here, do you think? God has favored our industry in such matters in the past. Might He not do so now? I know there is no sin in our poverty, but I do not like to see our monks ragged as beggars—I leave that to solitary mendicants and penitent pilgrims. It is said that the Romans of old had cotton planted in this region, but whether this is true or not, I have no way to know: there is no cotton here now.*

We have received the hand of Sanct' Procopius and have commissioned a proper reliquary for it. Fortunately a portion of the monies provided to us by the foreigner Sanct' Germain, who left Toletum many months since, remains and will allow us to have the hand reverentially displayed for the veneration of the people. It is altogether fitting that we demonstrate our piety in this way, let the Greeks say what they will. The sanctity of Procopius is present in the least part of him, and by being in the presence of his hand, Christians may share in his holiness. Those of your flock who may come to Toletum will be welcomed in Christ to receive the virtue of this hand.

Our hearts are full of gratitude that God has finally ended all signs of the Great Pox. Those who died of it are surely martyrs as those eaten by wild beasts in the time of the monstrous Nero, in whom the Devil moved to bring an end of our faith and thereby leave the world without Salvation. The Great Pox is the tool of the Devil, and as such it must be answered with fasting and prayer. Those who sought the help of soothsayers and perished have lost all hope of Paradise. The Christians of Toletum have decided that any who perished of the Great Pox without the Last Confession may not be buried with those who died in Grace. The Praetorius has levied a tax on all families seeking such burial for their kin. Because of this, many bodies have been taken outside the city walls and left at crossroads, where no tax may be imposed. A few monks have gone to pray for these unfortunates, but this is not encouraged, for the dead are beyond our help.

I anticipate the arrival of your tomus with the certainty that you will provide me information that will comfort all good Christians and assure the continuing strength of our faith, for surely your example will renew the devotion of us all. I have not yet heard from our Brothers in

*Gades or Corduba, but I await their promised communications with
the same tranquility of spirit that I expect yours.*

*May God bring you the joys of wisdom and the serenity of piety.
May He make your sons strong and worthy of you. May He lift up your
eyes to the wonders of His Realm. May He guide your flock in the ways
of virtue. May your worldly prestige enhance your faith. May your city
always be a haven for those who have affirmed their trust in Our Lord.
May you never know want or sin. May goodness be upon you from this
moment until the Last Days. May God keep you in His Sight on earth
and at His Right Hand in Paradise. Amen.*

> *Episcus Luitegild*
> *of Toletum and*
> *the Seat of Sanctissimus Resurrexionem*

*Written and sealed the 30th day of September in the 622nd year of man's
Salvation in the calendar of Sanct' Iago.*

9

"I am hungry," Csimenae announced as she looked across the main
room of Sanct' Germain's house. "The sun is down. How soon can we
hunt?"

"Not yet," Sanct' Germain warned. "There are villagers still awake.
If they saw you leave with me, some of them might become suspicious."

"You said I could visit them as they sleep," she reminded him, smiling in a way that revealed her determination. "You have said you will
tell me how it is done. There are many things you have said you will tell
me."

"Yes, and I will. But I also told you visiting your people in their sleep
is not safe. Your neighbors know you, and once they associate you with
dreams of the sort we give—" He broke off. "It would expose you to
more danger than is wise."

She thought about his answer. "Have you ever visited any of the villagers in their sleep?" Before he could respond, she continued, "I want to know; this is my son's place. Do not lie to me."

"I would not lie to you, whether Aulutis had anything to do with the village or not." He paused, making sure he had her attention. "No, I have not visited any of the people of this village in dreams. I never would; not in a place so small and isolated—I would endanger myself and any I visited. You are all untouched by me. People here are suspicious about me as a foreigner. How much worse would their fears be if they discovered that I was more of a foreigner than they knew. I would not be able to remain here were my true nature revealed."

"Are you certain of that?" Csimenae challenged. "You have power. Surely that would earn the respect and devotion—"

"I am certain," he said, interrupting her. "I have centuries of experience to guide me. This village is no different than any other in that regard, and the villagers are much the same as villagers everywhere. They, like you, do not want to be touched by anyone foreign. They do not trust your friendship with me, you know." He shook his head. "You risk enough coming here while the others are still about, and might see you in my company." He wished that Rogerian were back from his journey down the mountain to buy flour from the monks; he should be returning in the next few days if all went well. Sanct' Germain was still uncertain if he should have gone himself, as he had intended, but he had not thought it prudent to leave Csimenae on her own until she had learned how to deal with her vampiric state.

"Let them think what they wish. What can they do? This village is my son's assumption, and I hold it in trust for him. If I fail in that, I fail in all. As long as I am alive, my son is protected. These villagers know as much, and honor it." She held up her arms in a gesture of defiance. "They have too much to be grateful for. They should thank me, not question me. You will show me how to do it."

Sanct' Germain sighed. "There are more of them than there are of you."

"And they are cowards, all of them," she said, shrugging to show her opinion. "They will accept me so long as I am true to my child."

"Even cowards will act to protect themselves." He had seen that many times in the past, and had come to think that a coward fighting was as dangerous as a brave man.

"They are too cautious," she said, dismissing his concerns with a single motion of her hand. "They know how much they owe to me."

"Their lives are more fragile than yours," he persisted. "You must learn to respect that fragility."

"Why?" She faced him directly. "Because you tell me I must? You say that I have to follow your example. You tell me that because you brought me to your life, I must live it as you tell me. What arrogance! Your blood is not the blood of horses." She laughed without mirth, her hands on her hips. "You have been reading me lessons since the battle, and I have no more reason to believe you now than I had then. Your life is not my life." She took a step closer to him. "You have told me what I must do. I have listened. That is sufficient."

"But you are unconvinced." In the five weeks since she had wakened to his life, Csimenae had become more imperious, demanding respect and devotion, though she gave neither to anyone but her child. He wished now he had tasted her blood, for then she would be less of a conundrum to him; as things stood, she was too much a stranger to him.

"Why should I be?" she asked. "For Aulutis' sake?"

"Yes. He is as mortal as any of them," Sanct' Germain reminded her. "And we are not proof against all things. We can die the True Death."

"So you have said," she reminded him impatiently, and ticked off what he had told her on her fingers. "If our spine is broken, if our heads are chopped off, if we are consumed by fire. We cannot drown or suffocate or bleed to death. We cannot become ill. Or starve."

"True enough," he said, interrupting her recitation. "But we are not wholly proof against them and all those things are . . . not pleasant to endure. You would do well to avoid them when you can." He had personal experience with all five, and the memories still made him shudder inwardly. "Because you are able to withstand them does not mean they are desirable."

Csimenae held up her hand, continuing her enumeration. "There's more. We cannot be poisoned. Even the sun cannot entirely kill us, but it can burn us. Without our native earth, we are weakened." She stared at him, defying him. "See, Sanct' Germain? The things you have said— I have been listening. I have learned."

"You have learned lists, but you do not comprehend," said Sanct' Germain quietly. "In time, you will discover—"

"In time!" She laughed aloud. "In years and years and years of time!"

"That is my point," he said, not wanting to argue with her. "You may have the luxury of time, but you are not invulnerable. We must be careful of how we live, or we alert the living to our presence, and then we are at risk. Much as you may doubt it, you will need the people of the village—"

She interrupted him. "Not if you will not let me feed on them."

He did his best to hide his vexation. "You need them for your son's sake. You want him to have a village in which to rule, do you not? If you prey on these people, you prepare a cemetery for his inheritance. You want him to have a legacy that lasts more than his lifetime. Think of what you have dealt with to assure him of the fealty of the villagers. And you want him to be held in high regard, not dreaded and loathed."

"All right. That is what I want; chide me for it if you must," she allowed unhappily. "You say because your blood saved me from death that you are bound to me. Very well. I will hear you out."

"I am bound to you. The blood is a bond as strong as that of native earth," said Sanct' Germain, realizing that she did not understand what he was telling her.

"Yes, yes," she said impatiently. "No doubt you will hound me through all eternity."

He looked at her in silence for several heartbeats, then shrugged. "You do not want to accept what you have become. You will not learn—"

"But I am *hungry.*" She folded her arms. "If I wait much longer, I will set upon Gratius or Pordinae. They will sustain me. They will know I am honoring them."

Sanct' Germain regarded her gravely. "And I tell you that they will know you for what you are, and they will seek you out and give you the True Death. Do not doubt that they will. Perhaps not today or tomorrow, but in time." He saw her disbelief. "You think that because you have been one of them, they will permit you to raven among them? You have stoned mad dogs here: why do you suppose they would not do the same to you?"

"They are incapable of such perfidy," she said with a great deal of confidence. "You have not lived here long enough to know this."

"I know what those in my homeland are capable of doing to those of my blood," he said. "Your village is not much different from my homeland."

"No. You are wrong. Mont Calcius is not the same as other villages. No matter what you say." Her face was pale with hidden anger. "This village knows when it is guarded. They will not begrudge me an occasional sacrifice in exchange for what I can give them."

"Do you think so." Sanct' Germain looked steadily at her. "You are assuming your son will not mind, as well."

If he had hoped to persuade her with such an argument, he was disappointed. "Why should he? He will benefit the most of all." She turned away from him in a fine display of contempt. "You are always telling me of calamity and doom, as if I have become a monster. I am the guardian of this place as much as the horse-skulls are, and in time everyone here will know it." Csimenae tossed her head. "You do not know these people: I do. They will not deny me. For the sake of Aulutis."

"They would be more likely to visit the same fate on your boy than to permit you to make cattle of them." He held up his hand to keep her from interrupting. "Listen to me, for your son's sake if not your own. Try to understand what I am telling you without disputing everything I say: until you were fatally injured, I had not intended to bring you to my life, or to reveal my true nature to anyone in this village—indeed, I had been at pains to conceal what I am—but circumstances intervened. You would have died utterly, and your son with you had I not made it possible for you to change. For doing this, I am responsible for you, for the manner in which you live, because it is my blood that transformed you. I am only sorry you were unprepared, for now you must learn quickly how a vampire must live, or you will pose a danger to everyone living inside these walls."

Her face stiffened in ill-controlled rage. "I would not be so foolish! That would redound to my son's discredit and make him an outcast. You cannot think I would do such a thing. I will make the villagers glad of my presence. I will not make mistakes."

"Then you would be unique among my kind," Sanct' Germain said, unimpressed by her posturing. "None of those who come to this life unprepared—as you were unprepared—are innocuous to the living, little though you may think so. You have my blood in you, and although it is not the blood of horses, it is a bond, whether or not I have tasted yours. The bond cannot be denied. I am bound to you until you die the True Death, or I do." As he spoke, he saw her distrust. Only twice before had he experienced such perplexity, and now, as then, he was flummoxed by it: he did not know what he could do to remedy his predicament. He tried the most sensible approach he could think of. "You admit you are hungry. How long are you prepared to deny your need? Do you know what you hunger for? It is more than blood that sustains you. You have said already that you will permit the villagers to assuage your appetite, as if they were nothing more than sheep or goats. It is not what we ultimately seek." He paused, increasingly aware of the isolation that wore at him. Watching her pace the small room he sensed her inner conflicts. "Still, I am beholden to you, and your people, for giving me a refuge for so long. I would repay you egregiously if I were to treat the villagers as so much fodder, and you would be no less responsible for behaving in so dishonorable a manner."

"How noble you are," she mocked him.

"How pragmatic I am," he corrected her.

"Then, if I am not to feed on the villagers, let us go into the forest. There are goats and boar about. If we are fortunate, we will find the wild ponies, and drink the blood of horses. We may even find a marauder to feast upon." She gestured impatiently. "You may be used to this, but I am famished. I must feed."

"Lie back on the mat, the one with the blanket," he recommended, pointing to where it had been made up on the ground floor; it was where Rogerian slept. "Your native earth beneath it will sustain you for a time."

"Why should I? It is dark enough. We can hunt without fear." She frowned at him. "Or are you afraid?"

"Not in the way you mean," he said, growing apprehensive about her. "It is prudent to be careful. If you disdain thought, you may put yourself at more risk than you can handle."

Her eyes mocked him. "So you tutor me to model myself upon you."

He did not respond at once. "I have lived a very long time; I did not reach this age by being impetuous, or capricious; or foolish."

"So you say," she said, sulking. Then she sighed. "Oh, very well. We shall wait a little longer and then we hunt." She folded her arms. "Aulutis deserves my protection."

"Yes. He does." Sanct' Germain rubbed his chin with his thumb. "If he is to reach manhood, you will have to curb your desires, learn to control your appetite, and be willing to put his interests before your own, or he will answer for it." He hoped this argument might finally have some weight with her. "You are not the one who will suffer for your acts."

"But if I am weak, I cannot help him," she came back at him. "Hunger weakens me," she added pointedly.

He did not speak at once. "Tell me," he said, taking up his stance by the single backless chair, "how long do you expect to live in this place?"

Startled, she pursed her lips as she thought about her answer. "As long as my son is ruler here."

He nodded. "And you do not suppose that as the rest of the village grows old and dies, your unchanging youth will not be noticed? If the others age, and you do not, what then? Do you think Aulutis will not be aware of your nature?"

"It will be thought that I am fortunate, and my son will be glad of it," said Csimenae defiantly. "It will be thought that the horses have made me one of their guardians, if they think anything about my long life."

"A sign of favor from the horses, or the gods, or the angels," Sanct' Germain added for her, a deep exhaustion in his voice that came from the depths of his memories. "Or the newtri, or the Celestials. No doubt some would believe that, at least for a time. But as all your generation dies, and you do not; you show no signs of age—what then? Consider what I have told you: do you suppose no one will remark upon your unchanging youth? If not while your son is young, perhaps later? Then, when all of Aulutis' generation dies, and you do not, do you suppose the villagers will not have qualms about you?"

"I will deal with it when I must; you will not tell me how I will live," she said, dismissing the matter with a turn of her hand. "Now, have you finished? Can we go out to the woods to hunt?" From the tone of her voice, Sanct' Germain knew it was useless to try to talk to her anymore this evening.

"All right. But take the precaution of walking out through the barn. That way no one will suppose that you are going to hunt; they will assume you are tending the sheep and the goats." He straightened up. "I will join you at the edge of the olive trees in a little while. Wait for me there."

"Must I?" She frowned in displeasure. "I know how to follow animals in the forest."

"Certainly," he agreed. "But you have not yet learned how to catch them with your own hands and subdue them without killing them."

She pointed to him. "And why not kill them? It would be easier."

"Because we are nourished by life. Once the animal is dead, there is no virtue in its blood, not for us. It is life that sustains us, and nothing is more living than blood." He bowed slightly. "So wait for me. We will both be satisfied."

"How will we kill them?" she asked eagerly.

His answer was without emotion. "Bring a knife. It is no easy thing to bite an animal's neck while it lives." There were ways to immobilize quarry, but they took time to learn.

"Very well—I will bring a knife." For the first time she was eager. At the door she paused, taking the time to look out into the market square, making an attempt to ascertain if any observed her before she left.

Sanct' Germain watched her go with misgivings. He was failing with her, he knew; it was in every aspect of her, from the angle of her head to the contempt in her tone. She did not believe him, or any of the admonitions he gave her. If only he had some means of persuading her that did not sound as if he were reading her a lesson. He did not know any other way to convince her of the perils of her vampiric life, for although she claimed to comprehend all his warnings, she clearly did not think she had anything to worry about, and resented his repeated attempts to instill some sense of accountability in her expectations. He pondered her circumstances in this remote village and tried to discover some aspect of this place that would serve as an example to her—one she would heed. Nothing suggested itself, and finally he gathered up his dagger and a small axe before he left his house, going along the street swiftly and silently to the wall. He vaulted up on it, and leaped over it, landing with ease on the outside near the olive trees.

"How do you do that?" Csimenae asked as she came up to him.

"Those of our blood do not easily break our bones, nor do we harm our sinews." He saw the eagerness in her face, and added, "When we do break bones, they are as painful to align and as hard to knit as those of the living."

"But you, who tell me to be cautious, you would not make such a leap if you thought you would be hurt by it, would you?" Excitement shone in her eyes. "Do you teach how to do that, too, or only those things I am not supposed to do?" She had begun to stride toward the forest and the path that the woodsmen used.

"You will learn, in time," he said, knowing she was hoarding grievances against him. "It is like many other skills—you cannot do it well at the beginning, but practice over time will make you proficient." He lowered his voice. "The same with hunting."

"So you tell me," she muttered, ducking her head as the forest thickened around them. "What shall we hunt, then?"

"Goats. Boar," Sanct' Germain suggested. "Both are about tonight, and near enough to hunt with ease. It should not take long to find game to our liking." He raised his head and sniffed the wind. "The boar are eating acorns. You can smell them both on the wind."

She inhaled and tried to sort out what the scents and odors told her; shrugging her disdain, she said, "There is no need to snuffle the air, like mice seeking the pantry. I know where their favorite grove is. If we go there, we will find them." She motioned for him to follow her.

"Do not be reckless, Csimenae," he recommended, following after her.

Without hesitation she rounded on him. "Or what? Or you will chastise me?"

He held up his hands. "No. The tusks of a boar can cause real injury, and their hooves can break our spines."

"Oh," she said, somewhat mollified. "You wanted to keep me from being hurt, is that it?"

He decided not to answer directly. "The woods are no place to be hurt. We are not the only creatures drawn to spilled blood."

She laughed softly. "Wolves and cats, you mean?"

"Among others," he said. "Kites, vultures."

"And insects?" she suggested, moving quickly toward the narrow trail made by animals passing among the trees.

"Yes, insects. And rats." He could sense her shudder of distaste. "They all dine on blood and flesh."

"And we drink living blood," she said with pride. "Not like those who scavenge on the dead."

Puzzled, he made a gesture of agreement. "Does that matter to you?"

"Does it not to you?" She stopped and tugged at his arm in a show of exasperation.

He studied her face. "No. Not as it seems it does for you. I revere life; it sustains me. The rest is the nature of death." He wondered if she would tell him why this difference was so significant to her. Whatever her answer might have been, it was cut short by the sudden noise of a sounder of boar coming through the undergrowth. "Hold to the side," he ordered, all but thrusting her off the trail and into the cover of the thick-growing trees.

She moved with alacrity, crouching down behind an old oak, completely alert, as feral as any prey she sought. Her eyes glistened with excitement and she grinned, anticipating her kill. Although Sanct' Germain was only an arm's-length away, she paid no attention to him, her full concentration on the boars.

Listening to the forest around them, Sanct' Germain could hear the silence grow around them, and knew it was not caused by the boars. Something else was out hunting this night, and he strove to discover what it might be. He motioned to Csimenae not to attack, to remain where she was, and saw insolence in her gaze. "Something is coming," he whispered, hoping he would not disturb the boars.

One of the nearest lifted his tusked head and squinted into the darkness, then ducked back down toward the ground to root for acorns and mushrooms.

"Let's get him," Csimenae hissed. "I can reach him easily."

"Stay still," Sanct' Germain responded.

She was not listening; already she was moving into position so that she could drop upon the nearest boar's back. Her knife was in her hand, ready for use. She glanced once at Sanct' Germain, confident and expectant. Then she flung herself forward, attempting to straddle the boar and stab its neck at the same time.

The boar squealed in fury and pain, and began to run, heading into the deepest undergrowth, crashing headlong through the brush. The rest of the sounder panicked, and began to mill about, grunting and shrieking in dismay, a few of the larger boars slashing out with tusks and hooves, snapping branches and gouging the earth.

Forced to act before he was ready, Sanct' Germain slipped out of his cover behind the tree, moving with a speed greater than living men achieved; he was as surefooted as he was swift, unhampered by the uneven footing and the nervous boars. With his senses wholly engaged, he dodged his way through the sounder, striving to keep up with the one bearing Csimenae in spite of the close-growing branches that tangled around him, and the precarious footing.

Suddenly the boar Csimenae had caught slowed, then stopped just before it toppled over, blood welling from a long gash in his throat: the boar was dead. Scrambling to her feet, Csimenae began to kick the carcass, outraged at the boar's demise.

"Your people will get meals from the body," Sanct' Germain said as he came up to her.

"But *I* will not, and I am *hungry*," she protested with another kick to the boar's shoulder. "He ought to be alive."

"And it is unfortunate that he is not," said Sanct' Germain quickly. "But it is too late to worry about such matters."

The rest of the sounder was increasingly restless; one of the older males made a rush at the two of them, but stopped short of slashing at them with his tusks. Others in the sounder pawed the ground, grumbling.

"I will find another," Csimenae said, starting impetuously toward the nearest of the boars.

This time Sanct' Germain caught her arm in time. "No. We must move this animal and soon. We are not the only hunters abroad tonight. Once we have it inside the village walls, we may hunt for other prey. We have time enough to search for more sustenance. The goats will be out, some distance up the slope; they will suit us well." He released Csimenae and bent to lift the boar, which was more than half again his weight. Slinging it across his shoulders, he peered into the darkest part of the forest, still uneasy. "Something is coming."

The sounder wheeled and began to scatter, running down the mountain, ignoring Sanct' Germain and Csimenae in their sudden headlong plunge. The sound of their shattering escape filled the forest.

"What now?" Csimenae asked impatiently, annoyed that she had been denied more hunting.

Sanct' Germain motioned her to silence. "Now you run," he breathed in utter stillness. "Toward the village. Now."

She glowered at him, ready to protest, and lost valuable time. Confused by the flight of the sounder of boar, she had not heard the approach of the bear.

It shambled toward them, taller than the tallest man, standing upright, its front legs swiping the air ahead of it, emitting rumbling grunts as it came on.

Csimenae stifled a scream and sprinted away toward Mont Calcius; the bear dropped onto all fours and prepared to give chase, a chase in which the bear would surely prevail.

Sanct' Germain swung the boar from his shoulders and threw it at the bear.

With a coughing roar, the bear half-rose and snagged the boar out of the air, then struck out at Sanct' Germain as well, his huge, curved claws leaving four deep furrows along Sanct' Germain's shoulder and shredding his hippogaudion.

Sanct' Germain staggered and strove to stay on his feet as the pain sank into him. Only when he saw the bear tearing at the boar did he dare to move, and then at an unsteady walk, for he felt his back wet with blood.

By the time he reached Mont Calcius, the night was more than half over, and he was reeling with every step. He made his way around to the barn, hoping to get inside the walls without attracting any questions. Vaguely he wondered where Csimenae might be, but concentrated on reaching his house and the annealing comfort of his native earth. He had just rounded the goat-pen when he heard a voice from the slaughtering-shed.

"Sanct' Germain," Csimenae repeated a little louder. "Come."

Reluctantly he obeyed, his body so sore that it seemed each pebble underfoot was spiked and the air filled with sand. As he reached the shed, he saw a young ram hanging from the rafters, his trussed feet kicking feebly as blood spurted from the wound in his throat. Csimenae pointed to the ram with pride, her face smeared from her feeding. He nodded. "You have fed."

"So can you," she encouraged him. "I did not take all."

"This is from your herd," Sanct' Germain said.

"Yes. I chose carefully." She motioned to the animal. "He will last a little longer, and you are in need, are you not?"

His esurience was as much a part of him as the pain from where the bear's claws had raked him, but he made himself shake his head. "It is unwise to feed on your own flocks and herds."

"Why?" She was dumbfounded. "The villagers will get the meat when I am done. Where is the trouble in that?"

"The villagers will know you as a vampire if you feed on their herds and flocks," he said. "In time, they will resent what you do."

"They will understand, as they know why we sacrifice horses, to gain their protection." She went back to the ram. "I have earned this."

Sanct' Germain leaned on the wall of the shed and pointed to the ram. "You had better finish your meal. He is almost gone."

A single glance confirmed this, and Csimenae moved hastily to catch the last of his living blood as the ram kicked his last. "It is sweet, this blood."

"It is fodder," said Sanct' Germain. "It will keep you from starving, but there is no touching with it."

"Touching," she said, and laughed. "You keep talking about touching. You chide me because I will not have it, as if I have put myself at hazard by my refusal. Why should I want touching of any sort? What use is that to me?"

"It is the touching that nurtures. The blood is the least of our nourishment. We do not sustain ourselves without the humanity of touching." He closed his eyes, fighting the weakness that went through him.

"You have not had any touching here," she told him bluntly.

"No," he agreed, an emotion that was almost grief in his dark eyes.

"But the blood is necessary," Csimenae said pugnaciously. "You cannot deny that."

"No. It is necessary." He paused, trying to marshal his thoughts. "You do not understand what I mean because you had no chance to experience—"

"Why should it matter?" She cut him off. "You think you have found the only way to live this undead life. If that is the case, why should you have to teach me so much? Would I not find it out for myself, through compulsion?" Licking the ram's blood off her lips, she went toward Sanct' Germain. "Well? Wouldn't I?"

"In time you might," he said, longing to rest. "It took me several centuries to learn that I was feeding on despair, and to turn away from it."

She laughed. "Why would I despair? You lost all your family, and your homeland. I have lost neither, nor will I."

He shook his head. "You cannot remain here forever," he told her gently, for he could feel her fear beneath her defiance.

"You had better dress those wounds," she said, her abrupt change of subject indicating she was tired of their discussion.

"Yes; I will tend to them," he said slowly, righting himself as if all his body had gone stiff.

Belatedly she shot him a concerned look. "You will not take any lasting injury from the wounds, will you?"

"No; as are all vampires, I am proof against such damage. I have nothing to fear from these gouges. They are not pleasant, but they will pass." He paused. "If you will consider this awhile: soon or late, all those of us who have come to this life are vagabonds and exiles."

"I will not be," she declared, glaring at him. "You say this because it is how you live. I have this village and I will not have to leave it. This is where I live and die." She went back to the ram and began to gut it, taking care not to cut the intestines, but to pull them from the carcass intact. Soon her arms were red to the elbows; she finally turned to speak to him, but found he was gone. "Good," she said aloud before she started to quarter the ram.

Text of a letter in Imperial Latin from Ragoczy Sanct' Germain Franciscus to Atta Olivia Clemens, carried by Rogerian to Osca, there entrusted to a merchant bound by ship from Valentia to Ostia. Delivered on November 29th, 622.

To my most dear, long-time, long-treasured friend, Olivia, my greet-ings, and the assurance that I am still in this world, as you are no doubt aware through our bond.

My apologies for this dreadful vellum, but it is the best I have left in my sadly depleted supplies. There is no better to be had here. I have been in this out-of-the-way village for some time; you will not recognize the name: Mont Calcius. It is in the mountains north and somewhat east of Valentia, a walled group of houses and a barn, not much larger than the stable-yard at Villa Ragoczy. Presently twenty-nine people live here, although there is room for eighty or more. I will probably not leave until the winter snows are out of the high passes, but I will be gone from this place by May. I plan to go to Tolosa for a time, and then I may venture to Roma once again. Do not wonder at the route this travels to reach you—Rogerian is carrying this to Osca for me, where he is going to purchase grain for the village, and such other supplies as he can bring back on a mule. He will find a merchant or pilgrim bound for Valentia and Roma to take this to you.

For all its smallness and isolation, this place has been something of a haven for me, but it will not be so much longer, for it may be that I have erred in bringing another to our life, though I did so with the hope that in preserving her from death I would also bring her to cherish the liv-ing, a goal which thus far I have not achieved. Since she is determined to hunt without regard to touching or compassion, I will be prudent; for that reason Rogerian and I leave here when winter is done, as I have told you. I have already begun preparations against that day. Perhaps we should depart sooner, but that would mean traveling over water; considering what happened to me the last time I did that, I suspect it would be wiser to keep to the land, no matter how inconvenient it is. I have not vellum enough, nor the inclination, to tell you the whole of it.

If I am truthful, I must also admit that I am growing lonely. No one but Csimenae knows my true nature, and there is no one here who seeks me as a lover, or I would want to seek me thus. So I have sustained myself with hunting animals in the forest, and I long for the intimacy that is the heart of our life. To know a living being in totality, there is no greater gift, is there? As I cannot achieve that cognizance here—nor can I safely visit any of the villagers in sleep—I will seek it elsewhere.

*Have you fared better than I in these matters? I hope you have, for
that would remind me that fulfillment is not beyond reach, which now
I begin to wonder if it is. Tell me what your life has been these last
twenty years, and I will be grateful beyond anything I can express.*

*May all you long for be yours to your benefit. May you seek nothing
to your disadvantage. And until I send you word from Tolosa, may you
be content with this missive, brief though it is. Be sure that it comes
with my utter appreciation and the unfaltering bond that is the blood
we share, as well as my*

Love,
Ragoczy Sanct' Germain Franciscus
(his sigil, the eclipse)

on the September Equinox in Sanct' Iago's year 622

10

Csimenae stared in astonishment. "No," she said as she ran her hands
over Sanct' Germain's shoulder. "There are no scars remaining."

"It will be the same with you," Sanct' Germain told her, not expecting her to heed him.

"It was less than three months. Such furrows should leave deep
scars," she said, looking toward Rogerian with increasing respect. "You
are the one who did this."

Rogerian ducked his head. "No; it was not I," he said, his formality
indicating his purpose. "Those who are undead keep no record of injury on their flesh. All hurts are borne on their souls."

"Very good," Csimenae chuckled, applauding sarcastically. "You
both are trying to bend me to your will."

"Not my will," said Sanct' Germain as he pulled on his heavy black
woollen tunica with the long sleeves. "You have much to learn, and I
would like to spare you the most painful lessons. If you will only let
me." In the center of his house the fire shimmied in an errant draft.

"Again!" she protested, holding her hands up. "I am thankful you
will not be here much longer. You do nothing but talk and instruct, in-

struct and talk. I have been taught until my head is sore, and nothing has changed." With that, she went to where Aulutis was playing, scooping him up in her arms and holding him close against her. "When you tell me all the things I must do, you forget that I am here to guard and serve my son. When he is a year old, I will sacrifice a horse, as I should have done at his birth, and I will drink its blood so everyone will see and know the horse is within me, to protect Aulutis. Then I will have the power I need. I will hang the skull over the door of my house, and no one will stop me doing it."

Sanct' Germain paused in buckling his belt—he was thinner than he had been when he came to Mont Calcius—and considered her. "You do well to take care of your boy."

"How gracious you are to tell me so," she exclaimed, making no apology for her insulting tone.

Rogerian frowned. "He is not gracious," he said to Csimenae. "He is not flattering you."

"Is he not?" Csimenae achieved an expression of mock horror. "You cannot mean to slight my child, surely?" She put Aulutis down and began to pace the floor, her steps heavy with ill-concealed frustration. "The rain is endless. I have not ventured beyond the walls for three days." She rounded on Sanct' Germain, "And do not tell me that I will learn how to cope with running water. That will come. It is this night that troubles me."

Sanct' Germain said nothing for a long moment, then sighed. "I will go out and bring in game."

"But I *want* to hunt!" she protested. "You may despise hunting, but I do not. If you have no appetite, let me, at least, tend to mine. There are those in the village who are hungry, and they will share my feast. I know there are deer in the forest, and I want—" She stopped abruptly as Aulutis began to scream; she rushed to gather him up in her arms, soothing and chiding him as she looked over his head and arms. "What is on your floor? His hand is cut!"

Both Rogerian and Sanct' Germain hurried to respond to her cry. "Let me see," Sanct' Germain said, reaching out for the boy's hand.

"He's cut!" Csimenae repeated in dismay, shocked at Aulutis' determined shrieks. "He's bleeding!"

"Then the sooner he is treated, the better," Sanct' Germain said calmly. "He is more angry than hurt, which is a good sign."

Rogerian picked up a shard of pottery that was lodged in the earthen floor of the house. "This is the instrument, I think." He let the light shine on it, revealing a faint red stain on the edge of it.

"He is cut!" she said again, her voice rising with her son's.

"Then permit my master to care for the cut," said Rogerian, putting his hand on Csimenae's shoulder as he held out the broken bit of pottery to Sanct' Germain.

"Why? What will he do?" She stroked Aulutis' head. "Look at all the blood. If you would let me sacrifice one of your horses, he would grow strong from this."

"This is hardly enough to warrant killing a horse. There is not so much blood as that," said Sanct' Germain, unperturbed by all he saw but worried at her intentions for his two horses. "The cut is not deep. If I put a salve on it, the healing will be faster."

"Because he will be one of yours then, too?" Csimenae suggested, leery of him.

Sanct' Germain stepped back, appalled at her suspicion. "No. No."

"You would not share your blood with a child, is that what you mean, or that you would not share blood with *my* child?" This was an accusation. "You do not want him protected as you protected me, or is it that you plan to be rid of him, so you may rule in his place?" She waited defensively for his response.

"I mean I would not force myself on anyone, or bring to my life someone unable to comprehend it." He turned away doing his best to conceal his distaste. He put the pottery fragment on the small table where his boots were set out, their soles newly filled with his native earth. "Rogerian, old friend, if you will fetch my salve of pansy-and-willow?"

"It is in the lacquer chest?" Rogerian asked, although he was fairly certain it was. "What vessel?"

"Yes—the lacquer chest. In the chalcedony jar." He pressed his lips together as he went toward Csimenae and her son once again.

"You are angry with me," Csimenae said, her voice sharp and her eyes hot. "You think I am—"

"Not angry," said Sanct' Germain. "I am revolted by what you imply."

"And in time, no doubt I will understand and share your revulsion?" Her words were sweetly vitriolic. "When I comprehend what your life is?"

This time Sanct' Germain did not bother to take up the dispute. "I will treat your son's hand, and then I will find deer, two stags; I will bring them here alive. You will not touch my horses."

"You can find stags in spite of the rain." She made no effort to disguise her pouting; in her arms Aulutis was no longer howling, but now made furious coughing sounds, his face red and screwed up with passion.

"I will take precautions against it," he said, and remembered how little of his native earth was left in his chests; by summer he would have to get more or avoid sunlight and running water.

"Which I will also learn to do," she said in a scornful tone. "Even though this village is my native earth."

"When you go beyond its confines, or seek to cross running water, yes." He studied the child. "He is over the worst. Look for yourself, Csimenae. I do not think his hand is bleeding any longer."

"So you say," Csimenae scoffed, hitching her shoulder up as if to shield Aulutis from Sanct' Germain.

"If you doubt me, examine the cut as much as you want," Sanct' Germain recommended just as Rogerian came from the pantry with the chalcedony jar of salve.

Csimenae managed to contain Aulutis' little fist and coax it open; there was blood on his palm and the faint line of a cut angling across his palm. "He is no longer bleeding," she admitted after close inspection.

"Let me salve it," Sanct' Germain said as he removed the stopper from the jar. "It will not hurt him." He waited while Csimenae made up her mind, then quickly applied a thin film of the ointment to the cut.

"Is that what you used on the bear's cuts?" she asked as she watched him narrowly.

"No," Sanct' Germain replied as he finished his work.

"Then what is it?" She pulled Aulutis' hand away, prepared to wipe the ointment off.

"It is what I use for hurts suffered by living human beings; it is a very good medicine for cuts and burns and scrapes," he said carefully. "My flesh will mend without such treatment, his will not." He studied her for a long moment. "If you want to lessen his pain, leave the ointment in place; if not—" He shrugged.

Csimenae frowned deeply, her face set into hard lines. "I will do what I must."

Rogerian stepped back tactfully, going toward the pantry once more. "Of course," Sanct' Germain said, and moved across the room. "I will bring you deer tonight."

"Good," she muttered. "You had better, or I will select another goat or sheep to feed on." Her determination was plain, and her stance revealed more than her words did about her increasing hunger.

"The villagers would not like that," Sanct' Germain reminded her as he returned the chalcedony jar to its place in his red-lacquer cabinet; he noticed that Rogerian had opened the small window and was putting out a jar to measure the rain.

"You worry too much about the people of this village," Csimenae complained. "What have they to say about how I live? You are a stranger, and you will leave here one day." Before he could answer, she went on, "I know your views on this, Sanct' Germain, never fear. And I know you are wrong."

"Am I." He set the latch on the cabinet.

"Yes. This is my village, and these are my son's people, and I know them for what they are. They serve my son, and I serve him. He will be their leader, and I will stand beside him," she insisted, clutching her son in her arms. "Get the deer and there will be no reason for us to argue."

"All right," he said to her, and looked toward the door. "I will bring the deer to your house some time after midnight."

"I will be waiting," said Csimenae, imbuing this promise with great meaning. She picked up her long paenula, pulling it around her and raising the hood so as to protect Aulutis as well as herself. "After midnight."

"Yes," he said, and watched her leave.

"She is troubled," said Rogerian from behind Sanct' Germain.

He nodded. "That she is." He gave a single shake of his head.

"And that, in turn, troubles you, does it not?" Rogerian coughed delicately. "How are we to help her?"

"Until she is willing to be helped, we can do nothing," Sanct' Germain said in a remote voice. Then he shook off his apprehension. "I will need my birrus, I think, the one with the leather shoulders."

Rogerian accepted this change without comment. "How soon do you go out?"

"As soon as the doors are all bolted for the night," said Sanct' Germain. "It will not be long, given the rain."

"I will get it for you, and your boots." He nodded toward the table. "You will need them."

"That I will." Sanct' Germain managed a one-sided smile. "You think Csimenae will bring us distress."

"And so do you," said Rogerian. "At the least, she will want to sacrifice one of your horses."

Sanct' Germain did not respond, preferring to ready himself for hunting than to contemplate the problems that lay ahead of them. By the time he slipped out of the village to hunt, he had put his apprehension aside. There was no reason to expect the worst—Csimenae was unused to her new life and was still coming to terms with the demands it made of her. Her trouble was that she had much to learn and time was short. He told himself that Csimenae would come to appreciate his instruction, and would do herself no harm; convinced that he would prevail, he went into the forest.

His anxiety returned with greater force a month later, as the first snows fell higher up the mountains and three lost travelers stumbled into the village, half-frozen and exhausted.

"They are a gift, a *gift!*" Csimenae enthused as she came alone to Sanct' Germain's house after the strangers had been put up in one of the vacant houses. "It is plain that they have been sent here—the spirits of the horses that guard the village have sent them—so that I can learn how to take blood from the living without preying upon the people of this village." This last was sharp, directed at Sanct' Germain without apology. "Even you must agree they are a gift."

Sanct' Germain considered the situation. "What do you know of them, other than they are travelers who lost their way?"

She folded her arms. "Why does it matter? What else is there *to* know?"

His answer held a suggestion of exasperation. "Who they are, as a beginning. If they are expected anywhere, and by whom. What is their reason for traveling. You do not want others looking for them. One of them was speaking Greek when he arrived, the other two Frankish. You cannot be certain why they are traveling together, or where they are bound. It may be they are messengers, or factors. They could be in the service of an Exarch or Episcus or Gardingio." He saw her disbelief. "Do not think that travelers are without relatives and obligations."

"What does this mean to me? They have lost their way. Should a search be made. I need only deny they have been here; who is to contradict me," she said with studied unconcern. "There are still raiders in the forest. Who is to say that these travelers did not meet with the raiders?"

"The raiders could say the same of this village," Sanct' Germain told her.

"If any come looking for these travelers, then they, too, will serve my need." She raised her chin. "It will keep the villagers safe, and we will not have to kill our herds and flocks."

Sanct' Germain shook his head. "You do not understand. If you attack travelers, you must kill them all or eventually the world will learn of it, and you will find you are as hunted as the game in the forest. Travelers are wary, and if they know a place holds danger, they will not go there. If you are too blatant in your predation, you yourself will be hunted."

"Do you think so?" she challenged him. "If that is your fear, then you will be glad to be away from here, will you not?"

He was silent for a short while; her clear rejection of him did not surprise him, but it caught him up short. "Yes," he said quietly. "Yes, I will."

"Then you are going to leave?" She was happily astonished. "You will be gone after winter is over?"

"Yes," he said.

"You give me your Word? You will not change your mind?" Her questions came quickly, and she leaned toward him. "You are willing to leave?"

"Yes."

She smiled. "Then I will leave these travelers alone, for your sake. This time. Do not ask me again. And once you are gone, I will do as I think best. I cannot be forever running into the forest for deer or boar or wild goats, or netting birds." Looking toward the door, she licked her lips. "Before you go, you must show me how to visit sleepers and take what I want without discovery."

"You do not take what you want, you give a pleasant dream and participate in it. You share in the passion you have helped to awaken. It is what you exchange that gives the blood its virtue. If you pursue a man or woman for your benefit alone, neither of you will be furthered by what you do." He spoke as if by rote, certain that she would not heed him.

"You will have to show me how," she repeated slyly. "Who shall it be? If I cannot learn on these travelers, who among the villagers shall I—"

"Neither," Sanct' Germain snapped.

"But it must be someone, mustn't it?" Csimenae asked, approaching him with slow, determined steps. "And if you forbid me the travelers and my people, who is left?"

He sighed. "There is another village a day's walk away from here, is there not?" He waited for her to nod. "We will go there." It was not a solution he wanted, but it was the only one he could think of that would not put her in immediate danger.

"I cannot," she said quickly. "I would have to leave Aulutis here alone, and he would be at the mercy of the villagers. If they killed him while I was gone, it would not be safe for me to return."

Sanct' Germain studied her. "The villagers have sworn fealty to Aulutis; why should they kill him."

"He is a baby. He cannot defend himself. If I am not here, the villagers may decide that their vows have no meaning. Why should they honor a boy who cannot speak or fight, who has no horses to defend him?" She pointed directly at Sanct' Germain. "They would say you have done away with me, or have made me your woman, and abandoned my son."

"Why should anyone assume you would leave your son?" Sanct' Germain responded. "You have made his cause your own."

She shook her head. "What man would take another's son if he sought sons of his own? No, no; without me Aulutis would be lost. If he were bearded, that would be another matter, but that is years away." Her laughter was harsh. "I cannot leave Aulutis unguarded, and I cannot take him with me, for then we certainly could not return, for someone else would have risen to claim the village."

"If you are gone for a single day and night?" Sanct' Germain was incredulous. "Is the village as precarious as that?"

"A day and a night would be enough," said Csimenae darkly. "There are men enough in the village that they would claim the position of leader. If they did not kill one another attempting to maintain their place."

Sanct' Germain's dark brows lowered; she was forcing him to accommodate her, but he had no argument to counter her demands. "All right. If other travelers come before winter is over, I will show you what to do."

Her grim mood vanished, to be replaced by sarcastic gratitude. "Oh! Thank you. I am relieved. Then you can leave without worry."

"Of course," he said, aware that he would fret no matter what assurance she gave him.

"So the travelers will go away tomorrow, and tell others that they can find rest and shelter here." With a faint chuckle she rounded on him. "You are clever, Sanct' Germain. I begin to see your plan. These men will live to tell their tale. If other travelers hear that we will take them in, I will have a better opportunity to have what I desire." Before he could speak, she went out the door, leaving Sanct' Germain to try to sort out his emotions.

Rogerian found him later that night sitting beside his red-lacquer chest, his demeanor revealing his uneasiness. "Has there been another misunderstanding?" he asked when Sanct' Germain offered him a half-hearted greeting.

"I would not think it was a misunderstanding," said Sanct' Germain. "It is more a question of cross-purposes." He rose. "Csimenae continues to have . . . doubts."

"Have the travelers anything to do with it?" Rogerian coughed diplomatically. "As soon as the villagers agreed to give them shelter, I thought she was too conciliating, too willing to provide for the strangers. On her order I have seen the travelers fed and cared for. The villagers do not want to have dealings with them because it might bring misfortune; travelers are thought to be unlucky."

Sanct' Germain laughed once. "And so they might be, but not as the villagers fear." With that, he began to pace. "I told Csimenae I would teach her to visit sleeping travelers—no, not these, but the next ones."

"Do you think there will be others?" Rogerian made a sign of impatience. "There have been none before now."

"If you do not count us," said Sanct' Germain sardonically. "We were lost travelers, too, you remember."

"And think how much time has passed between our arrival and theirs," said Rogerian, his sandy brows lifting.

"Do you mean that others might not come before we leave?" Sanct' Germain asked. "It is possible."

"It would mean that Csimenae would not be able to claim what she seeks. Is that what you hope?" Rogerian's gaze was keen.

"Perhaps," Sanct' Germain admitted. "Although she will need to know how to bring sweet dreams if she is to continue to live among people." This admission shook him, and he turned away but not before Rogerian saw the shadow of trouble cross Sanct' Germain's dark eyes.

Winter deepened, bringing cold and darkness to the mountains.

Wolves howled in the night and the game in the forest grew thin as leaves, then bark and berries were stripped away. Hunting grew more arduous as snow and hunger made their claims on the animals of the forest. In Mont Calcius the sheepfold was built up with pine boughs to keep the worst of the wind from chilling the flock and blighting their wool. Two of the houses were torn down to provide materials for repairing others, and, on Csimenae's orders, men went into the forest every clear day to gather wood for the village fires.

At the end of January, four monks on two worn-out horses wandered into the village, one of the monks coughing and feverish, the others desperate for warmth and food which the villagers reluctantly provided for the sake of the horses. The monks called down blessings on Mont Calcius and thanked Aulutis for his kindness before setting about tending to their stricken comrade even while the villagers stabled their animals.

"You have heard about the strangers, haven't you—one of them is sick." She came toward him. "Will you treat the monk?" Csimenae demanded as she sauntered into the center of his house. "Is he going to recover?"

"I do not know how ill he is. If he grows worse, then I must care for him," Sanct' Germain answered. "In a day or two I will be able to tell you more."

"They came with horses," she said, clearly convinced that this was significant. "There haven't been horses in this village since the Great Pox. Other than your two horses." She gave him a sidelong glance. "I have let you have your horses."

"Does that make a difference? that they have horses," Sanct' Germain asked as he laid more wood on the fire.

"It is a sign."

"How do you mean?" Sanct' Germain asked warily.

She regarded him as if his question were foolish. "That the monks are a gift to us. You would not permit me to use the travelers, and I did not argue. You have said that I must respect those men I employ, and I will, I will, when it is earned. This is different. The horses mean the monks are ours." Her eyes glinted with purpose.

"In a day or two, we will consider what is to be done," he said, aware he was only postponing the inevitable.

But this time Csimenae would not be put off. "Why must I wait so long? You will show me how to visit these men in their dreams. You said you would."

"Yes. I did." He could not deny his promise to her. "If this is what you want, then I am bound to teach you."

"Good. Tomorrow night, then. I can wait that long. I will feed on one of their horses tonight, to show I am grateful for the gift." She spun around on one leg. "The horses will make me strong, and my son will flourish."

Sanct' Germain regarded her with dismay. "The monks will want their horses when they resume their journey," he said carefully.

"They will not begrudge us a horse in tribute," said Csimenae. "You have already sacrificed a mule, which is not quite as satisfactory." Her smile widened. "You may tell me that I have no claim on the horses, but you do not understand."

"No," he agreed.

"The men from the village know the horses are a sign that we have been favored at last." It was clear that she would not be swayed from her conviction.

"You are planning to kill one of the monks' horses?" The question was blunt but level.

"I will take what I need, and then the men will sacrifice it. They will see that I have taken the spirit of the horse as mine own, and they will know that I am protected by horses." She shook her head. "You will see the wisdom in what I do when I have done it."

Sanct' Germain cocked his head, studying Csimenae, wishing again that she did not perplex him so. "These are your people, and you comprehend them as I cannot. But I remind you that the monks will not see your actions as you do."

"Do you mean they will be angry?" She shook her head. "It is nothing to me."

"It may cause the monks to denounce you," he told her as calmly as he could.

"Let them. What can they say that would endanger me?"

"Some monasteries are powerful, with Gardingi to do their will." He saw her glare at him and added, "I would do you no service to leave you in danger."

"There is *always* danger," she said brusquely. "Men are never free of it. I am not such a fool that I do not know it? After everything you have taught me, can you doubt it? You have told me what I have gained and lost in becoming like you. You have laid out your manner of living, and showed me many things to guide me. I will honor what you have told me, so long as it permits me to guard my son and Mont Calcius. That is why we have the horses to protect us."

Sanct' Germain held back the retort that sprang to his lips, saying instead, "Yes, there is always danger." As she shrugged, he continued, "For the living and the undead; for those of our blood, care must be taken if we are not to be exposed, and pay the price for being discovered."

"Not this again," she said, starting for the door. "You will meet me tomorrow night at the house where the monks are, and you will show me how I am to bring them dreams. Once I have learned this skill, you will have no reason to teach me anything more."

"It isn't learned in a single night," Sanct' Germain told her, feeling an inner cold seize him.

"Well enough. The monks will be here for a while." She pointed at him; it was a gesture he had come to recognize as punctuation for an ultimatum. "You will not withhold anything from me."

"No; I had not planned to," he said.

She laughed at him. "And do not try to keep me from the horse, unless you want to give me one of yours in its place; I will do it, if I must. I will deal with the monks when it is necessary."

He said nothing as she went out of his house; he gave his attention to the fire, finding discretion in this common chore. He was still at it when Rogerian came out of the shadows of the pantry. "You heard?"

"It will be hard to travel in winter," was all Rogerian would say.

Text of a report from the monastery-fortress of Sancta Gratia, sent to the Captios of Duz-and-Exarch of Terraco.

To the most esteemed commander and leader of the forces of the Duz-and-Exarch, the Captios Willgeprand, the greetings from Sartrium Braulio through the good offices of the scribe Ildefonsus at the Sancta Gratia outpost on this, the 19th day of March in Sanct' Iago's year 623.

In observance of our duty, we combine our efforts to tell you of the events taking place at this place since the coming of winter, so that you may more readily provide for the welfare of your city, and these men who guard this pass at the will of the Duz-and-Exarch of Terraco.

In December, a company of men—Frankish merchants by the look of them—were found frozen to death in a defile four thousand paces from our gates. These bodies bore the marks of animals' teeth, but showed no other signs of misadventure. They have been placed in the lower crypt until the ground is thawed enough to allow for proper burial. There was nothing to identify these men beyond their garments, and so likenesses have been ordered drawn; these will be displayed in the Visitor's Hall in the hope that someone may be able to put a name to the dead men.

In December, five of the guards here were stricken with fever; all but one recovered.

In December, a man from the Greek outpost came here with news that Arab pirates have been raiding the islands off the coast, and requesting additional men to help in ridding the seas of these merciless sea wolves. Two men asked to go with the Greek officer, and permission was granted to them, provided they serve only the Greeks in this campaign. This oath being given, the men were provided with weapons and the assurance of employment upon their return. There is some fear that the Arabs are being aided by the families of Terraco and Valentia who have been in disfavor or driven from power, for which reason, our men have been commended to the Greeks, that they may not be lured into supporting those who are seeking their own ends without regard to their oaths of fealty.

In January, a severe avalanche made our road impassable for five weeks together, and as a result, we ran low on wood and certain foods. Rations were cut twice, as our hunting parties could only go on the slopes to the east of us, the west being too unsafe to traverse.

In January, one traveler arrived from the east, a weaver looking for work. He has put himself to work here, making cloth in exchange for a place to sleep and meals to eat. He has shown no inclination to leave this place, and has spoken of neither father nor son. His name is Sunna, and he claims to have come from Corduba in his youth. Whatever the truth may be, he has made excellent cloth for us, and so we are inclined to keep him here with us if he is willing to remain.

In February, the first travelers came from the south-west—pilgrims bound for Roma. They were twelve in number, to honor the Apostles. They told of floods at Caesaraugusta and Osca.

In February, a severe storm struck on the 13th day, lasting for the next three, and once again, this place and the pass it guards were cut off *from the world. When the storm was over, the road was once again impassable for many days.*

In February, the one-eyed ewe delivered a still-born lamb, much too early. The ewe was butchered and her flesh roasted. Her fleece has been made into saddle-pads and caps.

In March, a mountain cat attacked our flock of goats, killing a nanny and her twin kids. Men were dispatched to kill the cat, but were unable to locate the animal in the crags and the snow. Guards have been posted around the flocks to prevent any more slaughter.

In March, two men came from the south-west, with two horses and a mule, which bore three chests on its saddle. They were bound for Tolosa, and were coming from the mountains above Osca. They were not Greeks, nor Arabs, although one man claimed to be from Gades. As they carried only such weapons as a prudent traveler has with him, they were allowed to continue on.

In March, three widows from Aqua Sulla arrived from the east, bearing holy relics for the Episcus of Caesaraugusta, which they had vowed on their husbands' graves to see placed in the hands of the holy Episcus.

In March, a company of peasants brought two cartloads of cheese and bacon to us, as is their duty of old. Rations were changed and the garrison is once again eating like fighting men.

This concludes our account of activities at Sancta Gratia, the which we submit with our earnest prayers that you may be honored and praised for your excellence, and that you will always be deserving of such distinction. May your sons thrive and bring glory to your House. May you be spared misfortune. May you never flag in your strength or your purpose. May you please men and God in all things.

Sartrium Braulio
by the scribe Ildefonsus
at Sancta Gratia, monastery and fortress

PART II

CHIMENAE

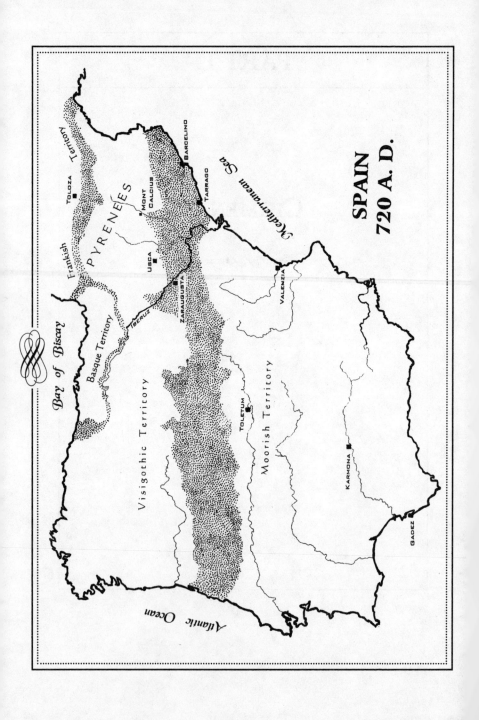

SPAIN
720 A. D.

Bay of Biscay

Atlantic Ocean

Mediterranean Sea

Frankish Territory

Basque Territory

PYRENEES

Visigothic Territory

Moorish Territory

TOLOZA

MONT CALCIUS

BARCELINO

TARRAGO

USCA

IBERUZ

ZARAGUSTA

VALENZIA

TOLETUM

KARMONA

GADEZ

*T*ext of a dispatch presented to Numair ibn Isffah ibn Musa from Timuz ibn Musa ibn Maliq.

In the name of Allah the All-Merciful, I, Timuz ibn Musa ibn Maliq, send this account and petition to you, my illustrious nephew, and inform you that a similar account will be provided to your august father, may Allah show him many years of fortunate life.

The slave San-Ragoz, who was a gift to you from the Emir, your most honored father, has truly escaped, although I have been unable to determine who helped him in this; as it stands now, this misfortune has brought much consternation to your soldiers, particularly those guarding your household, for it has been determined that San-Ragoz departed from his cell, apparently through the window, as one of the bars is missing. It is as yet unknown if anyone assisted him in his escape, although it is unlikely that anyone would be so reckless as to assist your slave in such an enterprise. The window is more than two full stories above the courtyard, so any fall from such a height should have injured—if not broken—his legs, making flight impossible, but there is no indication this has happened. The gate to the courtyard remains closed, so I must conclude that either he scaled the wall, or he found another means to leave the courtyard without alerting any of the guards, which leads me to suppose he was aided in his endeavor. I believe he must have disguised himself and passed out with others departing from this holding around mid-

night, but I have no proof of it. To determine the truth of this, I have put a dozen of your personal guard to the work of examining all those who were recorded to have left through the gates after sundown.

I must tell you, my nephew, that I disapprove of your intention to make San-Ragoz your personal physician and to blind him so that he might tend to your women without shame. Most particularly, I tell you again that a man who works only at night is a dangerous man to your women; had he not his remarkable gift, I would advise you to kill him and save yourself from danger. But San-Ragoz has saved men others could not. It is not for you to send such a one as San-Ragoz to tend your wives and concubines. Your father, my brother, had no such intention when he sent this slave to you, as you are well-aware. San-Ragoz is known to be an accomplished physician, and such skills as he possesses are too valuable to waste on women, and so you will realize if you sub-mit your will to Allah. You have many soldiers who require treatment for injuries and ills, and who have much greater call upon such a man as this slave than any of your women; it is fitting that you assign any man of such ability to your soldiers, who advance our faith and protect your family as no woman could. If it is Allah's Will that this San-Ragoz remain uncaptured, you may take it as an indication your intentions were contrary to the Will of Allah, which does not become a true fol-lower of the Prophet.

In these days since we have come to this city of Karmona, we have had to maintain our authority with the might of our soldiers and the favor of Allah. To deprive your men of San-Ragoz as a physician in order to have a slave for your women you show that you are not as de-voted to the glory of our cause as you have claimed to be. You have sworn an oath to advance the green banner until it is seen throughout the world, and all follow the One True Faith. Any act of yours that im-pedes this is an abjuration of your oath, and unworthy of you, or your father, my brother, to whom you owe all your allegiance and your ded-ication, in the name of Allah.

Your soldiers have been told to hunt down San-Ragoz and to return him to you, and insofar as they act as Allah Wills, it shall be done, and the slave shall bow to you again. Your soldiers are sworn to you, and they will not fail you, so long as it is the Will of Allah that they succeed. I have no doubt that they are capable of the task you set them. But if you then continue with your plan and have him blinded, I will no longer stand with your troops on your behalf, nor will I do anything to protect you in any regard, for you will have shown yourself to be be-neath my respect, and therefore of no consequence to me. If your father, the Emir—may Allah give him laudable years and many praise-worthy sons—should chastise me for this, I am willing to pay whatever price he demands of me, as is my duty and his right. Yet I warn you again: I will not and cannot support your wanton disregard for the good of your soldiers for nothing more than your women.

I have offered money for any information about this San-Ragoz and I will act upon anything I learn that will lead to his recapture. He has only been gone for two days and a night, and there is no report that he has been able to leave the city. I do not anticipate that this slave can go far, for his branded shoulder will surely be noticed, as is the brand on all slaves. It will not be many days before I bring San-Ragoz to you, and when I do, I ask that you reconsider your decision, and turn the slave to the tasks for which your father sent him to you: the care of your soldiers. Should you fail to do this, you know from this what I pledge to do. You must not doubt my purpose, for it is as firm as my adherence to the cause of the Prophet, and as the two are closely tied together, I will see that your father's intentions are served before your whim. You may defy me—you have surely done so in the past—but I beg you to reflect before you do so in this instance that it is not only your uncle and your father you betray if you do not release the slave San-Ragoz to me for the care of your soldiers, it is the battle for the souls of Islam that you forsake by depriving your men of the medicinal knowledge of this San-Ragoz. What can such treason bring you but disgrace in this life and perpetual darkness after death?

To this I set my hand in Radjab of the year 103 of the Hegira.

1

Now that it was dusk, he could move again; he had hidden all day, lying in the stupor that sunlight imposed upon him when he had no access to his native earth. San-Ragoz emerged from his hiding-place in the cor-ner of the abandoned Roman cemetery where even the new spring flowers had an air of decay and neglect to them; he made his way past the ancient tombs with care, to emerge in the Old Merchants' Quarter.

He was relieved that he still wore his black Byzantine dalmatica and black Persian kandys with black embroidery accents at neck and hem, for although they marked him as a foreigner, they also concealed him. The fading light had driven many of the residents indoors, away from the patrols of Umayyad soldiers with their lances and scimitars and whips. Concentrating intently, San-Ragoz kept alert to the approach of anyone still on the streets. Keeping to the narrowest of alleys and the darkest of paths, he took a circuitous route to the Byzantine Monastery of the Assumption, a squat, ancient building near the Eastern Gate of the city he still thought of as Corduba.

From the inside the stone walls came the drone of Greek chanting; San-Ragoz sank into the shadows of the short transept and waited for the evening prayers to end and the monks to retire to their dormitory. He reckoned these monks would leave one of their fellows in the chapel to guard the altar-flame, and all the rest would go off to pray and sleep, as Greek monks did. Their repetitive text and monotonous droning proved calming and he began to relax for the first time since he escaped the palace of the Emir's son. A pang of memory filled his thoughts with Charis and Cyprus, and his abduction to Tunis, followed by his sale into slavery; the enormity of his loss might have thrown him into melancholy but he forced such thoughts away: time enough for such recollection when he was out of Corduba—and to be out of Corduba he would have to achieve his goal here at the monastery. His opportunity would be brief, but he was determined to make the most of it, for if he could secure one of the habits, he could leave the city as a penitent before morning—not even the guards of the Emir's son stopped devout Christians in the practice of their faith.

The moon had risen by the time San-Ragoz slipped into the monastery and made his way toward the dormitory. He moved with unusual swiftness and so silently that no one heard him pass, or if they did, attributed it to the whispers of dreams. At the entrance to the dormitory corridor he paused, taking stock of his surroundings; there were only three oil lamps burning from one end of the hall to another, a reminder of the Trinity. What little illumination each shed was only enough to magnify the darkness beyond it. For San-Ragoz, this presented little trouble: he could see almost as well in the dark as he did in daylight, and just now night was his ally. Recalling other monasteries he had seen, he assessed the few, spartan furnishings, hoping to choose the one most likely to contain what he sought. Finally he made his way to the large chest in the alcove at the head of the corridor. He opened this with care and was rewarded with a stack of rough-woven, dark-colored dalmaticas that served as habits for the monks. Very carefully he took one from the middle of the stack and arranged the remaining garments so that no sign of any disturbance was noticeable. He worked as rapidly as he could, knowing that he risked discovery if he brought attention to himself.

As he was about to step back into the night, he heard a cough behind him; he froze.

One of the monks was making his way along the corridor, one hand extended to touch the rough stones of the wall.

It took San-Ragoz a long moment to see that the monk's eyes were white. Moving very slowly, he went around the corner and remained still until the old monk went past him, murmuring prayers in Greek. Once the corridor was empty again, San-Ragoz waited in stillness until he was certain he could once again move without detection.

When he was several streets away from the monastery, he stopped near a stable where he took his stolen dalmatica and tied it in knots, then rubbed the garment into the dusty stones paving the stable entrance. He continued to abuse the dalmatica for some little while, then removed his Persian kandys and subjected it to the same treatment as he had just given his penitent's habit. He began to fear he was risking too much time in his attempts to throw his pursuers off the track; he gave the habit one more energetic scrub on the stones, then stood up and untied the knots, then tugged it over his head, concealing the black silk dalmatica beneath. That done, he tugged one of the sleeves of the kandys loose and then pulled the eclipse-pattern embroidery off the neck before tossing the ruined garment near the stable midden. Satisfied that he had done as much as he could to make it appear he had met with foul play, he hurried toward the Eastern Gate, making sure to wipe his hands and face with soot as he went. By the time he was within sight of the gate he was grimy and smelly, just as he intended he should be.

"Halt," ordered the Moorish guard as San-Ragoz approached.

San-Ragoz did as he was told, remaining still while the guard came up to him.

"Are you leaving this city?" The guard wrinkled his nose in distaste.

"I am," said San-Ragoz in an attitude of resignation.

"Where are you bound?" asked the guard.

"I have been ordered to make a pilgrimage to Toloz, for a penance," San-Ragoz replied, adding, "I began at Gadez." Just speaking the name of Rogerian's city renewed his missing of his man-servant and valued companion; he hoped that Rogerian had not abandoned his search for him, in spite of the passage of more than thirty years.

"Why should you do penance?" the guard wanted to know. "If you wish to pass, you will answer me."

"I profaned the Church, and must atone for apostasy." As a good Moslem, San-Ragoz guessed the guard would be sympathetic to such an exercise, although he might deplore San-Ragoz's appalling condition: Christians, the guard was aware, equated filth with saintliness.

"So." The guard inspected San-Ragoz as well as he could in the darkness. "Let me see your shoulders," he ordered.

Although he knew the man was looking for a slave-brand, he asked, "Why?" in a truculent manner.

"That is not for you to know, dog." The last was an afterthought, a reminder that the Moors now held sway in Corduba.

"If you will tell me the reason you ask this of me, you will not offend me—unless that is your desire." San-Ragoz kept his voice even and his demeanor respectful, which made the guard consider his response.

"A dangerous slave has escaped and we are ordered to return him to Numair ibn Isffah ibn Musa for punishment," said the guard, reveling in this moment of self-importance. "No one may leave without baring his shoulders."

"To see if there is a burn-scar identifying him as a slave. I understand. Very well," said San-Ragoz, tugging at the neck of his two dalmaticas so that his left shoulder was exposed. "As you see, no brand." In all the years since his death, no injury had left a mark on his skin; the slave-brand had faded as soon as his skin healed.

"And the right one," the guard said.

San-Ragoz did as the guard required. "No brand there, either."

"True enough. You are not the man we seek." He stood back and was about to open the night-gate when something occurred to him. "Why do you travel at this hour?"

"It is required of me, and I must be obedient to my charge. I was given orders to begin my travels at the beginning of the Second Vigil, so that I would have to go in the dark, with only the stars and the Spirit of God to guide me," he said, providing the answer he had already prepared.

This time the guard made a gesture of approval. "Your superior is worthy of the Book. Profit by the lessons you are set."

San-Ragoz made the Sign of the Cross and bowed his head. "Holy is God," he said.

The guard lifted the brace on the gate and stood aside for San-Ragoz to pass. "May you learn wisdom, Penitent Christian dog."

With a gesture of humility, San-Ragoz went out of Corduba, into the cool, windy night, along the old Roman road that led eastward across the plateau and eventually, after many thousands of paces, into the mountains. He walked rapidly and steadily, seeking to put as much distance between him and the city as he could before daylight compelled him to seek out a shelter where he would not be discovered either by searchers or by mischance; he had no doubts that the soldiers of the Emir's son would soon follow him, for his ruse with the guard would not remain successful for very long: the morning inspection would list him among those departing, and that would put the soldiers on the scent. This certainty spurred him on. His efforts were exhausting, but he could not yet husband his strength, so he drove himself to keep on, to put as much distance between him and the soldiers of Numair ibn Isffah ibn Musa, the Emir's son

Shortly before sunrise he found a cleft in the rocks beside a small lake, and there he took refuge for the day, doing all he could to restore himself without blood or his native earth to nourish him; he sank into a deep, trance-like sleep that shut out most of the world around him. Once during the day he was vaguely aware that a flock of goats had come down to the edge of the lake to drink; their goatherd played an ill-tuned bagpipe to pass away the hours. The melody was still ringing in San-Ragoz's head when the sun dropped below the western horizon, and he once again continued his trek eastward.

By the third night he was famished; every step he took needed greater effort than the last, and as he trudged onward, he had to fight off the numbness of despair as he passed three razed villages, and anticipated worse ahead. He had seen the scars of battle across the countryside, and knew it would be increasingly devastated the closer he came to the actual areas of fighting; he had seen more than enough of war to seek it out now, but he was uncertain he would be able to avoid it entirely, for he had learned from Numair ibn Isffah ibn Musa the Moors were extending their invasion north and eastward. The thought of carnage sickened him.

Shortly before sunrise he managed to catch a large, white bird and take some of its blood, but this provided very little sustenance. He avoided places where people lived, especially if there were any signs of soldiers about: it had been nearly eleven years since the Berbers under Tariq had defeated the western Goths and the Berbers and Moors were still consolidating their territories even as they expanded their dominion; the destroyed villages gave testament to the continuing instability of the country, and the Moorish determination to hold what they had captured: soldiers could only mean trouble.

Finally, more by luck than cleverness, toward the morning of the next day San-Ragoz came upon a ruined villa left over from the days of the Romans. Most of the buildings were in disrepair, with vines and flowers running riot amid the broken marble. At the far end of what had once been the gardens, the large tepidarium of the old bath stood, rank with floating weeds and open to the sky; San-Ragoz was keenly aware of a beating human heart amid the wreckage of that vanished time; so keen was his need that the heartbeat seemed loud and compelling as a drum. He did not want to surrender to his craving, for he despised himself for his subjugation to it. Alone and enervated, for a moment he missed Roma keenly, and his Villa Ragoczy—it, too, was dilapidated, but just at present it was more inviting than any palace—then he put such things from his mind and did his utmost to determine who was living in the ruin, and why.

Moving silently, San-Ragoz made his way around the tepidarium toward the smaller, more intact frigidarium, for it seemed to him the heartbeat came from there. As he neared the frigidarium—thick-walled and dark to keep the water cold—he saw that a heavy, make-shift door had been constructed where the old door had been, and this one was marked with a cross. Someone had improvised a hermit's cell where the Romans had gone to bathe in cold water; the realization provided him brief, ironic amusement before he gave his attention to trying to work out some means of visiting the sleeper as a dream. He was so worn out that he began to doze before he hit upon any solution to alleviating his privation without exposing himself to worse than starvation, as well as bring horror and fury to the immured monk; so he was startled when, just before dawn, a young woman in a novice's habit came to the door of the tepidarium and called out to the inhabitant.

"Frerer Procopios, I have brought your morning bread."

"Deo gratias," came the answer in a muffled bass. "Why did she send you?"

"I asked for the opportunity," she said. "Are you well, Frerer?" she added, concern in her voice.

"I am as God wills me to be," Frerer Procopios replied.

"You do not sound wholly well," the novice persisted.

"That is God's business," said Frerer Procopios. "Whatever He send me, I will accept with humility for my failure in His cause."

"But if He should send you healing through—?" the novice said.

"He will do so," said Frerer Procopios. "His Angels will provide it." There was a long silence that was interrupted by birdcalls.

"And if the invaders come back? What will you do?" She sounded frightened.

"Die for the honor of Our Lord, as I should have done before," he said with the first enthusiasm he had shown. "I would win a Martyr's Crown with such a death. I should never have hesitated." His tone changed again, becoming flat. "So that splendid fate has passed me by. I lost that chance six years since." He was silent for a moment. "Go away. I must pray."

"And you must eat as well. My Sorrars have labored to make bread and cheese, and they do it for charity. Surely you—God sends us food to sustain us; you must not spurn it." She sounded plaintive. "For Mercy, you are my half-brother; you are the only one left alive." Now she was pleading, perilously near tears. "Procopios. Please. One mother bore us both. I cannot forget that."

"You must. I am not that man any longer." The words were abrupt.

There was a longer silence this time; finally the novice said, "I will bring you your evening meal."

"Deo gratias," said Frerer Procopios.

"Deo gratias," the novice echoed.

San-Ragoz listened intently as the novice left the make-shift cell. He could hear the man inside reciting prayers in a rasping tone. The sky was beginning to shine with the coming of day, and San-Ragoz knew he had to find shelter until nightfall, so he slipped away through the ruins to the old holocaust and settled into the maw of the ancient furnace, confident that he would remain undisturbed in such a secure hiding place. He set a slab of paving stone across the opening and let himself lapse into the torpor that passed for sleep among those who had come to his life. His last thought was that by the next time the sun rose, his appetite would be satisfied.

It was the novice's voice that wakened him once again, at sundown. San-Ragoz sat up, all vestiges of sleep gone from him; he listened as the novice greeted Frerer Procopios, her voice quivering a little as she spoke, as if her despondency of the morning was still fresh. "Are you all right?"

"I am as God wills me to be," he said. "That is all I ask, and all you should ask, Fountes."

"I am worried about you," she said.

"That is unworthy of you," said Frerer Procopios harshly. "You should pray for the conversion of the Moors and the Jews, not worry about me."

Listening to the two, San-Ragoz felt himself drawn to the melancholy novice, Fountes. He understood her sorrow with the solace of empathy; he listened more closely and moved a little nearer.

"I can't help it," said Fountes. When Frerer Procopios said nothing more, she added plaintively. "You are all the family left to me."

"I am not your family," he said. "You are one with the women of your community. I am one with my vocation. If you cannot achieve this understanding, you should leave your community."

The novice said nothing for a while, then coughed gently. "I will ask another novice to tend to your needs."

"If God wills it and your Superiora approves," said Frerer Procopios with deliberate indifference.

"Of course. If she approves. Deo gratias." Fountes began to move away from the old frigidarium, moving slowly along the ill-defined path that led out of the ruined villa to the rutted track that served as a road for this region.

San-Ragoz emerged from his hiding place and followed after the novice, all his concentration on her. He could sense her misery and loneliness as she tried to pray; as intense as his esurience was, his compassion for her in her dejection was greater.

Some two thousand paces from the old villa, the novice reached a long building that had been the stable for a long-fled Gardingio; it was now a small community of perhaps a dozen religious women, the box-stalls converted to cells, the central aisle to a chapel. Fountes went toward the nearest door surmounted by a cross, and spoke briefly to someone inside, then went along the building to a door that stood half-open.

In the shadows, San-Ragoz kept pace with Fountes, sensing her growing distress. He took refuge behind an overgrown berry hedge filled with blossoms and thorns; here he waited while the community finished chores and closed in for the night. When only the Vigil Lamp was shining, and the measured breathing of sleep sounded in the night, he moved out into the open, crossing the distance to Fountes' cell. He tested the door with care, determining whether or not it was barred from within. Satisfied that it was not, he eased it open, then entered the cell, pulling the door closed behind him.

The cell still had the look of a stall: the manger now served as a shelf for Fountes' few belongings, the palla that was her outer habit, and a single oil-lamp, now extinguished; the crucifix on the door hung from a halter-hook. The earthen floor had been carefully swept, and the cot that served as a bed stood along one wall; all three inner walls had been extended to the ceiling, closing off the cells as the stalls had never been. San-Ragoz stood for a long moment to assess his situation before he turned all his attention on Fountes, lying supine and asleep under a single worn blanket, to contemplate her before he spoke, his voice deep and soft. "You are dreaming, Fountes. You are pleased to dream. You welcome your dream. You are entering a wonderful vision, where you find comfort and solace. Everything you long for is yours, and all pain and loneliness have gone."

She murmured a few indistinguishable syllables and turned onto her side.

"In your dream, you are happy and carefree. No one troubles you. You embrace it with all your heart. This dream is an end to sorrow. You are in the house of your family, and all is well. You are deprived of nothing." He moved a little closer to her. "All your sacrifices have been rewarded, and you are restored to joy." A distant echo from his own life sounded deep within him. In the first few centuries after he had become a vampire, how he had yearned to be restored to his family, to life as it had been before the forces of the long-forgotten Hittites had come into the Carpathians, killing his father and enslaving him and his brothers and sisters. That had been nearly three thousand years ago, but the loss still caused a remote ache within him, and an abiding understanding of her loss. "You know delight, and you welcome it. In the gardens of your house, you have flowers and birds to gladden you; nothing diminishes your elation." He was at her side; he knelt down next to her cot as he sensed her enveloping herself in her dream. "You are overcome with unmarred happiness."

Deep as her sleep had become, her breathing slow and regular, she smiled, changing her careful, closed features to the enchanting face of a lighthearted young woman. Her body softened as well, one hand sliding off the edge of the cot, the palm upturned and slightly open.

"You are graceful and lithe as you move about your garden; you are warmed by the sun and caressed by the fragrant breeze. Everything you do is imbued with your radiance—plucking a flower from a branch, tossing your shining, red-gold hair, stopping to admire yourself in a pool of clear water." He touched her as he spoke, as lightly as the dream wind would, barely grazing her arm with his fingertips. "Your dream is so sweet, so filled with enchantment: you immerse yourself in it, so that every fiber of your being quivers to its pulse."

Her tongue ran slowly over her lips and her head rolled back.

His hands were gentle and persuasive as he roused her, opening her flesh to his touch as reverently as he would open a budding rose. "You are filled with raptures as with music. All of you is absorbed in fulfillment, in ecstasy."

Culmination came quickly, the first pulsations taking him by surprise; she gave a little cry, her body trembled as he bent to her neck. She sighed with contentment as he moved away from her; her breathing steadied and slowed.

Rising from her side, San-Ragoz stood for a long moment, then spoke again, very softly. "You are strong and kind, Fountes. You are worthy of all good things. No God would punish you for your fortitude, nor your humanity, no matter what others tell you. You do not deserve the pain you have been given; you have no sin to expiate." Turning away toward the door, he felt a pang of sadness for this young woman whom he now knew so profoundly, and to whom he was so grateful; he wanted to shield her from her fears, and understood he could not.

Dawn found him more than ten thousand paces from Fountes' cell, in the long, rising valley that led eastward, toward Zaraugusta. He was sufficiently restored that he did not look for shelter until the sun was risen; he did not take the first place he came upon, but settled at last on a cellar of an abandoned farmhouse some distance from the road. His rest was deep but without the ache of vitiation that had worn him down since he left Corduba, and for that, he thanked Fountes in his thoughts.

It was five days before he took nourishment again. By this time, he was close behind the Berber army that was holding the Eberuz for the Caliph as the soldiers of Islam struck across the mountains into Toloz and beyond. This time he was more hurried than he wished to be, and the woman—a potter's widow living on the outskirts of Zaraugusta— was fretful, the woes of her daily life pursuing her in sleep, intruding on the illusory exaltation San-Ragoz imparted, so that she nearly woke as soon as she had achieved her fulfillment.

Without his native earth in the soles of his houseauz, he did not dare to cross running water in daylight; it would be hard enough in darkness. So it was after sunset that he made his way down the banks to where a number of small boats were tied to a wooden wharf cobbled onto the old Roman stone supports. The place was used by fishermen and they did their utmost to be gone from it before dark. Insects hummed in the air, but none of them touched San-Ragoz as he untied one of the shallow boats, took its single long oar in his hand, and slipped into the river. By the time he reached the eastern bank, he was dizzy and nauseated from the running water, and becoming disoriented; he tugged the boat up the jetty and secured its bow-line to expose tree roots. Had he possessed any coins, he would have left some in the bottom of the boat under the oar to recompense the owner, but he had nothing. He climbed away from the river, unsteady as a drunken man, and headed away from the large encampment of the Moors.

"Halt," said a sharp voice in the Berber tongue.

San-Ragoz almost stumbled as he rounded the corner of the encampment walls. He blinked at the lamp the Berber carried as he answered in the language of the Visigoths, "What do you want?"

The Berber spat. "Infidel."

San-Ragoz pretended not to understand. "Your insults mean nothing," he said.

"Who are you?" The Berber drew his long, curved scimitar. "Where are you going?" His command of Gothic was clumsy, but he made his questions comprehensible.

"I am a pilgrim," said San-Ragoz. "I am bound for Roma, on orders of the Church." He spread his small hands over the front of his habit in a show of piety.

"Pilgrim, is it?" Again the Berber spat, as if such alien words had to be expelled from his mouth.

"Yes. From Gadez." He lowered his head to show respect.

"A beggar, in other words," said the Berber in disgust.

"I live on the compassion of good Christians," he responded, a trace of irony in his voice.

"A beggar," the Berber said. "Well, you'll get no charity this day, not the sort you hope for. We show charity to our own." He gestured with his scimitar, and spoke again in his native language. "You'll pass the time in our prison. We'll let you out in due course."

San-Ragoz looked puzzled. "What are you saying?"

"You are going to our prison," the Berber said in poor Gothic. "Your case will be heard before sunset."

"Prison?" San-Ragoz exclaimed. "Why are you imprisoning me?"

"I do not know you are truthful. You do not put your hand on your Book, or the Holy Koran." He made a prodding gesture with his scimitar. "Move along."

San-Ragoz hesitated. "This is unjust," he protested as he weighed up the possibilities of his predicament: he could overpower the Berber and flee, but that would bring unwonted attention to his presence at a time when his strength was depleted; he could go along and spend the day in a cell, which would afford him rest, but risked ending in capture or a beating.

"We'll give you justice," said the Berber, and slapped San-Ragoz's shoulder with the flat of his blade. "Move along. To the left at the gate."

"Where are you taking me?" San-Ragoz saw a dozen soldiers approaching and realized his opportunity for flight was over.

"Go through the gate," the Berber told him.

San-Ragoz complied, noticing that the low walls of this side of the encampment were recent and in some places incomplete. "Where now?" he asked as he looked at the neatly laid out tents of the Moors. This late at night, there was minimal activity; guards patrolled and a few officers hastened to meetings, but otherwise only the sounds of sleep and the occasional recitation of prayers were heard.

"To the right. To the wooden building at the end of the alley." He pointed to underscore his instructions.

Walking between the long rows of tents, San-Ragoz noticed the heaps of supplies that stood beside them, making the intention of the Moors plain: they were preparing another attack on Frankish lands;

this encampment was a staging area for the army of the Caliph to continue its conquest of Christian lands. He was careful not to make his curiosity too obvious as he continued down the brazier-lit alley.

"Halt," came the order from the doorway of the wooden building; San-Ragoz noticed that it was an old Visigothic guardhouse.

"Omma ibn Ali, may Allah give you long life and many sons," said the Berber who escorted San-Ragoz, salaaming to his superior. "The Christian dog is a pilgrim. Nothing to gain from ransom or fines. He's harmless enough, and he is of the Book."

San-Ragoz kept his expression carefully blank as he listened.

Omma ibn Ali sighed. "Put him in the usual place. It's nearly empty, so lock him in by himself. I don't want these unbelievers to talk together; they become defiant when they do." He cocked his head toward the side of the building. "You know where to take him." As an afterthought, he added, "Do not bother to feed him. It is too late for eating."

"What are you saying?" San-Ragoz complained, looking from one man to the other.

"He is saying," Omma ibn Ali said in very good Gothic, "that you will spend the day in a prison cell. You would do well to pray while you are held there. At the end of the day, the Imam will decide when you may be released. We cannot waste daylight on such as you; we have too many obligations to fulfill." He regarded San-Ragoz with distaste. "You might do well to bathe."

"I must not, except if God bathes me in rain," said San-Ragoz; many of the Moors knew that pilgrims were not supposed to wash their bodies or their garments until they reached their destination—he would not be caught in so obvious a trap.

"Just so," sighed Omma ibn Ali. "Tend to him, Jahdim."

"That I will," said San-Ragoz's captor. "You," he went on in Gothic. "Go to the side door. Then down."

"All right," said San-Ragoz, and made the sign of the Cross.

"It is as well that you pray," said Jahdim; he took San-Ragoz by the shoulder and shoved him along. The stairs were steep and narrow, their ancient wood creaked as the two made their way down. A strong odor of earth permeated the cellar, as well as a sour, latrine stench. Three doors were closed with bolts, two others stood open; Jahdim propelled San-Ragoz to the nearer of these. "Inside," he ordered, pushing the foreigner through.

San-Ragoz noticed the mound of straw that was clearly intended for a bed. "There is no window," he remarked.

"No, there isn't," said Jahdim, and shut the door, thrusting the bolt into place without further ado. He left the cellar quickly, going up the stairs two at a time.

Listening to Jahdim depart, San-Ragoz took stock of his situation and decided it could be much worse. At least he would be able to rest in this little cell, and although he would not lie on his native soil, he would garner some restoration here. He sank down on the damp straw, stretched out and let the night flow over him.

Text of a letter from Ruges to Atta Olivia Clemens, written in Imperial Latin and delivered the end of June 722.

To the most respected widow, Atta Olivia Clemens, the greetings of the bondsman Ruges who is presently bound for Tarraco from Neapolis.

I have finally been able to trace my master from Tunis and the Emir's territory to Corduba but I have lost the trail beyond that city. It has taken years to discover this, and I cannot tell you the relief I have felt on obtaining this knowledge. He is reported escaped and there is no notice of his capture. Had he been killed, notice would have to be sent to the son of the Emir who owned him; I have not learned of such notification, and therefore I assume he is still alive and free. Considering the current state in Hispania, it is possible he might have fallen in battle, or have been killed by soldiers of either side, but then you should be aware of it, due to the nature of your blood-bond. He could have suffered a misadventure and been injured, and may be recovering as I write this. There are a dozen misadventures he might have suffered, but I will assume he has made good his escape and will await me in the agreed-upon place. Unless there has been a change since your last letter to me, I believe that there is no reason to mourn him yet.

I am leaving for Tarraco, and when I arrive there, I will make my way to Mont Calcius, for that little village would afford him some protection—he left one chest of his native earth there, as he did in Toletum—and although there has been fighting in the mountains, it has been sporadic; the Moors have more important targets than small villages in remote places, which is another reason for my master to seek it out again. It would be far riskier for my master to go to Toletum than to return to Mont Calcius, and you and I know he does not take unnec-

essary risks. If he is not there, I will travel to Toletum. Once I have reached Tarraco, I will send you word of my arrival, and I will hope to have a letter from you. I will ask at the Sacra Lux monastery for any message that might come to me. The Moors will not forbid the monks receiving letters on behalf of travelers, but they will also read the letters the monks receive; you would be wise to be discreet in anything you send me there.

You have told me you intend to remain at Comus for some time to come, and so I will continue to write to you there, at your villa. If the lake is as beautiful as I remember, it must be a most pleasant retreat— surely far more lovely than Roma is now, and safer.

The ship leaves in the morning and I must put this in the hands of the courier, and load my chests aboard. I apologize for the brevity, but I know you will understand the reason for it.

Ruges

at Neapolis, the 2nd day of May, 722

2

Most of the old road had washed away, and the new path up the mountains was little more than a sheep-track. San-Ragoz had skirted the three Moorish work-camps he had seen since he left Usca; they had been busy places, where slaves labored to cut down trees for the Moors' ships as well as reducing the places where enemies might hide. He was still a considerable distance from Mont Calcius and already he was certain he would not find all he sought in that place. Still he kept on, trusting he would find some remnants of the village, and perhaps his native earth to restore him. As the mountain became steeper, he once again entered the trees, for the Moorish workers had not come this far up the slopes for their trees.

His hunting revealed that the game was much reduced in the forest, and he supposed the Moors had been feeding themselves from the woods; he supposed the wolves and cats had been driven out, as had the bear. Still, there were sheep and goats to be had, and he chose carefully, leaving the drained carcases near small farmsteads or religious houses as he continued upward. He was circumspect in his journey, traveling at night, and taking precautions to bring no attention on himself; this slowed his progress but gave him the opportunity to gauge the changes of the last century. There were far fewer people in the mountains than had been there a hundred years before; he attributed this to the privations brought by invasion. The few villages he had seen were largely deserted, many marked with crosses as if to ward off the followers of Mohammed.

A few evenings later, when he was roughly ten thousand paces from Mont Calcius, he came upon something that perplexed him: there was an ancient funereal barrow, and in the arch marking it stood a large cup filled with coagulated blood. Approaching it, he quickly ascertained the blood came from horses. It had not been there very long—only a few insects had discovered it—but it had been put there with ceremony, and San-Ragoz decided that it was an offering: who had left it and to what purpose? He recalled Csimenae and the horse-skulls over the village gates. Had the people in the mountains resumed their worship of horse-spirits? The puzzle haunted him as he continued on through the night; he noticed how still the woods were—game was thin and what remained was nervously alert. Who else was abroad in the forest, that the animals went in fear of them? Robber bands might account for it, yet he was not convinced that they alone could account for the missing game.

When he found a second cup set out in a ruin, he began to worry, for whatever the blood was intended to appease, it was more frightening than the Moors. He walked around the small clearing with its broken stones and hollowed boulders, taking stock of all the impressions the place gave him. Moonlight dappled the worn stones and limned the cup where it stood within an arch cut into the old stones. There were broken urns scattered about the clearing, and bits of bone were strewn beneath the arch where the cup stood. The site was very old; it had been made before the Romans came, and until very recently had been all but forgotten. Yet the cup was of metal, good-sized and well-made, and the blood was less than a day old.

San-Ragoz lingered in the clearing for a good while, hoping to learn more about it; only the tug of coming dawn sent him to find a place where he could spend his day. Reluctantly he moved into the forest again, taking care to go silently as he circled the clearing. He chose the deep overhang of a rocky outcropping not too far from the clearing, and he made sure he was not so far under the rock that he could not hear any unusual noises that might come from the clearing. As he sank into his vampire-slumber, he listened for the call of birds that usually greeted the sun; this morning the immediate forest was silent.

Around mid-day he was wakened by voices from the clearing; keeping to the shadow of the boulder, he moved as near to the clearing as he could without entering direct sunlight.

". . . and renew by blood," a shepherd was chanting, two other men standing with him. By the look of them, they were woodsmen, for both carried axes and saws.

"The protection of our own," said the two.

"To claim the Holy Blood, we give it you," said the shepherd. He held up another metal cup, not so fine as the one they had removed from the arch, but still of good quality and size.

"This we promise." The woodsmen laid their hands on the cup as the shepherd set it where the other had been.

"Tonight you shall feed elsewhere." The shepherd stepped back from the cup.

"Tonight you shall feed elsewhere," the woodsmen repeated.

San-Ragoz listened closely, trying to discern their intention by this rite.

"Spare us that we may serve you," the three said together as they backed to the edge of the clearing.

"I have a goat to leave out," said the older woodsman just as the shepherd was about to turn away.

"Good," said the shepherd, giving the woodsman his attention. "They had three of my flock last night. I cannot lose any more and feed my family."

There was an awkward silence among the three, and then the older woodsman said, "Since they took my younger daughter, it has been easier."

"It isn't wise to speak of those who have been taken," said the younger woodsman.

"It isn't wise to speak of any of them at all," said the older woodsman.

"I do not want to sacrifice my children as well as my sheep," said the shepherd. "Better to give them the flock than—" He stopped abruptly.

"They may take all," said the younger woodsman.

"If we had more horses," the older woodsman declared.

"It would only delay them," said the shepherd, fear and disgust making his voice harsh.

"Then why do we bother?" asked the younger woodsman.

"To buy time," said the older. "They will take others before they take us and ours so long as we prove our devotion."

"The Moors will deal with them, when they come to cut down our trees," said the shepherd: he was fidgeting now.

"That will not be for a while. They are still far down the mountains," said the older woodsman.

"And when they come, we will have to leave or turn carpenters," said the younger.

"That is for later," the shepherd said. "For now, we must deal with the night ones." He crossed himself. "They have kept us safe from the Moors and the Gardingi before them. It is the pact and they will honor it so long as we do."

"And so we will," said the younger woodsman. "Tomorrow I will bring the cup."

"Good," said the shepherd, shifting the one he held from hand to hand. "What blood?"

"We will butcher a shoat. There should be enough blood." He sounded uneasy.

"Well enough," said the shepherd, and swung around on his heel, going away from the other two as if he was too anxious to remain in this place for long.

"He fears for his woman," said the older woodsman.

"With good cause," said the younger; he coughed and stared off into the forest.

"Well, tomorrow," said the older.

"Yes. Tomorrow," the younger agreed before he strode off, walking rapidly.

The older woodsman lingered a moment, then he, too, left the clearing.

San-Ragoz emerged from the shadows, for the moment ignoring the discomfort he felt in the sunlight. How he missed his native earth in the soles of his houseauz! He shook his head impatiently as he went back to the clearing, disliking the foreboding that had begun to intrude on his thoughts. The ritual he had witnessed was not intended to rouse old gods for the protection of the people in the mountains, it was designed to placate a danger that was far more imminent than the Moors, a danger that was linked with blood. His strength was fading rapidly, leached by the sun; he stumbled back to the shelter of the boulder and tried to resume his rest. Sleep eluded him, for he kept casting back to what he had heard, and what it implied grew increasingly plain to him. "She cannot have been so reckless," he muttered as the forest fell into twilight and the creatures of the day surrendered the woods to the creatures of the night. Now that it was dark, San-Ragoz climbed to the top of the boulder and used this vantage-point to look out on the forest, his night-seeing eyes penetrating the deepest gloom.

There was laughter in the dusk, light and youthful; four young men came into the clearing. None was older than fourteen, and all four of them were dressed in peculiar assortments of garments, some of them Moorish, but most in the style of past years, as if their clothes were trophies or souvenirs. The apparent leader ambled over to the cup, sniffed at it and shook his head. "They are forgetting how to honor us."

The laughter came again as one of the four called out, "Aulutiz, we will have to remind them what we require."

All four laughed again, and the sound was not wholesome.

Aulutiz! the name rang in San-Ragoz's memory: that infant Csimenae had been so determined to save. There could be no doubt that they were the same, not with what he sensed of the young men, who had been young men for decades. The ritual the shepherd and woodsmen had performed put the seal upon his convictions. He came down from his perch, moving silently toward the four young men. He realized it was folly to challenge them, so he entered the clearing slowly, his attention focused on the leader; he was hungry for conversation, not conflict. He stood still, letting the four take notice of him in their own time.

One of the youths tugged at the leader's sleeve and pointed to San-Ragoz, whispering something before he stepped back.

"A stranger in the place of Holy Blood," said Aulutiz mockingly. He strolled toward San-Ragoz. "A pilgrim, by the look of him," he remarked to his companions. "With nothing to offer us but what we want."

Again the malign laughter sounded in the night.

San-Ragoz said nothing as he watched the dark-haired young man come toward him. When Aulutiz was an arm's-length from him, San-Ragoz said. "You are from Mont Calcius?"

Aulutiz stared at hearing the language of his people. "Yes," he said curtly. "How do you know?"

"I was in that place, some years ago," San-Ragoz told him calmly.

"Not recently," Aulutiz corrected him. "I do not know you. I know everyone who lives in this region."

"No, you do not know me," San-Ragoz agreed. "I have not been here recently." He made no move as Aulutiz circled around him, taking stock of what he saw.

"Who are you?" The question came from behind him.

"Sanct' Germain," San-Ragoz answered.

This time the laughter was incredulous. "He left long ago. He is dead." He rounded on San-Ragoz. "Do you say you are dead?"

"As dead as I was when I came here," said San-Ragoz. He turned to face Aulutiz. "You were still an infant, as I recall."

"You are not Sanct' Germain," said Aulutiz. "You look like a beggar. Sanct' Germain had horses and mules, and a servant. You cannot be him."

"Not just at present, no I am not." San-Ragoz said easily, his full concentration on the young-appearing man. He decided against giving him the name he currently used.

"This is a disguise, then?" Aulutiz suggested sarcastically.

"In a manner of speaking," San-Ragoz said.

Aulutiz shrugged. "My mother said you died."

"And so I did," San-Ragoz said with a cordial nod. "Thirty-seven centuries ago." He gave the four a short while to consider this.

"You are lying," Aulutiz accused, his jaw thrust out.

"I do not lie," San-Ragoz responded, his voice level as he contemplated the four.

Aulutiz continued to walk around San-Ragoz, his flinty eyes showing his age and nature if nothing else of him did. "Where have you been?"

"Away from here," said San-Ragoz, making no effort to appease the others.

"Why?" Aulutiz asked harshly. "You can find all you need in these mountains."

"Vampires become too obvious if they remain in one place too long." San-Ragoz paused. "Or if they gather in groups."

"So you say." Aulutiz howled his amusement. "Well. My mother will be surprised."

"She is still here?" San-Ragoz asked, more shocked than he expected to be.

"Where else should she be?" Aulutiz demanded. "This is her native earth. And mine. And theirs." He belatedly indicated the other three. "We are all hers."

"Hers?" San-Ragoz repeated as the whole implication sank into him. "Do you mean she brought you to her life?"

"Certainly," said Aulutiz contemptuously as if any other possibility were beneath his consideration. "She brought all of us to her life." This was a boast, and he smiled.

"She?" The enormity of the act shook him. "How could she?"

"If you are Sanct' Germain, you know." Aulutiz held up his hand in defiance.

"You say your mother brought you to her life," San-Ragoz repeated, his incredulity increasing. "How did she accomplish your change?"

"I drank her blood; what else should I do? So have all the others." He glared at San-Ragoz. "You had her drink yours."

San-Ragoz nodded numbly. "That I did." He could not think of anything more to say; he was too caught up in the tangle of his emotions: it was appalling to realize that Csimenae had done something so unthinkable to her child.

"What do you expect of her?" He folded his arms and faced San-Ragoz, his flint-colored eyes arrogant. "She has made this place ours."

One of the three sighed. "How long do we bother with this?"

"I say we hunt," seconded another. "This fellow is nothing if we do not feed."

"There is no point in it," said Aulutiz in disgust. "He has nothing for us." He turned on his heel, walking away from San-Ragoz. "Come. It is time we were on our way. There will be something left out for us, or we can claim what we want."

"Before you go," San-Ragoz called out. "How many of you are there?"

"You mean vampires?" Aulutiz asked. "Oh, forty or so." He signaled the others and led the way into the forest.

Remaining where he stood, San-Ragoz thought over what he had been told. Forty or so! This was the most dreadful revelation yet. No wonder the living called this region the place of Holy Blood: they would not intend the appellation ironically, no matter how richly it was deserved. He began to pace, his consternation increasing with every step. What had happened here in the years he had been gone? How could Csimenae allow so many vampires to be created? For he had to assume she had permitted it to happen: she had shown herself prepared to keep her position as village leader on her son's behalf. If she had made her son a vampire, she must have consented in the creation of the rest, directly or indirectly. But forty vampires! All the game in the forest would not be sufficient to feed them in these lean times, and every living human for many thousands of paces around would be in danger from them. Better to face ravening wolves in winter than have more than three vampires in one region—to have forty was catastrophic, and not for the living alone, but for the vampires. He tried to figure out what Csimenae had hoped to gain by this folly, and was left perplexed. He told himself that Aulutiz might have exaggerated the number, yet even half that amount posed a threat of such magnitude that San-Ragoz found it staggering. He halted in front of the cup of blood and shook his head. How much longer, he wondered, would the living be willing to extend themselves for vampires? Eventually they would refuse to accommodate, and then there would be carnage.

A breaking branch brought him out of his hideous reverie. Lifting his head, he attuned himself to the forest. He sensed a boar nearby, and he pondered for a moment going in pursuit of it; he was too distressed to have any heart for hunting; what else might he find if he went after the animal? He listened as the boar made its way through the undergrowth, then trundled off into the depths of the woods.

Deciding that he would spend another night without feeding, San-Ragoz started toward Mont Calcius—he knew he had to find Csimenae, to discover why she had done what she had done, and to try to persuade her to abandon so disastrous a course. He could not bring himself to believe he might fail in his efforts; he felt very much a stranger in unfriendly territory. The forest around him was no longer familiar, and so he went carefully, listening for every sound, aware of the vitality of the night.

By the time he reached Mont Calcius, night was almost over; the first birds were singing and the penned animals were growing restless. He circled the village, noticing that the olive orchard was smaller than before, and the sheepfold was larger; one of the out-buildings had fallen into ruin and the creamery showed a tattered roof. The village itself seemed to have weathered the last century badly—many of the buildings inside the walls were entirely roofless, and others showed signs of neglect. Whatever had become of the place, it had not been to the benefit of those still living there. He noticed an old building at the far end of the olive trees and for an instant considered hiding there for the day. Almost at once he decided against anything so obvious; anyone searching for vampires would know all the hiding places near villages and farmsteads, and during the day he—and all his kind—would be vulnerable. He went back into the forest and finally came upon a fallen shelter that had once protected logs from rain and wind. The bark and shavings made a rough bed, but he was glad to have it as he settled in for the day, and to be engulfed in torpor until sunset.

The woman minding the gate was marked by a life of drudgery; her hair was already veined with white, and her face was wrinkled although she could not have been more than twenty. There was no one else about; only the torches burning along the street hinted at other occupants of Mont Calcius. The woman moved nearer to the torch next to the gate; she glared at San-Ragoz, her brows drawn down in wariness as he approached. "Stop there, outsider." Her accent was somewhat changed from the one Sanct' Germain had learned, but he was able to understand her well enough to converse.

San-Ragoz did as she ordered him. "I am a pilgrim," he said.

"You are lost," she corrected him.

"Perhaps," he answered, and waited.

"You must be, to have come here." She studied him, making note of his self-possessed demeanor at such variance with his clothing.

"I speak your tongue: how can I be lost?" He did not quite smile but there was a softening of his eyes.

She frowned. "We have nothing to offer you. There is no inn, and no one here receives strangers into their houses. As you should know," she added in a testy manner.

"A wise precaution in such times," he agreed.

"And yet, you are outside this gate." She very deliberately looked away from him.

"I am on this path. I seek a way through the mountains, one that does not put me in the way of the Caliph's soldiers." He did his best to look reassuring in his ragged, dirty clothing. "I do not want to travel the obvious roads."

"We cannot help you. And I must warn you to leave this region as quickly as you can. The Caliph's soldiers are nothing compared to what hunts in these woods." She made a nervous gesture and coughed. "They have taken my brothers to be one of them."

"Outlaws?" San-Ragoz suggested, hoping she would reveal more.

"No. We have no outlaws anymore. They do not dare to come here because of the vampires. They know none of us will give them shelter, and they do not want to face the blood-lovers." She spat to show her anger as she squinted through the dusk at him. "Be wary. They are everywhere and their numbers are increasing."

"Vampires?" he repeated, letting the word draw out.

"Those who should be dead and are not," she told him abruptly. "Those who drink living blood. They live in the forest and we give them tribute in exchange for their protection."

"How do you come to have such a plague as this?" San-Ragoz crossed himself, and saw the woman relax a bit. He could sense the nearness of his chest of his native earth, and the pull of it was more intense than his hunger.

"It shames us, for it began here, in this village long ago." She faltered, then went on as if compelled to explain the whole of it. "A woman saved herself from the Great Pox by summoning a vampire to protect her." She sighed heavily. "In other parts of the mountains, they say it was Satan Himself who bargained with her, but in the village we know better. Chimenae was the first and she is still the most to be feared. She brought our village to the ruin you now see. She and all her tribe."

"Did Satan make the rest?" He wanted to know how distorted the stories had become.

"No: she did. They say she had to, that if she went a year without making a new vampire, her life would be forfeit." She glanced westward. "They will be abroad by now."

San-Ragoz had to force himself to ask the next question. "How did it come about that she had been able to do this? Did no one try to stop her?"

"Stop Chimenae?" The woman shook her head. "She said we would not starve to long as we sheltered her and her kind. We did not know what a bargain we had made. It disgraces me to speak of it." She motioned to him as if to shoo him away. "You must not linger here. The vampires will come soon. It is dark enough to be dangerous. Find yourself a secure place and close yourself in for the night. As I must." She started away from the gate, not quite running but moving faster than a walk.

"Wait," San-Ragoz called after her; he did not want to leave the village, and his precious cache of earth.

"No. It is no longer safe." Saying that, she ducked into one of the houses that still had a roof, and pulled the door to with a loud slap of wood on stone.

San-Ragoz did not remain by the gate; that would be useless. He slipped away into the forest, and found a vantage-place where he could watch the village. He promised himself he would find game before morning—at the moment, discovering the extent of Csimenae's folly seemed more urgent than his hunger.

Not long after midnight, his patience was rewarded: half a dozen figures emerged from the trees on the far side of the village, two deer carried hanging from wooden bars. The vampires brought the animals to the gates of the village, fixed them so that they hung over the wall, then went away, only to return dragging the body of a man with a stake driven through him. This they left sprawled near the midden. As soon as they had finished they went back into the woods once more; they did not return.

Apprehensive and curious, San-Ragoz came down from his watch-point and went to inspect what the six had left. The deer were drained of blood and perfunctorily gutted; they would have to be skinned and dressed shortly if all the meat was to be used. The dead man was another matter: he, too, had no blood left in him—indeed, he was pale as fine clay for lack of it—but the stake that severed his spine ensured he would never rise to join the ranks of vampires; he was a laborer, his garments like those of the slaves cutting down trees for the Caliph's navy. Either the vampires had extended their range dramatically or the man had run away from his work detail—San-Ragoz assumed the latter, and he could not conceal the pang of sympathy he felt for the dead man, who had sought freedom and found utter death.

Had he been at liberty to act out of conscience, San-Ragoz would have prepared a grave for the dead man, and put some description of him on a marker; but from what the woman at the gate had said, the bargain the villagers had with Csimenae's tribe made such an act unwise. He contented himself with tearing off the sleeve of his habit and dropping it over the man's face. This done, San-Ragoz hastened into the forest to catch a young sheep to slake his thirst. He put the gutted carcase with the deer, then returned to his resting place of the day before.

At nightfall, San-Ragoz came out of his lair once more, this time with purpose, for he realized he could not continue on his journey without securing some of his native earth to line the soles of his houseauz. There were streams up ahead, and towns with gates open only in daylight: his native earth would protect him from these hazards. He went back toward Mont Calcius, his stride soundless and rapid. This time he kept to the shadows until all the doors were shut and only the flames of the torches moved in the night. When he was certain he could proceed, he climbed over the wall and made his way to the tumbledown wreckage that had been his house, recalling the chest had been buried under the pantry.

The walls leaned at angles and the fallen roof littered the floor as San-Ragoz scrambled through the rubble to where he felt his native earth. He had nothing to serve as a shovel, but determination goaded him on as he dug with his hands, his strength increasing as he neared the buried chest. Finally he grasped the iron bands that secured the leather-and-wood body of the chest, and hauled it from its grave, revitalization surging through him as he opened the lid and laid his hands on the good Carpathian soil.

"No gold?" The light, jeering question came out of the darkness as Aulutiz sauntered toward him. "We've been told you buried a treasure."

"And so I did," said San-Ragoz. "As you will know if you ever venture beyond this place, and which I hope you will do, not only for yourself, but for all of your . . . clan. The longer you remain here, the more danger you will have. Our kind are not meant to live together as you do." He paused, seeing that Aulutiz was growing irritated with him. He stretched; his body was stronger, more resilient than it had been for all the years of his enslavement, his mind more acute. "What do you want, Aulutis?" He used the old pronunciation of the young man's name deliberately.

"I want to know what you are doing here." He straightened up and glowered at San-Ragoz. "You should not be here. My mother said you were dead, long ago. I asked her." His young face was shadowed with age as he pointed at the chest, "You have deceived us."

"Not I," San-Ragoz countered, his expression somber. "I never told you anything. You were an infant when I left. I told Csimenae what this chest contained just before my servant and I departed, and why I valued it."

"She said you buried a treasure," Aulutiz persisted stubbornly. "You have jewels hidden in the earth."

"No, I do not," said San-Ragoz. He laid his hand on the old metal claps; he saw that digging had broken two nails. "I have only the earth, which is worth more to me than emeralds and rubies." He did not add that for centuries he had made his own jewels alchemically.

"Search it," said Aulutiz to his companions, signaling them to lift their weapons. "And strike off his head if he fights you."

San-Ragoz felt a twinge of anticipated misery. "Will you at least pile the earth carefully, so I may make use of it?"

Aulutiz laughed. "Perhaps," he said, and stood back to permit his comrades to empty out the chest in their futile search for gold and jewels as San-Ragoz stood close by, his features unreadable, his dark eyes glowing with pain.

Text of a letter from Hassan ibn Fahsel ibn Hassan to Ermangild of Alta Usca, carried by Abran ben Rachmael.

By the will of Allah the All-Merciful and All-Wise, I, Hassan ibn Fahsel ibn Hassan, Marine Commander of the Caliph's ships, do send this offer to the Christian leader Ermangild of Alta Usca, with my most solemn vow to uphold the terms outlined here, if you, Ermangild, find them acceptable to you.

First, I Hassan ibn Fahsel ibn Hassan, promise not to imprison or enslave any of the family or household of Ermangild for as long as Ermangild is willing to give my men access to his forests for the purpose of cutting down trees to build ships. No claim shall be made upon Ermangild for concubines, or boys to pleasure me or any other officer of the Caliph. I, Hassan ibn Fahsel ibn Hassan, will supply such men and slaves as will be needed for the task of cutting trees and any other that may arise, so that the slaves and farmers of Ermangild will not be taken away from their labors on the land on Ermangild's behalf. In no other way shall Ermangild's authority be reduced or abrogated.

Second, for a period of ten years, I, Hassan ibn Fahsel ibn Hassan, swear I will raise no taxes beyond those I have already imposed, so long as it is shown that not Ermangild, nor any of his servants or family, has contrived to retain any of the money to be collected for the forces of the Caliph.

Third, that on my command, Abran ben Rachmael, who brings this letter, will inspect the records of Ermangild, his family and his servants, and his decision in regard to any question of taxation or other monies shall be final and unquestionable. Further, should Ermangild, his family or his servants be shown to be in arrears, the tax, double that of followers of the True Faith, shall be doubly taxed again. If there is not sufficient money and produce to discharge this or any similar debt, the servants and family of Ermangild shall be taken as slaves in such number as will discharge the tax debt in full, and the buildings owned by Ermangild seized and occupied by men of the Caliph.

Fourth, that such fighting men as Ermangild now houses will be given the opportunity of joining with the forces of the Caliph, for which service they shall receive the same recompense as any soldier of the True Faith without having to change their religion to be paid and enrolled, so long as they swear their loyalty to the Caliph. Should any fighting man prefer to remain in the service of Ermangild, he shall be subject to the same double taxation as all Christians and he will be made ineligible to take up the banner of the Prophet unless he converts to the True Faith.

Fifth, that all dowries and legacies are to be subjected to the review of Abran ben Rachmael, who shall determine how much of such monies may pass to the husbands and heirs of Christians, and how much is to be collected to the benefit of the Caliph. These amounts will be taxed but once, and after such debts are discharged, the money cannot be diminished by any follower of the True Faith. In the case of dowries paid for Christian women entering the religious life, as Christians are people of the Book, the religious dowries will not be subject to any taxation.

Sixth, that Ermangild shall receive, for the trees we have taken, ten measures of grain and two sheep every half year.

I, Hassan ibn Fahsel ibn Hassan, set my hand to this of the fifth full moon in the Christian year 722, 104 of the Hegira.

3

"It is a terrible waste," San-Ragoz said as he watched Aulutiz's companions empty out his chest and kick at the soil in their search for treasure. He hoped he would be permitted to gather up some of the earth once they understood that their labor was in vain.

"So you say." Aulutiz was growing edgy as the night drew to a close. Already a few birds were singing and the dimmest stars were paling.

"There is nothing here, Aulutiz," said one of his companions. "Just old dirt." He kicked at it, scuffing it into the ground.

Aulutiz flung up his hands. "Then it was all a lie," he exclaimed in disgust.

Erupting from the branches of the olive trees, birds flocked overhead, and a pair of bats, like scraps of soot, fluttered toward the old barn, to rest in the rafters.

"You may have no use for it; the earth is treasure to me." San-Ragoz bent to salvage as many handfuls of the soil as he could, pushing it into a mound and laying a bit of rotting cloth atop it.

"If you are mad enough to value it, take it," said Aulutiz, making no effort to conceal his annoyance at this disappointment.

"You are most gracious," said San-Ragoz, his irony unnoticed by the others.

Aulutiz was restless now, and he glanced at the eastern crags where the tarnished silver sky announced the coming sunrise; more sounds came on the breeze. "It is time to sleep; it will be full-light soon," he announced, and motioned urgently to those with him. "Hurry. We're late."

"What about him?" the tallest of the group demanded, pointing at San-Ragoz.

In the sheepfold, the animals were milling, ready for food and the shepherd to guide them out of the village for a day up the mountain.

"If he is who he says he is, he can fend for himself." Aulutiz pointed toward the forest. "Go. Go." He flashed a look in San-Ragoz's direction. "If you are still here tonight, my mother will want to see you."

"And I her," San-Ragoz said grimly as he continued to pile up the earth that had been spilled from his chest.

"It is nearly dawn," Aulutiz called as he ran toward the promised haven of the trees.

"I know," said San-Ragoz. He sat on the ground and began to unlace his houseaux, working the inner sole lose so that he could put a lining of his native earth beneath it, and replace the inner sole. He had finished both houseaux and was tying the laces when the silver edge of the sun sent long shadows over the land. San-Ragoz felt the annealing presence of his native earth spread through him as he stood up facing west, his shadow lying before him like a reclining giant. Using the old cloth for a bag, San-Ragoz scraped up the rest of the Carpathian earth he could salvage, unconcerned now with the brightening sun. Holding the bag closed with his hands, he began to walk toward the olive trees; behind him he heard the first of the villagers open his door and step out into the morning. Without haste, San-Ragoz went through the orchard, his spirits lifting and his strength returning. He was almost smiling as he went into the forest south of the village. When he came upon an outcropping of rock, he stopped, and found a hollow between two boulders where he could put his rescued Carpathian earth. Then he laid back atop the earth and let himself begin to regain his stamina and vitality.

Just before he lapsed into his intense slumber, two questions niggled at his thoughts: if Aulutiz and his companions were on their native earth, why were they inactive during the day? Why did they behave as if the sun drained them of all strength? Should they not have been as capable as he, on their native earth, of resisting the exhaustion of the sun? He had no answer when he woke, shortly after noon; rising and setting himself as much to rights as he could, he went back to the edge of Mont Calcius, determination in his stride.

This time there was a man with three missing fingers manning the gate. He had the bearing and body of a mason; he used his big shoulders to show he would not admit strangers to the village before he spoke. "Stop there." The animals of the night before were gone.

"Willingly," said San-Ragoz, keeping to his place by the wall.

"We do not welcome strangers here," the gate-warder said, adding unnecessarily, "I will not admit you."

San-Ragoz's demeanor did not change. "No matter. I do not seek entry; I ask only for some information, which you may give me without letting me in." He did not add that he could easily climb the stone wall, or that he had been in the village the night before.

"What information is that?" asked the gate-warder.

"Something I have heard in my travels—I understand your region of the mountains is called Holy Blood: why is that?" He saw that his bluntness had shocked the man, and went on smoothly, "I came this way some time ago and it had no such reputation then."

The gate-warder did his best to smile. "Lowland rumors," he said, dismissing the name and its significance with a wave of his hand.

San-Ragoz nodded. "It is always thus." He paused, then went on,

"And yet, I have heard the same in these mountains, from villagers living here. Why would they say—?"

"Because we fear the Moors," said the gate-warder quickly. "They are coming higher and higher into our forests. If you have been here before, you must have no doubt of that."

"They are taking many trees on the lower slopes," San-Ragoz agreed.

"We have no desire to give them ours. We encourage them to believe all manner of terrible things about our villages and our people. It is very useful." His expression was partly smug and partly worried; his explanations were not being received as he expected they would be.

"An excellent precaution," said San-Ragoz. "But I saw a cup filled with blood set in a ruin. That was not done before—not that I was aware of." He cocked his head. "Did I miss something earlier?"

The gate-warder shook his head several times. "No. No, you did not miss anything." He coughed. "With the Moors here, we have returned to the old ways. The god of the Christians has not protected us. The older gods might. We leave the blood of our animals. At feast-times we sacrifice a horse."

"Ah," said San-Ragoz, beginning to understand how this ritual had come about.

"Do not walk abroad at night, foreigner; there is a need of a goat tonight. Not all goats walk on four legs." He scowled.

"You are saying I may be one such," San-Ragoz said.

"If that is how you take it, you may be warned," the gate-warder recommended. "And do not return here."

San-Ragoz gave a single nod. "I thank you for your counsel."

"This is no place for you, or any foreigner," the gate-warder said for emphasis. "Tell any others you may meet."

"It is certainly no place for the Moors," said San-Ragoz, and stepped back from the gate. "Oh. One question more: have the old gods helped you?"

"We leave the cups of blood," said the gate-warder.

"Yes, you do," said San-Ragoz before he turned away. "And that is not an answer." He did not bother to look back as he went on to the north-west, crossing the little stream without hesitation or discomfort; he was aware of being observed for every step he took until he went back into the forest, and along the game trails and abandoned roads he had learned the century before. Once there, he kept on at a brisk pace, covering distance rapidly, following the faint but unmistakable pull of the blood-bond. This led him upward, to the long, bare ridge above the village; to the shepherds' huts that stood at every ten thousand paces as the mountain rose toward its crest in a treeless sweep of stone. He passed one, and saw another behind him on the ridge; by mid-afternoon, he had gone by a third; he estimated he was twenty-five or -six thousand paces from Mont Calcius; he could barely make out the cluster of buildings surrounded by trees below him in the distance.

Finally he saw one stone house larger than the others, much better-made and kept up than any he had discovered on his walk; it was at the end of a circle of ruins. There were old stone arches standing around the house, each with a cup placed within it. Approaching the door of the house, San-Ragoz saw that it was banded with iron and certainly bolted on the inside. He knew he would have to wait until dusk to speak to its occupant, and so he spent the late afternoon inspecting the cups, noticing how much the blood in each had coagulated, and determining what animal had provided it—most were sheep and goats, but two were boar and one was a horse. San-Ragoz put each back in its arch, then went back to the door, found a place to lean against the stones, and tarried there as the sun dropped lower and lower in the west.

By twilight, he was ready and alert, anticipating the arrival of Chimenae's band. They would be up by now, and they would travel swiftly. Chimenae herself would want to receive them; he was determined to see her first. He was sorry now that he had such a disheveled appearance, but there was nothing to be done; he brushed off the front of his outer habit with the missing sleeve, and straightened the hang of the garment.

There was the distinct scrape of a metal bar being drawn back and then the door swung open, the old hinges moaning, and Chimenae stepped out of the darkness, stopping at once when she caught sight of San-Ragoz, poised to attack, and staring as recognition dawned. "You!" she accused him. "You!" She was dressed in Byzantine silks that had once been a deep, vibrant red but were now faded to a dull pink against which the old-fashioned tablion of gold coins stood out luminously in the last echo of daylight. Golden coins hung from her ears and there was a narrow diadem of gold around her brow; she had belted her clothing at the hip and had many rings on her fingers. Her shoes were tooled leather and had once been red.

San-Ragoz made her a reverence. "My greetings, Csimenae."

"How can it be?" She recovered from her momentary stupefaction and was now glowering at him. "You left a century ago."

"That I did. Circumstances have brought me back." He paid no heed to her conduct.

"What are you doing here?" Chimenae demanded; there was no welcome in her voice or gladness in her face.

"I am hoping to get into Frankish territory," he said candidly. "I came here in search of shelter."

"And you thought you would find it? In this place?" She laughed and began to advance again, her movement swaying and sensuous. "I had almost forgotten you. I assumed you were dead. It was so long ago that you left."

"A century, as you said," he acknowledged with a shrug. "Not so long a time for us. The blood-bond will tell you when I have died the True Death. Until then, you may assume I am . . . alive."

She chose to ignore this kindly admonition; she raised her head with imperious style. "My clan is coming. You should be out of sight."

"Why?" he asked bluntly.

"Because they do not know you; you do not belong here," she told him, her hands on her hips. "You are a stranger."

Now San-Ragoz was genuinely shocked. "A stranger? How can I be that, when it is my blood that gives you life?"

"You left," she said, and came up to him. "You went away. My blood rules here now."

"As you should have done," San-Ragoz said. "You should have left these mountains eighty years ago at least."

Whatever her reply might have been, it was stopped as the first of her tribe came hurrying up the slope, two with raised swords; there were others close behind. Chimenae swung away from him and faced them. "Stay back!"

Aulutiz was in the lead, and he very nearly ignored his mother's command as he rushed at San-Ragoz. "You again!" he cried out.

Chimenae reached out and grabbed the young man's shoulder as he attempted to go past her. "You knew he was here? When did you see him?"

"We happened upon him," said Aulutiz. "Twice." He shot a look of reproach at San-Ragoz. "He said he is Sanct' Germain. I told him to leave."

"Why did you say nothing to me?" Chimenae demanded, forcing

Aulutiz to face her as she spoke. "I should have been told as soon as you found him."

"I thought he would be gone by now; most men obey us when we give them an order," he replied, looking shamefaced and annoyed. "Why should I speak of him? He is just a ragged stranger."

"Sanct' Germain returns and you do not suppose I would want to hear of it?" Chimenae asked incredulously.

Aulutiz feigned indifference. "If he is Sanct' Germain."

The others of Chimenae's tribe had arrived; they stood in a half-circle, many of them uneasy, as Chimenae announced brusquely, "He is who he says he is." This grudging concession brought a few of her clan anxiously watchful.

"He dug up an old chest last night, in Mont Calcius," Aulutiz went on. "It had earth in it, just earth."

"So that is what you wanted," said Chimenae as she rounded on San-Ragoz. "Well, now you have it, take it and go." She pointed down the slope. "There is a track over the mountains that will bring you into Tolosa. The snows are retreating and the passes will soon be open. It will be hard-going, but not impossible for you to cross. You are not wanted here any longer. I have no more use for you." Then she gave her full attention to the clan gathered around her.

Watching them, San-Ragoz saw that there were thirty-eight of them and that twenty-seven were male. None appeared to be more than thirty years of age; two looked somewhat younger than Aulutiz. He observed how Chimenae dealt with them, showing the greatest favor to her son and doling out smiles and frowns to the rest, modifying her praise with a challenging glance, her rebuke with a sympathetic tone of voice and always watching the others, measuring their reactions. He was troubled by her deliberate way of playing one off against another, and the eager, jealous manner in which her clan scrutinized every nuance of her attentions.

"What fare tonight?" Aulutiz asked, standing back from his mother.

"We hunt," said one of the younger men, grinning in anticipation as he reached out and slapped Aulutiz on the upper arm in a show of camaraderie. "It is our night."

"And for me?" Chimenae asked, looking past her son.

"Canthis is providing the two-legged goat tonight," said one of the older of her group. "The village has chosen him—he will be waiting at midnight. We will bring him here. For you."

"Very good; he should last a fair while," Chimenae approved. "We will leave more game at Canthis' gates for a time, to show our gratitude."

"Better be certain that the other villages do not expect such favor," warned another. "Some of the villagers are not complying with our wishes as they used to do. They say we have taken too much."

"They have brought their cups of blood," said Aulutiz. "Time to fear them when they no longer leave offerings."

Chimenae laid her hand lightly on his shoulder. "True enough. But better still, let us remind them now that if they do as we ask, they will benefit from our hunting. If they refuse the little we require, then they will pay the price."

Several of the clan around her laughed at her words; one man shifted uneasily, as if trying to summon up the courage to speak.

"The last two-legged goat was left as you ordered, in the circle where he was offered," said one of the females, a tall, angular young woman with a slight cast in one eye.

"You made certain he was fully dead?" Chimenae asked.

"Beyond all doubt," said the young woman.

"We took him to the shrine down the mountain," said Aulutiz quickly, all but stepping in front of the young woman.

"That was not a shrine," San-Ragoz said, his voice not loud but penetrating. "You left a man dead on a midden."

Aulutiz swung around to stare at San-Ragoz. "Do you say I lie?"

"I say you left a drained and staked corpse on the midden at Mont Calcius: you may have done something else with another dead man." San-Ragoz ducked his head. "I saw the body, or I would not doubt you."

"That was another," said Aulutiz, shrugging to show his indifference. "We came upon earlier, when we were hunting with Achona and Tamosh."

The angular young woman shook her head. "Aulutiz, you are a greedy one."

"Not greedy," Aulutiz countered. "I know it is good to hunt. You had other game to pursue; I went with Ennati and Cossadin and Wembo. We found better game than you."

Achona pointed her finger at him. "You know we must leave game for the villages or they will not put out the cups filled with blood to honor our pact."

"Well said, Achona," Chimenae approved. "And a good warning for all of you." She gave her son a reproachful stare. "How could you, of all of our blood, forget yourself so?"

"I did not forget myself," Aulutiz protested, his voice rising with emotion. "We were hungry. You do not let us have enough."

Chimenae spoke more severely. "You do not mean that you defied me, do you?"

The others were held in fascination as mother and son wrangled; San-Ragoz shook his head slowly, reading the situation with a practiced eye.

"I did not defy you. I hunted twice in a night, with two different bands, to feed this clan." He tugged at his ill-assorted clothing. "You have done the same yourself, many times."

She shook her head. "Not since our numbers grew beyond fifteen. It was different then, my son. Things have changed." She went and stroked his cheek. "You have been an impulsive boy for all your days."

Aulutiz tried to pull back, but without success. "I didn't do anything wrong." He was staring at the ground.

"Not purposefully, no; you would not," she agreed, her tone caressing. "But you still failed to obey me."

There was a subdued, general gasp. The man with something to say stared down at his feet, looking abashed.

"You never told me that I could not do this. You never did." Aulutiz seemed absurdly young as he stood before his mother, his youthful mien and breaking voice making it easy to forget that he had been a vampire for more than eighty years, and that he had been part of the clan since its founding. "I have a right to feed twice in a night if I have the chance."

"No!" She slapped him hard, twice, and then fixed her hands in his shoulders. "You do *not* receive favors beyond the rest of the tribe! You do not *give* preference. That is for me to do."

"Until I am leader?" he asked, suddenly very cool. "As it was in Mont Calcius?"

She released him, her temper controlled as quickly as it had flashed. "That was different," she said coolly, ignoring all but Aulutiz. "You and I held that place for as long as we could. We should be there still. It was yours by right."

"So you say," Aulutiz said, his sullenness returning.

"Well, and do you say you would rather have stayed, nothing more than a woodsman, until you died?" She looked up as if the others had just this instant arrived. "You must all pardon me. I have not received you well."

The clan responded a number of ways, some of them disclaiming any awkwardness, some with apparent disinterest, a few with avidity; the man who wanted to speak shook his head in frustration. Finally Achona spoke for them all: "You made us, we are all in your debt."

San-Ragoz felt disconcerted; he had no desire to witness any of this. For this, he agreed with Chimenae—he was an outsider and had no place in any dispute.

Finally the man trying to impart some news gestured clumsily. "You should know—all of you should know—that there are soldiers of the Caliph on the roads."

This information was welcomed gladly; as dismal as the message was, it was preferable to this dissension. The clan swarmed around the man who had spoken, eager to hear something that would end the confrontation.

"Why should they be here? Are they coming to subdue the villages of the region?" Chimenae asked the questions sharply.

"They say they are chasing a run-away slave, but that cannot be possible; there are too many of them and they are armed well," said the man with a knowing hitch of his shoulders. "There must be some other reason."

"What number are they?" Chimenae came up to the man.

"I saw them camped," he said, unable to conceal a smug smile now that he had finally made his revelation. "Last night. There were sixteen in the company I counted. That included sentries and slaves to tend to them and their horses." He looked around him, as if aware for the first time that he commanded so much attention. "They carry lances, and they wear silk," he added.

"And what more?" Chimenae pursued. "How many horses?"

"Twenty, that I saw," the man answered.

Chimenae's expression grew eager and sly. "Do you know where they are tonight?"

"Five thousand paces below Canthis," said the man. "I followed them this evening, as soon as I woke. They do not move as fast as we do."

"Then we must have the two-legged goat from Canthis quickly," said Chimenae at her most decisive. "And we must take some of the horses from the soldiers. But not quite yet; not tonight. Tomorrow, perhaps, or the night after." She glanced toward San-Ragoz. "If you can catch a horse, you may have it to carry you out of this region. We will not take it for our food."

"More Holy Blood?" San-Ragoz managed a sardonic smile.

"Yes," said Chimenae, turning around to face him. "Would you—of all men—say that blood is not holy?" She expected no answer, so did not wait for one; she faced her clan once again. "Fetch the two-legged goat, and see that you leave more game for Canthis tonight." She went up to Aulutiz. "I need you, my son, to go to with Edic to the Moors' camp. I want them watched at all times. Do nothing that will rouse them: that will be for tomorrow night. Tonight we watch and plan. You will be my eyes for me."

Somewhat appeased by this show of faith, Aulutiz nodded to Edic. "We will do it."

Edic, satisfied with himself, gave Aulutiz a sign of agreement. "I will show you where they are."

"Very good," Chimenae approved. "Then let it be now. The night is ours." She lifted her arms. "Bring me the two-legged goat, then show our gratitude to the villagers of Canthis." With strong gestures that San-Ragoz suspected were ritualized, Chimenae sent her tribe pelting away down the mountain into the night and the forest. When they were gone, she faced San-Ragoz. "You do not wish to go with them?"

"No," he said calmly. "I do not." He remained where he was, his thoughts still vexed by what he had seen.

"They will be back before midnight," she said, a speculative light in her eyes.

"With your two-legged goat," San-Ragoz said with distaste.

"You do not approve?" She was almost teasing him, as intensely aware of him as he was of her.

"You know I do not," he said. He saw a mocking satisfaction flicker in her eyes, then fade as quickly as it had come.

"Then are you intending to admonish me for what I am doing?" She achieved an edgy grin.

"Why should I bother, when you have no inclination to listen?" There was sadness under his banter; he waited for her to go on.

"You believe what we are doing is going to be harmful to us," she said. "Because it was harmful to you at some time in the past. You suppose your misfortune will be our misfortune as well."

The recollection of the oubliette two millennia ago, and the monthly victims, returned full force. "Yes." He gazed at her impassively. "But what is the point of trying to convince you? You have no intention of changing, or of listening to me, have you."

"No." Chimenae could not resist teasing him. "But who knows: you might change my mind."

San-Ragoz regarded her in silence for a short while, then said, "I may be of no use to you, not now, not here." His voice was unexpectedly gentle. "Those of us who live long travel far."

"So you have said, and yet, I am still alive, and I have traveled only twenty thousand paces from where I started out," she said, her feet set apart and her arms folded.

"You are only a century old," he reminded her with kindness.

"And that makes me a child in your eyes," she said, baiting him.

He shook his head, unwilling to enter the contest. "You have much to learn."

Again her temper ignited. "You, of course, are the judge of it!" She lifted her hand to strike him, then lowered it. "No. You will not best me. You will not."

"I am not trying to," he told her. "I am concerned for you, and for those you have made of your blood."

"You envy our numbers, and our strength, and the land we hold," she said, convinced she had the answer to his apprehension. "One day, we shall be an army."

His answer was low, almost soothing. "I envy nothing." His dark eyes met her black ones. "You will never be an army. The living will see to that."

"Ha! They cower at our name. They cull their villages for the weak and infirm and let us rid them of their burdens. We are as useful to them as they are to us. They accept the game we bring them." Chimenae gave a sigh of ill-usage. "You do not know how it is in these mountains. You do not—" She stopped. "What use is it to argue with you? You will not listen to anything I say." With that, she walked a short distance away from him and stood facing the flank of the mountain. "Here we have old ways; very little changes."

"You have been putting out cups of blood for centuries," San-Ragoz suggested, his eyes on her.

"We did, long before the Romans came—the Christians did not like it, so we did it infrequently and in places they would not go, but we never stopped, not entirely. It will not stop now that the Moors are here, or after they are gone." She lifted her hands above her head as if to call down the forces of the earth and sky upon her. "We have always known that blood is sacred."

"And you are not alone in that knowledge," San-Ragoz said, coming after her and speaking softly. "Csimenae, listen to me: you cannot continue to increase your numbers and your demands on the villagers and shepherds who live in these mountains. You may not need much to sustain you, but your numbers are too great to sustain. If those you prey upon do not revolt, your clan will."

"You are ridiculous," she said.

"It will come sooner than you think," he went on, striving to reach her, and certain that if he had tasted her blood all those years ago, he would be able to. "You believe Aulutiz will remain a child because you wish him to be, and because he retains the look of youth—but you delude yourself. He will not always be content to capitulate to you, and others will take their course from him."

"They may be rebellious from time to time, but they are loyal," said Chimenae in a tone of voice that closed the matter. "The Moors: what do you know of them?"

He did not try to return her to the previous subject. "The Moors in general, or the soldiers particularly?"

"Either. Both." She looked steadily at him. "Why would the Moors come into the mountains?"

"They wish to conquer the Frankish lands for their Caliph and their Prophet, as others have done before them," said San-Ragoz.

"Do you know much about the Moors?" she asked suddenly, her face revealing more than she knew. "You could tell us about them, if you went to watch them. You could let us know what their intentions are." She smiled and held out her hand to him. "You would be useful to us, if you would do that. We would not have to drive you out at once. Providing, of course, that you are willing to report all you learn to me. To me, Sanct' Germain, and no one else."

"And what will you tell your tribe?" he asked. "They heard you order me to depart. Do you reckon they will accept your change of mind simply because you have changed it?"

"I will tell them you understand the language of the Moors." She paused. "Do you understand it?"

"Yes," he said.

"Then you will be our watcher. I do not ask you to go among them, only too listen." She studied him. "If you will do this, you remain with us yet awhile."

He did not like the bargain, but he made a gesture of concession. "I will listen for you." He would have done as much for himself; to extend himself to Chimenae to this extent did not trouble him too greatly.

"My clan will understand. You are useful to us. When they bring me the goat, I will tell them." She nodded, confirming her decision. "They will appreciate that, and once they know you will watch the soldiers . . ." Her voice faded.

San-Ragoz could see her distress, and involuntarily took a step forward. "What is it?"

"You could betray us to them," she said abruptly. "You could inform the Moors that we are going to attack them, and they would be ready for us. Those who survive would be yours to command. This clan would follow you as they have followed me." She slipped away from him, keeping a distance between them.

"I do not seek a clan. You know this." He sighed as he recognized her disbelief. "There is another reason you may believe I will say nothing to the Moors, one you may find more persuasive."

This extenuation caught her curiosity. "What would that be?"

He took a deep breath. "I will not approach the Moorish soldiers because I am the one they are hunting."

Text of a report from Karif ibn Azim ibn Salah near Usca to Timuz ibn Musa ibn Maliq in Karmona.

In the name of Allah, the All-Seeing, the All-Compassionate, the All-Protecting, I Karif ibn Azim ibn Salah, set this down for the use and intelligence of Timuz ibn Musa ibn Maliq. May I be struck blind and dumb if I misrepresent my findings in any way, or seek to mislead Timuz ibn Musa ibn Maliq through my report, submitted at the new moon as required.

In regard to the escaped slave, San-Ragoz, we have, in accordance with the orders of Numair ibn Isffah ibn Musa, your nephew and son of the Emir—may Allah give him long life, weak enemies, and many healthy sons—continued our search for him. We have crossed the Iberuz at Zaraugusta and have learned that a man meeting his description was kept in a cell here some days ago. He said he was fulfill-

ing a religious vow, and had to continue for the sake of his faith. The Imam, Dawud ibn Jumah, saw him and heard him in his court. Because San-Ragoz said he had taken a boat to cross the river in order to preserve in a religious pilgrimage, he was given five lashes with the short whip and released; there was no reason to detain him at that time. The Imam further told us that there was no sign of any brand on San-Ragoz's shoulder or he would surely have been held in their prison.

It is said that this San-Ragoz is a great physician and if he is able to erase scars, this must be so. We will amend our dispatches regarding him to state that the slave-brands may be missing. However, if San-Ragoz is bound for Usca and the pass beyond—and it is the safest road—he may be far enough ahead of us to keep us from being able to catch him before he reaches disputed territory, at which point our task will be far more difficult. It may be that our horses have brought us here faster than he can walk, but in such mountains, it is unlikely that we shall overtake him if he is still ahead of us.

If Allah wills, our pursuit will succeed, if Allah wills otherwise, it will fail. I feel I must say that it is capricious of Numair ibn Isffah ibn Musa—may Allah give him long life and many worthy sons—to put so many soldiers at risk for the return of one slave, no matter how accomplished that slave may be. I do not intend to be insubordinate, but for the protection of my men, I am moved to ask you, and the Emir's son, to reconsider our task. Once San-Ragoz reaches the high mountains— which he may well have done already—our efforts must be redoubled and redoubled again to find him. There are many little valleys and remote towns where San-Ragoz may take shelter. Many of these places are so isolated that years may go by without any outsider coming across them. Some of them were hardly known to the Romans, let alone the western Goths who have held the region for generations. If San-Ragoz has found such a place, we might require a long time to root him out, time that could be better spent in the field under the banner of the Prophet. In searching for this one escaped slave, we may be inadvertently aiding the enemies of Islam. While I do not wish to make decisions for Numair ibn Isffah ibn Musa, I cannot help but believe the soldiers of the Emir and the Caliph may be better used than pursuing a single slave.

I have divided my men into three units of twenty each, with a horse-handler for each group, and I have assigned each group a portion of the mountains to search. A few have already suffered injuries and have been brought back to Zaraugusta for care, and we have lost ten horses. So long as it is the will of Numair ibn Isffah ibn Musa that we continue this hunt, we will do so, but I fear I must tell the Emir's son that the recovery of this slave may be costly indeed.

This will be brought to you, Timuz ibn Musa ibn Maliq, by courier, and your reply brought back to us by the same.

At the new moon, from the valley east of Usca,
Karif ibn Azim ibn Salah

4

From high in the branches of an oak, San-Ragoz watched the soldiers set up their evening camp; he had followed them most of the day, keeping well to the side of their march but remaining near enough to listen to them as they made their way toward Canthis. When they stopped to pray, he rested, when they sought out the game trails, he matched their progress while remaining out of sight. He had observed their cursory search of the village, and their departure from the huddled buildings; now he scrutinized their actions as he strove to hear all they said. Now that they were camped for the night and a few of them preparing for evening prayers, San-Ragoz had chosen a useful place as a look-out where he could be supported by branches and hidden by leaves. The wind was picking up and there were heavy clouds piling up against the mountains, both of which made the soldiers restive: scraps of their talk came back to him.

"—have taken some loot from the village," one complained as he inspected the girth of his saddle.

"Nothing to take besides onions and fruit," said the man beside him. "The beggars of Karmona have more."

"The bay mare is throwing a splint."

"Bandage her leg and let no one ride her for three days." The leader of the soldiers dismissed the horse-handler with a movement of his hand. "The white-footed grey is going lame, too."

"It's the mountains; it wears them out."

"Would you prefer to ride mules?" the horse-handler asked indignantly.

"—that cup filled with pig's blood. *Pig's blood!* The creatures are unclean!"

"Can you spare your whetstone?"

"How can I finish stitching my reins before nightfall?" This was addressed to the wind.

"—his buttock filled my hand—so!"

"Tomorrow I'll take my bow and hunt for birds; a dozen or so should feed us well," said the man who had brought back a wild kid for their evening meal.

"We have to refill our waterskins. There are streams here, but we need to carry water with us as well."

"At least there is game in the forest." The speaker was busy chopping up squash and dropping the chunks into a pot of lentils.

"Not as much as you would expect; they say malign ghosts drive the animals away."

"That may be so. I have seen no dogs in the villages, or with the shepherds." This from a man squatting near the fire, waiting for food.

"May Allah preserve us." He pulled out a string of onions seized at Canthis and began to peel them.

"—and no woman is worth nine horses, not even if she gives me nine sons! Find me another wife."

"Move that pot! Do you want sparks in the undergrowth?"

"This wretched country. The mountains themselves are against us."

"—and then return to Usca in two days." The second in command sounded bored.

"What will we report? We have discovered nothing of use."

"That may be useful in itself." The second in command reached for his wooden water-pipe and filled it with tary, acrid seeds and leaves. "Ah, the consolation of smoking."

Satisfied that the soldiers were set for the night, and with sunset not far off, San-Ragoz came down from the tree and slipped away through the forest, moving effortlessly at a pace faster than running deer. Soon he was on the treeless crest and hurrying toward Chimenae's stone house as the last of sunset slid away in the west. New cups of animal blood had been left out during the day, but one arch stood empty, mute testament to the presence of Numair ibn Isffah ibn Musa's soldiers in the region. The body of the man from Canthis had been taken away before dawn; the stone house preserved its splendid isolation.

Chimenae soon emerged shortly after San-Ragoz arrived, saying as she did, "I wish I could go about in daylight, as you do. I become feverish and listless if I try."

"That is very puzzling," San-Ragoz told her. "You are on your native earth, so you should be able to walk these slopes with impunity, day or night." He frowned. "I have been thinking about it, but I have no explanation to offer you as yet."

"And if you find such an explanation, will you tell me?" She pointed to his face. "I can see your doubts."

"You would have them, too, were you in my place," he said.

"As you have said. But you have reservations because you believe I am reckless. I tell you—although you should realize this—I am careful in whom I choose for my tribe," she assured him.

"And you allow none of the others to bring anyone to this life," he said, shaking his head.

"Yes. All the others I do not choose are staked or beheaded. Last night, the goat was beheaded. He was infirm, weak of gesture and slurred in his speech, of use to no one but me. He was relieved to die at last. All the two-legged goats die and only I add to our numbers: that has been the rule from the beginning. This way, I am certain the clan will remain loyal to me and no others." She smiled at him. "I have thought it out, and I know that so long as it is my blood they drink, they are mine."

"But you are not theirs," he said, giving voice to what had been troubling him. "They have drunk your blood, but you have not tasted theirs."

"And I have not tasted yours," she reminded him. "What is the trouble with that?"

"You lack . . . reciprocity," he told her. "There has been no exchange of intimacy, not of the intensity that establishes the link with the living earth as with blood. Perhaps that is what makes it difficult for you to cross running water or walk in daylight—you have not had colloquy with others and therefore cannot benefit from the protection of your native earth."

"Reciprocity? Colloquy? How can there be colloquy? Or reciprocity between the living and the undead? What ludicrous ideas. What would be the purpose?" She laughed, taunting him with her amusement.

"You are so ambiguous in the things you say; you delight in being so, I think. How should reciprocity give me that strength? What could I gain from colloquy?

"I cannot tell you, not in such a way that you would understand my perception that you have not fully embodied the totality of our blood; that is one reason for my reservations: I sense that there is some continuity you have not achieved, and it saddens me. You have tasted my blood, therefore you have me in you, and that brings about the blood-bond and all that it encompasses. I would not obfuscate with you even if I could, which I assure you I cannot, nor wish to. I have not tasted your blood, and therefore I cannot comprehend you as I would wish. I do not know if you wish me to understand you, although it seems you would rather I not." He saw her derisive smile. "You would do well not to mock the bond, for without it, our . . . humanity is lost to us. It is the same with your tribe. They know you far better than you know them." He heard a cry from the southern flank of the crest, and a moment later, the first of her clan arrived, rushing up the slope as easily as a goat and twice as rapidly. "If you could trust your knowledge, you would recognize this."

"And be more like you, I suppose?" Her words were barbed; she smiled as she saw him stand a little straighter. "That is your meaning, is it not?"

"No," he said. "What I mean is that you would be more like yourself."

She shook her head. "You delude yourself."

"Possibly," he allowed.

"We will speak of this later; if I remember." She turned her back on him to greet the new arrivals. "I am not satisfied."

San-Ragoz did not try to dispute her decision; he stood in the shadow of her stone house and watched while she gathered her clan about her as she had done the night before. There was the same ritualistic gathering, the same odd formality. Once again Chimenae bestowed approval and reprimand on those who addressed her directly, and treated the rest with a kind of flirtatiousness that had the others vying for her notice.

Aulutiz brought an end to this. "Did he"—he angled his chin toward San-Ragoz—"learn anything of use to us?" The bluntness of the question made the others pay attention to him. "Or did he fail?"

"I have information. You will decide what use it is," said San-Ragoz, addressing Chimenae.

"Yes. Tell us what you learned," said Chimenae in a general display of authority. "I want you to describe for all of us what you saw."

San-Ragoz waited a moment until he was sure Aulutiz would say nothing more. Then he began: "I followed the soldiers Edic found; they are part of a larger company that has been divided into three groups, at least that is what the leader said. They went though Canthis, killing one man and making free with a number of the women and two of the boys. They ransacked the village, leaving disarray behind for the villagers to set to rights. But they took only food and a length of rope for plunder, and they burned no buildings. Their search did not reveal what they sought and their demands got them no closer to it." He waited for Chimenae to challenge him on this point; when she remained silent, he went on. "They left Canthis shortly after midday and proceeded in a zigzag pattern through the forest. They made camp for the night about four thousand paces north-east from Canthis."

"So they are closer to us here than they were," said Aulutiz, grinning in anticipation.

"They will reach this place tomorrow if they continue as they went today," San-Ragoz said. "They will arrive by mid-afternoon—when the villagers bring their cups of blood."

Aulutiz spoke before Chimenae could. "We must not let them come nearer. We must stop them where they are. It would not be advantageous for them to find this place."

Chimenae gestured for attention. "We must not let the Moors see the villagers bring us their offerings. That would create questions that would not be to our benefit."

"Then we will stop them!" Aulutiz promised.

There were cries of agreement and a few of the vampires brandished knives and daggers to show their determination.

"These soldiers are armed," said San-Ragoz. "And they are trained to fight."

"Not such as we," Aulutiz boasted, looking around for nods of agreement. "No one knows how to fight us."

"There are many who do," said San-Ragoz, thinking of the people of his homeland, and of western China, who had long kept vampires at bay. "Your living neighbors will learn soon enough. You do not want to teach the Caliph's men how to best you; they are formidable enemies."

"Then we will kill them all," said Aulutiz, and earned a cry of support. "We will wound them enough to make them unable to fight, then we will fall upon them. We will *feast!*"

Chimenae raised her hands for quiet. "We shall decide that after we have a look at their camp. Nothing can be decided until then. If they are isolated enough, we can make them disappear completely."

"And the Caliph's soldiers will wreck havoc on everyone in this part of the mountains to revenge the loss of their troops," said San-Ragoz.

"If they can find us," said Achona, smiling at Aulutiz. "The villagers will take the brunt of it."

"And where will your two-legged goats come from, or your cups of blood, if the Caliph's soldiers have killed half and enslaved the rest?" San-Ragoz inquired with exaggerated politeness. "You have lived on the help of the villagers, but the attack of Moorish soldiers could end all that."

"We will find them when they come. We will protect the villagers and they will be more devoted to us than ever," said Aulutiz. "Will we not?"

"If I decide it is the wisest thing to do," said Chimenae with a warning glance at her son.

San-Ragoz felt himself running out of patience. "The soldiers hunt in daylight. If they find you, you will not be able to stand against them. They may not know how to fight those who are undead, but a scimitar can behead a vampire as easily as a living man, and a lance will break your spine. Do not expect the people of the region to interfere; the living people will do nothing to save you—why should they?"

"Because we can help them; we leave game for them and keep away robbers," said Chimenae. "They know where their loyalty is due." She pointed to Edic. "You will go with the clan to watch the camp, and to send back an assessment to me. Have Dorioz"—she indicated the youngest-looking of the clan—"carry your report. He will do what I require."

"Do you think it is wise to use a child?" Aulutiz asked, paying no attention to the cry of protestation Dorioz gave.

"A *seeming*-child," Chimenae corrected him. "He has been one of us for more than forty years, and has proven himself many times. He runs as fast as most of you, and he can slip through the forest almost invisibly. He can outrun even horses over steep ground. If they should see him, why would the Caliph's men stop him? He is nothing to them, less than a goatherd or a woodsman. No soldier would think a boy would be one of our number, or a messenger. They will ignore him." She was satisfied with her decision and wanted no contradiction to her strategy.

"All right," said Aulutiz, not quite sulking. "But it will be for us to decide if we must act quickly. If the soldiers become aware of us, we will strike, whether or not you have sent word of what you want."

There was a very short pause before Chimenae responded. "You may act if the circumstances demand it, but *only* if they demand it."

Aulutiz clapped his hands. "Well enough. We will do as you wish." He managed his most persuasive smile. "It might be as well to attack tonight, before the Moors can learn more. It would not be too difficult to arrange our assault before we go to spy on the soldiers."

San-Ragoz shook his head slowly, hoping none of the clan was watching. He was keenly aware of the contest taking place between Chimenae and Aulutiz, and wondered how long it would be before their contention became something more, for surely it would escalate as Chimenae brought more vampires into their life and their tribe. The trouble between mother and son was deep and it touched all those in the tribe. He stepped forward. "You will be wise to be careful around the soldiers. These are not farmers and woodsmen, who have no will for fighting. These soldiers have been in battle before and have their senses honed to guard them; they have learned to delight in war. You will put them on their vigilance if you press your watch of them. Once they know they are observed, they will take action; they will respond promptly, and severely."

"You are afraid of them?" Aulutiz asked, at once shocked and amused. "Do you credit them with so much because you are frightened?"

"Anyone who has seen them fight is afraid," said San-Ragoz. "Or he is a fool."

Aulutiz shook his head. "You say this, to explain your fear," he declared. "We are not so craven."

"I do not think any of you are craven. I do think you are impetuous, and that it is dangerous to be so in the face of this opponent." San-Ragoz went up to Aulutiz. "You have not seen these men fight. I have."

"I have seen the soldiers of the Gardingi, before the Moors came, and I have seen them defeated by simple ruses. Now the Moors are here why should their soldiers be any different?" Aulutiz faced him arrogantly. "We will fight to win—I will see to that."

"These soldiers believe that if they kill an enemy who does not share their faith, that enemy will be their slave in Paradise," said San-Ragoz very deliberately. "No Gardingio had such convictions."

Aulutiz laughed, and the rest laughed with him, except Chimenae, who spoke sharply to her son. "You would do well to listen to this man. It is true he is not one of us, but he is a vampire, and he has seen many things; among those things, he has seen the Caliph's soldiers fight and you have not. He can tell you what you need to know to hold your own against the Moors. You should learn as much as you can, for I want none of my blood to suffer because of what you face for being of my blood."

In that moment, San-Ragoz admired her; some of his apprehension diminished and he said, "These warriors are sworn to the son of the Emir, who is the Emir's deputy in this land. They are his personal troops, particularly chosen for their loyalty and their fierceness in battle. They have much to gain in conquering you and more than life to lose if they do not acquit themselves well fighting in his name. Do not underestimate them, or their devotion to the Emir's son." He paused, sensing the animosity that was he roused among Chimenae's tribe. "If they once identify you for what you are, they will pursue you until you are gone from here, either by flight or by the True Death."

"Who are you to say this to us?" asked Achona, her voice ringing, holding the attention of her clan-members. "You could be set on bringing us all to the True Death so that no one will be able to hunt here but you."

"I would not do that." San-Ragoz's voice was steady and his dark eyes met Achona's with a conviction that was all but palpable.

"Why not?" She looked from him to Chimenae and back again. "She will not deny you. She is blinded to your trickery."

"I employ no trickery, and I mean you no harm," said San-Ragoz as calmly as he could. "Neither would promote my cause with you."

"No, they would not. So perhaps you should lead us in battle, to show your allegiance to this clan." The challenger was Achona's companion Tamosh.

There were cries of support as well as accusations. Edic held up his hand. "I was the Fifth of the First Ten of Chimenae's tribe, and I had been the Captain of Gardingio Theudis when the Gardingio was too infirm to lead his men. I know how to fight. I will stand beside Aulutiz, not this outsider."

"Yes!" shouted one of the others. "Edic can lead us."

"Edic! Edic!" A few took up the cry while Edic stood, looking at once gratified and chagrined, for he knew Chimenae would not like this.

"No!" Aulutiz silenced the rest with an emphatic yell. "No," he repeated when the tribe was quiet. "I will lead you. I." He waited for objections; when none came, he said. "Edic is not the First—I am. It is only right that I should lead."

"Why is it right?" Edic asked, his manner pugnacious. "You have no experience."

"Nor have you, against these men if what Sanct' Germain says is accurate." Aulutiz glowered at Edic. "I will not disdain your skill and experience. You shall fight at my right hand. That will make it possible for our front to be as strong as the soldiers. Edic and I will bear the brunt of the attack. Will you agree, Matra?"

Chimenae shook her head. "You will do as you must do. We cannot let these soldiers find this place, and if the only way to prevent that is to kill them, then see it is done quickly and their bodies beheaded and hidden. There must be nothing left to find while they can be identified. Let the wild animals scatter their bones." She glanced at San-Ragoz. "Will you go with them, to show them the camp, or must they find it on their own?"

Before San-Ragoz could answer, Aulutiz said, "He will guide us, but he will not join us in the fight. Unlike Edic, I do not trust him to hold a weapon. And if he fails to bring us to the place we seek, we will know how to deal with him."

"What's one more beheaded corpse?" laughed Achona, stepping up to Aulutiz's side. "You are right, Aulutiz," she said, deliberately looking at Chimenae as she spoke. "If this stranger does not do as he claims he will, we shall be rid of him."

"And that shall make us stronger in the mountains," Aulutiz went on. "When the villagers learn that we have killed the Moors, they will look to us to guard them and keep them safe from the invaders." He was almost strutting now, as if he had already accomplished what he intended to do. "No one will question our authority then. No one."

San Ragoz remained silent.

Tamosh raised his hand in a show of endorsement. "Aulutiz is right. This outsider will prove himself or he will suffer the same fate as the Moors will."

"It is true," said Achona. "The outsider must prove himself, or we will see he dies the True Death." She put her hand on the hilt of her short sword; the weapon had not been well-cared-for, and its pitted blade revealed its age and neglect.

"That will not do well against the Moors," San-Ragoz warned. "They fight with the keenest steel to be had. Unless you have an equally strong blade, yours will break at the first clash with one of theirs." There were better blades in China, and the islands beyond, but that meant nothing to these eager vampires; he kept this reflection to himself. "If you plan to use that sword, you will fare badly."

Achona shook her head. "All I need to do is stun one of the men while he sleeps; no Moor will be able to draw a sword when we attack."

"It will be late at night, with only owls to witness. We will fight wisely, Matra," said Aulutiz, beaming at Chimenae.

"Very good, my son," Chimenae approved with a swift glance in San-Ragoz's direction. "You will be careful, I know."

"If I am not, I will pay the price," he said, and stood still while the tribe around him cheered him. "Now then, where is Dorioz?" Catching sight of the youth, he signaled the lad to come to him. "Do you understand what you must do?"

"I must bring word to your mother when you have attacked the Moors," he said at once, and although it was not the task Chimenae had described for him, Aulutiz laid his hand on Dorioz's shoulder.

"Excellent. Are you prepared to come with me, and my company, now?" He held up his hand as he faced Chimenae. "You will endorse this, will you not?"

"If you must attack, then do it quickly, and make the most of your opportunity. No half-measures here." In a histrionic gesture, she put her hands to her eyes. "I do not want to lose any of you."

"Nor do we want to be lost," said Aulutiz with a crow of laughter. "You." He pointed to San-Ragoz. "You will come with Edic and me. Achona and Tamosh will follow after with six of our number. Then another six will come. The last six will fan out in the forest to detain anyone who might have seen us attack, or to capture any Moor seeking to escape. No one is to get away from this night's work." He clapped. "Will that suit you. Founder of our Clan?" It was a title that Chimenae had assumed sixty years ago, and all of the tribe recognized the homage it conveyed.

Chimenae walked up to her son, moving deliberately. "Only if no one of our number is harmed by it. If anyone should fall or be hurt, you will answer to me."

"Of course," said Aulutiz. "You will see: we will triumph." He motioned to San-Ragoz. "Come. We must be on our way. Achona, you come after us when the moon has risen above the Ram's Head Peak. The others will come when the last lights are extinguished in the houses of Mont Calcius."

"Very good," said Chimenae, raising her arms in the ritual dismissal San-Ragoz had seen the night before. She stopped suddenly. "I fear Sanct' Germain is right—you cannot fight the soldiers without taking losses. They will not be driven away by a single rush at their camp. Once roused, you will have no chance to avoid hurt. So you will do as I order you. When you attack, stun the soldiers. You know how to give a blow to the head which renders the one struck unconscious. You may have one or two die, but most will live, but will be silent, and unresisting. Take your clubs to do the work. Behead them after you have slaked your thirst."

A few of the men made cries of disappointment, but most looked relieved as Chimenae finished the sign for dismissal. This time the clan did not all depart, although some of the group hurried away down the slopes; others gathered around Achona and Edic, preparing to seek out the Moors' camp.

"You will show us the way," said Aulutiz, plucking San-Ragoz by the torn sleeve.

"Yes." Edic looked more determined but less eager than Aulutiz. "And remember: we know these mountains far better than you do. We will know if you seek to mislead us." He looked in Chimenae's direction. "A blow to the head could repay your treachery."

San-Ragoz concealed his unsettled emotions, saying only, "It may be best if I describe the place, and let you decide how best to approach it. With the Moors coming into the mountains, I am no longer familiar with this region and you may know better ways than the one I came." He had not felt so much at a loss for more than two millennia and it perturbed him.

"I think it would be best if you retraced your steps," said Aulutiz. "In case you visited places you forgot to mention." He folded his arms.

Achona spoke up before San-Ragoz could answer. "No. Let him tell us." She stood directly in front of him. "You had better describe the camp—we who are coming after need to know where we are bound."

Chimenae came to Achona's side. "A wise precaution."

"One that may be useful," Aulutiz agreed spitefully. He lowered his voice. "Let each of you be ready to fight. Kill only if you must—otherwise, strike to immobilize the soldiers so that we may drink of them before we take their heads."

"What of their weapons?" asked Edic. "They have lances and scimitars and perhaps other arms as well."

"And the horses," Tamosh added. "It would be a fine thing to bring the horses to Chimenae."

"We must deal with the soldiers first," said Aulutiz, his brows drawing together. "We may need the horses to carry the bodies of the soldiers when we are done with them."

"And what then?" San-Ragoz asked. "You cannot mean to leave sixteen headless bodies on a village midden. The Moors would surely hear of it, and would send more soldiers to exact revenge on the villagers."

"Let them," said Aulutiz. "That will bring more fodder for us."

"No," said San-Ragoz. "You do not want the Moors raiding the villages and killing the people to avenge the death of their soldiers. And it is what they will do if you continue to hunt their men. They may not demand conversion of those they conquer, but they will not tolerate anything that hints of insurrection. You may survive, but you will not have men enough left alive to give you your two-legged goats, or to leave cups of blood in offering. They will no longer be willing to placate you." He turned to Aulutiz. "You can fight the Moors in skirmishes, and from time to time you will prevail, but once you start to war with them, you will have to continue until you or they are gone from these mountains. There are not quite forty of you. How can you hope to prevail against their army?"

"We are stronger than they, and we know the mountains," said Aulutiz. "This is our home, not theirs."

"Against those soldiers, you will have no chance of winning. They will identify you and then they will run each of you to earth." He had seen vampires hunted before, but never so many as could be found here. "Many innocents will die in your name before it is over."

"I suppose you would fly?" Chimenae suggested, a falsely sweet smile on her face.

"Yes; and I would advise each of you to do the same," San-Ragoz replied without hesitation. "I tell you to go in many directions, alone, and not to return until all who know you are dead."

"And be picked off like strays from the herd?" Aulutiz exclaimed. "What madness is this? You give them the advantage if you fight in that way. You may prefer such methods, but they smack of desperation. Why should we be so craven?" He shook his head. "You are one—we are many."

"Which is your greatest weakness," said San-Ragoz; as he saw he had wakened their interest, he explained. "One vampire, even two, might hunt this region in safety, undetected and unchallenged: with so many as are in this troop, the people know you are here, and they know your habits. You have come to depend on their familiarity with you, for with so many to tend to, you must follow a routine, so they know your movements and your needs. Your numbers make you vulnerable. You are exposed, whether you think you are or not."

"Where are your clubs?" Achona asked, deliberately cutting off anything San-Ragoz and Aulutiz might have said. "Ennati and Wembo have theirs already. They will come with me, along with Rinaul and Teric."

"You will need one more," said Aulutiz, looking about. "Walgild will do."

"And I have one," added Dorioz, holding up the club hanging from his braided-leather belt. "You will need them."

"Yes; we must fetch them," said Aulutiz. "We have been told how we are to subdue the Moors." Pointing to four of the men who lingered near Chimenae, he called out, "Blaga, Merez, Tacantiz, Prando: come with us." He began to stride swiftly toward the line of trees, not so much as glancing back to see if his summons was obeyed. "Each of you will bring two clubs. Except for you." This was directed over his shoulder to San-Ragoz.

Edic kept close to Aulutiz, his hand on his dagger. "You may have plans to escape, but they will not succeed," he declared.

"I have no such plans," said San-Ragoz with exaggerated patience. "I am not completely a fool." Even as he said it, he wondered if it might not be true: he had brought Chimenae to his life and was now caught in the folly of the consequences.

"Well, do not think to fool me," said Edic; they were in the forest now, and forced to go single file though the undergrowth, using the game trails to make their way. Edic was behind San-Ragoz, who walked immediately behind Aulutiz, with the others coming after them. They kept to a single line, an arm's-length between them. Only Dorioz made his own way, staying near but apart from the rest.

"There is a spring about five hundred paces ahead," said Aulutiz. "We will stop there so that you may go to get your club. As soon as you are all returned, we will be on our way once again." He increased his pace, not quite running, but going faster than most of the animals in the woods.

Edic turned to relay Aulutiz's orders to the four behind him, raising his voice to be heard. When he finished, he nudged San-Ragoz forward with this hand. "You will not be laggard. Keep moving."

San-Ragoz obediently increased his stride, paying close attention to the others behind him. None of the vampires ventured to speak until they reached the spring and Aulutiz called a halt.

"Bring your clubs and be sure you have short-swords or daggers with you. We may have to fight our way out. They will not be ready for us. If we do as we have planned, all will be well." He waved his hand in dismissal as he reached out and took hold of San-Ragoz's upper arm. "You will remain with me. I do not want you running away. Edic will bring my club."

Dorioz took up a place on the far side of the spring, serving as sentry; he made sure not to listen to anything that passed between Aulutiz and San-Ragoz. For a short while Aulutiz said nothing. Finally he sighed. "Was it really your blood that changed my mother?"

"Yes," said San-Ragoz.

"Why did you do it?" His voice was light, but the concern in his eyes could not be disguised.

"She was badly injured and you were both in danger," he said, then added in a lower tone, "and I was lonely."

Aulutiz chuckled, shaking his head in disbelief. "So lonely that you left before the summer was over. Oh, yes," he said, his grip tightening. "She told me how eager you were to leave her."

"I was not eager; it was necessary that I go. She herself was glad of it." He offered no apology or other explanation.

"Do you think so?" Aulutiz slapped his thigh with his palm. "Why would she be so reckless as that?"

"Not reckless," said San-Ragoz. "She wanted no one to impugn her authority." He shook his head. "It was better for both of us that I go, or so I thought at the time. Seeing what she has made for herself, I am no longer certain I was wise to leave."

"You disapprove of the clan," said Aulutiz.

"I fear for it," San-Ragoz corrected gently.

"And you disapprove of our mission tonight," Aulutiz added with a trace of smug satisfaction.

"Yes. This I do disapprove of," said San-Ragoz.

"Because you are afraid," said Aulutiz, shaking his head to show his contempt.

"Yes, I am," said San-Ragoz.

"You admit it!" He released his hold on San-Ragoz's arm and stepped back.

"Yes." San-Ragoz did not move.

Aulutiz tugged at his upper garment—a kind of tunica made of several fabrics and patched elaborately at the shoulders—and hitched his belt. "You will change your mind tonight."

Now the tribe fell back, approaching the soldiers with caution.

San-Ragoz said nothing in reply, and a short while later Edic came back, holding three clubs and a short sword in his hands.

"And the others?" Aulutiz asked as he took two of the clubs.

"They are coming," said Dorioz from the other side of the spring.

Merez was the first of the four to arrive; he had two clubs and a Roman dagger hanging from his belt. Not far behind him came Prando and Tacantiz, both hefting their clubs; Tacantiz carried a battle-hammer as well. Last to arrive was Blaga, who had included an axe among his weapons.

"Very good," Aulutiz approved. "You know what is to be done. Edic, you will bring down the sentries—they will be yours as spoils. For the rest, remember others are coming. Do not drain all the soldiers you stun. Move quietly. We do not want to alarm them." This last was a concession to San-Ragoz; Aulutiz stared at him while he gave those last instructions. "Dorioz, keep to the side of us. Do not fear. You shall share the spoils. Sanct' Germain. Tell us which trail to take."

Dorioz grinned. "You are good to me, Aulutiz." He went a few steps, then said, "Better than your mother."

The hush this remark brought stayed with the small group of vampires until they reached the edge of the Moorish camp and prepared their assault; they remained in the undergrowth, using the foliage as a screen. Satisfied they were protected, Aulutiz said very quietly, "You did well," to San-Ragoz and, "We know what is to be done," to the rest.

Edic slipped ahead of them, his club in his hand. He stayed away from the clearing where most of the soldiers slept, for he was searching out the sentries.

"There should be two of them," said Aulutiz. "If the horses do not whinny, we will soon have our work accomplished."

"Do not kill the horses," San-Ragoz said as Aulutiz prepared to lead his companions into the clearing.

"I will save a few of the for my mother, never fear," said Aulutiz sarcastically. At his signal, the others moved with him, leaving San-Ragoz alone in the brush at the side of the clearing.

At San-Ragoz's side, Dorioz said, "I have a club, too, and I am strong enough to use it. If you try to run I will break your legs and then smash your head; one of the others will cut it off. You might as well watch with me." There was no doubt that the youngster would do as he said.

So as Aulutiz, Edic, Tacantiz, Prando, Blaga, and Merez passed quickly from sleeping soldier to sleeping soldier, their clubs used with fatal purpose, San-Ragoz watched from the undergrowth, appalled and sick at heart.

Text of a report sent by Karif ibn Azim ibn Salah at Usca to Timuz ibn Musa ibn Maliq at Karmona.

In the name of Allah, the All-Compassionate—may He be praised forever and ever—I, Karif ibn Azim ibn Salah send this account to Timuz ibn Musa ibn Maliq, although it is not at the appointed time, to alert Timuz ibn Musa ibn Maliq to the dangers I and my men have encountered on this mission for Numair ibn Isffah ibn Musa—may Allah protect him and give him long life. May my tongue be stilled and my eyes blighted if I report in error, or mislead any of the officers of the Caliph, the Emir, or his son.

I have told you of my determination to divide my troops into three groups of twenty, the better to pursue the escaped slave of Numair ibn Isffah ibn Musa—may he have many years and healthy sons—who has fled into the mountains. It was agreed that all three groups would re-

turn to Usca after ten days if they did not succeed in capturing San-Ragoz.

The ten days have come and gone, and one of the companies has not returned. They have not been seen since they searched the village of Canthis. No one has seen them since then, not the men or their horses, and there has been no report on their disappearance. I have sent messengers into the region where they were last seen, but I have not yet gained any intelligence to reveal what has become of them. No one has given any information that has proven reliable.

I would not be worried were it not for persistent tales of those who live in the region of the mountains where the men vanished. The people who live in the villages and on the remote farmsteads call this part of the mountains the land of Sacred or Holy Blood. They offer chalices of blood to mighty beings who provide them with game and guard them from harm. It is said that there are sacred grottos where many jeweled cups stand in vaults to honor the heroes who continue to watch over those who are willing to show them homage.

Ordinarily I would not give credence to such rumors, nor would I think the reports anything more than legends repeated by these ignorant folk to persuade them they are not as much in danger as their life requires them to be. They are unwilling to hear the words of the Prophet, and they are not diligent in their worship of the Christian prophet. Many say that the cups are a tribute to defenders of Jesus who bled to death on the cross, but others say the gods are older and more terrible than Jesus of the Christians.

If the people who put out the cups are people of the Book, then they cannot be stopped from this practice without bringing shame on Islam. If they are not people of the Book, we would disgrace ourselves if we fail to stop this idolatrous adoration. I seek your judgment in this regard, for I am certain that the longer my men remain here the more reason we will have to be careful of the people of the Holy Blood; they are said to be brave fighters, and if they have bested my soldiers, I will have to agree that they are formidable opponents and if I am to campaign against them, I will need more troops and your permission for an all-out attack, otherwise we may all fall victim to whatever force has claimed the men who disappeared.

There is an ominous addition to my report; the bodies of two of the soldiers' horses have been found in the forest, their coats bloody, their flesh as bloodless as if they had been hung by a butcher. Both horses *were haltered, which suggests that they were assailed at night. There was no trace of tack or equipment anywhere that would indicate how the horses came to be dead. If it is as the people of the region say, and the devotees of the Holy Blood have done this, we may have to move quickly, which I must admit we are ill-prepared to do. However I will strive to do your will, and to discharge the mission given to me and my men by Numair ibn Isffah ibn Musa—may Allah show him favor for all of his days—when we were first sent into these mountains to find his escaped slave.*

In that regard, I must tell you that if San-Ragoz came into this region, he may well have suffered the same fate as my men appear to have done. I can see no good reason to continue the pursuit of the fugitive slave; if seventeen men can disappear without any sign, what must be the portion of a single unarmed man going on foot into this wild place?

This is being carried to you, Timuz ibn Musa ibn Maliq, by my most able second captain, Mainum ibn Kahlut ibn Akil, who will carry your reply to me as swiftly as his horses can bear him, if it is Allah's Will.

Three days after the new moon, from Usca,
Karif ibn Azim ibn Salah

5

"Look how many cups are offered," Aulutiz said exultantly. "There must be ten more than yesterday." He strode from one cup to the next, counting them off for the tribe that stood around Chimenae's stone house; his pride was obvious and he made no apology for the gratification he felt at this show of devotion. "This is better than when they brought us all their dogs as sacrifices."

Achona approached him, her smile fixed as if by rigor. "You have every reason to be honored; all of us are under obligation to you," she said before she gave her whole attention to Chimenae. "He has done more than anyone else for this clan."

"He has done what I ordered him to do," said Chimenae, unimpressed by Achona's enthusiasm. "He very nearly exceeded his mission, which none of you would have liked. If he had not had you and the others, three of the soldiers would have escaped, and then we would not have offerings but enemies to deal with. Fortunately, you arrived in good time, and you with your five companions saved my son from calamity. You are due as much a debt as he is." She approached her son, staring hard at Achona. "You do us no good, treating him as if he had no fault to correct."

"And what fault would that be?" Achona asked as she boldly put her hand on Aulutiz's arm while she met Chimenae's steady gaze.

"The sin of vanity," said Chimenae. "The Christian monks are correct in saying that it is a very great fault, because it blinds you to all others, and keeps you from learning. Be ware of your vanity, that it does not lead you to recklessness." She removed Achona's hand from her son's arm. "You did very well, but a good portion of that was luck. You cannot rely upon it."

From his place at the edge of the loosely defined circle, San-Ragoz could sense the discomfiture that was developing in the group, stronger than the night before, and more pervasive, for now it was apparent to him that the vampires were taking sides, and that it would not be long before loyalties were tested. He stared up at the stars emerging on the dark canopy of night, and wished he could leave without arousing suspicion in the tribe, escalating the tensions that roiled among them.

"All right," said Aulutiz. "I agree we were lucky. But we made the most of our luck; you cannot say we did not." He took Achona's hand in his. "Without her arrival, a few of the Moors would have got away from us. But she saw to it they did not."

"Most commendable," said Chimenae drily. "You have done what was expected of you, and you had the pick of the Moors for your efforts. You and those with you drank before any of the rest did."

"As you promised we would," said Achona.

"You seem astonished that I kept my promise." Chimena smiled at her son. "Yet I cannot deny it: you have shown your worth again, Aulutiz. I am grateful to you for all you have done. The clan should be as grateful as I."

Aulutiz grinned at this praise. "My companions are worthy, too," he said, with a quick glance at Achona. "It is a pity that two of our blows killed Moors outright, for it was a shame to waste such bounty, but in the excitement, it was not surprising that one or two of us should strike too hard." He ducked his head, as if acknowledging this error would spare him the recriminations of the others.

"It could not be helped, from what Edic says. The Moors were attempting to flee and only a sharp blow would be enough to stop them." Chimenae directed her nod at Edic. "You chose well in the Moor you brought to me. A fine, strong man, not so injured that he is wholly senseless. He is worthy to nourish me, to die for me. There is passion in him, to match his blood. He will last another night before he is drained, if I drink again tonight. Perhaps I will wait a night—let him enjoy another day." She indicated her stone house. "If he were not a Moor, I would be tempted to bring him to our number. He is the sort of man who would be a credit to our clan." She heard the quick muttering from those standing near her and shook her head. "Do not be shocked. And do not pretend it did not occur to you as well. You all had Moorish blood to drink, and relished it. To number one of them with us could provide us with information and other advantages. Surely you can see it would." She forestalled any objections from her tribe by executing a graceful turn and a light caress to Edic's arm; her brows arched roguishly, and she looked back at San-Ragoz with playful intention. "Do you not agree, Sanct' Germain?"

"I have nothing to say that would move you, one way or the other," said San-Ragoz, his expression unreadable.

But Chimenae was not daunted. "You could have a taste of him, and then you would know," she offered.

"Thank you; no," he replied, hating the sudden pang of need that shot through him.

"You would rather creep into the bed of a sleeping woman, and take no more than what fills a small cup, while wooing her with pretty dreams: that is what you do, isn't it?" Her contempt gave a venom to her courtesy that held the gathered vampires fascinated. "Well? Would you not prefer that to what I do?"

"If I had such an opportunity, if such a woman were accessible, yes, I would," San-Ragoz said without raising his voice; his expression was stern but without anger.

Chimenae laughed her scorn. "You hold yourself above us because you are not willing to hunt down your prey as we do. You have no appetite for the chase."

"Do you call your two-legged goats prey?" San-Ragoz inquired gently. "I would not hunt men as you do, but then, as you say, I am not like you."

"The two-legged goats are not the same at all. Everyone understands that. They are our tribute, for the game-prey we share with the villagers," Chimenae said, her temper flaring. She came up to him, her fury making her eyes shine. "The villagers love us. They know they are cared for. They have nothing to fear from marauders or bandits. We have rid the valleys and mountains of such vermin, and they show their appreciation with two-legged goats. Occasionally I honor their gift by making the goat a vampire. That is how most of my clan came into being. You cannot claim your way is better." She poked at San-Ragoz's chest. "You are too much a coward to accept such homage."

"It must seem so to you," said San-Ragoz, unwilling to be dragged into another fruitless wrangle.

"It *is* so," Chimenae insisted. "Let the living do what they will to change the day: come twilight the world will always belong to vampires."

San-Ragoz said nothing; he was caught up in memories of Nicoris, and how very different her response had been when she came to his life—she had been prepared for the change, and yet she could not bear it: Chimenae, who had changed with no readiness for the vampiric life had accommodated its demands with lamentable success in her own view, and in a manner that chilled San-Ragoz to the marrow. He became aware that Aulutiz had spoken to him and blinked. "Your pardon, Aulutiz. My thoughts were otherwise."

"I asked if you have your own clan? My mother says nothing of it." He gave a swift, defiant stare at Chimenae.

"A clan?" San-Ragoz shook his head. "No. Those of my blood are few, and scattered over the world—except for what your mother has done."

"How can you know?" Aulutiz asked, and took Achona's hand as he waited for an answer. "Some of the others might also have made clans of their own, as she has."

San-Ragoz fixed Aulutiz with his enigmatic gaze. "I know."

"What else would he tell you?" Chimenae demanded, stepping between her son and San-Ragoz. "He did not know about you."

"No, I did not," San-Ragoz conceded. "But we have not shared blood, you and I: you have kept yourself to yourself."

"And that is the reason you did not know about my clan?" Chimenae was incredulous. "How can you make such a claim?" She rounded on Aulutiz. "He lies."

Before Aulutiz could speak, San-Ragoz interjected, "How can she know?" He let the question hang as he took a step back, noticing as he did that Edic was watching him carefully.

"I can know because I know how I have had to make my way in the world. You cannot expect me to believe that it is different for any of the others, wherever they may live." Chimenae pointed at him. "You have lied and lied and lied. We should take your head and leave you as carrion for the kites and vultures."

"And if I have not lied, what then?" San-Ragoz asked, not responding to her threat.

She lifted her chin. "You lie." With that, she turned her back on him and deliberately walked away from him. "No vampire can survive without a clan and a leader. Left alone, a vampire is helpless. Everyone knows that."

"Because you have told them so?" San-Ragoz suggested gently.

Not understanding his intent, Chimenae said, "Why else—*how* else should they know it?" She looked back at her tribe and nodded emphatically.

A few of those gathered gave a ragged half-cheer; Aulutiz did not join in.

Finally Edic spoke up. "There are more Moors. In the mountains. At least one more company of them." As the tribe rounded on him as one, he said, "I have been searching for others, thinking that the group we attacked might not be alone in this region."

"What made you think to look for them?" asked Aulutiz, watching Edic closely.

"My years as a solider," was Edic's blunt answer. "When I led men into battle, I did not put all my men into the field at once, unless the enemy had done the same. These Moors were searching the mountains, not preparing to fight. Therefore I have assumed there must be other small companies in this region."

"And have you found any?" Chimenae's voice was sharp.

"I found traces to the south of Mont Calcius, Chimenae," said Edic. "They made camp there no more than two nights ago."

Suddenly Chimenae took hold of his short dalmatica at the center of his chest. "And why did you say nothing until now?"

Edic seemed shaken by her change of demeanor. "I . . . I did not know how to tell you."

Her grip tightened. "Why should I believe you? Have any of the clan—other than you—noticed the Moors you speak of?"

"I do not know," Edic admitted.

Chimenae released him. "Well?" She regarded the whole group gathered around her. "Have any of you seen Moors? Or heard about them?"

After a short silence, Wembo spoke up. "I have seen Moors on the old monastery road." He giggled; the road was little more than a goat-track. "A dozen of them, perhaps more."

"And when was this?" Chimenae was keeping her fury in check with difficulty.

"It was just after sunset last night." He pointed to Dorioz. "He saw them, too."

Dorioz held up his hands. "I saw them, but I saw they were going toward the high pass. I thought they were looking for a crossing into Toloz." He glared at Wembo.

"You saw them," said Chimenae in a dangerous tone, "and you did not tell me?"

"They were going out of our region," he said with a shrug. "Who knows, by now they may be at the monastery."

"We owe nothing to the monks," said Aulutiz hotly. "They leave no cups for us."

"And if they did, what then? They would give no two-legged goats to us, and the cup of blood is nothing more than a sign of respect." Edic held out his hand. "The monks have much to do to survive now that the remaining Christians no longer send them food and wine."

"Forget the monks," Chimenae ordered abruptly. "Edic is right. They are of no interest to us. The Moors are what we must think of now. The Moors can provide for us yet again, if we plan carefully. If they remain within reach, we will make the most of it." She stared hard at Wembo. "You will lead us—all of us—to where you saw the Moors. We will track them."

"When? Tonight?" Achona was avid, grinning hectically.

"Tonight, tomorrow, what difference so long as we all hunt?" Chimenae said with feigned indifference.

"Including you?" Wembo was caught off-guard by this announcement. "You never hunt with us."

"You are young among us," said Chimenae, her tone slightly less stringent. "While we were few, I led every hunt. Ask your elders if you doubt this. They will tell you that I hunted every night. When the villagers began to offer two-legged goats, then I ceased my hunting, so that you could have more."

"Was that the reason?" Achona kept Wembo from speaking. "Or did you grow afraid?"

Chimenae drew back as if struck. "I am not afraid," she stated, her mouth ugly. "Look what I have made of you. How can you say I am afraid?"

"I can and I do," Achona cried, taking hold of Aulutiz's hand.

This was too much for Aulutiz, who pulled himself free of Achona's grip and went to his mother's side. "You must not say such things. Have you no gratitude?"

Aware that she was suddenly in trouble, Achona did her best to brazen it out. "If any other of us refused to hunt, what would we think? Why is it any different for her?"

"Because she is the First," said Edic, settling the matter. "We are all beholden to her for our lives. Let none of you forget that." He stared at Achona. "You are troublesome."   .

"No more." Chimenae's voice was not loud but it carried her full authority.

There was a long silence this time, during which Aulutiz put more distance between him and Achona. The rest of the tribe was growing restless, and a few were looking angry. At last Chimenae lifted her arms. "Tonight you hunt as you will. Tomorrow night, if the Moors may be found, we hunt them. If they leave the region, well and good. If they do not, they are ours." She remained in her position of dismissal as the group broke up and scattered into the night. San-Ragoz withdrew a short distance so that he could observe what Chimenae would do when all her vampires were gone. Only Aulutiz lingered, looking as awkwardly young as his features would suggest he was. "What is it?" his mother asked of him as she made her way toward the stone house. "The Moor is waiting."

"You are not going to make a vampire of him, are you?" Aulutiz asked.

"Perhaps. It would be useful and he, at least, understands loyalty." She gestured as if to shoo him away, but he stood his ground.

"I think that would be very foolish. So do many of the clan. You could see that, couldn't you?" He attempted to keep her from entering her stone house without actually touching her. "You push them too far."

"You mean I push you too far," she said, more amused than annoyed.

"They will not always do as you order them. They are growing restive." Aulutiz shook his head. "If you make the Moor one of us, it will cause hard feelings."

"Is that so?" Chimenae challenged. "You would have no part of it, of course, would you?"

"I would not be happy, but I would do nothing against you," he said with subdued emotion.

"No; you cannot forget you are my child." She touched his face softly, seductively, and smiled at Aulutiz.

San-Ragoz wanted to speak but did not; Chimenae and Aulutiz had forgot he was still watching them and he knew it would be indiscreet to remind them of his presence. He kept his thoughts to himself even as he felt a twinge of dismay deep within. He was appalled at what he saw, and more appalled because he had made it possible. Little as he wanted to admit it, he also recognized an antagonistic fascination in this mother and son, who were of his blood but alien to him.

"No, I cannot," said Aulutiz, and kissed his mother's mouth.

Chimenae smiled and turned to face San-Ragoz. "I told you he is loyal to me." Then she laughed and said, "Go away. You have seen what you have come to see. But do not try to leave this region while the Moors are searching for you. I will not put my clan at risk so that you can reach Frankish lands. I will allow you to remain here for a time because of what you did for me, but do not ask for more, and do not fly. If you make such an attempt my clan will hunt you down and leave you staked on a midden. I will tell you when you may depart." With a flick of her fingers she dismissed him. "Be here tomorrow night, or be my foe."

San Ragoz made his way back toward Mont Calcius, to the place he had put his native earth. He had no wish to find food that night; he would regain as much of his strength as he could before daylight: with the powers of his native earth and darkness working together, he realized he would be almost as restored as if he had found living nourishment. What he lacked was solace, and now that troubled him, for he could not resign himself to what Chimenae had done, or his role in it. Living as a wild beast must had no satisfaction for him, and the raven-ous offspring Chimenae had created sickened him. As he followed the game trails through the forest, he began to grieve.

The next night Chimenae sent her tribe off through the forest, searching for the Moors. "Bring me any stragglers you may find— alive," she said before she dismissed them. "They will sustain us for a while. We must learn what has brought them into the mountains."

"But you know that already," said Edic, puzzled.

"No. I know what Sanct' Germain has told me. The Moor who left this world last night said nothing of use to me, or any of us." She began to pace. "I think there is a larger purpose here—that the reason we have been given is only an excuse, a means to conceal far more dangerous intentions."

Wembo pointed to San-Ragoz, standing apart from the circle around Chimenae and her stone house. "Why do you discuss this in front of him?"

"I want to know where he is, and what he has heard." She made another of her flirtatious turns. "You may guard him, if you wish."

Wembo shook his head. "You indulge him."

"If I do, or if I do not, it is of no matter to you," said Chimenae, staring him down. "It is not for you to choose for me."

Into this uncomfortable silence, one of the other female vampires spoke. "The Moors are more dangerous than this one wandering creature, are they not, at least to us?"

"Folma is right," said Edic, with a covert glance at Chimenae.

Taking this as a kind of truce, Chimenae allowed, "Yes; these Moors can bring us trouble if they ever recognize our existence."

"If we find the Moors are still in our region, will we attack them?" Dorioz asked, his eyes alight.

"If we may do it entirely," said Chimenae. "If we may not, then we must permit most of them to depart."

"Most of them?" Edic repeated suspiciously.

"We can pick off one or two of them" said Chimenae, taking full charge of the situation. "You may have one, and I will want one for my own use. Then we shall see what we shall see."

"This has no purpose," Achona complained as she came and put her hand on Aulutiz's sleeve. "We know where to hunt."

Chimenae's commanding tone stopped Achona. "You will leave when I give you permission, and not before." She waited while Achona glared and stepped back. "You do not comprehend what may be happening here. We must learn all that we can, and be ready to face what is coming." There was genuine apprehension in her eyes, and her voice shook.

"And what then?" Aulutiz demanded, hands belligerently on his hips. He had added a Moorish bangle to his trophy-laden clothing, one that had inscribed on it one of the many sacred names of Allah, intended to protect the wearer from enemies; Aulutiz's edgy movements revealed his hunger.

"Once we have gained information, I will decide how to deal with these interlopers." She regained her majestic composure. "You will do as I say. Tonight find them. If there are stragglers, seize them, and bring them to me before dawn." She raised her arms and waited until all her tribe had left and only San-Ragoz remained. "You see?"

"That they do as you order them?" San-Ragoz said as she came up to him. "Yes, I see that. I see also that many of them resent doing as you order them."

"But they do not defy me. Remember that," she advised him. "They will kill you if I tell them to. You are clever, but you cannot escape them."

"Very likely," he agreed with a slight, sardonic smile. "Do you want to kill me?"

It took her a moment to answer. "Of course not."

"Because," he went on in a level tone, "it appears to me that you want either my adulation or my death."

This time she coughed before she answered. "That's preposterous."

"Is it." He waited for her answer; when she did not deign to give one, he continued. "It seems to me that you want me on jesses so that you may show your authority to the vampires you have made; if I do not admire you, at least I obey you. If you are willing to kill me, they will know you are capable of killing them."

"You are a fine one to condemn me. You traveled with your servant—he was a vampire, and you both managed to live; you would sacrifice him if you had to." She made this an accusation, as if she thought such a sacrifice had already happened.

"Ruges—Rogerian is not a vampire; he was once truly dead, but he lives again. He is a ghoul. His needs are not mine." His enigmatic gaze rested on her face. "You want to keep me at your beck and call, until you can make the most of my True Death. Have I erred, Csimenae?" His use of the old version of her name startled neither of them.

"I will not dignify such drivel with an answer," she said. "Go find a sheep or a deer to feed on. I am not hungry tonight." She went toward the door of her stone house.

"Where are you planning to leave the body? The soldiers might find it if you do not conceal it well," San-Ragoz asked before she could enter. "The more Moors you kill, the more they will send to search for the missing. You cannot continue to attack them all. They will not cease their efforts until they discover what has become of their men." He knew she was listening although she did not turn. "Think, Csimenae: you must know that the Moors will come to find their own."

"And what is that to me?" she inquired with profound indifference.

"They will find the bodies, and they will hold the people of this region responsible." He took one step toward her. "The villagers will answer for your acts."

She shrugged. "Why should that happen? The villagers are cowards and the Moors will recognize their cowardice when they see it."

San-Ragoz considered her a moment. "Do you recall when the bandits attacked Mont Calcius?"

"You made me a vampire because of it," she said sharply. "Of course I remember."

"Those villagers fought well, even though they were cowards. Why should they not fight the Moors with the same determination? If they do, they will be taken as slaves, and you will lose . . . fodder."

"Fight the Moors?" She laughed. "How? It is more likely they will flee into the woods if the Moors come, where they will be ours." Opening the door to her house, she paused long enough to add, "You may want to think otherwise, but that would be foolish."

He watched her enter her stone house. When she did not reemerge again, he went away into the forest. He made his way to the outskirts of Mont Calcius, wondering if there was a night-guard at the gate. Although he doubted that there was, he kept within the shelter of the trees rather than move through the cleared land around the stone walls. The more he thought about Chimenae the more despondent he became; she had set herself on a path that could only lead to her destruction, and the destruction of the vampires she had made. If the villagers in the mountains did not turn against them, the Moors would track them down. There was nothing he could say to her to make her realize what danger she was in, and that was the most disheartening of all. She had made this part of the mountains her own and would believe in no will but hers. In the past, when he had had disagreements with others of his blood, he had been able to comprehend what they sought; he had no such understanding in regard to Chimenae, and as a result, no means of dealing with what seemed to him to be her headlong rush toward catastrophe. There was no question in his mind that she meant her threat: if he tried to leave before she released him, she would send her vampires after him to kill him. He was clever enough to evade them for a while, and he could foil them by traveling by day, but their numbers would make his escape more difficult, and more obvious, so for the time being, he was disposed to stay where he was, for Mont Calcius was one of the places Ruges would look for him. That consideration tipped the balance for him for the time being: in spite of the risk he assumed staying so close to Chimenae, he told himself it was more than a vain hope that he would be found, and together he and Ruges would be allowed to leave in peace. The last was cold comfort as he went to rest on his native earth with less apprehension than he had had for some time.

Shortly before dawn he was awakened by the sound of a mountain cat padding through the undergrowth. He sat up slowly so as not to alarm the animal, thinking as he did that this was the first of the kind he had seen since his return to the region. Cats and wolves were higher up the mountains now, and bear had retreated even further. He studied the cat with its tufted ears and short ruff, noticing it was thin, and that a half-healed wound on its flank suggested a recent battle. The cat caught sight of him; its head came up and it froze for an instant before sprinting away toward the deepest part of the forest. San-Ragoz watched the place where it had been, undefined sadness welling within him. Then the first birdcalls began, and he lay back to watch the sky brighten beyond the arch of trees.

By sunset that day, Chimenae had made her plans: she sent her tribe out to pick up any Moor still in their region. "If there are more than three together, leave them alone. But if you find one or two by themselves, secure them and bring them to me. We have much to learn." She paused. "The two-legged goat comes from Aqua Frates tonight. See that I have him before midnight."

The clan agreed automatically, but with an underlying tension that showed the clashes of the last days were unresolved. A few of their number did not depart on Chimenae's signal, preferring to choose companions before going into the forest. As they dispersed, Chimenae once again summoned San-Ragoz to her side. "You know the tongue of the Moors, do you not?"

"Yes," he said, uneasy as to why she asked.

"Then you will help me. I believe that hearing the Moorish tongue might cause any we capture to be more revealing." She almost touched him, but dropped her hand before she actually reached him. "If you will do this for me, I will look more kindly on your plight."

Ordinarily he would have challenged her choice of words: now he knew it was reckless to try. "I will do as you ask."

"Very good. Sanct' Germain." She sauntered away from him. "Then return after midnight. I have no use for you until then."

He left without saying another word. Tonight he would hunt, and by midnight he would feel no pangs when Chimenae received her two-legged goat.

Text of a letter from the Primos Blaziuz Gagin of Sancta Cruce in Usca to Timuz ibn Musa ibn Maliq in Zaraugusta.

To the most esteemed officer of the forces of the Caliph and of Numair ibn Isffah ibn Musa who rules in Corduba but is presently in Zaraugusta, the respectful greetings of Primos Blaziuz Gagin of Sancta Cruce, the Christian monastery of Usca. Know that the prayers of the monks here will never be to your disadvantage.

In answer to your inquiry regarding the region east of this place, it is my duty to inform you that, I, too have heard the reports you mention and have pondered the meaning of the chalices of blood: I have concluded that although this means of showing devotion is rare, the people of that region are reputed to be obdurate in their zeal, and for that reason, cups in memory of the Sacrifice of Our Lord are placed in sacred niches, to give thanks to God for Man's salvation. These cups symbolize the covenant of the Christians with our God which was secured by the blood of Redemption. The practice you described is not widespread, but it shows the degree to which the people in that part of the mountains will go to keep their faith alive.

You have dealt most fairly to us, as people of the Book, and surely you can understand the piety that spurs on these tributes. I myself would not encourage such extremes of worship for those not in Orders, but I admire the ardor of the people who remember their Savior in this way. You would be wise, I think, to respect their tributes and to make no attempt to stop their rites, for that could well bring about an uprising that would disgrace you and all Christians.

Many of the people in that part of the mountains cannot easily reach a church or monastery in which to worship, and these cups are signs of their worship in the absence of priests. I do not suppose you would hold these people in contempt if they prayed to Allah at the rising sun; so I beseech you not to stop them from making their offerings. These are humble people, esteemed Moor, most of them villagers, shepherds, and woodsmen; their religion is simple but powerful. If you succeed in putting an end to the leaving of these cups, you will not bring the people to your faith, you will only drive them to greater and more secret devotions, and perhaps fuel a rebellion that would not benefit anyone, Moor or Christian, in any way

You are in a position to honor what these people have done, and I beg you in the name of the God Whom we both revere, to spare the people from any act that would lessen their opportunity to venerate that sacred blood that was spilled for them. Do not impose restrictions on their demonstrations of fidelity to their religion, for that would do your own beliefs a disservice, as well as working against the just laws you have given to our people. If you truly intend to show a regard for the people of the Book, I ask you not to curtail this most conscientious of exercises. It is of the first importance for Christians that the blood of the Savior be honored. It is one of the central purposes of the Mass, so that Communion is achieved. To this end, we offer wine and bread as the blood and body of Christ. You must see that the people in the mountains are creating their own offering in their search for Communion.

As I have said, it is my belief that they do this in remembrance of the tale that says that after the crucifixion, the Apostle Sanct' Iago carried the cup of the Last Meal to the Iberian Peninsula, away from the strife in the Holy Land, and entrusted it to a company of warrior-monks, who have guarded it ever since. By leaving these cups of blood in sacred places, the people recall the story that has made them privy to the great mystery of Christians—transubstantiation. You cannot comprehend what power this gives to devout Christians, or the promise it secures them. These people of the mountains show us the depths of their faith in this way, for their homage makes them one with the warrior-monks, and gives them some hope of Heaven. You may force them to cease their humble celebration, but you will not silence the tale, for it is known that Sanct' Iago came to Hispania to preserve the Christian teachings and the way of Christ, and that he protects us even now.

Whether or not the tale of the warrior-monks is true, we of the old Roman provinces of Hispania know that there is much to gain from venerating the story as a means of preserving the faith which we, as Christians, know to be true. More than a tale recounted in every chapel and convent, church and monastery, it is recorded in our sacred chronicles that Sanct' Iago did indeed come here, with his treasures and his calendar—the one we use to this day. Our faith has survived thus far. I ask—out of respect for a great tradition—that you not deprive the mountain people of their offerings.

I pray that my accounts herein have moved you to show regard for our religion and opened your heart to the cause of the mountain folk, who have left cups of blood in tribute to Our Lord. Their simple demonstration of the promise of the Resurrection and the Life that is to Come is humbling to us all. May Our God bring understanding and compassion to your heart and move you to be merciful to the people of the region in question. It is important that you let it be known that you will not intrude in any way in this holy work, for otherwise my fellow Christians might well lose heart and, in the erroneous conviction that you would punish them for their piety, cease entirely their devotional offerings. They will gladly pay their double taxes for the surety that their religion will be allowed to continue unhindered.

May God open your heart. May you always know wisdom in your ruling. May God bestow high regard upon you, and bring you to grace. May your family always be thankful for you. May your children do you credit. May they speak of you from age to age as a worthy and compassionate judge.

With my personal approbation, and my prayers for your well-being in this life and the life that is to come,

Blaziuz Gagin
Primos, Sancta Cruce

At Usca, on the 16ᵗʰ day of June in the 722ⁿᵈ year of man's Salvation in the calendar of Sanct' Iago.

6

Two Moors remained of the stragglers captured in the last nine days. One of them was weak and disoriented, ready to leave the pains of the world for the houris of Paradise. The other had resisted and was now locked in a contest of wills with Chimenae.

"It is most entertaining," she told her clan when they gathered at her stone house. "And Sanct' Germain has been useful." This concession was as much praise as she was prepared to offer.

Overhead the sky was dense with clouds, and from time to time, thunder muttered in the higher peaks, heralded by sprinks of lightning. The air was close, heavy as a winter mantel, and still as an ambush. The clan was restless, wanting to be about their night's hunting before the rain came and immobilized them. The distant thunder provided an accompaniment to their gathering.

"It is nearly mid-summer," called out Achona. "We have not long to hunt."

Wembo seconded her. "And rain is coming."

"I will not hold you long," said Chimenae. "Which village supplies the next two-legged goat?" She knew the answer but wanted to be told as a reminder to the rest.

"Mont Calcius. Tomorrow. Possibly the night after." Aulutiz frowned in annoyance. "Is there anything we need to know about the Moors?"

"Then all of you will have what you want, and I will use the Moors a little longer." Chimenae could not conceal a quick, satisfied smile.

"Have you learned enough from them to make it worthwhile to keep them both alive another night? It is dangerous to let them live when they have seen so much, is it not?" Edic asked, a hint of criticism in his voice. "Would it not be better to finish them both and be done with it?"

Chimenae considered her answer. "I have found out a little—not enough yet. I know now there are parties of soldiers and slaves and slaves cutting down trees to the east and south of us."

"We knew that," scoffed Achona, encouraging others to share her scorn.

"They are coming higher into the mountains," said Chimenae. "They may eventually reach our region. Whether it is their intention, they are driving game higher into the mountains, and they will bring in their goats and sheep to graze after they have taken our trees to make ships."

"Still nothing new," said Edic with some concern.

Chimenae pointed to Edic. "Do you doubt me? Do you question what I have learned? Say if you do."

"I do not doubt you," Edic responded at once.

"Good." She singled out Dorioz. "You will bring the goat tomorrow, or the next night. Mont Calcius has yet to choose whom it will be; they may have to waylay a traveler or shepherd—no matter. And you may partake of him first." Then she swung around and looked directly at Wembo. "You will not share in the goat. Nor will you." This was to Achona. "You are treading near the edge, my girl. Do not press me."

If Achona was afraid, she showed no trace of it as she faced Chimenae. "Or you will make me a goat for the Moors?" A faintly derogatory smile curled her lips.

"Achona. Don't," Aulutiz said urgently.

"Very good, my son," Chimenae approved. "Now, all of you, listen to me. If rain comes, go at once to your resting places and secure them. We do not want the villagers to assume they can neglect their offerings. The storm will pass quickly and it may be that you may hunt still before dawn. If not, tomorrow night, or the night after, there is the two-legged goat and hunting to sustain us. I will have more to tell you when we meet then." She raised her arms and stood in that posture until all her tribe had gone and only San-Ragoz remained. "Come. I need you to speak with Yamut for me."

"Do you expect he will say anything more? He is very stubborn." San-Ragoz did not want to be part of the questioning; he was convinced that Yamut ibn Rabi could tell no more of the Moorish plans because he knew no more.

"All the more reason to persist," said Chimenae, and went into her stone house, holding the door for him to come inside.

Two oil lamps burned in the cave-like interior, lending their little flags of light and the smell of burning tallow to the place. High up on each wall there was a single, narrow window with a plank shutter; all four of them were open, but admitted little more than the oppressive night air; the flames of the oil lamps burned without wavering. There was a high table with two couches flanking it; the Moors lay on the nearer couch, kept in place with wide belts of braided leather and foot restraints of hinged wood. One of the Moors was pale and inert, his eyes beginning to turn upward in his head; his breathing was shallow and listless and his flesh had acquired a waxy texture. This was Marid ibn Ali, and he was dying. The other Moor was alert and angry, his body straining against his bonds, his face flushed with his emotion, his presence dangerous.

"Tell him I greet him," said Chimenae to San-Ragoz.

"She greets you, Yamut ibn Rabi," said San-Ragoz, his speech flawless but slightly accented.

"She should die. Allah must will it. She is a shameless woman and an unclean thing." Yamut ibn Rabi said through clenched teeth. "Jackals will eat her private parts and scorpions will nest in her hair."

"Tell him not to curse me," said Chimenae, correctly interpreting Yamut ibn Rabi's tone of voice.

"You should not displease her," San-Ragoz recommended. "She is a sharp-tempered woman."

"I do not need you to tell me," said Yamut ibn Rabi. "I have proof of it lying beside me." He angled his jaw toward Marid ibn Ali. "She has done unholy things to him, and he will die of them, may Allah send him a kind death." He set his face as if prepared to face the forces of Shaitan.

"What a fine, refractory heart is his," Chimenae approved sarcastically. "How worthwhile his obstinacy."

"He will not obey you," San-Ragoz told Chimenae while he scrutinized Yamut ibn Rabi's infuriated visage. "It is probably useless to try."

"I do not like being cursed," she said with false cordiality, inclining her head in Yamut ibn Rabi's direction. "I will make him pay for all his maledictions."

San-Ragoz faced Chimenae. "What do you want to know from him? I do not think he will tell you much, but I will ask."

"You keep telling me he will say nothing, but I hear many words," Chimenae said, her mouth pursing with annoyance. "You will not amuse yourself at my expense."

"No one is amused," San-Ragoz assured her before he once again spoke to Yamut ibn Rabi. "If you know anything about the military plans of your forces, it would be wisest for you to reveal them."

"Do you think so?" Yamut ibn Rabi glared at him. "Tell that she-devil that I know nothing, and if I did, I would never tell her." He spat to make his point.

San-Ragoz translated his outburst and waited while Chimenae prowled about the stone house. "Do you want me to repeat your questions?"

"No," she said, stopping still. "Tell him that if he will say what he knows, I will kill him quickly and cleanly, with a single stroke. He will not have to endure the agony his comrade is experiencing." Her smile was broad and insincere.

"That may be suitable," San-Ragoz said uncertainly.

"Tell him," she ordered, her smile vanished and her voice harsh.

Sam-Ragoz did as he was told, adding, "She may keep her word, or she may not."

"The offspring of a basilisk and swine!" Yamut ibn Rabi exclaimed. "She is made up of curses and infernal things."

Chimenae came closer. "Tell him," she said dulcetly as she reached out to run her fingers along his brow, "that if he will not earn himself a clean death, I will make him my lover and my slave before allowing him to die. What he sees in Marid is nothing compared to what I will compel him to do. He will be grateful to lick my foot."

"Do you think she can do such a thing?" Yamut ibn Rabi shouted out when San-Ragoz had finished his translating, his fear underneath revealed in the high pitch of his words.

"Yes; I do," said San-Ragoz as bluntly as he could. "I think she would enjoy doing it. You would be a fool to attempt to best her. Better to answer her questions than to put her will to the test." He did not like admitting so much, but he was appalled by the possibility of Yamut ibn Rabi becoming Chimenae's abject idolater.

"I would die first," Yamut ibn Rabi vowed.

"You would not have that opportunity," said San-Ragoz sadly.

"She is only a woman. How can she undo me? I have not been badly wounded, as Marid ibn Ali has been. I have more purpose than many others have." He bared his teeth. "She is a demon, and you are her servant."

"I am worse than a demon," said Chimenae when San-Ragoz repeated Yamut ibn Rabi's accusation. "A demon is a fable for children. I am as real as the blood in your veins." She came and leaned over the two Moors while San-Ragoz translated for Yamut ibn Rabi. When San-Ragoz stopped speaking, she bent down and kissed Yamut's mouth, maintaining the contact while Yamut tried to twist away from her.

"Stop it," San-Ragoz insisted as Chimenae took hold of Yamut ibn Rabi's shoulders. "Do not do this to him. It does nothing but make him resist you."

Chimenae lifted her head. "I know that," she said with a smirk. "That is why I enjoy it."

Yamut ibn Rabi was spitting epithets at her, condemning her in every way he could; there was fright in the back of his eyes now, as if he finally believed that she was capable of hurting him in precisely the way she promised she would. "You threaten me with death, but you do nothing. End this. Kill me and be done with it," he howled as she began to chuckle.

Beside Yamut ibn Rabi, Marid ibn Ali turned glazed eyes on Chimenae and whispered endearments to her, his breath fading even as he strove to speak her name.

"By Allah-the-All-Seeing, *you are despicable,*" Yamut ibn Rabi yelled, but whether he addressed Chimenae or Marid ibn Ali was impossible to guess; his condemnation was punctuated by a swath of lightning in the eastern sky.

"How good of you to rail at me," said Chimenae, once again caressing his brow. "You take away any doubts I might have in my plans for you." She pointed to San-Ragoz. "Do not tell him that."

"What is the she-swine saying?" Yamut ibn Rabi demanded when San-Ragoz did not speak to him.

"She is giving you compliments you would not like, as she intends you would not," said San-Ragoz, solving his conscience with the inner conviction that this was near enough to the truth. He looked at Chimenae as she touched Marid ibn Ali's hands and was rewarded with a faint, pathetic smile; thunder drubbed in the distance as if to underscore her actions. "Yes. Oh, yes. One day," she said dreamily, "very soon, Yamut will be as appreciative of my attentions as Marid is now."

Instead of translating Chimenae's toying with him, San-Ragoz said, "Your anger only tempts her to be more outrageous. You are goading her, and she is gratified when she can respond as keenly as your fury permits her. If you contain your emotions, she will not tease you as much. Believe this, for I am telling you the truth as if I held the *Qran* in my hand." He saw the astonishment in Yamut ibn Ali's eyes, and he added, "Say something derogatory to me—quickly."

Baffled, Yamut ibn Rabi blinked, then called San-Ragoz the spawn of afreets and vultures.

"Very good," San-Ragoz approved, telling Chimenae. "He thinks I am lying to intimidate him. I have said I am not; I doubt he is persuaded."

"Why should he think that?" Chimenae asked, her eyes shining like steel. "What have you been telling him?"

San-Ragoz answered indirectly. "Among his people, women do not lead. Csimenae. Women are supposed to devote themselves to their fathers, their husbands, and their sons. When they do, the men reward them by affording the same treatment they give their dogs: they keep them all together in a fine kennel and give them eunuchs to guard them." He recalled the women he had seen in Africa, who starved themselves so that their men might eat, and the women of the harem, who were kept in ignorance and idleness so that they could serve the whims of the Emir's son.

"That cannot be true," Chimenae burst out. "It is false. I know it is false. You are saying this to mislead me."

Recalling Charis, and the wives of Numair ibn Isffah ibn Musa, San-Ragoz shook his head. "No, I am not. I want you to know why he does not believe you, and why he cannot understand what you say." He looked down at Yamut ibn Rabi, saying to him, "You cannot frighten her with threats and curses. You can only give her pause if you take the time to respond sensibly."

"Sensibly!" Yamut ibn Rabi jeered. "Why should I do so much for her?"

"It is the only thing she will respect," San-Ragoz said, his voice dropping to a near-whisper.

This time when Yamut ibn Rabi cursed, it was under his breath.

"What is he saying?" asked Chimenae asked, disappointment turning the corners of her mouth down. "You have to tell me, Sanct' Germain."

"He says he is not afraid of you," said San-Ragoz. "He is afraid for his comrade."

Chimenae nodded once. "That will change," she said. "You had best go outside, Sanct' Germain. Marid is going to going to make his last offering to me." She paused, then said with deliberate provocation. "A pity that I have tasted this Yamut's blood as much as I have. It is too late to make him one of mine; I have too much of him in me now. It is a pity." She shrugged. "Still, I might make an exception for him, if he will become as much my ally as he is my foe. Tell him that."

Before San-Ragoz could speak lightning struck again, much brighter, showing vividly in three of the four windows, and followed almost at once by an eruption of thunder that bludgeoned the air.

Marid ibn Ali made a feeble effort to reach out to Chimenae, but he had no strength to sustain his exertion.

Very quietly and steadily, San-Ragoz translated for Yamut ibn Rabi, adding, "She may well do it."

"I could never surrender so to a woman." He squirmed as much as his restraints would allow so that he could see Chimenae. "You do not have the authority to bend me to your uses. I am above your threats, even death. Nothing you do could change that, for I am a follower of the Prophet of Allah." Then he looked at San-Ragoz. "You may tell her what you wish. I do not care if it is a lie or the truth."

San-Ragoz translated the first and last part of what Yamut ibn Rabi said, but omitted his condemnation at the middle. He gave Chimenae a long stare. "Do you still want me to go?"

"Of course," she said impatiently. "Unless you are curious enough to want to watch."

"I think not," said San-Ragoz, unable to mask his aversion. "Am I to remain nearby or may I depart for the night?"

"Hunt awhile if you like, but come back before dawn, for the spoils," she said at her most magnanimous.

San-Ragoz did as she told him, and saw as he shut the door that Wembo had come back to watch over the stone house.

"The lightning struck a way up the slope; there are trees burning," he said to San-Ragoz, as if that accounted for his presence. He kept his hand on the axe hanging from his belt.

"It may come again," San-Ragoz said, his thoughts in turmoil. Was Chimenae testing him once more, or had she already concluded he would never be part of her singular world and was prepared to be rid of him for all time? Was she informing him that she would not allow him to leave her region, that he would ally with her or die the True Death? She was capable of such finality, and her ambivalence was strong enough to impel her to kill him. Was she waiting for him to try to run, so that she could give her orders and justify them to everyone, including herself? Was there any way he could bridge the gulf that yawned between them without driving her to attack him? He did not like the way his ruminations were tending, but he could not ignore the likelihood that Chimenae would reach a point where she would demonstrate her authority over her vampires by killing him, for she wanted no ally who might prove a rival; his death would be a potent object lesson for those of her blood who had become restive. In the next few days he would have to leave or risk becoming a victim of her dreads and ambitions.

Finally the clouds gave up their burden in a display of rain, lightning, and thunder that shook the mountains even as the ground ran, carrying loose debris into freshets and rills, promising a gathering flood at lower elevations. The rain was dense, falling without wind in a direct line from the heavens, battering through the trees and soaking everything.

San-Ragoz's clothing was saturated almost at once, becoming heavy and clinging; he told himself that at least he would be cleaner when the rain stopped. With that philosophical observation for consolation, he started back the way he had come, letting the rain pour over him, not minding when it sapped a little of his strength. Giving himself a short time to hunt, he went past another of the improvised cup shrines located in a grove of trees where he noticed a few of the cups had been overturned and left; San-Ragoz could not determine if this had been deliberate or accidental, but it left him with an uneasy feeling that bore down on him with the rain as he continued up the slope toward the barren ridge and Chimenae's stone house.

Half a dozen of Chimenae's vampires had already arrived; they were prowling about the stone house seeking shelter from the misery of the rain. None of them spoke to San-Ragoz or to one another. As San-Ragoz hung back, a jagged blade of lightning gashed through the clouds, striking the largest of the cups and reducing it to misshapen slag while thunder pummeled the ridge.

Achona arrived in the yawning silence that followed. She did her best to swagger, but she could not hide the desperation that came from her like a stench. Staying a short distance away, she paid no attention to the rain or to the others as they came to the stone house.

Finally Aulutiz strode out of the woods and onto the exposed ridge. He had a stag slung over his shoulders; the animal was stunned but still alive. "Wembo!" Aulutiz called out. "Take this."

Wembo emerged from the shadows of the stone house and came to do as he was bid. "A fine animal."

"He had been running in fright. The storm panicked him. I brought him down without effort." Aulutiz was boasting and his boast was calm, confident.

"Are we all here?" Aulutiz asked nonchalantly as he gave the deer over to Wembo.

"Two are missing," said Wembo, taking up the stag.

Aulutiz was about to ask who they were when the door of the stone house opened and Chimenae stepped out. "There is a dead Moor to be disposed of in the mountains. This storm should make that an easy task." She looked about her. "Who shall do this thing for me?"

There was a clamor of voices, and one or two were bold enough to step forward to offer their services.

Chimenae motioned the impetuous volunteers back. "Tamosh," she said. "You and Ennati will do this. Make sure you choose a remote place. No one is to find any of the Moors for at least two generations."

Tamosh ducked his head. "I will see to it."

"And Blaga, you will bring the two-legged goat tomorrow. It must be this next night. Take Ennati with you." She pointed to the copper-haired man standing beside Blaga. "Tell them, Dorioz; tell them in the village what we demand. Go now, so you can speak to the guards. Make sure that they understand it must be ready by nightfall. I will accept no delays." Chimenae moved quickly to Aulutiz's side. "You have brought a stag, my son. That is good of you."

"You saw me?" He was startled, and disappointed with himself for being taken unaware.

"Certainly, Aulutiz. You should not doubt me." She walked away from her son, only to turn back to him. "Remember who I am."

"Yes, Matra." He scowled at her, to which she chuckled.

"Chimenae," said Edic, coming forward. "You must consider. You cannot continue to hide bodies in the forest."

"Edic," said Chimenae with exaggerated patience, "you are too timorous. Who is going to find them, but wolves?"

"I say you are growing too reckless. We have gone unchallenged for many years, and it has made you complacent. You have not been vigilant, thinking that you will not be tested by the villagers now that the Moors have come; that is foolhardy. You are no longer protected as you once were. These times are not as safe as twenty years ago." He shook his head. "You will draw attention to our presence, and the villagers will not protect us. They will be glad to be rid of—"

"Our kind," she finished for him. "Yes, yes, yes. You have said this before. And if it gladdens you to know, San-Ragoz agrees with you." She dismissed him abruptly. "You have heard my orders. That is the end of it."

San-Ragoz could see that Edic was disconcerted; he tried to form a protestation but decided it was useless. He shook his head in defeat and turned away.

"The storm may last through the morning, so choose your resting places with care, away from running water," Chimenae reminded them all. "Ennati and Tamosh, come with me. Blaga, Cossadin, Merez, you are to patrol the forest until dawn. Be vigilant. I will want your account at dusk. The rest of you, go with Aulutiz and feed on the stag. See that Mont Calcius is given the body, to remind them why they must give us our two-legged goat."

A few of her tribe attempted to catch her attention but to no avail; the downpour soon drove them off the ridge toward the place Wembo had taken the stag. San-Ragoz went off toward the place where his native earth was hidden, grateful he had not been asked to translate anything more for Chimenae that night.

By noon the clouds had passed and the sky was bright and hot; sunlight streamed down on the hollow where San-Ragoz had taken shelter, waking him from his stupor with the burning sting of its touch. He sat up, listening and alert, and wishing he had a change of clothing, for his garments were damp, ragged, and the hems were smirched with mud. The ground beneath him was slightly damp, cooling him enough to make him able to bear the impact of the sun. Rubbing his face, he felt the slow-growing stubble emerging. If he could find a weapon with a proper edge, he might risk shaving, but without such a tool, he knew the wiser course was to wait. He frowned, considering all that had taken place the night before, and again he wondered if it might be prudent to leave and take his chances being hunted. But he suspected that as long as Yamut ibn Rabi was able to speak, Chimenae would want him to translate for her, which gave him a few more days in which to plan.

With many hours of daylight still ahead of him, San-Ragoz felt at loose ends; he had none of his usual occupations available to him—he had no provisions for making medicaments beyond gathering herbs, and no place to store them once he had them; he had no books to read and no vellum or ink that would make it possible for him to write; he had no instruments on which to play; and worst of all, there was no companion with whom to talk. He had long valued his friend and bondsman, the ghoul Ruges, and not primarily for his service and attendance, but for his comprehension, his experience of long, long life. In the centuries since San-Ragoz had brought him back from death, they had been nearly constant companions; this separation of years had never weighed more on San-Ragoz than it did that day.

Finally making up his mind, San-Ragoz left his hidden native earth and began making a rapid trek through the forest, searching out tracks and trails that led upward and that could guide him out of the region without recourse to the few roads traveled by men. He came upon two more groves with offerings of cups of blood set out on stones or in ancient niches; he noticed that the blood was coagulated, and so the cups had to have been set out some time before. These remote groves served to provide him a rough estimate of how far Chimenae's region extended, and to gauge the distance he would have to travel to be out of the reach of her and those of her blood; it was an impressive range, and one he knew it was prudent to extend beyond the groves. To be safe, he decided he would need to be at least ten thousand paces beyond such shrines. He found it repellent to think of them as being of his blood as well, although he knew they were. It distressed him to think what might become of them, for clearly, they could not continue as they were. With the increasing acrimony and invidiousness, there would be a point where their rancor could no longer be contained, and when that occurred, San-Ragoz suspected that in spite of her strength of will, Chimenae would be unable to maintain the control she had contrived to exercise thus far; he did not know if she was appraising her tribe's devotion, but he reckoned if that were the case, she would fail. He realized that warning her would do no good, for it had not succeeded before now, yet he could not rid himself of the gnawing uneasiness that rebellion would be more catastrophic for the whole tribe than Chimenae's tyranny had been.

By late afternoon, San-Ragoz had covered more than forty thousand paces and was feeling the strain of his efforts. Turning his steps in the direction of Chimenae's stone house, some eight or nine thousand paces distant, he settled into the long, clean stride that was faster than it looked, taking him along the shepherds' trails to Aqua Frates and from there upward through the long shadows toward the treeless ridge.

Wembo and Edic were already at the stone house; they swung around protectively as San-Ragoz approached, the last glow of sunset fading behind him. Both of them held their weapons as if they were intending to use them. "The stranger," said Wembo to Edic. There were no greetings offered.

San-Ragoz went to where the cups had been let and noticed that there were fewer than the evening before. It was an ominous turn, he told himself.

Aulutiz was next to arrive, and after him, Achona. By the time the stars were fully bright, all the vampires but Dorioz were waiting for Chimenae.

She came out of her stone house with a force of purpose that was apparent from her stance to the way she moved the door. She paused in the frame of the open door, waiting until she had the full attention of all those gathered. "By sunset tomorrow," she announced, "Yamut ibn Rabi will be one of you."

There was an appalled silence; then Aulutiz howled, anguished beyond the scope of words.

"Chimenae!" Edic shouted, having recovered from his stupefaction an instant ahead of the rest. His cry was taken up by most of the others.

San-Ragoz felt a cold fist gather within him.

"It is done!" Her voice cracked over the others. "There shall be no questions." She took a step forward and closed her door behind her. "This is my will."

This time the shouts of protest were more angry than shocked, and a few of the tribe dared to curse.

"*That is enough!*" Chimenae commanded, and then waited for silence to return; when it did, it was sullen.

It was Aulutiz who braved her wrath. "Matra, you have wronged us," he said in quiet reproach. "You bring an enemy into our numbers."

"Not an enemy," Chimenae told him. "He will be our best friend."

"Your friend, perhaps," said Achona, taking a chance.

"Achona, you are being foolish," said Chimenae.

Very deliberately, Achona laughed. "I am not alone in what I think."

Some shouted words of encouragement, others of derision, and for a long moment, dissent took over the tribe.

Then Aulutiz stepped forward. "No. No. You must all stop! My mother has done this thing for a reason. Let her explain it to us."

Once again the vampires grew quiet.

The shift was subtle, but San-Ragoz sensed it as surely as if the ground had twitched beneath his feet; some portion of Chimenae's authority had passed irrevocably to her son.

"I do not have to explain myself to anyone," Chimenae insisted, pulling her arm away from Aulutiz's protective touch.

Into this conflict-ridden confrontation came Blaga; he was leading a hooded and bound man in traveler's robes. He brought the two-legged goat through the group, directly to Chimenae. "The villagers at Mont Calcius say they can spare no more of their own. They send you this instead."

At the edge of the gathering, San-Ragoz stood more observantly, a mounting sense he did not understand making him apprehensive; he saw the increased animation in Chimenae's tribe as the two-legged goat was turned to face Chimenae.

"Remove the hood. Let us see what the villagers have sent us," said Chimenae.

Blaga did as he was told, Ennati holding the bound figure while Blaga pulled off the hood and held it up as if it were a treasure.

The man revealed was sandy-haired and middle-aged, lean of cheek and austere of expression. He looked directly at Chimenae. "Csimenae," said Ruges.

San-Ragoz did not move as he stared at his old friend, apprehension changing to trepidation as he saw Chimenae's expression set in one of fury. "*You!*" She made the word a curse. "A thousand devils! It is not enough that *he*"—she flung her hands in San-Ragoz's direction—should be here, but now *you!*" She signaled to her companions to come closer to Ruges. "What use are you to us? You are no two-legged goat." She pointed to San-Ragoz this time. "You are execrable. How can you do this—having this creature of yours come here? I cannot endure the sight of you—of either of you. Mont Calcius will pay for this affront."

Those gathered around her were confused and distressed, seeing the depth of her rage; their whispers were a susurrus against the bluster of the wind. Finally Edic dared to raise his voice. "Who is this man?"

"He's not a man at all," said Chimenae, dismissing the notion with a shrug. "He is the tool of Sanct' Germain. He was here with his master, long ago."

"Another vampire," groaned Aulutiz, and was echoed by the protests of a dozen of the others.

San-Ragoz had recovered from his first astonishment and was now scrutinizing those gathered around Chimenae, trying to discern how they were reacting to this latest phenomenon.

"No, not a vampire. He is something other." Chimenae walked up to Ruges and poked at his chest. "What are you? What are you?"

"I am a ghoul, as well you know," he said without emotion, looking only at her. "I have come to help my master; I have been seeking him for five years and more. When he was taken away, he said he might be found here. The villagers in Mont Calcius took my chests and my horses when they seized me."

Chimenae scowled. "You will have it all back again, every bit of it," she announced with grim determination. "And you shall be permitted to leave here, for all you have done for me and mine in the past; I do not forget these things, and I know my obligations. We shall choose a two-legged goat from among their numbers for ourselves. They have lost the right to select the goat. It is now our right." This evoked a cry of approval from those around her. "Let us make the hunt worth our while. We will choose *two* goats, so that they will know not to disgrace me and mine again."

Aulutiz led a ragged cheer. "Finally you give us sport," he approved, and was echoed by most of the rest, although Achona hung back, her face sulky.

"This is troublesome," Edic said as the enthusiastic noise died down. "The people of Mont Calcius have defied us before."

"It is because that was my village," said Chimenae, "the one I held for my son. They never recovered from my departure." She pointed to Aulutiz. "You will bear the news to them—that we will come soon to take what is owed us."

"But they will not want us to do anything so . . ." Aulutiz sought for the word, and said finally, "like fighting. They will fight back."

"Not against me," said Chimenae. "They will not have the courage. They owe me too much. That village is *mine*. They *owe me* fealty. If they have forgot that, I will remind them." The fury in her eyes dissipated. "I do this for you, my son. I held the village so that it would be yours."

Aulutiz nodded in response to this old theme. "So you say."

"Do you doubt it?" Chimenae studied him intensely, dismay building within her. "How can you doubt it? After all I did? Ask this person"—she pointed to Ruges—"if you doubt me after all this time. He saw what I did. He knows." She touched Aulutiz's cheek gently. "This is for you, my son."

"If it is," said Aulutiz, his doubt becoming a challenge, "then do as you have just promised and send Sanct' Germain and his servant away. They do not belong with us." As Chimenae stepped back, Aulutiz pressed on. "You say that you are obliged to show him gratitude. Well, then, send him away. Send them both. Do not go back on your word. So long as he is here, I do not think you will be free of his influence."

"How can you expect treachery of me? I have said they may go, have I not?" Chimenae demanded, shaking her head adamantly.

Aulutiz was ready with his answer. "I can question you as your son. Do not pretend you have never countermanded an order in the past. If you intend to protect me as you say you intend to—and if you hold our clan in the regard you claim—you will have them leave and soon, as you should have let the Moor die rather than make him one of us."

There were whispers among the gathered tribe, and an uneasy movement toward the stone house, as if to get closer to Chimenae and Aulutiz. Ruges was shoved up against the door and pinned there while the confrontation continued, San-Ragoz moved as near as he dared, knowing how volatile the situation had become.

"This is intolerable. How can you question me?" Chimenae cried out. "You have no notion what I have done for you—for all of you."

"Then do one more thing," Aulutiz said. "Send those two away. Or give your Moor the True Death. Here. Now. So we may see it happen."

"That is what you want, isn't it? That is what you want me to do: kill the Moor. These two do not matter. They are nothing to any of us, nor should they be more than that. You're after Yamut ibn Rabi, aren't you?" Chimenae asked cynically. "You want Yamut ibn Rabi truly dead, so you make this absurd request." She laughed without mirth. "Very well, my son, I will play your game this once." With that, she reached out and took Ruges by the shoulder. "You and your master will leave. At once. With no more than what you came with. You will have two days to depart the region, and then, if you have not gone, I will not vouch for your safety. My clan will honor my word for two days. Will you not?" This last was to Aulutiz.

"We will," said Aulutiz, his voice raised enough to carry. "They will have two days and two nights to get beyond this region. Two days and two nights, no more and no less." A muttered agreement from the rest served to encourage him. "The Moor will have nothing to fear from us." It was a graceless concession, and one that evoked fewer sounds of compliance.

"It is done, then." Chimenae thrust Ruges into the crowd, saying as she did. "You and your master will leave at once. You will take what is yours from Mont Calcius, and if anything is refused you, I will make them answer for it. You will have two days and two nights to get beyond our reach. When the two days and two nights are over, you will be hunted."

A bellow of anticipation came from the gathered vampires as Ruges, his hands still bound, stumbled through them toward San-Ragoz. As they met, Ruges managed to smile. "Well met, my master."

San-Ragoz managed a chuckle as he freed Ruges' hands. "By all the forgotten gods, I hope so." Was he actually dismissed? he wondered as he clasped Ruges by the shoulders. Had Chimenae decided to be rid of him at last? Was this mercurial determination genuine, or had she some deeper intrigue in mind? He would not wait to find out. "Are we able to travel?"

"I have two horses and a mule, in Mont Calcius; I came with them, and therefore I should be allowed to claim them," said Ruges. "If the villagers will part with them, we may be gone by mid-day." He looked around circumspectly, asking just above a whisper. "What has happened here?"

"I will tell you, but later," San-Ragoz assured him.

Chimenae raised her voice again. "Sanct' Germain must have his things. And we must have an accounting. We go to Mont Calcius!"

This time all the tribe roared approval, and stood aside for Chimenae as she started away from her stone house toward the slope that led down the mountain to the village she had claimed for her son a century ago.

Text of a letter form Timuz ibn Musa ibn Maliq in Usca to Numair ibn Isffah ibn Musa in Karmona.

Before Allah, the All-Compassionate, I tell you, my nephew, that your soldiers are chasing a dead man. I have received the report of Omma ibn Ali from his own lips, and I tell you that it is impossible for

San-Ragoz to have survived; there is no report of such a man at the passes we control, nor has any ship's captain taken the fugitive aboard a ship. We know he did not flee to the north, perhaps to avoid the fighting there, or perhaps because he did not think he could escape us in that direction. We do know he left Zaraugusta headed east and north into the mountains, but we can find no trace of him beyond that, in spite of the determined searches of your soldiers. You have ordered a thorough search, and your men have done all they can to carry out your wishes. It is not by accident that these mountains have proven a barrier to our efforts. The mountains are steep and difficult to travel and the villagers are not friendly. Furthermore, Omma ibn Ali has lost forty-two men in the region known as Sacred Blood: they have vanished as if into a void. If your soldiers have disappeared in those mountains, armed and mounted as they were, how little chance is there that San-Ragoz could succeed where they have failed?

I know you have sworn to have this San-Ragoz back, and I know you have declared that he will answer to you for his perfidy, but I ask you to think: it is possible that this man will not be found, except, perhaps, as a corpse, or a scattering of bones. Your men have better things to do than to tramp about these mountains, taking risks that endanger their lives, all so you may be satisfied in your vengeance. Not even those cutting timber on the lower slopes go willingly into the higher valleys, and the peasants say it is dangerous territory.

This is one man, my nephew, and a slave. What has he done that has made him worthy of your wrath, but put himself into danger? If by some quirk of fate he has managed to stay alive, he must be living like an animal, and among such people and beasts as would turn survival to torture. I do not think he is still alive, nor does Omma ibn Ali, who has said that he is certain San-Ragoz is not alive. Even the Christians here in Usca say that they are wary of the Sacred Blood region, and they do not venture there. If they are in accord with Omma ibn Ali, do you not suppose that it is futile to continue this search? How many of your soldiers must you lose before you are willing to accept San-Ragoz's death as unquestionable?

It is my intention to begin my return to Karmona in three days, for I have neglected my duties for too long on this fruitless quest. I will stop in Zaraugusta for a few days to see if I can garner any more information about San-Ragoz; I have offered rewards to Muslims and Christians alike for information that will bring this escaped slave to heel. There may be word brought from the mountains, or from the passes, that will tell us something of use, and if that should happen, I will pursue the matter as diligently as I can. But if I should learn nothing more, I will continue on to Karmona, where I shall present all my findings to you upon my arrival, and await your decision in their regard. Your soldiers are willing to do your bidding, although they have little stomach for this hunt.

For the sake of your father, let me urge you to consider carefully what you are doing. Forty-two soldiers are a high price to pay for a single slave. Let this be enough. If you keep on, you will surely bring disgrace to your father—may Allah send him many good years and healthy sons—and to our family. You cannot be willing to sacrifice so much for so little, when we have a grand opportunity before us, to claim this land for the Prophet—may He be praised forever—and to complete our campaign against the Franks. It would be folly to persist in this venture when there is so much more to gain in other emprise.

Timus ibn Musa ibn Maliq

four days after the Summer Solstice

PART III

CHIMENA

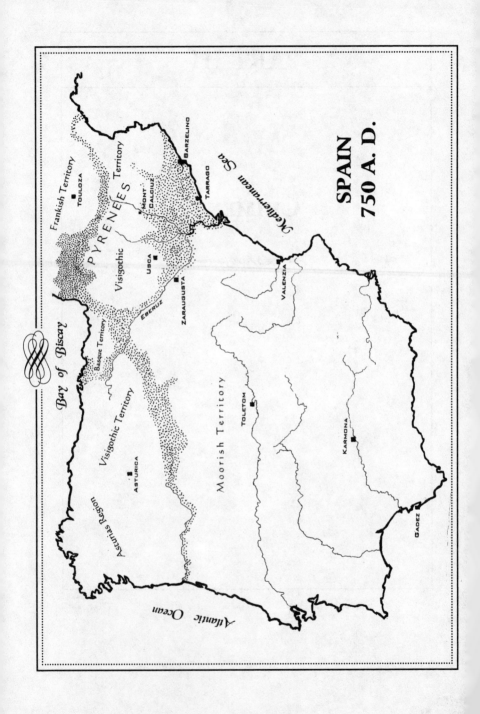

SPAIN
750 A. D.

Mediterranean Sea

BARZELINO
TARRAGO

MONT
CALOUZ

Frankish Territory
TOULOZA

PYRENEES Territory

Visigothic

USCA

EBERUZ

ZARAUGUSTA

VALENZIA

Basque Territory

Bay of Biscay

Visigothic Territory

Moorish Territory

TOLETOM

KARMONA

ASTURICA

Asturias Region

GADEZ

Atlantic Ocean

*T*ext of a letter from the Comites Egnacius of Touloza to Manrigo, Dux of Asturica.

To my most dear, my most esteemed brother in faith, the high-reputed Manrigo, Dux of Asturica, the greetings of Comites Egnacius of Touloza, for so I style myself in the certain knowledge that my claim to the title will be upheld and I will finally come into the honors and dignity my father sought to bestow upon me at his death. Since you have the respect of me to address me thus, I will uphold my claims in these pages.

Were it not for this most pressing matter of securing my inheritance that keeps me here, I would bring men to help you in your fight against the perfidious Moors who have everywhere striven to claim these good Christian lands for their own, and have brought suffering and trouble to the world. I am unable to say what distress I feel at this necessary disappointment, but you must doubtless comprehend the reasons for my decision in this matter, for your position is secure, and you have no interloper of a half-brother attempting to claim what is yours. Had my mother lived, her testimony would have ended this whole absurdity at once, but as she has been called to Heaven—the result of poison, administered, no doubt, by my half-brother's agents—she has no voice with which to plead my case. I am unable to trust any of my kin, for they are under the spell of my half-brother, who is said to be a great warrior instead of the coward he has shown himself to be.

It is the opinion of the holy hermit Meurisse, I must put my case to the Pope if ever I am to resolve it, and so I am committed to go to Roma and put my case before the Vicar of Christ and ask him to settle the matter once and for all. My half-brother might defy Moors and his peers, but he will not lose all by defying the Pope, if the soldiers truly fear the great man's power. I am prepared to fight for what is mine, and I am certain that no one will wonder at my determination to do this, although it does mean I will not be in Touloza again for more than a year, and in that time, I cannot help you as you would like, for which I ask your understanding. Were you in my position, I know you would do no differently than I must do. Our fathers fought side by side, and that is a most worthy thing, and I am aware of the obligation under which such vassalage places me. Yet until my land and my soldiers are truly mine to command, I cannot comply with your request, for I am to set out in nine days' time and already my preparations are underway. I can spare no men from my company to aid you, for they are escorting me.

Instead I am sending you a most worthy man: he speaks the language of the Moors and has traveled in their lands. He is called Ragoczy Germainus, although he is not German but from mountains far beyond the German lands. He is a learned and useful man, capable of smelting metals for weapons and treating wounds with medicaments of his own making. My men hold him in the highest regard, saying he is more formidable than a Moorish horseman. He journeys with a manservant called Rotiger who is from Gadez, or so he says. Ragoczy Germainus accords this servant great liberty and treats him as if they were comrades and not man and servant. He allows Rotiger to sleep in an antechamber on a bed rather than on a pallet outside his door; the two actually converse from time to time. You should find these two most useful, and capable of aiding you in your fight against the Moors at a time when I cannot. Man and master are devoted to one another, a devotion which you may be able to turn to your advantage, as I have done in the past. If you will look upon these two as indicative of my wish to aid you in your time of need, I will be most thankful, and will tell the Pope that I have done as much as I am able to in my present diminished state to put forth the cause of our people and our faith.

For bona fides, Ragoczy Germainus will bring with him a wax impression of my sigil, and by that you will know him. I must tell you he was at first reluctant to undertake this journey, but I have persuaded him through diverse means that his gifts would be far more useful to you than they presently are to me, and that his efforts on your behalf will earn my gratitude. Doubtless he has come to understand how crucial it is that he comply with my wishes in this regard, for if he fails to serve you well, he has friends here who will answer for his laxness. I should also tell you that the man plays a number of musical instruments, and will grace your court with songs and tales if you have need of such entertainments. He carries an Egyptian lyre with him; my men have listened to his singing many an evening, and joined in the better choruses. I have been glad of his service, and I am reluctant to sacrifice it, but either I must bring him to Roma with me, or I must send him to you, for if I leave him alone here, he is likely to be the target of my half-brother's malice, who has sworn to kill all those who support me. Be good to him for my sake and you will be amply rewarded. He is more of a treasure than you know, and so you will discover for yourself. Do not think I have done a paltry thing in sending him to you, for nothing could be further from the truth.

I pray God will guard and protect you and all you hold dear. In these hard times, we must put our trust in the justice of God and the strength of His Son, Who has defeated the Devils in Hell for the sake of those suffering in Hell. I will remark on your fortitude to the Pope and speak well of your deeds everywhere I go, you have my pledged word on it. We both know what it is to have enemies in this world. No doubt you will come to think of them as the means by which God tests our souls and determines our worthiness as Christians, even as we undertake the great tasks the world imposes upon us with purpose. May God defend my claim and reduce Perpontus to beggary and disgrace.

> *By the hand of Meiric the scribe,*
> *Comites Egnacius of Touloza, his mark*

four weeks after the Feast of the Kings, in the Year of Salvation 752

1

All day they had been heading uphill into the wind, hunched in their saddles over the bowed necks of their horses, their pluvials flapping around them like tethered wings, the three mules on the lead behind them laboring steadily along the merchants' road. Of their week of hard travel, this day had proved the most demanding, for the climb was steeper now than it had been, and the weather more severe. Shreds of clouds streamed overhead, and grass and trees thrashed in the onslaught; the high peaks, still snowbound, leached the gentle spring warmth from the day. The noise was so great that both men refrained from speaking, knowing they would not be heard. When they finally stopped in late afternoon, picking a site near a stream at the edge of a copse of pine where they would have a good view of the road in both directions as well as a modicum of shelter, they came out of their saddles as if they had been in battle.

"What do you think?" Rotiger shouted as he loosened the girths and eased the saddle off the back of his dun mare. He was almost numb with fatigue, and knew their animals must feel much the same as he did. "Are we going to reach the pass by tomorrow night?"

It was a long moment before Ragoczy Germainus answered, and when he did he seemed preoccupied. "I think the horses will need a day of rest once we're through the pass. I know I will." He pitched his voice to carry. "At least we have not encountered snow yet. That would slow us down." He was dressed in Byzantine fashion, in a short, belted dalmatica of heavy Chinese silk brocade showing phoenixes rising from their own ashes, surrounded by blazing red halos. His Persian leggings of heavy black silk had a decorated band down the center-front of his legs, on which was embroidered his eclipse device in silver. His pluvial of black wool was lined with wolf-fur. Only his thick-soled Frankish heuse revealed where he had begun this journey.

"Rest may be more difficult to get than you anticipate," said Rotiger. "What with the fighting still going on."

Ragoczy Germainus paused in his fixing the hobbles to his gray's front legs. "I would like to think you and I have learned to avoid fighting." The light, ironic note concealed his darker intent.

"When it is possible," said Rotiger, repeating it more loudly when he realized Ragoczy Germainus had not heard him.

"Do you think it will not be now?" Ragoczy Germainus asked, standing upright again to reach into his saddlebag for a handful of grain; he offered this to the gray, who whuffled in pleasure. "See that they all have a measure of oats," he said to Rotiger. "I will try to find wood enough for a small fire." He stared up into the tattered sky. "Although it may be unwise to light one in this wind."

"Truly," said Rotiger, nodding to show he understood. As he took oats from Ragoczy Germainus' saddlebag, he asked, "How long do you plan to remain here? Or have you decided yet?"

He came up behind Rotiger and spoke loudly over the moaning gale, "Oh, no more than half the night. The horses and mules will be rested enough by then and the moon is nearly full. We should get across the crest tonight if the wind dies down. If not, we will seek shelter in one of those monasteries on the crags."

"If they have not been razed completely," said Rotiger, the melancholy tone making his voice hollow.

Ragoczy Germainus halted. "You are not sanguine about this venture, are you."

"No, I am not," said Rotiger bluntly. "I am troubled that we are returning to Hispania so soon after we left; you say it is necessary that we do, and that may be so, but I believe it is too soon. It could lead to difficulties." He offered a handful of grain to his mare, and, while she ate, went on stubbornly. "This is unlike you. It is all well and good to say that it has changed a great deal in the last thirty years: the mountains, and those who dwell in them, have not."

"Perhaps not," said Ragoczy Germainus. "But it is unlikely we will have much contact with them. They are still east of Usca, and we are going to the west." He looked up the slope. "I am more concerned about snow."

"So am I, if there is no fighting," Rotiger pointed out.

"Of course; if there is no fighting." He went off to find dried bits of wood, letting his pluvial fly out around him as he walked. The cold bite of the wind had no impact on him, nor had the gathering darkness. He made his way into the copse, looking for downed branches and dry scrub. His arms were soon laden with bits of tinder and enough dry wood to fuel their fire for half the night. He carried his gleanings back to where Rotiger was brushing down the mules, having stacked their saddles and their burdens a few steps away.

"The younger jenny has a swelling in her off-side hock," said Rotiger as Ragoczy Germainus prepared to lay a fire for them. "I don't know if she can carry her packs."

"How bad is it?" Ragoczy Germainus asked as he put down the rest of his wood and tinder more haphazardly than he had intended. He went to inspect the jenny for himself, and found the hock hot to the touch and somewhat enlarged. "I will make a poultice for her," he said as he patted the mule on the rump.

"Very good," said Rotiger, to make it clear he had heard his master.

"I am going to make a shelter for the fire. There are stones enough to do that," Ragoczy Germainus said, and began at once to select stones of fist-size and larger. When he had made a pile about as high as his knee, and darkness was full upon them, he scraped on the earth, sweeping away leaves and twigs, then laid out a pan of stones, making a rim at the edge. There he put his tinder and fuel, then took flint-and-steel from the wallet that hung from his belt and patiently worked to strike a spark to the tinder.

As the first wink of brightness took in the loose material, Rotiger came nearer to it, his hands held out to the promise of warmth. "Do you think we will attract trouble with the fire?" he asked uneasily as he saw the flames rise.

"I think it is better to have the fire than not," Ragoczy Germainus said. Although cold did not bother him, he found the small blaze comforting, and he sank down on the ground between the fire and the stream, relieved to have a chance to rest.

"That may be," said Rotiger dubiously as he flipped back his pluvial and smoothed the front of his blue-gray woollen dalamtica; he moved nearer to the fire. "You have been unusually quiet, my master, and it is not because of the weather. Something is troubling you, and has troubled you since before we left Touloza." When Ragoczy Germainus did not speak, he added, "If you continue to tell me nothing, I will guess, and assume my guesses are correct."

"You know Comites Egnacius made threats," said Ragoczy Germainus as if to dismiss any concern Rotiger might have.

"He made certain all your household knew. His own servants told us that we might all be held accountable for any wrong you did." Rotiger shook his head, showing his distaste at so obvious a ploy. "Do you think that Comites Egnacius would truly put Ambroisus and Ubertuz in jail if you do not present yourself at Asturica?"

Again Ragoczy Germainus hesitated, his manner remote; then he sighed. "Very well. We are far enough away from Touloza. You might as well know." He sat up, his hands locked in front of his knees. "Egnacius needs money to pay for his fight with Perpontus, and vintners like Ambroisus and Ubertuz have money and land that would be very useful for him to have. I would be a poor friend to give Egnacius the excuse he is seeking to confiscate as much of their wealth as he can." He stared into the fire. "What he would do to Lavetta would be much worse."

"And she is the crux of the matter, isn't she?" Rotiger said, comprehension dawning at last. "I have been puzzling about this since we left Touloza. I should have realized that Lavetta was part of the tangle, though you only visited her in dreams." He nodded. "So we must at least go to Asturica."

"Yes. If Manrigo has any use for us—which I doubt—we will serve his interests for a year or so, and then find good cause to leave." Ragoczy Germainus got up and began to pace, his restlessness as eloquent of his apprehension as it was uncharacteristic of him; it was the first hint Rotiger had that more worried him than he admitted. "That will keep Ambroisus and Ubertuz from risk, and Lavetta out of the hands of Egnacius' soldiers."

"Would Egnacius do that?" Rotiger asked, doubtful that so ambitious a man would do such a reckless thing.

"It depends on what the Pope decides," Ragoczy Germainus said. "If Egnacius has the Pope's support, Perpontus may risk everything to keep his position. Egnacius may have to show his ruthlessness to maintain his claim."

There was more to it than Ragoczy Germainus was saying; Rotiger tried another approach. "Perhaps we should be grateful that Valenzia is in Moorish hands, so that we do not have to cross the Pyrenees in the east. That could be very dangerous. It would be unfortunate to go from Egnacius' clutches to Moorish ones." Rotiger did his best to turn this to a jest, but he did not succeed; when he saw no response in Ragoczy Germainus' face, he tried again. "Is there anything else? What haven't you told me?" He had been with Ragoczy Germainus long enough to recognize his reticence for what it was. "No matter what Egnacius does, you need not answer for it."

"But I must live with myself," said Ragoczy Germainus.

Rotiger had no response for that, so he said, "What more? You might as well tell me, for I will discover it eventually."

Ragoczy Germainus sighed again, this time drawing the air out slowly and looking away. "He sent men to imprison you while you were gathering herbs for me. I paid them in pearls and they left. But I knew they would be back. I have assumed that Egnacius was planning to torture information out of you that he would find useful in his drive to claim Touloza." He shook his head. "I gave the men-at-arms that I would say nothing, so that if you were taken and tortured, you would know nothing to their discredit."

"So *that* is why you decided we must leave quickly. I thought it was Egnacius' preparations for departure that—" He stopped. "Am I still a hunted man, then?"

"Probably not, at least not until Egnacius comes back from Roma. Then we may both be in disfavor, if not with Egnacius, then with Perpontus. Those two will not cease their disputes any time soon, no matter what the Pope decides. I hope Ubertuz has the good sense to go back to Primuntiaco, and to take his cousins with him. He can put the vineyards in the hands of monks and neither Egnacius nor Perpontus will dare to touch them; it is not what any of them would want, but it is better than falling into Egnacius' hands." He was quiet for a short while. "I apologize for telling you so little."

Rotiger nodded. "I supposed something had happened, but I did not—" He stopped and coughed. "Never mind. We are where we are and we are bound where we are going." With this concession, he hunkered down by the fire. "Why did it have to be Asturica that asked for aid? Why not Aquileia? Or Paderborn?"

"Why not Tun-huang?" Ragoczy Germainus suggested, recalling that distant outpost on the Old Silk Road with mixed emotions. "The Moors are a threat all Franks understand. As you know."

"But surely—" He broke off. "Of course. He wants to tell the Pope that he is defending the Christian cause." He smiled with a touch of rancor. "In a way, it is clever. He had to compel you to do his bidding and this was one way." He rocked back on his heels. "Must we go to Asturica? Can we not choose another place?"

"I have to suppose that Comites Egnacius has spies at Manrigo's court, as Manrigo does at his. If we do not arrive and there is nothing to account for our absence, others will be made to pay. Hardly the recompense I would want for friendship." He frowned, the firelight accentuating the angle of his fine brows. "It is not fitting that any of them should suffer on my behalf."

"Lavetta most of all, but Ambroisus and Ubertuz as well," said Rotiger. "And you find that unacceptable."

"Do you not?" Ragoczy Germainus asked, surprised at Rotiger's tone.

"Not in the way you do," Rotiger conceded. He shook himself. "The poultice."

"Oh, yes," said Ragoczy Germainus in another tone of voice. "If you will fetch a pail and fill it with water, I will make my preparations." He was relieved not to have to say anything more about anyone in Touloza, but he did not mention it.

Rotiger hastened to do as he had been told, and decided to postpone any further inquiries for a while. He had learned enough to know he would have to spend a little time mulling over what he had been told. Taking care of the jenny was more urgent, in any case. He took the pail from their supplies and went to the stream to fill it.

"A pity we have no hens' eggs; mustard and boiled nettles will have to do," said Ragoczy Germainus as he opened the chest of red Roman lacquer he used to hold his medicaments. "Do we have strips of linen?"

"A small roll of them," said Rotiger. "Look in the middle drawer."

"Ah. Of course." He found the roll and took it out, peeling several of the long strips from it. "Will she try to eat this off?"

"If you have mustard in it, I should think not," said Rotiger, then, wise in the ways of mules, added, "but she may try."

"Then keep her on a close lead so she cannot," Ragoczy Germainus said, and went back to the fire where the pail of water was heating.

The wind was much colder now, and keener, cutting through clothing to flesh as if made of tempered steel. Two steps from the fire and its warmth was entirely lost. Rotiger pulled his pluvial more securely around him, saying, "It is a hard night."

Ragoczy Germainus squinted into the wind. "Yes. But tomorrow will be easier. I think the storm is blowing itself out."

"Not before time," said Rotiger with an impatient shake of his head.

"No," Ragoczy Germainus agreed as he put dried nettle-leaves into the pail. "This should be hot enough. I will make a mustard paste." He retrieved a small metal cup from his red-lacquer chest, measured out a palmful of ground seeds and carried them back to the fire, where he added a little of the hot water to the mustard, stirring it with his finger until it was the consistency of carpenters' glue. "This will draw out the heat from her hock. The nettles will help to keep the swelling down." He wiped his finger on the linen strips so as not to waste any of the mustard and set the metal cup on one of the rocks rimming the fire.

"Very good," said Rotiger as he finished giving grain to their animals. "I'll shift her load to the others until the hock is improved. No sense in forcing her to carry a pack when it would only serve to slow us down." He laughed once. "Such attention to a jenny-mule. What would Egnacius say?"

"He would consign the jenny to the stew-pot and call us simpletons for bothering with her." Ragoczy Germainus' voice was flat, but that did not conceal his disparagement of such attitudes.

"No doubt," said Rotiger, and came back to the fireside.

Using a stick to stir the nettles in the pail, Ragoczy Germainus waited for a bit before he spoke again. "What would you have done, old friend, had it been your decision to make?"

Rotiger was well-aware that Ragoczy was not asking about the mule; he considered his answer carefully. "Eventually, I would do much the same as you; I admit it. But I would not so readily accept the necessity." He lowered his eyes. "And I would resent being coerced."

"Ah." Ragoczy Germainus pulled a wad of nettles out of the water. "If it will console you, I do not like being coerced either." He let the nettles drop back into the pail. "This will be ready soon."

"You do not resent it," Rotiger pointed out.

"It is all so petty, such resentment, and the rancor that causes it," said Ragoczy Germainus. "I cannot demean the lives of those who have befriended me by resentment." He folded his arms and settled back to wait.

Rotiger nodded slowly. "I understand, but I do not share your state of mind." He expected no response, and so was somewhat startled when Ragoczy Germainus said. "That, old friend, is not necessary."

By the time the jenny's hock had been poulticed and bandaged there were cries of wolves from above them, and Ragoczy Germainus built up the fire to keep them at bay. The two companions sat by the fire, wrapped in their pluvials, drowsing away the first half of the night.

When they resumed their traveling, it was by the bright light of a moon just on the wane; the wind was dying, no longer fierce but brisk, touched with snow from higher up the range. The distant cry of wolves mixed with the cry of night birds and the steady clop of their horses and mules. When they stopped again to rest and water the animals, the sky was growing light in the east, promising a limpid spring day.

"How much longer to the pass?" Rotiger asked as he checked the jenny's poultice. "I think she is improving."

"Very good," said Ragoczy Germainus. "She is young and her blood-line is strong." He had long ago developed a high regard for mules, having bred them by the hundreds for the Roman Legions. He patted the jenny's neck, saying, "Olivia will be pleased." For the mules had been bred at Olivia's stud farm near Fruttuaria, and had been one of a dozen she had presented to him on his last visit.

"Is she still at Roma, do you think?" Rotiger asked as he handed an angled pick to Ragoczy Germainus, watching as his master bent to lift the mule's hoof for cleaning.

"For a while yet, I would guess. She is expanding her holdings there, and for that, she must be present." Ragoczy Germainus moved to the next hoof—the on-side rear—holding the leg tightly so that the jenny could not kick him. "Make sure the girths are tight. We have a long ascent ahead of us."

A short while later they were underway again, heading through the changing forest toward the snow-mantled peaks; before long they saw patches of the snow, and then whole meadows of it. Breath steamed out of the horses' and mules' nostrils and the light dazzled off the snow.

It was nearly mid-day when a small group of mounted, armed men headed toward Ragoczy Germainus and Rotiger, their scale armor glinting against the blazing snow. They held their lances peacefully, point up and flapping pennons to show their purpose was not bellicose. The man in the van of the company held up his hand to halt his men as well as Ragoczy Germainus and Rotiger.

"Draw rein," Ragoczy Germainus said to Rotiger in vulgate Latin. "I want to hear what these men have to say."

"They may not be as peaceful as they look," said Rotiger in Greek.

"All the more reason to be cautious," Ragoczy Germainus agreed in the same tongue.

The company head spoke a version of Latin, too, but it was much coarser and mixed with a number of Frankish words. "Good day to you, stranger," he said.

"And to you, Capito," said Ragoczy Germainus.

"Are you bound for the Roncesvalles Pass?" The Capito rapped out his question as if addressing men-at-arms.

"That is where this road leads, to Roncesvalles and the north of Hispania beyond," said Ragoczy Germainus mildly. "We are bound for Asturica on behalf of Egnacius of Touloza."

The Capito shook his head. "You may well have such a duty, but you will not get there by this road. The pass has been blocked by an avalanche, and it will not be open again until late in spring, when the worst of the snow has melted." He indicated the crusty drifts around them. "It will be some months yet before you can complete your journey."

Ragoczy Germainus took a long, steady breath. "And to the west? What of passage there?"

"You may try if you like, but it will lengthen your travel, and you may not be allowed to pass into Asturias. The people there are not kind to strangers, no matter who they are. If you want to reach Asturica, before the end of summer, go east and take the Septimania Pass. You will have to cross Moorish territory, but you are not soldiers. You should be permitted to reach your destination with only double tolls paid." He made a sweeping gesture with his lance. "If I had to make such a choice, I would elect to go by the Septimania Pass."

Recognizing this as an order instead of a recommendation, Ragoczy Germainus said, "Comites Egnacius expects me to travel through Roncesvalles Pass."

"He expects you to reach Asturica," said the Capito.

"Yes. But—" He did not go on; it was clearly useless to bother. "Are you certain the Septimania Pass is open?"

"Travelers have used it recently," said the Capito in what was not quite an answer.

"Isn't there fighting on the southern slope of the mountains?" Ragoczy Germainus persisted in a tone that implied he knew something of the matter.

"It is not enough to stop travelers," said the Capito, becoming less cordial.

"That you know of," Ragoczy Germainus pointed out.

The Capito said nothing; the tip of his lance swung in Ragoczy Germainus' general direction. "A wise man would go back to the fork at the bridge and take the eastern path."

Ragoczy Germainus closed his eyes briefly, his thoughts tumbling. "Are there other patrols in this part of the forest with the same errand as you have?"

"The Dux of Garomma has companies of men like this one on all the roads leading to Roncesvalles Pass. He has the plight of many travelers to consider, and has ordered out patrols to warn those on the road. Eight men and a Capito in each company. All travelers are told the same thing. It is the Dux's intention that all travelers be protected from harm." Under his helmet, his eyes were stern. "Any man of honor must bear the responsibility that has fallen to him."

"No doubt," said Ragoczy Germainus. "And no doubt you have good reason to keep watch for him."

"It is his order that we do." The Capito was staring straight ahead now.

"And sending travelers through Moorish territory will serve the Dux's purpose, will it not." He turned his open hand up. "Since there is no choice, I suppose I must, perforce, do as you require."

"The Dux of Garomma," the Capito corrected, and kept his men behind him as he watched Ragocz Germainus turn around, his manservant and mules following after; he and his men followed them down the trail for four or five thousand paces.

"Do you really think that there are more companies patrolling the forest roads?" Rotiger asked when the soldiers were no longer behind them.

"I wouldn't be surprised if there are a few," said Ragoczy Germainus. "Perhaps not as many as he claims, but three or four."

"Is that why you did not challenge him?" Rotiger asked, unable to conceal his disappointment.

"No. I did not challenge him because I did not like the odds, and there was little to be gained from fighting."

"And who is this Dux of Garomma? I have never heard of him." Rotiger had come up beside Ragoczy Germainus, for the road was wide enough to accommodate them both if they rode close together.

"Nor I. He has probably bestowed the title on himself." He shook his head. "I am surprised we do not see more of that."

"But Dux of Garomma? Is he claiming the river for himself?" Rotiger was too indignant to be amused, but he did his best to diminish his anger. "How can he claim a river?"

"I suspect he has carved himself out a fiefdom with the river for a border, and has struck some sort of bargain with the Moors to send travelers through their territory so high taxes can be levied in exchange for the Moors respecting the Dux's boundaries," said Ragoczy Germainus. "It will save him from having to fight on two fronts, which I reckon he has insufficient men to manage, or supplies. If he can keep his lands and his claim intact, his sons will make the family's reputation, and the title will be accepted. In four generations, the family will be honored by all. If he fails to hold it, the family will be disgraced." He pointed ahead to the old stone bridge that straddled the river they were approaching. "There it is."

"We can still turn westward," Rotiger suggested.

"We can, but it would not be wise," said Ragoczy Germainus. "I assume we are still being watched. If we fail to cross, the soldiers will return."

Rotiger cursed in Greek, adding, "Could we not elude them?"

"Yes, but it would bring more attention to us, which I would like to avoid." He set his horse toward the bridge. "Well, old friend, come on. We have a long way yet to go, and the day is far advanced already."

At last Rotiger voiced the one concern that weighed most heavily upon him. "The Septimania Pass will take us into the region of Holy Blood." He had to raise his voice to be heard as Ragoczy Germainus led his mule across the bridge. "Directly into it."

Ragoczy Germainus turned in the saddle. "Yes," he called back. "I know."

Text of a letter from Habib ibn Rayhan ibn Timuz in Karmona to Akil ibn Dawud ibn Timuz in Valenzia.

In the name of Allah, the All-Merciful, and by His Prophet Mohammed, may I have no sons to live after me if I report to you, my kinsman, in error, or in any particular fail to give an accurate account to you of the recent demise of our most illustrious cousin, Numair ibn Isffah ibn Musa, who died at the new moon immediately before the Spring Equinox, in the fifty-seventh year of his age. May Allah show him the glories of Paradise, and rejoice in his coming.

*Our cousin took ill at his palace in Karmona shortly before the Win-
ter Solstice. He had been hale enough before then, and it did not appear
that age had laid too heavy a hand upon him—thanks be to Allah—or
that he had lost any of his reason or memory. The first appearance of
the illness that felled him was deceptive, hardly more than what any
man might expect in winter. But what had begun as an occasional
cough soon became a profound weakening of the lungs, which left Numair ibn Isffah ibn Musa in a debilitated state. His physicians treated
him with lemons and wasps, but he did not rally, and at last sank into
a stupor that lasted for four nights, and ended shortly before dawn on
the day described. It was a cold, blustery morning and turned later to
rain, as if the heavens mourned his loss with us. His body was prepared
with honors and his burial was held with all the men who served him
in life attending him to his grave. Even a Christian priest blessed his
body so that Christians might not show disrespect to his grave.*

*In his accounts of his service to Numair ibn Isffah ibn Musa, our
grandfather says that in his youth he was given to sensuality and the
pleasures of the harem, but that certain disappointments hardened him
and made him a leader of fighting men who was renowned for his re-
lentlessness in battle. It is shown that once Numair ibn Isffah ibn Musa
had a taste of battle, he fought valiantly at the head of his own soldiers
for twenty years—a most distinguished career. Timuz ibn Musa ibn
Maliq served Numair ibn Isffah ibn Musa for nearly twenty years, and
his records show that once Numair ibn Isffah ibn Musa discovered the
joy of battle, that he never flagged in his devotion to the spread of our
people and our Faith. The campaigns in which these two participated
bring fame and esteem to all our family, distinctions for which we must
show ourselves worthy.*

*It may be that you and I will be summoned to fill the office left open
by the death of Numair ibn Isffah ibn Musa, and if that is the outcome—may Allah show favor to us in our lives—we must thoroughly
acquaint ourselves with all our cousin has done, so that we may more
truly fulfill the goals to which he dedicated his life. There have been
many who depended upon Numair ibn Isffah ibn Musa's good-will, and
who would continue their support of our family and ourselves if we are
well-informed. To that end I propose to go to the palace here in Karmona and spend many days learning all that I can, so that if the Caliph
should decide to have our family continue in this office, I will be ready
to assume the responsibilities promptly. If you agree to join me in this*

enterprise, I believe we may expand the good work we have done and add to the high repute our kinsmen have already gained.

There are many officials to whom I must apply for endorsement, a task that might as easily fall to you as to me if you were here with me, my cousin. Working together, we can accomplish far more than either one of us can do working alone. I ask you to consider how we may mutually benefit ourselves in this time, and I beg you to take the plunge and come to Karmona.

It is true that Numair ibn Isffah ibn Musa had many sons, and three of them have spoken out for his post, but they are highly placed men in the army, and they have not the time or the learning to undertake the administration of his post as he carried it out the last decade of his life. They do not understand the demands of commerce, for they have given their lives to war. We, on the other hand, are well-schooled in commerce and have traveled for reasons other than war, which make us particularly useful in the position that is being left empty. Let his sons continue his battles for him, as they did while he lived, and let us undertake his other tasks. My heart is willing. I pray yours may be, too.

There are accommodations for you and your wives in the palace, as there are for me and mine. If we neither of us add too many concubines, it is possible that the palace will suit us both for many years to come. Think of the advantages of working closely together, and consider how our shared efforts will improve all our fortunes. I am acutely aware that I am no fighting man, and I know you are not, either; our strengths lie in other abilities. Therefore, let us make the best of our situation and accept the advantage that is presently available to us. Our talents are complementary, and if we do not become too greedy, we may yet control the fortunes of Numair ibn Isffah ibn Musa. You cannot deny that our interests are better served in concert than at cross-purposes. Our grandfather benefitted from his long association with Numair ibn Isffah ibn Musa, and why should we not do as he did?

Send me your answer by messenger as quickly as you may. I tell you it is folly for you to remain in Valenzia when there is so much to gain here in Karmona. This at the first full moon after the Spring Equinox.

Habib ibn Rayhan ibn Timuz

2

"What has happened to all the trees?" Rotiger marveled aloud as they continued their descent from the Septimania Pass. They were well below the elevation where the forest had grown yet they found only empty slopes; where the snow ended there were patches of sparse grasses and low-growing weeds, but the trees were gone.

Ragoczy Germainus pointed off to the west, where in the far distance, many ridges off, they could just make out the dark green smudge of forest against the sky. "There," he said, his tone as devastated as the mountainsides around them. "They are not completely gone."

Rotiger could find no words to express his sorrow for the vanished forest. He rode on in silence, only once speaking up when he saw a vast flock of goats at the end of one of the narrow valleys. Immediately above the animals was a scar on the land where a section of the slope had slid away, exposing the bare, rocky soil beneath. "Is there more of this, do you think?"

"Oh, much more," said Ragoczy Germainus, pointing to the goats. "And as they strip the land bare, there will be more."

The next day revealed more of the same, and the toll it was taking, for a stretch of the road had dropped into the gorge on the east side of the track. Ragoczy Germainus and Rotiger had to dismount and lead their animals along a precarious, improvised path to where the road began again. There were signs that other travelers had reached this place and turned back.

"How many do you think have crossed?" Rotiger asked when they were safe.

"Very few," said Ragoczy Germainus. "It is not surprising."

"What is the point of this . . . this ruin?" Rotiger demanded as he got back onto his dun mare.

"The Moors need wood to build their ships," said Ragoczy Germainus with quiet certainty. "And open land for their flocks."

"And it is harder for enemies to hide on an open hillside than in a

forest," said Rotiger, nodding savagely. "No doubt it serves their purposes."

Ragoczy Germainus said nothing; he was staring at the line of trees
so far to the west, a minor frown forming between his brows. Finally he
said, "We will not be able to travel at night, not with the road as it is."
He pointed ahead where the ruts in the road became rivulets, erasing
the track for several hundred paces. "We will have to lead our animals
awhile longer."

Rotiger signaled his concurrence. "How much more damage will we
find? Is it as bad further down?"

"It depends on how hard the winter was, and how many merchants
want to use the Septimania Pass," said Ragoczy Germainus, his dark
eyes fixed on the far distance. "And how many goats have grazed here."

"True enough," said Rotiger, tugging on the rein and the lead as he
continued after Ragoczy Germainus.

"There could be bandits, too," Ragoczy Germainus called back to
him as he picked his way ahead of his horse and mule.

"I should think not," said Rotiger, keenly aware of the dangers they
faced.

"What about villagers?" The question was deliberately provocative.
"You expect trouble from them."

"And you do not? Think of where we are." Rotiger swept out his arm
to indicate the desolation around him.

"I have thought of little else," Ragoczy Germainus admitted.

"You are apprehensive about Chimenae's tribe, aren't you?" He
halted his horse and two mules, then turned to face Ragoczy Germainus as he waited for his answer.

"I would be reckless not to be," said Ragoczy Germainus with a tranquility that was little more than an urbane veneer. "I have also thought
about Ubertez and Lavetta and Ambrosius. The longer our arrival is
delayed, the more danger they will be in, I fear. So Csimenae or no
Csimenae, we must pass through her territory, and quickly."

"You think they are still abroad." It was as blunt a statement as
Rotiger could make.

"It seems likely." Ragoczy Germainus' manner now was diffident.
"Unless there has been a campaign against them, we must assume
there are more of them."

"All still of her making and doing her bidding?" Rotiger asked, getting to the heart of the matter.

"That is what we cannot know," Ragoczy Germainus replied, and fell silent as he crossed a small stream, wincing at the brief sensation of vertigo it gave him. At least, he thought, he had his native earth in the soles of his shoes to shield him from the greatest discomfort running water created. The hooves of his horse and mule splashed and slithered on the gravel bed, and they scrambled up the far bank with more efficiency than grace, but Ragoczy Germainus kept pace with them, glad to be away from the water.

"This is annoying," said Rotiger as he hauled his horse and mules over the stream and up to where Ragoczy Germainus and his animals stood. "The road will disappear by summer if something is not done."

"Another will be made," said Ragoczy Germainus as he remounted at last. "We have some time until dark. We should keep a lookout for shelter."

"A village, a camp, what?" Rotiger asked as he climbed back into his high-canteled saddle. He pulled the lead up so that the mules had to follow closely.

"A place that is safe enough to pass the night without having to defend it," said Ragoczy Germainus as he tapped his mount with his heels.

"From whom?" Rotiger asked, repeating the question when he received no reply.

"I do not know: that is what troubles me," said Ragoczy Germainus.

Rotiger studied the rugged landscape for a little time, then ventured, "It isn't just Moors you're fretful about, is it?"

"No," said Ragoczy Germainus. "Not just Moors."

"But surely you cannot think that Chimenae has made more of her kind? Not after what we saw?" He was alarmed by the notion. "If she has done anything so foolish, the others would—"

"Exactly. The others would not accept it. It would be divisive." He held up his hand to show his predicament. "Moors are not my only concern. Nor are the villagers, though their lives have been disrupted by what the Moors have done to the forest."

"They must have enlarged their flocks," said Rotiger doubtfully. "Do you not think they have?"

"It is possible," said Ragoczy Germainus without conviction. "Chimenae's clan would prey upon flocks, the larger the better."

They went on a way in silence, their attention held by the miserable condition of the road; the daylight began to fade as the shadows length-

ened, then disappeared, leaving the barren slopes eerily silent but for
the steady sound of their horses' and mules' feet.

"Up ahead!" Rotiger shouted in relief and surprise. "Is that an inn?
Here? Surely it cannot be a farm—there are no fields or pens. There
are no watch-towers, so it cannot be a fortress." He rose in his stirrups
for a better look at the place. "It is right next to the road. It must be an
inn."

"It may be," said Ragoczy Germainus, his enthusiasm less than Rotiger expected. "If there is anyone still in it."

"There is a lamp burning in the window." Rotiger pointed at
the three squat buildings that looked so much like the rocky hillside
around them that they might have been mistaken for an outcropping of
stones. "There, on the building nearest the road, on the corner window."

"I see it," said Ragoczy Germainus. "And perhaps you are right. We
will stop there for the night."

Rotiger was well-aware of Ragoczy Germainus' reluctance, but he
was not willing to accept it unquestioningly. "You are not pleased to
have shelter for the night?"

"I am not certain it *is* shelter," he said, his voice distant. "I wonder
at a place in so desolate a location that still offers a haven to travelers."

"Oh," said Rotiger, chastened. "You are remembering Baghdad."

"I am puzzled that you are not," said Ragoczy Germainus, no hint of
reproach in his tone. "There are so many similarities."

Now that Ragoczy Germainus had reminded him, Rotiger was very
much struck by them. "A remote place, the only building for thousands
and thousands of paces, and the land empty around it. I do see why
you—" he stopped. "Do you think we should go on? We might find a
place to make camp beyond the next ridge."

"No," Ragoczy Germainus said after a short silence. "No, I think we
might as well stop here. We cannot travel much farther today, in any
case; our animals won't stand for it. We might as well make do with this
place as with a camp of our own."

Rotiger was now apprehensive. "How do you wish to deal with
this?"

"I assume we should ride up to the door and ask for a night's lodg-
ing, as any traveler would." He looked back at Rotiger. "There is no
point in putting them on their guard, particularly here."

"No," agreed Rotiger, and settled into the last of their day's ride.

The three buildings were almost wholly undistinguishable by the time they reached the door of the one with the light; only a faint glow in the west provided any light to the land, and it was vanishing.

"Landlord!" Ragoczy Germainus called out as he dismounted. "If anyone is here!"

There was no response for a short while, and then a second light was struck inside the stone building, and there was the sound of the bolt being drawn back. Then the door swung open and a youth just on the verge of manhood stepped out, bending over in welcome. As he straightened up, he stared, then swore in the old tongue of the region as he kicked at the door in a display of petulance and aggravation. "What are you doing here, Sanct' Germain?"

Ragoczy Germainus recovered quickly from his shock. "Aulutiz," he said. "Is this place yours, then?"

"You haven't answered my question." Chimenae's son went to stand in the doorway, arms folded, legs apart. "And it is Olutiz now," he added, the subtle difference in pronunciation another reminder of the time that had gone by since they had seen each other.

"No, I have not answered your question," Ragoczy Germainus conceded. "Nor have you answered mine." He made a gesture to show he had meant no offense. "It was not my intention to come here, but circumstances have brought me. I must suppose that you were hoping for—" He walked around the front of his horse, pulling the reins over his neck and leading him forward with him.

"There are travelers enough on this road to keep us from starving, if that's what you mean." Olutiz glowered at the two arrivals. "You have horses and mules. That's something."

"I am afraid that we need them," said Ragoczy Germainus. "If we must make some arrangement, let us discuss it first."

"Why should we not take what we need?" Olutiz asked, his posture insistent.

"Because you are not a fool," said Ragoczy Germainus as he came to stand directly in front of the door. "Consider: you have lost the element of surprise. If I must, I will have Rotiger stay in the stable. He will not permit any of your numbers—and there cannot be too many of you in this remote place—to harm our animals. If you make it necessary, I will join him." He paused, letting Olutiz think about what he was saying. "On the other hand, we will take nothing from you."

"You must be hungry," said Olutiz, suspicion making him snap.

"Yes, I am, but it is nothing I cannot endure," said Ragoczy Germainus.

"You would have to fight us for any blood." Olutiz pointed directly at Ragoczy Germainus. "You know that."

"It will not come to that," Ragoczy Germainus said calmly.

Olutiz shook his head. "There are six of us here. Do you think you could defeat us?"

"Do you think I would not?" Ragoczy Germainus let the question hang between them, then went on in a more affable manner, "You are a long way from Chimenae's stone house." Ragoczy Germainus pointed to the building. "You have made one of your own."

"She!" He swore again. "She has banished us. More than twenty of us." He spat to show his disdain for her. "A few she killed, as an example."

"How long ago?" The question was kindly asked, without any suggestion of inculpation.

"Years. Many years." He shrugged and relented. "You might as well come in."

"We have animals to attend to first," said Ragoczy Germainus firmly. "If you will tell me which of those two buildings is the stable?"

Olutiz snorted in self-mockery. "That one. I'll tell Dorioz to leave you alone. We had a goat last night. He shouldn't mind too much. Have your man lead them there. You will not need to guard them." He held out his hand in greeting. "You may come in while your man takes your horses and mules to the stable; they will be cared for."

"No doubt, but I will ask Rotiger to remain with them, I think," Ragoczy Germainus said as he paused on the threshold, reins and lead in his extended hand and called back to Rotiger, "Stay with our animals. I will come to speak with you shortly."

"That I will," said Rotiger with purpose as he reached down for the reins and lead Ragoczy Germainus had been holding out to him. "And I will not sleep."

"Nor will I," said Ragoczy Germainus, his eyes never leaving Olutiz's face.

"So you say," said Olutiz, not very graciously. "You are determined to watch, then we must be satisfied."

"Very wise," said Ragoczy Germainus as he stepped into the front room of the inn. It was an unprepossessing place, small, with a low ceiling supported by sagging beams with a fireplace built into the western wall. There was a counter where barrels of wine sat, and a few rough benches set out, offering a minimum of comfort to the traveler. "A most . . . simple place," he said as he looked around.

"Well, it is the only inn for ten thousand paces in any direction, and the monastery no longer takes in travelers: the Moors collect a tax on them if the monks feed them." Olutiz went to stand in front of his fireplace, his head held up at an arrogant angle as he called out, "Dorioz!"

Almost at once the boyish creature appeared, bright eagerness in his cynical old eyes. "Yes?" He stopped still, seeing that Ragoczy Germainus was in the room. "Gods of the horses!" he swore.

"Yes," said Olutiz. "He has returned. His man is taking care of his horses and mules. You are to leave them untouched." He added, more forcefully, "Do you understand me?"

"You are ordering me to go hungry," said Dorioz, a defiant edge to his voice.

"Or find a goat," said Olutiz. "Just leave this one and his alone."

Dorioz glared at Olutiz, then turned and left the room without another word.

"He may not like it, but he will obey," said Olutiz. "He does not want to hunt alone."

A number of questions burgeoned in Ragoczy Germainus' mind, but he kept them all to himself, aware that Olutiz was enough like his mother to resent inquiry; he contented himself with saying, "Thank you."

Olutiz ducked his head once in acknowledgment, then once again met Ragoczy Germainus' gaze. "What are you doing here?"

"I am on my way to Asturica; I have been delayed," said Ragoczy Germainus. "It was not my intention to come by the Septimania Pass, but as it turned out, I was unable to use Roncesvalles. I had hoped to be in Asturica within the month." He went to the longest bench and sat down on its far end. "There are those who will suffer if I fail to arrive in Asturcia, and in good time."

"That is supposed to move me?" Olutiz asked.

"Apparently not," said Ragoczy Germainus dryly.

Olutiz raised his voice. "Or am I to assume you expect me to help you because of it?"

"I want you to know why I am here; it has nothing to do with you, or your mother." Ragoczy Germainus put the tips of his gloved fingers together. "She is not with you."

"No," said Olutiz, his mouth surly. "Not she."

"Because she banished you." He nodded. "You were not telling tales when you said she and you had fought."

"I was not." He folded his arms.

"Are the others with you?" Ragoczy Germainus inquired as he looked around the empty room.

"A few—six are here now. Many of them scattered. Some were caught and killed by the Moors, and some by the monks. Perhaps there are a dozen of us still on our own." He frowned, recalling the things he had seen. "Even Edic came with us, in the end, for he did not like to see her prey on Moors. It was bad enough that she made three of them of our blood, but when she ordered us to hunt their logging parties, we refused, saying we would not hunt slaves, and she . . . she would not tolerate it."

"But that was an old dispute among you, whom to hunt," said Ragoczy Germainus patiently. "Why did it worsen?"

This time Olutiz did not answer as readily. He tapped his fingers on the barrel nearest the fireplace. "I see what it is. You want to draw me out. You want to make me tell you what I know." He was about to leave the room when Ragoczy Germainus' answer stopped him.

"Of course I do," he admitted openly. "I have not been in this region for thirty years and it is much changed; the forest is gone, and the road is dilapidated. It would appear that there have been other changes as well, ones that are not so visible as the ravaged forests, and I want to know what they are. I must travel through the region. Were you in my position, you would do the same thing." He sat still while Olutiz made up his mind. "You do not have to say anything, but eventually I will hear something from one of your number. This is an opportunity for you as much as for me."

"You say you want to know what happened?" The challenge was as much hopeful as belligerent.

"Yes, I would."

Olutiz paced to the fireplace, then stood there for a while before pacing toward Ragoczy Germainus. "It had to come. Everyone knew it. After you left, it became worse with her, as if she had to keep control of all the region, villages, Moors, and all. She would brook no opposition from anyone. Her demands increased, and she required more cups of blood and more two-legged goats." He was talking more readily now, as if glad to have someone to listen to him. "She also forbade us to make others of our blood. She said any such vampire was to be killed; that had been her rule from the first, but now she was more adamant than ever, as if she suspected the rest of us were going to raise a clan of our own to stand against her, or to challenge her for . . ." He sought for a way to express his emotion. "I did not agree with her, and I said, if she had done so much to preserve us, and that I, as her son, would rule after her, that I should be permitted the chance to make a company of my own."

"So you defied her," said Ragoczy Germainus, thinking how inevitable that was.

"Well, I had to," he said. "There was no bearing it." He slapped his hands on his thighs. "She wanted almost to be worshiped. How could I go along with her demands when they were so outrageous?"

"And so demeaning," Ragoczy Germainus suggested.

"Yes, that as well." He stared into the fire, then roused himself once more. "But not only for me; she belittled us all, particularly those who had been with her the longest. She held them all in contempt for their devotion to her."

"I see," said Ragoczy Germainus, to encourage him to continue to talk.

"Why am I telling you this?" He swung around to confront Ragoczy Germainus. "You are tricking me!"

"I am listening to you," said Ragoczy Germainus without revealing his inner alarm. "And I understand."

"So you claim," said Olutiz sullenly. "But why should you?" Before Ragoczy Germainus could answer, Olutiz went on, "You disapprove of how we live. How can you understand?"

"Because I am a vampire, and I have lived nearly three thousand years," he said.

The quiet statement brought Olutiz up short. He stared and struggled with a response, finally thrusting his hands through his belt and sinking onto the nearest stool. "That may be," he allowed in an effort to maintain his sense of command. "And you know my mother."

"Not as well as I would have preferred," Ragoczy Germainus said.

He did not add that he thought Olutiz was very like her; that observation would not be welcome.

"That is part of it, isn't it?" said Olutiz, chagrin twisting the corners of his mouth. "She does not want anyone to know her too much."

"It appears so," said Ragoczy Germainus as he lowered his head.

"Do you intend to see her?" Olutiz asked cautiously. "I should warn you that she will not be—"

"No," said Ragoczy Germainus. "That is not my intention."

"That's right," said Olutiz with a quick smile. "You said you were planning to go by Roncesvalles Pass, weren't you?"

Ragoczy Germainus ignored the note of doubt in Olutiz's question and said, "Yes. I was."

"Fewer Moors up that way," Olutiz suggested slyly.

"Yes." Ragoczy Germainus got to his feet. "I should go to the stable. Rotiger may need my help."

"Somehow I do not think so," said Olutiz. "I will have Achona make up a bed for you."

"So Achona is with you," said Ragoczy Germainus, not truly surprised.

"Yes. She is." The justificatory note was back in his tone again.

"Do not bother her," said Ragoczy Germainus with a wave of his hand. "I will sleep with Rotiger, in the loft."

Olutiz shrugged. "If you prefer. There are rats in the stable."

"No doubt," said Ragoczy Germainus wearily. "There are rats everywhere."

Olutiz did nothing to stop Ragoczy Germainus from leaving; he remained seated, his chin sunk on his chest, his whole aspect one of indifference. As Ragoczy Germainus closed the door, Olutiz finally moved, but only to set the bolt in place.

The stable was not large, but the stalls were well-made and there was hay in the mangers for their animals. Ragoczy Germainus found Rotiger busy with their chests, which he had piled up in the center aisle between the stalls.

"The jenny is better," he said as he saw Ragoczy Germainus approaching.

"Good. We will have to travel far tomorrow," said Ragoczy Germainus.

"Is there trouble ahead?" He stopped in his work, concern in his faded-blue eyes.

"There is trouble here," said Ragoczy Germainus, coming to sit on one of the chests that contained his native earth.

"With Chimenae's tribe?" he asked, knowing the answer already.

"And who knows how many others," said Ragoczy Germainus heavily. He glanced at the nearest stall. "Where are the brushes?"

"In the leather case, where they always are," said Rotiger, recognizing a sign of worry in Ragoczy Germainus.

"Hand it to me, will you?" Ragoczy Germainus asked as he got to his feet once more. He took the case and went into the stall where he began to brush his grey, working down the glossy neck to her chest and withers. "Have you seen Dorioz?"

"You mean that little ferret of a boy? Yes. He slipped in here to bring buckets of water. He is a guileful one." He resumed his work while Ragoczy Germainus went on grooming his horse.

"Did he say anything to you?" Ragoczy Germainus asked a short while later.

"Only that there was a well behind the inn," said Rotiger, feeling uneasy.

"Did he." He stopped working the brush and looked directly at Rotiger. "We must be on guard this night, old friend."

"From that boy?" He showed no sign of amusement. "How can that be?"

"Not only the boy. Olutiz said there are six of them here, but admitted that a dozen still remained: I saw only him and Dorioz." He rested his arm across the grey's croup. "This makes me suppose there may be many more of them."

"How many more?" Rotiger asked without any indication of distress.

"I wish I knew." Ragoczy Germainus went back to brushing his horse, then picked out the hooves. "Olutiz said we would not be disturbed, but—"

"—but you are not convinced of it," Rotiger finished for him.

"Exactly," said Ragoczy Germainus as he came out of the stall, the leather case in his hand. "It might be best to build up a small fire near the door."

"I take your point, my master," said Rotiger. "And when that is done, I will keep watch from the loft."

Ragoczy Germainus laid his hand on Rotiger's shoulder. "That should be my task, old friend. If you will guard the animals, I will be sentinel for us."

Rotiger nodded. "As you wish," he said, and began to set up tinder and wood near the entrance to the stable while Ragoczy Germainus climbed into the loft to keep watch.

Report from Yamut ibn Mainum to Khallad ibn Baran ibn Fadil, carried by military courier.

In the name of Allah, the All-Compassionate, may I be struck dumb and blind if I report inaccurately in any detail; may my family be beggars in lands of famine, and may no son of mine bring honor to my name if I fail to present all the information you, most revered official of the Caliph—may Allah give him long life and many sons—have asked of me.

The detail of slaves and guards you have assigned to me have been set to work in the hills to the north of the Iberuz River, for the purpose of logging trees and clearing land, to which task we have devoted ourselves for the last sixteen months. The labor has been demanding, for as we have continued up the mountains, we have faced more opposition than was expected. The villagers here do not often fight us, for they have few weapons, and nothing to bargain with but their few flocks. Some have even sold themselves to us so that their children might be allowed to leave. Most of those who have departed have gone toward Christian territory, or the city of Usca, where many villagers have sought refuge.

But we have encountered other difficulties. The villagers in the higher valleys are not like those on the lower slopes. They have rituals that make them stubborn to our advances, and they tell us of demons that come in the night to drink the blood of unwary men. These tales have been told for years, and some of our men have heard them with fear. I put little faith in such fables, for surely anyone could understand how it was that the villagers would claim such an evil in the hope of protecting themselves from what our tasks demanded we do. Those men who claimed to have seen these night-demons all said that nothing could be done to keep safe but to set fires or behead the vile creatures. To keep our slaves from being made weak with dread, I ordered that fires be lit and maintained around our camps at all time. I also ordered the guards to behead anyone they caught sneaking around our camps at night. For a time this sufficed, and all those under my command were willing to work without fear.

But that has changed. In the last month we have been cutting trees in the region called Holy Blood, and there have been problems we have never encountered before. Not only is it more difficult to log in these mountains, but we are no longer able to count ourselves safe from the night-demons, for it would seem—Allah witness that I speak truth—that some of the night-demons are Moors, for only Moors could approach our guards and not be stopped or beheaded. In the last month, four of our guards have died, bled white and left with wooded stakes driven through their chests. The slaves are no longer willing to work, for they are afraid that they will die as their guards have died. The number of logs we have cut and sent down the slope is halved because of this fright that I cannot combat or fault.

I have sent to Usca to ask the Imam there what we must do to save ourselves from these night-demons that are all around us. We have taken refuge in a walled village called Mont Calciuz, and we have made the villagers work for us, both in cutting trees and in tending the flocks that follow, for they have long dealt with the night-demons and are wise in their ways. It is an abomination, but we have allowed the villagers to leave men at the gates on certain nights as offerings to these night-demons, and thus far we have not had any more of our guards or our slaves killed. It is wrong of us to do this thing, but—may Allah bear witness—I can think of nothing else to save those consigned to my care.

The land we are to log is in this region of Holy Blood, and I cannot suppose that we will not encounter the same difficulties we have experienced here. The land is steep and the villagers leave tribute for the night-demons and kill pigs to make offerings to them. If we are to persuade our guards to stay at their posts, I must be allowed to continue this policy of appeasement to the night-demons, not only to save our slaves and guards, but to end their terrors. I ask you to allow me this liberty, or you will have to send many soldiers to root out and slaughter the night-demons, which would be a costly venture at a time our soldiers are needed elsewhere.

Also, I must warn you that if you are to send flocks into this region, the animals as well as the herders will be in danger from the night-demons. You may think that this is readily avoided, but I assure you it is not. I have been told that the night-demons are of several warring clans, and that unless some arrangement is made with all of them, none of our flocks or men will be safe.

It is my ardent hope that our production of logs will increase through-

out the summer, but if we cannot keep the night-demons at bay, I may be forced to withdraw from this region until the soldiers have elimi-nated the monsters from their havens high in the crags and deep in the forests. It is the cutting of trees that most distresses them, we are told, for the woods have long been a safe harbor for them. Our slaves say that to go into the forest now is certain death, and the villagers encour-age them in this belief.

Advise me, O Khallad ibn Baran ibn Fadil, for I do not know what to do that will fulfill my duty and protect those under my command. The night-demons are many and we are few, and our fears increase with every passing day. Soon we will be at a standstill if I cannot be permitted to mollify the night-demons so that we may do the work we are assigned to accomplish. As Allah knows the truth, I tell you that I am at my limit. This at the full moon before mid-summer, in the village of Mont Calciuz.

Yamut ibn Mainum

3

"They are following us still," said Rotiger to Ragoczy Germainus three nights later as they made camp in a shallow ravine some forty thousand paces from the remote inn. The crags around them looked much the same as the slope where they had found the inn—swaths of exposed rock with occasional dead stumps serving as memorials to the lost for-est. Patches of tough grass showed here and there, fodder for the goats that roamed the mountains in large flocks.

"Tomorrow we will reach the forest and they will find other game," said Ragoczy Germainus with a tranquility that was only superficial.

"Do you think so?" He shook his head. "We could travel tonight, and put more distance between us."

"And encounter who knows what in the effort," said Ragoczy Ger-mainus. "No, I would rather be on the road when they are all at rest. If there are as many vampires in these mountains as Olutiz implied there were, I have no wish to encounter them unprepared." He glanced at the goose Rotiger was plucking and achieved a wry smile. "You may not think this is much of a meal, old friend, but it was not taken from any shrine to Chimenae's get."

"No, it was not," Rotiger agreed as he continued to pluck, shoving the feathers into a canvas bag and grinning in anticipation of his meal.

"If only the road were better, we would travel faster," said Ragoczy Germainus, revealing his anxiety in a quick frown. "With so many trees gone, the road may fall away completely in another year or so."

"We have traveled over worse terrain," Rotiger reminded him.

"And in greater haste," Ragoczy Germainus said. "But I do not want to be driven through these mountains in panic if we need not be so." He struck flint to steel and set the spark to the tinder he had gathered. "I do not like the notion of having to kill my own kind, but it would be wisest to be ready for that, as well." He had three straight branches as long as his arm lying near the incipient fire. "I'll get these sharpened when the flames are steady."

"Do you think you will have to use them?" Rotiger asked, doing his best not to sound worried.

"I hope we will not. But it may be necessary, and I will prepare these to be both torches and stakes." He frowned, grief at the back of his dark eyes.

"They would not hesitate to use those, or other weapons, on you," Rotiger pointed out, understanding Ragoczy Germainus' hesitation.

"Perhaps not," he conceded. "But I cannot be easy in my mind about the possibility."

Rotiger said nothing as he continued his plucking. When he was finished, he split the goose and sat down to eat it, after leaving the organs in a small pile a short distance from their camp. "There may still be cats or martens or weasels on these hillsides who will be glad of such food."

"So there might," said Ragoczy Germainus as he busied himself sharpening the last of his branches. He worked in silence, his thoughts carefully kept at bay as he worked, his determination showing in the set of his jaw. How long had it been, he asked himself, since he had had to face other vampires? It was half a lifetime ago, at least, in Judea, and the vampires were thought to be demons; then it had not mattered to him, for the killing gave him a rush of terror that filled him with a furious satisfaction that cut through his despair and left him intoxicated with the potency of the emotion. Only later did he discover the nourishment of love, and came to seek it instead of the inebriation of abject fright.

"What is it?" Rotiger asked, regarding Ragoczy Germainus with unsettled feelings; the expression he saw on his master's face was haunted, and Rotiger knew the memories he had summoned up were ancient.

"It was before your time." He looked up into the sky, studying the stars. "They change so little, even after centuries."

Rotiger accepted this with a philosophical nod. "Egypt, I suppose."

"Before Egypt. Judea." Ragoczy Germainus finally lowered his head and met Rotiger's eyes again. "You would not have known me then."

As always, when Ragoczy Germainus recalled those long-departed times, Rotiger felt a qualm that could not be hidden; his shudder was strong enough to make the goose in his hands shake. "If you tell me so."

Ragoczy Germainus laughed once, so sadly that Rotiger shuddered again. "I hardly know myself as I was then." He took care to build up the fire, using this chore as an excuse to say nothing more.

"Are you going to stay awake all night?" Rotiger asked when he had finished his meal and tossed the bones far off into the darkness.

"I think it would be best," said Ragoczy Germainus, his manner slightly remote. "I will look after the horses and mules. We do not want any misfortune befalling them."

"If you mean Olutiz, no we would not," said Rotiger, spreading out his Roman bedroll on the ground.

"Olutiz or any of the others." Ragoczy Germainus dragged one of his chests of his native earth nearer the fire; it was an easy task for him, though ordinarily it would take two grown men to handle the heavy object. He sat on it, one of his stakes in his hand. "Go to sleep. You have nothing to fear."

"If you say not," Rotiger told Ragoczy Germainus, almost convinced of it himself.

Not long before dawn, Ragoczy Germainus awakened Rotiger; the fire was low and their animals were beginning to be restless. "There are men on horseback coming this way. If you listen you can hear them. We had better be prepared to meet them. Rise and arm yourself quickly." He went to build up the fire and to saddle their mules and horses.

"Are you certain they are men?" Rotiger asked as he tended to his bedroll, securing it with braided thongs before tying it to the cantel of his saddle where it stood on its pommel-end for the night.

"No doubt whatever. They all have pulses and by the sound of their orders, they are Moors." The self-possession he displayed was familiar to Rotiger, who shook his head.

"You have no apprehension about Moors?" He went to find his short sword and thrust it into its scabbard before buckling it onto his belt.

"Of course I do," said Ragoczy Germainus. "But not as I have about vampires." He was strapping his Byzantine long sword in its scabbard across his back, and he had taken his double-curve bow from its place in their packs and now strung it with an ease that would have shocked its Mongol maker. That done, he slung the quiver over the opposite shoulder to his sword, saying as he did, "I think I will leave the cross-bow packed. The Moors are not likely to think it a hunting weapon."

The sound of the approaching horseman was louder, now, and their pace had picked up from a walk to a trot.

"They have seen the smoke of our fire," said Ragoczy Germainus, and began to saddle their mules, starting with the jenny he had treated a few days ago. "Keep on with your tasks, old friend. Do not appear too ready to fight. That would encourage them."

Rotiger's dun whinnied suddenly and was answered by four of the approaching horses.

"If that is what you want," said Rotiger as he picked up the long stakes Ragoczy Germainus had fashioned the night before. "What about these?"

"Put them into the pack with our weapons. We will not need them during the day." He secured the breast-collar to the girth and began to buckle the girth. "Put the lightest packs and chests on this one. I'll saddle the jack next." He picked up the largest pack-saddle and its sheep-skin pad and went to the second mule—a strengthy mule whose neck and shoulders revealed his cart-horse dam—and put the pad in place on his back. The jack immediately inhaled and held his breath. "Very funny," said Ragoczy Germainus and went on with putting the saddle in place, then the breast-collar, and then began to tighten the girth, leaving it slightly loose. He was saddling the third mule when a company of Moorish soldiers topped the rise of the ravine in which he and Rotiger were camped.

The leader of the troop shouted out a greeting that was also an order for immediate attention in a language that might have been Frankish, and was surprised to be answered in his own tongue.

"May Allah bring you good fortune and many sons," said Ragoczy Germainus, offering the Moors the traditional salaam.

The leader of the Moors held up his hand to halt his men. "How does an Infidel dog know this?"

"I have spent some years among your people, when I was younger," said Ragoczy Germainus, not mentioning that he had been a slave and had escaped from his owner thirty years before.

"And you follow the ways of the Franks?" The leader spat.

"Because it suits my purposes, yes, I do. I am not a Frank." Ragoczy Germainus did his best to maintain a cordial manner, but his dark eyes were flinty.

"You do not follow the Prophet?" The leader's bearded chin jutted forward.

"I have not learned enough of your faith to embrace it with under-standing," said Ragoczy Germainus in his most cordial tone.

The leader nodded and sat back in his saddle. "Then how is it you are on this road? You are not a merchant, by the look of you."

"No, I have other business that occupies me." Ragoczy Germainus pointed to his three mules. "A merchant would have more goods than I carry."

"Tell me what your business is." The leader drew his scimitar and held it at the ready.

"I am a messenger for the Comites Egnacius of Touloz"—he used the Moorish version of the name of the territory deliberately—"bound for Asturica at the Comites' behest. He has ordered me to attend on the Dux of Asturica on his behalf."

"And you have come by this road?" The leader looked doubtful as he moved his horse a little closer.

"The road in the north is blocked, by avalanches, we were told," Ragoczy Germainus said. "We would have preferred to go that way, but it would have meant a long delay, perhaps into the summer, which the Comites would not approve for I must present myself to the Dux with all haste."

"So you have come this way. Did you not think there would be fight-ing?" The leader held up his scimitar as if to underscore his remarks.

"From what we have been told, fighting is the least of what we have to fear," said Ragoczy Germainus. "Everywhere we have heard tales of terrible attacks on the unwary. This region is said to be afflicted with demons." He cocked his head as if considering the possibility.

"It is," said the leader, his face revealing more than he intended, for as he glanced over his shoulder, his expression was tainted by fright.

"How can that be?" Ragoczy Germainus asked. "Have not holy men come here? Is the place not protected by prayers and amulets?"

"They are not enough," said the leader uneasily. "Many have disappeared, and nothing found of them again. Not even bones."

"Could not that be the work of bandits?" Ragoczy Germainus suggested. "If men disappear, it would seem to me that other men would be suspect."

"Not in this region," said the leader. "Scoff if you will, you will see for yourself if you continue through the mountains."

"You have men in these mountains," Ragoczy Germainus pointed out, indicating the remnants of logging that marked the slope. "You have had many men here, and not so long ago. Why should we fear to go where you have gone?"

"Our slaves were under guard, and even then, some of them vanished," said the leader.

"They ran away," Ragoczy Germainus countered. "Slaves will do that."

"Not here," said the leader. "Here they are glad to stay with their overseers and to work where they are ordered to go, so long as they are guarded day and night." He leveled his lance in Ragoczy Germainus' direction, saying forcefully, "If you do not go east to the coast, we will not protect you. You will be on your own against the demons that hunt here."

"Why should we go away from Asturica rather than toward it?" Ragoczy Germainus asked, his smile as affable as if he spoke to a comrade. "It may be that there is danger in these mountains, but that does not mean that demons are the cause. I have a crucifix with me, blessed by the Pope, that no demon can withstand." He pulled a small silver crucifix from his wallet and held it up. "For Christians, it is proof against all evil."

"Then you have nothing to fear," said the leader, not quite concealing his sneer.

"So we think," said Ragoczy Germainus as he made sure he was able to keep an eye on all the men in the troop.

"If you should discover otherwise, we will not be able to help you," the leader warned, pointing toward the distant ridges where trees still grew. "And once you are in the forest you will be beyond all help."

"No doubt," said Ragoczy Germainus, salaaming again. "I thank you for telling me of the risks I may run. My manservant and I will be cautious in our choice of companions as we go."

"If you think that will be enough," the leader said, "so be it, and Allah witness what we have said."

"Amen to that," Ragoczy Germainus said, crossing himself and motioning to Rotiger to do the same. "You have nothing to worry about, good Moor. We are grateful to you for your coming to inform us of what lies ahead. Our crucifix will protect us, now that we know we must have it to hand."

The leader shifted in his saddle, making a sign to his men. "We ride on," he announced. "There is nothing more for us here." He wheeled his horse, then swung it back toward Ragoczy Germainus. "When you reach the wood, be on guard: there are patrols that may kill you before they know you are nothing to fear."

"Thank you again; I am twice in your debt," called Ragoczy Germainus, and stood, watching the Moors ride on, their horses leaving a cloud of dust hanging in the air to mark their departure.

"Do you think they accepted what you told them?" Rotiger asked when the Moors were far enough from their camp that the dust of their passing was settling once again.

"I think they were disgusted enough to decide not to question us any further. We have nothing they want, and that makes it easier for them to leave us to our fates." He did his best to smile, but his eyes were bleak. "If they should change their minds, we may find the going rather harder than before."

"How do you mean?" Rotiger paused in his work of breaking camp.

"I mean they could waylay us up the road and detain us." He shook his head. "Once in their prisons, we would be hard-pressed to conceal our true natures, for they are inclined to look for vampires and ghouls in these times, and in this place. They would be done with us quickly." He went and tugged the girths on the jack-mule's tight, smiling briefly as the mule huffed indignantly.

Rotiger looked appalled. "Surely not. You and I have been in prisons before and nothing happened worse than torture and hunger."

"Ah, but then our captors assumed we were living men. That would not be the case now." Ragoczy Germainus lifted the largest of their chests—one filled with his native earth—onto the pack-saddle on the jack-mule—saying as he did, "Now they would be watching us closely, and we cannot find ways to hide our . . . appetites." He began to strap the chest in place before reaching for the second, working with an ease that belied the weight of the chests.

"Then perhaps we should find another road, or make our own," Rotiger suggested. "They will not want to pursue us into the forest."

"They might not want to, but they would." Ragoczy Germainus shook his head. "If we deviate from the road we declared we were following now, they might come after us because of it. Having professed myself unconvinced of the presence of . . . eh . . . demons . . . I cannot now behave as if I believed in them. No," he said, setting his second chest of earth on the other side of the pack-saddle. "I must continue as I have begun with them."

"Do you think they will bother with us?" Rotiger asked, puzzled by Ragoczy Germainus' apprehension, "They left readily enough."

"Perhaps too readily," said Ragoczy Germainus as he lifted the third chest—his red-lacquer one—onto the other two and began to secure it in place with the broad, buckled leather straps that held the load and kept it from shifting; it was Ragoczy Germainus' own design, developed over centuries, combining elements of Roman, Scythian, Hunnic, and Mongol pack-saddles, made on a flexible, partly Roman, partly Moorish tree that adapted to almost every load.

"Then you are not satisfied that they accepted what you told them." Rotiger drowned the last of the fire with a pail of water and finished strapping bed-rolls and sacks of food to the second jenny's saddle, then went back to brush down his horse.

"No. That is why I have not removed my weapons," said Ragoczy Germainus. "I recommend you do not remove yours, either." He put their case of weapons on the larger jenny's pack-saddle, adding, "Keep her close to you. We may have to fight."

"You are expecting trouble," said Rotiger as he removed the hobbles from his dun's legs.

"I think it is possible," Ragoczy Germainus countered. "I hope the

Moors will find more to occupy them than two foreigners traveling alone. Had we come with an escort we might as well be at a clash of arms now." He took his bridle from where it hung over the cantel of his up-ended saddle and put it on his horse, taking care to be sure the bit lay properly in the grey's mouth.

"You are going to fight these Moors, aren't you?" Rotiger demanded, his patience worn thin.

"Only if I must," said Ragoczy Germainus, and went on tacking his horse.

By mid-day they were in a deep valley cut by a stream. Along the distant ridge they could see gangs of men working to cut down the few remaining trees. Although they were many thousands of paces away, the sound of their labors came back to them.

While they watered their horses and mules in the stream, Rotiger looked about. "We are not far from Mont Calcius," he said, using the old version of the village's name.

"No, not far. It is a bit to the south of us, and, as I reckon it, Usca is directly west. The forest around Mont Calcius must be gone by now; I can think of no reason to go there. Once we reach Usca, we will have a direct road to Asturica. If there is no fighting between Usca and Asturica." Ragoczy Germainus glanced up at the men laboring high above them. "They are determined to clear out the trees."

"You do not approve," said Rotiger, recognizing the neutrality of his master's tone for condemnation.

"Not as they are doing it, no, I do not." He pointed to where a section of slope had slid. "Mountains need their trees, or they crumble. The Moors should have left the younger trees to grow, so that there will be more in fifty years, and they may build more ships. If they cut down much of the brush, they could graze their flocks in the forests as well as on the hillsides. But they will not do this, for they want the land cleared. So as it is, when those trees they are logging are gone, they will have no more generations, and the mountains will fall away. Remember what happened around that Byzantine outpost after the Huns came through. That was four hundred years ago and the forest is only starting to grow again."

Rotiger could think of nothing to say in response, nor did Ragoczy Germainus appear to expect anything, so he nodded once and turned away from the activity on the ridge, and a little while later was glad to move on.

By the time they made camp that evening, it was dark, and the place they found was a remount station where horses were kept saddled in the courtyard for the couriers and officers who used the road. For a piece of silver and two of copper, the Moorish landlord gave them room in the field behind the stables, and a paddock for their animals for the night.

"Will you hunt?" Rotiger asked his master, growing uneasy on his behalf for his long fast; he had just finished eating a haunch of lamb he had bought from a shepherd who had brought some of his stock to the remount station for the kitchen there.

"No. We are too close to the station for that, and there is not one within I can safely visit in sleep." He was lying back on his bed-roll, laid atop his largest chest of earth. "A night on this will restore me."

"How long can you continue this way? And do not remind me that you have gone much longer without sustenance of any kind." He held up his hand to show he had not yet finished. "I have seen you in those times, and I know what they do to you."

"Well and good," said Ragoczy Germainus. "I will hunt once we reach the forest. It will be safer there."

"With only Chimenae's minions to trouble you," Rotiger said, his sarcasm more worried than angry.

"I know what to do about vampires," said Ragoczy Germainus. "Little as I may know Chimenae herself, she is of my blood, and to that I am no stranger."

"I am sure this will serve to make allies of them all," said Rotiger.

Ragoczy Germainus chuckled sadly. "I doubt it, though it would please me to think so." He smiled up at the brilliant sky. "If only the nights were not so short, I would take the chance and hunt, but—" He lifted a hand in resignation.

"Speaking of hunting," said Rotiger in a different voice, "I have not sensed that we are being followed any longer."

"No," said Ragoczy Germainus. "We are not."

"Perhaps Olutiz has grown tired of the chase and gone back to his inn," Rotiger suggested, spreading out his bed-roll.

"No," said Ragoczy Germainus.

"Then what has become of him?" asked Rotiger as he settled himself down to rest.

Ragoczy Germainus' answer robbed him of his equanimity. "He and

Dorioz are hunting the Moorish soldiers now," he said, continuing to study the night sky.

Text of a letter from Atta Olivia Clemens in Roma to Ragoczy Germainus in Touloza, written in Imperial Latin and never delivered.

To my most dear and oldest friend, Ragoczy Germainus—as you now call yourself—my affectionate greetings from Roma at the beginning of what promises to be a miserable summer here at Sine Pare.

I can but hope that this will reach you before you go on to another country with another name, for then I would have to wait until you have the inclination to write to me, and hope that I will still be here to receive it. You have been unusually peripatetic, even for you, since your escape from slavery in Hispania. You would think that the forces of the Emir's son could pursue you even now, and that if you remain anywhere for more than five years, you will be taken again. Yes, I am chiding you, for you know you could come here and have nothing to fear but the whims of the Pope, or from the soldiers who claim to garrison the city. Not that the Pope and the soldiers cannot be dangerous in their way, but I have found that a sack of gold is most salutary in its effect, and these days the Pope has other things to worry about than those raising horses on the outskirts of the city, and the soldiers are willing to accept money so they can gamble and whore.

Yes, I am truly now on the outskirts of the city. I have, in the last ten years, purchased land from the old limits of Sine Pare to that first line of villas, three thousand paces beyond the north gate of Roma itself. I have more than trebled my holdings, and I am about to purchase more. Or rather, my absent-but-very-wealthy-husband is about to purchase more, and to leave it to my care while he travels the world for the purpose of enriching our household. Niklos has twice gone to fetch the gold necessary for this expansion, and twice has managed to return with the whole sum intact. I am most pleased with him. Not simply for his skill at preserving treasure, but he has proven apt in keeping alive the myth of Servius of the Orsinus gens, my supposed husband. Even now, so many centuries later, I cannot bring myself to use the name of Cornelius Justus Sillius, though he was truly my husband, for fear that in so doing I might once again find myself hostage to a man. So Servius Secundus Orsinus is my spouse, far-traveled that he is, and Niklos is able to convince everyone in Roma that he has seen and talked to the man a year ago. How else, he says, can anyone account for my increase in wealth? No one here knows of the three stud farms I have, or the mills I have built in the Frankish territories. So now as no more wars ransack my holdings, I should have a good period of prosperity, which I am more than eager to share with you.

Very well, I admit it. I am lonely. I am lonely and I hate it. I have had lovers who have pleased me, but it is not the same as having you, for you know the demands of long life, as well as its delights, and with you, I may speak of the past without fear that I may reveal too much, and thereby bring myself and all I have worked for into danger. Niklos is a help, for he, too, is familiar with this gulf that yawns between us and the living, and he is willing to speak of it with me, but it is not the same. I know you have learned to accept the separation from the living, and to accommodate in a way I have not mastered. If you were here, you might be able to teach me how I might achieve the acquiescence you have acquired; as it is, I cannot keep myself from railing at the loss of rights that have forced me to invent husbands and fathers to enable me to have what is mine. When I was young and living, I would not have required such a ruse. No one here can comprehend my feeling of disadvantage that continues to thwart my ambitions, for they have never known another way; I am left to fret on my own, without the comfort of shared indignation. I do not mean to cark at you. It is good that you are willing to bear with me when I do, for you understand how one can miss what has been lost so many, many years ago: bear with me now.

Roma is not as you remember it, of course. It is not as I remember it, either. The walls are broken in several places, the baths are used for very little bathing, and those that are still standing are more brothels than anything else. The farmers raise pigs and sheep and cattle inside the walls, and where many great houses stood there are now only ruins half-buried in the earth. There are days when I wander the streets— with Niklos to escort me—and try to recall how it looked when I was growing up. It is at those times that I can comprehend why you return to your native earth, no matter who lives on it now, or what has become of your own people, for I know what was here seven centuries ago, and I know I am still part of that.

How maudlin of me. How can you bear to read this? Well, if I have not succeeded in putting you off entirely, let me say again how much I would enjoy your company at Sine Pare for as long as you care to remain. I am aware that two of our kind cannot stay in close proximity for many years, for it draws attentions to our habits and alerts the living to our presence, which is never useful. Still a year or two would not put either of us in danger, and it might be worth the chances we would have to take. I cannot promise you much better conditions than you have in Toulosa, but I can make sure you and Rotiger are protected from all but the forces of nature.

This by my own hand on the 6th day of June, according to the Pope's calendar, at Sine Pare.

Olivia

4

They crossed the river on a rough bridge of logs, and entered the trees two thousand paces beyond, into the welcome shade that blocked the relentless summer sun. Gradually the light dimmed as they moved deeper into the forest; now the sunlight came only in dappled flecks where the leaves gave enough opening for it to reach the floor of the woods. Here the heat was less, and a welcome breeze strummed the leaves.

"It's quiet," said Rotiger when they had followed the narrow road for some distance. "Just the wind." He was in his linen gunna over Persian leggings but he was still warm.

"The loggers are driving the game away," said Ragoczy Germainus, "and the hunters follow the game." He was alert as he listened to the sounds in the woods, paying attention to every shift and change that came through the branches. His clothing was lightweight: a gonel of black, loose-weave wool with deep-pleated sleeves over Frankish tibialia, with thick-soled brodequins of soft black leather laced to the knees.

"The road isn't much," Rotiger observed. "Hardly wide enough for deer."

"It is still the only road to Usca in this part of the mountains," said Ragoczy Germainus. "The Moors want travelers to go toward the coast, to Terrago, and Valenzia, not west to Usca; they have no inclination to maintain this road. The western Goths still hold much of that north-western territory: why would the Moors keep this access route in good repair?" He raised his arm to push aside a low-growing branch. "Watch out. It will snap back when I release it," he warned Rotiger.

"I'm prepared," said Rotiger, holding back his horse and the mules he led as the branch thrashed toward him. "Not bad for a trap," he re-marked as he held the branch as he went by, seeing it whip back behind him. "It could knock a man out of the saddle if he were inattentive."

"I was thinking much the same thing," Ragoczy Germainus said, turning in his saddle to be sure Rotiger was unharmed.

"Do you think anyone would try such a trick?" Rotiger wondered aloud.

"If you mean Chimenae and her tribe, I think it may be possible," said Ragoczy Germainus, looking around with care.

"Then you think they have expanded into this area," said Rotiger. "We are well beyond Mont Calcius."

"They have not remained in the open; I suspect they have followed the forests, back into the mountains, where they are hard to find." He made a gesture, taking in the tangled undergrowth and the narrow path they followed. "This is safer for them, particularly if Olutiz was right, and there have been more added to their numbers."

Rotiger said nothing more for a good stretch of their travels until they came to one of the old shrines. "Cups," he said, pointing to the of-ferings in the ancient niches.

"Filled with blood; some of it has not fully coagulated yet," Ragoczy Germainus remarked. "There have been men here not half a day ago."

"And vampires?" Rotiger asked, sitting more upright in his saddle.

"If these offerings are fresh, the vampires cannot be far away." He studied the shrine, counting the cups and making note of the empty niches. "Most of the blood comes from goats, but one of the cups has horse's blood in it."

"Chimenae would like that," said Rotiger ironically.

"No doubt the reason they left it," said Ragoczy Germainus som-berly, his dark eyes fixed on the middle distance. "I must suppose she still believes in the magical powers of horses' blood." He glanced around the old shrine one last time. "It would be ill for us if we are discovered here."

"By men or vampires?" Rotiger inquired, not quite amused.

"Either. Or both." Ragoczy Germainus tapped his grey with his heels and they moved on along the road, into the deepest part of the forest.

That evening they found a glen with a spring making one end marshy, and grassy enough to give their animals a chance to graze. They made camp at the dry end, in the widest part of the meadow so that they had a little distance between themselves and the cover of the trees. Ragoczy Germainus made a point of building up enough of a fire to keep them in its glare all night. "I do not want to have any uninvited visitors to contend with unless we are ready for them."

"But you see well in the dark," Rotiger reminded him.

"And so do they," Ragoczy Germainus declared as he laid another branch on the blaze. "I will not sleep, so that they will have no opportunity to stalk us without detection."

"Are you expecting them to do that?" Rotiger asked as he set their tack up for the night.

"Not particularly, but I am not going to assume they will not. If they can get nothing from you and me, they can drain our horses and mules, and I must suppose they will try." He rubbed his face. "When we reach Usca, I will need you to trim my beard again. And probably my hair as well."

"Of course. I could tend to that now," Rotiger offered, wanting something to do other than wait for an attack that might never come.

Ragoczy Germainus considered it. "Why not?" he said at last. "It is not as if you need a mirror, and I—" He stopped with a one-sided smile.

"It will not take long. My shears and razor are in the pack with our weapons. I can get them out now," said Rotiger as he pulled the leather case from the stack of chests and sacks and packs. "I know where they are," he announced as he unbuckled the good Padovan leather and took out a small case. "Here. Sit on that chest and I'll have this done quickly."

"You have combs as well, or must we borrow from the horses?" Ragoczy Germainus asked, half in jest. "I know; I know. You always have combs and a Greek brush with your shears."

"True enough," said Rotiger as he pulled out the ivory comb and set to work, pleased to have this work to do. He went about the task quickly and expertly, combing and shearing with the fluidity of long practice.

"When I was newly come to this life," Ragoczy Germainus remarked when Rotiger was half-done with cutting his hair, "I used to try to see myself. There were few mirrors then, and most of them were polished metal, although still water was always preferred. It infuriated me that I could not see myself: that was a long time ago."

"But you miss having a reflection," said Rotiger, knowing it was so, although Ragoczy Germainus rarely spoke of it; that he did now told Rotiger that his master was uneasy.

"Of course. But it is one of the many things I have become accustomed to, over time." He held still while Rotiger began to trim his beard—already short and sharply defined—cutting it close before using the razor to neaten the line of it.

"There," said Rotiger, standing back. "That should do for another three months at least." He began to put away his tools.

"Should I not return the favor?" Ragoczy Germainus asked.

"Perhaps, in a week or two," said Rotiger. "I can tend to my beard myself."

"Because you can see yourself," Ragoczy Germainus said. "From time to time I envy you that."

This admission gave Rotiger pause, for in his seven centuries with Ragoczy Germainus, he had been told this only twice before—once on the road to Baghdad and once in the mountains of northern Greece; on both occasions it had signaled trouble. "Why?" he managed to say with a modicum of composure. "My face has not changed since you restored me from death."

"But you can see that it has not changed," said Ragoczy Germainus, and then he reached for his short sword, responding to a crackle in the bushes.

"What is it?" Rotiger asked, his voice dropping to a whisper.

"I cannot make it out yet," said Ragoczy Germainus in an undervoice; he spoke in Byzantine Greek.

"What do you think it is?" Rotiger said in the same tongue as he tried to squint to see beyond the shine of firelight.

"I have a fair notion; I sense no pulse." He was concentrating now, focused on what moved under the trees beyond the firelight.

"Chimenae, do you think?" Rotiger carefully put his case down and reached for his dagger.

"It is possible, but I doubt it." He pulled one of the long, sharpened branches from the pack. "Still, I want to be ready."

Rotiger nodded, poised to fight off any attack.

"Keep an eye on the animals. I think they may try to circle behind us. The mules and horses are a very tempting target."

"How many do you think there are?" Rotiger was alarmed at the implications of what Ragoczy Germainus said.

"Half a dozen, perhaps more," was the tranquil answer. "Yes; a few are moving toward the far end of the glade. Drive the animals into the water. That will afford them some protection."

"Will you be able to manage alone?" Rotiger asked, preparing to obey.

"I would hope so," said Ragoczy Germainus. "Make a torch and take it with you. The fire will be more helpful than swords and daggers."

Rotiger seized one of the sharpened branches Ragoczy Germainus proffered him, thrust the blunt end into the fire, held it there while it caught, then hurried off toward their animals. He had almost reached the nearest mule when a strangely dressed man wielding a small axe burst out of the trees, yelling and waving his arms in an effort to panic the animals; had the five not been hobbled the attack might have worked, but as it was, the horses, unable to flee, or to rear, began to kick instead, neighing in distress. A moment later, the mules did the same.

The man with the axe was caught on the hip and tossed half-way across the clearing where he found himself looking up at Ragoczy Germainus, who stood over him with his sword at the ready.

"Well, well," he said cordially, although the point of his sword did not move. "Blaga. Still using an axe." He saw shock in Blaga's face, and went on, "Why should you be astonished to see me? *You* are still alive: why should I not be?" He carefully stepped so that his hand was on the supine man's wrist, just above his weapon. "It would be reckless to try to attack me," he went on without any loss of good-will. "I am your equal in strength and I have my sword."

"So you say," Blaga responded in fury as another man came hurtling out of the forest, holding two short swords, and running straight at Ragoczy Germainus.

Quickly Ragoczy Germainus stepped back, but only to kick Blaga's axe away as he turned to face the second vampire; he saw by the copper-colored hair it was Ennati, and that Rotiger had come up behind him and set his clothes afire with his torch.

Ennati screamed and flung himself backward, rolling to put out the flames, his shrieks making the horses and mules whinny in distress, and mill at the edges of the marshy stream, churning up mud and occasionally striking out with their teeth.

Blaga reached out to grab Ragoczy Germainus' leg, but cursed as the older man eluded him.

"That ploy is too old. I have learned to avoid it," said Ragoczy Germainus. "If you do not wish to be hurt, stay where you are."

"I am not afraid of you," Blaga stated, unwilling to look at Ennati, who had finally put out the fire on his clothes and was trying to sit up.

"Then you are a fool," said Ragoczy Germainus, looking about him. "Where are the rest of your comrades? I can sense them, as you can sense me."

"They are waiting to attack," said Blaga with more bravado than certainty.

"And do you think they will? You have lost the element of surprise and they will have seen that we know how to manage you." He motioned to Blaga to sit up. "You will not be able to harm either Rotiger or me, though you may try."

Blaga rose, his demeanor sullen and resentful. "We will kill you yet, and we will make sure you do not rise."

"If that is your plan, it has not succeeded; I am grateful for the warning." He glanced toward Rotiger, who was keeping a wary eye on Ennati. "What do you think, old friend?"

"I think this must be settled, and quickly." He pointed to Ennati. "They will not all be so reckless as this one."

"No, they will not," agreed Ragoczy Germainus. "They are watching us still. Four or five of your tribe." He rounded on Blaga. "Did Chimenae send you to do this?"

"She does not send us. We go where we wish to." Blaga folded his arms and stared beyond the firelight.

"Then you have broken with her?" Ragoczy Germainus asked, thinking of what Olutiz had told him.

"No. We do not let ourselves be ruled by her as many do. We will provide our help in need, but we will not be her chattel." He laughed. "Some of the others are still under her spell. They would have killed you at once."

Ragoczy Germainus regarded him steadily. "Do you think so."

Blaga retreated into silence while Rotiger brought Ennati over to the edge of the campfire.

"The animals are all right; they are frightened and restive, but they are all right," Rotiger told Ragoczy Germainus.

"Thank all the forgotten gods for that," said Ragoczy Germainus. He turned to face the two they had captured. "I think it is time I called upon Chimenae."

"She says Chimena now," Blaga corrected him smugly, as if he were certain that this would embarrass Ragoczy Germainus.

"Does she so. I will keep that in mind." He listened to the sounds of the forest. "Your comrades are departing."

Blaga tossed his head. "They will find you again, and you will not be ready for them."

But Ennati was not so cocksure. "They will have to tell Chimena," he said to Ragoczy Germainus. "We have not wholly gone from her. We have our own ways, but we are not like Olutiz is: we know our obligation."

"Then she will be expecting me," said Ragoczy Germainus. "We did not part well, thirty years ago."

"No one parts well from her," said Ennati. "She dislikes to have anyone leave her, even for the True Death." He was pale from his ordeal, and his manner remained subdued.

"Merez was gone for a time, and when he came back, she punished him for more than a year." Blaga looked about him in agitation. "She will be angry that we have been caught. Better we are killed than captured."

"She will understand that I made your attack untenable," said Ragoczy Germainus.

"No, she will not," said Ennati, mumbling a little as if anticipating a rebuke for his remark. "She never understands failure."

"Then she is being foolish," said Rotiger before Ragoczy Germainus could say anything. He had gone to get two lengths of rope and now used them to tie Ennati's and Blaga's hands behind them, saying as he did, "If you test these bonds, you will notice they have wire through them. You may be able to break them but they will cut your wrists in the process, and even vampires suffer when they bleed."

Ennati nodded dumbly; Blaga cursed.

"Is Chimena still at the stone house on the ridge?" Ragoczy Germainus asked, his manner conversational.

"She is not. She has gone to the next crag; the Moors have been logging on the slope below the stone house, and she could not risk discovery. She has found a safer place, near an ancient altar." Blaga sounded proud of this even as he winced while Rotiger secured his hands behind him.

"And do the villagers still bring her cups of blood?" Ragoczy Germainus asked.

"They have brought the cups to old shrines, but only a few climb to her new dwelling, and then only on special days," said Ennati.

"Do you think she will be there tomorrow night?" Ragoczy Germainus did not sound as if this made much difference to him, but he listened intently to the reply.

"I think she will be waiting for you," said Blaga. "Merez will warn her."

"So you said," Ragoczy Germainus conceded, then went on more briskly. "Well, you may as well make yourselves as comfortable as you can. We will travel in the morning—"

"There will be sun," exclaimed Blaga in shock. "You cannot—We will not live, nor will you."

"We will carry you with the packs on the mules; you will be wrapped in heavy hides, so you will not burn." Ragoczy Germainus nodded to Rotiger. "Take the bears' hides from the wooden chest. Those will serve our purposes."

"But they are gifts to the Dux of Asturica," Rotiger reminded him.

"This will not harm them," said Ragoczy Germainus.

Blaga looked panicked; he took an unsteady step in Ragoczy Germainus' direction. "You cannot do this. What will become of us?"

"You will have to rely on us to keep you safe," Ragoczy Germainus said, his voice tinged with irony.

"Keep us safe." There was a long pause while Blaga considered this. "You must surely think we are gullible—keep us safe!"

"You have my Word that we will," said Ragoczy Germainus in a tone that was beyond question. "Come. Find yourselves a place near the fire. There are more than vampires to be held at bay tonight."

"If you mean wolves, they have gone farther into the mountains," said Ennati. "So have the cats and bears."

"Because the Moors are cutting down the forests," said Ragoczy Germainus. "That much is obvious. But if any wolves or cats or bears remain here, they must be hungry, and they have a taste for horses and mules, as you do."

"You have the fire for *them*?" Blaga said in disbelief.

"Certainly. They are as much under my protection as you are." Ragoczy Germainus began to pace. "How many more of you are there since I was here?"

Ennati and Blaga exchanged glances. "Perhaps twenty," Ennati said.

"Far too many," said Ragoczy Germainus, shaking his head in worry. He thought back to what Olutiz had told him, and he felt cold growing in him, in spite of the fire and the summer night. "The wolves and cats are not the only ones who will feel the loss of the forest," he said to Blaga and Ennati.

"This is nothing to us," Blaga insisted, although Ennati looked thoughtful.

Ragoczy Germainus shook his head. "You are not thinking of what may come in time. You tell me that Chimena has had to move higher up the mountains, and yet you do not think the logging has deprived you of hunting ground and game?"

"We do not hunt game, except when there is no choice," said Blaga arrogantly. "And the loggers are men."

"For which we are pleased," added Ennati, but less forcefully than Blaga had spoken. "We hunt them as they rest from their labors."

"And some of you are apprehended and killed," said Ragoczy Germainus for them. "You need not deny it."

"Very well," Blaga allowed. "Some have been killed."

"And more recently than in the past," Ragoczy Germainus persisted.

"Yes," Ennati said slowly as Blaga glared at him. "That is true."

"I feared so," said Ragoczy Germainus as much to himself as to Ennati and Blaga.

"Why should you fear?" Blaga challenged him. "You have deserted Chimena and all that is hers."

"I was unwelcome, and I have learned it is unwise to remain in one place too long." He stopped his pacing and faced Rotiger, and once again spoke to him in Byzantine Greek. "What do you think, old friend? Do we plan for a trap along the way?"

"It would be prudent," said Rotiger. "You may have much to deal with when we reach this crag they speak of."

"You are probably right," Ragoczy Germainus agreed. "Well, let us plan to depart shortly before dawn."

"How will we find this place? The villagers cannot be asked without rousing suspicion, and the Moors would not aid us at all. If we must find our way without any directions, we may become completely lost, and be unable to reach Chimena's place or the road to Usca." He seemed unworried but there was an edge in his voice that revealed his misgiving.

"I think that one of these two will tell us," said Ragoczy Germainus, once again speaking in the language of the region.

"Tell you what?" Blaga demanded.

"The way to find Chimena, of course," said Ragoczy Germainus blandly.

"Never. If you want to carry us to her in disgrace, you must find your way on your own." His face set in hard lines and his brow lowered obdurately.

"Then you will ride, wrapped in bearskins over the backs of our chests and packs, until we are trapped or we reach a road or village. We may have to leave you then," said Ragoczy Germainus, and smiled wryly. "The villagers know what to do with you, do they not?"

"You would not!" Blaga yelled. "How can you leave your own kind to be killed at the hands of men!"

"So now I am your kind after all," Ragoczy Germainus marveled.

Ennati looked up. "I will tell you how to find her crag."

"You will not!" Blaga shouted. "You will not betray her, or us!"

Ennati shrugged. "He is right. If we leave him to wander, then sooner or later we will fall into unfriendly hands. All of us." He nodded. "You will have to reach her before the end of the day, or you will be attacked again, and by many more than the seven of us who came here tonight."

"Is it possible to do that?" Ragoczy Germainus asked, his demeanor serious and attentive.

"If you keep a good pace, it should be. The worst of it is that there is only one trail leading to the crag and it is carefully guarded at night." Ennati ignored Blaga's furious gaze. "The mountains are rugged, and you may find that it is more difficult to climb them in the heat of the day. The Moors and their slaves rest through the worst of it."

"Do you think the animals can endure the heat?" Ragoczy Germainus was not at ease about the effort that would be demanded of them, but he concealed his concern behind a composed mien.

"They are your stock," said Ennati indifferently. "How have they fared thus far?"

"They have done well enough," said Ragoczy Germainus as he thought of the jenny's swollen hock.

"Then you must decide if you can risk it," said Ennati. "The last part of the path is the steepest—and it is narrow." He looked gratified at this, as if the severity of the climb made his revelations less a betrayal than they would have been if the road were an easy one. "The canyon is deep and not even you could survive a fall into it."

"Very likely not," Ragoczy Germainus said. "So we will have to be diligent. It would not do to lose you and our mules on such a climb."

Blaga spat out an obscenity and glared at Ennati. "You will answer for this."

"He may well do so," said Ragoczy Germainus, "but only if we all arrive at our destination without mishap."

Sighing, Ennati said, "I will tell you what I know. You must decide if you are willing to risk the journey." He squatted down, making himself as comfortable as possible. "You must go to Canthiz and take the track that leads to Querzus Scopuluz. Do you recall where that was?"

"Above that old monastery?" Ragoczy Germainus asked. "Is there anyone living there anymore?"

"Owls and badgers," said Ennati. "The monks left long ago—before the Moors came." He coughed as if embarrassed by what he had said.

"So we take the trail up the mountain to Querzus Scopuluz. What then?" Ragoczy Germainus was doing his best to recall that part of the mountains, and wondered how much he might discover in that region if he had time to explore; he suspected he would learn more about the extent of the changes in the forest in that area than he might in many another.

Ennati avoided looking at Blaga as he continued. "You go to the old shrine on the flank of the mountain there, and proceed along the side of the cliff to the fork in the way near the waterfalls: there are three of them, one beneath the other. There you cross on the rope bridge and keep on until you reach the old tombs built into the caves." He went silent, his face without expression. "That is where you will find what you seek."

Blaga muttered under his breath, the words inaudible to Ragoczy Germainus; Ennati winced.

"That must be sixteen thousand paces at least," said Rotiger. "A hard day's journey in such territory as this."

"Yes," said Ragoczy Germainus. "But one we must make." He looked past the fire to the enormous shadows of the forest.

"Is it really so necessary?" Rotiger asked. "This will take us far from the road to Usca."

"If we do not face this now, we will not be safe from it," said Ragoczy Germainus. "It will follow us everywhere."

"But why should it? Do you not want to be away from here?" Rotiger persisted. "You said you did not want to come this way, yet we came. You said you did not want to deal with Chimena's tribe, yet here we are."

"Yes; and since we are here, and so are they, I cannot dismiss my part in this." Ragoczy Germainus shook his head slowly.

"Because you feel responsible for what Chimena has done, do you not?" Rotiger said, his expression keen.

"If I do nothing, many living and undead will pay the price," he answered gently and indirectly.

"You will not change Chimena," said Blaga, all but boasting.

"Perhaps not," Ragoczy Germainus agreed, "but I must make the attempt to persuade her."

"You are not answerable for what she does," Rotiger insisted as he tightened the braided thongs holding Blaga's wrists.

"No; but I am responsible for making her what she is," said Ragoczy Germainus in a voice of finality.

"You will not succeed," Blaga said with certainty.

"I may not," said Ragoczy Germainus, his smile as bleak as it was fleeting; he put another branch on the fire and watched with enigmatic eyes as it began to burn.

Text of a letter from Ursino Baroz in Asturica to Comites Egnacius in Toulosa, carried by pilgrim monks and delivered four months after being entrusted to the monks' care.

To the most excellent Comites Egnacius of Toulosa who is rightly entitled to the recognition and dignity of that position, and who has been

a most gracious patron to the clerk Ursino Baroz, his greetings and ex-
pressions of regard from the beleaguered city of Asturica.

 Surely you have heard of the campaigns being waged against the
Christian north of Hispania by the godless forces of the Caliph, and
you know how desperate the position of the soldiers of Christ has be-
come, so you will not be astonished to learn that the Dux Manrigo has
gone to join other Christian knights for the purpose of mounting a
proper counter-attack on the Caliph's men. This place is filled with
men-at-arms and belted knights who seek the favor of God and the
Dux, and who are sworn to accompany him on his campaign. It is said
all the cheese for ten thousand paces around the city has been seized by
the Dux's growing army, and that wine barrels have been brought by
the wagon-load to fill the tankards of the men going off to fight.

 You pledged your support, and vowed to send aid to this place, but
no such aid has arrived, and it is feared that some terrible fate has be-
fallen the men you have sent here. We know the Roncesvalles Pass has
been closed, but it is now open enough for men on horseback to venture
through it. Yet there has been no report of any such men coming here
on your order. We pray that they were not caught in the avalanche that
blocked Roncesvalles and that they will come soon, so that they may
join with the others in this drive to reclaim this land for the good of
Christ and His people. So long as there is no report, we must hope that
they will arrive.

 It is known that you have men here in this court who report to you;
from them you will learn that I describe the situation here truthfully.
You will have no reason to doubt me, or them, in regard to the plans of
the Dux. You are in a good position to help us, and Manrigo will see
that your aid is lauded everywhere Christians fight the hoards of the
Caliph. You will be forgiven many sins for your assistance in this time,
and should the Caliph's men breach the Pyrenees and strike into
Frankish lands, the Dux would be obligated to show you the same rein-
forcement that you provide him now; should you fail him in this time of
greatest need, you may not be confident of his participation in your de-
fense, or in his willingness to send his own troops to fight your battles.

 In the name of the Savior and of all Christian Kings, I tell you the
Dux must have every man you can send him, and I ask you in his name
to respond in haste. The armies of the Caliph are massing to drive us
north and into the sea. Those men you have dispatched are urgently

needed, and any more you can send to us will be needed in the efforts
of the knights and men-at-arms. You will be glad of the honor you will
bring to your House, and you will enjoy the gratitude of Dux Manrigo
and all his sons and their sons for your devotion to this highest cause.

I am bidden to express the thanks of the Dux, in anticipation of your
donation to his war.

In the name of Manrigo, Dux of Asturica and of Christ our Savior
Ursino Baroz
Clerk to Dux Manrigo

at Asturica on the 20ᵗʰ day of June in the 752ⁿᵈ year of Salvation, by the
calendar of Sant' Iago

5

This was the second time they had stopped to rest their mules and
horses, letting them drink from the stream their path followed in a
steadily upward climb toward the crest of the mountain. The additional
weight of Blaga and Ennati in their muffling bearskins slowed the
mules, making them increasingly reluctant to go on.

"I am grateful that this is a long day," said Ragoczy Germainus in the
language of the Poles, so that neither Ennati nor Blaga could understand him, should they happen to be roused from their daylight stupor
sufficiently to overhear them. As he checked the girth, tightening it a
little before getting back into the saddle, he went on. "Were we in winter, there would be no chance of completing our mission; if the way was
not made impassable by snow, the shortness of the day would give us
insufficient time to complete our travel before nightfall."

"I would not like to have to fight on this trail," said Rotiger in the
same tongue as he patted the pommel of the sword slung across his
back, and fingered the other weapons on his broad leather belt.

"Nor would I, in any season," said Ragoczy Germainus. "But still, we
ought to be ready for anything once the sun is low."

"And that will not be long. Once we cross the bridge—" Rotiger began only to be cut off by his master.

"We will not cross the bridge," he said as he gathered up the reins and the lead-rope in preparation for moving off again.

"Why not?" Rotiger asked in surprise.

"Because Ennati was giving us . . . shall we say, poor information," Ragoczy Germainus replied.

"Are you certain of it?" Rotiger pulled on the two leads he held, bringing the mules up behind his dun.

"As certain as I am of anything I do not know as a fact." He took the lead up the steep, winding trail toward the jutting crags at the top of the mountain. "Consider how difficult it is for Chimena's brood to walk in daylight or cross running water—in spite of being on their native earth. Would they make so crucial a traverse over a series of water-falls?"

"It does seem unlikely," said Rotiger, and, after a brief silence asked, "Why does their native earth not shield them, I wonder?"

"I do not know," Ragoczy Germainus admitted. "I have thought about it for a long time, and all I can arrive at is the same conclusion I reached decades ago: that since there is no reciprocity between Chimena and her . . . offspring, there are none of the benefits that come from that exchanged intimacy, with anything. They have lost their sense of . . . mutuality." He coughed in warning. "There is an overhang ahead of us."

"I see it." Rotiger peered at the stone brow and frowned. "I wish I had a hand free for my sword."

"And I," Ragoczy Germainus confessed. "It is an ideal place for an ambush. I cannot use throwing weapons in so confined a place."

"Or there must be a watch-post," said Rotiger, holding the leads more firmly. "I would expect them to try to stampede our animals. On a trail this narrow, and over a ravine, that could be fatal."

"So it could," Ragoczy Germainus said, recalling just such a trap in the Greek mountains; then the enemy had been Huns and the pack-train had had a dozen mules and six riders in it, but the results were the same as they would be here if the animals were panicked: disorder and disaster.

Rotiger held his horse and mules back on the trail to give Ragoczy Germainus and his horse and mule some room to maneuver or retreat if that became necessary. He knew his nervousness was being communicated to the animals, and there was nothing he could do about it but keep his grip on the reins and lead while hoping nothing untoward would happen.

The high screech of a hawk sounded overhead; a pair of the raptors were circling in their last hunt of the day.

Ragoczy Germainus laughed once. "Do you think we are their prey?"

"The mules might be, if the birds could carry them off," said Rotiger, watching the hawks slide through the sky.

"We cannot rush the mules, not so high up. The air is thinner here, and they must not be pushed beyond their endurance. It would be folly to exhaust them." Ragoczy Germainus recalled crossing the Celestial Mountains, and the difficulty he had experienced on the high passes when he tried to speak; so high and cold was the road they followed that the ponies carrying their chests were fed hot gruel with bits of meat in it so that they would not collapse on the journey.

A while later they reached the bridge; it was cooler now, and the shadows cast by the peaks around them moved over more of the mountain, creating a kind of twilight in the canyon. They took the goat-track that led up the mountain instead of crossing the falls.

"At another time I would admire them," said Ragoczy Germainus, looking down at the spectacular display in the gorge; the rumble of the falls, magnified by the stone walls around them, made it necessary for him to shout.

Rotiger made a sign to show he heard and agreed as they continued upward, toward the long, brilliant rays of the westering sun; behind him, tied over the packs and chests the mules carried, the trussed figures of Ennati and Blaga began to move as the coming of the end of day stirred them from their sleep.

Finally they emerged from the shadows of the narrow canyon to a plateau where scrub grew in place of trees and rocks poked up everywhere. "It should not be far now," said Ragoczy Germainus as he looked around them with shaded eyes. "I think I see one of those old shrines, there"—he pointed—"at the end of that escarpment."

"You mean those large white stones?" Rotiger asked as he did his best to follow Ragoczy Germainus' line of vision.

"Immediately to the right of them. There is a standing arch, about half my height, by the look of it, making a niche." He sat back in the saddle, grateful—as he often was in the last nine years—for the stirrups that he had had fitted to his saddle a decade ago. On a climb like this, stirrups made all the difference.

"Is that a tomb?" Rotiger asked, and turned in his saddle as Blaga roared in fury.

"The two are waking up," Ragoczy Germainus noted, his face set in an amiable smile that did not touch his eyes. "Blaga, be still," he ordered in a louder tone, and in the dialect of the region. "You are not improving your situation by making so much noise." He spoke to Rotiger in Persian, "Let us wait until he is ready to be sensible. I do not wish to have to fight him on this trail."

Blaga muttered incoherent threats as he struggled against the bonds that confined him in the bearskin.

"Rotiger will be forced to subdue you if you keep on that way. If you hope to alert Chimena of your coming, that has probably already been done." He waited until Blaga calmed down. "That is much better. Continue in this manner and all will be well. I am afraid there is nothing I can do about the heat in those skins. It is summer, and even up high in the mountains, it has been warm."

There was a long silence this time, then Ennati said, "We will not fight you."

"We will not have to," Blaga finished for him.

"No doubt," said Ragoczy Germainus, and moved off again, trying to discern who was following them—if, indeed, anyone was.

"You are edgy, my master," Rotiger remarked in Persian as they approached the ancient tombs with their arches for protecting offerings.

"With good cause, I fear," Ragoczy Germainus said as he drew in his horse. Although he took his saie from its ties on his saddle and slung it around his shoulders more for the protection it afforded than against the first evening chill, he remained in the saddle; Rotiger followed his example.

"This is a very exposed place," Rotiger said.

"And there is just the one path out of it," Ragoczy Germainus added.

Rotiger nodded, glancing over his shoulder toward the fading sun. "It will be night in a little while."

"Then it is time they emerged," Ragoczy Germainus said as he pointed to the high niches.

"How many?" Rotiger asked.

"I have no idea," Ragoczy Germainus replied, and put his hand to his belt where a long chain hung, with a fist-sized iron ball at either end.

Rotiger saw this, and said, "You expect to fight."

"No; I am prepared to." He waited as the light behind them went from gold to red to lavender. "Are you ready?" he called out to Blaga. "You and Ennati will soon be back with Chimena."

"She will be angry," said Ennati fatalistically.

"That she might," Ragoczy Germainus said, making no attempt to deny the possibility.

"And then what?" Blaga demanded abruptly. "Will you keep us safe from her anger?"

"My master," whispered Rotiger before Ragoczy Germainus could answer Blaga.

"I see it," said Ragoczy Germainus.

"The nearest tomb . . ." Rotiger trailed off.

"Is opening; yes, I see." He rose in his stirrups and loosened the fine chain holding the metal balls to his belt. He swung down out of the saddle and went to unstrap Blaga and Ennati from their places, handling them with no sign of effort as he lifted them from the packs to the ground, saying as he did, "I am not going to release you yet. There is much to be decided before I do. You may struggle if you wish, but I would hope you have better sense than that."

Blaga mumbled an obscenity and wriggled against his bonds, then did his best to sit up, but without success. Ennati lay supine and inert, which made Ragoczy Germainus more wary of him than Blaga.

The first door was open now, and the occupant emerged. The figure was dressed in Moorish clothes, wearing a tunic of leather stitched with metal scales; he had a scimitar thrust through his broad green sash and there were metal points on his tooled-leather boots. Ragoczy Germainus recognized Yamut ibn Rabi; he recalled the steady hatred the Moor had shown for Chimenae, and wondered how he had become the guard of Chimena.

A second door opened, and another Moor came out, also dressed for combat. The two swung around to face Ragoczy Germainus.

"I remember who you are," said Yamut ibn Rabi in the language of the region flavored with a strong Moorish accent. "How is it you have returned?"

"I remember you as well," said Ragoczy Germainus, offering him a salaam. "My travels brought me here. I am on my way to Asturica; the roads forced me to come this way. I am in a hurry to reach my destination." He secured the lead-rope of his mule to his saddle.

"Of course," said Yamut ibn Rabi sarcastically. "I should have realized that you would not come here for any other reason. How do you come to have two of ours trussed up like lambs going to slaughter?" He indicated the struggling figures tied inside the bearskins.

"They will tell you if you ask them," said Ragoczy Germainus. "I have brought them back to Chimena—for so I understand she now calls herself—to ask her not to set her tribe on me."

"Do you suppose she would do this?" Yamut ibn Rabi asked, unconvinced. "For what reason would she?"

"Those two have . . . persuaded me that it is a possibility," said Ragoczy Germainus, indicating Ennati and Blaga. "They and a number of their comrades attacked my manservant and me. They wanted our horses and mules for blood and rituals, it seems, and they attempted to kill us. Since the others fled, I decided it would be best to settle this now, before they all gather again." He nodded toward his two captives. "I could easily have given them the True Death, but I did not, to show that I mean Chimena and her descendants no harm."

"So it is you," said a voice off to the left.

Ragoczy Germainus turned to see Chimena approaching. She was as magnificent as ever, her silken finery better than most that could be found from Gadez to Roma. Her stole was of thick, pleated silk in a deep, wine-red, belted with golden links, and draped around her shoulders was a loros set with rubies and pearls and embroidered with gryphons—fine enough for an empress to wear. Her shoes were sewn with golden thread and she had added a golden fillet to her brow.

"You are very splendid," said Ragoczy Germainus as she approached.

"Yamut and Sayed have been busy getting tribute for me; it is only right that I should display it," said Chimena, nodding to her two Moorish guards. "They have brought me things." She fingered the loros. "They know what I like most."

"How unfortunate more of the world cannot behold your grandeur," said Ragoczy Germainus, no hint of condemnation in his voice. "You have come far into the mountains."

"They are cutting down the forests. I could not rest safely in my own house; they are emptying the mountain villages, too, and that has driven me here." Resentment simmered in her eyes. "One day, they will regret what they have done. They all will—the villagers who have forsaken me as well as the Moors."

"For your sake, I hope not; for in that day, they will know you enough to find you and kill you." Ragoczy Germainus glanced toward Blaga and Ennati. "They are doing you no good, hunting travelers like wolves."

She shrugged, then asked, "Why do you think so?"

"Because they cannot catch all of those who have offended you, and eventually the tales will be pieced together and you will be hunted as you have hunted them. Had the Moors not come, you would have been known before now, and you would have been forced to flee or die. Since you have increased your numbers, you have made yourself a reputation that may be your undoing." Ragoczy Germainus let the small chain slide through his fingers as he saw Yamut ibn Rabi and Sayed coming toward them. "Tell your Moors to keep their distance."

"This is where I belong." Chimena sighed and held up her hand to them. "Stay where you are. For now." She looked back at Ragoczy Germainus. "Very well, you have brought them back to me. For that, you must suppose I will be grateful?"

"No," said Ragoczy Germainus.

"No," she seconded. For a short while she said nothing more, then, "Have you thought about how you will leave this place?"

"I am aware that this could be dangerous," said Ragoczy Germainus, "but I could not think you would be unworthy of trust."

"How delicately you put that," she said, false approval making her demeanor overly respectful. "You were counting on my sense of obligation to you, were you not? to ensure your safe passage from here."

"Rather say I was hoping for it," said Ragoczy Germainus quietly.

She laughed, throwing back her head as if she were baying at the night. "Very deft, Sanct' Germain. You know just how to appeal to me, do you not?"

"I am not trying to—" he began, only to be interrupted.

"You are trying to shape me to your desires, as you have from the first, and I have no patience with it any longer. I am not subject to your pleasures or your strictures, no matter how much you suppose I ought to be. Will I never be rid of you?" She pointed to Ennati and Blaga. "Release them at once, and let me deal with them."

"If you are planning to harm them in any way, I will not; I did not bring them to you for that," said Ragoczy Germainus.

"But look at them," said Chimena as she went to stand over them. "They are useless." She kicked out, striking Ennati in the leg; Ragoczy

Germainus moved between her and the two bound men. "How can you protect them when they have done nothing worthy of it?"

"You do not know they have done nothing worthy," said Ragoczy Germainus.

"You bested them, did you not?" she countered. "They are useless to me if they fail."

Rotiger spoke up, "Chimena, you may be their master"—he used the masculine word deliberately—"but you should not hold your clan in contempt."

She looked up at him. "You would say that, for *his* sake!" She flung her hand in Ragoczy Germainus' direction. "It has nothing to do with me. I make members of my clan as I need them and I rid myself of them when they defy me or have proved themselves useless, as so many have." She paused. "Yamut and Sayed know what to do."

"And who will know what to do with them when you decide to be rid of your Moors?" Ragoczy Germainus asked.

Chimena laughed. "You are very clever, trying to make them think I will turn on them so that they will not do my bidding now." She held up her hands. "You will go now, and you will be unharmed. If you stay, you will have to answer for it."

"Why do you do this?" Ragoczy Germainus asked, changing his grip on the chain in his hand. "You demand devotion and you reward it with disdain."

"They are all weak, every one of them," she said. "What is there to admire in that?"

Ragoczy Germainus shook his head. "You do not understand—"

"Reciprocity," she finished for him. "And *you* do not understand that I do not want it. Why should I? Reciprocity is for equals, and I have yet to find one, living or undead, who is that. Not even you—especially you, no matter what you think. You haven't the courage to defend your territory." She tossed her head, her golden fillet shining in the pale starlight. "Still. You have brought my followers back to me. I acknowledge your service." It was clearly a dismissal, but Ragoczy Germainus made no move to depart. "I do not want my guards to kill you, but if you insist . . ." She shrugged, finishing her thought with the action.

"I have no desire to fight you, or them," said Ragoczy Germainus, stepping back to find better footing away from Blaga and Ennati. "If you cannot be satisfied any other way, then so be it."

"They will kill you," said Chimena, smiling in anticipation.

"They may try," Ragoczy Germainus responded, getting more distance between himself and the two men on the ground. "Rotiger, guard them."

"I will, my master," said Rotiger, and drew his short sword from its scabbard.

Chimena pointed to her Moors. "Yamut. Sayed." With that, she got out of the way, choosing the haven of an arched niche from which to watch the fight.

Ragoczy Germainus pulled the chain out between his hands and set the balls on the end to spinning; they made an eerie moaning as they swept through the air. "Come. Let us get this over with," he said, sounding tired.

The two Moors separated and tried to move in on Ragoczy Germainus from the sides, their scimitars held up at the ready, but the whirring balls kept them at bay, giving them no opportunity to strike.

"What is happening?" Blaga shouted, trying to maneuver the bearskin off his head so that he could watch.

"There is a fight going on," said Rotiger, his whole attention on the engagement taking place before him.

"The Moors?" asked Ennati. "Is he fighting the Moors?"

"That he is," said Rotiger.

Sayed made an experimental slash with his scimitar, testing to see how much it would trouble Ragoczy Germainus; the metal ball hummed past his head and forced him to withdraw a step. At the same time, Yamut ibn Rabi tried to get behind Ragoczy Germainus, only to discover the foreigner had swung around on his heel and now faced the Moor, driving him back with the weighted, whirling chain.

"The first passage ends in no advantage," said Rotiger to Ennati and Blaga.

"Did the Moors draw their swords?" asked Blaga, a note of incredulity in his voice.

"Oh, yes," said Rotiger.

"How strange that they could not—" Ennati interrupted himself as another sound—metal on metal—claimed his attention. "What was that?"

"One of the Moors tried to catch my master's chain on the blade of his scimitar," said Rotiger.

Sayed jumped away, struggling to hold onto the hilt of his weapon, and discovered that it was well and truly caught in the chain. In a quick movement, Ragoczy Germainus jerked the scimitar out of the Moor's hands, shook it free of the chain and kicked it so it went bouncing and clattering down the mountain.

Yamut ibn Rabi rushed forward, hoping to turn this misfortune to advantage and was stopped as the one metal ball still spinning slammed into his shin with an audible crack; Yamut ibn Rabi howled and went down, holding his leg.

"I am sorry," said Ragoczy Germainus, stopping his chain from moving. "The break will heal over time, but it will be long, and you must keep it splinted and bound for all the months it heals or it will be weak." He looked toward Sayed. "You may draw your dagger if you wish, and we can battle on, but you will not prevail."

"Attack him!" Chimena ordered, pointing to Sayed. "Do not stand there!"

Obediently Sayed pulled his dagger from his sash, raised it and rushed at Ragoczy Germainus only to be stopped as Ragoczy Germainus seized his arm and pulled it sharply around behind him, all but lifting him off his feet.

"If you drop your dagger I will not have to hurt you anymore," said Ragoczy Germainus gently.

"What has happened?" Blaga demanded.

"My master has broken the leg of one and may wrench the shoulder of the other from its socket," said Rotiger with no display of emotion.

Any remarks Blaga might have added were silenced as Chimena came rushing out of her niche, screaming in outrage, a spiked club swinging in her hands as she approached Ragoczy Germainus.

"You will not do this," Ragoczy Germainus said, and released Sayed to face her, stepping aside as she swung at him so that her club hit nothing and the force of its weighted swing nearly pulled her off her feet. As the club began its arc back, Ragoczy Germainus moved in and stopped it, lowering it out of her hands and letting it fall to the ground. "Enough," he said.

Chimena faced him. "You are going to kill me, are you not?"

Ragoczy Germainus stared at her. "Of course not," he said, still nonplused. "You are of my blood, and I do not kill those I have brought into the world."

"I kill those I have made," she said with pride. "I have the right." She studied him. "I know what it is. You are afraid." She looked down at Yamut ibn Rabi. "You should not live for this."

"He fought well," Ragoczy Germainus said quickly. "He did not know how to counter my weapon."

"He did nothing to stop you," Chimena persisted. "Now he will need a year of being crippled at least to be able to defend me again."

"What is a year to you?" Ragoczy Germainus asked. "You have more than a century behind you, and many more ahead of you. A year—it is such a little time." He waited for her to speak, and when she did not, he went on. "I have my medicaments with me. I can splint his leg and show you what must be done to keep it from being injured again."

"Being injured again?" Her voice rose in acerbity. "Why should I do anything for him? He disappointed me."

"As will many others before now and after," said Ragoczy Germainus, taking a risk in reminding her of what she did not want to consider. "You brought them to this life—why can you not accept them as they are?"

Chimena's lip lifted in an expression of disgust. "He is no better than Ennati and Blaga. I should have Sayed strike off their heads and leave their bodies in the forest of vermin to forage on."

"Because they were unable to kill me?" Ragoczy Germainus asked, not quite incredulously.

"Because they let themselves be bested," she said, unwilling to look at him. "They are worthless."

"Worthless," Ragoczy Germainus echoed, shaking his head. "They have given you all their loyalty and you want them slaughtered."

"I will find others who will do what I require of them; they will not be as cowardly as these are." She went to Yamut ibn Rabi and spat in derision. "It is bad enough that you refused to punish Olutiz for me, you now fall to a weapon that is little more than a toy." She was about to kick him again when Ragoczy Germainus restrained her, pulling her away from the fallen Moor.

"You must not," he said as she struggled in his embrace. "For your sake, you must not."

"Let *go* of me!" she ordered, trying to scrape her heels down his legs without success; her attempt to smash his arch was also thwarted, leaving her fuming.

"You are doing an injustice to your people, Chimena," he said steadily.

With a final wrench she broke out of his arms; panting and square-mouthed in fury, she rounded on him. "Get away from here! You have no authority over me. Go. Go now. This is nothing of yours. *I* am noth-

ing of yours. Leave me and do not come back, for you are now my
enemy, and you will be my enemy until one of us is truly dead." She
was trembling with rage and her voice shook. "If you come back, you
will be killed."

"By whom?" Ragoczy Germainus asked, knowing his challenge was
futile.

"I will have those around me who will not fail me." She pointed
down the mountain. "This is *my* place. You do not belong here."

He took a step toward her only to see her draw a long, thin poignard
from her deep sleeve. "Chimena," he said.

"If you come any nearer, I will use this on Yamut ibn Rabi, and then
on Sayed—" She looked around and discovered Sayed was missing.
"The craven—how *dare* he—he will be made to pay for his perfidy."
She went silent, then pointed at Ragoczy Germainus. "I will not punish
the two you brought if you go at once," she said in a tone that was
coldly remote. "If you linger, they will suffer for it." She held her
poignard up, ready to use it.

"Give me your Word, Chimena," Ragoczy Germainus said, aware
that she was prepared to do everything she promised.

"You have it. If you go. Now." Her rictus smile was dire.

There were so many things Ragoczy Germainus wanted to say to
Chimena, and he realized that all were useless. He walked back to his
horse and got into the saddle, an emptiness yawning within him so profound that it held him like pain. A jumble of parting words rose in his
mind, only to be abandoned; she had no desire to listen, nor inclination
to hear. If he tried to press an advantage with her, the three vampires
on the ground would pay the price of his failure. "Come, Rotiger," he
said as he signaled his horse to turn, and the mule with them. "Ambrosius and Lavetta and Ubertuz are waiting. We have a long way to go."

Text of a dispatch from Dabir ibn Badr ibn Jumah at Terrago to
Ibrahim ibn Husain at Zaragusta.

*In the name of Allah, the All-Seeing and All-Merciful, this request
from the leaders of our great fleet, that must surely triumph for the
Glory of Islam, and to which end this petition is presented to Ibrahim
ibn Husain on behalf of those devoted to the Caliph and the Prophet of
the One God. May I be struck blind and impotent if I report in error.*

As the officer given the task of supervising logging in the mountains east of Zaragusta, you are without doubt aware of the severe storms that have cost us so many lives and ships since the Spring Equinox. Not only have we been unable to provide the admirals' needs, we have many ships still awaiting repairs that cannot be completed unless you undertake to increase the lumber that is needed to restore our navy and our merchants to their preeminent position on the seas. Without the enterprise of those over whom you have authority, we might lose the advantage we have enjoyed for more than twenty years; should that happen at so crucial a time, there is little chance that we could soon recover what we had lost, for our momentum has not altered until now, and as a hunter more urgently pursues a prey when he knows it is wounded, so our enemies will hound us should they come to discover how extensive our damage has been to our ships.

Therefore it is imperative that you increase the number of logs you deliver and the speed at which you deliver them. To that end, you are being allocated twenty more work-gangs of slaves to enable you to provide us with what is required. We are also allocating more barges for the purpose of carrying cut logs down the river to the port, and the crews to man the barges as well. These crews will need to be quartered and fed, and will therefore require tents for barracks and tools for their work, all of which they shall have with them. The work-gangs for cutting trees will be provided tents as well, against the desertions that have been the bane of overseers in the mountains.

Your reports of demons have been noted, and appropriate talismans will be issued for the preservation of the slaves cutting trees. We will also increase the flocks feeding on the hillsides once they are open; it may prove then that the demons are Christians who have become outlaws and bandits, hiding in the forests and preying upon those venturing too near their hiding-places.

So that the remaining villagers will not be tempted to side with these lawless creatures, we will excuse all taxes for a year, and charge Christians the same taxes as followers of the Prophet for five years, so that they will not be beggared by aiding us. This may well put an end to the rumors of demons and the tales of the living dead who pursue the living for the purpose of draining the life from them. It is fitting that we should bring such fables to an end, and to cease the rites of Holy Blood that have been in the traditions of those mountains for many years, for *to encourage anyone in those beliefs is to turn them from Allah and His Prophet, by indulging the ignorant in their superstitions. Let the villagers and shepherds see that we will not deny them charity, or refuse them the means of making a living, and they will no longer seek the favor of the creatures of legend. If there is more talk of demons, then burn the hillsides once you have taken the trees: that will destroy many hiding places as well as put an end to all this talk of demons and it will show the villagers that we are not going to accept their excuses, or it will send the demons—if demons there are—back to Shaitan, and show that the followers of the Prophet and the One True God have nothing to fear from demons, particularly Christian demons.*

You will soon have these new crews in your city, and you are urged to prepare for them; you will have to lay in additional foodstuffs and cloth, as well as the leather and metal these work crews require; the bargemen will be able to tend to themselves so long as the Eberuz is kept clear of debris, to which end watermen must be set to work. If we are to maintain control of these mountains, the work-gangs may well prove to be a double blessing, for in cutting trees for our ships, they will also open the mountains for our soldiers. You are being given a great honor and a great responsibility in this time. May Allah grant you strength and wisdom to make any adversity a victory for our people and our God.

This at the first full moon after the Summer Solstice, in Tarrago,

Dabir ibn Badr ibn Jumah
Scribe to the admirals of the fleet

6

"You have been silent for nearly three days," Rotiger said to Ragoczy Germainus as they made camp for the night; gathering clouds overhead promised rain before morning and the air was still and close. The leaves hardly stirred.

"I am thinking," said Ragoczy Germainus distantly.

"You are brooding," said Rotiger.

Ragoczy Germainus gave a sad laugh. "Perhaps. Lavetta and Ubertuz and Ambroisus are on my mind. I hope I have not caused them pain, being as late as we are."

"There's more to it than that," Rotiger said. "You blame yourself for all Chimena has done."

"I am not without some responsibility," said Ragoczy Germainus.

"Why? Did you think she would do what she has done when you made her a vampire?" He was sitting on one of their chests and staring into the fire that burned in a desultory fashion, as if anticipating the wet to come. Their travels had been hard, for the road was neglected and the forest difficult to penetrate where it had grown up around the road; more than once they had had to detour to avoid armed camps or hostile villages and as a result they had not covered as much ground as they had intended. Rotiger reached down into the leather game bag at his feet to pull out his dinner. "Did you expect to have her for an enemy?"

Ragoczy Germainus sighed. "You know the answers; no to both." He looked up through the branches of the trees. "Nothing I can say will change her now. Perhaps it never could." He rose from where he had been squatting on his heels and walked over to where their animals were tethered to a long, braided-leather rope stretched between two trees. "They will be restive tonight."

"Until the storm passes," said Rotiger. He held a skinned hare in his hands, but he held off beginning to eat, watching Ragoczy Germainus with troubled eyes.

"Yes. Until it passes." He patted the jenny on her neck, then bent to examine her hock. "The pace is causing her trouble again. I will make another poultice."

"And tomorrow or the day after we should be out of the mountains and on the plateau, headed for Usca. The forest will not slow us down as much once we are on flatter ground. There should be more travelers about, as well. No doubt we can find an inn where we may all rest for a day or two," said Rotiger with determined optimism, hoping Ragoczy Germainus would consider his suggestion.

"Perhaps," said Ragoczy Germainus; he looked away from their animals toward the stack of packs and chests they carried that were now stacked in three neat piles near the fire, ready for loading in the morning. "We will have to be careful of bandits, so near the Usca road to Zaragusta. They, too, know where to find travelers."

"They have not troubled us thus far," Rotiger remarked, and an instant later wished he had not spoken.

"That is the doing of Chimena's vampires. Once we are beyond their range, the bandits will take their place again," said Ragoczy Germainus with a wry glance toward the forest.

"And soldiers, there will also be soldiers," added Rotiger. "Christian and Moorish."

"Oh, yes—most certainly soldiers." He nodded to the dressed hare in Rotiger's hands. "Aren't you hungry?"

"Of course I am," Rotiger said, feeling a bit foolish.

"Then eat, will you." Ragoczy Germainus smiled slightly. "I had its blood; now it is yours."

Rotiger took his wide-bladed knife from his belt and began to carve the hare. "You have had nothing but the blood of game and animals for . . . for many days," he said, not wanting to admit he had been keeping count.

"So I have," said Ragoczy Germainus, continuing. "And will for many days more, I suspect. Before you tell me that I need . . . richer sustenance, I will agree. There; I have said it. But even had I the opportunity, here, in Chimena's region of Holy Blood, I would not make any attempt to visit a woman, knowingly or in sleep." He stared into the middle distance. "It would not be safe for her, or nourishing for me."

"Because of Chimena and all of her followers?" The last word was uncertain, as if he could not think of one that would more accurately describe those who had become vampires of her making.

"Yes. I could not achieve even the most fleeting intimacy with any of them, not after what her lot has done." He shrugged. "So I will wait. Game will suffice me yet awhile; I have gone decades on worse."

"That you have. But why should you—once we reach Usca, you should have some chance of finding a woman who will be glad of the dreams you bring." He took a bit of hare off the point of his knife and began to chew.

"Ah, but we have not reached Usca," said Ragoczy Germainus.

"It will be soon," said Rotiger with conviction. "Three, four days at the most, and we should arrive there."

"But we have not got there yet." Ragoczy Germainus picked up the thick headstall that was added to the jack-mule's halter when he was being led. "This is beginning to fray. I will have to replace it at Usca."

"Is it beyond repair?" Rotiger asked, resigned to the dismissal of the subjects they had just been discussing.

"It is not, but it is old. This one was made in Cyprus, and that was what? seventy years ago? It has been oiled so many times to keep it supple I am surprised it does not drip." He put it down again. "It is time it was replaced."

"There should be saddlers in Usca," said Rotiger as he cut more flesh from the hare's carcase. "No doubt you can purchase one there, or the leather to make your own," he added, for he had seen Ragoczy Germainus make every kind of tack over their centuries together.

"Very likely," said Ragoczy Germainus, his attention now on the braided-leather straps they used to hold their packs and chests in place. "These need oil and wax," he remarked.

"Something more to purchase in Usca," said Rotiger, trying to plumb his mater's enigmatic mood.

"Yes." Ragoczy Germainus was inspecting a girth now, scrutinizing the broad leather belt, looking for wear around the holes for the tongue of the buckle. "This will do," he said a little later, and went on to the next with the same air of perplexing calm. He had finished perusing three of the girths when there was a disruption in the woods a little beyond the firelight. Immediately he dropped the girth and reached for his chain with the iron balls that hung from his belt.

Rotiger set the half-eaten hare aside and drew his short sword, turning to face the dark mass of trees. "Can you see?"

"Not well enough," said Ragoczy Germainus, intent on the direction from which the sound had come.

"How many, do you think?" Rotiger wondered aloud.

"Not many," said Ragoczy Germainus, beginning to twirl one of the iron balls.

"One, in fact," said Ennati as he stepped out of the forest, holding up empty hands and moving slowly.

Rotiger did not lower his sword. "Just you?"

"Just me," Ennati confirmed, continuing quickly. "I have come to warn you—Chimena changed her mind after you left. She killed Yamut ibn Rabi and Blaga, and she ordered Sayed killed as soon as he is caught. Merez is now her guard, and she has said that the clan must hunt you down, for our protection. She told us all that you have put us all in danger. You must die or none of them is safe." He glanced about uneasily. "I left as soon as I could. She is determined to do this."

"Is she," Ragoczy Germainus said quietly, looking directly at Ennati, scrutinizing him.

"You do not know how she is when she has been thwarted," said Ennati. "It is her pride, and her Right that speaks." He kept glancing behind him, as if he feared the trees might attack.

"And her Word?" Ragoczy Germainus asked bleakly.

"She said it could not hold her in this case. She said you coerced her into making a promise, and because of that, it was not binding." He clasped his hands together to stop them shaking.

"And you could not endure it," Ragoczy Germainus said, his voice flat.

"She told us that you would bring our enemies down upon us if you were not stopped and silenced. She said you know too much, and that we would all be hunted because of you." He came a step closer to the fire. "I mean you no harm. I only want to warn you, because you spared me and Blaga when you could have killed us easily. She may feel no obligation for that, but I do." He stumbled and caught himself on the nearest pile of chests; Rotiger instantly raised his sword.

"There is no one else with him," said Ragoczy Germainus, motioning to Rotiger to lower his sword. "And look—Ennati is burned."

"I have been up since mid-afternoon," said Ennati, gingerly touching his face where his skin was blistered and torn.

"To reach me?" Ragoczy Germainus said dubiously.

"In part," said Ennati candidly. "I am also afraid that Chimena may decide to have me killed, as well, as she killed Blaga. She is in a bloody mood now, and that can only be satisfied with deaths, True Deaths. You are not the only one she would like dead. If she could lay her hands on him, she might well do away with Olutiz." He looked up at Ragoczy Germainus. "I saw what happened. She took Yamut ibn Rabi's big curved sword and with her own hands severed Blaga's head in two blows." He swallowed hard. "After she had done the same to Yamut ibn Rabi."

"He did not try to escape?" Ragoczy Germainus asked, more doubtfully than before. "I would have thought he would have fought her."

"How? He was on the ground with a shattered leg," said Ennati. "I think he did not expect her to kill him, not after all the time he has served her." He stared into the forest again, his expression desolate. "And Blaga was still corded up in the bearskin and never saw what she intended to do."

"Why did Yamut ibn Rabi not protest?" Ragoczy Germainus was mildly surprised, thinking back to the Moor and his determination. "I would think he had seen her do as much to others, and for less cause."

"He was devoted to her. He told her he had lost all chance of Paradise to be with her, and she said she was gratified. He made her his deity when she gave him undead life. From that time on, he has been her most ardent slave." Ennati shook his head. "I cannot weep. I wish I could."

"Vampires have no tears," said Ragoczy Germainus, his tone revealing his own anguish at this loss. He saw Ennati attempt to compose herself, and some of his suspicions of the man diminished.

"So we have all discovered," said Ennati as he put his head in his hands. "I do not grieve as I need to." He stared out through his fingers. "I fear I will see her kill him for as long as I walk the earth."

Rotiger asked the question Ragoczy Germainus would not. "Why did she spare you? With all her killing, how did you escape?"

"She said she needed someone to be a witness, so the rest of her clan would know the consequences of shaming her." He crossed his arms and clutched his elbows as if to shield himself from a blow. "I cannot take it all in, not yet."

"You will," said Ragoczy Germainus with such utter conviction that Ennati was driven to silence for some little time.

It was Rotiger who broke the silence. "How far behind you are they?"

"I cannot say for certain: they could reach this place before dawn tonight. They will be here tomorrow beyond question. If they come tonight, they will be tired– that is something in your favor." He shivered as if struck with sudden cold. "If there is rain, it would slow them down with running water."

"And there will be rain tonight." Ragoczy Germainus looked up at the leaves overhead and tried to make out the sky beyond. "It will not be much longer before the clouds open."

"Are you certain?" Ennati asked, half-relieved, half-apprehensive.

"Fairly certain," said Ragoczy Germainus. "I can smell it."

Ennati shook his head. "I am not so sure, but—" He shrugged. "At most you gain yourself a night. And then you will have more than ten of us on you."

Ragoczy Germainus seemed unfazed by this. "And you? Will you attack us then?"

"No," said Ennati. "I am now Chimena's enemy as much as you are; she has made me that. She will want my True Death as passionately as she wants yours, witness or not. I have left her side and she will consider that treason, no matter what I did, or why." He was no longer distraught by this realization. "If I thought it would do any good, I would flee with you."

"Why do you not?" Ragoczy Germainus asked, his dark eyes on Ennati.

"Because it would only prolong what is coming." He paused a long moment. "Besides, where would I go?"

"You could come to Asturica with us," said Ragoczy Germainus. "I think the Dux would be glad of a fighting man who knows something about the Moors."

Ennati chuckled desolately. "And how long would that last? I cannot fight in daylight, and I cannot eat with others." He fingered his copper-colored hair. "I could not be a spy among the Moors."

"You may not need to be," said Ragoczy Germainus. "There are many other services you could perform." He thought back to his own past and his many improvised occupations that served to disguise his true nature. "If you are willing to guard the dead, no one will ask many questions of you, or if you can supervise the sick and wounded at night."

"Why should I do either of those things?" Ennati asked, appalled at the suggestions.

"Because no one else wants to, and those who can do these things are not scrutinized. If you are not blatant, you may manage very well. Tell the Dux that you have taken a vow to do these things, and he will not interfere with you." Ragoczy Germainus saw Rotiger nod in agreement. "You see? I am not the only one who has found such work to be useful."

"But I would have to go away from here," said Ennati, with such desolation of spirit that Ragoczy Germainus felt it as keenly as a knife-thrust.

"So you would." Ragoczy Germainus paused. "I, too, have gone far from the mountains where I was born. I return there from time to time, but now I am as much a stranger there as I am anywhere in the world."

"You did not rule there?" Ennati asked, amazed that this would be so.

"My father did." As he said it, Ragoczy Germainus remembered his father—a man who had survived to the incredible age of forty-eight, half again the age most men attained then. "He was regarded with respect for many thousands of paces beyond our borders." Until, he added inwardly, the long-haired, green-eyed foreigners in their chariots had come out of the east and laid waste to all his father had built and made Ragoczy Germainus a slave, to serve as an example to all his people. "I did not leave of my own volition."

Ennati knew he had touched on something much vaster than Ragoczy Germainus had told him. "How long ago?"

"Nearly twenty-eight hundred years," said Ragoczy Germainus, and knew the sum was too enormous for Ennati to grasp. "There was no Roma yet; Egypt was mighty." How inadequate that sounded, even to him.

"Long ago," Ennati said, trying to show he understood, knowing that he did not.

"Yes," said Ragoczy Germainus, and shook off the ephemeral bonds of memory. "There is nothing for you if you remain here. You have an opportunity to decide how you will live now you have left Chimena. Better to go where you wish now while you can choose for yourself than wait until you are forced."

"Listen to him," Rotiger advised.

"I cannot go from here." Ennati looked around as if to assure himself he was safe. "Even here, in this place, I begin to feel uncomfortable. If I go to Usca, I will be sickened. None of us can go beyond Chimena's lands."

"Because Chimena said so," Ragoczy Germainus suggested, but with less conviction than he wanted to have; the lack of bonds among Chimena's vampires was as familiar to him as it was perplexing; perhaps their bond to their native earth was stronger for that reason.

"And because when I have traveled beyond the region of Holy Blood, I lose strength and become almost as helpless as a babe." He shrugged.

"I have thought I might go to one of the old hermitages and take up living there. I know of such a place near the road to the Septimania Pass. The only difficulty is that Olutiz rules there, not Chimena, and he may not allow me, or anyone who has served his mother, to stay in territory he has made his." For the first time his tattered face showed despair as he paced from the fire to the tether-line and back again.

"The Moors might not like such a thing, either, if they discovered you," said Ragoczy Germainus sardonically. "This is most . . . vexing."

Rotiger noticed the slight hesitation in Ragoczy Germainus' words and he wondered what his master had intended to say. "How much farther can you travel?" he asked Ennati.

"Another ten thousand paces, perhaps twelve thousand," he answered uncertainly. "Not in daylight, certainly. Daylight is too difficult for me now." He indicated the state of his skin.

"That doesn't put us at the Usca-Zaragusta road," said Rotiger. "He would be five to six thousand paces shy of it."

"No, not quite that much; it would be too far in any case," said Ragoczy Germainus. "And it is all moot since you are unable to leave the region of Holy Blood." He faltered, considering. "Where the hills are barren, the earth is sliding away, so such places will not sustain you. You will have to stay in the forests, as far from the loggers and the goats and sheep as you can."

"The Moors are fighting the Christians in the mountains. The Moors want the Frankish lands as well as all of Old Hispania." Ennati sat down suddenly, as if suddenly deprived of all energy. "If I must fight, I suppose I might as well fight the Moors. Better them than my own kind."

"With the intention of dying in battle, I would guess," said Ragoczy Germainus, his tone dropping, his dark eyes shrewd.

"It would solve many problems," said Ennati.

"Possibly," Ragoczy Germainus allowed. "It is a drastic step to take." He thought, suddenly and poignantly, of Nicoris, and how readily she had embraced the True Death.

"But you do not think so," said Ennati, seeing Ragoczy Germainus' countenance and intuiting some of the reason behind his expression.

"No. I do not," Ragoczy Germainus admitted. "It has little to do with you, Ennati, but it does remind me that departing our life is no more conclusive than leaving the realms of the living." His smile had no hint of mirth in it. "You would be rid of your burdens, beyond all doubt, but others would have to shoulder them for you."

"That may be," said Ennati. "I do not want to die yet, not after all I have done to remain undead. Still, if I am to live only to serve Chimena, then death is more welcome to me. I do not want to live in daily fear of her anger."

Ragoczy Germainus nodded emphatically. "Yes. You take my meaning. It is more appropriate that you live as you decide you would like to than to leave you to struggle with Chimena's demands." He gestured to Rotiger. "Come. We must prepare lanthorns: we have a long way to go tonight."

Rotiger made a fatalistic gesture. "You do not want to remain here."

"No, not after what Ennati has told us. Do you?" He indicated their mules and horses. "We cannot go rapidly; our animals are too tired for speed, but we can put another six or seven thousand paces between us and Chimena if we travel all night and into the day."

"I cannot come with you," said Ennati. "I am near the limit of my tolerances." He cocked his head toward the animals. "If you left the jenny with the sore hock behind, that would slow your pursuers down. They would feed on her, and that would delay them." His smile was a mixture of eagerness and uncertainty.

"That may be," said Ragoczy Germainus. "But I do not leave animals behind unless there is no choice whatsoever. We are not at such a point yet, and with a little care, we will not have to be." He went to the tether-line. "We are not so desperate that we must sacrifice these creatures to Chimena's tribe."

"But that could gain you several hours, perhaps as much as a night," Ennati objected. "I am hungry, and I know were I hunting you, I would not hesitate to feed on the jenny first."

"That may be," said Ragoczy Germainus as he reached for the saddle-pad for the jack-mule and put it in place on his back, smoothing it so that it lay smoothly. "Finish your dinner, Rotiger, and douse the fire. We will not rest tonight."

"Do you need any help?" Ennati offered. "I cannot do much, but if you will tell me what you would like—?"

"Be at ease," said Ragoczy Germainus as he went on saddling the jack-mule, securing the breast-collar and girth with the ease of long practice; the jack-mule stamped his on-side hoof and nodded his head to express his annoyance, but did not balk at this new development.

"The mules must be worn out," said Ennati as he watched Ragoczy Germainus continue his work.

"They have come a long way, but they are able to go farther," was the answer he received.

"The breeder is an old friend of my master's," said Rotiger as he ate the last of the hare, and flung the bones away into the dark. "The animals are the hardiest and strongest that she breeds."

"Do you not fear what may happen to them at night?" Ennati asked, his disquiet increasing.

"Not so long as I am guiding them," said Ragoczy Germainus as he hefted the first of his chests onto the jack-mule's pack-saddle and set it in place. "My eyesight is not much hampered by dark—just as yours is not."

"But what shall I do?" Ennati blurted out. "If you are going on to Usca, what will become of me?"

"Come with us as far as you can," Ragoczy Germainus suggested as he began to saddle the larger jenny-mule. "We will not be going faster than a walk, so you will not have to press yourself to stay with us. If you would rather go into the forest, away from the others who pursue us, then go with my thanks."

Rotiger was stacking their goods for loading onto pack-saddles. "If you decide to keep up with us, you will have our protection, should it be necessary. If you would prefer to flee into the woods, you might as well go now."

"That is all very well," said Ennati, sounding a little despondent. "You will leave and I will still have to find some way to live in these mountains." He frowned as Rotiger poured water on the fire, then poked it to be certain it was out; the sudden darkness made him apprehensive.

"Then pack some of your native earth and come with us," Ragoczy Germainus said, continuing to ready their animals for travel. "You may be able to go beyond the region of Holy Blood if you have your native earth with you—not far but far enough to be safe."

"Do you think it would be possible?" Ennati asked, daring and dreading to hope.

"It may be." Ragoczy Germainus loaded the second mule's pack-saddle, taking the time to give the animal a handful of grain before he finished his work.

Ennati paced the dark clearing. "You do not understand how difficult this is."

"No, I do not," said Ragoczy Germainus, saddling the smaller jenny last of all, and making sure she had the lightest load. "Her hock will need treatment when we stop again," he said to Rotiger while he adjusted the packs she carried before strapping them in place. "Remind me if I do not remember."

Although there was little chance of Ragoczy Germainus forgetting, Rotiger said, "Of course, my master."

Ennati swung his arms in exasperation. "What am I going to do?"

"That seems to be a troublesome question," said Ragoczy Germainus with real concern in his voice. "Your constraints are such that my advice would have little value, I fear." He was brushing down his gray now, working over the shoulder and flank, moving down and back. "It is unfortunate that you are not able to leave the region, for then you would have all the world open to you."

"You think I should try to leave in spite of my discomforts, do you not?" Ennati asked sharply.

Ragoczy Germainus answered carefully. "I think that if you remain you will have to confront Chimena eventually; she will require it even if you do not. I can comprehend you not wanting to live an exile's life, but I fear that may not be in your power to decide. Ultimately it is Chimena who will control this region for as long as she is vampirically alive."

Ennati stopped, his head lowered in misery. "Yes. No doubt you are correct." He began to pace again. "If I stay away from her and her clan, she should not bother with me; I am only one man." He waited for agreement that did not come. "I could find some of those who have broken away from her. They might accept me as one of them, and I would have protection then. She would not come against us as readily as she might hunt down a solitary vampire." Again he was silent.

Rotiger stopped his packing, saying, "Either way, you are in her path the longer you stay here." He glanced toward Ragoczy Germainus, who remained unspeaking. "Leaving the region may be unpleasant, but what is coming may be horrendous; you would do well to be clear of it."

"Do you think I—?" Ennati broke off. "I will come with you as far as I can, and then I will decide what to do."

"Very good," said Ragoczy Germainus. "You can lead one of the mules and follow Rotiger on my grey. I will bring up the rear on foot, in case we are pursued."

"On foot?" Ennati exclaimed, astonished.

"My master can move as swiftly as any horse, especially in this forest," said Rotiger as he went about saddling his dun.

"There are a few things I can do to discourage our pursuers," said Ragoczy Germainus as he reached into his weapons pack for a broadheaded axe and several lengths of leather thongs.

"Then you believe me—you are being followed," said Ennati with a suggestion of relief in his tone.

"I will bend a few branches as spring-traps for the unwary, to slow them down," said Ragoczy Germainus as he went back to his horse, putting the saddle-pad in place before lifting the saddle onto the gray's back.

"Will you fight them?" Ennati's eyes shone with the prospect of battle.

"Not if I do not have to." Ragoczy Germainus stared into the forest behind them.

"But she wants you dead, the True Death," said Ennati, his fear making his voice strident.

Ragoczy Germainus secured the girth of his saddle. "Many another has wanted that as well, and yet I am still . . . living." He went to bridle his horse, saying to Rotiger as he did, "Do not push the pace; once it starts to rain, keep on as long as you can. If we get separated, I will meet you at the Usca-Zaragusta road. Come," he said to Ennati, and helped him clamber into the saddle. "Follow Rotiger for as long as you are able. If you must leave, give him my horse's reins before you go."

Rotiger swung onto his dun, and took two of the mules' leads from Ragoczy Germainus. "I will wait for you."

"I know you will, old friend," said Ragoczy Germainus, then slapped the dun's rump before handling the third lead to Ennati; as they moved off, he vanished into the forest.

Text of a letter from Frer Serenus at Santus Spirituz, near Usca, to Ebiscuz Dominicuz in Calagurriz on the Eberuz.

*To the most reverend Ebiscuz Dominicuz, at Mader Deuz in Calagur-
riz, the blessings and prayers as greeting from Frer Serenus at Santus
Spirituz on the road to Usca, with the pious hope that this finds you
well and your flock in good heart in spite of the trouble of these times.*

*This is to introduce to you a man seeking a hermitage where he
might live in isolation from his fellows for the expiation of his sins,
which he says are many. He has vowed to walk abroad only at night,
and to take no food but what God sends him, so that he will not become
a cost on any of the Christians who, staunch in their faith, may seek to
aid him in his withdrawal from the world. His name is Ennati and he
came to Santus Spirituz in the company of a man of dignity and learning, and his servant, who were bound for Asturica, and who have departed this place ten days since, leaving a donation of four golden
Angels in thanks for the hospitality we extended to them all. As the man
and servant both vouched for this Ennati's worthiness, I have taken the
liberty of writing this to ask you to make a place for this penitent man;
I believe you may acquire much knowledge from him, particularly
in regard to the activities of the Moors in the mountains to the west of
Tarrago.*

*As you must be aware, this region has seen fighting for several years,
but the Moors have not yet wholly subdued that part of the mountains
known as Holy Blood. We have been fortunate that the people in those
valleys have remained devoted to our cause, for it is bruited about by
the Moors that demons live in that place, demons who drink blood that
is left for them in chalices of gold. I have heard many travelers tell of
cursed places and empty villages, but it can only be that the Moors
themselves have done the things the travelers report, for it is not possible that those who worship the Blood of Our Savior could ever commit
the crimes that have been attributed to them.*

*Of late we have noticed that the Moors are still determined to con-
tinue to press into the mountains in an effort to claim Frankish lands
beyond; if they can gain control of all the roads and passes so that the
Christians in the north, beyond the control of the Caliph, are cut off
from the Christians of the Frankish lands, then we might well be
doomed. You must see that the link between the churches of the Franks
and our churches must be maintained at all costs. Here we have already made our walls higher and thicker, and are now building dormitories for Christians seeking a haven from the Moors. In this respect I*

commend this man Ennati to you, for as one who has fought the Moors, and in the mountains, he can guide your efforts and help you to prepare travelers for all the dangers they might encounter, as well as aiding us to defeat the foes of our faith.

With my assurances of my continuing devotion, and my prayers for your soul and for all Christian souls in this dark time, I sign myself,

Frer Serenus
Santus Spirituz

on the last day of July, in the 752nd year of Man's Salvation, by the calendar of Roma

PART IV

XIMENE

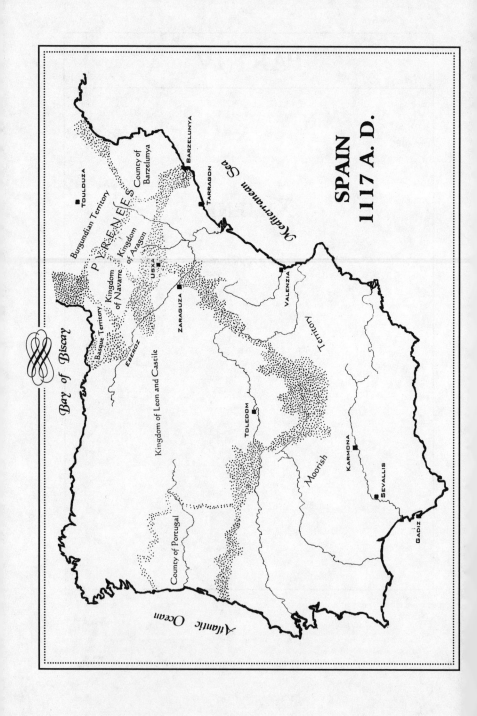

SPAIN
1117 A.D.

Bay of Biscay

Atlantic Ocean

Mediterranean Sea

TOULOUZA

Burgundian Territory

PYRENEES

County of
Barzelunya

Kingdom of Navarre

Kingdom
of Aragon

Basque Territory

USKA

EBERDI

ZARAGUZA

BARZELUNYA

TARRAGON

VALENZIA

Kingdom of Leon and Castile

TOLEDOM

Moorish

Territory

County of Portugal

KARMONA

SEVALLIS

GADIZ

*T*ext of a summons from Idelfonzuz I, known as The Warrior, King of Aragon and Navarre, son-in-law of Adelfonzuz VI, King of León and Castile, to Germanno, Comide Ragoczy at Burgoz.

To the most excellent foreigner, Germanno, the Comide Ragoczy, currently resident at Burgoz, the felicitations of Idelfonzuz called The Warrior, who bids you leave Burgoz and travel to Toledom, for such is my pleasure.

I have been informed that you have experience with Moors and Jews, that you speak their languages and know something of their ways. Those from Burgoz who know you and have given you high praise have said you have conducted various negotiations with Moorish traders on behalf of Christians, and that neither the Christians nor the Moors have had reason to complain of your dealings. I am also told that you have been in the lands to the east of Egypt, and therefore have seen the heart of the followers of Mohammed; many of the Moors in this land cannot say as much, which surely should earn the respect of those Moors with whom you have contact here.

Now that Toledom is once again in Christian hands, it behooves me to put all the knowledge I possess to bringing this place to order with as little new disruption as may be managed, for now that this city is mine, I seek to have peace restored here so that I may continue the great work of Adelfonzuz of León and Castile, and secure all of the Spanish territory for Christians.

You may aid me in this effort, and to that end, I ask you to make your skills and knowledge available to me as shortly after your arrival as is practical. I have included the order of safe passage to ensure you are not delayed in your travels. I will authorize you funds to purchase any reasonable supplies for the journey, and give you the right to requisition quarters with any Christian between here and Burgoz. You are to retain soldiers to escort you. You may be relieved of all anxiety that anyone will deny you service, for it is given to my benefit. Should you encounter any opposition to my commands, discover the instigator of that opposition and inform me of the miscreant after you are come.

When you have arrived in this city, you may select from many fine houses where you may begin a household. As a member of my Court, you will be allowed to choose from any of the houses left empty by the Moors who have fled Toledom; the only cost for you will be the cost of occupancy—the house itself will be my pledge of support to you. I will not require you to have servants accompany you, for that would slow your travels and give you more risks of losses and delays. There are slaves in plenty here, and experienced servants eager for new masters now that the Moors no longer rule there.

Once you have made yourself a life to your liking, then I will ask that you help me to deal with serving out justice to the people of Toledom, and so that the Moors and Jews do not suffer overmuch, I will designate you to attend to them, and to be certain that their needs are met and they are given every chance to conduct themselves appropriately in a Christian court of judgment. Surely it must not be said of us that we came only to end the upholding of the right.

I want to give them no occasion to rise against me now that this city is secure. At the same time, I want to be certain that the laws of the city are enforced with all rigor. Let the Moors and Jews show themselves willing to accept Christian rule, and let them give fealty to me, and they will go as honorably as any Christian priest. My soldiers are under order to leave the women of Toledom alone—they will have opportunities aplenty for venting their lusts when we begin the campaign for Zaraguza in the spring. It should ease our occupation of this city if the Jews and Moors know they need not fear for their women.

My later plans will demand more effort from you; Zaraguza is just *the beginning of my plans to see Spain free of Moors from Aragon to Gadiz. The Comide of Barzeluna is willing to aid us in driving the Moors from all of Gotalunya, and the new Comide of Portugal will also lend support to this cause. I will explain all to you upon your arrival here. Suffice it to say that I am not going to rest content until I am certain that I have done all that may be done to secure these lands. Once all of Spain is again in Christian hands, the divisions of the lords may be settled in a mutually satisfactory manner. In this, I have the support of the Comide of Barzeluna, who defends all of Gotalunya from the Moors, as well as other enemies.*

In the name of Santiago, amen. Do not linger upon receiving this, but hasten to obey. You are not my vassal, but you are a nobleman and you live or die at my desire. It is to our mutual benefit that you serve me in this; if you are prompt in your coming, I will uphold my promise and reward you handsomely for it, beyond what I have already pledged to you. Therefore, with the prospect of such favor awaiting you, I look to see you here before the Nativity.

> *Idelfonzuz the Warrior*
> *King of Aragon and Navarre*
> *By the hand of Fre Jimeno*
> *Carried by Toedonadoz, Knight*

*at Toledom on the 21*st *day of September in the 1116*th *year of Christian Salvation*

1

The sound of his boot-heels was loud on the marble floor of the primary reception room; a fountain in the courtyard behind them softened the noise with a constant musical chuckle. The scent of lemon trees sweetened the afternoon breeze. It was warm for late November, and the light lay brightly golden over the hills; Toledom basked in it, although it clearly revealed the scars of war on walls and buildings. In the markets the last of the slim harvest was being sold to the highest bidder and to the forces of Idelfonzuz of Aragon and Navarre who were beginning to enjoy the fruits of their victory as well as the advantages of their occupation.

"I hardly recognize the place, with all that has been done to it. The street is no longer as it was, either," said Germanno, Comide Ragoczy in Byzantine Greek as he went into the next room. "Ah. This is more familiar." He had been surprised that his old house was still standing—although much modified by subsequent owners—and his inspection of it was reassuring and startling by turns. "It is half again as large as what I had built, five hundred years ago."

Behind him, Ruthor nodded. "At least it is not a ruin." He paused, glancing at the fireplace. "That should be cleaned and inspected before anything is burned. You do not know that it is safe."

"I was thinking the same thing." He passed through the room into a gallery that had not existed the last time he left this house. "I like the columns: red granite—and it is pleasant to be open to the garden. At mid-summer this must be a welcome haven from the heat."

"It is also good that the garden is walled," said Ruthor, looking beyond the courtyard to the stretch of trees and shrubs beyond. "And, if it comes to that, the outer gates are very imposing."

"I thought so, too," said Germanno. "What building did they take down to make this garden?" Before Ruthor could answer, he said, "It was that grain emporium, was it not? Yes, that and the barn of that carter." He smiled. "The garden is much handsomer, and longer, than either of the buildings were."

"That it is," said Ruthor, shading his eyes against the sun. "A fine place, this."

"It is," said Germanno. "The emporium was no great loss, but the carter had a family—" His expression darkened.

"After five hundred years or so, I doubt anyone remembers them," said Ruthor pointedly. "They surely must have scattered when the Moors came."

"Very likely," said the Comide, his voice level as he glanced at Ruthor.

"Yes. As my family certainly was when I had been away from Gadiz for several centuries," Ruthor said in a tone to match Germanno's.

Germanno nodded once. "At least we came to Burgoz from the Breton March port of Noirmoutier. Little as I like traveling by water, I am less eager to go through Chimena's territory, even now. Who knows what has happened there." He paused in the door that led to a wing of the house he had never seen before. "This must have been the women's quarters. You see those screens."

Ruthor paused at the mention of her name. "Do you think Chimena is still there? It is almost four hundred years since you saw her." He saw Germanno glance away. "Aragon is in the territory she held, is it not?"

"Yes, a portion of it is," said the Comide. "The rest is in Gotalunya, in the Comidie of Barzeluna. I must assume that she is where she was before, since she was disinclined to travel. I have no sense of her True Death, although it is remotely possible that she could die and I not know of it; the bond of blood with us has never been strong. I must admit I am curious about those around her, and I worry that there may be far too many of them by now. But I am not going to ask Idelfonzuz if he knows anything of a group of vampires in his kingdom."

"He might be offended," said Ruthor automatically.

"Or worse," said Germanno, and did not elucidate.

Ruthor came to the doorway and peered in. "That pool is very nice."

"If I can line its bedding with my native earth, I will keep it; I would like to have such a bath. If you will discover how it is fixed in the foundation and if there is room for my native earth?" He left the wing and went toward the corridor that had led to his laboratory. "I hope they have not ruined it."

"Why should they?" Ruthor asked, his curiosity piqued.

"I have no notion. I have not set foot in this city since we left almost five hundred years ago. It is unknown to me now." He went down the corridor carefully, as if to reassure himself that he had chosen the right direction. When he reached the door he opened it carefully, troubled by what he might find beyond. "By all the forgotten gods," he murmured as the door swung back, revealing a chamber with a ceiling higher than the rest of the roof with a circular staircase of metal leading up to a high balcony under a skylight hatch that now stood open. "An observatory."

"So it is," said Ruthor, astonished by the discovery. "What an extravagant addition. The former owner must have been a wealthy and educated man."

"Or he employed a teacher," said the Comide, assessing the room with narrowed eyes. "You see that there are pigeon-holes in the north wall for scrolls, and chains by that book-rest, so there were Arabic and Roman books here." He looked about, a wistful turn to his mouth. "A pity I will not have more time to use this place."

"Do you think you will not?" Ruthor asked in some apprehension.

"Idelfonzuz did not order me here so that I could study the stars," said Germanno.

"You are to assist in the running of his Courts," said Ruthor, sounding unconvinced.

"So he has told me. I am sure there is more to it," said the Comide.

"But if he expects you to deal with the Moors and the Jews, would not this room serve that purpose admirably? Could you not show that it would increase your acceptance by their learned men? Most of them would be pleased to have such a place as this in which to work." Ruthor pointed to the high desk against the south wall. "If you offered the opportunity to study here to many of the scholars in the city, might not you earn the respect and trust you need to fulfill the King's mandate? Your library could be brought here, as an added incentive."

"It is possible, but that will depend on the King," said Germanno, making himself turn away from the wonderful transformation of his long-ago laboratory. "My books are the least of it; I will need to have at least half the rooms suitably furnished. That means in Roman fashions, or Frankish ones. Idelfonzuz would not appreciate divans and carpets in the Moorish style." He shook his head as he closed the door. "Perhaps I can use the observatory to explain my nighttime habits. It will be more readily understood why I am up late if this room is known." Going back down the corridor, he added, "It would be wise to do a full inspection of that room."

"Why? Does anything seem amiss?" Ruthor was troubled by this remark. "Do you suspect something has been done to the room?"

"No, but I remember the scorpion, and I would not like to have such a surprise again." He paused, listening to the fountains. "Be sure the water flowing in the wells is wholesome. A few of the cisterns in the city had dead rats sunk in them, as a departing token of the Moors who have gone. Those who have stayed may still ally themselves with those who left, and seek to do mischief to all of those here with Idelfonzuz."

Ruthor stopped still. "If you are so apprehensive about such ruses, how can you enjoy your homecoming?"

"But this is not a homecoming," said Germanno, Comide Ragoczy rather sharply, going on in a gentler tone, "it is a return, and one that has been long in coming. I would be soft-witted if I mistook this place for the one we left so long ago; think of all the work that must be done on Villa Ragoczy in Roma. This is not much different, except that it appears never to have fallen to ruin." He resumed walking, this time bound for the part of the house that once held his library, and faced a solid wall of jasper and malachite. "I want to know what is on the far side of this wall. Then tomorrow morning, when it is appropriate, I will dispatch you to Idelfonzuz to tell him the house suits me very well."

"Because it is your house. You had it built," Ruthor said, annoyed and not knowing why he was so.

"The King does not know that," the Comide said gently. "He will want to be thanked for his magnanimity."

"Which you will do," said Ruthor, smiling in spite of himself.

"Of course." He went back to the courtyard where the larger fountain splashed over large white stones into a large marble basin. "If the wells have not been tampered with, you may start hiring servants tomorrow; do not hesitate to pay well for quality. I would prefer not to purchase any slaves unless it is absolutely necessary. Find me good servants and offer them decent wages; a bit above the usual, but nothing so high as would imply we are naive in such matters. If those you hire have families, offer a little extra for housing, and make the servants' quarters available to those who are alone in the world." He paused, staring in the inlaid frieze of *Qran* text that filled the wall of the main reception room. "*Peace be upon you, for you have endured patiently; how splendid a recompense is paradise,*" he read aloud, translating. "From the *Chapter of Thunder,* I think. Noble sentiments, and yet I would rather have a painting of the city. Shameful in Moorish eyes, but tempting to me."

"Will you hang paintings?" Ruthor asked.

"I think not. It would offend any Moors visiting here. I may make an exception in my own apartments. There are those Byzantine mosaics, you know, the ones Olivia had commissioned for me when Justinian ruled." He went to the stairs that led down to the cellar and the kitchens. "I will probably have to choose my decorations carefully; a saint's statue in the smaller fountain, so that the Christians will not become suspicious, but I will keep the frieze from the *Qran* in place, so that the Moors will not be insulted by a slight to their scriptures. I will have to hope the Jews will be tolerant. Perhaps a prophet instead of a saint in the fountain would be better: Isaiah, I think; his prophesies are acceptable to both Jews and Christians." He looked around at Ruthor and said crisply, "This place is grander than when we left it. I suppose it would be foolish not to take advantage of the improvements."

"Then you will open it for scholars," Ruthor said, grinning his satisfaction at the notion.

"If the King will allow it, yes. Thank you, old friend." He began his descent into the kitchens, making note of the niches in the wall for oil lamps. "It seems that the kitchens have been expanded, too." He stopped at the opening to the cavernous room, looking at the two large open hearths where spits were in place for turning meat. "It would be wise to have more than one cook, judging by the size of this place."

"And assistants, perhaps two or three," said Ruthor. "If you have fewer than that, someone will remark upon it."

"I would not doubt it," said Germanno, walking through to the door leading into the small kitchen garden. "Herbs and squashes, by the look of it. That should suit any cook you hire." He closed the garden door and went back through the kitchen. "This is going to be an expensive household to run as the King will expect."

"Then you are going to refuse him?" Ruthor asked, wanting only to know why Comide Ragoczy would do such a thing.

"Of course not," said Germanno, ascending the stairs again. "I will have to build my athanor as soon as possible. I think one of the side-rooms will do for it. I will decide which one when we have taken up residence here in the house and may arrange to install it with a minimum of attention. I would rather not have it where everyone in the house—staff and guest—can see it; that could lead to questions I would not like to have to answer." Now that he had reached the top of the stairs, he set off moving quickly, walking with a deceptively easy grace that covered distance more swiftly than most men could run. "I wonder of my old apartments are still intact."

"Do you want to occupy them?" Ruthor found it difficult to keep up, but did not ask Germanno to slow down.

"That depends on how they have been maintained," said Germanno, starting for the stairs and climbing the narrow, steep steps two at a time. "If the occupants have used them well, I cannot see why I should—" He stopped as he reached the door and touched the latch.

"Do you not want to open it?" Ruthor inquired when Germanno did nothing more.

"Yes and no," said the Comide, and with that, lifted the latch and looked inside.

The room was in poor repair, with an uneven floor and scaley walls. What little paint had not flaked off the wood was so faded that its original color was nearly impossible to determine. A single stool lay on its side near the tall windows, and the door to the inner chamber hung askew on its hinges. There was no parchment in the windows, and the sill showed damage from weather.

"I am sorry to see this in such poor repair," said Ruthor after a brief silence.

"I have known worse," said Germanno. "This is not remarkable, considering how long Toledom was fought for. I am grateful that more has not been done. You saw what dreadful condition the old church was in." He pulled the door closed. "This will have to be repaired; I cannot use . . ." His words faltered as the skittering of rats was heard above them. "While the wells and rooms are being checked, the attic should be, too. If there are rats there, who knows what else we might find among the rafters." He rubbed his chin thoughtfully. "This will take money. I am in no position to barter for work."

"That will be expected of you, will it not? Servants are not peasants, to trade labor for a share of their harvest. They will expect housing and food, and some payment besides." Ruthor went down the stairs ahead of Germanno, not bothering to turn back to look at him. "You have more than enough gold to fill this house with servants, if you want, and to pay them double the usual wages."

"It is just as well that this is not generally known," said Germanno drily. "Foreigners with money are easy targets. Idelfonzuz or the Church would invent a new tax if they found out."

"Are you certain of that?" Ruthor stopped at the corridor leading into the newest addition to the house.

"As certain as I am that campaigns are expensive," the Comide answered with a wry smile.

"And this one is long," said Ruthor. "It has lasted for generations."

"Not as openly as recently, but, yes, it has," said Germanno, adjusting his black cote of Sicilian silk so that it swung more loosely around his legs, sheathed in dark-red bamberges; his black-leather solers were thick-soled and high enough to reach the base of his calves. "I will need my silver-embroidered surcote for this evening," he remarked to Ruthor. "The King has said he seeks to learn what I know of Toledom."

"Will you tell him why you were interested in this house over many another?" Ruthor asked mischievously.

"I have already told him there were records that one of my blood had lived in this house many decades ago. It may incline him to accept my living here without question. He, himself, can make such a claim to other properties here in Toledom, and so he could be inclined to approve my request." Germanno frowned slightly. "I do not know how long he will expect me to wait upon him tonight. I trust it will not be too late.

"Do you think you might spend some part of the night with a woman longing for a dream?" This question was not lightly asked, nor was it lightly answered.

"I think it would be a tremendous risk to make such an attempt until I have had the opportunity to establish myself and learn something of the way the city has changed. It is not the place we left so long ago, and Viridia is long turned to dust." He looked directly at Ruthor. "I appreciate your concern, but I am not yet so desperate that I would hazard so much."

Ruthor said nothing for a short while, then said, "You will not neglect yourself again, will you?"

"It is not my intention," said Germanno enigmatically as he started to move again. "If you will use my absence to prepare notes for what we will require to furnish this place well, but not too lavishly, I would be most grateful." He went out into the courtyard to the larger fountain. "We must ready ourselves quickly, for I have no doubt that Idelfonzuz will have plans laid out for me by now. He will reveal them as suits his purpose, and we will have to respond quickly."

"Our host at the hostel will have men and carts to carry your belongings here, will he not?" Ruthor asked, knowing that such tasks were his to perform. "Assuming your occupancy is granted."

"Pay him enough and he most certainly will," said Germanno, sardonic amusement in his eyes. "There are any number of men searching for employment who would welcome a handful of silver for labor." He pulled his gloves from his belt and drew them on; it was a signal of departure.

"That is apparent," said Ruthor as they passed through the outer gates to where a youth of about twelve was holding their horses at the edge of the busy street. He averted his eyes, as he was required to do, as he handed the reins over to Germanno and Ruthor.

The Comide tossed the lad three copper coins, saying, "Thank you for your service," as he swung into the saddle and gathered up his gray's reins; the horse was still heavily dappled, revealing his youth, and he pulled restlessly, eager to be going. A moment later they set off through the rough-cobbled streets toward the hostel where they were staying.

Most of the streets were busy enough, but there was little camaraderie to be seen, for the peoples here were still uneasy in their dealings with the new masters of the city. Although the number of Moors in Toledom had decreased since the Castilians conquered it, there were still many of them about; artisans of all sorts remained when the military and nobles had fled, and now those artisans were busy expanding their businesses to accommodate the men from the north in spite of the uncomfortableness that still existed between them. The Jews were more apprehensive than the Moors, for they had been targets of Christian hatred before and were keenly aware that it could happen again; they tended to keep their businesses to their own parts of the city and were careful when they went into the central markets of Toledom. Ruthor remarked upon this as they passed a busy street in the largest Jewish quarter.

"Do you think they will be accepted now that the Christians control Toledom again?" He sounded uncertain. "They would have good reason to fear."

"Still," said Germanno as they approached their hostel, "given how long and bitter the campaign for this place has been, there is more sufferance here than I would have expected." His memories welled: the slaughter of his own family, the deliberate decimation of the Assyrian captives in Egypt, the comprehensive butchery of the Huns, the Magyars sending thousands of their captives off into the forests to starve . . . He put his hand to his eyes to stop the visions from coming.

"Would you remain, in their situation?" Ruthor asked as they entered the front court of the hostel.

"I might," said Germanno. "But it is not the same, is it?" He pulled his gray to a halt and dismounted, handing the reins to a groom who stood waiting to take them.

Ruthor did not bother to reply to the Comide's question. He came down off his horse and surrendered his reins to the groom, then followed Germanno through the confusion of the courtyard to the entrance of the hostel where the landlord was waiting to give them a message.

Germanno took the reverently offered roll of vellum with the seal of Idelfonzuz on it, tugged the seal off and read the message. "I will have to leave soon," he told Ruthor. "There is someone Idelfonzuz wants me to assist him with. The man is from the south and in need of someone fluent in the Moorish tongue."

"A spy?" Ruthor suggested as they went toward their chambers at the top of the stairs.

"Possibly, but I think it may be more complex than that." He rolled the message up and thrust it through his belt. "I will leave you to begin arranging the transfer of our belongings."

"Certainly," said Ruthor.

"I do not suppose I will return much before midnight." He went into their chambers and reached for the chest containing his clothes. "The surcote with the eclipse embroidery in silver, and my pectoral. This is going to be a grand occasion, from the tone of Idelfonzuz's missive." He unfastened the buckles holding the chest closed, and pulled out a camisa of black silk. "I will change as soon as I can wash the dust off. It is too warm for the full cote under the surcote: in such clothes you would think we were back at Leosan Fortress, not in Toledom. The camisa will suffice." With that he strode into the rear chamber leaving Ruthor to make his garments ready.

By the time Germanno emerged from the inner chamber, his short-cropped hair still glistening with water, the oil-lamps had been lit and his outer garments were ready for him. Ruthor held up the surcote so that Germanno could shrug into it, then helped him shake out his sleeves.

"Do you want the solers of red leather, or the black?" Ruthor asked, both pairs set out for use.

"The red, I think. They are more festive." He removed his dusty pair and donned the tooled-leather red ones, handing his riding solers to Ruthor. "The soles will need more of my native earth soon."

"I will take care of it," said Ruthor. He handed Germanno his device-pectoral—a black sapphire disk surmounted by raised, displayed silver wings depending from a ruby-studded chain of broad silver links—and watched as Germanno set it carefully in place. "Do you need anything more?"

"Probably," the Comide allowed. "But it is not so important that I can call it to mind." He took a fist-sized piece of red amber from a leather case that contained a number of jewels. "This should be a suitable sign of appreciation—Idelfonzuz will expect something of the sort. At least I did not make this," he remarked as he held it up to the lamp. "Good Baltic amber. Idelfonzuz will be pleased." With that, he put the amber into his wallet and straightened up.

"Have a care coming back; the streets are dangerous at night."

"So they are," Germanno agreed as he picked up the short staff given him by Idelfonzuz to secure his passage everywhere in Christian Spain. "I will bear that in mind. At least we are not in Gotalunya, or in Aragon." He had intended it as a wry jest, but Ruthor responded somberly.

"No. But that day may yet come." He held up a warning hand to the Comide. "Idelfonzuz is from Aragon. You would do well to remember that."

"And has made common cause with the Comide of Barzeluna. Yes, I know." He touched his shoulder with his baton in a gently ironic salute. "Still, old friend, we are not in the region of Holy Blood yet." Saying this, he nodded to Ruthor and left him in their apartments while he hurried down to the stable.

Text of a letter from Fre Carloz of the Monastery of Santoz Ennati the Martyr near Usxa, to Idelfonzuz, King of Aragon and Navarre at Toledom.

In the Name of the Father, the Son, and the Holy Spirit, and in honor of our Santoz Ennati: Amen.

To the illustrious Christian King, Idelfonzuz of Aragon and Navarre and ruler of Castile and León in the name of Urraca, daughter of Adelfonzuz of Castile and León, the greetings of Fre Carloz of Santoz Ennati the Martyr, for whom you have a special devotion, and in whose name I now appeal to you.

You know how much strife we have seen in this place, and how much is soon to come. As Santoz Ennati battled the demons of Hell, dispatch-

ing five of them with his axe before he gained his martyr's crown at their hands, we, too, must stand and face the horrors of war as your valiant knights join with other good Christians to reclaim the land of Santiago for Our Savior. This is a most worthy goal, and one that we most heartily endorse, but we are cognizant of the dangers that can come from such enterprises. Those of us not schooled in battle are often the most damaged by it. Great clashes often bring ruin in their wakes, and for this, those who must live where the fighting has been are left to deal with the trampled crops, burned forests, contaminated wells and streams, and the confiscation of livestock and poultry as well as all foodstuffs for the purpose of feeding the soldiers of both sides.

As the leader of great armies, I implore you on behalf of all those who live in this region to mitigate the demands of your men as best you can so that famine and dishonor are not the legacy of victory in this place. Think of Santoz Ennati and his valor in the face of an over-whelming enemy, how he strove to save his Brother hermits from any harm from his heroic action. He faced the demons alone, purposefully leading the group of them away from his hermit's cell and the monastery to which he was attached, so that none of his Brothers would suffer because of his battle. If that one good, holy man could be mindful of his Brothers when entering into a fight against the minions of Satan, should not you and your soldiers keep in mind this pious ex-ample, and strive to preserve the land and the people thereon as a show of Christian charity?

If you do not come this year, yet we know you and your armies must arrive before many years go by. When you do, we beg you to keep in mind our situation. The Moors have taken many of our trees and the great forests we are told once spread from the Ebroz across the moun-tains into France have been gone for centuries, leaving bare hillsides that cannot support anything but flocks of sheep and goats. The few forests that remain are small and remote. Your own Kingdom of Aragon has felt this privation for decades. Surely you can spare us the few things we must have to survive? Our vineyards have been our greatest treasure, but if we cannot save our harvest of grapes, then we will have nothing more than squashes and peas for sustenance, which would not be sufficient to keep the monks here from starving, let alone provide for others in need. We have opened our doors to your people when wars forced them to flee to us, and in the name of Santoz Ennati we have shielded them from harm and want.

The Church has called for the end of Moors in Spain, and we have, in fealty, sworn to assist in this effort in whatever capacity we can. To that end, we have gathered stores of cloth, foodstuffs, and bedding so that soldiers may be cared for in their campaign. If these things are seized indiscriminately by the first company of knights that comes this way, we will be unable to lend assistance to any of the others who may come later. For that reason alone, I beg of you, keep your knights from looting and raiding the countryside when they come here. Remember the inspired example of Santoz Ennati, the Visigothic warrior who would not bring misfortune upon those who could not defend themselves; surely he has shown the way that all good Christians should conduct themselves when going into battle for so great a cause.

Let me remind you that in this place, we are at the very border of the region known as Holy Blood, where no one can count himself safe from the predations of night-hunting demons. Over the years, their numbers have increased and their boldness as well, for their hunger is unrelenting. We are hard-pressed to manage this place against such foes, and no Santoz Ennati has come forward again to rid the land of those pernicious creatures that pursue all living things to the same contemptible end. Surely it is enough that we do our utmost to contain those vile beings. Were you to add the force of your armies to our humble attempts, the night-demons might finally be routed from our mountains, and we would once again live in the state of Christian hope that all devout souls seek. If you cannot rid us of the demons, then I ask you to remember the many trials we of Santoz Ennati have already endured in our stand against all the foes of our religion. Do not bring more burdens upon us, I beseech you even as I warn you of the dangers that wait in the mountains for all those careless enough to venture there.

You are King of Aragon and Navarre, and thus some of these blasphemous creatures are within your borders. Nothing you have caused to be done thus far has rid us of the blood-demons. If you cannot stop them, then do not increase their lusts by sending us, without food or shelter, into their territory, whither we must flee if your soldiers do not conduct themselves charitably toward all those who live here. If you cannot do that, send us another Santoz Ennati to defend us from the demons once our monastery has been razed by battle. It is not so much to ask, when the enormity of the trouble we face is weighed in the balance. Your assurances will bring us more relief than any guards or men-at-arms would do. Give us your Word that you will abide by our

*requests and we will offer thanksgiving in your name at the Feast of
Santoz Ennati this year and every year to come.*

*We who serve you as well as the Church give you our most solemn
oath that we will devote our labor and our prayers to your success in
this campaign you have undertaken. Our doors will always be open to
you and any deputy you deign to send to us. It is our most ardent hope
that you will once again bring all of Spain back into Christian hands,
as God intended it should be when he sent Santiago to minister to this
land, in the days when all yearned for the true light of God, and welcomed His Savior and his Apostle Iago. For so long we have lan-
guished, torn between our religion and the Moors that despair stalked
us as fatally as the demons from the region of Holy Blood. Now hope
has sprung up again, and we rejoice that you have done so much to restore us to our position that our devotion has earned.*

*In the certainty of your triumph and mercy, I am your most truly
faithful vassal, but for God.*

*Fre Carloz
Santoz Ennati the Martyr*

*By my own hand on this, the 14th day of February, in the 1117th Year of
Grace, near Usxa. Deo gratias.*

2

"There is something I must ask you to do for me," said Idelfonzuz to
Germanno, Comide Ragoczy as they dismounted after a morning of
hunting in the hills around Toledom; the escort of guards and courtiers
had been left at the entrance to this inner courtyard and now only the
two of them were met by grooms. "It would be helpful to me if you
would consider it while the others go to eat." He was so nonchalant
that Germanno was immediately on the alert.

"I am, of course, at your service," said Germanno, making a reverence as he entered the palace a pace behind the King.

"That you are," Idelfonzuz approved. Dressed as he was for hunting, he still gave a military impression; his cote short and lined with fur, his pellotes was equally short and made of wolf-pelts that might have been mail. His bamberges were of boiled wool and clung to his legs; his estivaux were of tooled leather and had a broad, flat heel to support his foot in the stirrup, and his spurs rang as he walked. "Unlike many of those around me, you have the wisdom to know it. You make this much easier for me." He headed down a broad, colonnaded gallery, striding through a series of parti-colored stone arches, paying no attention to the servants and slaves who hurried to get out of his way. "I have to tell you what you are going to do for me."

Germanno studied the King as he followed after him. "I will be honored to do whatever I may; I am grateful for your hospitality." He understood now why the others had not been permitted to join them.

"Grateful. I hope you will be." Idelfonzuz increased his stride; Germanno kept pace easily. "You are said to be wealthy. No," he went on, his hand up to show he was not to be interrupted, "do not disclaim. I have seen how you have fitted out your house. You must have gold in plenty to do so well. If you have funds left over, I want you to use them on my behalf." They had now arrived at a grand hall with tall pillars holding up an ornate ceiling; there was a formidable hearth in which blazed a massive log to lessen the chill of the east wind that scampered through Toledom that day. Three slaves scurried off as Idelfonzuz and Germanno approached the fireplace. "You will have my gratitude if you do this," the King added.

"You are most courteous to a foreigner," said Germanno, continuing cautiously, "If you will tell me what it is that I am to do, I might better answer you."

"Ah, as to that," said Idelfonzuz, taking off his gloves and rubbing his hands before the fire, "you are to purchase another grand house."

Germanno maintained his calm. "What house, good King? And to what purpose? Mine has proven most satisfactory, as I thought, to us both."

"True enough," said Idelfonzuz. "But the grand house I want you to purchase is in Sevallis." He kept his light tone but turned to regard Germanno with a keen gaze.

"Sevallis is still in Moorish hands," Germanno reminded Idelfonzuz in a steady tone, no indication of surprise or dismay in his manner, although he was startled.

"Just so. That is why it would be most useful to me for you to do this," said Idelfonzuz, once again giving his attention to the fire. "If it is not possible, then tell me, and the thing is forgotten."

The Comide considered his response carefully, knowing once a King asked a favor that a refusal would always be remembered, and unfavorably. "This is a most unexpected request, and one I must have more information about before I decide if I may be able to do as you request, although I hope it will be possible, for I owe you, Liege, a great deal. I do not know what price is being asked, for what dwelling, nor do I know why it is being sold, or by whom." He held out his hands apologetically. "If I can discover these things, then I can answer you."

"What a canny fellow you are," said Idelfonzuz with a chuckle. "No wonder they tell tales about you." He wagged his finger at Germanno. "You need not ask who tells tales. You know what courtiers are—no fishwife gossips more than they, and you, being foreign, are an ideal target, the more so because many of them envy you."

Germanno ducked his head. "They do so without reason."

"Nonsense," said Idelfonzuz. "You have gained my confidence, which most of them would lose a foot to have. They would envy you for that alone, but there is more. You are wealthy while most of them are not. You cannot think they would not be jealous of such a one as you are." He turned his back on the fire and let its warmth sink into him. "Just the act of keeping you with me while the others of the hunt go off to have a meal will cause them to resent you. None of them would be willing—or able—to do what I have asked you to do, but they do not know this, and so they are given to rancor where you are concerned."

"No doubt you are right," said Germanno, his thoughts preoccupied: why had Idelfonzuz asked this of him, and what did he expect to gain from it? "As an exile, I have learned that not all foreigners can hope to be welcome everywhere."

"No, they cannot," said Idelfonzuz. "Nor can all rulers." He laughed aloud at his own wit, and cocked his head when Germanno did not echo him.

"I beg your pardon, Liege. I have had too many years wandering the world to be amused by them." He lowered his head to show he was abashed by his inability to share in the King's amusement.

Idelfonzuz considered this, frowning a little. "I suppose I would share your burden had I been forced to carry it. God has not imposed such a weight upon me, for which I am most truly thankful to Him, and serve His Cause." This was a significant concession, as both men knew.

"I cannot think of what you have endured. You must tell me of your travels, one day when there is time."

"So I shall," said Germanno, knowing neither he nor Idelfonzuz meant this.

"Anyway," Idelfonzuz went on with a wave of his hand to show this minor lapse was forgotten, "the house I want you to purchase would be a most useful addition to the other Christian holdings in Sevallis."

Germanno strove to keep from telling Idelfonzuz that he was no Christian, but held his peace, aware that such an admission was dangerous. "What makes this particular house of such importance to you, Liege?"

"It was once a Roman villa, where the great generals of Rome lived, and where horses and mules were bred for the Roman Legions. It was highly reputed everywhere, even after the Romans left. The Moors took it over and made it into a palace. The people of Sevallis will know that the rule of Rome is coming again if that house is in the hands of a Christian. Even the Moors will understand my meaning." He looked up at the Moorish embellishments in this palace and he sighed. "They understand well enough why I have made this place my own."

"If that is the case—that the palace would become a symbol of your intentions—why should they permit this sale?" Germanno inquired in a tone of curiosity rather than criticism.

"That is why I want *you* to buy it. You are not one of my Court as most are, and you have your great house here, and a fortune for traveling. There will be no reason to refuse you, no matter how suspicious they might be." He smiled broadly, pleased with his strategem. "You can see the advantage in all this, can you not?"

"I can see disadvantages as well," said Germanno as bluntly as he dared. "Do you plan to send me to Sevallis to live in the house or do you want me to remain here?"

"That is a problem." Idelfonzuz conceded, taking a few steps away from the fireplace. "I want you by me, but if you are, you cannot do what must be done in Sevallis." He sighed again, more harshly. "Well, I shall work it out in time. Not that we have much of that to spare." He swung around to face Germanno. "So you must purchase that house, and soon. The owner will not wait for much longer to secure his price. He has only just arrived in Toledom but he will not remain here much longer. He is bound for Burgundom at the end of Lent."

"I see," said the Comide, wondering if Idelfonzuz had approached any of the others of his Court for this service and been refused. "I would have to present my claim to the house in Sevallis or Corduba."

"Yes. I will give you leave for a period of time to do this. But I am pressing eastward soon, and I would like you to accompany me. I will need someone who can talk with the Moors we capture, and whose knowledge I can trust." He said it lightly enough, but the look in his prominent hazel eyes made it obvious this was an order.

"I am at your service, Liege," said Germanno, making a reverence in Idelfonzuz's direction.

"That you are," said Idelfonzuz with satisfaction. "So you will purchase the house. We are understood on that point."

"I will try to," Germanno agreed. "If the Moorish authorities will accept the sale, then all will be well. If they refuse, then—" He lifted his hands to show he would be unable to do more.

"Bribe them well enough and there will be no opposition," said Idelfonzuz, dismissing Germanno's reservations with a slight shrug. "You can afford a bribe, can you not?"

"I can afford a bribe," said Germanno, thinking that he would have to build an athanor, and quickly, to make the gold and jewels he would need for this transaction. It had been centuries since he had been in Moorish-held territory, but he was certain the expectations for bribe had not decreased from his last time there.

"Then you may rest assured I will grant you occupancy of your house in Toledom for as long as you may wish to live there. You may have any other that suits you as well—except this one and the Obispus'." He showed his teeth in a kind of smile. "Send your servant along to me in the morning and my clerks will tend to the matter at once; we will settle our work this evening. By morning, you will have all the permission you need to purchase the house; I will see to it."

"Liege is most gracious," said Germanno.

"I am nothing of the sort," countered Idelfonzuz. "I am demanding because I am at a crisis and I must find a way to win through or lose much of what I have gained. I have sworn an oath to God that I cannot break without sending my soul to perdition. I will reclaim Spain for Christ or I will perish and become a martyr with Santoz Ennati. Anything else is unthinkable."

Germanno blinked. "Santoz Ennati?" he repeated.

"You may not be familiar with him: he is not much talked of outside of Aragon and Barzelunya. It is a most exemplary story: he was a Visigoth warrior who became a hermit and fought demons, killing a number of them with his axe—some say he killed five, some say he killed twelve, one for each Apostle—before they killed him, and hacked him to pieces. He saved his monastery and fellow-hermits by his act, and gained Heaven." He touched a small pendant decorated with seed-pearls that hung from a chain around his neck. "I have some of his hair in this, to give me his protection and guidance."

"What color is it?" Germanno asked, inwardly resisting the urge to laugh: it was a great irony, he thought, to have Ennati enrolled among his martyrs.

"I have just a little of it," said Idelfonzuz as he opened the little reliquary with his thumbnail; a lock of copper-colored hair lay coiled in the pendant-box. "It is said he was a great champion, driving back Moors and demons with equal valor until he withdrew from the world. Then the demons mustered and came to drag him to Hell. His valiant battle earned him his place at the Right Hand of God." He snapped the little reliquary closed.

"A most . . . edifying legend," said Germanno, and went on, "Not that I question you, Liege, but I know that over time the reports of such heroism can change, and the truth may be lost in the telling of the story."

"No doubt that is true," said Idelfonzuz stiffly.

Aware that he had over-stepped, Germanno said, "But that does not deny the underlying truth." He recalled Ennati's fear of being taken by Chimena's followers, and wondered if he would be offended or amused at the turn his story had taken, could he know of it.

"It may be so," Idelfonzuz said, relenting a bit.

"Where was the monastery or hermitage?" Germanno asked, trying to discover how Ennati's tale had been handed down.

"It was near the road between Zaraguza and Usxa; it was long ago, three centuries at least. The monastery served as a hostel to travelers, and there were hermits' cells in the hills and the forest around the monastery. Having been a warrior, Ennati knew how to fight the demons." Idelfonzuz stopped his recitation. "It is as I have told you."

Germanno ducked his head in a show of deference. "A brave man, whatever his situation."

"An inspired man, filled with zeal in God's cause, as I would hope all my men will be," said Idelfonzuz, and changed the subject. "I want you to prepare for your journey, for delays will only impede my cause. You must be ready to go to Sevallis as soon as the sale is agreed upon. You will have at most a week to make ready. I want you to go there and se-cure the place. You are to appoint a care-taker—I will tell you whom to select—and then you will return here to aid me in my campaign in the east." He stared at Germanno. "If you betray me, I will order you killed. Running would avail you nothing. Do not think you cannot be found, for my arm is long."

"I will return from Sevallis if I am permitted to do so," said Ger-manno, a bit wearily. "It is not my wish to be hunted by anyone, Liege."

"A wise decision," said Idelfonzuz. "You may yet prove as useful as any of my knights." He clapped his hands suddenly, and a moment later two slaves came, their heads lowered in abasement. "Bring Fre Genisioz to me. Tell him to fetch parchment and his implements and his ink. I have need of him now." He clapped his hands again and the slaves departed. Looking directly at Germanno, he went on, "Writing is not work for a man, and we must declare our purpose in writing."

So that you can make all my property forfeit to you, should I fail in this task, Germanno thought, even as he made another reverence to this broad-shouldered, bristly man who was half a head shorter than Germanno. "That is not necessary, Liege. If you have them fetch ink and pens and quills and parchment, I am willing to serve as your clerk," he offered.

"No; no reason to do that," said Idelfonzuz as if the notion was slightly distasteful. "No man of position should do clerks' tasks."

"As you wish, Liege," said Germanno, adding to himself that Idel-fonzuz did not trust Germanno sufficiently to allow him to write a binding agreement between them; this, he supposed, was because the King of Aragon and Navarre could read very little and was wary of the written word.

Suddenly Idelfonzuz gave a broad, affable smile. "You must be chilled. Come stand with me; let the fire warm you."

Although he was not cold, Germanno obeyed promptly. "It is a treat to have so large a fire." He found the heat pleasant, and remarked to Idelfonzuz, "A morning in the saddle on such a day as this can leach the warmth from a man's bones."

"That it can," Idelfonzuz agreed. "And it is prudent to take warmth where it can be found."

"Amen to that, Liege," said Germanno as he made a show of appreciating the warmth. "You are good to let me share your hearth this way."

Idelfonzuz laughed aloud. "You are a man of some wit, Comide Ragoczy—wherever Ragoczy may be."

"It is a place far away, in mountains called the Carpathians, east of the Frankish lands, and south of them. The Magyars claim them now," said Germanno seriously. "My family lived there for more generations that I can easily count," or, he added to himself, than you believe. "I left when my father was killed and have been making my way about the world ever since."

"Your father's loss must have weighed heavily upon you," said Idelfonzuz. "It is a cruel thing to lose a war and a father."

"That loss was hard, and the killing of our High Priest." It was the blood of this High Priest, who was also their god, that had made Germanno what he was. "The deaths of those two was almost more than I could endure."

"Then you understand my battle, how I must embrace the cause of Christians in Spain, and the campaign of Adelfonzuz, my father-in-law, who wed me to his daughter Urraca for the purpose of ensuring his fight against the Moors would not falter with his death." He glanced over at Germanno. "I mean nothing that would offend you when I say I would not like to wander the world as an exile."

"I do not blame you," said Germanno levelly. "It is not always an easy life."

"That must be so, the more for me, if I do not defend the Christian faith along with the sacred soil of Spain." Idelfonzuz gave Germanno a quick smile. "You have a deftness that must have served you well in your travels."

"Liege, you are kind to a stranger," said Germanno, and stepped away from the fireplace. "I am honored that you are willing to entrust a mission to me. Let me know when I am to sign the deed for the grand house in Sevallis and I will do it willingly." He made a reverence again. "It pleases me to serve you in this."

"So long as you do not linger in Sevallis, all will be well; you are not to be there over half a year, at most, and for a shorter time if you are able to arrange it," said Idelfonzuz curtly. "You have too much to offer for me to want you to remain where my enemies might learn of your skills and employ them against me. Not that I doubt your many protes-

tations of loyalty." He pointed to Germano. "You have a place, and that
is by my side. Secure the palace in Sevallis and come back. That is the
whole of what I require of you at this time."

This insistence caught Germanno's attention. He bowed in the
manner of the Chinese. "I will do what you require of me, Liege, not
only for the good name of my House but to show you that you may well
depend upon me in this."

This assurance served to awaken Idelfonzuz's suspicions. "You have
no reason to make such pledges to me."

"No; that is why you may believe them," said Germanno.

Fre Genisioz arrived at that moment, and hovered in the arched
doorway, his short-sighted eyes peering into the room hesitantly as he
clutched his writing supplies to his chest, against his pectoral crucifix.
Finally he coughed to make himself noticed, and ducked his head as
Idelfonzuz hailed him.

"Come forward, good monk. I have a task for you to perform." He
pointed to the low table on the far wall, and frowned when Fre Genisioz did not move at once in response to his order.

Germanno, however, realized the cause of this and went to lead the
monk to the place the King had indicated. "There is a chair, but it is
low," he said as they approached the table.

"Ah. A Moorish table then," said Fre Genisioz, trying to smile in
thanks and almost succeeding. "You have done me a kindness, foreigner. I will not forget it." He set his parchment and implements
down, then looked in the general direction of Idelfonzuz.

"Sit; sit," said the King impatiently, waving his hand as if to shoo
away a pesky insect. "Make your ink ready."

"It will not take me long, Liege," said Fre Genisioz. He set to work,
adding water to his ink-cake and beginning to work it with the spatu-
late end of his pen. When he was satisfied with the texture and density,
he chose a crow-quill and began to trim it to the shape he needed, all
the while whispering bits of prayers.

"You will write," said Idelfonzuz loudly, pausing frequently as he
spoke so that Fre Genisioz could keep up, "that on this day, the foreigner, Germanno, Comide Ragoczy, resident in Toledom, has sworn
to me, as King of Aragon and Naverre and son-in-law of Adelfonzuz of
León and Castile, to undertake a mission for me, to be conducted in
the city of Sevallis in the Moorish-held part of Spain; to wit: he will pro-

cure the grand house known as Al Catraz and set up Antoninus the Greek as his care-taker there. He is also charged with bringing back to me any and all such dispatches or other items as Antoninus may entrust to him. He is further to leave sufficient funds for Antoninus to run the household of Al Catraz for a period of two years at a standard that will give the Moors no cause to rescind the terms of sale. Failure in any particular will constitute an act of treachery and will bear severe penalties. Attempts to flee from Toledom or Sevallis will bring a death sentence and the seizure of all holdings now owned by Germanno, Comide Ragoczy in all Spain currently in Christian hands. This is my will, and to these terms, Germanno, Comide Ragoczy consents without reservation." He stamped his foot as if to punctuate his dictation. "There must be a place for our names, and a witness, in case anyone brings the agreement terms into question."

Fre Genisioz scribbled as rapidly as he could and still make a presentable page; he blew on the ink lightly before sanding the sheet. "There, Liege," he said, and looked up at Idelfonzuz, his expression as ingratiating as that of a kicked hound.

The King clapped again, calling out, "Send two of my courtiers to me. Choose any two of those who have sat down at my table today, so long as they can sign their names." He laughed as the slaves hurried off, saying to Germanno, "I wish I could be there to watch them scramble. As hungry as they are, they are more eager to serve me, in the hope of gaining my favor."

"And will they, for doing this?" Germanno asked.

"If it suits me," Idelfonzuz answered, his head cocked to the side as he strove to read the words Fre Genisioz had written, sounding them out from time to time. "Very good," he allowed at last. "You have done well, monk."

Fre Genisioz ducked his head. "For that, give thanks to God."

Idenflonziz shrugged. "If you want."

"Tomorrow my servant will come to receive all permission for the sale—is that what you intend, Liege?" Germanno asked in the awkward silence that followed.

"It is," said Idelfonzuz. "You will bear the parchments with you, and the assurances we will have from the owner, and that will allow you to purchase Al Catraz. It is named for the—"

"Seabirds," Germanno finished for him. "I recognized the words."

"Yes. Seabirds," said Idelfonzuz with a broad smile. "You do know the tongue, then. You have said you do, but that is not always an assurance to be trusted. I am much encouraged to know you have spoken accurately. Others have told me the same thing, and in the end, it has turned out that they had no such understanding; at most they spoke a few rudimentary phrases that might suffice in the marketplace, but would be of no use elsewhere." He scowled. "And, unlike many I know, I will not ask Jews to undertake such missions for me."

"But why not?" Germanno asked. "Surely you may put greater trust in Spanish Jews than in one foreign exile."

"Jews betrayed Christ; the Church teaches us that. If they will turn against the Son of God, how much lesser a thing is it to betray me?" He glared in Germanno's direction. "Too many of the Castilians have come to trust their Jews, to give them high office and great powers, in the mistaken belief that they will serve their Christian rulers with devotion. But the Jews are not faithful to their Word, and when they go to the Moors, they become like them, given to opulence and luxury, and they forget their vows and purposes, and their Christian rulers come to grief."

It was tempting to argue with Idelfonzuz, but Germanno kept silent, aware that he knew too little of such things, and convinced that Idelfonzuz was referring to a specific Castilian and a specific Jew. "The Moors have had their share of betrayals as well, have they not?"

"It is not a betrayal when a man seeks salvation," said Idelfonzuz in a tone that did not encourage more remarks. He pointed toward the inner archway. "Where are my witnesses? This must be done today."

Germanno wondered why Idelfonzuz was suddenly so determined to have this agreement on record, but he only said, "You feed them too well, Liege, and they are loathe to leave their meal."

"Sluggards, all of them," Idelfonzuz declared loudly. "What King is as poorly served as I am?"

Since Ragoczy had seen Idelfonzuz embrace the notion that he was ill-used on other occasions, he was not alarmed by this outburst, although he was not eager to have the King continue nursing slights and injuries. "They should come at your bidding, Liege, whatever they may be doing when you summon them."

"Except they are being shriven," Idelfonzuz corrected Germanno. "No King can call a man from his religious duties."

"Of course," said Germanno, and looked up in relief as he saw two courtiers approaching eagerly. "There, you see?" he said to Idelfonzuz. "Your men know their obligation to you."

Idelfonzuz did not deign to answer the Comide, but signaled the two to come and put their names at the places Fre Genisioz marked as soon as he and Germanno, Comide Ragoczy had signed the agreement.

Text of a bill-of-sale recorded in Toledom for presentation in Sevallis.

On the authority of the Church and that of Idelfonzuz of Aragon and Navarre and son-in-law of Adelfonzuz of León and Castile, I, Rachmael ben Abbas, formerly of Sevallis, do hereby acknowledge the receipt from Germanno, Comide Ragoczy the sum of forty gold Apostles and seventy silver Crowns as payment in full for the great house known as Al Catraz in the city of Sevallis, to which I have full title and the right to sell it for any amount that I deem acceptable. The monies paid for Al Catraz are sufficient, and in reasonable accord with what a reasonable man would expect to pay in Sevallis, and therefore are not to be challenged by any of those living in the city, or who may believe they should be entitled to occupy the great house Al Catraz.

I have prepared statements for all the authorities having interest in such a transaction, bearing witness to my decision to sell the great house and to accept the money paid to me by Germanno, Comide Ragoczy, who will present these proofs upon his arrival in Sevallis. Such furnishings as I have left in the house are his to use or dispose of as he likes. He is to install his own staff, and to that end, I give him permission to sell my slaves for such money as may be reasonable, or to continue to house them in accordance with the laws of Sevallis.

Let no one think that this sale is the result of gambling or of coercion or any other sort, for I give my most solemn Word that is not the case. To settle any suspicions that may be attached to my sale of Al Catraz, I will explicate my reasons for offering this great house to a foreigner. This sale was sought by me for the purpose of permitting me to move all my goods and chattels with me into Toulousa, where I have long maintained a factory to transfer goods and spices for me. Now that it is possible for me as a Jew to own land in Toulousa, I intend to operate my business from that location rather than from Sevallis, for Toulousa is more central to my profession than is Sevallis.

The lands and grounds of Al Catraz are included in the sale, and all produce of those fields are to become the property of Germanno, Comide Ragoczy. It will be his task to decide how such crops are to be handled, how they are to be planted, changed, rotated, discontinued, or used in any way that suits him. I have placed no binding conditions upon Germanno, Comide Ragoczy, as a condition of this sale, and I hereby forbid others from imposing any such conditions upon him. The lands and grounds of Al Catraz are to be turned over without question to the Comide Ragoczy, and any decision he makes in their regard is to be obeyed as binding and final.

In the event that any claim be made against this sale, I stipulate here that the person bringing such an action is to be given one copper Ship for his trouble, and that no other recovery be granted him now or in the future. I further declare that no heir of mine will at any time seek to recover this great house, nor its lands, nor its contents, and that those who proceed in spite of this shall be disinherited entirely, and be as if they were not ever heirs of mine in any capacity whatsoever.

To this I set my hand in the City of Toledom in the Christian year of 1117, on the day after the Paschal Mass.

Rachmael ben Abbas
Spice merchant

witnessed by Idelfonzuz, King of Aragon and Navarre and son-in-law to Adelfonzuz of León and Castile

witnessed by Malachai ben Doron, advocate of Toledom

3

Night was falling when they reached the walls of Sevallis; the hills around them loomed over the city, blotting out the swaths of stars that spread over the sky above the last embers of twilight. After a short search, they found a place to make camp, about two leagues from the city, at the edge of a large stand of oak trees. Here they were far enough away from the other travelers waiting for admission, and could make use of the time they spent without attracting unwelcome attention. Around them the green, fecund smell of spring gave the night air a presence that was profoundly tempting.

"Will the gates open at dawn, do you think?" Ruthor asked as he prepared a sleeping place for himself.

"Immediately after the first call to prayer," said Germanno, finishing up rigging a tie-line for their four horses and nine mules where the animals contentedly ate the grain in their nose bags.

"I prefer the cries to the clanging of bells," Ruthor said, only half-jesting.

"No night hours to ring, as well," Germanno agreed. "That is something to be thankful for." He took a long reel of twine and stepped out of the range of their firelight and began to set up a trip-line around them.

"You do not think we will have to fend off thieves so close to Sevallis, do you?" Ruthor was mildly disgusted at the notion. "No thief would be so bold: it would be too great a risk."

"Perhaps," came the Comide's voice from the darkness. "But thieves may not be the only danger in the night."

"Oh, no." Ruthor shook his head vigorously. "None of Chimena's tribe could have spread this far, not with all the fighting that has gone on these last thirty years."

"You may be right," said Germanno just loudly enough to be heard. "But neither of us would like to be wrong in that estimate." He was now almost half-way around the camp. "I am suspending the double-chime Greek bells. They are not loud, but they cannot be mistaken for anything but what they are."

In their journey from Toledom to Sevallis, Germanno had made use of a trip-line from time to time, but never so close to a city; Ruthor wondered why Germanno should be so careful now, then shrugged and went on with his work, only saying when the Comide came back into the light of their campfire, "I hope you will rest well tonight, my master."

"So do I," said Germanno, taking his bed-roll from its canvass wrapping, and spreading it out on the other side of the fire. "I'll stand the first watch; and I'll remove the nose bags so the animals can graze a little. You need sleep more than I do tonight."

"Wake me at midnight," Ruthor told Germanno. "I do not need to be coddled with extra hours of slumber."

"Of course," said Germanno, so readily that Ruthor could not hide his doubts of this. It was after midnight when Ruthor felt Germanno shake him slightly, whispering, "To the east," as he did.

Ruthor came awake at once, reaching for his dagger that he kept under his husk-filled pillow. "What is it?"

"There is someone circling our camp," said Germanno in an under-voice; as if in confirmation, one of the horses chuffed and a mule gave a nervous half-bray. "He's moving."

"But where is he?" Ruthor asked, trying to see into the dense dark-ness of the trees.

"Over there," said Germanno, cocking his head instead of pointing. "I think he may be a leper. He has a clapper with him."

Shaking his head in sympathy, Ruthor listened attentively. "He's going around."

"To the south," Germanno agreed. "There," he said a moment later. "Did you hear the clapper?"

"I heard something," said Ruthor. "I cannot be certain it was a clap-per."

Germanno stood up slowly, his hands empty, and called out, "You. Out in the darkness. You!"

There was a sudden stillness, as if not only the person beyond the firelight but all of the animals of the forest had come to a halt. Then there came the sound of the clapper, this time loud and deliberate. "I mean you no harm." The voice was hoarse but far from weak. "I hoped you had some food I could . . . take."

"Do you mean steal?" Ruthor asked bluntly.

"You would not starve because of it," said the voice; the accent was that of a learned man from Barzelunya, the timbre suggested age, but that could as well have been the result of the disease. "I might, if I can-not find something to eat today or tomorrow."

Germanno took a step toward the voice, ignoring Ruthor's signal for caution. "How long has it been since you've eaten?"

"Three days," the voice answered. "I took a handful of almonds from a sack day before yesterday. I have had nothing since then."

"I fear we have little to offer you," said Germanno. "Sevallis is the end of our journey, and our food is almost gone." It was a plausible enough explanation for their lack of provender. "I can offer you some gruel, but it will take time to prepare."

"I am patient," said the voice, less urgently now. "God has left me that, at least."

Germanno motioned to Ruthor. "Two handfuls of oats in a pot of water. Boil it up so that our visitor need not be hungry on our account."

"That I will," said Ruthor, wondering what Germanno was up to now. He got out of his bed-roll and went to their piled up goods to take out a metal pan in which to cook the gruel. "Two handfuls of grain, you say?"

"Two. Our guest is hungry," said Germanno, and glanced toward the darkness.

Ruthor shrugged, and did as Germanno had requested, all the while keeping an eye on the place from which the leper's voice came, for such miserable unfortunates were also desperate men who might lash out.

"Would you like to share our campfire?" Germanno asked while Ruthor tended to the cooking.

"I am not permitted to approach," said the leper.

"Who is here to forbid it?" Germanno's voice was gentle and his manner persuasive.

"The disease—"

"I have no fear of it. I have some knowledge of medicines and although I can offer only a little succor to you, I am willing to extend what benefit I can to you." He paused to allow the leper to think about this. "We are strangers here, my man and I, and you must know a great deal about the region."

"I know the land from Pyrenees to Gadiz, from Burgos to Valenzia," said the leper with a combination of pride and contempt.

"The very man to instruct us," said Germanno without a trace of hesitation. "Come, man. We will not tell anyone of this meeting."

"They will exile you with the rest of us if anyone learns you have spoken to me," the leper warned, and moved forward to the edge of the firelight. He was tall—almost half a head taller than Germanno— and lean under his dusty rags; the cowl of what had been a shortened habit was raised to conceal his face. He held the staff and clapper that were required of him, his water-gourd depended from his rope-belt, and his hands and feet were wrapped in bandages.

"We will say nothing," Germanno told him, "and as to exile, I am that already."

"But you have possessions beyond a staff, a gourd, and a clapper," said the leper, and faltered. "I may still turn away."

"There is no reason to. Your gruel will soon be cooked, and I have no wish to waste it." Germanno moved one of his chests near to the fire. "You may sit here."

"May God bless you for this charity," said the leper, but not in the formalistic recitation that was usual for this traditional acknowledgment; he spoke with genuine feeling as he came to sit on the chest.

Germanno made a reverence to the leper. "I thank you for your willingness to speak to me."

The leper sat very straight, with no trace of shame, as he watched Ruthor tend the mixture in the pail over the fire. "I have not had much to eat, these last few days. People are more generous around the Holy Days, but afterward they forget." There was more resignation than anger in his words. "Many of us starve."

Ruthor went to a large bale and pulled from its protective wrappings a bowl of shiny metal which he gave to the leper, noticing as he handed it over that the leper had only three fingers under the bandages.

As the leper studied the metal bowl, he said, "More than twenty years ago, Ruy Diaz—the Cid himself—founded a haven for us. Cruel and treacherous he may have been to many, but he was kind to lepers." His voice dropped and he sagged a bit where he sat. "The haven is not what it was since he died."

"You have been there," said Germanno.

"Oh, yes. I sometimes go that way for the winter, to stay out of the Bloody Mountains. No one wants to go there in winter. Not even lepers are safe there." He laughed a bit wildly. "It is not just the fighting that kills there. No."

Germanno and Ruthor exchanged a quick glance; Germanno said, "The Bloody Mountains—I do not think I know them."

"They are north and east, near Aragon and Barzelunya, in the mountains between Usxa and the sea. They say it is renegade soldiers who prey on travelers, but it is not." He pointed to Germanno. "Do not go there unless you have a company of armed knights to guide you and a goodly supply of weapons."

"Surely merchants travel there," Germanno suggested.

The leper nodded. "That they do. Those who go without escort do not always reach their destination."

"What of the rest of Spain?" Germanno asked.

"There you need only fear soldiers and monks and bandits." The leper shivered suddenly, as if a cold wind had gone over him. "From time to time a few of the creatures are caught and burned. Nothing is so sure of killing them as burning."

Germanno nodded in slow agreement. "Burning kills almost everything." He studied the leper for a long moment, then said, "Have you seen such burning?"

The leper nodded eagerly. "Yes, I have. Twice I have seen it." In the shadow of his cowl, his eyes glittered.

There were many questions Germanno wished to ask, but he realized it would be unwise to press his guest. "The Church praises such efforts, does it not?"

"It does," said the leper. "It also praises giving alms to lepers and other beggars, but . . ." He stopped, continuing a moment later. "God has chosen this for me, and it is my duty to accept His Wisdom."

"Do you miss the life you had?" Ruthor asked as he stirred the thickening oat-gruel.

The leper nodded. "Who does not miss being one of the living?" He took up the bowl and held it.

"Who indeed," said Germanno, who had witnessed the Mass of the Dead celebrated for lepers as they were shut away from most of humanity.

Ruthor tested the gruel. "It is nearly ready."

"It smells as if it were baked meats in saffron," said the leper. He put the bowl out, cradled in his muffled hands. "I will remember you in my prayers."

"That is kind of you, but it is also unnecessary." Germanno went to another of their crates and tugged a stoneware jar from its contents. This he held out to the leper. "It is wine from the Rhosne Valley. I have a little of it, and I can spare this; the followers of the Prophet do not drink it. Take it with you."

The leper sat very still, listening intently as if he had misunderstood Germanno's words. "You will give me *wine*?" His astonishment was so total that for a long moment it seemed he was not breathing.

"Certainly," said Germanno, wondering why this gesture should be so remarked upon.

"It is nine years since I tasted wine," the leper said. "The last was the Communion the night before they sang the Mass of the Dead for me." He stared at the stoneware jar. "Is it sealed properly?"

"With wax," said Germanno, showing this to the leper. "You will have no reason to fear it has lost its savor."

"Wine," the leper crooned. "I pray it is as sweet as I remember." He lifted his head and the light struck his face enough to reveal a face ravaged as if by fire: his nose was almost gone and his mouth no longer had defined lips; his cheek was a mass of sloughing tissue and the lobe of his ear was in tatters. Aware that he had been seen, he ducked his head, hiding his visage in shadow once more.

"A terrible scourge, this leprosy," said Germanno as neutrally as he could.

"That it is," the leper agreed, and, after a short silence, asked tentatively, "Will you still give me the wine?"

"Of course," said Germanno. "I have seen more severe cases than yours."

"And you are still clean?" the leper asked incredulously. "How can that be?"

"I cannot explain it," said Germanno, knowing that being undead, he was proof against any sickness that could touch the living. "But as there are those who are untouched by the Great Pox, so there are those who cannot be lepers."

"I pray that is so," the leper agreed after a thoughtful silence. "It is as God Wills in all things." He crossed himself without putting down the bowl.

"Here," said Ruthor, lifting the pail from the spit over the fire, his hand wrapped in a scrap of leather. "Hold that out."

The leper did as Ruthor told him, and bent forward to smell the odor of cooked oats rising in the steam. Behind him, one of the horses whinnied, tempted by the fragrance. "How wonderful, to have this."

"Let it cool a bit before you eat it," Germanno recommended. "You do not want to burn your tongue."

"What difference would it make?" the leper asked with sudden bitterness. Then he set the bowl down beside him and said, "When I was whole and clean, I wanted nothing more than to be able to pass freely down the length and breadth of Spain. Now I am a leper and I may go wherever I like. No one stops me. I have my wish, I suppose."

"You were a man of some position, I take it," said Germanno as kindly as he could.

"I? Oh, yes. I had lands and a title, and I served with Adelfonzuz before he died. I had been the student of a learned man, and I made a journey to Roma when I was thirteen. My son has the title and lands now, and he fights with Idelfonzuz; his son will have the land and titles after him." He looked down at his swathed hands. "Who knows what they will know of me in another generation?"

"You are dead to them, are you not?" said Germanno. "They will remember only that." He knew this was most likely, for few families were willing to admit that any of their number had contracted leprosy. "You have fought in battle—very likely they will say you died from old wounds."

The leper laughed; it was a rusty, harsh sound. "You are probably right. God will cause them to forget." He stared into the fire. "It is just as well."

Germanno could think of nothing to say in response to this. He glanced at Ruthor and said to him, "Is there a blanket we can spare this man?" knowing full well that there was.

"Of course," said Ruthor, and went to take one from their goods.

"You are being most generous to a dead man," said the leper as he lifted the bowl with one hand and pulled a large wooden spoon from the back of his rope-belt with the other. "Whatever your reason, I will thank you in my prayers." He paused a moment in anticipation and then began to shovel the gruel into his ruined mouth.

Ruthor came back carrying a rolled blanket under his arm, a long braid of leather in his hand. "So you can tie it across your back," he said to the leper as he set the blanket down beside him.

The leper nodded and continued to eat in desperate haste as if he expected to have the bowl snatched from his hands.

"Where are you bound?" Germanno asked when the leper finished his gruel. "Do you have a destination in mind?"

"I think I would like to go to Gadiz," he said. "North and east there is fighting. Gadiz is peaceful, or so I have been told; I have not been there, and they say the ocean is good for lepers."

Ruthor looked up at the mention of his ancient home. "It is a fine place," he said adding, "I have not been there in many years, but it was splendid when I last saw it."

Germanno nodded his agreement. "You might like the ocean."

"So I think," said the leper, and touched the blanket he had been given. "At least no one will steal this. Once a leper has a thing, not even thieves will take it." He rose, putting the bowl down on the chest. "Do you want to keep this?"

"You may have it if you like," said Germanno.

"So you have respect for this disease after all," said the leper, and picked up the bowl. "It will be useful. Thank you." As he spoke, he rigged the blanket with the leather braid, then slung it over his back. "I will not stay. Dawn is coming, and you do not want it known that you gave hospitality to a leper, for they will not admit you to the city if they learn of it. That would be poor recompense for all you have done for me." He slipped the bowl into one threadbare sleeve and the wine-jar into his other, then began to move off into the woods. "May you travel in safety, foreigner."

"And you, leper," said Germanno.

"He is planning to drown himself," said Ruthor when he was sure the leper was out of earshot.

"Yes I know," said Germanno.

"Then why give—?" Ruthor began, and stopped at almost the same moment.

"Because he has lost so much. He is utterly alone. What is a blanket, a bowl, and a handful of oats, after all."

"And a jar of wine," Ruthor reminded him.

"A jar of wine," Germanno allowed. "It is all so little."

"He thought you were afraid of his leprosy, and gave him the bowl on that account." Ruthor shook his head.

"Why should he not?" Germanno looked into the forest. "It is probably just as well I did not hunt tonight."

Ruthor understood him. "Probably. Though few people listen to lepers' tales."

The stood together in silence for a short while, then Germanno stretched, saying, "I will sleep for a while. It is going to be a busy day."

"Very good," Ruthor said, and began to restore order to their chests and bales while Germanno went to his earth-lined bed-roll and stretched out supine upon it.

Birdcalls began as the sky started to lighten, and very soon after the wood was full of rustlings and murmurs as the creatures of the night gave over the forest to the creatures of the day. A light breeze sprang up, strumming the leaves of the oaks and bringing new scents from the camps down the road, closer to the city walls. On their tie-line, the horses and mules became restless, wanting their morning feed. From the river came the sounds of fishermen calling from boat to boat, and the first summons to prayer was carried on the wind from Sevallis.

Germanno woke abruptly, and rose at once, stowing his bed-roll so quickly that it surprised Ruthor, who was used to the Comide's rapid recovery from sleep. "I'll take care of the mules," he said to Ruthor who was readying pack-saddles for the last leg of their journey. He went to give them their nose bags again, with oats in each of them. When he had finished that chore, he went to take down the trip-line around their camp, rolling it carefully so it would be ready for use again.

"Do you expect trouble in Sevallis?" Ruthor asked, indicating the line.

"I have no idea what to expect in Sevallis," said Germanno. "Or what to expect on our return journey."

"That concerns you, does it?" Ruthor nodded. "There is a great deal of contested territory between here and Toledom."

"There is," said Germanno, and set about saddling the mules and loading their pack-saddles.

Some little while later, Ruthor gave voice to his thoughts. "Will you go to the great house first, or to the central tribunal?" He felt uncomfortable asking the question but he could not keep from wondering how Germanno would proceed.

"I think it would be most prudent to present myself to the tribunal, so that it will not appear I am attempting anything underhanded." He shook his head. "I do not want to create any more suspicion than I must. If it seems I am unwilling to respect the tribunal, who knows what stumbling blocks they could put in my way."

"All right," said Ruthor, and pointed to the dusty clothes Germanno was wearing. "Then you may want to don a clean cote and surcote, to show the extent of your respect to the tribunal. Come before them in smirched clothes, and you may well make them think you are deliberately slighting them. It will not take long. You have not yet put the chest of clothing on the mule. Let me choose something for you."

Germanno sighed, nodding. "You are probably right, old friend. Very well. Find me something that will not be disreputable. If I am going to do this, I want to do it thoroughly. There is no point in trying to impress with half-measures." He chuckled, and unbuckled his belt so that he could remove the dusty black surcote and dark-red cote beneath. "I might as well have the pectoral, too."

"So I think," said Ruthor. "Hand me what you have on and I will give you clean garments."

"The Moors put great store by cleanliness," said Germanno thoughtfully as he tossed his surcote to Ruthor, and then the cote, "almost as much as the old Romans did."

"As the Christians abhor it, for glorifying the flesh," said Ruthor. "On the whole, I like the Moors' position better." He held out a cote of black damask silk from Antioch. "This should impress them."

"If anything would," Germanno said, and pulled the cote over his head. "I wonder how much I will have to pay in bribes to settle this purchase?"

"They will want a good amount," said Ruthor. "You have bought a great house and you have means. That will influence the officials." He gave Germanno his second-best surcote—a wide-shouldered garment with a high collar of black silk shot with silver thread and lined in a wine-red brushed satin that came from Constantinople. "It will be hot but there is no cure for that."

"Alas," said Germanno lightly as he shrugged into the surcote and secured his belt once again before accepting the eclipse pectoral from Ruthor. "There," he said as he put the pectoral in place. "If this will not gain me some respect, then nothing will." He took his black gloves from his wallet and pulled them on. "This should do it."

"That it should," said Ruthor, and motioned to the last two chests. "I'll manage these if you'll saddle the horses."

"Do you want to ride the chestnut or the bay?" Germanno asked as he picked up his brushes.

"The bay, I think. He's showier. And you would do best on the lighter gray." He shifted the chest to his shoulder and carried it to the mule. "This will be a short journey."

"Yes, it will," said Germanno. "I wish I knew how I am to find Antoninus the Greek."

"Did Idelfonzuz not tell you?" Ruthor set the chest on the pack-saddle and strapped it on.

"Not specifically, no." He finished his cursory brush-down of the bay and took up the saddle pad.

"Then perhaps Antoninus will find you," Ruthor suggested. "You cannot be the only man Idelfonzuz has ever sent to Sevallis."

"No; nor am I likely to be the only one of his spies here now," said Germanno, and remained silent until they were ready to mount up and leave their camp. Then, as he swung up into the saddle, he said, "I do not like being put in such a vulnerable position."

"Who would?" Ruthor remarked, and took up his lead lines as his bay moved out.

They entered the gates of Sevallis before the sun was a quarter way up the sky; the city—Hispalis to the Romans eight centuries ago, and showing a few remnants still of their occupation—was busy filling up for market-day. Vendors and buyers all crowded along the narrow streets toward the central square. Most of the people were in Moorish dress, but a few wore Byzantine garments, and fewer still were dressed in the style of Castile and León.

"What do you think?" Ruthor asked as they made their way to the central square where fountains cooled the air and provided drink for man and beast.

"I think it will be a long day," said Germanno as he pulled his second horse and the string of mules to order. He shouted suddenly as a youth attempted to pull one of the bales off the pack-saddle of the last mule; the youngster faltered, then bolted. "There will be more of that, I fear," he said as he watched the would-be thief vanish into the crowd.

"I will watch them all," said Ruthor.

"It would probably be better to pay a handful of coppers to one of the horse-minders to help you. He will know the real thieves by sight; we do not." Germanno smiled quickly as they finally reached the genial chaos of the market square. "Look about for horse-minders."

"There's a likely looking group over there," Ruthor said, pointing to a dozen young men, a few with horses already in their care. "What do you think?"

"I think it would be wise to speak to them," said Germanno, dismounting and leading his horses and mules toward the group. He called out to them in their Moorish tongue, his accent old-fashioned but understandable. "Good minders! What will you charge a stranger to watch four horses and nine mules?"

One of the group looked around, his eyes narrowing as he sized up the man in black, red, and silver. "Three silver Mercifuls," he said at once; they both knew it was an outrageous sum.

"Two, and a copper Wisdom for each animal at the end of the day if nothing has happened to them or their loads," Germanno countered, knowing it was a generous offer and one the young man was not likely to turn down.

"Done," said the young man, and spat in his hand to seal their bargain.

Germanno did the same. "Excellent. My manservant will remain with the animals; I trust you will not object."

This time the young man scowled but gestured agreement. "Very good," he said in a tone that meant the opposite.

Turning to Ruthor, who was still in the saddle. "You heard?"

"I did," said Ruthor in the language of Persia. "I will be alert for thieves."

"That would be appropriate," said Germanno in the same language. "If I have not done these young men a disservice, they probably augment their earnings by pilfering from chests and bales."

"So I thought," said Ruthor as he climbed down from the saddle. When he spoke again, it was in Castilian. "I will be sure they are watered and fed, my master."

"Thank you," said Germanno in Castilian. "I will return from the tribunal as soon as I am allowed to leave." He looked around and settled on the most impressive building next to the mosque as the likeliest place for the tribunal. "Let us hope this will not take all day." As he started to walk away through the thickening crowd, he called back to Ruthor. "You may want to buy a chicken or two, for your supper."

Ruthor waved to show he heard, and thought to himself that it was a far simpler matter to deal with an outcast leper than with a single city official.

Text of a letter from Antoninus the Greek at Sevallis to Idelfonzuz, King of Aragon and Navarre, son-in-law to Adelfonzuz of Castile and León; smuggled in the false bottom of a casket of saffron.

To the most excellent, most Christian King, Idelfonzuz of Aragon and Navarre and protector of Castile and León, the most devoted greetings from Antoninus, the Greek, trader in spices and oils, living in Sevallis.

Your man Germanno, Comide Ragoczy has arrived; I saw him myself on the last market-day. He spent most of the day closeted in the tribunal, but in the end, he was allowed to take up his residence at Al Catraz, with his servant and much property, carried here on mules; not so many that he roused envy, but enough to show he has substance. He went to Al Catraz at once, and made himself known to the household.

There is a difficulty in that regard that none of us had anticipated: Rachmael ben Abbas did not mention he left his second and third wife at Al Catraz, nor did he mention his irregular daughter, Lailie, a woman of sixteen, who is also living in the great house.

The tribunal has declared that Germanno must care for these women as if they were his own, and provide a living for them when he leaves the city. There was also a large bribe required of him. I have heard it said that it was supposed he would be unable to pay the whole of it, and there was surprise when he complied with the order.

I have not yet contacted him. I have much to report, but I do not want to draw attention to our dealings, for that would surely result in a scrutiny that would please none of us. In time, I will, as a spice merchant, visit him to learn of my old colleague, Rachmael ben Abbas. That will not be regarded as anything but good business.

When I call upon Germanno, I will try to find out what he intends to do with the two wives and the daughter. He must abide by the tribunal's order, but that does not mean he must do more than what is spelled out for him to do. It is most unfortunate that my colleague should have decided to leave without including all of his household, but as Christians frown on more than one wife, he might have been wise to leave these behind. As to the daughter, she is without a dowry, and that may be a problem for her. To be sixteen and yet unmarried is most un-usual.

There seems to be trouble brewing among the Moors. Apparently some of their people in Africa are at odds with those in power. It may come to nothing, or it may be only a rumor, or it may lead to more civil unrest, which may well weaken the Moors in Spain. When I know more, I will send you word of it.

May God speed your cause, great King, and give you the victory we all pray for day and night. For the sake of us all, hasten to deliver us.

This at sunset, by my own hand,

Your most humble servant,
Antoninus of Sevallis

on the 3rd day of May in the blessed Christian calendar, in the 1117th year of Christ's Coming

4

"Why are gardens always so much sweeter at night?"

The sound of the young woman's voice caught Germanno's attention and he turned to face Lailie as she emerged from the women's quarters into the cool of the walled garden of Al Catraz. "I did not mean to intrude," he said, bowing to her.

"I am the intruder," she said, smiling at him. "I am a guest in my father's house. Because my father is no longer master here." Her clothes were loose and pale, made of sheer cotton and suited for house-wear; they provided contrast to her dark hair and fine olive skin.

"Perhaps I should leave the garden to you," he suggested. "If you think it would be advisable."

She shook her head. "I am a Jew, not a Moslem. My father's other wives would not come out here if they even suspected you were here." She shrugged. "My mother was a Jew, but not my father's wife." Her stare was hard, as if she expected condemnation from him. "I should be more conciliating, shouldn't I?"

"I am sorry you have had so . . . so difficult a time," said Germanno, trying to read her mood, for she was at once sweet and angry.

"Why? It is not your fault that my father decided to leave us here. Or that he made no real provision for us beyond the most minimal. He said the sale of Al Catraz would give us money to live." She picked up a pebble from the carefully groomed pathway and tossed it into the nearest of three fountains that sang their liquid songs to the warm spring night. "He could not afford to do more, he said. And then he left."

"I know very little of his circumstances," said Germanno. "I met him only once, to pay him for this house." The darkness did not obscure her features to his eyes, and he sensed a deep sorrow within her, disguised as wrath. "He told me very little about Al Catraz."

"Then why did you buy it?" This challenge was made without apology; she waited for his answer.

"It was available and it suited my needs," he replied, knowing he was not to speak of Idelfonzuz's involvement in the transaction.

"He said nothing about his wives, did he? He took his first wife and her children, but left us here." She picked up another pebble and shied it into the largest of the fountains. "He should have said something."

"Perhaps he was afraid of what the Church would say," Germanno suggested gently.

"He is a Jew. What does it matter what the Church says?" she asked as she paused to pick a flower and pull it to bits.

"In the Christian kingdoms, the Church is as strong as the rule of Islam is here," he said, resuming his ambling pace. "As the tribunal is tied to the mosque, so the law is tied to the Church." While he spoke, he picked a five-petaled rose and held it out to her. "I am sorry that you should have to bear the brunt of this."

"Why should you be sorry? What does it mean to you? You knew nothing about it, from what I have been told." There were tears in her eyes; she dashed them away with the back of her hand. She ignored the rose.

"It means that I have been made party to a fraud, and I dislike being in such a position." He stared out over the garden, following the flight of a night bird.

She studied him for a moment, and then, as if making up her mind, she said, "My father did not deal well with you, either, keeping us unknown to you."

"No, he did not," Germanno said.

Lailie chuckled sadly. "He educated me. I can read Hebrew and Arabic and Greek. I can do sums and figures. If I had been a son, he would have taken me with him, even though I am illegitimate. Wouldn't he?"

"It is possible," said Germanno, who agreed that it was likely. Capable sons were not as hampered by bastardy as daughters were.

"He would have had to take me if he and my mother ever married," she said, more sorrowfully than resentfully. "He thought that if my mother were pregnant, they would be allowed to marry. It had happened before. But this time they were refused. So, I am what I am and my father has left me behind."

Germanno considered her, wishing he knew how to comfort her. "Your mother? What happened to her?"

"She died, oh, nine years ago now. She became listless and lost flesh, and no one could treat her." Lailie walked on in silence for a bit; finally she said, "I had my studies to console me."

"Did you also learn Latin?" Germanno asked, thinking that Lailie was not the only person who found succor in learning; it had sustained him many, many times in the past. Her knowledge would also stand her in good stead now: she might find acceptable employment knowing languages.

"No," she said, downcast. "He said it might corrupt my faith if I knew Latin."

"Now, why is that?" Germanno was truly perplexed.

"He said I would read Christian writings and lose my Jewishness," she told him, ending on a hard, short sigh.

"That seems . . . unlikely," he said. They had reached the third fountain and they stopped there to consider the night. "Would you like to learn? to read Latin?"

She looked up at him. "Are you mocking me?"

He answered softly. "No; not I. I want to know if you would like me to teach you Latin."

It took her a long while to reply. "Yes. Please."

His smile was quick and one-sided. "Very good," he approved. "Shall we begin tomorrow? After the mid-day rest?"

Lailie thought about her answer. "Tomorrow? Can it not be the day after? I should explain this to my father's wives, so they will not be too appalled." She sensed his puzzlement, and went on, "I am an unmarried woman being given instruction by a man who is not a blood relation. They will be shocked. I will have to ease their minds. They are very frightened, for they are certain you are going to make them your concubines."

"You may tell them they have nothing to fear from me." He said it in a level tone and with no hint of duplicity.

"Then they will be afraid that you will turn them out to be beggars." She held up her hands to show how useless it all seemed to her. "They are both without fathers and only Rabiah has a brother alive, and he is across the sea, with a household of his own and no place for her in it. Neither of them has uncles willing to take them in, or sisters' husbands with room in their households."

"No wonder they are frightened," said Germanno.

"They fear they will have to become prostitutes in order to live," said Lailie. "It is not a fate I would wish on anyone." She looked at Germanno, as if expecting him to respond to her doubts.

"Though they are known to be without means, they will not suffer if I can prevent it," said Germanno. "Abandoned wives are at the mercy of the city and that often makes them beggars. You may tell your father's wives they need not turn to such a life, not while I am here. That would be a trifle . . . impractical, would you not agree?"

"Do you mean this? I know that you are in a position to mitigate their compromised position: I also know nothing compels you to do so." She looked up at the stars. "If you would extend your protection, they would not fear you as they do, nor worry that they will be cast off."

He reached out and took her hand, kissing it in form, as if she were a Frankish woman of high degree. "That will be attended to. All I ask is that you try to reduce their anxieties. Use your influence on them."

"I? How could I influence them?" Lailie asked, not quite shocked by the suggestion. "I am no different than many other women in Sevallis."

"Amen to that, Lailie," said Germanno wryly, his eyes crinkling as he glanced of her. "All women in Sevallis speak several languages and—"

"No, they do not," she interrupted with mild petulance. "You know what I mean."

"I have some inkling," he said, his demeanor conciliating. "But I think you may find the women will listen to you more than they would listen to me. I am a stranger, I am not of their country or religion, and it is known I will not remain here for very long. I do not blame them for distrusting me."

"It isn't as bad as all that," said Lailie. "But they . . . they have good reason to worry, and they have not trusted anyone but my father in the past, for that was what they were taught. And you see what has come to pass on his account." She let her fingers dangle in the cool water of the fountain.

"I see you are annoyed, and that you feel helpless now that your situation has changed." He studied her for a long moment, then said, "Do consider coming with me when I leave to Toledom. It is not as elegant a place as this—war has made it rough and stalwart, not graceful—but there would be work for you."

"Translating?" She tasted the word carefully.

"Yes," he replied. "There are not many in Toledom who can read and write their own vulgate, let alone any other language. If you will learn Latin, you will never want for occupation there."

"Toledom," she said as if it were the farthest point in the world.

"Or other cities in the north." He saw her doubt, and added, "You might go as far as Toulouza and find work, but you might also find your father."

"I should probably do as you suggest," said Lailie, her doubt making her remark a question.

"But?" he prompted.

"But I am worried that you will be unable to do as you say you will, and then I, too, will be a stranger in an unfamiliar place, away from my religion and my family, and who knows what will happen to me." She met his dark eyes steadily. "This is too much to think about at once. Yet I have been waiting all day, gathering the courage to talk to you. I thought you would not listen to me."

"Why should I not," he responded.

She hesitated as if trying to sharpen her thoughts to answer him. "You are a stranger, and you were deceived by my father."

"Yes," he said, and let her go on.

"Many another would think that because you had been deceived, you had no reason to do anything for me, or my father's wives," Lailie declared.

"Yes," Germanno said.

"Then why are you so ready to assume responsibility for us? We are obligations you did not have to accept, but you have." Her voice rose with exasperation. "You have no reason to do anything for us."

"Yes," said Germanno. "I have reasons of my own."

"Ah!" She pointed at him. "I *knew* it! You are making arrangements without consulting us."

Germanno shook his head. "I understand that you are worried: you need not be. I will do nothing that any of you dislikes." He wanted to touch her hand in reassurance but did not, aware that she would not be relieved of anxiety by such a gesture, "Nothing is settled yet but I am reasonably certain I have made suitable arrangements for your father's two wives. You are a bit more . . . difficult."

"Because of my birth," she said, and this time there was bitterness in her voice.

He chuckled softly. "No, Lailie, because of your learning." He saw her startled look, and explained. "I have found a very respectable family of considerable means in need of capable servants for the women's quarters. It struck me that your father's wives would be more comfortable there than left here on their own. It is what they have known all their lives, and what they expect. But you?" He shook his head. "No. I cannot see you living happily in such a setting, spending your days at sewing and bathing and tending to infants. That is why I suggested coming to Toledom with me, where you can put your education to use."

"You mean that none of the Jews in Sevallis want their sons to marry a bastard daughter of a man who has fled the country." She slapped the marble rim of the fountain.

"No one has told me so," he said gently.

"Of course," she said. "Do you think they will come right out and tell you that you have made an intolerable invitation, proposing any kind of match for me? My father tried to find me a husband and could not."

"He told you about this, did he?" Germanno asked.

"Oh, yes; tearfully." She began to pace away from the Comide. "He apologized more times than I care to recall, and always with such feeling that I would have believed him had I not listened to precisely the same apology so often. I could recite it along with him, had I wanted to." Turning back toward Germanno, she shook her head. "I should not be telling you *any* of this."

"I will keep your confidence," said Germanno, knowing she meant something else.

Lailie slammed her hands together in frustration and glowered at Germanno. "I was a fool to talk to you. I should have kept to myself."

"I do not think you foolish," Germanno told her. "I think you are a very brave young woman who has had to deal with more than she can manage for some time, and I think you are afraid of what lies ahead."

She walked directly up to him. "And you think it is wrong of me to fear this?"

"No. I hope it is unnecessary." He saw her wince. "You want to have the life you used to have—and who can blame you for that?—but with your father gone, that is not possible. With your father gone you cannot remain here on your own, because the law would not allow it. You have no relatives who have offered to take you into their households. You have not found a husband to your liking, and admit you are not likely to find one. So what else is available to you here? Very little that you would like."

"That is harsh," she said in a small voice.

"Is it wrong?" The question was suspended between them as if it were a filament in the air.

She shook her head. "No."

"Very well, then," he said. "You are an intelligent woman. What are you going to do instead?"

"I am going to think for tonight, and tomorrow, what might be best to do, and then I am going to let you teach me Latin," she said, squaring her shoulders and swallowing her grief. "There is no point to mourning what is lost."

At another time he might have argued that point with her, but he saw how fragile her self-possession was, and did nothing to reduce it. "I have books and writing implements with me."

"I have pens and vellum and ink," she said, somewhat defensively.

"Very good" he approved. "Since you already know Greek, you will learn quickly." His confidence in her capacity buoyed her spirits; she smiled and nodded. "You have something to look forward to."

Lailie's mouth quivered but she managed not to lose her smile. "Yes. Yes, I do. And I will tell Rabiah and Amine that they will not be beggars, if you will permit it."

"Far better that they hear it from you than from me," said Germanno. "I fear they would assume some deception if I told them; from what you have said tonight, they think me a monster."

"Not a *monster*, exactly," said Lailie, flushing a bit at the recollection of all she had told him. "A foreigner and a—"

"Man?" he suggested.

"Yes," she conceded, and, growing bolder, said, "and an interloper."

"Of course," Germanno said without shock or condemnation. "All the more reason for you to tell them. I would be most grateful to you if you will do this for me."

Color spread through her cheeks again. "Certainly."

"That is a kindness on your part and I thank you for it." He inclined his head to her.

"I do not do it to be kind," she admitted. "I wanted you to do something for all of us, and so I came to talk to you." She licked her lower lip with inexpert provocation. "I would have done . . . more."

"I realize that," said Germanno, his voice low.

"I still will, if you want." She looked at him hesitantly, expectation mingled with distress in her posture.

"You do not need to bribe me, Lailie," he said, knowing how much he wanted her.

"I know how men are," she said, tossing her head. "You do not need to fear that I would demand more of you than you have already granted."

He sighed slowly. "You do not know me, Lailie," he said to her at last. "There are many things about me that would not . . . suit you. If you are to be my student, it would be just as well if you were not more than that."

"Why should I not be?" She turned to take hold of his arm.

"Because I am a foreigner and you are a bastard and neither of us are trusted." He was deliberately blunt, and had the dubious satisfaction of seeing her blink in reaction. Taking advantage of her shock, he continued, "You could find yourself condemned and imprisoned, which neither you nor I would like. You could be deprived of a place to live because the tribunal confiscates Al Catraz. You could be made to accuse me of assaulting you in order to protect yourself from harlotry. You could be stoned for seducing me. If I were a follower of the Prophet, or your father were here to give countenance to what passes between us, then I would be glad to consider your offer. But as things are . . ." He lifted his free hand to show how constrained he was. "I am constantly under scrutiny. You and I both know that. So you must be watched as well. If you took me as your lover, you might be held in error by more than the Jews of Sevallis: the tribunal could decide that you had committed a crime, and I have no power to save you."

"You could marry me," she said defiantly.

"No, Lailie," he said as gently as he was able, "I could not."

"You may have more than one wife here. My father had three," said Lailie, her attempts at seduction gone.

"That is not the issue." He lowered his voice. "Your father has used you ill, leaving you as he has, with no adequate provision for your maintenance."

"He had to do it," said Lailie urgently. "He did not mean to put us in danger. You are not to speak against him."

Germanno raised his hands in a sign of truce. "You misunderstand me; I do not question his decision; I know very little about the circumstances that led him to leave Sevallis," he said, choosing his words carefully so that Lailie would not feel compelled to defend Rachmal ben Abbas. "I only say that because of what he had to do, you and his wives have borne the brunt of his necessity."

"He wanted to handle our situation better, but he could not. He was not allowed to. Everything happened so quickly. The tribunal told our teachers that action had to be taken. There were questions being asked, and insinuations made." She averted her eyes as if her next admission were too shameful to voice while looking at the Comide. "He had to depart sooner than he planned, without time to do all that he wanted to for us." She caught her lower lip between her teeth, then said, "Sometimes I think he could have waited a day or two longer, just to put our situation right."

Knowing that agreeing would be precarious, Germanno ventured, "Perhaps he was afraid that if he lingered, you might be at a greater disadvantage than if he left." He doubted this was the case, but he could not deprive Lailie of the consolation of that possibility.

"Perhaps," she said, a forlorn note entering her voice. She hit her thigh with her fist. "This is nothing like I had planned."

"As is often the case in life," said Germanno quietly.

She rounded on him. "You have been reasonable, and courteous," she accused him. "You should be a barbarian, without conduct or compassion and you are *not!* You are not!"

In spite of himself, he laughed. "I must apologize for disappointing you, Lailie," he said. "You have much to endure from me."

"Well, I have," she said, pouting and trying not to share in his amusement.

"I am not disagreeing," he pointed out.

"If you would, I could remain angry," she said, and managed a single chuckle. "Oh. I didn't want to do that."

"Of course not," he said. "You need not cease being angry on my account."

"That makes it worse; if you do not mind my anger, what is the point of having it?" she complained without heat. For a long moment she said nothing, then she glanced at him. "You'll still teach me Latin?"

"I will," he promised. "Beginning the day after tomorrow."

"And you will take me to Toledom if you cannot find me a husband here?" She sounded a bit less confident now.

"Yes; I have said so," he told her.

"Well. Since you are reasonable and unseduceable, I will wish you a pleasant night and return to the women's quarters." She walked away from him, her pale garments wraith-like in the night.

When he was sure she was gone, Germanno turned to the back of the garden and called softly, "You can come out now."

The plants rustled, and then a thin man of middle height and middle-age stepped out of the cover of plants. "You knew I was there?"

"I knew *someone* was there. I did not know it was you, Antoninus," said Germanno at his most affable.

The Greek merchant stared at him in amazement. "How did you guess—?"

"Your clothing is Byzantine and you are armed only with a dagger, a dagger with a Greek crucifix on the hilt. Whom else would you be?" He approached Antoninus, sizing up the Greek and mistrusting what he saw. "I have been expecting you."

"Have you?" Antoninus said, raising his eyebrows to show his disbelief.

Germanno was not tempted to play at whatever Antoninus seemed to want to do. "Idelfonzuz said you would contact me. Why have you waited so long, and what possessed you to choose such a manner to make yourself known?"

"I was afraid we would be watched, and I knew if I approached you directly it might alert those whose business it is to know what foreigners like you and me do. This is the third night I have waited in your garden." He pursed his lips in disapproval. "I did this for your benefit, you know."

"Do you think so." Germanno shook his head once, and indicated the sprawl of the great house at the other end of the garden. "In which case, we would do well to stay away from there. Slaves watch everyone."

"They say you have sent away most of the slaves in the house and hired servants of your own," said Antoninus, probing awkwardly.

"I do not like having slaves. I prefer to employ servants," said Germanno. "Part of my foreign ways."

"Um. Yes." Antoninus coughed experimentally. "That is the sort of thing that sets tongues wagging, not having slaves."

"So be it," said Germanno. "Did you come to tell me gossip?"

"No, I did not. I came to tell you that word has come from Karmona that more soldiers are needed to defend the eastern front. This is urgent, not like the other summonses of the past. The fighting is getting worse there, and the Caliph's forces have taken heavy losses. The soldiers of Castile and León drive from the west and the soldiers of Aragon drive from the north-east and the Moors are caught in the wedge. There will be a summoning of men to fight, and everyone in the city will be given an extra tax to pay for the soldiers." He looked about in sudden apprehension, as if he expected officers of the tribunal to appear out of the garden.

"That is to be expected," said Germanno, who had been through many such taxations in the last three thousand years. "War is a costly business."

"Many of the soldiers do not want to fight there. That is why they want new men for the army." Antoninus flung up his hands in dismay. "These are sturdy men, but they dread those mountains east of Usxa."

A cold grue ran down Germanno's spine as his memories flooded in. "Why that place more than any other?" he made himself ask. "Is it the Aragonese?"

"No; or if they do, that is the least of it." Now Antoninus was in his element; he launched into the juiciest part of his news. "They say that a huge cache of human bones has been found in the mountains between the Caliph's forces and the soldiers of Aragon and Barzelunya. They say night-demons killed them and are killing still. In the place that is called Holy Blood."

The Comide closed his eyes as if to absorb a blow. "Holy Blood," he repeated. "Tell me more of this."

"It is just rumor, of course," said Antoninus hastily. "But the soldiers are troubled. There are more and more tales of these discoveries, each more incredible than the last. It is said there were two high canyons, very remote, where these skeletons were found. Some were very old and others still had enough clothes on them that it was plain they were Christians or Moors." He paused dramatically and went on, relishing his story. "A few of the bodies found were only recently dead, and their flesh still showed the marks of the demons. The few people who live in that region say that it is the work of a demon-woman and her demon-children. The people have sacrificed to them forever."

"And how do you come to know this?" Germanno asked, feeling very weary. He waited for the answer with reluctant curiosity.

"I told you. The soldiers are talking. I make a point of going to the same eating places the soldiers go, and I listen to what is said. That is why Idelfonzuz values me." He put his hand to his chest in pride. "I go about the market and I listen. I go to the eating places and I listen. I go to the houses where women and boys and pipes are offered and I listen."

"For which you are well-rewarded," said Germanno, regaining his inner composure.

"And for which rewards I am thankful," said Antoninus, ducking his head in a show of submission. "But I must tell you, Idelfonzuz will have to act swiftly if he is to take advantage of this disruption in the Caliph's army. You must transfer this great house to me and leave very shortly. No more than two weeks, or the advantage will be lost." He glanced a Al Catraz again, a greedy smile on his lips; the great house was half-hidden behind the splendid hulk of the fountains so that its graceful domes and spires seemed to float on the spray.

"What of the night-demons? Would they not be as dangerous to Idelfonzuz's army as the Caliph's?" Germanno asked, recalling Chimena's anger the last time he had seen her, more than three hundred fifty years ago; had it diminished, he wondered, or had it grown over time?

Antoninus stared at Germanno incredulously. "Idelfonzuz and his men are *Christians*," he said as if this explained everything. "God Himself defends them against all evil." He made the sign of the cross. "Christ gives them victory."

"Ah," said Germanno, and crossed himself.

"So you must make haste," said Antoninus, trying to recapture the momentum of his information. "The army will soon be raised and you must inform Idelfonzuz where to strike, and when, so that the new troops will not reinforce the Caliph's soldiers."

Germanno considered this. "The army will not be called in a day, nor a week, especially not if the older troops are reluctant to fight." He tilted his head back, watching the display of stars.

"But Idelfonzuz needs to know of this now. *Now!*" Antoninus insisted. "You cannot delay."

"That would leave you to pay the taxes," said Germanno sardonically. "But if what you say is right, I agree I must depart earlier than I had planned." He regarded Antoninus for a brief while, trying to weigh the report against what he knew already. "Do not worry; I will keep the title to this place, and leave money enough for the tribunal. Oh, you will occupy it, but it will remain mine."

"And you will leave soon?" Antoninus grinned expectantly.

"Come to me in two days and I will tell you what I have arranged." He started back toward the great house. "And, Antoninus, come to the main door, as a proper merchant."

"Of course. All right," said Antoninus, bobbing his head in deference.

"In two days," Germanno reminded him, and then the marble expanse of the main fountain rose between them and the Comide was again alone in the night with only his thoughts for company.

Text of a letter from Germanno, Comide Ragoczy to Atta Olivia Clemens at Oriaga on the Dalmatian Coast, written in the Latin of Imperial Rome.

To my most treasured Olivia, my greetings from Sevallis in Moorish Hispania—as you would no doubt call it—before I once again depart to the north and the Christians, as indeed, I must do in the next ten days, or risk the displeasure of Idelfonzuz of Aragon and Navarre.

This part of Hispania is not what it was when I was here last, and that saddens me, although I do not miss being the slave of the Emir's son. It is as if something has sapped the life from the place and the people: it may be the long years of strife, it may be the struggles among the Moors themselves, or it may be something I have not been able to recognize, yet whatever the cause, the vigor is gone and in its place is a kind of luxury that leaches purpose from the people and leads to petti-

ness and cruelty if it is not checked. When last I was here, there was an eagerness to embrace the new, to seek beyond the limits of knowledge, but now, such studies are frowned upon and can lead to ostracism and condemnation. Even the Jews, who have long been a bastion to learning have begun to close their doors to that which is dangerous, or may become dangerous.

And you, Olivia: how is it with you? Is the Dalmation Coast as you remember it, or has it, too, been touched by this strange debilitation? Your estate is remote enough that I hope you remain untouched by the troubles that have risen among the Byzantines, for you have already endured more at their hands than even one of our blood should have to face.

Which brings me to my other purpose for writing to you. Do you remember the young woman Csimenae? She became of our blood some five hundred or so years ago. It would appear that she has continued to add to her tribe, and now both Christians and Muslims know of her and her group and are determined to be rid of them at last. I am torn between a desire to warn her, and the conviction that she has put herself and all of her people in harm's way, against which my warning will be as nothing. Still, as I am to campaign with Idelfonzuz in her region of the mountains upon my return to the north, I suppose I must try to do what I can to guard her. When I last saw her she made it plain she wants no part of me, but in these circumstances, I hope she will relent sufficiently to hear me out. If not, then at least I will have made the attempt.

Once again you have helped me to clarify my thoughts, and for that I thank you. I will now imagine the acerbic response you would be likely to give me, and my missing you will be complete. I also thank you for your good sense and your unswerving loyalty over the centuries— it is more than a millennium now since you came to my life. Little though I may say so, I value it, and I value you as I value my soul.

To you, and to Niklos Aulirios, my wishes for joy and prosperity in these parlous times.

Sanct' Germain
(his sigil, the eclipse)

by my own hand on the 9th day of June in the Christian year 1117, at Al Catraz in Sevallis

5

Ruthor bowed the guest into the central hall of Germanno, Comide Ragoczy's house in Toledom. He took care not to look Idelfonzuz in the face, for such an affront to a King by a servant was punishable by death. "I will bring my master directly," he said at his most subservient.

"I am eager to see him. I know you did not arrive in Toledom until sunset last night, but I cannot afford to wait on the ceremony of three days before I speak with him," he declared, striding down the room as if practicing for conquest on the field. It was late in a hot afternoon, and so he had dressed in a light-weight cote of rust-colored linen with only a minimal damask auburn surcote over it, and still he was sweating; his beard and hair were newly trimmed and he wore only a gold circlet on his brow to show his rank.

"I will hurry," said Ruthor, and made his way down the gallery toward the study with its observatory in the ceiling. There he found Germanno showing Lailie the books stored there, and the place where writing materials were kept. "My master," he said, knowing he was interrupting.

"Yes, Ruthor?" Germanno said, turning around; beside him Lailie looked up, a touch of anxiety in her eyes.

"The King is here. He intends to speak with you." He nodded to Lailie. "Perhaps it would be more sensible if you were to come to him."

"Ruthor, old friend, you are the master of tact. Certainly it would be . . . more sensible." He stepped away from the trestle table and said to her, "Do as you like while I am gone. There is nothing you cannot open in this room."

She ducked her head, showing her hair was still bound up from traveling; her mantel of Sicilian silk was as fashionable in Toledom as it had been in Sevallis. "You are very kind, Comide."

He made a little reverence in her direction and then left the study. "Why on earth is Idelfonzuz here? I should have visited him in three days, as required."

"He said he does not have time to wait," said Ruthor. "He seems impatient, even for him."

"That does not reassure me," said Germanno. "What can have happened to make him behave so?"

"He would not tell me, my master," said Ruthor, so neutrally that Germanno turned to look at him.

"Then more fool he, old friend," said Germanno as they turned and entered the gallery that led to the main hall. "If you will go to the kitchens and have something suitable sent up? A jar of wine, as well, I think. Idelfonzuz puts great store in such niceties."

"And it takes me out of his way," said Ruthor. "I will tend to this at once," he said, and slipped away toward the kitchens, leaving Germanno to greet the King on his own.

Entering the main hall, Germanno made a deep reverence to Idelfonzuz, such as he might offer the Emperor in Constantinople. "What honor to me and my house, Liege, that you visit it."

"Comide Ragoczy," said Idelfonzuz, flattered by the distinction Germanno had shown him. "How good to have you here in Toledom again." He smiled briefly, then addressed the reason for his visit. "I am planning my campaign to take control of the disputed regions to the east. You may advise me on what the Moors will do when I move my men into Usxa."

"You do not need me to tell you they will fight," said Germanno, a bit nonplussed by this obvious situation.

"That they will. But whom will they fight?" He paused and arched his brows. "My informers tell me that there are demons in the mountains."

Germanno nodded. "Yes. Antoninus said much the same thing." He then repeated all that he had been told, adding when he was through, "I must tell you, Liege, that I do not place much confidence in rumors. Most of them turn out to be unfounded, and those that have a grain of truth are—"

"Yes, yes, yes," said Idelfonzuz, waving his hand to dismiss the matter. "And Antoninus can turn a pair of mules into a mounted company of horsemen." He walked away a short distance, then came back. "Still, those mountains have an evil reputation. When I was young, there were tales of rivers running with blood, and travelers and peasants disappearing. Some said it was robbers who killed the unwary, but others said that all the robbers were long-dead, killed by the demons."

"And what do you believe, Liege?" Germanno asked, watching Idelfonzuz more narrowly than he knew.

"I believe that many are being killed in the mountains, particularly where the forests remain. There are roads that are dangerous, and places where they have fallen away altogether, and in such places a man might come to grief. Where the trees no longer stand, there are fewer disappearances, but the land is hard, and crumbles with rain, so many do not want to live there. Even the shepherds do not graze the flocks on such shifting ground." He sighed abruptly. "So the danger is in the forests. The Moors have proved this many times, and if they have truly found many skeletons, then it can only be that the killings were deliberate and not the cause of accidents or other misfortunes."

"You have given this much thought, Liege," said Germanno, trying to discern what it was that the King wanted from him.

"I, and others." He folded his arms. "When I was very young, I recall hunting boar and coming upon a grove in which many cups of blood were left. The priest said that this was to honor Christ's Cup, but I did not think it was. The huntsmen said it was for the demons. I believed him more." He looked around at the sound of footsteps. "Ah. How pleasant to have something to eat."

The cook and two servants approached carrying trays on which were set out cheese and a tub of butter and another of honey, new bread and hunks of smoked fowl and ham. A jar of wine stood open beside a silver cup. Taking care not to look directly at Idelfonzuz, they set their trays down on the table beneath the window and then backed out of the main hall, their eyes directed at their feet.

"It is little enough," said Germanno, thinking that his household had done extremely well on such short notice, "but if it pleases you, Liege, then we are honored by your graciousness."

"Prettily said," Idelfonzuz approved as he snapped his fingers for a chair; Germanno brought the best for him. "And nicely done."

"A man learns things in his travels," said Germanno, stepping back from the King.

"So," said Idelfonzuz, taking a wedge of cheese and smearing it with honey, "what do you think is in the mountains? You said you had crossed them."

"That was years ago," said Germanno, looking away from Idelfonzuz.

"These stories have been handed down for generations," came his response in a tone that insisted on an answer.

Germanno paused, gathering his thoughts and considering his memories. "I think the forest can conceal many things, and that no matter what they are, someone will call them demons to explain them. I think that travelers may be injured, or become ill, and so do not reach their destination, and some credit demons with their misfortune."

"A careful remark, but not an answer," said Idelfonzuz around the cheese as he chewed.

"I apologize, Liege, but I have not knowledge enough to deal with these matters in a way that would serve you," Germanno replied, hoping that Idelfonzuz would be content to eat and ask nothing more.

"That is wise, to consider my wants." He swallowed the cheese and reached for another wedge of it, this time spreading it with butter before shoving it into his mouth. "Still, you have more experience of the world than most, and therefore your knowledge is useful to me."

"Liege," said Germanno patiently, aware that he might be offending the King without meaning to, "I do not seek to tell you of your own country."

"Oh," said Idelfonzuz, pausing in his chewing to regard Germanno skeptically. "Do you mean that because some of the Holy Blood region is in Aragon, you have no wish to speak disparagingly of it? You may do so without fear; I know the reputation of that part of my country."

This assurance brought Germanno no relief. He cleared his throat and said, "For centuries, Christians and Moors have fought in that region, and each has believed that God favored them. When the others triumphed, it was most satisfactory to account for this by saying demons were responsible. That has played a part in the stories over the years. And many of the people living in the mountains have been slow to give up their old faith, and although they may pray to Christ or Allah, they also leave tribute to their ancient gods, in the form of offerings." He had a brief, intense recollection of Pentacoste tying red twine to oak trees; then he thought of Chimena. "Those people, the ones who keep to the old ways, are glad to honor their ancient gods, and they do not care if Christians and Moors call them demons, for that recognizes their power." He wondered if there was any purpose to protecting Chimena, but could not bring himself to expose her and her followers.

"Then they are faithless, and deserve to die for it," Idelfonzuz said as he pronged a hunk of smoked goose. "I will instruct my soldiers to destroy their shrines. Then God will show His Might in our behalf."

"That could turn the folk against you," Germanno remarked, careful not to sound too apprehensive about it.

"What can peasants do?" Idelfonzuz asked. "They scatter like fish when they see a mounted soldier; it does not matter for whom he fights." He bit into the goose, then reached for the wine to wash it down.

Two of the household servants appeared and began to light the lamps that hung throughout the main hall; they did not look at the King, but they managed to take longer than usual to accomplish this simple task. In a short while, the glimmer of lamplight vied with the setting sun in gilding the columns and arches of the hall and gallery beyond.

"Then why not leave them to their own devices and keep your men after the Moors?" Germanno recommended. "They have much more important foe than villagers and farmers."

Idelfonzuz shrugged. "And besides, if they are chased off, whom shall I tax to continue the war?" He swallowed and laughed, took a deep draught of wine, and laughed again. "You should have been in the Church, Comide. You are subtle enough for it."

"Liege is gracious," said Germanno, keeping his thoughts on the matter to himself.

"I have forces in Zaraguza now, and they maintain our lines, but as soon as I have readied my new soldiers, we will press the Moors from above and below. Men are being sent by the King of France—if arrangements are successful, and they will reinforce the men of Aragon and Navarra, as I will lead the men of Castile and León. The Moors will have to withdraw to the east and the south, and all of the north of the country will again be ours."

"When do you suppose you will accomplish this, Liege?" Germanno asked, aware that coordinating so tremendous a campaign would be an imposing task.

"Next year. And you will aid me, for you speak the language of the King of France as you speak my tongue and that of the Moors. You will be my courier." He smiled fiercely, aware of the great respect he was showing Germanno. "You will move between our lines, through the region of Holy Blood." His smile became a wolfish grin. "So you must hope your assessment is right, and the forests are held by nothing more than soldiers and peasants, for you will be going through them with some regularity." He dug his two-tined fork into a lump of ham. "This is all very good."

"I shall inform my cook that you are pleased," Germanno said flatly, his mind now fully occupied with what lay ahead.

"You acquitted yourself well on your mission to Sevallis. This is most satisfactory, for now I know I may rely on you to act on my behalf when you are beyond my Court. This is essential for my courier. You are also not one of my subjects, so there will be less jealousy among them for the favor I show you." He reached out to the trays again, as if trying to make up his mind what next to eat. "I am relieved that you will do this for me, as many of my courtiers have lands in Aragon which they will seek to defend preferentially. You have no such constraints upon your service to me, and no relatives to make demands of you in such regard."

Although he doubted that last, Germanno said, "Liege is most generous."

"I know a worthy man when one is proven to me," he said, a bit smugly as he helped himself to bread. "You are expected to be at my service every day starting five days from now. That will allow you time to reestablish yourself in your household. Then I want you to devote your skills to me."

"Of course, Liege," said Germanno automatically.

"You will have many opportunities to demonstrate your value. I will be glad to advance you in accordance with your service. There is no reason you should not come out of this very much the better for being my courier." He bit off a wad of bread, then drank his wine to swallow it down.

"Then I will hope to be worthy of distinction," said Germanno, an ironic note in his courteous words.

"I am not a fickle King, to demand service and later renege on my obligations. I have said I will reward you: do not think I will forget. You have come through your first test in fine form." He drank more wine. "This is very good."

"Thank you; it is from my own vineyards," said Germanno, then returned to what troubled him. "Was my journey to Sevallis by way of a test?"

"In part," said Idelfonzuz. "In part you have provided me a needed base there, and for which I thank you most heartily. But generally I wanted to be certain you would do as instructed even while beyond my realm, and that you would report aright when you returned. I have read Antoninus' accounts and heard yours. I am satisfied."

There was no reason to be surprised, Germanno reminded himself. "Then I am well-rewarded," he said.

"You see?" Idelfonzuz remarked, holding up his hand. "That is where you are above most of my courtiers. You do not chide me, nor do you sulk that I tested your devotion to me."

"Would it matter if I did?" Germanno asked, a bit impatiently.

"No; but it is to your credit that you do not." He finished the wine in the jar and shook his head. "Is there more of this?"

"Certainly." Germanno clapped his hands, and when Ruthor appeared, said, "Bring another jar of wine for the King."

"And one for you, as well," Idelfonzuz exclaimed, lavish with his host's supplies.

Germanno made a gesture of dismissal to Ruthor, then sketched a reverence in the King's direction. "Liege is all kindness, but I do not drink wine."

"Learned that from the Moors, did you?" Idelfonzuz was not pleased to hear it.

"No," Germanno said. "I learned it from the priest who taught me in my youth." It was true enough; the priest had been a god to Germanno's people and when he had brought Germanno to his undead life, he had taken all such appetites from the young initiate.

Idelfonzuz nodded several times. "Yes. Some priests do abstain from all pleasures. No wives, no wine, no meat, no silks, no horses. All for the love of Christ. They might as well be hermits." He belched and smiled. "Excellent food."

"Liege does me honor to say so," Germanno said.

"Still, if you do not want to drink, I will have your portion," said Idelfonzuz with such innocent greed that Germanno lost all irritation with the man, and offered him another reverence.

"And welcome, Liege." He was prepared to maintain the conduct Idelfonzuz expected, but was growing tired of the necessity.

"The Moors, now, they are said to be opulent hosts," said Idelfonzuz speculatively.

"They may be," said Germanno. "They do not so extend themselves to a stranger who is not long among them." As he said this, he wanted to make an attempt to lessen his apparent dissatisfaction with the Moors. "They live with much grandeur when they can, just as Christian seigneurs do. They have men of learning around them, and they extend themselves on behalf of those less fortunate than themselves."

"Admirable," said Idelfonzuz in a tone of utter condemnation. He licked his fingers and swung around to stare at Germanno just as Ruthor arrived carrying a large jar of wine. "You would be well-advised to keep such praise to yourself. There are many Christians who would view such paeans as contemptible, and, as you say, you are a stranger here." He signaled to Ruthor to give him the wine. "You are fortunate that I appreciate your observations, and will keep them to myself."

"As you say, Liege," Germanno told him as he offered another profound reverence.

"You have much that is praiseworthy about you, Comide Ragoczy. Why endanger it with reckless comments that would give rise to general execration?" He approached Germanno. "When you wait upon me, guard what you say."

"That I will," Germanno assured him, and lowered his head as Idelfonzuz prepared to depart.

"Set your household in order, and then answer my call. You will have duties to attend to before autumn is here." He looked about him as if he had only now become aware of the vanished day. "My escort must have torches. See to it."

Ruthor spoke to Germanno, bending from the waist. "I will attend to it at once, my master."

"That is a good servant you have," Idelfonzuz approved as Ruthor hastened down the gallery. "You must beat him often."

"He gives me no cause to do so," Germanno said without any inflection whatsoever.

"Does he not?" the King asked in mild surprise. "Well."

Germanno knew it was his obligation to escort Idelfonzuz from his home; he did so in proper form, staying slightly behind the King and maintaining a subordinate manner. As they reached the courtyard, half a dozen mail-armored men stood waiting, holding the reins of the King's horse, a big, rawboned light chestnut with two white socks. "My servants are bringing torches, Liege," Germanno reminded him.

"Then bring them quickly. We cannot linger here." Idelfonzuz signaled to one of his escort to get on his hands and knees to provide him a living mounting block; the man who obeyed this silent order smiled as he dropped on his knees and leaned forward onto his arms. While the King settled into his saddle, three servants hurried up carrying the requested torches. "In good time," Idelfonzuz approved, and pulled his horse around.

Germanno reverenced the King again as he left, surrounded by his armed men, who would walk him back to his castle at the highest point of the city. When the doors to the courtyard were closed, Germanno turned on his heel and went back inside his house, his head bent thoughtfully. Only when Ruthor appeared did he break his reverie. "I am going to be sent on a mission for the King."

"Again?" Ruthor exclaimed. "What have we just returned from?"

"That, it seems, was a test," Germanno said with a faint, wry smile. "This is what Idelfonzuz truly wants of me." They walked together into the main hall. "I am to carry messages from Zaraguza to Usxa into Aragon, and bring messages back from there." His expression was mildly abstracted but there was a look in his dark eyes that Ruthor found disquieting.

"You would have to pass through Chimena's territory, would you not?" he asked knowing it was true.

"Yes, I would," said Germanno. "Idelfonzuz claims I am the only man he can trust with such an enterprise." He paused and looked directly at Ruthor. "Which I take to mean that he considers me expendable. If I fail to get through the region of Holy Blood, there will be no one to demand blood money from him, or any Christian."

"Did you expect otherwise?" Ruthor asked.

"No. Yet I was a bit . . . taken aback at how obvious he was." He fixed his gaze on the middle distance. "I will have to think on this."

Ruthor nodded, then looked closely at Germanno. "What of Lailie?"

Germanno sighed. "Yes. I have brought her here. I owe her more than leaving without explanation." He glanced at Ruthor, saying in the Persian tongue. "Yes, I know. You are troubled that I have only visited her in sleep."

"That has occurred to me," said Ruthor in the same language.

"You believe that I should make her my lover." He shrugged. "She does not seek me, she wants a husband, or, barring that, someone who will keep her properly, care for her, and show her respect."

"You can do these things," Ruthor observed.

"Not while I am running errands for Idelfonzuz. And it may be that we will have to depart hurriedly." Germanno took a deep breath. "No. That would not do, not for Lailie. She has had her father leave her already; she does not need a lover to do the same."

"You will visit her in sleep again?" Ruthor said, doing his best not to make this a suggestion.

"I will," said Germanno. "Once certainly, perhaps twice." He rubbed his chin with his thumb, right along the line of his close-cropped beard. "I would rather she knows me, but that would be unwise."

"She would accept you," said Ruthor.

"In time, she might," said Germanno. "But always with reservations, and eventually with disgust, though that would trouble her. She is true to her religion, and that does not give room for friendship with vampires." He paused, and added, "I have not said that word aloud for a long time, I think."

"A prudent thing, as you have often told me," Ruthor reminded him.

"True, but sad, nonetheless." He started away from Ruthor, then hurried back. "You have many tasks to attend to, have you not?" This time he spoke in the language of Castile and León. "You are apt to be occupied with them for a day or two, are you not?"

"As we have just returned, yes, I have, and I will be." Ruthor was puzzled; it was unusual for Germanno to ask about something so obvious.

"Then I will not bother you with going to the Jewish quarter and speaking with the elders there on Lailie's behalf." He laid his hand on Ruthor's shoulder, a familiarity that was unique in Toledom households. "You may have to supervise visits here while I am gone."

"Gone? I am not to go with you?" For the first time since Idelfonzuz had arrived, Ruthor was alarmed.

"I doubt the King will allow it," said Germanno. "Besides, if it comes to that, I would prefer only one of us be killed."

Ruthor found it difficult not to argue. "If that is your wish," he said stiffly.

"For your sake, old friend, I wish it." He dropped his hand and began to walk away. Halfway down the gallery, he paused and looked back. "There is no reason to be angry. It is no punishment to be kept from the fray. And you are for more useful to me here: I rely on you to keep all in order until I am able to return. We have some little time, after all; I do not have to leave instanter."

"You leave at the pleasure of the King," said Ruthor in a steady voice, knowing it was useless to press the Comide.

"Of course," Germanno said with a quick smile. "What other reason is there."

Text of a letter from Ximon ben Mazo to Germanno, Comide Ragoczy, written in the Toledom vulgate and delivered by messenger.

To the most respected foreigner who enjoys the favor of Idelfonzuz himself, to Germanno, Comide Ragoczy, the greetings and deep esteem of Ximon ben Mazo, clerk-advocate of Toledom and Reader of Texts at our synagogue; it is in the latter capacity that I am moved to address you, in answer to your visit of the immediately previous week.

We do not generally admit women to our numbers. There are many good reasons for this exclusion, all to be found in the Texts of our faith that advise men and women to be as God made them, and not to try to venture to the proper realms of the sex to which one does not belong. I would be glad to cite those references which are the authority in these matters, if you are not familiar with them for your own perusal of sacred writings.

Still, as you have said, an educated woman is a rare thing, and as such, requires nurturing and protection beyond that which is usually extended to women. It would be most helpful to our scholars to have one among us with such broad knowledge of tongues as you say this woman possesses. We ask you to bring her here that we may test your claims of her knowledge, so that we may decide if it is appropriate to forgo our usual exclusions and permit her to assist us, and on what terms.

You say she has only a rudimentary command of Latin. This is unfortunate, for now that Toledom is once again in Christian hands, such capability is especially valuable. Still, it is possible that she might, in time, learn enough of that language to increase her worth in our eyes.

I must tell you that I, myself, am not sanguine about having a woman-scholar in our numbers. Women are a distraction, and can lead to jealousies and intrigues that would serve to disrupt the standard of study we have sought to maintain here, no matter who occupied the palace. What Moors and Christians could not accomplish, I fear a single woman might, for the men who study here are not eunuchs, and they are not unmoved by female wiles.

How much easier this would be if she were old, or disfigured, or deaf, or in any other way unattractive, for then it would be an easy task to discourage all improper thoughts. But you tell me she is young and handsome. This could be intolerable, no matter how great her scholarship. Many of our scholars have wives who would be moved to anger if their husbands should be in the company of a woman—let alone a young and personable one—during their hours here. Do not argue that wives would not protest her presence, for they have occasionally spoken against the beautiful Moorish youths who would come here from time to time in the past. If a young man can stir such opposition, think what a young woman would do. The discord that might result from this appalls me as I write.

You inform me that this young woman has lived in Sevallis and therefore has knowledge of the society of that place, and that such knowledge may well prove useful to us in time, when the Christians reclaim the south. While I agree that it is likely such a thing will happen, I am not as convinced as you are that it will happen in a decade. I base my opinion on the knowledge that Idelfonzuz has been concentrating on the east, not the south, and until he has the boundaries of Castile against the boundaries of Aragon with no Moorish holdings between them in any part, he will not be content to claim any other lands.

No doubt this is a more sensible strategy; to capture Sevallis and yet see his own kingdom fall to the Moors would be a blow that would be inclined to cripple him as leader of the Christian forces, and would provide the Comide of Barzelunya an excuse to ally more with the forces of Toulouza, a most undesirable possibility. In sum, the young woman's affiliation with Sevallis is of minor importance at best, and will not mitigate our decision in her regard.

Still, I will not immediately tell you that her cause is wholly lost. We have high regard for learning here, even in so unlikely a representative as a young woman. However, I would advise you to speak to a matchmaker for her, so that she will be known to be ready to marry. That may well diminish the hard feelings that she would otherwise encounter. Let her find a man, one of our number, to make her his wife, and then, if he is willing, she may accompany him to study with us. That would not be entirely welcome to many, but it would also not be as unacceptable as the presence of an unmarried and unbespoken woman. If she has a dowry of reasonable size—and you tell me that she has—it should not be too difficult to find her one among these young scholars who will be glad of her comfort and aid. If you seek a husband for her among the Christians, I must tell you that the chance of her acceptance here would be slighter than it is now.

I doubt whether it is entirely wise to leave the choice of a husband wholly in her hands. Such a decision cannot be made by a woman. She must be guided by those more prudent than she, more knowing of the character of the men who might offer for her. I also do not think you have been entirely wise to allow her to bestow her dowry as she sees fit. Still, that is your position, and we have your intentions in hand, so if she comes to grief over your ill-considered liberality, it will be on your head, not ours.

Let me and my colleagues examine her, to find out if her scholarship is as fine as you say it is. Then we shall render our decision. If you will permit me to tell the others that she will soon be married, I think you may hope for a better response than if she is seen as wholly independent.

I await your response with respect and patience.

God give you praise and plenty, Comide Ragoczy.

Ximon ben Mazo

6

Lailie regarded Germanno through narrowed eyes. "You brought me a long way to desert me," she said in a voice as cold as the summer evening was warm.

"I am not deserting you," Germanno said, knowing how futile it sounded. "The King has ordered me on a mission, and it would be unwise to disappoint him."

"So you say." She looked up at the window in the ceiling of the study. "You have to obey the King."

"If I want to remain in any of the Christian countries, yes, I do." He chose a high stool near his unfinished athanor. "I would not do this if it were not necessary."

"Would you not?" she challenged, taking two hasty steps toward him, then turning back.

"No," he said in a tone that was entirely convincing. "I would not."

She thought about this as she made a circuit of the large, open chamber. "Do you think they will let me study with them?"

Oblique as the question was, he understood it, and answered, "We should have ben Mazo's answer tomorrow or the next day. Then you will know. Until then, I see no point to constant guessing."

"I surprised them, did I not?" She smiled a bit at the memory.

"Yes, you did." His face softened a little. "You did very well."

"They thought I would have only rudimentary knowledge." Her chuckle was tinged with justifiable pride. "I read those Greek texts with ease, and that shocked them. I wish you had more time to teach me Latin."

"And I," he said.

For a short while there was silence between them, then she said, "I thank you for providing a dowry for me."

"It is my honor to do it," he responded with an elusive courtesy that was at once flattering and maddening.

"And you have done it only because you hold me in high regard," she said sharply.

"I have done it because you would find it difficult to live here—or anywhere—without a husband." He thought briefly of Olivia's long parade of fictitious husbands to make her widowhood acceptable, and added, "Think carefully, before you marry; find an ally, if you can."

"You say this because of your wives?" she asked, and put her hand to her mouth in dismay. "I did not mean . . . I spoke . . ."

"It is because I have no wife that I can tell you this." He waited until she managed to recover herself. "Consider what you seek, and find a husband who will seek the same thing for you. Otherwise, marriage will be as much a prison as a protection, and you will not thrive."

"You have decided on the man?" She stared at him, as if trying to determine if he meant what he said.

"Of course not; you are the best judge of what will suit you," he said. "I will not select the man. That is for you to do. If I were your father or your brother, I would still want you to choose—it is you who must live with the man, not I."

"Very generous," she said sarcastically.

He did not answer her for a moment, and when he did, his voice was low and gentle. "Why do you want to fight with me?"

She made a gesture of exasperation. "You are going away. You are my only protection in Toledom. Anything might happen."

"And you think it will be less frightening if you are angry," he finished for her.

"No. Not less frightening. Less . . . strange." She swung her arm to take in the whole study. "This is a wonderful place. Not as grand as Al Catraz, but more engaging. There is so much to do, so many things to learn. If you go, how can I know I will not have to leave?"

"For one thing, I have provided for you. For another, since the matchmaker is looking for a husband for you, you will have the protection of the Jewish quarter as well as the word of Idelfonzuz that you will not be required to leave this place." He did his best to smile, and for a brief moment achieved one. "I did not anticipate the King's orders, or I would have arranged matters differently. But there is no reason for you to fear. You have Ruthor to guard you and this house to live in; there is money enough to keep you, and the household, and to satisfy the tax collector, when he comes."

She shook her head. "But you will not be here."

"That is unfortunately true." He met her eyes, his compelling gaze holding hers as surely as if he clasped her hands. "If I were to refuse Idelfonzuz, then you would be in danger because of me. If I obey, you are safe."

"Does that matter to you?" she asked.

"Yes, it does," he answered.

She considered his reply. "Why?"

"Because you are a most remarkable young woman, and life has not treated you well." He rose from the stool. "But no, you cannot use my affection for you to keep me here."

"You are as bad as my father," she said, determined to hurt him for what he was about to do.

He accepted this condemnation without argument. "I hope I will not always seem so," he said as he went toward the door.

"Sometimes," she called after him, attempting to halt him, "sometimes I dream about you."

Germanno reached the door and turned back. "If they are pleasant dreams, what can I be but flattered."

"They are the best dreams I've ever had," she said, at once pleading and boasting.

"Then let them comfort you while I am gone," said Germanno, and left her alone in the study.

Ruthor was waiting in Germanno's apartments, putting together the last of the traveling gear in two large leather satchels; one contained clothes, the other had weapons and a small casket of medicaments. Catching sight of Germanno's face, he wisely remained silent until Germanno went to change to his short barbaresque riding cote of black leather. "I have put your native earth in all your soles, and in the lining of these cases; you may not be able to keep the chest of it with you."

Germanno gave him a knowing glance. "You are an excellent fellow, old friend."

"She does not want you to leave," Ruthor observed.

"Can you blame her? She has been abandoned by her father and up-rooted from the only home she has ever known. Her future is uncertain, no matter what I hope to achieve for her; I would be unkind if I did not understand how much she has been forced to change, and the role I have played in it. Now I am going away to a place where there is fighting." He pulled on his estivaux, tapping the soles as he did. "Thank you for this."

"It was mine to be done. You will have to be careful with the supplies you have, for it will not last more than six months," Ruthor said.

"A pity I can no longer use my cache near Mont Calcius," he said, using the oldest name he knew for the village.

"If you could find Mont Calcius at all," said Ruthor. "There have been many landslides in that area, where the trees were taken." He put a massive roll of linen into the satchel with Germanno's clothes. "You may need this."

"So I might," Germanno agreed as he laced up his other estivaux. "I could wish it were cooler."

"It is July; it is heat or storms," said Ruthor, shrugging at the choice.

"The staff?" Germanno asked, referring to his courier's staff that was intended to give him safe passage through the fighting lines.

"I put it in a sheath on your saddle. You will not have to search for it." Ruthor began to buckle the satchel closed.

"You are not pleased that I am going, either, are you?" Germanno gave Ruthor time to answer.

"No, I am not. I cannot forget the years it took to find you at Leosan

Fortress." He put the first satchel on the floor and began to buckle the second closed.

"This is hardly a similar case," Germanno pointed out. "I am not going on a sea voyage but a mission for the King."

"To the region of Holy Blood," Ruthor reminded him. "It is as dangerous as the ocean, in its way."

"Yes." Germanno frowned at his feet. "However, time has gone by. Who knows what I shall find there now."

"More vampires, if Chimena has had her way," said Ruthor bluntly.

"Perhaps," said Germanno as he picked up one of the satchels and started toward the door. "Will you see me off, or would you rather not."

Ruthor picked up the other satchel. "I should never have asked you to help me find my family, all those years ago. I should have left well enough alone."

Germanno stopped in the doorway. "By all the forgotten gods, Ruthor, you do not still hold yourself accountable for what happened then, do you?"

"It set things in motion—" he began, but would not go on.

"So did the Goths, so did the Moors, so did the Franks. You are not responsible for any of it," Germanno assured him.

"You would not have known Csimenae." He used the archaic form of her name deliberately.

"Very likely not," Germanno said at once. "But it was my decision to give her my blood to drink, not yours. And you did not tell her to bring others to this life; she came to that against our advice, as I recall."

"True enough," Ruthor allowed as he began to lead the way along the smaller gallery toward the stable yard. "I have selected the blue roans for you, and the two spotted jack-mules." He walked a little faster.

"Very well, we will not discuss it any longer," said Germanno, increasing his stride to match Ruthor's. "The blue roans, you say?" It was a much safer topic.

"Yes; the mare and the gelding. Same sire, different dam; the sire is that stallion Olivia provided when we came here. We have half a dozen of his get still in the stable, and another three more in foal to him. Of the two you will ride, the mare is the older by a year or two." Ruthor went on a short way, then added, "I'll say this for Spain: the horses are wonderful."

"That they are," Germanno agreed. "If not for the horses of Lusitania and Andalusia, the Romans would not have been as eager as they were to keep control of the central part of the peninsula; they would have contented themselves with the coasts and left the interior alone. But the horses were too good to ignore."

"Their shoes are new. You will not have to worry about that for another six to seven weeks." Ruthor opened the door for his master and together they walked out into the warm dusk.

"I am sure I shall find a smithy somewhere," said Germanno, and glanced toward the stable. "The spotted jack-mules: how old are they?"

"Six and seven, I believe," said Ruthor as they went into the stable, into the long broad aisle between the box-stalls. "They are all in the exercise arena."

"A good place for them," said Germanno, sounding a bit remote.

"They should be ready for you." He paused. "A few of the stable-hands have asked why you are leaving at night."

"Raises their suspicions, does it?" Germanno considered, then said, "The King has given me urgent orders—"

"That he has," Ruthor agreed.

"And I am eager to discharge them. Also, there are fewer eyes to see my leaving if I go at night, which serves the King's purpose, too." Germanno smiled. "Tell them that. It should be enough."

They had reached the exercise arena at the rear of the stable, and found, as Ruthor had promised, two blue roans, one saddled, the other haltered with a lead, and two spotted jack-mules, both their pack-saddles moderately laden. Grooms held the animals, and one of them said to Ruthor, for it was unacceptable for him to address Germanno directly, "They are ready. They have eaten and been watered. They are fresh and should go well into the night before they have to rest."

"You have done well," said Ruthor with a glance at Germanno. "These two satchels are to be secured to the master's saddle. Then you may have extra bacon with your evening bread and cheese."

The grooms all looked pleased and a bit embarrassed by so lavish a reward; one of them brought a stool for Germanno to use to get into the saddle; no simple task, for both the pommel and cantel were as high as his waist once he settled into it. Then they secured the satchels to the rings fixed in the back of the cantel and stepped back, saying to Ruthor, "All is ready."

"Then I am away," said Germanno, taking the leads of the mules and the horse, and starting them toward the door in the outer wall.

One of the stable-hands was there to open the door, and did so promptly, closing and barring it after Germanno had passed through.

The streets of Toledom were nearly empty; a few beggars and some monks were still about, and, as he neared the eastern gate in the city walls, Germanno encountered two small bands of roving soldiers, clearly out for adventure and mischief; only their recognition of Germanno's obvious position caused them to hesitate approaching him. The guards at the gate were surly, but did not argue with Germanno's courier's staff.

"God save King Idelfonzuz," said the guard as he opened the gate sufficiently to permit Germanno to leave.

"Amen," said Germanno, hearing the gate thud closed behind him. He started off into the night without looking back. He had elected to travel without lanthorns to light his way, for night did not trouble his eyes, and the mules did not need the extra illumination to find their way. It seemed to him that having lanthorns would only serve to mark his passage and alert those who might be his enemies to his location. So he went without any lamps, enjoying the anonymity this afforded him: he was a shape, a shadow passing, a sound among other sounds. Occasionally he looked up at the stars, scattered bits and clouds of light against the darkness. One day, he promised himself, he would take time to study the stars, not for omens, as so many others did, but to discern their nature. "Who better than a vampire to study the night sky?" he remarked to his horse as they went along the broad, dusty road that led to Zaraguza. By the time he stopped for the day, in an old Moorish way-station, now half-charred and deserted, he was more than seven leagues from Toledom, and a small, square fortress lay half a league ahead of him.

Late in the afternoon, he resumed his travels, passing the fortress before sunset so that no one would seek to halt him for the night. The road was in good repair as it rose toward the broad plateau that would take him east. There were signs of fighting in many places, from the absence of trees to the ruined houses and empty farms, many of which were black from fire. Even at night the air was hot, and when the wind blew it did not offer relief, as if to remind him that the calm of night was illusory at best.

On the third evening he come upon a group of wounded men, more than a dozen of them walking slowly in a group for protection and assistance; they were making their way toward the monastery to the north in the hope of finding a haven there, and monks to treat their injuries without holding them for ransom. Germanno paused long enough to give them some food and water, to find out where their battle had been, and to receive news of the Moors.

"You will have to bear northward a way if you want to avoid them completely," said the man who had clearly become their leader; he had a bandaged arm that smelled of infection and a cut on his face that would leave a bad scar.

"How far to the north?" Germanno asked.

"Two leagues should be enough. They are sending only raiding parties for now. Our forces have held the greater part of their soldiers at bay. They remember the Cid and they retreat." The man indicated the men with him. "We have lost three men since we started walking. There was nothing to be done but bury them."

"Was the battle very hard?" Germanno asked.

"It was fiercer than it was hard," said the leader. "The Moors fight like madmen. I was sure they would have a second force behind them, the way they came hurtling at us, lances and spears filling the air. But they were alone, without reserves. It took most of the morning, but we beat them back. We captured their captain and had his hands struck off so he could never again lift a weapon against a Christian."

Germanno said nothing: he was no stranger to these appalling acts, but he had lost his indifference to them more than two thousand years before. "The King will rejoice," he said at last, knowing it was true.

"That he will, as will all Christians." The leader motioned to the men behind him. "I hope the monks will not have so many wounded that they cannot take us."

"I have some medicaments," Germanno offered, ready to dismount and treat the most severely injured.

"No, no. You are a courier; your staff says so. You have far more important tasks to perform than tend to a handful of wounded men." He waved Germanno on.

"It would not take me long," Germanno said, hoping the man would accept his offer.

"Go. Idelfonzuz has entrusted you with his orders. You must not be distracted from your work. You may lose hundreds because you stopped to help fifteen." He walked a little faster, showing he was determined to have his little company on its way again. "Thank you for the water and the food. That was charity enough."

Germanno watched them go, thinking they would be lucky if half their number made it to the monastery alive. When he continued east, he bore to the north, in case the warning had been correct, and the fighting had spread again. The roads were narrower and less well-kept, but he made steady progress traveling by night and resting by day, and when he finally saw Zaraguza in the distance, he sighed with relief and allowed himself a night of hunting before entering the city, which he did shortly before sunset the following day. The city was larger than Germanno remembered it, and better fortified. It had spires built by Moors, and gardens; here and there some of the old Roman brickwork was still visible, but most of it had been lost in the last five hundred years. The markets had changed, being laid out on Moorish lines, and ancient churches, once in disrepair, now showed the start of fine new fronts to the people who flocked to them.

The Guard at the gate directed Germanno to the great house of Radulphuz of Sant Palampito, saying, "He commands here, no matter what anyone tells you."

"Of course," Germanno said, and handed the Guard a copper Ship for his trouble; he found the house readily enough, brought his horses and mules into the courtyard, and told the startled groom that he was here on the King's business.

"I will bring the maior domuz to speak to you," said the groom with properly averted eyes. He did not help the Comide to dismount, but hurried off, seeking a servant with more authority than he possessed.

By the time the maior domuz arrived, Germanno was out of the saddle, his courier's staff in hand, and his expression so neutral that no one could accuse him of rudeness. He raised his staff as the maior domuz approached, saying, "I trust you know what this means."

The maior domuz looked startled and put his hand to his forehead and then his heart in respect, a gesture borrowed from the Moors. "I know, and I revere it," he said to Germanno. "My master is at supper and ordinarily he would not allow an interruption, but he will receive you as his guest."

"That is not necessary; I have taken nourishment," said Germanno, waiting while the groom returned. "See they have grain and are rubbed down," he ordered. "The jenny is mouthy, so be careful around her."

"I will strike her nose—" the groom said, only to be stopped.

"You will not do anything to my animals but what I tell you to," Germanno said, his voice kindly and soft; the groom stood in terror. "You will use caution around my jenny. If you strike her, I will strike you."

The maior domuz looked shocked. "If you do not beat them, they will not submit to you," he said.

"Nonetheless, if anyone is to . . . beat my animals, it will be me. They have labored hard and have earned their keep handsomely, as any servant would." He gave the groom a long, hard stare. "Keep in mind what I say and you will be rewarded. Forget, and you will be punished."

The groom shook his head, and reached for the leads and reins to take the horse and mules away. He did not dare to speak again.

"If you will come with me," said the maior domuz, indicating a colonnaded gallery that led to the front of the house. "My master has brought his lieutenants here tonight, and dines with these men."

"May God bless them all," said Germanno, aware that every word he spoke would be heard and noted.

"May God bless them," echoed the maior domuz. "As your animals will have tribute for their efforts, so my master is thanking his subordinates. They have been holding the Moors in the hills beyond the river, and my master is moved to reward them."

"As a good commander will do," Germanno agreed, curious where this might be leading. He noticed four barred doors leading off of the gallery and asked himself what this might indicate.

"He entertains them, and praises them," said the maior domuz.

"Which is to his credit," said Germanno.

"Woe betide him who says otherwise," the maior domuz declared.

Germanno was still digesting this obscure warning when the maior domuz threw open the door to the main hall, revealing twenty or so men, all of them drunk, most of them naked, roistering amid the ruins of a banquet. Dogs and cats vied with one another to glean the fallen meats that littered the floor; half-a-dozen servants carried trays of cooked meats and new fruits to those still eating, and two musicians, at the far end of the hall, did their best to be heard against the general uproar.

From his place at the high table, Radulphuz of Sant Palampito watched his guests with bored, lascivious eyes; he was dawdling over his meal, keeping a handsome young page by his side to serve him. A man of middle years—perhaps as old as thirty-five—Radulphuz had the grizzled hair and scarred features of a field commander; his left hand lacked three fingers and there was a cicatrix along his shoulder where a Moorish scimitar had missed his neck by less than a handsbreadth. His surcote was of berry-colored velvet and he wore no cote beneath, allowing it to hang open from his neck to his knees. He looked up as the maior domuz escorted Germanno into the hall. Lazily he motioned the two to approach.

Germanno did as he was required to do: he made a deep reverence to Radulphuz, holding his courier's staff out to him. "In the name of Idelfonzuz of Aragon and Navarre, and guardian of Castile and León, I am Germanno, Comide Ragoczy."

The foreign name caught Radulphuz's attention. "A mercenary?" he asked in surprise.

"An exile," Germanno corrected courteously.

"I suppose there is a difference," said Radulphuz, whooping and pointing as two of his men began competitive masturbation; a few of the others stopped their various amusements to watch. Radulphuz waited a moment before looking back at Germanno. "And what am I to do for Idelfonzuz?"

"You are to provide me with all your latest information on the territory to the east of you currently in dispute," Germanno said.

"Ah," Radulphuz said, pulling his lower lip between his remaining thumb and finger. "So you are the one he is sending into that godforsaken region."

"I am the one," said Germanno, a hint of wry humor in his voice.

"I do not envy you that mission; I would not authorize any of my men to undertake it. I cannot afford to lose any of them," said Radulphuz as he reached for his goblet and drank, signaling his page to refill it.

"It will be less hazardous if you will provide me with the information I will need when I am there," Germanno suggested firmly.

"Naturally," said Radulphuz. "I have no doubt that you are correct."

"Then you are minded to give me what I need?" Germanno asked, ignoring the howls and cries below him.

Radulphuz was staring at his men; he ran his tongue over his lips.

Wholly preoccupied with what he was watching he said, "Yes. Yes. Come to me in the morning and I will provide you with all the information I can. I have a letter that you should see. If you cannot read, my clerk will read it for you."

Germanno was not surprised at this order. "I can read," he said. "Where will I find you in the morning?"

"My maior domuz will know," said Radulphuz, his gaze devouring the debauchery that was increasing; the naked men had begun plundering one another's bodies in a variety of ways, most of which would have got them burned at the stake if any Churchman had seen them.

"I will seek him out," said Germanno, preparing to rise and leave.

Abruptly Radulphuz turned and stared at him. "You are taking a great chance, going into those mountains."

"The Moors have many soldiers there, I know," said Germanno as if he were aware of no other danger.

"Moors are nothing. They say the Viexa Armoza lives there, with all her brood." He smiled unpleasantly. "Rather a hundred Moors than Ximene."

"Ximene?" Germanno said, fully alert now. He could not convince himself that the name was coincidental.

"They say the Viexa Armoza is called Ximene. Whatever her name, she is very dangerous," Radulphuz said, and glanced back at his men. "If one is to believe peasants, she, and her children, are vampires. The Moors call them night-demons." He laughed, but whether at the antics of his men or the notion of vampires or the Moors' name for them was impossible to discern.

Germanno considered his next question carefully. "How many of them are there: do you know?"

"Vampires?" Radulphuz shrugged, irritated at having to listen to Germanno any longer. "If the peasants are to be believed, there are hundreds of them." Saying that, he waved Germanno away and went back to staring at the orgy he had created.

Text of a letter from Gildoz, Knight of Usxa to Radulphuz of Sant Palampito at Zaraguza.

To the most excellent Radulphuz of Sant Palampito, commander of troops in Zaraguza and champion of Christians throughout Spain, the most respectful and devoted greetings of Gildaz, Knight of Usxa, with the heartfelt prayer that you may heed my words for the sake of our King and the Christ Who has bought our Salvation with His Blood.

In my years in this city, I have fought the Moors with the singularity of purpose that only faith can provide, and although I have sought neither riches nor advancement for my dedication, I have hoped that I might, at some point, provide crucial support to one such as you, who has given so much hope to those of us who have fought so long in our shared cause.

To that end, I have gathered such intelligence as may aid you in your battles. I send it to you in the care of the monk, Fre Benedictuz, who will vouch for its accuracy and truth, for he, too, has seen many things that will make your work here more true to our goal than if you came here fully unprepared. Fre Benedictuz is known as a pious man, and one who may be relied upon not to lead you or your forces astray, as so many others might, for the good of their own community, but the disadvantage of the King.

It is his report that the Moors have been burning the forests again. They say it is to rid the region of night-demons who are reputed to inhabit the area, but there are those who are not convinced that this is their only motive, for wherever there is burning, soldiers are exposed to a terrible death, and they lose the protection the forest affords them. Whether or not the charred bodies found afterward are Moors or Christians or night-demons, no one can say, although the Moors contend only their enemies are hurt in these exercises. I cannot be as sanguine as the Moors claim to be, for I know that each death brings damnation and perpetual fire to those who have not embraced their Salvation, and have died without the blessing of Christ's Church to protect them. Thus far the burnings have not been carried out in summer, for the heat of the day and the aridness of the mountains could well cause the fires to burn beyond the limits the Moors have set. It is hard enough when summer lightning sets the mountains ablaze, as has happened many times before. However, the Moors are increasingly desperate and therefore are not willing to show any caution for fear it will lead to greater losses among their numbers.

It is my own belief that the Moors would embrace any excuse to harm Christians, including martyring them with fire. I am certain that if they can claim fear of night-demons they will do so and they will scorch the earth from the Eberoz to the heart of Aragon, for the chance *to rid themselves of any centers of resistance that might have escaped their vengeance until now. I am fearful that there may be losses of an intolerable nature if the Moors are allowed to do as they wish. In Usxa we see every day the extent of the Moors' determination not to release their hold on this region. I pray that they will not be so adamant in their efforts that all any of us will have in the end is burned forests and barren hills, but in spite of hours on my knees, I find all my hope is fading with every day that passes without the warriors of Christ driving back the Moors.*

Nor is destroying the forests the end of their perfidy. In this city, we see young men taken as slaves every day; their fate is in the hands of our enemies, and all of us know that these young men will not return here. For this alone I ask that you bring your soldiers soon, so that these young men are not lost to Christ through the cruelty of His enemies. As I yearn for Christ, I beg you to come soon, while there is a city to rescue and lands to hold for more than a graveyard.

In the fullness of devotion, and with an esteem for you that is offered for no man on earth, save King Idelfonzuz, and with my continuing prayers for succor, I sign myself,

Gildaz, Knight of Usxa
Son of Bauthizta, cousin of Adelfonzuz of León and Castile
By the hand of Fre Patrizoz

At Usxa on the 1ˢᵗ day of July in the 1117ᵗʰ of Grace. Amen.

5

Everywhere the night smelled of burning; smuts carried on the capricious wind were a constant reminder that the fire was not yet wholly extinguished in spite of the rainstorm that had drenched the mountains in the middle of the afternoon. Charred carcases of small animals—mice, hapless birds, voles, toads—littered the smoking ground; here and there a larger creature—a badger, a fox, a goat—lay blackened amid the remains of the woods.

Germanno's horses were nervous and the mules balky. They made their way through the early night, with the horizon behind them still tarnished with the last smudge of sunset. The animals moved in that precarious precision that was eloquent of fear; Germanno could feel their tension through the reins and the leads he held, and realized it would not be wise to force them to go much farther. "Just as well," he remarked to the night. Dawn was coming, and it was time for him to find shelter—assuming there was any to find. His quick survey of his surroundings was far from promising, and he wondered if he would be better off improvising a shelter in this desolate place or pressing on toward the faint line of sparks that lit the edge of the surviving trees. Although they were dying, there was always the chance that the flames would rise again, and that was an unwelcome prospect that Germanno feared as keenly as any living thing.

According to the rough map Radulphuz had provided him, Germanno should now be a short distance from the Usxa road that led up into the heart of Aragon and linked Idelfonzuz's kingdom with Zaraguza and Castile beyond. In the burned landscape, the road was indistinguishable from any other fairly flat stretch of ground, and the map was not specific enough to make finding his way possible; distances were estimated and geographical features were placed as much for design as accuracy on the vellum sheet. He crested a small rise and peered into the slight depression beyond, where the fire had stopped short of a copse of oak and pine. No red ember eyes winked at him from the branches, and the gust of wind carried no new ash on it. This was the first encouraging sight he had had since mid-day, and he was absurdly glad to see it. He clucked his blue roan forward, and tugged the other three animals after him.

Immediately before the stand of trees there was a small summer-low brook, sliding along as if hoping to avoid notice, almost silent, and giving little shine from between its banks. Insignificant as this band of water might be, it appeared to have been enough to halt the fading fire. As uncomfortable as running water made him, Germanno was relieved as he crossed it, pausing on the wooded side to allow his horses and mules to drink while he listened to the sounds of the forest behind them. At first he noticed little more than the continuing sound of rustling leaves and branches, but then he became aware of the chitterings of those creatures that had survived the fire, and sensed their barely subdued panic.

Without any transition, the woods were still, only the wind making noise. Something had come into the stand of trees that had troubled the creatures within it; the jack-mule raised his head, long ears working to pick up the shift in sound. Germanno's blue roan whuffled nervously.

Nothing happened for a long moment, and then a terrible scream, one that came from the deepest part of the man whose voice it was, cracked the silence. Immediately birds flew out of the safety of the trees and many animals rushed away from so mortal a sound. For a short while Germanno struggled with his horses and mules, all of which wanted to bolt. As the last of the cry shivered away, Germanno swung his horse around and went into the forest, drawing rein only when he heard shouting ahead of him.

"He is finally dead!" a voice crowed. "He can die!"

Another voice, less excited than the first, said, "You knew that. You chased him to kill him." Their dialect was so unfamiliar that it took Germanno a long moment to comprehend what he heard. "Make sure he is dead. His kind are harder to kill than most of the living."

"And we did not have to burn him," the first exclaimed. "The lance was enough."

"So it seems," the second agreed, but with less conviction.

"We should chop off his head!" the first said, nervous and thrilled at once. "That will make sure."

"We have nothing to do it with. I did not think to bring an axe, and neither did you." The second sounded disappointed. "If we run him through with the lance a few more times, that should be enough."

"I'll do it!" The first rushed through the underbrush and began to wrestle with the body, thrashing noisily as he strove to do his self-appointed task. "Let the Viexa Armoza howl for this."

"Make sure the backbone is broken. That keeps them from rising," said the second, coming after the first in a less hectic pace.

"I will," the first said, panting with his effort.

Germanno decided it was time to end this assault. He pulled his horse around and tugged the horse and mules after him as he rode into the wood, making sure to be loud enough to alert the two men to his coming, for by the sound of it they would not respond well to being surprised. The gloom of dusk deepened to enveloping darkness in the shelter of the trees, but Germanno continued on without much difficulty, using the urgent voices to guide him.

"Do we bury him?" The second voice was sharper now, and holding a hint of dread beneath its apparent control.

"No; he might recover if we do; they say the Viexa Armoza has been buried before, and risen," the first said breathlessly; he grunted with effort, then said, "There!" This was followed at once by a bludgeoning sound. "Got his spine that time. I heard it break, and I felt the bones give."

"And his hostel? What about his hostel? The fire did not reach more than its barn. Should we not destroy it before it is found empty?" the second asked, then stopped.

"Someone is coming."

The first cursed fulsomely, but the sound of his activities ceased. "Horses. Is it Moors?"

Deciding it would be better to answer than not, Germanno called out, "No, it is not Moors. I am a traveler bound for Aragon."

The two men whispered to each other, and were standing a bit apart from the man they had killed when Germanno rode into the small clearing.

One of the men was spattered with blood, his colobion torn from shoulder to waist, and his chaperon hanging by a frayed cord. He was breathing fast and his knuckles were skinned from fighting. Although custom forbade the men to look directly at one so clearly their superior, the two men stared directly at him, anger and fright making them bold. "You are a long way from the road," he said, and Germanno recognized his voice as the first he had heard.

"There was a fire on that road," Germanno said gently, almost apologetically. "And a battle, not so many hours ago."

"He has the right of that," said the second man, a fellow somewhat older than the first, wearing the same peasant garb as the first, but with a leather belt instead of a corded one, showing his relative prosperity. He coughed and spat, not taking his eyes from Germanno as if he expected treachery. "The soldiers came through our village two nights ago. They took all the geese and all the cheese."

The first nodded. He moved a little, as if to screen the body that lay beyond them, prone and battered, a lance leaning through him. "Soldiers take food and wine, they take our donkeys, and they use our women," he said resentfully but with wariness; he was having trouble understanding Germanno's speech. "It does not matter what side they fight on."

"And that unfortunate—" Germanno indicated the body without appearing overly curious—"what had he done? He does not appear to be a soldier, Moorish or Christian."

"He is not," said the first. "There are other dangerous men than soldiers abroad, good traveler," he said.

"Yes, and there would appear to be one less of them," Germanno said at his driest. "What did he do, to earn your enmity?"

"My what?" the first asked suspiciously.

"Your hatred," Germanno replied.

"He kept a hostel—he and his harlot—and preyed on those who were foolish enough to stop there," the second said smoothly, but with ill-concealed rancor. "The Moors killed her, and welcome. We have done for him. He and his kind are not like other men. He brought misfortune to those of us who live in this region, where the Viexa Armoza and her children drink of men."

"So when the battle came, you thought no one would bother with one body more or less?" Germanno suggested, saying nothing about the Viexa Armoza. "Or that the Moors could be blamed, since they killed his companion?"

The second man narrowed his eyes. "The same could be said of two bodies."

The first made a hissing sound and gestured to his comrade. "No. He is not—"

Germanno interrupted, achieving an amused smile. "Do I understand you: you think you could kill me?"

The first did his best to appear brave. "I have a lance."

"Which you must first pull from that man's body," Germanno pointed out.

"There are two of us," the first bragged.

"And I am on horseback, with swords and daggers," Germanno said, sounding bored. "Why should you threaten me? I have done nothing to you. This is useless. Listen to me before you regret your words." He looked at the two, seeing their terror behind their posturing; they knew they had gone too far. "What you have done to this man is of no importance to me. I tell you that I will say nothing of this; I have no reason to. My mission is too essential to be thwarted by this one incident. I am a courier for King Idelfonzuz. I carry his staff. You know that lends me the King's authority." He indicated where it hung in its scabbard. "If you have any regard for your King, go away from here at once, and forget you have seen me, as I shall forget I have seen you."

"So you say," the first blustered, but was stayed by the second.

"Why should a man of your rank bother himself over what we say or do not say?" He studied Germanno carefully.

"Exactly my point," Germanno agreed affably. "You have no reason to think I would trouble myself with the likes of you when I have the King's mandate to fulfill."

The first was growing apprehensive. "You could order us killed for what we have done although we have spared our people, and many travelers, from a hideous death. You do not know what we have known."

"Then you will have to let your own people decide what is to be done with you," Germanno said calmly. "Go on your way now, and do not return here."

"Why should we not?" The first man took a stance that showed he was ready to fight if he had to.

"Because there will be more soldiers coming. If you are found near the fighting, or near a body, the soldiers may well hold you to account, and they may not be as willing to listen as I am." He spoke with the ease and certainty of conviction. "Believe this."

The second man had taken his companion by the arm and was tugging of him. "This is the King's man. We must not stand between him and what he is sent to do."

"But—" The first pointed to the corpse.

"His back is broken. It will suffice," the second said, still pulling the other man away. "We are leaving," he announced to Germanno.

"Go in God's care," said Germanno, and remained where he was as the two men fled the clearing.

Germanno sat in the saddle until he was certain the two men were gone, then he got out of the saddle and went to look at the body, already anticipating what he would see. He dropped on one knee next to the dead man and wiped the dust and bits of leaves from the blood drying on his face, nodding grimly as he recognized the bruised features. "Olutiz," he said aloud. For an instant he recalled the dead man's birth, nearly five hundred years ago, and for that instant, Germanno felt as keen a pang of grief as if he had a true bond of blood with him. Then it passed and he sighed, wanting to leave Olutiz where he had fallen, but knowing he would have to return him to his mother.

Gathering up the body, he carried it to his second horse, and using the spare set of straps from his pack-saddles, he bound Olutiz to the horse, hoping as he did that they would prove sufficient to hold the dead man in place for the journey ahead. Then he remounted his horse and tugged the second horse and mules to follow him as he set off through the night, bound toward the high peaks where Ximene still held sway. As he went, he considered his mission for Idelfonzuz; he would resume it, he told himself, when Olutiz was finally home.

By morning Germanno had put the burning far behind him and was at the border region between Aragon and Barzelunya, climbing steadily into the mountains. He had seen a number of small, hidden shrines with offerings of chalices of blood; these indicated to him that he was still within Ximene's territory. A few of them had been destroyed, their cups overturned, their niches broken, which evinced the conflicts that raged in this border region. At dawn he had found an empty village, with tumbled walls and collapsed roofs on the houses. Choosing the safest of these to stall his animals, he searched out a cellar for himself and Olutiz's body, reminding himself that even the undead decay, and that he did not have much time to find Ximene before he would be forced to bury her son himself, and bring her only the sad news.

As he reclined on his earth-lined bedroll, he let his thoughts go in search of those of his blood, hoping as he did that he would not be distracted by other vampires—Ximene's vampires—that were in the region. Usually he applied this skill with animals, to gain a level of control over their activities, but now he let the extension of his mind roam in search of the long-denied blood-bond with Ximene. Finding the sense of her was as elusive as piecing together scraps of song borne from far away on the wind, but gradually he gained an impression of where she had gone. As he did, he recalled the two Moors who had guarded her, more than three centuries ago: what would protect her now? How many of her numbers had been ordered to ward her eyrie, for he had no doubts now she was high in the mountains, away from the wars and the sliding hills.

He wakened just before sunset, a bit disoriented by what he had done, and feeling depleted in a way his native earth could not wholly ameliorate; what he lacked was a connection to life, the intimacy that the living could provide to the undead. The only compensation for his reaction to his exercise was that he now knew where he had to go, and how he would be able to get there. Removing Olutiz's body from the cellar, he took the time to wrap it in a length of cloth before securing it to the blue roan Germanno had ridden the day before. When he had saddled the mules and loaded their pack-saddles, he groomed and saddled his horse for a long night of travel. He was in need of nourishment, but there was no relief for that possible, and he resigned himself to waiting for the opportunity to feed after he had discharged his self-appointed obligation; he was no stranger to such deprivations and he followed his habitual discipline now.

A band of erosion swathed the rising flank of the mountain where the trees had been cut down, and the night air whistled with a rising wind that was still hot from its passage over the high plateau to the west. Germanno let his horse pick his own pace along the edge of the landslide; he neither hurried nor checked the pace the blue roan set for the others, knowing that the horse understood their perils better than he did. Once the unstable shoulder was crossed, Germanno guided his animals along the crest of the mountain, going toward the next rise beyond that led toward one of three high passes in the mountains, for his dream-like explorations had shown him that Ximene had gone to the highest of the three passes and made a kind of fortress for herself in that harsh place.

Those villages he saw—those that were still inhabited—Germanno avoided, recalling the temper of the men who had killed Olutiz: they had known enough of the vampire's nature to be able to kill him without misstep, and so might many of the others in those small, walled towns. Being a stranger might give them sufficient cause to act against him. It was best to stay away from the villages, especially at night. A few isolated shepherds' huts stood near springs on the rising face of the mountains, each one empty; Germanno encountered no flocks: no goats, no sheep. There were four more shrines he discovered as he went up the mountain, all ruined and with no sign of attempts of repair. Had war devastated these high canyons and peaks so utterly, he wondered, or was this on account of something else?

Daybreak found Germanno well into the upper peaks, his animals laboring in the thin air that was warming rapidly now that the sun had risen, sending crimsons streamers up the sky from the horizon to mark its arrival. He was nearing the place he sought, aware that it was three or four leagues beyond the spring where he had halted to rest the horses and mules. It was tempting to press on, but his animals were tired and the way was becoming more elusive, the trails narrower. He checked Olutiz's body where it lay bound to the horse, unwrapping it enough to inspect the skin of his face and shoulders: the skin was dry and flaking as Egyptian paper, as if Olutiz had lain in the desert for months; Germanno knew that it would soon become brittle and would fall apart. For that reason alone, he finally chose to continue his journey into the morning, when the path could be more readily seen; he told himself that any guards Ximene had posted would surely be less alert when the sun was up. Wearily he continued on into the morning.

At mid-morning he passed an isolated monastery where he saw habited monks gathering wood and stacking it in a huge pyre. This aroused Germanno's curiosity, but he did not stop to ask about it; instead he resolved to come by the monastery after he had given Olutiz to his mother, to find out what the monks were intending to do. It would be safer then, without the body, and he had the King's staff to lend him a degree of palladium the monks would respect. Still, the sight of the pyre made him uneasy, and he was relieved when it was lost to view around the shoulder of the mountain.

The sun, hot and implacable, stood low in the west when Germanno finally reached the place he sought: the stone fortress was not large, but it was formidable, set in the very top of a canyon, perched on a ledge that made it unassailable from any direction but the sky; at this time of day it was nearly hidden in shadows. A path, cut out of the living rock and only wide enough for one horse, led up to the narrow gate. Germanno dismounted and retied the leads of his horse and mules, then, walking ahead of the four, led them along the precarious trail to the stout wooden gate.

There was a brass bell that hung near the gate, the sort that a traveler might find at many fortified sites in the Christian world. Germanno hesitated a moment, then rang it, hoping to hear a quick response. When none come, he rang again.

"Who is there?" a voice bellowed down from above, cross at being disturbed. He repeated the question in the language of the Moors.

"I bring something to Ximene," Germanno answered, speaking loudly enough to be heard down the canyon, then added, taking a risk, "Tell her Sanct' Germain has come."

"Who?" the watchman demanded.

"Sanct' Germain. She will know." He stood patiently, grateful for the long wedge of shadow cast by the brow of the crest above him, for his skin was already burned by the sun and he had no wish to make it worse.

"You will be admitted," the watchman yelled down a short while later.

"Thank you," Germanno said, loudly enough to be heard but no longer at herald's pitch.

There was a brief wait, then chain groaned and crumped as the gate was slowly opened, revealing a long, narrow courtyard in front of a bailey built into the mountain.

"Enter," said the guard who worked the spoked windlass; he was of mixed heritage, with satiny olive skin and dark, slightly curling hair, but having pale-green eyes. He pointed to the door at the front of the bailey. "Go there."

Germanno inclined his head slightly. "I will. Is there water and food for my animals?"

"I will tend to them as soon as I have closed the gate." The guard did not look directly at Germanno as he spoke.

"You are most generous, but I think it would be best if I kept them with me for now," Germanno told the guard in his most courteous manner; without waiting for the guard to speak, he led his horses and mules forward.

The door of the bailey stood open, and in its shadow, a woman in wine-red cote of Antioch velvet beneath a surcote of brocaded crimson samite stood, her luxurious hair bound up with bonds of gold and silver; her face was hardly changed from the last time Germanno had seen her, more than three centuries ago. She stepped gingerly into the light. "I told you never to come here again."

Germanno offered Ximene a profound reverence. "I have not come to flout you, Csimenae," he said, speaking the tongue she had spoken when they first met.

"Well, you must have some purpose, or you would not be here," she said sharply, frowning at him. In the uncompromising glare of the sun, her clothing was shown to be threadbare and slightly old-fashioned, but she was still a splendid figure, and she dominated the courtyard and the occupants of the fortress as surely as if she held a sceptre. She surely deserved being called Viexa Armoza—the beautiful old woman.

"Sadly, yes, I do." He pointed to his second horse with its silent, well-wrapped burden. "You may not have made peace between you, but I thought you would want him with you."

"Him?" Ximene repeated, continuing at once, "You have brought me an offering?"

"This is no offering, I fear," Germanno said as gently as he could.

"Then what is it?" Behind her defiance there was a trace of recognition, as if she understood what he had brought, but had not yet permitted herself to know it.

He could think of no way to soften the blow. "It is Aulutis," he said, using the name the boy had been given at birth.

She stared at Germanno as if he had uttered an incomprehensible sound. She blinked as if against the sunlight, then bit her lower lip. "He defied me," she said. "He should have been dragged to death by horses."

"He was killed by villagers, many leagues from here," Germanno said, his voice low. "They knew what to do: they used a lance to break—"

"Stop!" She raised her hand as she took a step toward the shrouded figure. "Goroloz! Herchambaut! To me!"

Two men—one in the garb of the Castilian court a century ago, and one in still older Frankish clothes—come out of the bailey, each with weapons drawn, and both ready to attack. They paused at a sign from Ximene, coming to her side and facing Germanno with determination.

"Stand away," Ximene ordered Germanno, watching as he led his mount with him to the side of the courtyard, leaving the mules and the second blue roan where they stood.

"Take the . . . body down," she said, pointing.

"Be careful with him," Germanno added. "He is fragile."

Goroloz and Harchambaut exchanged uneasy glances, but hastened to do as they were told. The roan side-stepped at the approach of these unfamiliar men, but at a word from Germanno, she stood while the body was taken down.

"He's very light," said Herchambaut, his Frankish accent strong.

"He has been dead a long time," Germanno said, loneliness coming over him like a cloud over the setting sun.

"Put him down," Ximene said, pointing to the step below the one on which she stood. "Gently."

The two guards obeyed, then stepped back to retreat to the shadow of the bailey door.

Ximene stood over the body for a short while, unmoving and silent. Then, as if pulled by invisible strings, she knelt down and pulled back the heavy cloth that concealed his face: the desiccated features were still recognizable, though they began to crumble as the waning light struck them. Ximene crossed her arms on her breast and wrawled her torment; the sound echoed, ululating from the stones until all the mountain rang with her grief. Her keening went on as she strove for the anodyne of weeping, but could not achieve it. When one of her men approached her, she motioned him away abruptly.

"But Viexa Armosa—" Goroloz protested in dismay.

"Stay back from me," she commanded him. "This is my son. I have done all for him, and now he is gone." Her mourning resumed, the sound of her voice more eerie than before.

The guard at the gate had secured it again, and now he stood as if bound, appalled by what he saw. He glanced at Germanno, and cried out, "He deceives you, Ximene. He killed the boy. He is to blame!" Taking a step forward, he reached for the short-sword that hung from his belt.

"Stay where you are," Ximene said, and the guard halted.

Herchambaut and Goroloz remained in the doorway, their weapons drawn once more; they hesitated as if trying to make up their minds. Finally Goroloz spoke. "Shall we kill him?"

At first Ximene did not respond—she continued to wail over the rapidly collapsing corpse of her son. Then she looked over at Germanno and said with tremendous fatigue, "No. No, he is not to blame. Leave him be." She rose, and without looking around, said in a flat voice, "He must be buried quickly, or there will be nothing left of him."

Goroloz moved first, coming out into the light, sheathing his sword. "Where shall we take him?"

Ximene shook her head slowly. "Wherever you can make a grave." She stared up into the sky without squinting. "It was for him. Even when he betrayed me, it was all for him."

Herchambaut came to help Goroloz, trying to contain as much of what remained of Olutiz in the cloth in which Germanno had wrapped him. "The stable, do you think?" Herchambaut suggested.

Ximene overheard and said, "Not the midden. Make him a proper grave."

The two uttered sounds of assent as they carried the nearly empty cloth away, leaving Ximene standing alone on the steps to her bailey.

Text of a letter from Fre Carloz of the Monastery of Santoz Ennati the Martyr near Usxa, to Idelfonzuz, King of Aragon and Navarre, at Toledom.

In the Name of the Father, the Son, and the Holy Spirit, and in honor of our Santoz Ennati: Amen.

To the most excellent and illustrious Christian King, Idelfonzuz of Aragon and Navarre, and ruler of Castile and León in the name of Urraca, daughter of Adelfonzuz of Castile and León, and champion of Christian knights everywhere, the thankful greetings of Fre Carloz of Santoz Ennati the Martyr, in whose name I address you and rejoice with you.

Most estimable King, delight with us in the victory God has given to His most humble of servants, His monks and the peasants who are in our care, for today we have done that which seemed impossible but four days since. We are filled with gratitude to God, Who is the source of all wisdom and strength, both of which He has bestowed upon us in our darkest hour.

Know that the war which continues to rage in this disputed region has lately added to its perils a plague of night-demons and vampires who have come to the battlefields to drink the life's-blood of those who have fallen but not died. This horror has outraged all who have witnessed it, and caused many to lament for the lost souls of the prey of the vampires as well as to appeal to Heaven for succor, not only from the soldiers ravaging the land, but from the vampires that have followed in their steps, destroying all those they find. No peasant and no monk could be safe from such foes. In this predicament, when all hope seems lost, a misfortune pointed the way to our triumph: the Moors set fire to the woods where Christian forces were said to be lying in wait for them. This has happened before, but not in high summer; the Moors dread the fire as profoundly as Christians do. The fire sprang up quickly and raged through the forest for two days until a rainstorm ended it. Then it was revealed that most of the bodies were not those of Christian knights, but of night-demons and vampires. The bodies were little more than piles of ashes, like ancient husks with brittle sticks inside them.

We have now found a way to burn more of these baleful creatures and finally rid our region of them. We may burn them out as we would burn out all Godless things. We need not offer blood to them again, nor go abroad at night with fear in our souls. Had the Moors not done so shameful a thing to our good Christian soldiers, we would not have been given to see how this great enemy is to be destroyed. With renewed purpose, we have determined to lure as many of these vampires into the heart of the woods where they have been known to gather and that have not already been burned, and there we will surround them with flames, and let them perish as they have delighted in our deaths down the generations. Surely Santoz Ennati will aid us from his place among the blessed in Heaven.

Our one concern now is that this may destroy one of your forests, for Liege, the best stand of trees for our purpose is within the boundary region of Aragon. This is yours by right and lineage, and therefore we know you may well think such an act as this is treasonous, if you did not know the whole of the circumstances, of which this letter informs you. Your forests are protected by your right, and we may be held to account for any mishap that occurs there, not only as it pertains to the loss of the woods, but as an insult to your dignity. We intend no affront to you, Liege, in our efforts to rid the mountains of the vampires who have for so long preyed upon the peasants, clergy, merchants, and soldiers unlucky enough to cross their vicious paths. It is the one thing we can do that will spare us the depredations of these damned creatures, and if there must be a sacrifice to accomplish so worthy an end, then we are prepared to make it, and take the consequences of our act. But I beg you to forgive us for burning your forest. Do not condemn us for doing what must be done in order to save ourselves and your people from further decimations at the hands of these remorseless beings.

You have it within your power to demand our lives for what we are going to do, but I pray in the name of Santoz Ennati, who faced these same demons and earned himself a place at the Right Hand of God for his battle, that you will condone our righteous cause and the means we have employed to achieve them. I must tell you that other monasteries have agreed to stand with us in this, and find some way to end the long sovereignty the vampires have claimed in this region known for so long as Holy Blood. Your soldiers will soon fight in this very region; would you rather they fall to the Moors or to vampires? If they die from

Moorish blows, they will achieve Heaven; if they are set upon by vampires, they will be consigned to Hell if they are not shriven. Think on this before you objurgate us for what we are about to do.

In the certainty that justice will prevail in our cause and that you, Liege, mindful of the sacrifice of Santoz Ennati, will pardon us for emulating him in his fight, I bless you and your reign, and sign myself

> *Your most deeply devoted subject, save for God Himself,*
> *Fre Carloz*
> *Santoz Ennati*

near Usxa, by my own hand on this the 17ᵗʰ day of July, in the 1117ᵗʰ year of man's Salvation. Amen.

8

Although they were almost a league away from the monastery, Ximene and Germanno could hear the shrieks and other grisly sounds as the flames rose in the pyres on which more than twenty vampires were tied. The westering sun lit the clouds from beneath as if the horizon were burning, a grander version of the smoke rising above the monastery walls with the glare of red on its underside; fortunately the wind was blowing across them, to the east, and so they could not smell what the smoke carried.

"How did they do this?" Ximene whispered as she stared at the smoke from the shelter of the trees. "How did those stupid, cowish monks manage to trap so many of my clan?"

"It hardly matters how," Germanno said, keeping in the shadow of the forest, reaching across his mount and hers to lay his hand on Ximene's shoulder both as comfort and restraint. "They have done it."

"But they are nothing—*nothing*." She pushed his hand away. "And still, they have done what they could not do, what they have never done before. How is that possible?"

"Ximene," Germanno said quietly, "I know you grieve for your—"

"Grieve?" she repeated, then laughed suddenly and harshly. "I cannot grieve for any who are so lax as to be caught by living fools, and monks at that, not soldiers. No, Sanct' Germain. They do not deserve mourning: I *despise* them for such a death. Had I thought they would fall in so headless a fashion, I would have killed them myself, and spared the monks their trouble." Her face was set in a kind of rigid fury, her hands knotted on the horse's reins.

"You told them to come down from your fortress," Germanno reminded her, troubled by her outburst. "When the others sent word of their fears, you dispatched . . . them"—he nodded to indicate the victims of the flames—"to aid the rest."

"Yes, to aid them. I did not think they would fall into a trap, especially one so clumsy as the one the monks set. A goat would not be so easily duped as they were." She shook her head. "No. They brought this on themselves. They have shown me that they are too reckless and gullible to live."

He contemplated her face, noticing the shine of anger in her eyes; he realized she was sincere in her condemnation, that she had no comprehension of her loss. "You are too severe."

"Why? They have been loathsome." Her mouth twisted with the word.

"I do not mean severe for their sake, Ximene: I mean for yours." He shook his head as the nightmarish screams suddenly stopped. "If you hold them in contempt, you will be haunted by their deaths; if you can accept their bond to you, and yours to them, you will release them and yourself."

"Do you think so?" she asked, gesturing to the smoke as it drifted away to join with the gathering clouds.

"I do," he told her.

She rounded on him. "What kind of idiot do you take me for? They are gone as if they were as mortal as the monks who have burned them. No affection, or any other feeling, remains." Her eyes met his. "And you cannot understand why I want you to leave here."

He put his hand out to her. "I will leave, but not on your account."

"Oh, yes," she said with heavy sarcasm. "You and your wandering. It is safer to wander. You have told me before. You are content to be alone in your travels, you have said. You make few vampires in your wanderings, and you console yourself by deciding that those whose blood you drink love you." Tugging the reins she pulled her bay mare back into the trees. "The monks will start chanting soon, and I will not listen to them. Come away."

Germanno perceived more emotion in her than she was willing to accredit, but said nothing more than, "All right."

"There is nothing more for me here," she said. "Not for such as they were."

"Ximene, they are dead. This was the True Death." He hoped to see some indication of compassion in her eyes, but there was none.

"All the better. My son is dead, and his was the True Death: none of them were worth a nail on his hand." She signaled her horse to walk on. "We have a distance to go tonight before we can feed."

Germanno wanted to bring her to a realization of what had happened, but decided that she would not listen to him now. "And where are we—"

"Follow me and do not ask me ridiculous questions anymore," she said, her back stiff and her voice edged. "There will be game to hunt tonight. Tomorrow night we will hunt men."

"No," said Germanno, quietly but with absolute conviction. "You may, if you must, but I will not."

She turned in the saddle to stare at him; even in the dim light of the forest he could see her taken aback expression. "You refuse to do as I require?"

"I will not stop you from hunting, but I will not join you. I do not prey upon men," he said, adding to himself that he had not done so in more than twenty-five hundred years.

"And if I order you?" She sounded dangerous now, angry enough to be reckless.

"I will refuse." He pointed ahead. "There is a river nearby. How do we cross it?"

"We follow the banks to the cattle-ford, and ride over. The water is low; it will not be too painful." She coughed, suggesting he was too fastidious to expose himself to running water.

"My soles are filled with my native earth," he reminded her. "The water will not bother me." That was not entirely true, he admitted to himself: he would still have a faint sense of vertigo and lassitude while crossing the river, but it was bearable.

"So you say," she mocked. "If you must keep yourself untainted by what you are, I will not compel you join me."

"Thank you," he said sardonically.

They went along in silence but for the steady clop of their horses' feet. When they reached the river, they turned westward along its banks, following a trail made by game; hoof-prints of deer and foxes marked the soft earth, and once there was the unmistakable impression of a bear's clawed pad, and at another place, the whole of the trail was scored by the marks of boars' hooves where a sounder had passed.

"The game has been moving away from our region. The fighting and the fires have made them afraid," said Ximene, her voice distant, as if none of this touched her. "The shepherds have taken the flocks to the other side of the mountains, beyond Aragon, so they will not have to lose any more of their sheep to the soldiers."

"That must interfere with your hunting," Germanno remarked, recalling the many times in the past he had seen just such a pattern emerge from war.

"All kinds of hunting," Ximene agreed. "The villagers have turned against us, and there is no game."

"Yet you remain here," Germanno said.

"Better to stay where you belong than become an exile, an exile from home, and from daylight." She sounded bitter now, and resentful. "Do not tell me it is a wise way to live, for I know it is not."

"You do not wish to consider what I have told you." He knew it was fruitless to argue, that no matter what he said, she would regard it as wrong.

"You have said nothing worthy of consideration," she responded, then held up her hand. "The ford is not far ahead. I think I hear cattle." For a moment she thought about it, then said, "If there are cattle, there will be men." A sly smile lifted the corners of her mouth as she swung around to look at him. "What do you say? Will you change your mind and hunt with me?"

"I will hold your horse," he answered. "Hunt if you must."

"I am *famished*," she exclaimed, keeping her voice low. "If you are not, then you must be more monkish than the monks."

"I hunger," he said quietly. "But blood alone will not suffice."

She waved him to silence again just before she swung her horse around to face him, slipped out of the saddle, tossed him her reins, and slunk off into the cover of the trees, moving more like a wolf than a woman.

Germanno heard the lowing of cattle just before a man screamed.

There was a swift, intense brawl, mixed with the distress of the animals, then the sound of cattle scattering. He held his horse and the reins of Ximene's more tightly, not wanting them to bolt with the cattle.

A short while later, Ximene returned, her clothes wet to the waist, a smear of blood on her lips. Her pace was unsteady, as if she were slightly drunk. She was panting a bit; she shot a resentful glare at Germanno. "Do not trouble yourself about this one. He will not rise into our life. I made sure he was truly dead." She pulled herself into the saddle. "I will continue on in a short while. For now, I am sated and I need a little time to restore myself."

It was useless to protest. Germanno handed her the reins she had given him. "If you have to rest, so be it."

She glanced of him. "If Aulutis had been as knowing as you, he would still be alive and we would never have quarreled," she said dreamily.

This seemed highly unlikely to Germanno, but he kept his thoughts to himself, choosing instead to listen to the night around him, and watch over Ximene's rest. He would have to leave her soon, he knew, and return to the task Idelfonzuz had set for him. Would she rejoice or be saddened by his departure? he wondered, or would her fury blot out any other emotion?

Shortly before midnight she wakened, rousing gradually, stretching as much as the saddle would allow. "There," she said slowly, deliciously. "Now I am ready."

"Where do you want to go?" he asked as he put his horse in motion.

"Well, first we will go pick up your mules where you left them. If Goroloz has managed to control his hunger, the mules should be ready to come with you. I know you do not like to leave them too long in our care." She offered him a snide smile, as if his concern for animals was as foolish as his regard for living humans.

"Would you want to, were you in my position," he countered, bothered that she had managed to drag him into a dispute with her.

"If I did not think I would ever find mules again, I might." She threw back her head and gave a crack of laughter. "We will cross here," she added in a different tone as they reached the ford.

The ford was shallow, coming no higher than their horses' knees, but the water was fast-flowing, which made it more precarious to cross; Germanno held the high pommel of his saddle to compensate for the queasiness that filled him. As soon as they were on the far bank, relief washed over him with an intensity that almost made him dizzy.

"It is two leagues to where they are waiting. They have your mules safe, or they will answer to me." If this assurance was intended to please Germanno, it failed.

"Why do you punish your own?" he asked. "I find it baffling that you do."

"Because they are my own," she said as if this was obvious. "It is for me to make them, and having made them, it is for me to keep them in order."

He considered her answer, and was nonplussed by it; he had expected a blunt answer but not this one. He had to curb his desire to challenge her certainties, to contain his inclination to make another attempt to show her there was another way for vampires to live. "Yet you are disappointed," he said at last.

"How could I not be? You would be, too, were you willing to command those you have made," she countered, turning as much as the high saddle would allow. "You have seen for yourself how I must deal with those around me, how much care they require. What can I be, but disappointed?" There was a trace of emotion in her voice now that suggested she might allow herself to mourn her son, but when she spoke again, it was gone. "They all betray me, in the end." They went the greater part of a league without speaking, each alone though they rode together. They passed a village with half its buildings burned, and only pigs left in the pens. "Moors did that," Ximene said. "They do not eat pigs, so they let the peasants have them."

"At least they did not slaughter the pigs, so the villages would lose most of the meat in any case." Germanno said, having seen that done from China to Britain, from Poland to Tunis.

The track they followed went into the forest again; here the underbrush was thick and the trees half-grown. "There was fire here, twenty years ago. Some of the mountain washed away, but here, on this plateau, there will be real forest again in sixty years, if they do not burn it anew." She gave the place a look of disgust. "There used to be many bear here, and deer. Now they are fewer in number and harder to catch. I have not seen a wild cat in this part of the mountains in forty years. It is said that they have all gone to Toulouza."

"And have they?" Germanno asked, knowing the answer.

"No one has seen them there, either," she said, and sighed. "I remember how it was when I was young, and the mountains were all forested. A few of my clan also recall those times, but most came to me after the Moors began to fight, and to cut trees, and to burn. The Christians learned from them, and now we watch the mountains fall away in the winter."

"It saddens you, does it not, Ximene," Germanno observed, feeling a touch of satisfaction that something—anything—could make her sad.

"When I see familiar places vanish, it does," she admitted. "But then, I know that the living are asinine."

"You lived, once," he reminded her gently.

"And when I did, I was as witless as any of them." She stared into the half-grown woods. "Something is wrong." Reining in her horse, she stared intently into the night.

Germanno rose in the stirrups and looked ahead. "What is it?"

She swung her horse around. "The forest is on fire. Three leagues or more. It will burn this way."

"But three leagues—" Germanno began.

"Yes. That is where most of my clan gathers each night," she said grimly. "If Herchambaut and Goroloz have any sense, they will run for the far side of the mountains. Two of my clan have long since gone to the north, and will give them shelter. You have lost your mules, Germanno, it would seem."

Germanno signaled his roan to crouch and half-rear, then turned him back the way he came. "Do we cross the river?" he called out to Ximene, who had put her mount into a steady trot.

"And follow the far side until there is another valley," she said.

"You will tire your horse," Germanno worried her. "Let them walk as long as they can." He had kept his roan from trying to run, and held him back as Ximene urged her horse to go faster.

The first, distant trace of smoke fingered the night wind; two deer came crashing through the scrub, all but blundering into Germanno's roan in their panic. As if goaded by the fleeing deer, Ximene pushed her horse into a canter, and was soon lost to sight on the narrow path.

Germanno kept his horse to a steady, rapid walk, not letting the increasing number of scared animals frighten him into bolting with them. "We will get there," he assured his horse, patting his neck as he watched the woods around him. He was nearing the small village they had passed when he brought his horse to a halt; men were rushing out of their houses, many of them bearing torches, and shouting, "The Viexa Armoza! The Viexa Armoza!"

Ximene's bay mare stood, flanks heaving, by the pigsty; from the way she stood, her off-side foreleg was broken. Ximene was just getting to her feet, one hand to her head.

"Burn her! *Burn her!*" the villagers shouted.

"You would not dare!" Ximene raised her voice in command. "You will not *touch* me!"

Three or four of the men surrounded her horse and clubbed its head until it fell over, kicking once or twice before it died.

"Burn her!" The words were becoming a chant, as hypnotic as any cycle of prayers.

"You killed my horse!" she shrieked. "You will answer for that!"

"Burn her!" The cries grew louder and more frenzied as the men crowded around Ximene. One of them thrust a torch at her.

With a scream of rage she rushed at the man, throwing herself on him and trying to bite him. Most of the men drew back, aghast, but three did not retreat, and one of them actually struck her across the shoulders with a crudely made whip. Ximene bellowed and pushed herself away from her victim, her hands raised like talons to rip at anyone who came close enough to be touched.

Germanno clapped his heels to his horse's side, putting the roan to a gallop. He charged at the center of the men, keeping his whole attention on Ximene. As he reached her, he pulled his roan to a rearing halt, reached down and swung Ximene up into his saddle across his lap, then set his roan galloping away from the village toward the river. He held her in place with one hand and guided his horse with the other.

"The Devil!" one of the villagers shouted as they shrank back from Germanno's blue roan. The others around her took up the cry, and a few of the men sank to their knees and began to pray.

At the river, the roan splashed across the shallows in a series of plunges and half-jumps until he made his way up the far bank, where Germanno stopped him, dropped Ximene out of the saddle onto her feet and let the horse shake himself. Only then did he look back. "They are not following us," he said.

"Why should they?" she demanded. "To be carried away like a sack of flour—" She finished her thought with a gesture that showed aggravation and disgust.

"At least you were carried away," Germanno said. "They were prepared to burn you."

"And of course I am grateful," she said, making him a reverence of such submission that it was insulting.

"You had some other plan for escape?" Germanno suggested, not surprised by her response.

"I would have made them release me," she muttered, looking down toward the river. "The fire will reach them by dawn, in any case. And they have their village to look after before they pursue us."

"You would have been ashes by then, yourself. Vampires are swift runners but even we cannot outdistance flames." He dismounted and went toward her.

"They will burn, and I will be glad of it. I will rejoice." She folded her arms and dared him with her stance to contradict her. "Or will I have erred?"

"You may be right," he said in a tone that ended their dispute. "And you need to recoup your strength before dawn comes, as do I."

"So we can run from the fire, too," she said. "We might as well be one of the living, trying to flee every misfortune."

"You may stay and die the True Death if you would rather," Germanno said with an ironic smile. "You are not safe here, Ximene. The villagers may soon be looking for you."

"They will soon be trying to save their houses and their rigs," she said, tossing her head to show she put little stock in his warning.

"Possibly, but they will hunt you, as well. The fire will not deter them unless the wind picks up." He touched her arm in the hope she would look at him. "You cannot wait for the fire to reach them, in the hope that it will save you. We must go, and quickly."

"Go where? I will not leave my region." She glanced at him, her eyes flicking away from his. "If they are hunting me, as you say they are, then I would be numb-witted to go back to my fortress. If the fire gets into that defile, the fortress would be a death-trap in any case." She put her hands on her hips, trying to show her usual authority. "I will have to find another place."

Germanno saw her desperation. "Have you any place in mind?"

"Not just at present," she replied, glaring across the river. "All the usual places are no longer safe."

"Then pack some of your native earth and come with me; you may not want to leave this place, but what is left for you in it—your fortress is lost and your clan is gone. What more keeps you here?" Germanno said, doing his best not to sound impatient. "It may not be the same for you in the wider world, but you will not be hunted."

"As you are not?" She gave him a speculative look. "You wander the world because you are welcome everywhere?"

"No," he admitted. "But I am not often despised." Because, he added to himself, I am not often known for my true nature.

She came up to him. "You are tolerated by men because you hide your power, you make yourself less than you are to reassure them." She spat to show her opinion of such compromise. "Think what you could do if you had a clan like mine everywhere you have gone."

"I have thought of it, and I know we would be destroyed by the living." He saw the doubt in her face and went on, "No clan of vampires is large enough to stand against the living. There are far more of them than there are of us, and they are not as hindered as we are. There was a time, when I was far younger than I am now, when the living called me a demon and I was blind enough to take pride in that name. But over time, I saw the vainglory of it, and I learned to value the brevity of life, and to honor the living. Then I found that power is nothing if it has no use beyond its own perpetuation." He knew she did not believe him; he fell silent.

"You are ridiculous, Sanct' Germain, do you know that?" She took a dozen steps away from him. "What use is sympathy for the living, when most of them would kill you if they could? Has your compassion brought you anything but loneliness? We are enemies, the living and the undead. Nothing will change that. I did what I could to preserve my clan, and you know what has happened to them, but I do not deceive myself with pity for those who killed them. By sunrise most of them will be gone, slain by the living whom you say you honor." Her voice shook with contempt. "You are worse than any of the living."

He knew it was useless to take issue with her condemnation; he cocked his head in the direction of the river. "Should we not at least get back from the bank and into the trees?"

"Where the fire can catch us more quickly?" She kicked at the sodden hem of her cote. "I will go into the highest peaks where they cannot find me."

"And start another clan?" he asked, feeling a sudden hopelessness as he watched her.

"No. Not until I can command the region again. It would insult my son's memory to do less than that." She squared her shoulder, determination once again taking hold of her. "I will keep myself away from the living for a time; I will live in the highest peaks, where few men venture. I will not leave the crags; they—the living—will forget me in a century or two, and the Viexa Armoza will become nothing more than a tale, a story to frighten naughty children. In time they will bury their knowledge of vampires as they will bury their dead, and none of them will remember how to kill us, or what identifies us. When they are no longer able to fight me and mine, I will come again, restore my clan, and reclaim the region of Holy Blood."

Germanno considered what she said, and decided not to question her resolve. "How will you live?"

"There will be occasional travelers, or outlaws, or shepherds, or hermits, or knights who will wander into my realm. Not lavish fare but enough to meet my needs. I will be careful. They will all die the True Death from their first time with me." Her smile was self-satisfied. "It will not be as it has been, but I will not starve. Vampires cannot starve to death, can we?"

"No," Germanno said, recalling the times in his life when hunger had driven him mad; he shuddered inwardly at the memories.

"Then I have nothing to fear. But you." She swung around and pointed directly at him. "I told you I would kill you if you ever came to this region again. You disobeyed me, but you brought my son to me, so I pardon you this one lapse. However, you have no more means to bargain with me."

"Nor do I want one," Germanno said.

"Therefore in future if you seek me out you had better be prepared to give me the True Death, for I will be ready to give it to you." She stared at him for a long moment. "If you still think anything binds us, put it behind you; it has no substance with me." With that she put her back to him and began to walk away from the river.

"Ximene," he called after her. "Csimenae."

She did not turn around. "Go away, Sanct' Germain. The fire is coming. You are not wanted here."

He watched her until she was lost to sight; there was an emptiness within him, the ache of failure as well as the first pain of loss. Only a shout from the far bank jolted him from his morose reflections; then he looked up and saw half-a-dozen peasants rushing toward the river. "Time to leave," he said to his roan, and vaulted into the saddle, heading downstream, away from the fording and the path of the wind. Behind him he heard the curses of the peasants and the sound of rocks thrown after him. Would the men be reckless enough to follow him? He doubted it, as he doubted they would track Ximene in the morning. There would be too much to do then, and so long as the Viexa Armoza did not return, the peasants would have more than enough to occupy them. Perhaps, he thought, Ximene was right: in time she would be forgotten if she remained in isolation.

The river grew deeper and faster, and the canyon narrower. Germanno dismounted and led his horse along treacherous trails. He could see the first billows of fire to the north, and knew that by afternoon it would reach him. Overhead the sun hung like molten brass. There were animals at the river already, swimming across the current, attempting to find safety; marten and bear and deer swam with badgers and foxes and ferrets. Some were carried away by the current but many of them straggled ashore near a wide plateau that held the remains of a Moorish watchtower.

Making up his mind almost before he grasped the thought behind it, Germanno swung down from the saddle, untied his two satchels from the cantel, and reached up to pat the smooth dark-blue neck of his horse. "Someone will find you," he told the animal. "And you can graze on your own for a night or two." He reached up and unbuckled the throat-latch and pulled off the bridle, flinging it away down the slope. "There. Nothing to catch your head on now."

The roan nuzzled his arm, knowing something was wrong.

Germanno patted the smooth neck again, then stepped back and slapped the horse on the rump. "Off you go," he said, waving his arm to signal the horse to move away; the roan obeyed reluctantly, then began to trot in answer to Germanno's sharp command.

Taking up the satchels. Germanno rigged a kind of harness that tied them to his body. He hoped that they would retain enough of his native earth to keep him from being completely paralyzed by the running water. Then, before he could change his mind, he went to the bank and threw himself into the river; the current caught him and carried him away.

Text of a letter from Lailie, daughter of Rachmael ben Abbas to Teodoziuz Gratziaz, knight of Toledom: written in Greek.

To the most excellent Christian knight, Teodoziuz Gratziaz, the respectful greetings of Lailie, natural daughter of Rachmael ben Abbas.

Esteemed knight, I have in hand your generous proposal of marriage, and I am filled with gratitude that so highly reputed a knight as you would stoop to offer for one so unworthy as I am. I will ask God to show you special favor and to guard you in battle for the goodness you have shown to me.

Because I am fully aware of the splendid tribute you have shown me, I am doubly chagrined that I must regretfully inform you that I have recently accepted the proposal of Bildad ben Uzziah, mercer of Toledom, who has been recommended to me by the elders of the synagogue. He is a widower, with three children, and he has need of someone skilled in languages to advance his business. As great an honor as it would be to become the wife of a belted knight, it is a more sensible decision to marry one of my station in life and who shares my religion.

Were Germanno, Comide Ragoczy, who has been my guardian, here to advise me, I might have made a different choice, but he has been gone for many months, and with only the elders to guide me, I have chosen that which is familiar. With other council, I might have been swayed by your fame and your title, but as it is, I beg you not to despise me for my decision; you may put it to my woman's frailty, that I cannot convince myself to accept so fine an advancement as you offer.

I cannot help but think your Confessor will be relieved to know you will not take a Jewess as your bride. The Church has not encouraged men of your rank to marry women of my religion, no matter how much of a fortune we might bring with us as dowry. I know my portion is a generous one for a woman of my rank and position, but it cannot be so attractive that you and your Confessor would set aside concerns about marriage outside of your faith.

If you cannot forgive me, then at least I pray you will not take revenge upon me, or upon my affianced husband, or upon my religion. It is I who offends you, no one and nothing else. If anyone deserves your odium, I do. Spare the others your hard feelings, I beseech you, and know you will always have the heartfelt thanks of

Lailie, daughter of Rachmael ben Abbas

at Toledom, by my own hand, on the 9th day of November in the Christian calendar, in the Christian year 1117

9

Winter had taken hold of Toledom, setting its icy seal on the streets and blotting the sun from the sky for days on end. The odor of smoke hung heavily over the city, some of it from wood, some from tallow. Few travelers ventured out of the gates and fewer still came in. Even the steady flow of soldiers into the city had slowed to a trickle as snow claimed the roads beyond the walls. From the Court to the meanest hovel, the residents wrapped themselves in muffling layers of cloth to keep the cold from numbing their bones and spent as much time before their hearths as they could, drinking hot wine or ginger tea to ward off the worst of the cold.

In the house of Germanno, Comide Ragoczy the fires blazed and lamps shone their little, bright eyes in the encroaching darkness that came early and stayed long. The place seemed empty now that Lailie was married; the Comide himself had not been heard from since the King received a report from him in August; that had come from near Usxa and his silence was considered ominous. Those who feared the worst took care not to mention it to Ruthor, who ran the house for its absent master. Under his order the place was maintained as if its master would return shortly, and be received with appropriate ceremony.

Three days after the Mass of the Nativity, the Comide of Meior Pandexa came to the house; he arrived late in the afternoon on a showy blood-bay. He condescended to speak with Ruthor, although men of high rank did not usually converse with servants, there being no one of a more superior position to receive him. The Comide was very grand in a cote of heavy, leaf-patterned deep-green wool beneath a surcote of damask bronze silk lined in fox-fur; his chaperon framed his face in marten-fur, and he wrapped the hood's long tail around his neck for extra warmth. He went down the gallery with nods of approval until they reached the main hall, where he stopped. "You are in your master's confidence, I am told."

"I have that privilege," said Ruthor, trying to maintain the subservient manner the Comide expected.

"Privilege it is," the Comide approved. "Yes. If that is the case, the King himself has asked me to put a most . . . delicate question to you: do you know if your master has prepared his Will." He coughed once to show the question embarrassed him.

"Yes," said Ruthor. "He has."

The Comide was encouraged by this response. "Was it witnessed?"

"It was," said Ruthor.

"By whom?" This could be awkward, for if Germanno had not used a Christian witness, the Will could be excluded by the Church.

"By Fre Ebertoz and by the knight Maurixio of Linnomanjo. They saw the Will shortly before my master left on his mission." Ruthor spoke clearly, so there could be no misunderstanding.

"Both of them can read?" The Comide wanted to be precise on this, for it could prove a sticking point to the Church.

"Yes; the Fre better than the knight, but both knew what they witnessed," Ruthor said, and added, "My master was most careful to fulfill all the requirements of the Church."

"And do you know where that Will is to be found?" the Comide asked, doing his best not to demand it.

"Yes, I do." He reverenced the Comide.

The Comide waited a short while, saying nothing. Finally he spoke. "Well? Where is it, then?"

Ruthor did not answer directly. "May I send for some refreshment for you? We have fresh bread and some excellent wine." He lowered his head in a show of respect. "On behalf of my master."

It was minimal hospitality for one of such high rank; the Comide nodded; to refuse the offer once it had been made would be an intolerable insult. "Out of respect for your master, I accept."

"On his behalf, I thank you for your courtesy," said Ruthor, and clapped his hands for a servant.

"Is it true that Germanno keeps no slaves?" the Comide asked, as if he could not bring himself to believe such rumors.

"It is," Ruthor said, and issued a series of orders to the servants who came to the door; they took care not to look at the Comide.

The Comide shook his head. "Most unusual. But he *is* foreign, is he not?" He chose one of the Moorish chairs and sat down. "Is it also true he gave a dowry to a young woman not of his blood?"

Ruthor could not keep from smiling at this observation. "That is also true," he said, thinking to himself that it was accurate in the sense the Comide intended as well as in the sense Germanno would mean it. "Your wine and bread will be brought to you directly."

"Very good," said the Comide, who was not in the habit of talking with servants. "While I wait, you may fetch the Will."

"Now that, I am afraid, is a difficulty," Ruthor said diffidently. When the Comide of Meior Pandexa looked up sharply, he added, "I offer neither you nor the King any insult when I tell you that my master ordered me to deliver the Will to the King when he—that is my master—has not sent word to anyone for a year, for he has stipulated that he is to be regarded as among the living until a full year has passed. That would mean that in the first week of next August, I will carry the Will to Idelfonzuz myself, if there has been no message from my master in the meantime."

"That is a most unusual arrangement," the Comide said, his manner making it clear he did not approve.

"Perhaps, but it is what my master required of me." He made another reverence.

"But the King has other demands," the Comide said as if mentioning Idelfonzuz would change Ruthor's mind. "Should you not obey the King in the absence of your master?"

"Were I to betray my master's command, how could the King repose any confidence in anything I do?" Ruthor countered.

The Comide sat very straight. "You will not give it to me now?"

"Alas," said Ruthor. "I have pledged my Word to my master and I am bound by it, as you are by your oaths."

Realizing that they had reached an impasse, the Comide rose from the chair and began to pace. "I have my duty to discharge," he said as he went down the room.

"As I have mine," Ruthor replied.

"But surely your master, who serves the King, will allow his orders to be superseded by the King's," the Comide suggested, at pains not to look directly at Ruthor as he did his best to establish his own authority.

"It may be that he would: he did not so instruct me," said Ruthor.

"But *he is gone!*" the Comide exclaimed. "There has been no word from him for months. No one expects him to return."

"That may be, but I must abide by his orders whether he returns or not," said Ruthor, noticing out of the corner of his eye that the servants were returning with the bread and wine for the Comide. "If you will be seated again, Comide, I may have the honor of providing you with refreshment in my master's name."

The Comide gestured his exasperation, but he sat down again, and waited while the servants brought a table to him and put down the tray. "New butter as well as new bread. I hope your master would approve such profligacy."

"For the sake of guests, my master has instructed me to receive them as his equals." Ruthor stepped back so that the Comide could eat in the appropriate isolation.

"You may stand in the doorway," the Comide said magnanimously. "There are matters we still must discuss."

Ruthor did not sigh, although it was an effort not to. "As you wish," he said to the Comide in a humble manner.

"You see, I must inform the King that you have not been willing to do as he requires, and that will go against your master." He broke off a piece of bread, spread it thickly with butter and popped it into his mouth.

"If my master does not return, how can that be?" Ruthor asked as politely as he could.

"The Will could be set aside," the Comide suggested. "Such things have happened before"

"No doubt," Ruthor said. "Yet more servants have suffered at the will of their masters than at the will of the King."

"Are you being impudent?" The Comide paused in the act of pouring wine into the silver cup the servants had brought.

"I am trying to serve my master," Ruthor said.

"Exactly. Your master would not want you to refuse the King," the Comide said as if Ruthor were a bit simple. "If you will not do as the King has ordered—"

"—it will discredit my master." Ruthor finished for him. "I understood that."

"You will do as Idelfonzuz demands?" The Comide lifted his cup to drink.

"I do not know that I can. Were my master Spanish, there would be no doubt what I must do; he is from the Carpathians, and his title is an ancient one in that land." He ducked his head in apology.

"That cuts both ways," the Comide pointed out. "If Germanno were

Spanish, he would be assured of the King's protection. As it is . . ." He left his thought unfinished.

"In August I will gladly surrender the Will," Ruthor said, taking care not to give the guest any reason to be affronted.

"Incidentally, the wine is very good," the Comide remarked, then said, "I do not want to bring unwelcome news to Idelfonzuz."

"Nor do I wish to give any such," Ruthor said.

"In August, the King will be on campaign, driving back the Moors from the borders of Aragon. He will be within the walls of Zaraguza, with men in the field to command. He will not want to stop his fighting to send to Toledom for a Will." He dipped the bread in the wine and ate it.

Now Ruthor understood what was being required of him. "I can make a generous contribution to the costs of the fighting on my master's behalf. This would be.as a sign of my master's service to the King. He left me gold enough to cover any such obligations, and his authorization, permitting me to act in his stead without the need to obtain the endorsements of others." He made a reverence once more. "That way the King and my master are attended to without slights to anyone."

"What an extraordinary arrangement, to leave gold in the hands of servants," marveled the Comide.

"Given the nature of his mission, he thought it best that I be able to act for him when the occasion required it," said Ruthor modestly.

The Comide considered this, munching a bit of the bread as he did. "I could explain to the King, try to persuade him to let this most remarkable arrangement stand—if there was gold enough to assure him of your master's devotion."

"No doubt," Ruthor said, keeping the amusement from his voice. "I will arrange for two bags of gold to be delivered to the King, and half a wallet for you, for your efforts, to show the appreciation of my master." It was the only way to be sure Idelfonzuz received the full amount, Ruthor knew; he was also certain that this amount was at least double what Idelfonzuz had hoped for.

"Two bags of gold." The Comide almost choked on his bread; he recovered himself. "A handsome donation."

"My master would do no less were he here to tend to it himself," Ruthor said. He paused. "Will that suffice?"

The Comide swallowed hard. "For now, I am certain it will." He topped off the wine in his cup and drank it down hastily. "Well, you have done credit to your master. When shall I tell the King the donation will arrive?"

"Tomorrow morning after Mass," Ruthor answered. "If it does not, tell the King he may send armed men to claim it."

"Be sure I will," said the Comide, and got to his feet. "The King does not like to wait upon the whims of others."

"Certainly not," said Ruthor. "I will prepare the gold tonight. You may inform the King of what has been done in my master's name."

"That I will." He paused and studied Ruthor's face. "I have heard you are from Gadiz."

"That is so." Ruthor answered, not adding that when he had left his family for Roma, Nero's reign was coming to an end.

"You have not the look of it," said the Comide.

"So I have been told," Ruthor responded.

The Comide waited, as if considering something more, then said, "I will tell the King what you are providing him."

"Yes; so you have assured me," Ruthor said, reverencing the Comide. "On behalf of my master, I express his gratitude."

"Good," said the Comide, and abruptly left the hall; he sauntered down the gallery, obviously well-pleased with himself.

Ruthor watched him go with a knowing look in his eye, an expression that, had the Comide seen it, might have lessened his satisfaction in accomplishing his task, for this was the third time Idelfonzuz had dispatched one of his courtiers to demand money—however indirectly—from Germanno. He was fairly certain the Comide would not be the last. With a sigh he took up the tray with the last of the bread and the tub of butter on it and carried it down to the kitchen, where he handed it to the scullion who had been squatting by the massive hearth where a side of pork turned on a spit, filling the room with the aroma of roasting meat.

The senior cook, a massive fellow with muscular forearms and a broad belly, came up to Ruthor, his manner uneasy. "There is trouble," he said.

Ruthor chuckled. "Not from that fellow. Idelfonzuz does not want to take all the money at once, he would rather ask for it in discrete portions."

"It's not the courtier," the cook said, his voice dropping. "There is a leper in the garden." He covered his mouth with his hand as if to show he wanted no part of this."

"What are you saying?" Ruthor asked.

"He come last night, very late. I cannot think how he was admitted; the guards turn lepers back at the gates, except on the night of the Mass of the Nativity." He crossed himself. "What are we to do?"

"I suppose I should go see for myself," Ruthor said, feeling exhausted suddenly, as if the long months of waiting had put all their weight on him at once.

"Do not touch him. If you touch him, you will be a leper, too," the cook warned him nervously.

"I will be careful," Ruthor assured him as he went out into the twilit garden. He paused near the terrace behind the house, listening for the leper's clapper. When he heard nothing, he made his way toward the small stone cabin near the walls where seeds and supplies were kept. He had almost reached the narrow doorway when he heard the clapper. Pausing, he wondered how he would be able to get the leper out of the cabin, for he could not let it be known that one so afflicted was living in the garden. When the clapper sounded again, he called out, "Who is there?" and felt foolish for asking.

An arm swathed in the linen wrappings that marked leprosy motioned him to come nearer.

Ruthor sighed in annoyance. "That would not be prudent," he said.

The arm beckoned again, but nothing was said.

"Tell me what you want." Ruthor took a simple step nearer the cabin, hoping that none of the kitchen staff was watching.

"Another chest of my native earth to sleep on," said Germanno, and stepped out of the door. He wore the rough woollen habit of lepers over the bandages; what Ruthor could see of his face revealed patches of scraped skin and healing wounds.

"Oh!" Ruthor exclaimed, gladness wiping the austerity from his countenance. "Oh, my master. You are back."

Germanno held up his hand. "No, I am not. A leper has come, and that leper will soon depart—"

"But you are no leper. Disease cannot touch you," Ruthor said, his enthusiasm barely contained. "You have returned."

"No," Germanno repeated. "The Comide Ragoczy is still missing, and will continue to be so." He gave Ruthor a serious stare, his compelling eyes stilling the exuberance of his old friend.

"What is the matter? Has there been some treachery?" Ruthor looked about as if belatedly concerned about spies.

"Nothing out of the usual," Germanno said, "but it is just as well that I am gone."

Ruthor accepted this. "Did you fail to get the King what he wanted? Do you fear his anger?"

Germanno's fine brows flicked together. "No. He had what he wanted from me, and money as well. How much more direct it was when the Gardingi simply demanded twenty horses from me. Gold was not so important then. Now, without gold a war is impossible."

"Do you think the King will claim all you own?" Ruthor was alarmed at the prospect.

"I doubt it. However, that was not the reason I have dropped from sight." He indicated the low stool by the bed of sweet herbs. "Sit down. The cook will be able to see you, and he will know you are not touching me."

"As you wish," said Ruthor, and sank onto the marble stool, paying no heed to how cold the stone was.

It took Germanno a little time to gather his thoughts to speak. "I found Ximene and her tribe still in their old region. There were more of them."

"Not surprising," said Ruthor. "You did not think she would refrain from making more, did you?"

"I hoped she would learn," said Germanno heavily. "The people— the living—have grown tired of her predations, and they have struck back. With the war going on around them, the battles serve to cover what they do." He fell silent, thinking back to the fires. "They know to break our spines, to burn us, to cut off our heads. And they are better at recognizing us."

At this last Ruthor nodded, comprehension coming at last. "You say that someone in that region might realize that Germanno, Comide of Ragoczy is a vampire."

"Yes. So Germanno, Comide Ragoczy must be no more," Germanno said.

Ruthor nodded slowly. "And Ximene? What of her?"

He answered quietly, his thoughts inward. "She blames me for all that has happened, I think. She has gone far into the mountains to wait for a time she and her clan are forgotten so she may once again rule in the region of Holy Blood."

"And Aulutis?" Ruthor used the original version of the boy's name deliberately.

"Dead. I took him back to his mother." He moved out of the angle of the cabin and looked directly at Ruthor. "Two peasants drove a lance through his back."

"They knew," said Ruthor.

"Clearly they did." Germanno agreed.

A sudden sound came from the barnyard as one of the scullions tossed the kitchen slops to the half-dozen pigs in the sty behind the stable brought both Germanno and Ruthor on the alert.

"I should not stay much longer," Ruthor said, getting to his feet. "I will return later, near midnight."

"I may not be here by then," Germanno said.

Ruthor stood still. "Where will you be?"

"With any luck I will be on a mule bound for the north," said Germanno.

"A mule from the stable?" Ruthor asked.

"If one should wander out of his stall," Germanno answered. "I will need a monk's habit and a begging bowl."

"I will see that they are put in the stable as soon as the household has sat down to dinner." Ruthor took a few steps away. "What happened to your face?"

"I scraped it on a river-bottom," Germanno said in so casual a way that Ruthor stared at him.

"You were thrown into a river?" His shock made his voice louder than he had intended.

"I jumped into one. There was a fire behind me." He sounded almost apologetic. "I could not outrun it, so I set my horse loose and took my satchels—"

"Which had the linen strips and your native earth," Ruthor interjected with a nod of approval.

"Yes. It is steep country there, and the river carried me more than eight leagues before I washed up on the shore." He held out his bandaged hands. "They are bruised and scored. So are my legs. The bandages have served a double purpose."

"That was a dangerous thing to do. You are immobilized in running water," Ruthor said.

"Was burning less dangerous?" Germanno's voice was lightly ironic. "In my position, I had few choices."

Ruthor took a deep breath. "So you are going north as a monk." He cocked his head. "What am I to do?"

"Stay here until Idelfonzuz marches to Zaraguza in the spring. Then declare you are going to search for me. Make sure you include generous donations to the Church and the King in my name before you do—"

"I have done so already. Just this evening I promised two bags of gold to the King," Ruthor said, trying to mask his faint frown. "He sent a courtier to inquire about your Will."

"Did he." Germanno shook his head once.

"He was most insistent," Ruthor said. "I supposed he wanted to find out the extent of your fortune here. I denied him, but I offered him recompense."

"Was it more than he wanted?" Germanno asked.

"I think so," Ruthor replied. "Certainly more than the King expects. The bribe I offered him should keep him from seeking more, at least for a while."

Germanno gave a mercurial smile. "Very good. I knew I could rely on you, old friend."

Ruthor shrugged off the praise. "So. I am to look for you when Idelfonzuz's campaign begins. What then?"

"You will find me at Olivia's horse-farm, outside of Orleanis, well beyond Idelfonzuz's campaign, or his reach."

"He may seize this house," Ruthor cautioned him. "It is likely he will ignore your Will and confiscate your holdings."

Germanno shrugged. "I have lost more than houses on his account. Let him take what he wants; you and I will not soon return here."

"So Germanno, Comide Ragoczy will completely vanish?" Ruthor asked.

"It is better so. When you find me, I will be a scholar from Poland." He held up his hand to keep Ruthor from making an indignant protest. "No one remembers Hiermon Ragoczy now. Carl-le-Magne is long dead, and the Poles do not care what happens beyond their borders."

"So you hope," Ruthor countered ready to defend his position. Then, as quickly as the impulse had taken him, it was gone and he studied Germanno intently. "You are bothered by Ximene, are you not?"

"More than bothered." Germanno said.

"Because of what she became," Ruthor said.

"And what she remains. She is adamant against—" Germanno broke

off and nodded in self-condemnation. "I failed her," he said, his
voice low. "She has not learned that it is touching that nourishes us, not
the blood. We seek life and she has contempt for the living."

"From what you told me, so did you at first," Ruthor said as sympa-
thetically as possible.

Germanno said nothing for a while, then coughed once. "Her losses
have been great, but she will not mourn them."

"In time she may," Ruthor said, sensing the anguish Ximene was
causing his master.

"Perhaps." Germanno shook off his melancholy with a single, decisive gesture. "There is nothing to be gained by dwelling on this; it is beyond my remedy." He took a moment to marshal his thoughts. "I will
leave by the Santoz Guion gate. Monks may pass through it at any hour
of the day or night."

"It may be snowing," Ruthor warned as he glanced up at the sky.

"The cold will not bother me so long as I have my native earth to
shield me," Germanno reminded him.

"I will see to it that you have a satchel of it with the monk's habit,"
Ruthor promised him.

Germanno gestured his approval. "I cannot thank you enough, old
friend." He glanced back toward his house. "You had better be getting
back. Tell the staff you have persuaded the leper to leave."

"That I will," Ruthor said. "And I will decry the missing mule in the
morning."

"An excellent plan," Germanno said, and stepped back into the
stone cabin while Ruthor made his way through the garden and into
the house.

Text of a dispatch from Idelfonzuz, King of Aragon and Navarre, son-
in-law of Adelfonzuz of Castile and León.

*Be it known: I, Idelfonzuz, King of Aragon and Navarre, son-in-law of
Adelfonzuz of Castile and León do hold the city of Zaraguza and the control of the Eberoz River for twelve leagues in both directions from this
city, and will hold it for the honor of my Crown and the glory of God.*

*Moorish captives tell us of contention among the numbers, for there
are ambitious men serving Allah as there are those who claim to be devoted to Christ. It is my intention to take advantage of this unsettled*

situation among the Moors and advance my claims on the lands that are rightly ours. Let the Moors spend their strength among themselves—I will turn their strife to my cause and gain triumph over them. Well it is said that confusion among the enemy brings victory to the purposeful. That will be my motto, and it will serve to keep my soldiers and knights at their keenest.

I have received word from the monastery of Santoz Ennati near Usxa that the people of that place await our coming with prayers of eagerness; I have already sent word to them that I will hasten to free them from the Moors. I am told that their other foes have been routed as well, a sign that God has given His potency to us, and has blessed our endeavors. In His Name we will persevere to the ultimate victory.

Many have shown their devotion to this cause, and have not been praised for their efforts. Their fates remain unknown, and for their sacrifice, I will offer up the Masses of priests throughout Spain, so that they may be rewarded in Heaven for their forfeiture here on earth in this cause. Most of these unknown soldiers will be nameless anywhere but in Heaven. I am certain that God is Just and will receive their souls among those who have died in Christ's Name over the centuries. For those who are known and who labored for me, I declare that their heirs shall have ten gold Angels for their loss.

This is a worthy fight, and one that will not end in a year or a decade. Our enemy is an old enemy, and for that reason we must be prepared to remain steadfast and to fight on for as long as a single Moor stands upon Spanish soil. I have dedicated my life to this battle, and I will continue to war on. Let men call me The Warrior: I take pride in the name, and I will strive to earn it many times over before I fall in God's cause.

Let all be diligent in this effort. Priests and peasants are as useful to God in reclaiming His land as soldiers and knights. I will praise those who support my army and I will punish those who do not. If you are not willing to aid me, you are aiding our enemies, the Moors, and you will receive the same penalty as all enemies must expect from me.

To this I set my hand on the 20th day of August in the 1118th year of man's Salvation,

Idelfonzuz, King of Aragon and Navarre
Son-in-law of Adelfonzuz of Castile and León

EPILOGUE

*T*ext of a letter from Atta Olivia Clemes in Roma to Hiermon Ragoczy in La Chappelle; written in the Latin of Imperial Rome.

To my dearest, most worrisome friend, greetings from the new Circus Romana where the Church has been providing the entertainment in place of the charioteers, gladiators, and wild beasts of old.

Anacletus II has taken over San Pietro's while Innocentus II has occupied the Lateranus. One has a choice of Popes, and that has brought a looseness to Roma that has not been in the city for many years. I tend to see Anacletus as the better of the Pontiffs whether or not he is a converted Jew; he is better educated and far more capable of handling the complexities that are encumbering the Church, particularly the uproar that has resulted from the new prohibition on priests marrying. Innocentus is little more than a tool of Lothair II, the Holy Roman Emperor, but he has armed men to support his claim. What an array of II's we have, to be sure; two Popes and an Emperor, all the second of that name. Were I an Arab mathematician, no doubt I should find some significance in this. As it is, I find it both diverting and lamentable.

What is there in the edge of the Low Countries that offers half the amusement of what we now have here in Roma? You may say what you like about the change in trade, or the civil war in Britain, I know I am having a livelier time than you. Consider coming to join me here. I will not be departing for another year or so—I am too much delighted by the chaos being stirred by the Church, and all in the name of preserving the succession from San Pietro to the present. At least the Caesars were open in their ambition.

Are you still planning to try to find the last of Ximene's tribe? I will tell you again that such an act would be absolute folly. Let well enough alone. If they enlarge their numbers, then you will have every reason to seek them out, but until then, trust that they profited by her errors and have learned not to flood the world with vampires. I have heard nothing from the Toulousa region, where you say you think they have gone. Why draw attention to them by searching them out? The Church would take immediate advantage if it was discovered that there were undead creatures to hunt; think of how much more important the Church would become if people thought they had to be protected from our kind. I understand that you believe you are under obligation to them because Ximene has not instilled in them a sense of proportion. Why you should have such a responsibility, when it is she who did not show them the danger of their nature, I cannot comprehend. Still, I am not astonished that you have taken the duty upon yourself.

Consider the risk you will run to do this, I ask you. They may be able to manage without your instruction, but I am not certain that I can. If not for your sake, then for mine, do not expose yourself to the wrath of the living. Barring that, give me your oath that you will stay on the north side of the Pyrenees. As dangerous as Toulousa may be, Spain is infinitely more so. Promise me you will not cross into that thrice-cursed region of Holy Blood. Ximene may be right, and the peasants there may forget her and her tribe in time, but even you would agree that not enough has passed. Help those in Toulousa if you must, but leave those in Aragon and Barzelunya to their fates.

You may think me hard-hearted to ask this of you, and truly, I may be. But, Sanct' Germain, I would be neglecting my obligation to you if I did not caution you in this venture of yours. You are not the only one who has a debt to honor; since you brought me to life, I have known that I owe more to you than I can ever repay. So, if you insist on placing yourself in harm's way, I will take it upon myself to inform you of the hazards you face. Do not chastise me for it: you have earned my concern.

I have sent Niklos Aulirios to Alexandria to find out if there is any way I might arrange to purchase property there. I would like to have a place to go that is not in the lands of the Church, but I am worried that the followers of the Prophet are no more reasonable that the followers of Christ. There are many things I miss about the Roma I knew when I was one of the living, yet I miss none so much as the laws which once allowed women their own estates and property. To have to continually invent late husbands or missing brothers is not only an annoyance, it is an insult as well. But at least Niklos is capable of smoothing over those inconveniences as much as may be done. If he discovers a way for me to secure property that is not too convoluted, then I shall go there, and hope I will be able to avoid any of the intrusions that religion continues to make on those of us who would rather not be bothered by it.

What I shrew I have become, and a carker, as well. I would not be amazed if you stopped reading before you reached this point. If you are still with me, I must tell you that I miss you, and I would be glad of see-ing you at any time, in any place you may select, even in the distant lands of the Silken Empire—where you have gone, although I have not. Choose where you wish to meet and I will find the means to be there. In spite of the confusion in Roma, I would be delighted to have you with me, and would sacrifice my entertainment here for your company.

With my affection and my—however unwished-for—guardianship, I sign myself,

> *Your most enduring, most fond,*
> *Olivia*

by my own hand at Roma on the 14ᵗʰ day of September in the Pope's year 1133